Infernal Providence:
Heir of Destruction

J. Armand
www.jarmandbooks.com

*In loving memory of my grandmother.
She stood stalwart against the current of time for more than
a century to become an enduring pillar of inspiration for
three generations of family whose lives she touched.*

*And dedicated to my mother, for all your unwavering support
and always being the cheerful light in my life that drives
away the dark times.*

*Also to Dan, without you I never would have been able to
pursue this dream, let alone realize it.*

Table of Contents

"The path to paradise begins in hell."
— Dante Alighieri, "The Divine Comedy"

"For small creatures such as we the vastness is bearable only through love."
— Carl Sagan, "Contact"

Prologue

Life was never the same after the gates of Hell opened on Earth. Humanity was powerless to defend itself against the Infernal hordes that poured through dimensional fissures and sowed chaos in their wake. Seven of the world's major cities were leveled in mere moments, with over a hundred million lives lost to the fiery pits.

Earth's only hope rested on the shoulders of a long unseen supernatural population. Deities, human mages, and ancient undead were called to arms in a reluctant eleventh hour truce forged by the power players and figureheads of their respective factions—myself included.

I am Dorian Benoit, God of Destruction.

A coven of enigmatic undead, known as the Strigoi, brought me to life in one of their arcane laboratories to be a vessel for the Infernal Kings. After my creation I was sent to live as a human until maturity, when I would be reclaimed; however, that plan didn't unfold as expected because they ultimately failed to contain me. The once-great Strigoi were now at risk of extinction, and I stood more powerful than ever in open defiance of Hell's occupation on Earth as the patron deity of the Alabaster Order.

My people were no ordinary humans either. They were of old blood, for the most part. Old and magical. They had spent generations grooming their heirs to become elite spellswords worthy of serving the one they called the Ascended, who was prophesized to deliver them from apocalyptic ruin. According to their elders, I was that one.

The ascension to godhood was a violent, meteoric rise for me. Only five years ago I unwittingly began my foray into the supernatural as a naïve and sheltered mortal. I was so afraid of my own meager powers at the time that I came close to death during my first hostile encounter. Since then I have slain demon lords, vanquished evil gods, and shattered a falling moon in my telekinetic grip.

Still, none of my previous exploits compared to the magnitude of carnage in the world today, or what was causing it. The Infernal Kings were seven demons of the highest distinction with absolute sovereignty over their domains in Hell. We had yet to confront them by direct means, but mention of their name alone was enough to make the heavens cower. If we were to stand any chance at success in opposing these Infernal interlopers, we would need more than the current uneasy alliance between a few immortal beings and our followers. We would need an indomitable coalition of the absolute best that Earth had to offer.

"Have you found anything useful on this Horned God that's supposed to have risen?" I asked the young white-haired knight who stood before me in my bedchamber.

I resided with the Order in an abbey on a tiny island just outside the Cyclades archipelago of Greece. Leadership didn't come naturally to me, but a settling in period was a luxury I wasn't afforded at the time of my inauguration. From the moment I joined the Order I was thrust onto the proverbial throne; an introverted and unassuming twenty-five-year-old from Boston was now worshipped as both monarch and deity with all the expectations that came along with it. The Order's impressive magical power and infallible loyalty made them too much of an asset to let reticent behavior get the best of me and so I played the part as best I could, even if I had greater trouble convincing myself of the role than them.

"The druids remain tightlipped despite your hospitality, Ascended. Liam's mother is a Wiccan. They may be more willing to speak with her."

"No, I don't want to involve anyone outside the Order. They don't trust us, but one of them is bound to talk. Eventually."

Before I took over the Order they had a history of silencing other humans who dabbled in magic, for fear that their potential incompetence and lack of discipline would draw dangerous attention. It came as no surprise that word spread of the Order's authoritarianism, making any attempts at peaceful negotiations that much more trying. We had convinced several geomantic druids to join us for a while, but they scattered shortly after divulging a few evasive, yet pointedly dogmatic opinions. Personally, I think they fled in fear after witnessing the Order's rigorous training, which would cause even a Spartan to cry foul.

"I doubt they could be of much help even if they wanted," the young knight continued. "Like most religions, their belief system has become more personal than centralized, which makes for almost as many variations as there are followers. We do know that any place steeped in untouched wilderness is considered sacred to them and most legends point to the far north as an origin. I've scouted some areas, but return empty-handed."

"Are we looking at Norse mythology?" I asked. My eyes wandered to the seaside cliff outside my window where my other half was practicing with his swords, drenched in sweat under the high noon sun. The last real bastion of sanity I had on this Earth was within his embrace. There I was just Dorian, without the responsibilities of a god or ruler bearing down on me.

"Celtic, but there is a measure of crossover with Wiccan, Norse, and even Roman lore. I was able to uncover a possible name for the Horned God: Cernunnos. Of course, there *are* four or five more names associated with him that all coincide with their own unique legends. He might even be a demon."

"We can't afford to make a single mistake with this, Claudius. I need to know without a doubt if we're dealing with an ally or a threat, and if it's the latter I want to know how to put an end to it fast. We're in no position to take on another god when we've got Hell closing in on all sides. I don't care if we have to raze an entire forest to the ground in a preemptive strike if that's the case."

"At once, Ascended. I am ever at your command," Claudius said with a bow, leaving me to my thoughts.

When the world was already ablaze, how much more harm could a localized scorched earth tactic do if it meant preventing a worse inferno from spreading? The days of pretending that the supernatural was nothing more than a fairytale were a fading memory. All the effort I had put into being someone I wasn't seemed wasted now. I longed for a different world back then, but now that I had it, all I felt was its burden. I was a fool to think life would be easier without all the restrictions of having to hide from humans. Seven billion screaming voices, each one louder than the last, drowned out good sense and rational thinking once the end of the world started.

Almost every day Hell's forces made an effort to gain another foothold by deploying a steady stream of fodder and shock troops to wear us down. Their army was infinite. In only three months we were already weighted by the exhausting repercussions associated with a war of attrition. We had lost an estimated four hundred million lives after the initial assault and the situation was only continuing to slide further downhill despite our resistance. One boon in our favor was the fact that Infernals could not sustain their presence on Earth unless Hell had bled through the interdimensional veil where chaos ran the most rampant. This kept most battles contained for a while, until neighboring areas caught wind of the invasion, sending them into hysteria.

The only modicum of peace in the human world came in the form of ironic reassurance from one of the most nefarious undead in history. Aurelia de Saint-Pierre, Queen of the Archios, was the first to make public contact with mankind. Her transcendent beauty and near-limitless telepathic control made her the ideal representative to pacify mortals and any interference we might have met from their armies on the battlefield.

Her act of goodwill ended there.

I had revealed a plot by her and the other undead Ancients to frame one of our strongest allies as a scapegoat for the apocalypse, since he was the biggest threat to their plans of taking over after the war. She also happened to be the sadistic former master of my lover Noah and, despite her self-indulgent peacekeeping efforts, I found it difficult to not end her reign in violence. We were so desperate that there was no other choice but to sit and watch as she fed her ravenous superiority complex, assimilating one government after the next into her rule with a disarming smile.

I would have to be patient and wait until an opportunity to eliminate her arose, but first and foremost I needed to ensure my own survival along with those I cared about.

Part I

"Dust"

Current world population: 7.1 billion

Chapter One

Mumbai was on the demons' menu today—a city of over twenty million that was falling fast in a smoldering pyre of hellish flames. The stench of charred flesh was inescapable and unable to be forgotten. One more metropolis was now a scrapyard. One more civilization a graveyard.

"Nathaniel, take these survivors across the bridge to the rest while we clean up here," I instructed my protégé as he flew past me.

He changed direction in midair to retrieve the family of four I had uncovered from the ruins of an apartment building. The infant with them was inconsolable. The young doe-eyed brother and his parents were frozen in a thousand-yard stare I had witnessed numerous times during these rescues. Looking into their vacant eyes as they struggled to process the day's events caused memories of my first experiences with losing everything to surface.

Nathaniel crouched to speak with the trembling child covered in soot and plaster dust. "You don't have to be afraid anymore. I'm here to help."

When did I stop being afraid of monsters for the second time? The problem with overcoming fears is that there's always something worse waiting around the corner.

He conjured a crystal in his palm that sparkled with a dazzling light and offered it to the boy. "Here you go. This will bring you good luck."

After a moment of hesitation, the child reached from behind his father's leg with a shaky hand and took the crystal.

"Would you like to fly to someplace safe with me and your family?" Nathaniel asked, opening his arms in welcome. The boy nodded his head vigorously and wiped the stream of tears rolling down his face on his dirty sleeve before approaching. Nathaniel picked him up and let the parents hold on as he flew out of the city amid their thankful praise.

Nathaniel never failed to make me proud. He had grown so much since our paths first crossed. He was a child of the Order who had endured years of horrific abuse and neglect due to a corrupt few who disapproved of his right to succession. Their final act against him was to inflict a curse that eroded his health by the day while he was forced to obey them.

When I arrived he didn't have long to live, yet he took it upon himself to sacrifice what time he had left to aid me during a decisive battle. I returned the favor by granting him a fragment of my transcended soul that restored him to life to serve as my champion. This not only gave him the immense power of a demigod but also created an empathic link between us. Now at a mere twenty years old he is known across the world as a hero of the people.

"We can't keep this up." Noah appeared beside me atop a collapsed office building. "Soon you're not gonna have an Order left if you let these kids burn themselves out anymore than they are already."

"I know."

The magic used by the Order was fueled by aether—an ambient spiritual energy that many considered to be the lifeblood of the planet. Harnessing this energy taxed the body and soul of the caster, depending on the strength and frequency of the spells. The Order had outstanding resilience to this toxic effect due to their training, but even they had their limits. There were only around thirty combat-ready adults available, which stretched us thin during these large-scale incursions. We had to start rotating out members so that others could rest, leaving us with half that number during optimal conditions for most battles.

We were not entirely on our own though. My best friend, Lyle Turner, was a leader of an independent military organization called PROJECT: UNITY that specialized in supernatural incidents. Although their members were non-magical human beings and they were down to little more than a few hundred trained troops, they possessed advanced technology the most well-funded governments wouldn't have access to for decades.

PROJECT: UNITY's high-tech arsenal, working in tandem with the Alabaster Order's theurgic magic, was invaluable at saving lives, but it wasn't enough. Conservative estimates tallied losses at two-thirds of a city's populace once invaded. Firepower was not the issue for us. I could reduce a city to dust if I wanted, but that wasn't any better than what we were trying to prevent the humans from doing by hitting the button on their nuclear contingency plan and eradicating innocent civilians.

Evacuating millions of frantic people from overcrowded cities around the world at a moment's notice was impossible, but to add to that, many of the first strikes weren't detectable until they had already started. As Hell's influence seeped in through the interdimensional veil between worlds, the demons could steal the souls of those affected by the chaos before even setting a claw on Earth. The results were mindless and hostile empty husks known as the Abhorrent that sought other souls to fill the void within them and snowballed into an ever-increasing wave of fodder.

We needed a new strategy.

I floated through the war-torn streets, parting the mountains of wreckage by telekinesis to open escape routes as I searched for one of my appointed councilmembers. A group of the Abhorrent climbed out from the rubble and headed straight for me, but was struck down with impunity before making it within a few yards. Their twisted forms with elongated limbs and hollow, glowing mouths and eyes were tragic to look at. The scraps of clothing still draped over their bodies indicated that only a short while ago they were perfectly normal people. It was easy to imagine what they were doing when their lives came to an abrupt end: mothers on their way to the market, gas station attendants assisting patrons, children playing ball at recess...

The sound of intense battle grew louder as I closed in on a rather grandiose railroad station resembling a Victorian castle. A peculiar feeling, like an updraft without wind, launched me higher into the air. At first I thought it was Noah using his signature superhuman speed to be mischievous, but then I heard a councilmember's voice.

"Ascended!" Knight Marianna yelled from the ground nearby after I regained my balance. "I'm so sorry! Please forgive me!"

"What was that?" I asked.

"A reverse gravity trap. I forgot to dispel it when we moved on." Marianna was only eighteen and yet one of the Order's best and brightest. She never made a mistake and had a wit sharper than the bastard sword she wielded. This uncharacteristic oversight further proved the toll that these campaigns were taking on everyone.

"You should mark it next time," I said.

"Then it wouldn't be a trap."

"Good point. Tell everyone we're done here. If you find Lyle, have him give the okay to the local military so they can start the recovery."

"What about the remaining demons? We still have a whole section of the city left up ahead," she said.

"Has it been evacuated?"

"Yes, although there weren't many survivors. Ingrid and Quinn's cabals are on their way there now."

"Tell them not to bother. I'll take care of it."

"By your leave, Ascended." A translucent energy bubble engulfed her, and Marianna teleported away.

I flew up to survey the surrounding streets. Sure enough, they were packed with the denizens of Hell for as far as the eye could see. Some stood twelve to eighteen feet tall with reddish-brown bulletproof hides and large horns protruding from their skulls. Their incredible strength could shred a heavily armored tank; they breathed putrid green hellfire that burned away the very souls of their victims when they didn't ingest them for sustenance.

The beasts that fought alongside them were hellhounds. These sinister canines were the size of a small car, with dark, shaggy fur and multiple crimson eyes that sent shivers down the bravest soul's spine. Like their bipedal brethren, the hellhounds' blood was akin to molten lava, making them as dangerous in death as they were alive, if one was not careful about how they were killed. At first sight their intimidating countenance made any chance at survival seem unlikely, but both of these were only lesser demons—one step up the ladder of Infernal hierarchy from the minor Abhorrent. If fighting them was wearing us down we had no chance at holding out against what came next.

"What're you planning on doing?" Noah shouted up to me.

"Getting rid of what's left in one blow."

"You sure that's not gonna tire you out?"

"It might, but this has gone on long enough."

The Order and PROJECT: UNITY were covering each other as they retreated with minimal assistance from me. I watched Knight Alexandre stare a rampaging demon and hellhound companion into submission by flaying chunks of flesh from them with an unseen force.

Is he learning telekinesis now too?

Although I disliked fighting I felt guilty for not participating as much as I used to, but even the little I did was more than it should be. I was one of four deities active and awake in the world today. We were arguably the most powerful beings to come to Earth's defense, and so we had made the tough decision with our allies to conserve our strength for only the greatest threats. Should any one of us fall, we feared that Hell would take the opportunity to overwhelm us.

Despite our agreement I had wiped out legions and rebuilt basic city structures more days than not. For gods and mortals both, repeated use of supernatural powers caused substantial friction, like striking a match. I might not be able to die, but my thoughts became scattered and my patience was fading.

"We're clear, Ascended." Marianna reappeared, levitating next to me. Without any opposition the demons weren't wasting time spreading toward the city limits to find fresh victims to fuel the chaos. They couldn't die in uncorrupted areas on Earth, since any fatal damage would simply send the damned back to Hell only to return again, but here they were vulnerable.

"Wait for me across the bridge where Nathaniel led the survivors and we'll evac from there."

Marianna departed for our rendezvous point and Noah followed me through the decimated ruins toward the horde. The demons turned their focus to me but didn't advance. They stared, circled, and backed away.

"Looks like they're scared of you," said Noah.

"I didn't know demons could feel fear. I must be doing something right."

"Kill a thousand demons and become one yourself; kill a hundred thousand and live to be their king."

"Is that a warning or a wish?"

Noah shrugged his broad shoulders. "Neither, really. Just don't want you pushing yourself when there'll be plenty left to kill tomorrow."

I freed my mind and unleashed a wave of devastation upon everything in sight. The molecules of my enemies were dispersed across the city and the sundered landscape disintegrated down to the soil underneath. Even the noxious stench of sulfur and brimstone was cleared as the particles were erased from the air. Destruction came as natural as a thought to me. I realized that it was a frightening amount of power I wielded and the stronger I got, the more discipline it required to keep the consequences in mind.

"Tired?" Noah asked as I floated back down to him. The barren field that surrounded us now was serene.

I rested my head on his chest and closed my eyes. Fatigue was setting in, but I didn't want to admit it. Noah still knew me better than I knew myself many times and the same could be said the other way around.

"I just want to go home."

We delayed joining everyone for a moment to enjoy the calming silence together, but that was too much to ask. The ground quaked and a fault line split the field in two. A shadow soared out from the depths and landed not far from us, where it revealed itself with a courteous bow. Another demon, different from the rest. I recognized its sleek biomechanical form from a previous encounter. A synthetic musculature that articulated with the fluidity of living flesh was an unforgettable sight.

"I'll take care it," Noah said, stepping up to challenge the multi-armed demon one-on-one.

"No." I grabbed his hand to warn him. "It's a demon lord."

With a thought I willed the Infernal into microscopic pieces, then scattered them through the air and closed the fault.

"I could've handled it." Noah pulled me back into his embrace.

"I didn't want to take any chances," I told him. "It's a *rakshasa* from Hindu and Buddhist folklore. I thought I killed it when I was in Yomi."

Our fear that Hell was waiting for a sign of weakness wasn't an irrational one. They had done it before.

Empress Kamakura was one of the other four deities in our wartime pantheon. She guarded the Asian underworld—Yomi—and was incapacitated for a time after coming to our aid during a battle on Earth. The Infernals didn't waste a second invading Yomi in her absence.

"Let's go home." Noah swept me off my feet and grinned down at me. "I think we earned some alone time."

He was about to take off at lightspeed when there was a crack of thunder and the sky tore open in a sea of swirling red. The ground ripped apart all around us, spewing magma from beneath the bedrock.

"How...?" I flew above Noah to get a better look and my question was answered. "You shouldn't be able to survive here for more than a minute without the chaos."

"This world is yours no longer." The rakshasa was back and it could speak English, though it sounded like it was talking through a mask. "Your travails, the very nature of your plight is chaos. You fight us with one hand and invite us in with the other. Do you not see that the more you resist, the more you doom those you try to protect?"

"I guess I'm a slow learner." I blew the rakshasa to pieces.

The demon reemerged from the ashes coughed up by the persistent eruptions. It was accompanied by a second and then third copy of itself, each drawing swords burning with hellfire in all four of their hands. "The damage is already done. There is no going back. We are here to stay and progress will be made no matter how much you continue to struggle. The Earth is on fire and only we can walk through the flames."

"There is nowhere left we cannot go," said the second. "The hope you so desperately spread is a poison that only increases the suffering as it fails those who believe in it. You make our job easier with every broken promise of salvation."

These weren't illusions of the one rakshasa. We were facing three individual demon lords—leagues above the fodder from earlier and obviously not as simple to keep down as I had thought.

I obliterated the trio with a withering glare, but they kept coming back.

"Stop. They're trying to wear you down," said Noah.

"What am I supposed to do? They shouldn't be able to do this."

"Our bodies are every bit as immortal as yours, but we can end your frustration if you so desire." The trio swung their flaming swords in a choreographed battle stance and launched a barrage of attacks against us with surprising agility. It was like they had wanted me to get used to dispensing of them easily so I would be caught off guard when they were ready to do serious combat.

The rakshasas were masterful swordsmen and the extra set of arms made them twice as deadly. I didn't have much trouble tagging them and only one strike was needed to kill, but they began staggering their return to the field so I never knew if one, two, or all three would be ambushing me. I might have been immortal, but I still had a soul and that meant the hellfire on their swords could prove fatal. The enchantments on our armor mitigated hellfire, but not if it pierced the skin.

Noah was faster than the rakshasas by a significant margin. He covered me by deflecting one swing after the next barehanded with effortless grace until I could react.

"I want one of those swords," Noah said, breaking the first rakshasa's cybernetic arm.

"Great idea, actually. You might want to duck in about two seconds."

Instead of fruitlessly blasting away the rakshasas, I claimed the swords from one and whirled them around me. The rakshasas were fast, but not enough to dodge the turbine of metal and hellfire I created. They also contained a soul and even a damned one was affected by hellfire, the same as any other. I severed their bodies at the waist and they flopped to the ground where their molten blood poured out. The flame on the swords was extinguished along with the rakshasas' miserable lives.

Noah had transformed into a cloud of mist to avoid the blades. "You're not *that* slow a learner," he said with a smirk after he changed back.

"Gee, thanks. That still felt a lot easier than it should've been. Maybe they weren't demon lords. I remember the one in Yomi being pretty easy too."

"Or maybe they just suck."

I picked up one of the swords and handed it to Noah.

"I don't want it if it isn't shiny anymore."

"You can be such a child—"

The rakshasas' bodies turned to ash, mixing with the layer already at our feet. Their blood kept moving along the charred ground making unnatural turns like it was following a track. I went up higher to see what was happening. Once I recognized the pattern in the ashes I knew we were in trouble.

"It's a summoning circle!" I yelled to Noah. "Move!"

He leaped into the air and grabbed me to retreat to a safe distance posthaste. We stopped just outside the circle's blast radius as a colossal hand breached the gateway to our world.

"This is gonna be interesting." Noah cracked his knuckles, ready to dive in again. I wished he had brought at least one of his katana with him.

"Go meet up with Marianna and get out of here," I told him.

"Where's the fun in that?"

The towering demon stopped rising halfway through the portal, but it was already taller than most houses.

"Judging by that thing's aura we might actually have to try with this one," Noah said as we both gazed up at it.

This six-armed monstrosity seemed inorganic like the rakshasa, but it was also morbidly obese and jiggled like real fat. Taking Hell's spiteful nature into account, this may have been a blasphemous perversion of a local cultural or religious icon. Not only did its cat eyes glow ruby red, but what could have been exposed veins or simply ceremonial patterns snaked along its body like circuitry.

"Ah, to be free again," the Infernal's voice bellowed from its grotesque tusked mouth. "I knew the rakshasas would fall eventually and release me."

Noah raised an eyebrow and I shared his confusion.

"You're a *demon*," I shouted up to it. "Why would you be trapped by your own kind?"

"Who cares? It's gonna be dead soon," said Noah.

The behemoth let out a belly laugh that split the land even further. "Traitorous lot, are we not? No worse than humans. The rakshasas you defeated were generals of my forty legions. They sealed me away with each one of their bodies a part of the seal. It appears all three failed to collect enough souls to become the next lord of my domain. Teamwork and ruthless ambition never were a productive combination. I suppose you deserve a reward for freeing me."

Noah and I glanced at each other. This was different. The demons we had encountered so far had always attacked us on sight.

"Go back to Hell, never return, and we'll call it even," I answered.

"No, no, I don't believe I will. There is much work here to be done after so long and the atmosphere is...perfect."

"Then you're going to die the same as your generals," I said.

"Am I? You speak with Demon Lord Vināyaka the Sophist, Maharishi of Obstacles. Simple concepts such as life and death have little meaning to me. All things in existence are a gateway to another and I am the key bearer." It held the palm of one enormous hand over the ground and summoned three more identical rakshasas. "They are mere greater demons in this state, but your souls will do them well as the first step to a fresh start."

"Get the swords and go for the big one's eyes," Noah said to me under his breath. "I'll go from behind and keep the others busy."

He pegged the rakshasas in the head with throwing knives and vanished, allowing me to claim the hellfire swords from them while they were stunned. I knew I couldn't kill them or the fire would go out, so I encased myself in a telekinetic shield and flew away. Noah reappeared in a blur, breaking a knee from each one to further hinder any attempt by them to interfere. The swords shot through the air and snapped against the demon lord's ruby eyes without so much as making it blink. I tried again using the broken shards, but it was no good.

"I will still honor my debt of gratitude," Demon Lord Vināyaka said, smacking away the rakshasas I threw at him like leaves on the wind. "The mortals across the water despise you. I can taste their fear and hate boiling over. They blame you for bringing war to their home and think you a portent of oblivion. Soon they will be your enemy and we will be on the same side."

Demon Lord Vināyaka raised a hand up to the blood-red sky in a swooping motion. Over the bridge where the survivors were gathered, the land ignited in a miles-wide conflagration of hellfire.

"NO—!" I screamed in horror. Retaliating with a shockwave did little more than ripple through the demon lord's corpulence. It projected a shield from another hand, blocking my stronger follow-up attack.

"No more false hope, no more hate." Demon Lord Vināyaka laughed. "A true sacrifice for one of my creed, but I have kept my word."

I sensed such anger pushing its way into my mind. It was stifling, yet it wasn't mine.

A beam of light streaked across the sky from the billowing clouds of smoke in the distance; a roar of fury came along with it. I only caught a glimpse of Nathaniel's enraged face as he approached. His fist was clenched, drawn back and ready to strike. He shattered the barrier without effort and landed a right hook between the eyes that exploded Demon Lord Vināyaka's head off its shoulders. I watched in disbelief as the lifeless body crashed to the ground and fell back through the portal from where it had arrived. The rakshasas disintegrated in Nathaniel's blinding illumination as he floated down to confront them. The look on his face was more threatening than any demon.

"Nathaniel—" I started, approaching him with Noah.

"They're all dead." Nathaniel's fists were still clenched, but the light around him dimmed.

"Marianna? Lyle?"

"No. They went together to make contact with the military."

I breathed a sigh of relief, but it was tempered by how many other lives were lost.

"I told them it would be okay." Nathaniel hung his head to hide behind his long hair. "The children clung to me even when I promised them it was safe once we crossed the bridge. They said I was their hero. I tried to wrap as many of the smaller ones in my cape as I could to protect them, but I wasn't able to save a single one…"

There was nothing left for us to do in Mumbai.

We had failed.

Chapter Two

"We're reporting live from outside the city of Mumbai to give you a look at what's left after a long battle between supernatural beings left no survivors. Now, we're told that the Indian government has officially banned anyone from coming within five miles of the city limits, but there has been no military presence put in place to enforce that. Again it seems that local and world leaders are too paralyzed with fear to make a move or even begin recovery efforts.

"As you can see behind me, the sky is still churning bright red. This is the first time one of these battles has concluded without some return to normalcy and it begs the question what additional consequences we should expect from this loss. I'm here with Preston Nichols, a representative from the Department of Homeland Security, to get his input on these tragedies and what response to expect from our government should this happen back home."

Nathaniel walked into the kitchen where I was cooking on a fire crystal-heated granite grill and noticed the tablet on the counter playing the news. He was still in his white and gray leather bodysuit from yesterday. I had designed his armor with flavors of comic book superheroes in mind to make him approachable as the public face of the Order. The knights shared the same color scheme, though they favored brigandines, hauberks, and plate mail pieces, along with cloaks and surcoats depending on the occasion. Humans were so quick to judge based on appearance and the more relatable style had gone well with Nathaniel's humble demeanor, but I could tell that he wasn't feeling quite as heroic anymore.

"Did you fall asleep like that?" I asked him.

"No. I haven't slept."

"If you're hungry, I'm making steak," I offered.

"No, thank you."

I didn't feel much like eating either, but cooking kept me busy until the next disaster. Besides, Noah ate more than a starving grizzly bear regardless of the fact that, as with all sanguinarians, he gained sustenance only by drinking blood. He wasn't typical of his kind anymore, however. After he died fighting for his freedom from the Archios, the Order helped me resurrect him. The ritual to do so broke most of the undead curse and restored his body to true life, which allowed him to eat again, if only for pleasure, along with no longer being harmed by sunlight.

"—What we're looking at is a full-scale invasion by two or more opposing factions of these creatures," said the man being interviewed on the news. "This is the stuff of conspiracy theorists' greatest nightmares come to life. These aren't just monsters. They're monsters with plans and motives. We're looking at alien life that has been observing us for long enough to mimic our religious icons and legends and use that against us in psychological warfare. Who's going to pull a gun on God? No country wants to be the first one to pull the trigger. No one wants to give the order to open fire on their savior. That's what these creatures are banking on, and it's working.

"We have to keep in mind that these are imposters exterminating us like vermin. They are not our heroes, they're damnation taken form. Just look at Mumbai. They've begun terraforming our world by erasing parts of it from the map and replacing it with this toxic red atmosphere we can see behind us. We have real, tangible evidence now that these monsters will kill our children and leave markers of their victory like in Egypt—"

Nathaniel crushed the tablet in the palm of his hand.

"PROJECT: UNITY is going to stop loaning those to us if we keep breaking them," I said, half-joking. There was no wireless connection in the abbey, so we were set up with a more expensive version that was satellite capable.

"I'm sorry, I just—"

"It's okay. People are going to talk and make false accusations as they try to figure us out and cope with what's happening. Some of it will be hurtful, but we're strong and they're not. We also have each other, so we have to keep moving forward to win this because we're the only ones who can. You're still a hero no matter what they say and you've never let me down."

"Thank you. I know I don't have to tell you that I enjoy helping people and seeing happiness return to their faces. I just want to make a lasting difference..."

After the constant misery Nathaniel had experienced throughout his life it was no wonder he gravitated toward what little joy he could find in the positive reactions to his help. He was like a flower still reaching toward the sun after being stepped on so many times.

"You have." I took his hand and could tell he was starting to feel better. There was a familiar comfortableness whenever we touched because of the link between our souls. "You can't hold yourself accountable for things that happen outside of your control either. You're the most selfless person I know. People recognize that about you right away, so don't let one person's ignorance get to you."

"Maybe I should find this man so he can see that and know we're not the enemy," he suggested.

"I wouldn't bother. You can't concern yourself with trying to change everybody's mind. Let your actions speak for you. Millions of people adore you already."

"They would feel the same about you if you dealt with them directly too. I know it makes you nervous, but I would be there with you."

"Hey, don't flip this on me. I'm not nervous. I just don't like crowds—human crowds. I'd rather deal with a horde of demons than people gawking at me. Besides, I'm not the gorgeous glowing demigod with a lion's mane. I'm the pale guy with the freaky black and white eyes when I use my powers."

A bashful smile came across Nathaniel's face. It was no secret that many swooned over him, even if he was oblivious to it or pretended to be.

"No, you aren't. I know they'd like you if you gave them a chance," he said in an impassioned tone.

"Maybe, but I'll let you have all the fun for now," I said as I stacked four steaks onto a plate. "Why don't you try to sleep if you're feeling better?"

Like any immortal, neither of us could die from lack of sleep, food, or air, but we could still experience the nonlethal effects of their deprivation. I had been told that would eventually pass the longer we lived, but it could take decades or even centuries.

"I will. Thank you." Nathaniel went to leave, but paused at the door. "Do you believe we can win?"

"It's the only option there is." And that was the only way I could word it without revealing my true, less optimistic opinion. "As long as we keep fighting because we love each other more than we hate our enemy, we won't be blinded by rage and lose sight of victory."

Nathaniel nodded and exited in silent contemplation. I headed to my room to give Noah his lunch.

The stone halls of the abbey were unoccupied for the moment. Unless I called for them, the Order allowed me my privacy as a show of respect, though I had verbalized more than once that I would prefer the casual interaction. Each member was raised on the same stringent values and customs as their ancestors and were that much harder to reprogram. A few months ago I had started to build a rapport with some of the younger knights only for all of them, with few exceptions, to begin sliding backwards into their "comfort zone" as anxieties over the war mounted. At the very least I was relieved when they had stopped kneeling and offering to do everything for me as often. The fantasy of having people at your beck and call who would do *anything* you ask without question was misjudged. The reality was worrisome to me in that I could never be sure if I were requesting something against their will that they felt unable to refuse.

Regardless of the formalities, this was the first place I felt at home since my faux-human days. During my travels I drifted everywhere from a wooded mountainside in Japan, to an apartment and then the streets in New York City, and a military base in Greenland with PROJECT: UNITY. Having roots somewhere that I could call my own was something that I often pined for prior to settling down here.

Noah wasn't in our room when I got there. If he wasn't sprawled out in bed watching his TV, rigged to work with an electrically-charged aether crystal, he could usually be found somewhere outside. I checked the row of windows. Sure enough, he was sitting in the orchard near the log cabin he had made for the Order children, so I set the plate down and went to see what he was doing.

The abbey was cozy, for an old medieval building. Much of the masonry was covered by burgundy rugs and scenic oil paintings, or tapestries of the Order's emblem and heraldry of the most prominent bloodlines. Everything was handmade by those who had lived here throughout the years: the dark wood furniture, the fur blankets and leather upholstery. Each room was cast in the warm radiance of candlelight or enchanting twinkle of aether crystals.

I walked instead of floated across the lawn once I got outside. Sometimes it was nice to act human and ground myself from the lofty expectations of supernatural life. We lived on a hill a distance away from a small village that I always said I wanted to walk around more often, but I never followed through. The people had some idea of who we were before everything was revealed to the world. The Order still dressed to blend in out of habit, though they stood out anyway. Their homemade clothes had a distinct modern medieval style that was attractive and passable in public, but a better fit for a Dark Ages-inspired runway show, with linen or cotton tunics and blouses, vests, and leather pants and satchels. They didn't use zippers and buttons were rare. Everything fastened with buckles or knots, and the only colors were black and earth tones. It was a result of using old patterns passed down from that time, which were considered too formal for casualwear today. Every generation tailored and embellished them with some variation that caused the incidental trendiness.

When I approached Noah was sitting with his eyes closed, shirtless and barefoot in the grass, looking quite peaceful. "You smell delicious," he said without moving.

"I made you steak. Are you meditating out here?" I asked, taking note of his cross-legged pose.

"I *was.*" He smirked and opened his stunning green eyes to look up at me.

"Sorry. I don't think I've ever seen you meditate."

"I used to all the time when I was in Japan. It's been a while. Good way to clear the mind."

I took a seat next to him, but he picked me up and sat me sideways on his lap instead.

When we first met I was terrified of Noah. He was an aggressive six-foot-three killing machine with biceps peaked like Mount Everest and the predatory stare of a wild animal on the hunt. Now I couldn't picture anyone I'd rather be curled up with or who could make me laugh like he did. In all fairness, he wasn't as bad as his crass behavior and imposing exterior would suggest if you weren't on his bad side, and there were only a small number of people for which that held true.

"How's the kid?" he asked, referring to Nathaniel.

"Better. He took our loss in Mumbai harder than any of us."

"His problem is that he cares too much. He's like you. If he wasn't four years younger than you he could be your kid."

"Five years younger. I'm twenty-five. Remember I just had a birthday?"

"Oh, right. I forgot how ancient you are now."

"Maybe not like you, but I'm not a kid either, you dirty old man." I sat up to straddle him with a teasing grin.

He groped the seat of my pants with a devilish grin. "Dirty old man? I thought I was your tiger."

"You're a bit of both." I put my hands on the sides of his face and stroked his stubble with my thumbs while we gazed into each other's eyes. We moved in for a kiss at the same time and didn't stop until all of my worries faded away. I didn't think I'd ever grow tired of noticing how soft his lips were compared to his rock-hard body. The world could have ended right then and there without any resistance from me.

"We should go in before your steaks get cold," I whispered with my eyes still shut.

"I'd rather eat you," he growled into my ear. He got up and carried me to our room in a flash.

"You're not gonna eat?" he asked, setting me down and noticing the one plate.

The troubles of the world flooded back. "No, my stomach isn't feeling well."

Noah put his hand up my hoodie. "Feels fine to me."

"I'm worried about everything that's been happening." I held his hand there for a moment, his touch relaxing me. "It's like this tide that keeps pulling people under and there's nothing we can really do to fight against it. By the time we even get to these cities most of the people there are already gone. I just don't see us winning this."

"Not if you set unreasonable conditions for victory."

He zipped into the bathroom and came out with my hairbrush, which he used to scratch his back. "What do you mean?" I asked.

"You can't expect to save everyone or we've already lost. Be realistic. Work on minimizing casualties, not eliminating them, and prioritize your targets. My only priority is you."

I poked his chest as he went over to wolf down his food in bed. "You're just talking tough. I know you care about everyone here as much as I do."

"You're cute when you're wrong, you know that?" he said through a mouthful of steak.

"Too bad it doesn't happen more often then. I think I should speak with the other gods about changing our approach toward victory."

"We don't need them, but go ahead if it makes you feel better."

"I'll start with Gianluca since he's the easiest to deal with."

Noah grunted. "He better not touch your butt."

I ignored his comment, although it wasn't unwarranted. "Keep an eye on Nathaniel for me while I'm gone. I'm worried he might do something that gets him in over his head."

"Babysit the kid who can bench press the moon. Got it."

"Noah, I'm serious."

"I know." He held an arm out to me. "Come here."

I got in bed next to him for one last bit of relaxation before business. The feeling of his skin against mine and even his scent was always such an effective panacea for whatever upset me out there in the world. Just one of his sculpted pectorals offered more than enough room for me to lay my head. Our size difference made it easy for us to fit together, although it was not uncommon for him to be amused by how he could pick me up or lie on top of me with his full body weight. I was of average height yet he made me feel half that.

"We'll find a way to protect this place like they did in Egypt," he reassured me. "The rest of the world is going to shit no matter what, but if we can keep this piece to ourselves it's the best chance we've got."

Egypt had fallen to one of its old gods, Set, who was tricked by the Infernal Kings. After we banished him, his sister and our ally Isis took over what was left of the land. The country was a veritable sandbox until the winged goddess and I worked together to rebuild it. She showed me visions of what Egypt had looked like during the peak of her worship and I filled in the blanks by manipulating matter in the area. An unexpected aesthetic from the use of modern materials—such as glass, plastic, and steel—created a pseudo-futuristic throwback to ancient times. A temple in her honor made from glass etched with hieroglyphics let her light shine across the reborn kingdom.

Refugees from nearby countries flocked to this new kingdom of light to bask in her spellbinding radiance. This was not natural light, however. Divine light deterred hellspawn and soothed the mortal soul. Mirrors were erected to extend her influence and she enchanted large aether crystals to spread throughout the kingdom like streetlamps. It might be possible to safeguard the abbey the same way by substituting Nathaniel. The dilemma was the rest of the world finding out and trying to force their way in after we had managed to keep our location fairly well hidden. Egypt was beginning to have that problem—influence of any kind could only be spread so thin before losing all functional effectiveness.

After a few more minutes of indulging in Noah's iron embrace I pried myself away to get dressed.

"You're not having coffee before you go?"

He was stalling, but I couldn't blame him for trying.

"I will when I get back."

"You're gonna be grumpy."

"No I won't."

"That's a filthy lie and you know it," he said with his fork pointed at me.

I kissed him goodbye. "I'll be back soon, tiger. Be good."

Chapter Three

A cabal of elder knights from the Order escorted me to Rome where they had located Gianluca.

The title of elder was a bit of a misnomer that defined status more so than age. The oldest among them was not yet fifty and maintained the same impressive fitness as their younger counterparts. One became an elder simply upon their heir completing the rite of passage to attain knighthood, although it also seemed to come with an entitlement to some degree of leadership regardless of talent or interest. I didn't mind telling them what to do as much as with the other knights, since most had a reputation for being uncompromising and downright harsh with enforcing their archaic principles. I resigned myself to meet them halfway, but made it known that I wasn't going to accept placing duty and tradition above morals.

"Stay here and be on guard," I commanded the cabal once we reached the outside of the Colosseum. The surrounding streets were desolate, but that could change in an instant. "I shouldn't be long."

I shared a brief, yet passionate history with the charismatic Roman soldier turned God of Darkness. Gianluca and I remained close friends after the romance ended, although I wasn't ignorant of the fact that he would rather it hadn't. This was my first visit since he claimed the Colosseum for his own. Nostalgia brought him to prevent its further destruction during the apocalypse, and he had restored it to its bygone glory by molding tangible darkness into impregnable obsidian architecture.

I soared over the outer wall and down to the emperor's podium, where Gianluca sat on a throne dressed in slacks and an unbuttoned dress shirt made of the same dark matter as the repaired architecture. Scaffoldings, restricted entry signs, and security were gone. Any remnants of the Italian government's presence had been driven out, as it was no longer a tourist attraction. Only sentries of living shadow made in the image of Roman soldiers stood watch.

"Ah, I did not think an angel come to see me this day," Gianluca's thick Latin-Italian accent greeted me along with a kiss to both cheeks. "Roma is never more beautiful than when my light in the darkness is here."

"It's good to see you too, Gianni," I said, still calling him by his pet name, yet not knowing the best way to answer without sounding flustered.

He flashed a charming, infectious smile. "Why you do not come for so long then?"

"It's only been two weeks at most."

I always thought that he first made popular the description of tall, dark, and handsome, with his olive skin, jade-green eyes, and jet-black facial hair. At six-four he had an inch on Noah and a physique not far off in comparison.

"Maybe more, I think." He summoned a bottle of wine and two glasses through the shadows from somewhere else. "Sit, come and drink."

Gianni ushered me to take his throne with such enthusiasm it was impossible to refuse.

"I'd love to relax, but I'm here on business," I said, although I accepted the seat.

"Alone?"

I looked him in the eyes while toying with the prayer beads on my wrist. They were Noah's only remaining personal possession from his past and he had given them to me when we became a couple. "Do I need anyone else here to talk with my friend?"

"No, of course you are always safe with Gianni." He caressed my cheek with the back of his hand before creating another throne out of darkness for himself across from me.

"Good, because that's why I'm here." I cleared my throat and took a sip from my glass to refocus. His eyebrows perked, likely thinking I meant getting back together with him. "Things are getting worse. The Order is exhausted and there aren't enough of us. I know we're supposed to conserve our strength, but I already blew it and got too involved in India."

"You are too impatient, little one. I hear from Kamakura about the demon lord. We still need to learn much about our enemy and make more allies before we fight. You only cause more danger if you challenge the demons too soon."

The worst part about needing patience during war was that it wasn't like I could rest in the downtime and wait to be called. Remaining hyper-vigilant for extended periods was almost as tiring as combat.

"I can't let people die when I could be doing something, especially not *my* people," I explained. "They're family to me now and there won't be anybody left if we don't help hold back the tide."

A flash of golden light to my left and a bolt of lightning to the right brought goddesses Isis and Empress Kamakura into the conversation.

"It is imperative we work solely through mortals at this time and this is why, Young One. Your haste has cost us." The dragon-eyed empress's voice resonated in our minds with the sound of tinkling bells matching those adorning her headdress. "The rakshasa are power hungry cannibals and opportunists. They waited for a tempting enough target to be lured into the carnage and you took the bait."

"Whatever happened to saving the world? Why do I feel like I'm the only one who cares anymore?"

"You are not alone in your concern, Ascended." The faint chirping of birds in my head accompanied Isis's speech. Her face was concealed behind an avian-inspired mask and Ra's solar crown in the shape of a miniature sun hovered above her head. When she placed a compassionate hand on mine the soothing feeling of a mother's touch placated some of my agitation. "Our task is no longer to stave the inevitable end now that it is here, but to blunt the impact to those we cherish and empower the humans to act while working through them."

"So just sit at home and watch them do the fighting?"

"Until these kings appear, yes," said Gianni.

"Which may occur prematurely should we continue to invite conflict," Kamakura said. "This is the time to shore our defenses. Let us not further squander the opportunity on overzealous behavior. And be wary of your champion's involvement. To vanquish Ganesha's shadow is no small feat that will surely draw more attention yet."

"Ganesha's shadow?" I asked.

"Vināyaka was the dark side of the deity known as Ganesha. While he creates obstacles, be they physical or destined, Ganesha removes them by passing on wisdom and knowledge. Despite thriving worship among Hindu and Buddhists, Ganesha has disappeared and the demon Vināyaka endures."

"How is that possible?" I asked. "Spiritborn deities manifested from aether like you and Isis form and rely on the prayers and beliefs of their followers. Why doesn't Ganesha reappear from the aether somewhere else he's worshipped?"

"My thoughts were that Vināyaka had trapped Ganesha within himself, but with his defeat Ganesha has not returned. It could be that they became one at some point in time."

"Gods can become demons too?"

"Beings such as the Infernal Kings are on a level superior to any deity," said Isis. "They already exhibited the power to corrupt gods when they possessed my brother."

"Fantastic." I thought about the information Claudius had given me on the Horned God possibly being a demon. It appeared I wouldn't be getting the support I came for, so I decided to make an exit. "I should return to the Order. Thank you for your time."

The goddesses departed ahead of me the way they came, lacking interest in small talk after having conveyed their messages. I was most disappointed with Gianni. He lived for the thrill of battle and conquest. It was what put an initial wedge between us and now that I was petitioning him to embrace it, he'd rather sit around. The goddesses didn't surprise me though. Spiritborn often came across as something more than impassive behind their cold logic meant to portray enlightenment. Getting them to agree to anything outside their immediate sphere of influence was a trial. I had to ask myself on more than one occasion if they really cared about what was going on or if they were simply doing a job.

Gianni stopped me before I flew off. "You leave so fast. Stay, relax with me a small time."

"I'd love to, but—"

"You are angry we do not fight."

"No, well, yes, but...I don't know."

Gianni took my hand, prompting me to sit with him again.

"I love the people too," he said, looking out at the empty Colosseum while we sat. "Roma is not Roma without them. The people make a life in this world worth better, ah... more worth? Better to live, you know?"

We both smiled over his endearing stumble.

"See? I need to talk more with you." He gestured to his mouth with his free hand. "I need a practice with this to make my English sound nice."

That was when I realized his other hand had been holding mine this whole time. The only excuse I could think of to take it away, without being obvious, was to run it through my mess of hair like it made a difference.

"It's okay, I understood what you meant."

I had actually forgotten what we were talking about for a second.

"We always have a pain in our heart when we lose," he continued, facing me now. "To lose one we love is worst and because we make a mistake is more. But tears will make us blind so we cannot see another victory. I fight many battles and I see to win is not always the same. Some time you fight for one. Some time you fight for many."

"You think we shouldn't be fighting for everyone this time?"

"If it is not possible. We do not know our enemy very much yet. When we do know is the time to decide. For today what is most important is the people close in our heart. I will do anything for these people."

"Even if it means waiting and doing nothing?"

"Yes."

"That's not what you used to say," I reminded him.

"Because I learn."

"Oh?"

Gianni paused.

"I am a stupid man, a fool. I think I know what is best and it is a mistake that make me lose the most important one in my heart," he confessed. "When I am a soldier I practice to have a victory no matter what and this means to wait too, but I do not listen. All I think is with a passion I never feel before, but a true love is to learn to be a better man."

I noticed he was holding my hand again, his fingers between mine, but I couldn't recall for how long. My heart was racing. I was caught in the tide and being carried out to sea. There wasn't a doubt in my mind that Noah was the one for me, but Gianni's magnetism was difficult to ignore when he wasn't trying and when he *was*...

"I see," was all I could muster, drawing a blank on how I should separate us this time. "I should get going."

It wasn't my smoothest exit, but it beat announcing that I needed to use the bathroom. Gianni didn't seem to mind.

"I take you home, okay?"

"You don't have to do that. The Order is waiting for me outside."

"Okay." He stood and kissed my hand before letting go. "Visit Roma again soon."

I left without another word and rejoined the cabal waiting for me. After my head cleared I realized something was wrong.

"Tobias. Why are your swords drawn?" I asked the salt-and-pepper haired man.

"We were confronted, Ascended. The residents are under the impression that our presence heralds the coming of death."

"And what did you do with them?"

"We disarmed them and they retreated." He indicated the melted remains of guns and knives left in the street. "None were harmed as we assumed would be your will."

I had to tell myself that the humans were confused, but it still stung of betrayal and was hard to ignore. We had given our everything to fight for the longevity of their kind when I could've kept to myself and rode out the storm.

"Yes, let's just return home and put today behind us."

"A word please, Ascended." A sparrow swooped down in front of me and took Isis's form with a flourish of feathers. "There is more you must know about our enemy, or rather where they come from, that I have gleaned from Thoth's scrolls."

She cupped her hands and showed me the image of a lotus blossom with Earth in its center. "Hell is not a destination in the way we think of our world. 'Tis not a singular location, but multiple realms in dimensional layers like the petals of this flower."

The vision of the lotus closed around Earth one petal at a time and then went black.

"What does that mean for us?" I asked.

"The invasions are not only breaches in the veil as we had once thought. I fear the first layer of Hell is beginning to envelop our world and with every new layer comes new perils. Seven planes of existence—while still vast or even infinite—converge on top of one another until the world we once knew becomes unrecognizable. As it stands now, there is nowhere on our planet the Infernal denizens cannot travel. I believe they merely restrict their campaigns to where it is most convenient and feign limitations."

"The rakshasas talked about the spread of false hope to make their job easier. We've been setting ourselves up to be caught off guard by giving people a false sense of security."

"The mortals should be allowed the dignity of defending themselves should they choose not to seek our aid. Be vigilant of an ambush in your lands should you draw their ire or the demons' eye."

"Thank you, Isis."

We bowed to each other before she departed. The bad news eased an ounce of my tensions in a morbid fashion. I realized that the situation had evolved and there were more definitive justifications for our retreat from the frontlines that I could agree with. Noah was right about changing our focus to defense. I hated when he was right.

"Back to the abbey, please," I said to the cabal. In a blur we were transported across the planet's network of aether streams. Traveling through these "ley lines" at close to light speed made reentry jarring for those not in control, but it was worth the time it saved.

We arrived at the inner courtyard cradled by flora and epitaphs to the fallen throughout the Order's history.

"How else may we be of service, Ascended?" Tobias asked.

"That'll be all for now. Thank you, everyone."

I flew up and out of the courtyard to find Noah sparring in the training grounds with Tobias's son, Liam, and Rafael at the same time. They had turned eighteen only a few months ago and yet were in peak physical condition, superior to any competitive athlete due to the strict diet and intensive training regimen they had maintained since the earliest years of their youth. I found it funny how the entirety of the Order was in better shape and generally more combat experienced than I, yet still considered me their superior. Too bad my immortality prevented growth beyond what I'd attained by twenty years old. My followers would always have the potential to look more impressive not long after puberty because of their training.

Still, Noah had both Liam and Rafael out of breath even without the use of his powers.

"Go easy on them, Noah. They should be resting," I shouted from the fence. He and Rafael were exchanging jabs until Rafael became distracted by my arrival and was pinned in the dirt by a figure-four armlock. Liam was caught on their way down and trapped by Noah's arm constricting around his neck.

"You kidding me? These shitheads were asking for it," Noah called to me, applying more pressure to Rafael's arm. "Tap already or I'll break it!"

Noah had trained me, so I knew that wasn't an idle threat.

His terms of endearment might have sounded condescending, but they were far from it. He loved to be kept on his toes and shared the same fondness I had for the Order's younger generation. They exalted him almost as much as they did me, once they got used to his personality and unorthodox methods.

"Come on, I need to talk with all of you," I said.

Liam managed to teleport free, trying not to appear winded as he stood at attention with his chest out, shoulders back, chin up, and hands folded behind him. He was one of the fiercest, most versatile warriors I had met, the strong silent type with a clean-shaven face and head, always maintaining perfect posture on top of a stoic expression no matter what the circumstances.

"Having fun?" I asked him.

"I am, Ascended. Thank you." He nodded politely. I could tell by his face that he was searching for more to say. "I always enjoy when sparring feels like real combat."

"Liam, we've known each other for months. When are you going to relax around me? You're more calm around Noah and I'm not the one that bites."

"I apologize. It's only that I'm used to my father speaking for me—"

"You're not your father and he doesn't lead the Order anymore. I put *you* on the council. Lighten up!"

Liam relaxed his shoulders and showed a fleeting half-smile. "Did your trip to Italy go well?"

I shrugged. "Could've been better, but that's what I wanted to talk about."

Noah caught Rafael again right as he teleported free, throwing the six-foot teenager over his shoulder like a towel while sauntering up to me. "What?" He grinned at my look of disapproval.

"Put him down."

His grin widened at the excitement of being naughty, but he did comply.

"You guys are a mess," I said of their bruised, dirty, and sweaty bodies. "Get cleaned up first and we'll meet with everyone in the courtyard."

Rafael attempted to be nonchalant about flexing while he picked grass off of himself. The perceptive side-glance Liam gave him was comical.

"Are you going to be okay, Raf?" I asked after he winced and stopped to rub the elbow that was still recovering from Noah's hold.

"Yes, thank you. Just a bit sore."

A number of the younger knights had begun to imitate how Noah would show off as a way of trying to impress me, but the clash with their usual behavior was somewhat amusing and it didn't stop there. Rafael, who had used magic to turn his hair neon red, even returned it to his natural brown, which happened to be the same shade as mine. I had overheard more than a few "he favors me more than you" debates behind closed doors, and there was constant competition among them to get me to acknowledge who was the strongest, fastest, smartest, and even who knew the most about me.

Every day the hallway leading to my bedroom was decorated with fresh white hyacinths. I wasn't a flower person, but I happened to linger around some in the garden one day while lost in thought. From then on a new tradition was born, which I didn't have the heart to end. It was bad enough I had to make sure each person I encountered throughout the day was greeted in the exact same manner or else it would be perceived as a slight. Heaven forbid if I were to nod at someone without noticing another right away, or I failed to finish a cup of coffee prepared for me because I needed to deal with some ancient horror that had risen to threaten the world.

"You're back fast," Noah said to me as Liam and Rafael walked inside at my instruction. "You must've missed me."

"Always. You were right, by the way."

"Not surprising."

I flicked his arm. "I mean about playing defense. The goddesses showed up for an impromptu group meeting and are in agreement that we should pull back. Hell is already here, everywhere, so they can attack us at home if we're unprepared. I guess it explains why the rakshasa were able to appear even after the city was cleared out. I'll get in touch with Lyle after this so he doesn't charge into anything expecting us to provide backup. Then we've got to worry about the humans going nuclear—"

Noah put his hand over my mouth. "Slow the fuck down a second."

"I can't."

"We're gonna be fine. Trust me. You and I always pull through and these are good kids. We'll come up with something." He put his big arms around me. We kissed until I had to pull away.

"You smell awful," I said. I recoiled and removed the grass from his hair. "And you're getting me dirty."

"I made you a Noah salad."

"You made a mess." I laughed.

"Only downside to having a living body again is how something's always leaking from somewhere and most of it smells."

"That's gross."

"It's true though. You wanna know what else's gross?"

"Not real—"

He raised his arm and went to shove my face under it.

"Ugh! Stop!" I pushed him away and retreated through the front door.

"Those two kids were better at fighting hand-to-hand than I figured they'd be from how they rely on magic tricks and fancy gear," he admitted as we headed to our room. "They're too stiff though. They've gotta loosen up to adapt to the flow of battle."

"They should've been resting. They're two of our best and they've been on almost every mission for the past two months."

"Only more reason it was the perfect time to push them harder. You know our enemies aren't gonna cut them slack because they're tired. They should learn to fight in any condition so they don't get panicked when shit goes downhill or they get disarmed."

"Is that why you've been leaving the katana and wakizashi I made you at home?" I asked.

"Part of it." He closed the bedroom door behind us before continuing. "It's also because I haven't earned them yet."

"What're you talking about? They were meant to be a gift."

He went over to the wall by the fireplace where the swords were mounted and unsheathed one from its scabbard. Constructed from the mystic metal orichalcum embedded with aether powder, the polished surface of the blade shimmered like water and the cutting edge had been refined down to a single molecule. The Order helped infuse it with my telekinetic energy to let loose a short-range, razor-edged projectile with every slash.

Noah handled the blade with a more delicate reverence than anything else he laid hands on, except maybe me.

"You can't wield a blade without earning it," he said. "That was one of the very first lessons I was taught in Japan. I got my ass kicked by an unarmed old man in a robe because I was unprepared to use the blade he gave me to fight him for demonstration. Same reason I lost fighting for my freedom using the Muramasa. You handed it to me and it knew I didn't deserve it."

"You didn't lose, we won together. And the fact that I got the Muramasa from Kamakura for you has nothing to do with it. I didn't think you were so superstitious."

"It's not superstition," he said, looking at me in the reflection of the blade. "A sword is the extension of oneself. You bond with it like a person until you understand each other, but to be worthy of that bond you have to earn it. Skill without a connection to what you're channeling it through is pointless and that becomes more obvious when it matters most. We're just gonna have to agree we have different opinions on this, but I'm always right so, there's that."

His smirk returned.

"What are you going to do then? Handicap yourself by not using a weapon until your ego is even more overinflated?"

"Go back to basics. Build up to what I want to be—*need* to be—to be the best again. Maybe I'll start with Shotokan, throw in a little mix of Tiger style kung fu."

"Are you planning on confronting the Infernal Kings with just your fists?"

"Watch me." His expression turned grave. "She's gonna come for me, only this time I won't be making any mistakes."

Aurelia. Noah never mentioned her by name since he had been freed from her tyrannical grasp.

"No, she's not." I placed my hand on his arm. "It's over."

I knew he suffered from regular night terrors although they were becoming less frequent. It broke my heart knowing from experience how it was to suffer inescapable night terrors whenever I closed my eyes after one too many brushes with death and losses of loved ones. I found that the only thing I could do to console him was to place my hand on his chest until he held it firmly over his heart while returning to a peaceful slumber. I didn't understand the exact reason behind that trigger, but it inevitably worked every time. Trying to wake him tended to result in a hole being punched in our headboard or some other unintentional violent reaction not directed at me. He never remembered the incident when he woke up later. It reminded me of what I had heard about sleepwalking. I wondered if it could have been Aurelia torturing his subconscious while he was vulnerable, so I had the Order ward our room against telepathic intrusions without his knowledge.

They swore with absolute certainty that there was no getting through their spell, but nothing was certain when dealing with the Archios queen, except for the misery she spread.

Chapter Four

The announcement to the Order about our nonparticipation in global affairs going forward went as I had expected. Ninety-five percent of them nodded in unquestioning agreement as any god-fearing religious congregation would. However, the palpable frustration emanating from Nathaniel was about to give me an aneurysm.

"But what about all the people counting on us?" a weary Nathaniel blurted out as I was finishing.

"They'll need to start defending themselves so we can meet in the middle once everything is secure here," I explained. "Hellfire is the only thing that's a danger to me and you. If we get ambushed there's no saving anybody."

Nathaniel's anxious outbursts continued, causing unease among the more reserved members. "How do we protect the abbey so we can return to helping people?"

"We could enchant aether crystals with your light." The suggestion came from the freckled fifteen-year-old, Connor Coetzee. I had given him his first "adult" mission when I came to the Order. Although a bit premature, I couldn't deny his zeal, and as Noah put it, "the kid can take a real beating."

Rhys, one of the elder knights and ex-councilmembers, was quick to shoot down his idea. "Crystals can easily be shattered and those of divine strength cause a cataclysmic backlash when disturbed."

"Easier to defend a bunch of crystals than a whole building during an ambush," Noah shouted from his perch on the overhang above the courtyard. "Light's not gonna do much to us, but it could fuck up some demons."

"Permanent blindness for many at the very least," Rhys said. "With respect, it may be more advantageous for us to erect wards around the perimeter."

"Any demon worth their salt could dispel even our best wards," said Tobias. "Should they come for us they will surely come prepared and in sufficient force."

"Could we not do both?" Rafael asked.

"The wards would likely interfere with the raw energy of the crystals and vice versa," said Marianna.

"Hell's top priority should still be highly populated areas," I said. "Being on a remote island works in our favor as long as we don't do something to alert them. In the meantime we'll make a schedule so one cabal is always on guard duty while we figure out a more effective defense."

The knights bristled with excitement at the chance to make a name for themselves, yet all hesitated to speak out of turn and risk coming off vulgar until one had the courage to step up. "It would be my honor if you would allow me to volunteer for first patrol, Ascended, or perhaps as your escort while the others rest," he proclaimed with a closed fist over his heart in salute.

"Thanks, Quentin. I'm going to leave it up to Marianna though."

"By your leave," she said with a bow and coy smirk at the chance to command her peers. "I'll make sure that our strongest are on patrol when the majority of us are sleeping."

Noah dropped down beside me. "Just put the crystals in metal like you did with my swords so they're more durable. Build guard towers or something to put them in."

"That sounds like it could work," I agreed.

"I know, that's why I said it, *and* you get to build stuff."

I rolled my eyes at him and looked to the others for confirmation.

Tobias answered, "That will certainly increase durability and prevent the disastrous effects of shattering, but embedding aether powder is new to us since it's only something you're capable of, Ascended. I feel it may limit the desired range. We won't know until such an effigy is created to test it."

"Bring me whatever orichalcum you can spare then and I'll try it out with Nathaniel right away. Marianna, I'll leave the rest here to you." I was in a rush to end our meeting, knowing that Nathaniel couldn't hold in his emotions any longer and we needed to talk in private before he imploded. I left with him and Noah while Marianna discussed schedules.

"Hey." Noah stopped me in the hall. "While you're busy setting up mouse traps I've got something I need to do."

"Okay—"

He vanished without saying anything else.

What's that about? It's not like him to be so secretive around me anymore.

Nathaniel absent-mindedly followed me to my room and stood silent in the doorway.

"All right, let me have it," I told him.

"I don't understand."

"I know you're upset about my decision."

"No...I'm not."

I waved him inside and closed the door. "You can't lie to me and it isn't necessary."

"I can't take knowing that so many more people are going to die while we sit here and hide. Children *burned* to death in my arms and we aren't going to do anything but worry about ourselves. Where's their second chance?" He looked at me out of the corner of his eye. "It was a bad decision."

I was shocked at how vocal he was being about his convictions. Shocked, but pleased.

"It was the only decision I could make—"

"No, it wasn't. You can do *anything*. That's what being the Ascended is. You let the elders get to you, the same ones that ignored what happened to me when I was a child because I was in their way. They don't care about anything else but getting themselves through the war."

"They have nothing to do with this," I said. "Keeping our family safe will always be my priority."

"They're not my family and they never will be. When I'm here I feel nothing unless you're with me."

"I didn't know you felt that way. What about Liam's cabal?" I asked. "You seemed to be getting close to them like I was."

"I'll never be one of them even if we might get along. You're the only one I'm blessed to call family and our relationship is everything to me, but I still can't agree with you on this."

"You don't have to agree," I said. "I just want you to understand that I'm in this for the same reason that you are. I didn't tell the Order, but it's my fault that those demon lords appeared in Mumbai and we lost the survivors. The Infernals aren't all mindless beasts. They waited for us to take it to the next level to match our challenge and I fell for it. Just my presence on the battlefield puts everyone in more danger now and the same goes for you. You may have witnessed the deaths, but I have to live with knowing I caused them. I can't let that happen again even if it means you disagree with me and may wind up hating me for it."

"I could never hate you."

I hadn't thought about it with everything going on, but although I had brought Nathaniel back to life and purged the Order of evil, he was still living within the same walls that confined him as a child and sleeping in the same room where he had been abused for years. Every time he left the abbey was a gasp of fresh air to drive out the old wounds.

"When was the last time you slept?" I asked, noting how worn out he sounded.

"I'm not sure." He sighed. "A couple of days ago perhaps?"

"You should sleep here from now on. I think you'll be able to relax better someplace where there aren't as many negative emotions lingering."

The only two available bedrooms were the ones that had been occupied by his attackers before I sent them to Hell. Not much of an upgrade.

"I won't be in the way?"

"Not at all. We're going to be sleeping in shifts anyway."

Rafael knocked at the door, coming to deliver an orichalcum ingot. "This is all we have prepared at the moment, but I'd be glad to ready more whenever you need it."

"I can work with this for now. Thanks," I said.

"My pleasure."

"Can you make a crystal for me before you fall asleep?" I asked Nathaniel once Rafael left. "Don't enchant it yet though so I don't blind myself."

"Of course." He removed the top half of his body suit and took a seat that he appeared ready to sleep in.

"I think the bed would be more comfortable, wouldn't it? Or the couch."

"Oh." He looked at me with an innocent smile. "You don't mind?"

I silently handed him a pillow in exchange for a sparkling aether crystal.

If only there were some way to balance Noah's personality with everyone else's humility.

"I apologize for my anger earlier," he said. "I don't want you to think I blame you for not doing enough. You shouldn't feel responsible for what the demons have done."

"Then don't blame yourself either. We know that hellfire destroys souls so there's no afterlife or reincarnation. The only positive thing we can take from what happened is that at least all those people weren't captured and brought to Hell to suffer."

"I suppose." Nathaniel finished getting undressed and got in bed. "Wow. I never noticed how many pillows you have."

"Yeah, Noah likes to hoard them all on his side like there's a pillow embargo no matter how many I get. I'm pretty sure if the Infernal Kings don't cause the end of the world, the Great Pillow War between us will."

"I can't imagine a more reasonable cause for war."

"Keep that sense of humor. It's something I had to work on to help get me through the past couple years."

"I'll try."

"Get some sleep. I'm going outside to work on the effigy."

I left the room and went up to the roof where the salty sea air off the Mediterranean and bright afternoon sun set the perfect stage to get to work. The first step was breaking down both materials into powder, but I had to be sure not to refine either one too much or they would lose their properties.

I separated the particles and swirled them in the air in front of me, then orbited them around me as a spherical lattice. It gave me an idea of how I could use enchanted powder to create barriers with larger surface area to block energy I wouldn't be able to on my own. For now, I finished merging the two components back into the shape of the ingot.

"I'm sorry to interrupt." Rafael appeared, standing at attention on the roof beside me. "Do you have a moment?"

"Don't worry. What's up?"

"It's about the VIPs you instructed me to watch after. Should I try to make contact with them again and see if they'll join us once we fortify the abbey?"

"Nah. They know how to keep their heads down and are probably somewhere the demons aren't likely to hit. Do me a favor and check up on them though, in case they need anything."

"Right away," he said with a bow.

I had almost forgotten about the Outsiders—a ragtag group of undead not affiliated with any of the three main covens. One in particular who we called Grampy Octavio was once a member of the Strigoi and responsible for my creation in some way that I had yet to discover. Something had turned him senile since then, but he always had cryptic advice to offer, as if he were trying to help me through the fog in his mind.

He—along with two other Outsiders I had become friendly with—survived the initial demon attack on Manhattan that leveled the landscape and divided the island in four. They declined my offer to stay at the abbey to instead help the survivors in New York recover, but I didn't plan on leaving them to fend for themselves after all they had done for me prior to my ascension. Grampy could also prove useful by sharing clairvoyant intel, if we ever figured out what was going on in his atrophied brain.

"How's the arm?" I asked as Rafael went to leave.

His face brightened into the friendliest smile I had seen from anyone here in quite some time until he seemed to become aware of it and stopped. "It's doing well, thank you. It wouldn't be a problem if you need me for something more."

"Nope, I was just checking to see how you were."

"Oh." He sounded disappointed. "Should I leave for America then?"

"Sure, if you have time to do it now."

"Yes, of course, and if you do need anything else once I return I'm always happy to serve."

I nodded, the only response I had left to all the subservience. He bowed again and vanished into the aether.

I glanced over at Nathaniel's room, which was isolated at the end of a short wing branching off the east side of the abbey, and I had an idea.

Hm, I should scrap that and build a tower for the effigy along with a new room for him. I'd need more materials though and we still have to test the enchantment.

I went back inside to find my third councilmember, Alexandre. If I knew him as well as I thought I did he would be in one of the meditation chambers. The tall, dark-haired prodigy was a master alchemist and whisperer who studied and communed with spirits. Despite his size and the almost five-foot-long sword he wielded, he was a gentle soul who preferred building relationships with aetheric beings to people. He lacked Nathaniel's raw power, but his precision in enchanting crystals was second to none and could provide the best chance at a stable prototype.

"How can I help you, Ascended?" Alexandre sat on his knees in one of the hazy candlelit rooms designated for spiritual alignment, a blindfold covering his eyes.

"I came to see if you could enchant the effigy for me—"

The walls and ceiling were dripping blood. This was not normal.

"I'd be honored." He stood and removed his blindfold.

The blood disappeared.

"What's going on in here? Was that a spirit?"

"Yes. You haven't seen me with it in battle?" He sounded more suspicious than I felt.

"I don't really know what you do in battle. It's confusing. I thought spirits were only elements or animals though."

"Many also represent various concepts like their divine evolutions. I was in the process of communing with Massacre, Pain, and Vengeance. Spirits work best in threes and I've coined this trio the Trinity of Carnage."

"That sounds a bit...demonic. Why would you be talking to a massacre elemental in the first place?"

"We are essentially massacring demons every time we go to war with them. The spirits gather whether we can see them or not, drawn to a location by notable events and emotions. I would rather they be allied to us instead of taking indiscriminate action and we know our adversaries can make use of them as well. They're simple and, unlike the Spiritborn gods, only able to perform one or two feats associated with their concept."

"Massacre can just kill things then?"

"Massacre carves fatal wounds directly into the flesh of large groups, which has been invaluable for bypassing the armor of defensive units, although useless against other spirits and inorganic things, or those with instantaneous regeneration like yourself."

I guess that's what I saw in Mumbai when I thought he was using some form of telekinesis.

To demonstrate, Alexandre called forth a scarlet fog palpating with several bloodshot eyes. "Pain here inflicts no actual damage, but causes the body and mind to seize, opening up opportunities to strike or disable crowds when the pressure is too great. And once Vengeance has been evoked it uses a possession technique that retaliates on its own if I'm struck. I don't need to identify the target or be conscious for it to act."

There was still so much about the Order I was learning that nothing surprised me for long. Everyone had their own flavor of magic and I think they sometimes forgot I wasn't all-knowing as most gods advertised themselves.

"Seems advisable not to anger them. I hope they don't have a short fuse."

"Spirits don't experience real emotions, although they can recognize them and respond to aggression. I believe even the Spiritborn gods only emulate them in the way a painting can portray an emotion without the canvas and paint actually feeling anything. We have the late scholar Paracelsus's unpublished manuscripts in our archives if you have interest in the subject. He was someone I would consider to be the grandfather of modern spirit phylogeny, despite the many attempts by the Order to discredit him, as with any nonmember."

"I'd be willing to giving it a look when life settles down, but I'd probably need you to interpret it for me."

"I would enjoy nothing more."

"Why were you wearing a blindfold?" I asked. "And what's that smell?"

"Dittany of Crete. It's an herb native to these parts that aids in astral projection when burned as incense. The blindfold helps to tune out distractions while seeing through the eyes of spirits. There's a minor distortion of the spacetime continuum in the upper thermosphere I was hoping to get a look at from the Astral Plane."

"What kind of distortion? Is it dangerous?"

"From what I can tell it seems more of a trivial anomaly or a quirk in the fabric of our universe. I'm sure Hell's invasion will have many strange effects and I'll be looking to catalog them all for posterity." Alexandre took the effigy from me after I molded it into a sphere. "What would you like the enchantment to be?"

"I'll let you decide. It's only to test the range."

"With some further study we may be able to apply your telekinetic power as a defensive shield to surround the abbey."

"But the demons could still spawn past the shield."

"That is true. Perhaps a twofold defense by triangulating the psychic effigies around the property and housing the one of light inside the abbey as mentioned earlier. Keeping them far enough away from each other should avoid any disruption."

"Sounds good to me. I have to go to Greenland to meet with Lyle about our change in strategy, so you can be responsible for setting it up after testing is done, since it was your idea."

"Thank you. I promise you will not be disappointed." Alexandre bowed and charged the effigy with an azure sparkle. "While I have you, Ascended, will you be needing any more rose incense?"

"No, it was, uh, more than enough. I was under the impression it was just for setting the mood and didn't think the effects would be so *potent*. It didn't really do anything to me, but Noah..."

"Common incenses have their properties magnified when treated by an aetheric infusion, similar to how orichalcum and other alchemical reagents react. How much of it did you burn?"

"It wasn't a one time use thing?"

Stricken with reserved, yet obvious amusement, Alexandre explained. "No. I gave Noah a word of caution along with instructions to burn only a small amount and waft it about the room."

"Yeah, he used all of it at once like a smoke bomb. Noah likes to run head first through caution signs, but this was more of a marathon than a sprint. I have some acquaintances in England that would probably pay a king's ransom for a vial."

"I wouldn't doubt it. It's known to be popular here with knights experiencing certain anxieties when looking to produce an heir."

"Anxieties are something I have plenty of, but fortunately that's not one of them."

Chapter Five

My next stop was PROJECT: UNITY's underground base in Greenland, where a plastic-coated wonderland of technological marvels was hidden beneath the permafrost. After finding out that Aurelia had a porcelain hand in their establishment I stopped visiting as often, but their commander was someone who I called a brother and he wouldn't abandon his team no matter how I tried to convince him.

I brought Connor with me as an escort for this trip. I could be sent across the ley lines to a destination but couldn't navigate them on my own, and long distances had a wider margin of error. Teleportation was a high-level magic that took an enormous amount of energy to use on someone as powerful as myself, and Connor was too inexperienced to traverse the ley lines as accurately as say, Liam, but it was better than nothing. I didn't want him to feel he was in the way back at the abbey because I had jumped the gun at granting him knighthood. He was also perhaps the one slight exception to the Order's solemnity for whatever reason.

"Hey, snowflake," Lyle teased as he came down the hall from his office to greet us. I almost disappeared against the backdrop in my Alabaster ensemble. Anywhere not covered in white plastic was either chrome, glass, or an interactive hologram recently installed to start replacing the "old" touchscreen computer terminals. Lyle, on the other hand, was in his usual T-shirt, jeans, and trusty NYPD cap from a past life.

"Laughing at your own jokes doesn't mean they're funny," I said, hugging him hello.

"Ouch. Someone's in a rough mood. Did Noah forget to put the toilet seat down and you fell in or something?"

"Close."

As we headed into Lyle's office he suggested to Connor, "Why don't you get something to eat upstairs, man, or play some video games in the rec area?"

"Video games?"

"Like, games on the TV?"

"Oh, no, I know what they are. I should stay on guard though."

"It's fine, go enjoy yourself," I told him. "He has no idea," I mumbled to Lyle as we walked away.

"He's not gonna believe what he's been missing. He might hang up his sword for a controller."

"About that. I came to tell you that the Order is out of the fight, especially me and Nathaniel."

"Tell me you're kidding," he asked, clearing a seat for me after the door closed.

Lyle's office, much like every other living space he had ever occupied, was a complete mess. I didn't know how it was possible here since most everything was computerized and automated, but somehow he found a way.

"The Order is burnt from overusing the aether," I said. "More importantly, what happened in Mumbai was a direct result of my participation. Hell's been waiting to bait the gods so they could kick things up a notch and I fell for it. I already spoke with the rest and they all said the same thing, even Gianni."

"I meant to talk to you about Mumbai, but you haven't been answering my calls."

"Yeah, I need a new tablet. The last one you gave me was, um, defective."

"Bullshit," Lyle said of my transparent attempt to cover for Nathaniel.

"I might've dropped it."

"From space?" He retrieved another from his desk for me. "These things have a titanium alloy casing and are covered in the same polymer used in our suits. You could run it over with a truck."

"It might need more testing." I played idly with the icons on the screen. "I've been meaning to tell you that I'm getting into your morning motivation videos."

Lyle hesitated to see if I was poking fun at him. "I didn't think you watched those."

"I thought they were corny in the beginning, but they've been growing on me. My favorites definitely have to be when it's obvious you overslept and don't have a script."

He grinned. "I try not to make those a regular thing."

"What made you start doing videos?"

"I came up with it after we talked about how I wanted to operate my part of things here as a community, like how it felt back when I was on the force. With how much we've been growing it's not possible for me to recognize everyone as fast as I'd like to though. A lot of times I'll return from the field to reports on a breakthrough or a failure that I can't address right away, so I decided to use vlogs to reach out, acknowledge the team, and offer a few casual words to reassure everybody and let them know I'm proud of the work they're doing."

"My leadership style mostly involves me hiding in my room to avoid the cult worship," I said.

"You're not gonna get them to treat you like family by demanding it. You gotta lead by example, the same as you do in the field, and it'll catch on sooner or later. Letting somebody know you're proud of them is one of the best ways to motivate and bond as a team. Hearing those words at any job I've had often meant more to me than the paycheck."

"Compliments are a double-edged sword with them, but I'll give it a shot."

"All right, man. Let's get down to business. How does this play out for us if you guys are bailing?"

"The others gods were saying to 'work through the humans' and 'empower them.' I suppose I could float around after you with a megaphone shouting inspirational messages."

"Dude."

"Sorry. I'm just fed up that whatever I come up with there's always a problem from our own side. Humor is all I have to keep me going."

It was refreshing to speak with Lyle as equals. He was the only one beside Noah with whom I could be a twenty-five-year-old guy and not a deity. Lyle and I had been through everything together since the very beginning, when I could barely levitate a sword and he was the one taking point with an ordinary handgun.

"I have the Order working on setting up defenses around the abbey. Isis dropped some knowledge on me that Hell isn't just breaching the cracks to enter our world; it's starting to overlap us entirely. That means the demons can spawn anywhere they want at any time. We're guessing they'll still be focused on major populated areas to keep collecting souls with as little resistance as possible before coming for us."

"You're *guessing*?"

"Well, yeah. It's not like we have someone on the inside telling us their exact plans."

"And you're okay with leaving it up to less than a hundred troops—counting myself—to save every city in the world?" Lyle said. "That doesn't make any sense. You don't combat attrition by dragging it out even more. Eventually their numbers will be depleted enough to get a shot at who's in charge, but we need the big guns to get that far. I was thinking you were gonna come here upset about the Mumbai massacre and I was gonna tell you I thought you did a great job taking over what we couldn't have done on our own."

"I'm trying to hold back with everything I've got from letting what happened in Mumbai get to me. It's bad enough that Nathaniel is destroyed over it and I have to keep cheering everyone on like it's all going according to plan.

"If I don't make a move, millions will die. If I do make a move, millions will die. I think it's time for the militaries of the world to fight for themselves, hopefully without going nuclear right off the bat. I'm sure Aurelia will figure it out and send them in after we're absent for long enough."

"Actually, she's backed off a lot." Lyle leaned back in his chair with his feet up on the desk and rubbed his forehead. "The heads of state she's been entertaining for months have returned to business as usual this week."

"Why would she do that? Aurelia doesn't give up power. She takes it by the throat."

"Beats me, man." He sighed. "The other Ancients have completely disappeared into hiding like they said they would once the apocalypse got serious. My best guess is that she's a step ahead as usual and trying to smoke you out to take the blame for things as they fall apart, like she wants to do with Gianluca."

"We'd have no reason to keep her around then," I said. "So what if Hell gets her soul? We're way past that. She's not stupid. There has to be another reason."

"Whatever it is, she's the least of our worries. Politics aren't gonna kill us, demons are."

"Don't be too shortsighted, Commander. More lives have been lost to politics than monsters. Figuring out what Aurelia's motivation is has to be a priority, but first can you get in touch with your local government representative and kindly ask them to send some armed forces?"

"I can try. No clue if anyone will listen. Military diplomacy was Rudgar's forte."

"Is 'he' still around?" I asked.

"Haven't heard anything in a while."

Commander Rudgar led PROJECT: UNITY before Lyle and was his mentor from the time Lyle joined. What we didn't know was that Rudgar later died during the mission that introduced us to the Carpathian Ancient, Vyrlakalos. The eldritch horror used his body as a flesh puppet to masquerade around PROJECT: UNITY and gain access to Aurelia's chateau as her liaison. It wasn't until Vyrlakalos allied with another Ancient who took control of Rudgar's mindless visage that we found out. Whether or not Aurelia was aware of Rudgar's new identity remained unknown.

"You know this means you're going to have to share your toys with the rest of the class," I said. "Nothing in any of the militaries' arsenals can reliably take down the Infernals. I'm not sure nuclear weapons can either since they're immune to fire and heat."

"I'm more afraid of the consequences from that than the nukes."

"Why? Nothing you have is capable of mass destruction or radiation."

"You realize what it means to arm the world with weapons that can kill demons?" Lyle said. "It's not a big jump until they figure out a way to kill gods too."

"It's a long shot—no pun intended—to say that magnetic rifles would cause us problems any time in the near future. I've come back from being reduced to atoms and Gianluca is a living tank even without his armor. We'd die to the demons long before that."

"I'm not so sure, man. They're cooking up some insane stuff in the labs. Mag rifles and our standard combat armor are about to be outdated junk. This is more of a STEM research facility than a supernatural peace corps lately. We've got three thousand across all fields and only a hundred troops."

"Three thousand?" I said. "You had, like, twenty a few months ago. Where are you keeping all of them?"

"Dude, we've expanded like crazy. We've got infinite funding from every government that pooled their money into us at Aurelia's command. We have all the best in every field working around the clock."

"And she decided to abandon that legacy? I'm not buying it. How are you keeping track of leading all these people?"

"I'm not. I co-lead the troops with Commander Timmons."

"Sober?"

"Yes." Lyle frowned. "Don't be a dick."

He might not have liked it, but I had good enough reason to ask given his prior history.

"I'm just looking out for you. I know how stressful leadership can be."

"The only things I've been chugging lately are energy drinks and protein shakes, so you can relax."

"And are you eating all your vegetables?"

He threw a balled up paper at me from his desk and we started laughing.

"*Anyway.* We promoted four lieutenants to help out with running drills and local stuff," he said. "Science is its own separate area now. There are connecting facilities for each field—science, tech, engineering, and math—and each of those is divided down into departments with department heads. Totally self-governed too, so no red tape or waiting on approval from anyone to start a project."

"What kind of projects do you have going on right now?" I hesitated to ask. Human ingenuity could be a terrifying thing when motivated by fear or desperation.

"Every day is some new breakthrough and I never understand most of it. The math eggs are studying the dimensions to figure out how the demons travel."

"Eggs?"

"Eggheads," he clarified. "Math shouldn't have letters in it, that's all I'm saying."

"Obviously."

"The weapon tech is more my speed. We've got bullets that release an acid able to melt bone in seconds and another that creates a pressure vacuum inside the body. One headshot from that will take down any demon we've come across, except the rounds are the size of your forearm and can only be launched from a stationary turret. They're working on mobilizing it."

"Anything biological?"

"Nah, but they are doing autopsies in the field when possible to find out weaknesses. Medical Engineering designed a cold laser that fuses broken bones instantly. They've started using it along with limb replacements to get wounded warriors back on their feet. They can clone a limb and then attach it after it grows to full size or use one of the new advanced prosthetics from the Robotics Division."

"My god, you guys have become the new Strigoi."

"We're not that bad," Lyle said, getting up to leave. "Come on, I'll show you around."

Not much had changed in the areas I was familiar with, except for the Medical Ward on the floor above, which had been expanded to replace the neighboring R&D labs with additional triage.

"Do you *ever* walk anymore?" Lyle asked jokingly as I floated alongside him.

"The floor is lava."

"I haven't heard that since grade school." He laughed. "I don't know how a holy order of knights takes you seriously."

"Like you're any better," I said, sneering.

"You got me there."

There wasn't a hard edge or right angle anywhere in sight. The base was set up in a cylindrical open floor plan with a reinforced glass elevator and circular staircase running down the center. Rounded symmetrical hallways radiated from the main rotunda on each level, illuminated by backlit plastic that simulated the helpful rays of the sun for those whom seldom left the base.

"We had to make the hangar twice the size after getting all those donated jets and ATVs," Lyle told me as we took the elevator up from the bottom floor. "It's out along the coast now by Engineering. I was kinda hoping the U.S. would give us an aircraft carrier. Those things are so cool."

"I still can't believe how fast you got this done."

"Believe it, man. Aurelia convinced everyone that humanity's fate depended on it. Manpower and resources haven't been a problem since."

Above Medical were the Barracks and then the Armory.

"We can cut through here to Math." Lyle stopped the elevator so we could get out and head down a new corridor that was still under construction beside one of the Armory's mechanized vault doors.

"Commander," said an older Indian gentleman wearing a UNITY Engineering lab coat as he hustled toward us from an adjoining hall. "Commander, a word?"

"What can I do for you, sir?" Lyle asked.

The man looked uneasy, his eyes darting between us. "With my respect, do you feel it wise to host someone...someone like *him* in a place meant for our safety? Their kind can be unpredictable outside of containment."

Lyle turned to check my reaction, but I had none. "I think you might be confused. Dorian isn't a werewolf."

"I know this, sir. There is no confusion. Their kind all have the same tendencies, however." He smiled at me as if that would blunt his underlying tone.

"Hang on a second," Lyle said. "I just want to make sure I'm hearing you right. You're coming to me requesting I kick out or lock up my friend and our closest ally based on what exactly?"

The man sighed in annoyance. "Please, sir. This is not a matter to take so personal. I speak only in the interest of our security, which is your job to ensure. Certainly I mustn't be the only one to share this concern."

"Forget it, Lyle," I said and started to walk away.

There was a change in the man's face after hearing me speak English. He seemed worried that I had understood him. Perhaps he thought Lyle was taking his pet for a walk or using the base's artificial intelligence, PARAGON, to translate. Either way, it was obvious that he was woefully uninformed. I knew anything I said to rectify the situation would be twisted to make me the aggressor and I couldn't be bothered to waste my breath. PROJECT: UNITY had always been a welcoming place, so I wasn't going to let one person ruin it for me.

"No, hang on because we're gonna make this right." Lyle held me back. "I'm going to take it personal when you're talking about my friend like that and you don't have the authority to dictate what my job is to me. For your information, you're more secure *with* Dorian here than without."

"I do not need authority to have common sense, sir. Inviting a dangerous element onto the premises invites danger. Please understand this, okay? I know you are a soldier, but this is very simple."

This guy is really pushing it. I'm getting angry over him insulting Lyle instead of whatever's being said about me.

"Common sense would be not antagonizing someone you're afraid is dangerous or the person you expect to protect you from them," Lyle retorted. "Have some class at least and express your concerns in private, not right in front of him like he's not even there."

"I'm sorry, sir, very sorry. My concern lies mostly with the company that might be attracted. My city back in India was destroyed only days ago by the monster fights. They shouldn't be allowed so close to us where we are trying to work."

"Watch how you're speaking, man," Lyle said. "You're really starting to piss me off. He's not one of those monsters or an animal you put behind glass. And Mumbai was a tragedy, but he wasn't the cause of it, indirect or not. I was there."

"I see, sir. Thank you for your time. I am very sorry if I may have offended you both." He smiled again, which only came across as more insincere than the previous effort.

"No, you're not. Just get out of my sight until you can either come up with a real apology or need a one-way flight somewhere."

I can't remember seeing Lyle get so heated, except maybe in a barking match with Noah.

The gentleman decided to make an exit instead of a more genuine appeal.

"Sorry about that." I could still hear the anger in Lyle's voice as we moved on.

"It's not your fault. I thought I'd have to stop you from shooting him though. You had the forehead vein going and everything."

"Shit like that is what pisses me off the most. We're not gonna rebuild a halfway decent world with cracks like that in the foundation and it's not what PROJECT: UNITY is about. It's one thing to be afraid or cautious, but we have extensive files on you and everyone else supernatural and all you've done to help. Most of it's mandatory reading, so that's plain willful ignorance on his part. The way he went about it is what really pushed me too far."

"I've heard worse, but thanks for sticking up for me."

Lyle faced me and put his hand on the back of my head for a heart-to-heart. "You just gotta know that for every one of *them* there are a thousand more like me who appreciate and accept you."

"Don't kid yourself. There's no one like you."

"You'll find plenty out there, but remember I always got your back. I don't want you to feel unwelcome here, or anywhere else."

"Thanks, Bromander." I smiled.

"It already sucks that I can't come by you with Noah there. Don't need anymore drama keeping us apart."

"This is all very Romeo and Juliet. Are we about to kiss?"

"I'd rather skip to the end—wait, that's the one where they off themselves, right?"

"Nope. They get married and live happily ever after, so I'll take that as a proposal. I accept."

He laughed. "Good thing I don't have a ring on me, so it doesn't count. While we're on the subject, there's this girl in Math—"

"Here we go." I ran my hand through the leaves of potted plants along the way to wherever he was taking me.

"I'm serious, man. She's something."

"You do love the smart ones, but what happened with Rebecca?"

"She's running Med Engineering."

"I mean between you two."

"We called it quits like two months ago. You'd know that if we saw each other more than in the field lately."

"You know why that is and you could always come to Greece too. Besides, I feel like I'm always asking this and even though it's the same answer every time it keeps happening. I can't keep up with your relationship. I can't keep up with *mine*! But that's because my other half has super speed."

"Rebecca was..." Lyle let out a heavy sigh. "I was in love and wanted to be a couple, but she kept pushing me away whenever we got too close. She cut me off completely right when I thought things were looking up after meeting her folks. She always claimed she was afraid if we got serious and something happened to me out on the field it would affect her too much to keep focused on her work. I considered stepping down to a less active role to compromise, but even that wasn't good enough."

The two of them were in a constant on-and-off cycle. Rebecca was as clinical in her approach to romance as someone administering an eye exam from what I had seen, except for maybe once or twice when there were hints of warmth. I respected her wanting to remain professional and tried to stay neutral since Lyle swore it was different in private, but after a while it became ridiculous. The two of them were never on the same page at the same time.

"No harm in moving on then," I said. "You deserve to be happy. You are mortal and have an expiration date."

"Jackass." He laughed. "But you're right. No point in waiting for the end."

"I wouldn't open with that as your pickup line."

"We're a little past those," he said with a grin.

"As if I haven't heard that almost as much as Noah telling me 'don't worry' right before getting into trouble."

"Yeah, yeah. So, how's it going between you two?"

We reached the mathematics conservatory, which was a building of similar size and aesthetic to the original base, but the feel of a futuristic university. The few differences in layout were a hexagonal floor plan mirrored on both sides with an office, a lecture area, and a touchscreen whiteboard display going down for three floors. At the bottom was a cafeteria and above us were dormitories. For math nerds there were an awful lot of elevated voices and heated debating in various languages. I could have closed my eyes and pictured myself in an airport sports bar during the Super Bowl.

"I can't imagine anyone who could make me happier. It's so weird how much I miss him whenever he's not around." My heart soared just mentioning Noah. "Gianluca—he was romantic and attractive and suave, but aside from the other issues, when he wasn't in front of me, drawing me in with his, well, *everything*, we felt like two separate people without much holding us together. We were always trying to feel each other out yet never quite blending. It's a lot more natural with Noah. No matter what mood we're in, we still seem to get along. Even when he gets on my nerves, he manages to make me love him more."

"I'm glad to hear he's treating you right," Lyle said as we took the stairs down one floor. "He does seem pretty smitten with you."

"*Smitten?*"

"It was the first thing that popped into my head. The dude can't seem to take his eyes off you anytime I see you together. I never would've thought he could stop checking himself out in the mirror long enough."

"Come to think of it, in all the time we've known him I don't think I've ever seen him do that."

"I'll take your word for it. He's been a douchebag to me in every encounter I've had with him."

"He's calmed down a lot lately."

"Probably because he's getting laid."

"I mean since gaining his freedom, but yeah I guess that helps too. He'll come around. That whole arrogant machismo act was really all he had to stay strong during a long period when he felt powerless. Now it's become more of a source of humor from him."

"Hope he keeps that sense of humor if things ever start going south between you two and I need to have a talk with him."

I laughed at the thought of it. "Taking the big brother role seriously, huh?"

"Yeah, man. I did it with Gianluca."

My laughter came to an abrupt halt. "You did?"

"I took a shot at leveling with him when I saw the red flags. It was around the first time you told me you were having issues. He came to me with questions once before that, so he was the one to open the door."

"What questions?"

"Small stuff. Things you might like and whatever. I could tell he wanted to do right by you, so I sat him down one day and tried to lay it all out how things aren't like they used to be. He seemed receptive, but even with PARAGON translating I don't think it really clicked. I mean, obviously it didn't."

I was touched, although not surprised. "You're a really good friend. You didn't have to do that."

"Protect and serve, little bro. Gotta look out for the little guy and no one I know fits that description better than you."

He tousled my hair, which wound up escalating into a scuffle to see who could mess with the other's worse. After calling a truce I returned his cap, and he took more than a passing glance at the first reflective surface he could find to primp himself.

"I think *you* might be the real narcissist, not Noah," I said. "A closet narcissist."

"Sometimes I almost wish I had that much confidence. I'm just trying to work with what I've got."

We stopped our tour not much farther ahead at the office of several strung out scholars. I had managed to make it through the crowd without being on the receiving end of a single inquisitive stare. If this were the biology lab I wouldn't have been able to make it three feet past the doorway without getting hounded for a blood sample or organ donation. The math elites looked more sleep deprived and over-caffeinated than anyone who had seen actual combat. My mouth watered at the sight of coffee cups littering every available space.

"Sierra," Lyle called to get the attention of a woman lost in thought over her notes. I counted at least three writing utensils stuck in her hair, which was tied back in all directions.

"Oh!" She got up with a smile and came to the door to give Lyle a peck on the cheek.

Maybe Lyle wasn't exaggerating about a woman's interest in him for the first time.

"I was passing through to show Dorian around and thought I'd introduce you," he told her.

"Hi, it's a pleasure to meet you!" Then she greeted me the same as she did Lyle.

Yikes.

Sierra just seemed to be a warm and friendly person with less personal boundaries like Gianni.

"You too," I said, glancing toward Lyle. He didn't pick up on what I did, as I'm sure his head was swimming with endorphins.

"I've heard and *seen* such great things from you," she continued without her enthusiasm wavering in the slightest.

Lyle gripped my shoulder. "Yeah, I'm proud to call this knucklehead my best bud."

"Yup, that's me. Although I couldn't have done most of it without Lyle. He's the one responsible for taking down the demon lord in Iraq."

"C'mon, man."

"You never told me that!" she exclaimed, tapping him on the arm. "There weren't many details in the official report either."

"It's not something to brag about. We worked as a team; we won as a team. Probably the most dysfunctional team in history, but we got the job done."

Lyle seemed annoyed that I had brought it up; yet as farfetched as it might have sounded I wasn't exaggerating the importance of his participation.

"He's humble about the wrong things," I said. "But I bet he doesn't hold back the lame jokes or doing that move where he wipes his face with the bottom of his shirt to show he almost has a six-pack now."

"No!" She giggled, so I lifted his shirt to display the goods and her eyes lit up.

"Hey, let's not make this all about me," he said, but I knew he was thrilled to have her attention.

"Sure. Do you mind if I ask a few questions, Dorian?" Sierra shifted gears as if addressing a teacher after class. "I've taken a real interest in where you come from after going over your history."

"Boston?"

She and Lyle laughed more like they were in on some personal joke than at what I said. I was always happy to play his wingman, but he was in trouble if he made it at my expense. I could take him down a peg by revealing how he pretends to answer a text from his mom because he needs to use the calculator on his phone to figure out what to leave for a tip when going out to eat.

"She means the Rift," Lyle said after coming out of his enamored daze. Sierra had a natural beauty even at critical levels of fatigue, and the hint of a Spanish accent complimented that, but Lyle needed to cool it.

"Hilbert space, or rather, what we've started to call Hilbert's Fault," she said with another laugh and touched Lyle's arm, which removed his brain from the conversation all together. "A little word play."

"Who the heck is Hilbert?" I asked.

"David Hilbert, the German mathematician who expanded on the concept of Euclidean space to an abstract vector space of infinite dimensions."

"I went to public school. I have no idea what you're saying," I stated flatly.

"I'm sorry, I didn't mean to sound condescending," she apologized. "Sometimes I forget how to speak like a normal person after being chained to my desk for so long.

"What I'm trying to understand are the principles of multidimensional beings such as yourself or these Infernals. My theory is that immortality is not biological perfection or magical, but mathematical. For instance, the Infernals can't be permanently killed in our world, yes? But they can be in their native dimension."

Sierra retrieved a mostly blank piece of graph paper from her stack of notes and began to draw demonstrations as she explained.

"Okay, so, basic geometry: a line is one-dimensional because it only has length from one point to the next. A plane is two-dimensional because it has length and width, like a square. A three-dimensional object is a cube and that has length, width, and height, which gives it volume because something can fill it. Now, we can say that we are three-dimensional objects too, but in physics we live in four-dimensional space because we are bound also by time, or Minkowski space. Does this make sense?"

"Uh, sure," I answered without bothering to attempt sounding confident.

"I'm not the greatest at communicating my ideas," Sierra said. "It's why I never became a professor. I'm leaving out too much and so much of this is only based on theories.

"If we set the length and width of a square to infinity it will always be 'smaller' than a cube with a length, width, and height value of one, since the square's height is always zero and therefore has no volume or third dimension. No matter how big or powerful we are in our three or four-dimensional universe, we will always be smaller and weaker than a being from the fifth dimension. Molecules, atoms, time, none of it is a permanent solution against them unless we have a way to interact on a higher dimensional space. I believe the demons aren't magical evil monsters, but beings surpassing the limits of mortal comprehension from a higher plane, the fifth dimension.

"Take this stick figure I drew. It's two-dimensional. I can draw it with a sword, or an atom bomb, and it will never be able to hurt us. We can still 'hurt' or destroy it though by erasing it since we are on a greater dimension able to interact with it, much like the demons crossing over to kill us. But even when we 'kill them' we are only killing their representation in our dimension while they still continue to exist on a higher plane.

"I've read the file about how you became an immortal recombinant organism through fusion with some non-Euclidean horror able to crossover and interact with our dimensional realm from the bowels of the multiverse. No matter what state of death your body is in here, your higher self is never actually damaged and keeps manifesting you over again, maybe from shared memory or subconscious will."

"I can be killed by hellfire because I have a soul though," I said. "So can other people with a soul. It erases them from existence. My soul is what was merged with the parasite from the Rift to make me immortal, so hellfire and souls must both be fifth dimensional."

"Yes!" Sierra exclaimed. "And my theory is that the Infernals cannot manifest here not because of any correlation to chaos, but the process of intersecting with our dimension must be very jarring and limits their power. Picture rearranging your atoms to become two-dimensional on this piece of paper to fight my stick figure. The mass-energy loss is tremendous, which would also mean they are much stronger in their native dimension too."

That was a more scientific definition than what Isis said about Hell overlapping our world.

"Dr. Adler has a theory of his own expanding on that. He believes their translocation abilities come from them moving beyond the x, y, z axes of three-dimensional space to reposition themselves. When moving a chess piece on the board it can technically be considered not to exist once lifted in the air, since as a two-dimensional board representing the playing field it has no height value in play. To the other pieces that would look like it blinked in and out of their reality from one point to the next. You would have to ask him what he thinks happens to the energy displaced by it. I'd guess that they maintain some flow to a source within their higher selves capable of absorbing the backlash that would seem almost unperceivable to them."

"Why would they want to be bothered if they're so great then?" Lyle asked after finally catching up. "Just erase us from their dimension like we can do to the stick figure and win instantly."

"They must want something," she said.

"Our souls," I answered. "They feed on them, but our souls aren't any good to them if they're erased. They have to come here and kill us to free our souls from our bodies, or steal them directly."

"Like picking fruit from a tree," Sierra said.

"That demon lord in Mumbai didn't seem to mind using hellfire to erase all those souls there," said Lyle.

"Fear and chaos are still their best weapons," I said.

"Fear weakens us," Sierra added. "No one wants to pick fruit from a tree with thorns. When they come to our plane they must want everything in their favor to unbind our souls, even if it means losing a few to do it."

Alarms and red warning lights went off around the conservatory and on the tablet I was carrying, interrupting our conversation. Lyle took the tablet from me and with a quick response from PARAGON we had our reason why.

We were under attack.

Chapter Six

Lyle was casual about dismissing the alarms.

"Again." He sighed. "It's werewolves. Two of them are outside the main entrance."

"I've still never seen one in person, and the Order gave me a rug and two blankets made from their fur. Why would they be attacking here?" I asked. "I thought UNITY used to help them?"

"We do." A yes/no option was flashing on the tablet screen in Lyle's hands as he contemplated his next move. "About a week ago we heard reports of 'Big Foot' lurking near a town twenty miles west of here. When some of the troops went to check it out they found it was a wounded werewolf. They tranq'ed it and brought it back here to get patched up."

Lyle clicked "no" on the screen, which brought up a second prompt.

"We got attacked that night by what we assumed were the wounded one's packmates thinking it was in trouble, so we had to tranq those too. We released them all into the wild about seventy miles north. They keep coming back though. We thought they could've been starving based on how aggressive they were acting so we left them a mountain of deer carcasses, but they won't stop. I don't want to have to put them down, but I think they've gone rabid or something. I'm worried about our team getting hurt."

Lyle chose "yes" for the second option after another pause.

"I activated the defense matrix," he said with remorse. "PARAGON's AI has been upgraded to handle targeting our turrets and drones on its own. We can watch from the screen on here."

I was impressed by my first glimpse of these bestial juggernauts. You could feel the raw savagery behind the roars that shook the security cameras. They were exactly as they had been described to me in the past: eight-to-nine-foot walls of muscle and fur, with fangs and claws like railroad spikes.

"They just ate your drones," I said. The speed and efficiency with which they rushed their opposition was startling for something so animalistic. "They just ate your turrets too."

"Shit." Lyle grabbed the tablet back from me and left the office to avoid showing his irritation in front of Sierra, who was watching anxiously with some of her colleagues. "The drones weren't loaded with silver ammo, but PARAGON should've reloaded the turrets fast enough. We've got more though. They won't get through those doors."

"You sure about that?" The beasts' claws had already torn through UNITY's special metal alloy with ease—the same metal that also protected them from the lesser demons.

"I don't want to send troops out there for this— Who the hell is that?" Lyle stopped to take a closer look at the screen. "Uh, that's Connor out there!"

"We have to get to him."

"Back this way." Lyle headed for the stairs, but I decided on the more direct approach before my escort was eaten, so I crashed through the ceiling to get outside.

I thought it would be safe here. I won't be responsible for anyone else's death.

Connor was several hundred yards away, engaging both werewolves at the same time the secondary turrets were coming online. I had never seen him fight aside from sparring, but I doubted he had the reaction speed to stay out of the crossfire and evade the beasts' attacks.

It all happened so fast. In the course of a single second Connor slid under one of the werewolves as it lunged at him. I could feel the weight behind its swipe just watching it part the bitter cold air. Connor's sword sliced clean through its wrist as he passed under it and then spun around to cut through the ankle on the opposite side, leaving the werewolf reeling in pain. Its roars cracked the frozen ground around it, but Connor leaped up and over the second werewolf coming to help its friend. He grabbed it by the fur on its neck and plunged his sword through the back of the skull, pinning the beast to the ground and freezing its head in a solid block of ice with a spell.

The level of skill on display within that snapshot impressed me; however, Connor was too slow to dodge the first werewolf's wild flailing. Its remaining front paw struck him in the stomach and smacked him into the hangar doors before he could teleport away. The turrets activated, buying him an additional second to regroup. He froze the werewolf's good foot and conjured a spike of ice, impaling it through its muzzle as it fell forward. The beast couldn't save itself, but its thrashing caught Connor with a claw between the ribs and shattered the ice encasing its friend's head.

Connor's sword snapped at the hilt. That remained a remarkable feat of strength even for a supernatural being, but orichalcum, like many legends, was overstated in its greatness. When orichalcum was discovered centuries prior to the invention of synthetic materials and modern manmade alloys, it might have seemed impervious to weapons of that period.

The blade came free from the second werewolf's skull, whose roar then freed the first from its glacial impalement. Before the situation could get any worse I blasted them both into chunks of meat and stopped the last hail of bullets from the turret in midair.

"Are you all right?" I shouted as I flew down to him.

"My sword is broken."

"You're bleeding." I peeled away the blood-soaked leather and chainmail of his armor to get a better look at the gaping puncture wound. "Can you heal yourself?"

"Yes, I'll be fine." He flinched and held his hand over the wound to mend the skin with a sapphire glow, but it didn't heal all the way.

"Why did you come out here by yourself?" I asked. "You could've been killed."

"I was to guard you. That was why you brought me as your escort, wasn't it?"

I didn't want to tell him it was so he wouldn't feel useless at home, although his combat skills *were* leagues beyond what I had expected.

"Yes, but you should've found me first. What if the enemy had already made it inside?"

"Forgive me, Ascended, I hope you aren't cross. I thought to head them off before that happened."

"Not at all, I was just worried, but I'm proud of you. I never knew you were so good."

"Thank you!" Connor smiled from ear to ear and showed no signs of still being in pain. "I broke my sword though. It took me months to forge it properly."

"I'll fix it for you." I took it from him after he retrieved the pieces. "Let's get out of the cold and get you patched up."

A door to the side of the hangar opened. Lyle finally made it to us, along with a number of troops. He was wearing his futuristic helmet, which interfaced with the base's AI through an implant in the back of his neck. I noticed he hadn't removed the smiley face sticker I put on the side during one of my previous visits.

"That was something else," Lyle said to Connor. "You cut right through them."

"Thank you, but orichalcum can cut through anything."

"Well, the way you cut off both paws like that was pretty cool."

"Oh, I was only doing what I was taught. You're supposed to sever an appendage on each side where it's weakest to keep it off balance if you don't have silver. Everybody knows that."

"Everybody knows that, Lyle. *Everybody*," I said. Lyle put his middle finger in my face. Connor was trying so hard to conceal that he was still smiling.

"Commander, we've got more company," one of the troops said. I flew higher to see where they were looking through their visors. On the horizon was a line of werewolves. "They're backing off."

"They're scared of you," Lyle yelled to me.

"I get that a lot lately," I said. Once they were gone I floated back down.

"Glory to the Ascended!" Connor cheered, holding his side in pain.

"Be calm, knight." I smiled back at him. I repaired his sword with a motion of my hand, including some of the silver bullets strewn across the ground and a few decorative engravings. "Here. Now you've got a blade as sharp as any of Noah's. Don't tell him about the silver though or he'll steal it."

"I'll treasure it forever." He beamed.

"I'm going to set up a repair ticket with Engineering. Take Connor down to see Medical," Lyle said to the troops.

"You can't stay here," I told Lyle once everyone was out of earshot. "Come with me to the abbey."

"Not this again, man." He groaned. "I've got a good thing here that I want to see through. You have your team and I have mine. I think it's kinda cool that you and I are both leaders in this. Giving that up would only mean weakening our joint effort."

"This doesn't scare you?" I pointed to the claw marks on the hangar door.

"After what we've been through? Not a bit. These were young. You can tell by the light brown fur. The older ones are darker or gray depending on where they come from and Connor would've been a smear on the ice."

"That doesn't convince me that you'll be safe here. There were tons of them out there."

"It's not a big deal. The hole in the ceiling you made might be an issue though."

"I can fix it, but that doesn't stop whatever's going on."

"We'll keep a few turrets loaded with silver rounds and have better stuff online soon. They can be loaded up with tranqs pretty easily too. Maybe all the craziness in the world got to them. That might be why they're on the move in the first place."

"What if they're teaming up with the demons?" I asked. "I don't like it."

"You don't have to because it's not up for discussion. Remember you came here to tell me how I'm on my own with the invasions now."

"I didn't mean *you* specifically. Get off the frontlines like you were saying and go get yourself a girlfriend."

Lyle headed inside with me chasing after him. "You're not gonna talk me out of this, little bro. Someone's gotta keep this train on the rails."

"At least stick to recovery missions!"

He turned and tossed me the tablet as he continued down the corridor, walking backwards with a sarcastic expression on his face. "Hey, enjoy your time off, all right? Maybe use that to send me a pic of you on the beach drinking from a coconut so I know you're not pushing yourself too hard."

"That's not fair and you know it. My hands are tied."

"What were you saying about politics taking more lives than monsters? And besides, you don't even use your hands!"

It was early in the morning when Connor and I made it to the abbey where the Order had been keeping busy under Marianna and Alexandre's instruction. Lyle set us up in one of UNITY's hypersonic jets so the flight wasn't long. Connor spent the first half of the trip sleeping off the painkillers he was given and the second half jabbering about anything that passed through his mind, from his performance against the werewolves to the war. Before I could respond to one topic he had already moved on to three more until I gave up and questioned if this was really an improvement over the others' reticent behavior.

Marianna and her aunt Helena were standing with the effigy on the cabin roof in the orchard. Once the jet departed for Greenland they came over to greet us along with

Alexandre. There was a good chance that they had been working through the night, but the Order typically woke up everyday around four in the morning like they had a barn to raise.

"Welcome back, Ascended," Marianna said with a bow. "We've just finished testing the positions for the effigies and are ready for the real ones to be made."

"Great. I'll be building a short tower off the east end of the abbey where Nathaniel's room is now. We'll place the effigies with my power at the ranges you narrowed down and one in the tower with Nathaniel's light."

"Like a lighthouse," Connor chimed in.

"Connor, please prepare the children's breakfasts and then take the list Pavel left in the kitchen to the butcher for this week's stock," Helena said to his dismay.

"Can someone else do it?" I suggested to help him out. "Connor's had a long day and should rest."

"But I'm not tired," he said. "I slept on the plane."

"Okay, fine. Go do your chores."

"Actually I am a little tired. I did just fight off *two* werewolves," he boasted with about as much subtlety as one could expect from a typical fifteen year old.

Alexandre, Marianna, and Helena stared at him in distrust. They wanted to challenge his claim but were waiting for my response first.

"He did," I said. "I was impressed, especially with the ice magic."

"Ice?" Marianna questioned. "Connor hasn't mastered cryothurgy to combat levels. Ice is a secondary element that takes more communion with fire and learning to negate heat than he's ever experienced. Unless it's ice channeled through a spirit like Alex can do, but he's not a whisperer."

"I saw it with my own eyes."

"We don't doubt what you saw, Ascended. You were in Greenland where ice is prevalent," Alexandre added. "Connor was most likely essence tapping from the environment."

"What's essence tapping?" I asked.

"It's how we teach the children to conjure elements by first learning to induce their effects in a natural setting,"

Helena explained. "Aether is a unique energy in that it takes on the properties of other energies that it synergizes with. It's the basic principle behind why we can enchant aether crystals. To make fire in a place that is already sweltering, or ice in a frozen tundra, is a remedial application of aether that complements natural laws. True conjuring goes against nature by bending it to your will, such as creating ice in a desert."

"What color fur did these werewolves have?" Alexandre asked.

Connor was about to lose it. There was anguish in his eyes as he tried to control his frustration. "What does it matter?" he said through gritted teeth. "I still fought as hard as any of you could."

"It doesn't matter, Connor." I patted him on the shoulder. "Results are all that matter and you did great."

"Thank you, Ascended. May I be excused?" he asked quietly, not making eye contact with anyone.

"Sure." I waited for Connor to leave before addressing what happened with the group. "What was that about?"

"Our apologies. Connor is far too emotional and impulsive," said Helena. "He's every bit of his mother and father."

"I meant why did you have to tear him down like that? We should be proud of his accomplishment."

"We meant no harm," Marianna said. "Connor always talks himself into predicaments that are over his head and it can be dangerous. A lack of modesty is a prescription for failure."

"I'd rather you were more gentle about it. I think you underestimate him. I know I did."

"We're sorry," said Alexandre.

"Tell him that, not me." I couldn't think of anyone else in the Order that he looked like, or had his last name. "Who are his parents?"

"They aren't with us anymore," Helena said. "His father was taken from us last year and his mother only months later with several others. It was a tragic loss. They were brilliant, *brilliant* spellswords who specialized in hexes."

It was rare for both parents to be in the Order. Most only had a single family member that raised them and it wasn't always a parent. Some didn't have any and were taken care of by an assigned guardian. The Order mated—as primitive as it sounded—only to produce offspring with the best magical aptitude. Since you could only be born into the Order or recruited as an infant, significant others were left out in the cold. It was frowned upon to remain in contact with them for fear of sharing secrets or tainting their isolated lifestyle.

"I'm not familiar with hexes."

"Most aren't," she said. "Many attempt to learn, but usually only one comes along every few generations who is able to grasp them with any proficiency.

"Hexes are the most complex system of aether magic that work through conditional triggers and a substantial level of creativity and conceptual knowledge. A spell is inscribed onto the personal reality of a target, which uses their own energy to activate instead of the caster's. It's exceptionally troubling to dispel since it exists behind most defenses. We've witnessed them vanquish a demon lord by stacking layers of hexes that made any action it took cause instant necrosis, passing amnesia, painful mutated bone growth, or a purifying light burst. Sometimes it all happened at once. The beast couldn't so much as blink or take a step without a horrible fate befalling it."

"I see. So how did they die?" I asked.

"His parents were eccentric and boisterous," Helena continued. "They didn't fit in well with most and refused to be part of a cabal with anybody other than themselves. It isn't something our traditions allow under normal circumstances, but they were an extraordinary talent and not many wanted to cooperate with their excitable ways. Connor was mostly isolated from the rest of us during his younger years because of this, not unlike Nathaniel, only with very different intentions and results.

"Sadly, they got in over their heads one too many times, as Connor is prone to do. His father sacrificed himself to save his mother during a trip to the Astral Plane. She was never the same after and that distraction cost her when she conceded to working in a full cabal. Instead of learning from their mistakes, Connor has done everything to emulate them in what I can assume is an attempt to keep their memory alive."

"I think he still sleeps with that pillow doll his mother made for him—"

I shot Marianna a look to stop her from turning that into an insult.

"I know what it's like to lose both parents unexpectedly," I said. "All the more reason why you should be lifting him up, not putting him down. I do agree I don't want him or anybody else getting in over their head. That's my biggest fear with just about everybody. Let him cool down for now while we finish out here."

"I'll fetch more orichalcum and then prepare the children's breakfast, if Connor hasn't already," said Alexandre.

"I'm going to find Nathaniel so we'll be ready to enchant."

I almost made it to the door when I was tackled from behind. As we went tumbling across the grass I could tell by the size of the arm around me that it was Noah. He was careful not to hurt me.

"Hey," he said, locking his tree trunk-sized legs around me too.

"This is not a normal way to greet somebody."

"I don't see the problem."

"I'm about to give you one if you don't let go."

"I got something to show you first." He released me and lay back on the ground so I could turn to see him. I noticed what it was immediately. His entire right arm had been tattooed in a colorful Japanese style sleeve. "Like it?"

Starting from his rounded deltoid was a tiger facing down the side to a fish in a pond with cherry blossoms on the surface.

"Very sexy. It definitely suits you."

"It's me and you," he said in a far more sincere tone than usual. "Careful, the ink still needs to finish setting."

"Why am I a fish?"

"Koi have a lot of symbolism behind them, but I chose it for the strength and luck you bring me. There's also a legend that if one is able to prove itself by swimming up a waterfall it'll turn into a golden dragon, so I thought it fit with your ascension."

I couldn't take my eyes from the ink. "Wow, Noah, that's really sweet. I never would've thought a fish could be made into such a romantic gesture."

"See the tiger reaching to eat you?" He flashed a roguish grin that showed his fangs.

"I don't think that one needs any explanation."

I pressed my lips to his to express my gratitude and passion. Sadly, that indulgence only lasted until I remembered I had to find Nathaniel and finish the effigies.

"Hey, get back here. I wasn't done with your face," Noah protested when I got up to leave.

"Then come with me and you can have the rest after I do something."

Chapter Seven

Alexandre had already dropped off a stack of orichalcum ingots by my bedroom door when Noah and I went inside to check for Nathaniel. I didn't have much faith in the effigies getting us through an Infernal onslaught. I didn't think Noah did either. The plan was busy work and I knew it. Everyone needed something to say we were taking an active role in our fate, but when the end came we'd still need to think on our feet no matter how many walls we built in advance. Each second we spent with those we loved was more precious than any magic crystal, because we never knew if that moment would be our last.

We found Nathaniel sitting in his room at the edge of the bed. He was dressed for battle and his hands were clasped to his forehead in prayer, but he stopped once he heard us.

"Everything okay?" I asked.

Noah closed the door behind us and leaned against it with his arms crossed.

"Yes."

His face told a different story. I had thought I sensed something odd coming from him on the way over, but I pretended to buy his unconvincing answer for the time being.

"How'd you sleep?"

"Very well," he said, brightening up a little. "I don't think I've ever slept that well in my life. Your bed is a lot more comfortable than mine."

"That could be it. Yours is too small for you," I said, even though I knew it had more to do with the bad memories in his.

I hadn't been in Nathaniel's room too often, but I did notice a change in the sparse décor. He had a plethora of new knickknacks and papers. Most of it looked like junk: bottle caps, a worn string bracelet, an old MP3 player, a piece of candy, and a ratty doll made of straw and cloth. The papers had notes scribbled on them and drawings in bright primary colors...of Nathaniel.

"Where did you get these?" I asked. There had to have been dozens.

"They're from the children we've helped. I go back to visit them in the refugee camps whenever I get a chance."

"When did you have time to do that?"

"When I should be sleeping, I suppose, or after a mission when I fly back instead of teleporting with everyone else."

"That's why you're so tired? I thought it was because—"

"I know what you thought—and you're right—but there was more to it that I didn't want to say. I was afraid you'd tell me to stop. The more I am away from here the better I feel. Not only the children, but everyone I've met, I give them hope just by seeing me and they give me peace. I'm doing what you did for me."

"I wouldn't have stopped you." I sat on the floor across from him.

"Even if he did, you have to do what *you* feel is right for you," Noah told him. "You're nobody's slave. People weren't meant to follow orders, even from a god. Someday you might see or know something he doesn't and if you don't act it could cost you everything."

Nathaniel was silent, taking in what we were saying. He picked up one of the crayon drawings of him.

"Shanghai is under attack," he said.

"How do you know?" I asked.

"I overheard it when I was in town earlier. I went to see if anyone needed my help. Some people have homes where they feel they belong. I feel I belong wherever people need me. It's what makes me feel alive." He looked me straight in the eyes. "I want to go to Shanghai. Please."

"Then go, kid," Noah answered before I could.

Nathaniel didn't take his eyes from me, waiting for my consent.

"You have to go where you feel complete, but promise me one thing," I said. "Focus on saving the civilians and leave engaging the demons to the army. No matter how they try to antagonize you, be in control."

"I swear it."

Something about him changed in that moment. I could see it in his eyes. The last remaining shackles of his past crumbled away. The final remnants of the damaged little boy inside faded, giving rise to the adult he had become but always shied away from embracing.

"And if Lyle is there—"

"I'll look after him."

"Have the others teleport you, but first I need four crystals. One of them with your best light enchantment."

Nathaniel conjured the most flawless aether crystals that made the light around them dance like diamonds in the sun. It was a shame I would be breaking them down into dust.

He clutched the fourth crystal and charged it with his power. The light surrounding his hand was different than the usual stellar glare—it shone in a hypnotizing fractal pattern of white, yellows, and very pale blues.

"That's new," I said.

"I see it all the time in my dreams right before I wake up," he said. "I'm not trying to do it. This is the first time I've seen it appear in person myself."

During the ritual meant to resurrect Noah, an ancient relic of the Order known as the Empyrean Jewel of Light had fused with Nathaniel's soul by accident and given him the rest of his powers. We didn't know much about the jewel except that it was the crystallized essence of a Spiritborn god who had been defeated by the last Ascended centuries ago.

Nathaniel had a bit of a unique connection to the aether to begin with due to the curse meant to kill him. It allowed him to increase his resilience to most forms of damage with the more he absorbed, but not without the risk of constant lethal aether poisoning. After the life-giving energies of the Rift I granted him made him immortal, there seemed to be no limit to the amount of aether he could take in safely and use as a secondary source to grow his powers.

"It's a mandala," said Noah. "They're a spiritual symbol in Buddhism and Hinduism used for meditation or to mark sacred places. Kid must have seen it when we were in India."

"I saw it in my dreams before that."

"As long as it isn't harmful we can discuss it another time," I said.

Nathaniel went back to enchanting the crystal. The light shone with increasing intensity until I could no longer see the scintillating mandala. Closing my eyes and turning away didn't help. It felt as if the light was penetrating the back of my skull.

"Way too bright," Noah said. I could hear similar complaints coming from down the hall.

Nathaniel placed the finished crystal in my hand and left before my vision returned. I used my powers to feel around the room and tried hiding the crystal under the bed, but the light cut through it the same as glass.

I worked fast, still without my sense of sight, and merged the crystals with the orichalcum. It had no effect on dimming the one of light, so I figured now would be as good a time as any to build that tower and get it out of the way.

"Stay close," I told Noah as I started tearing up the walls.

This was simple construction that only required me to reorganize the stone building blocks already present. I could feel that nobody was in the hall, which let me take what I needed from there without concern. I built a spiral staircase two stories up and moved Nathaniel's room on top of it while Noah and I were still inside, then went higher to give him a vaulted cathedral ceiling and wider, circular perimeter walls. Above the ceiling I made an enclosed platform to isolate the effigy. To complete the new layout I placed the spare windows from the old hallway around the room to give Nathaniel a full view of the island in all directions. From up here it was almost as if you weren't in the abbey at all.

"That was easy enough," I said, disintegrating everything in the room except for his clothes and the gifts.

"Still can't see shit."

I flew us out to the cliff with the rest of the effigies where we could see again once our eyes adjusted. At this distance the mandala was visible and engulfed the entire abbey. Marianna came out to escape the light with Alexandre and two other cabals that gathered around us.

"Can you bring me more orichalcum? I can polish it down into mirrors to deflect some of the glare," I said. "Then I'd like you to furnish Nathaniel's new room up there with the best of everything."

"That could take a while, but we'll all work on it," she said.

"I'm ready to enchant these too," I said to Alexandre and moved the effigies in front of me. He cast a spell that activated the crystal portion to accept energy.

"Just like when enchanting Noah's blade, you'll need to be careful how much force you put in or the effects could be disastrous," Alexandre warned.

I interacted with the effigies the same way I would if I were trying to crush them. They absorbed the kinetic energy from my powers until they began to vibrate.

"Perfect," Alexandre said, signaling me to stop. "We'll take them to their positions and add regulating wards to channel the energy into a barrier."

Noah rolled on his back in the grass next to me to sun himself while I oversaw the completion of our defenses. "Not to ruin your joy, but can you ever go outside without getting dirty?" I asked with a laugh and rubbed his stomach. His abdominals felt like smooth stones under his golden tan skin, the lower pairs set between the accentuated taper of his waist that created a suggestive V leading downward.

"Nope." He winked at me and stuck his bare foot in my face.

"I have some unfortunate news." Marianna approached with the orichalcum. "Our reserves are running low."

"How low?" I asked.

"We only have six ingots left. We haven't sent a cabal to gather ore in some time with everything going on. I should have planned for this better."

"It's all right. Where can we get more?"

"It can be found on Earth in veins along the bottom of the Mediterranean, but we get most of ours from the Astral Plane where it's more common. The ore looks like dull gray crystals there instead of rocky metal lumps. It comes already saturated with aether, giving it its super durability. It saves a step, but is more difficult to forge because of it."

"We'll conserve what we have for now. I don't want to send anyone too far in a time like this and we can always reuse these later. I just want to make sure we don't have mirrors that can break."

I flattened and polished the ingots, then set them up to divert some of the brightness into the sky. Even with the mirrors in place, the luster penetrated its way into the abbey but was not anywhere near as harsh. I could see the dust particles in the air and the flecks of minerals in the stone walls glittering clear as day without the need for any other light source.

"Everything is in place," Alexandre said.

"I don't see anything."

"Your powers don't have much visual effect, but I assure you the force field is up. Only slow-moving gasses without significant resistance to the kinetic energy can permeate it so we won't suffocate."

I could feel the barrier reverberate when projecting my telekinesis against it. The most I saw was a ripple in the air similar to a heat wave, which was no different than any application of my powers unless I was affecting an object.

More of the Order came out to see what was transpiring, including Connor, who looked like he had just fallen asleep in his pajamas.

"They should get that metal while things are quiet," Noah said.

"We could break down your swords if you're not going to be using them," I said, swatting his foot away when he put it in my face again. "I guess we can send a small group. Marianna, where's Liam? I thought he'd be more interested in this."

"He's...in town bringing his mother flowers. I told him he should be here for this."

As the former leader of the council, Liam's father had bent the rules quite a bit, such as allowing Liam to have a relationship with his mother. Both traditionalists and their more progressive counterparts within the Order were never too thrilled about being forced to accept the obvious nepotism.

"Are you talking about orichalcum?" Connor asked. "I can go fetch some."

"I've never been to the Astral Plane. How dangerous is it?" I asked.

Connor's enthusiasm faded when he realized he had offered to transcend the mortal realm and not just take a quick run to the storeroom.

"Much of it depends on random chance. However, there are bird and mouse spirits there, which could kill him instantly upon entry," Marianna answered.

"Are you teasing him again or being serious?"

"I'm serious. Everything is deceptive there. We never go alone and without a clear plan and supplies for that reason. You never know exactly where you'll wind up when you enter either. It's like falling asleep and entering a dream. None of reality's laws apply, so it's extremely disorienting even to someone with experience."

"The Ascended and I kill werewolves. Birds and mice don't scare us, right, Ascended?" Connor grinned and flexed like we'd seen Noah do countless times. He was only fifteen and he already had bigger arms than me.

"When did you kill a werewolf?" Noah sat up in interest.

"Two of them attacked the UNITY base when we were there," I said.

"Yes, and there was a pack of them watching, but they ran off with their tails between their legs when they saw what the Ascended and I could do," Connor added.

"That's pretty much how it happened," I said, seeing Noah's doubtful expression. "Lyle's team brought one in for medical treatment and they've been pissed about it since."

"Damn, I wanna fight some of the big dogs," said Noah. "It's been a while."

"Lycanthropes are intelligent and honorable creatures." Tobias came to join the conversation with the other elders. "They are not ones to bite the hand that feeds them, so to speak."

"I was told they may have been driven into a frenzy because of Hell's presence."

"That's a reasonable assumption," said Tobias. "Although in much fewer amount than the legion of Infernals, the wolves can be equally bothersome should they begin to interfere."

"If these effigies work out then we can pass some on to UNITY."

"You should make them look like me," said Noah.

"I'm sure Lyle would love that. When Liam gets back we'll talk about a trip to the Astral Plane. Connor, if you're not going to sleep, why don't you train with Noah?"

"Really?" Connor was ecstatic. Noah had neglected him recently to spar with Nathaniel, Liam, and Rafael instead. I knew it bothered Connor, but he was too scared to speak up and get on Noah's bad side.

"Yeah, I'll smack him around for a bit," Noah agreed.

"Good. You guys have fun. I need to check on something."

Our defenses in place, our roles defined, all that should be left to do was sit and wait for the worst. There was so much that could be done around the world to help it recover and I was here hiding. Part of me was afraid that history would repeat itself as it usual did and something would happen to my new family should I leave them unattended. The other part was afraid for the world.

I returned to my room and retired to the big leather chair across from the fireplace, with UNITY tablet in hand, and turned on the TV to get a glimpse through my window to the world. Channels had begun disappearing as the cities they broadcasted from were wiped off the map or the people running them abandoned their posts to spend what time they had remaining with their own loved ones. There was always something on the news though and it was never good.

This time was no exception.

Chapter Eight

Any innocent death was tragic, but for some reason it was especially jolting when a newscaster was killed on live TV during a field report. The brief moment of shock and excruciating pain on her face as the cameraman ran for his life was soul crushing. The image gnawed at my conscience. Millions had already been lost in Shanghai and the invasion was only just beginning. This was a more aggressive advance than we had seen from the demons in the past.

Shaky cellphone footage was circulating the internet and it provided a better scope than most of the news stations. The Chinese government had rolled tanks onto the fractured streets, but all they did was create obstacles for fleeing civilians before they were stomped on or fell into the hellish pits. The inaccuracy of the military's air raids likely killed more of their own than the real targets.

Empress Kamakura's serpentine dragon form could be seen flying overhead in many of the shots. Plenty of the air force accidentally got caught in her crossfire or crashed into her, with no greater effect than a paper airplane colliding with a brick wall. I hated to think how many of her own were roasted by her flaming breath or lightning storms as she laid waste to entire sections of the city at a time. Her guardian spirits—The Black Turtle of the North, Vermilion Bird of the South, Azure Dragon of the East, and White Tiger of the West—were no more careful cleansing the area. They had grown so powerful from the sudden influx of worship after centuries of withering that I doubted they realized how strong they were now, or they were so determined to eliminate all threats that they didn't take collateral damage into consideration.

So much for not escalating, Kamakura...

I scanned every source to find some sign of Nathaniel. The best I got were some flashes and blurs of light that I had to tell myself were him.

"They're all monsters and they deserve to be dealt with like them." Another TV lunatic like the one yesterday was ranting to a reporter somewhere else in the world. "The government isn't doing anything so we have to rise up and take back our homes one town at a time. This world is meant for humans, not freaks of nature."

"How do you propose anyone does that when many of them can lift cars and knock over buildings?" the reporter asked.

"They can be killed all right. My boys and I have killed plenty back home. The ones posing as humans don't put up much of a fight when you fill 'em with bullets or take them down with a nailed bat. Some can just be dragged out into the sunlight. We've started a militia and started a website where you can read up on how to fight back and watch videos showing some of our kills."

"I've seen your website and I have to say, some of it is very disturbing. It isn't for the faint of heart. Many of your subjects look completely human and don't appear to fight back."

"You have to be tough if you want results, tougher than the enemy. It's fine if people are bothered by what they see as long as they know we're on the same side and stay out of our way."

"How can you be sure someone is supernatural?" the reporter asked. "You have to admit they put on a very convincing performance."

"You can always tell which ones are the freaks by the look in their eyes or if they get twitchy around you. They'll say anything to keep their cover so you can't trust a word they say."

"What if it's someone wearing colored contacts, or has a disease, or simply is socially awkward? There is graphic footage on your website of your militia dragging a young man from his home who looks terrified as you beat and cut him open in front of his family. What are the chances that you're wrong and make a bad call? Shouldn't we focus on those we're certain about like the ones with horns growing out of their skulls?"

The militia leader twisted his face in anger. "You'd know if you were there staring these monsters in the eyes, but maybe thanks to us you'll go another day without having that chance. It's a gut feeling and my gut is always right. Sympathizing with these freaks is what they want. They're the ones calling in their big friends to come wipe us out after they infiltrate our homes and learn about us. We're doing God's work—the real God—by making these tough calls and we encourage others to do the same. That creepy neighbor who never leaves their house, the store clerk who looks at you strange across the store, your queer uncle, question everything and open your eyes. Better that you strike first before they do—"

My blood boiled. I changed the channel in disgust. Leave it to humans to find something else to blindly hate. It wasn't like they didn't see us saving lives from the obvious demons. There was a pretty big difference between someone like me—even with my "freaky eyes"—and the hellfire giants that spoke in tongues.

I went back to looking for Nathaniel sightings and was glad I did. My champion was on video being kissed on the lips by a very pretty female survivor for a full three seconds. The lingering stunned expression on his face when it ended and people gathered around to try to take pictures with him was priceless.

Watching Nathaniel's interlude prompted me to check on Lyle.

"PARAGON, locate Commander Turner," I said to the tablet's voice-controlled AI.

"Commander Turner is in the Minhang District of Shanghai, China," PARAGON answered, bringing up a map of his exact position. *"Shall I connect you to his communicator?"*

"Sure." I was surprised when PARAGON accepted my casual reply and didn't require a "yes," but then again what was a several billion-dollar computer program good for if it couldn't understand conversational English?

"Lyle," I said over the background noise on his end.

"Are you really not coming?" he shouted back.

"We talked about this. I can't."

"Can't or won't? We could really use your help. The Chinese have the numbers, but they're not doing much in the way of damage. There haven't been much of the Abhorrent though. I guess the people putting their faith in Kamakura have stopped them from turning."

"Get out of there and let Kamakura take care of it," I said. "The military can evac the people."

"Not gonna happen, man." Lyle patched me into his visor so I could see what he was seeing. "Look at this mess. We just got here and already lost half the city. Hell ain't joking around anymore. Your boy is flying around here somewhere and you should be too."

"I sent him so I could stay here. I'm not risking an attack at home while I'm away. We have little kids here as young as four years old."

"There are millions of kids here in danger right now who don't have an army of magic knights to protect them or teleport to safety. I'm sure you could find something to do that wouldn't piss off Kamakura."

"I'm not coming, Lyle."

"And I'm not leaving, so let me get back to work and you enjoy your vacation. Have that drink for me or something and don't forget your sunscreen."

Lyle disconnected.

"PARAGON, can you show me how many Infernals are in Shanghai?"

"Yes, Dorian."

"How did you know it's me?" I never logged in to use the tablet.

"I run a three point verification check on all users for maximum security when primary biological sensors at home base are not available. I can see you. This unit can also read fingerprints, and I ran a syntax diagnosis on your conversation with Commander Turner cross-referencing it with his own speech patterns for authenticity."

"Spooky. Just show me the map of Infernals."

The demons were marked in orange, highlighting the whole city and starting to spill west across the city lines. This was bad.

I took one of the decorative aether crystals from the fireplace mantle and rolled it in my hand while watching Noah spar with Connor. He wasn't going as easy on Connor as I would have preferred, but Connor couldn't be kept down. Some of the younger children came out to play and stretch their short string bean legs, which made a very strange contrast between the two scenes.

I'm making the right decision staying here. These are the people I have to protect. The rest of the world isn't my responsibility, especially if they don't want my help. I have to push all doubt from my mind and stick to the plan.

Noah had Connor running back fist drills to help him build speed, occasionally tripping him or throwing him over his shoulder several yards away to mix things up. Noah was the king of dragging people outside of their comfort zone. I could remember us having a calm conversation and then being hurled off a roof mid-sentence when learning how to fly.

The news interrupted my idle spectating.

"The Shanghai massacre has begun to cross the Yangtze and spread into Nantong. Fearing for their lives, many have fled north ahead of the invasion. Officials are encouraging those in densely populated areas to disperse and head into the countryside. It appears the military is having little effect against these monsters and containment is a lost cause."

I shut off the TV and crushed the crystal I was holding to dust, subconsciously twisting and turning it into the images I had seen.

"That kid's got potential." Noah's voice came from behind me as he entered the room. "He's not as stiff as the rest of them. Should train him in Snake style kung fu to work on his movement. Then again kung fu stances are pretty rigid. He has a pair of balls on him too. Little shit tried putting me in a headlock. So, what're you doing in here by yourself?"

"Watching the news." I turned the aether dust into a small statue of him.

"Sounds fun, but why play with that when you've got the real thing right here?" He stepped around in front of my chair with his hands on his waist to put himself on full display.

"Because the real thing is covered in mud. Again."

"Just for you. Now we have an excuse to go take a bath. I'll even let you sit on my lap."

"I'm thinking of going to Shanghai."

"Why? We got a tub here."

"The situation seems worse than the other times. I'm torn between staying here to protect my family or going there to save millions, and my conscience is telling me to do both."

Noah crouched down to look me in the eyes for a moment of seriousness. "They're both the right decision. When your heart presents you with two paths, let a clear mind lead." He turned the beads around my wrist. "Think of what bothers you the most. If you're scared about losing these kids, you have to trust in what they're capable of. Make an escape plan with them to bail if things get too hot while you're away."

"That's what Lyle said."

"I hate him so it doesn't count."

I smiled and pushed Noah over. "I'll go talk to them and then head to Shanghai."

"After our bath." He wiped my palm across his muddy chest, zipping into the bathroom before I could retaliate. I heard him run the water and shout over it. "I'll go with you. At least come wash your hand."

"I'm not falling for that." I cleaned my hand on my cloak and dumped it in the laundry before going to talk to Marianna outside.

While Knight Paige chopped wood, Marianna stood nearby watching the children play like she was a prison warden. It wasn't the first time.

"Stop scowling at the kids, Marianna."

"I'm not scowling! I was thinking."

"You were doing both," said Paige.

Since taking over their predecessors' positions on the council, Alexandre, Liam, and Marianna had become even grimmer than the rest. The pressure of leadership was getting to them as much as it was to me, although I was aware that Marianna was the only one doing any actual leading. Liam had always been less than proactive, but now he slipped away to his mother's house at every opportunity. Alexandre retreated to the meditation rooms more often and stayed longer.

"Do you know why I chose you to help lead the Order?" I asked her.

"My aunt was on the council before me and you wanted someone new."

"No." I sighed. "You're intelligent and you're bold, you all are, but you were always the most vocal about the changes you wanted to see in the Order. Lately I see you falling in line with old traditions because they're safe instead of stepping forward, and that's not the Marianna I first met. Stop being scared of your own footsteps."

She stared straight ahead as she considered what I said against her own perspective. "I don't know what to say. I'm truly sorry if I let you down—"

"Don't apologize. Just be yourself and you won't have any regrets. Listen to your own ideas instead of running to scriptures for answers or doing what your aunt would do."

"Thank you. I suppose you're right. I lost sight of that with everything in the world being so terrifying. I wanted it all to be stable again like when I was a little girl."

"We're going to get through this. I have nothing but confidence in you."

"Thank you," she said again. Her face warmed and she looked like she might start crying, hopefully in relief or happiness, but I couldn't take anymore emotion for one day so I changed the topic back to business.

"We need an evacuation plan if these effigies fail. I'm going to Shanghai and I want to be sure everyone here will be okay. The youngest children should be taken out first and go up the line from there. Is there anywhere you can go back and forth from easily that's also unpopulated?"

"There's an uninhabited island east of here that's smaller than this one. We duel there at times," she said.

"That'll do. Now, off to Shanghai."

Connor ran over to us. I didn't even see him sitting in the shade. Maybe because he was so black and blue he blended in. "Wait! Take me with you!"

"Not this time," I told him. "I don't want anyone going. Not even Noah. Besides, you need to take some time off. Don't you ever get tired?"

"Not really. But Marianna can heal me and then I'll be ready to fight. I can take a decoction with me for energy in case."

"I want you here," I insisted. "You need to finish learning how to travel the ley lines, heal yourself better, and conjure elements so you can come with us when needed."

"Yes, sir."

"Don't give me that. You sound like Marianna, who won't even call me by name anymore."

"I do!" she exclaimed in shock. Connor had a wily smile painted across his face seeing her get called out. "I thought it best to lead by example on how to show respect."

"We can discuss protocol later. I need to get the elders to send me to Shanghai, but in the meantime, don't forget what we talked about."

Chapter Nine

Night had completed its descent upon Shanghai when I arrived at what was left of a recently abandoned beach resort. My exact location was unknown. I could have been almost anywhere along the coastal city and there was no one around to point me in the right direction, not even the sound of screams to follow. The only noises were a low, irregular rumbling and occasional popping so far off in the distance I couldn't pinpoint from where it originated.

Bodies lined the sand down to the shore; some were being dragged away by the dark tide along with scattered beach chairs and umbrellas. The power was out for as far as I could see, but inland the fires raged on, casting a ghostly flicker across the field of corpses.

I thought I had seen death before, but this was on another level. The previous invasions were dominated by the Abhorrent that didn't leave corpses, and those who escaped being transformed were minimal compared to this, usually dying from being trampled or struck by falling debris.

The Far East was rooted in tradition perhaps more than any major modern culture and so they embraced the return of one of their old gods unanimously. Hell couldn't take the souls of those claimed by another, such as Kamakura, so instead they resorted to outright slaughter.

Floating over the bodies was the only way to move across the beach without stepping on them. Whole families—or pieces of them—were piled up against fences. They had been cut down while trying to flee. In the parking lot blood pooled into a lake deep enough to partially submerge the remains of those who had made it that far.

I flew higher and kept heading further into the city. The stillness was getting to me. I could hear only the wind rushing past my ears as I soared above the cooling trenches carved through the streets by a catastrophic attack. It was the hardest to see the shelled schools and hospitals, their occupants in lifeless poses. Corpses hung from broken office building windows, those who chose to take their inevitable deaths into their own hands but were caught last second.

The scenery didn't change for miles until downed military vehicles were added to the upheaved landscape. Corpses lined the roads as they did the beach. While flying by I tried to find patterns in the way the colors of their clothes overlapped to disassociate them from real people, but then I'd see a face in the crowd, its eyes open, staring up at me, and I'd have to remind myself they were dead. There was no life here. Not anymore.

Magma pits grew larger and more frequent the further I went. There was still no sign of Nathaniel, but I could feel I was getting close. A wriggling, fleshy mass was climbing out from the flames. There were several of them in the street gathered around a group of corpses. They were maggots. Ginormous maggots chewing through the flesh and bone of the deceased to engorge their bloated bodies.

I smashed the revolting bugs to stop their desecration of the dead and moved on, but soon realized there was no end to their numbers and nothing I could do to reverse the tragic outcome of the fallen. What life might be left elsewhere deserved the whole of my attention. The husks suffered no longer.

A sudden whistle distracted me from the nauseating feeding noises coming from the corpse eaters. It came from up ahead where a human figure stood on an overpass. The figure called my name and I recognized the voice.

"Noah?" I called back. "I told the Order I didn't want you coming with me."

I slowed my flight to land in front of him. His presence was a welcomed break from the gloom of the haunting atmosphere, which could have been made better should he have brought a sword.

"I can be pretty convincing. You didn't think I'd let you take this on alone, did you?" He rested his chin on top of my head.

"This is the worst I've seen from these invasions. I don't want you to be here. If anything happens to you—"

"I know you think you're going to make the same mistake that cost you your parents, but you can't control everything—especially not me. You're not supposed to. You can't take on the whole world alone while you hide everyone you care about behind glass."

"It's true." I sighed. "I should have come sooner."

"Nah, you're here exactly when you're supposed to be. You can only look forward to what needs to be done."

"Do you know where everybody is?"

"Yeah, back the other way." He laughed at the contradiction. "About ten miles northwest by the Yangtze. I guess I got dropped off closer to the action than you did. It doesn't get any prettier though, so be prepared."

Noah turned his back to me so I could climb on and he could bring us to the battlefront using his super speed. The world whizzed by faster than my brain could comprehend. All I got were out of focus snapshots miles apart as we crossed the city.

"Why'd we stop?" I asked. I could see Kamakura snaking through the cloudy night sky in the distance whenever a flash of lightning struck from the heavens. The screaming and gunfire had become so commonplace in the soundtrack of my life that it felt natural to hear them again after the initial jolt from the silence.

"Look at these moths." Noah pointed out the small featureless insects fluttering in swarms near the dead.

"They're a symbol of death in China, believed to be the souls of loved ones, but I've never seen them actually have auras on Earth before."

Noah brought us to the staging area where UNITY and the Chinese army had been cornered on a main avenue between a toppled skyscraper and a magma pit. A good number of them had burns and other injuries worthy of serious medical treatment.

The demons here were shorter in stature. They were both more and less terrifying when human-sized, teetering closer to the edge of the uncanny valley yet less of a physical threat than their larger counterparts. Some were diminutive versions of the *oni* that I had witnessed invade Yomi with their horrible tusked mouths and blunt weapons.

After tossing away the wave of Infernals clawing their way toward the army I yelled for Lyle, but there was no chance either of us would hear each other over the confusion. The Chinese opened fire on me while I hovered over them searching for Lyle, thinking I was one of the demons. The bullets and rocket-propelled grenades were useless against my telekinetic barrier. Noah barked at them in Mandarin to ceasefire.

Finally I saw the helmet with the smiley face sticker. It looked like Lyle had taken a hit or two.

"Thought you weren't coming," he yelled. "It's bad, man. It's real bad. We're stuck here until Nathaniel returns, if he ever does. Ammo is running dry, our aircraft have all been destroyed, and communications are being jammed by something."

"What do you mean 'if he ever does'?" I asked.

"He flew off to find survivors, I don't know, maybe fifteen minutes ago, and we haven't seen him since."

I didn't sense that Nathaniel was in any trouble or pain, but he was close—most likely busy with civilians.

"Tell me what you need me to do," I said.

"Just bring the whole fucking place down." Lyle removed his helmet so I could see his face. He was rattled. "We lost half our team."

"What are the odds on any more survivors?" I asked, raising a part of the road in front of us to act as a barricade.

"Low, but if there are any they're in these buildings," Lyle answered. "We were in pursuit of a group of demons that broke off to escape the city and about to cross the river when we realized we were the ones being pursued. We ducked in here to hold our ground, but that pit opened behind us. The last I heard from Nathaniel the bridge out of Shanghai is down now though."

"I can fly all of you to safety, but anything more than that is going to draw a lot of attention. I don't want to spread this anywhere else or summon something worse like in Mumbai."

A second wave came up from the pit. I dispatched them and tried closing it, but it opened again immediately.

"These guys said the navy should be arriving soon so we can evac and hopefully reestablish communications from their ship."

"If we had a way to secure these buildings fast I could demolish them once they're clear and let you move on your own while I covered your backs," I suggested.

I called to Nathaniel in my mind. It was the only telepathic power I had, thanks to our soul bond. He could cause just enough of a distraction to let me evacuate everyone.

"I'll check them," Noah said.

"Some are crawling with demons, dude," said Lyle.

"No shit," Noah snapped. "Just give me something to signal the all clear."

Lyle handed him a flare gun from his leg holster. "It's got ten rounds. Keep heading east until you hit the coast. And...thanks."

"I'm not doing it for you." Noah grabbed the gun.

"Don't all your firearms require that neural implant UNITY members have?" I asked.

"Not the nonlethal stuff."

Noah came in close to exclude Lyle. "Bring down the buildings when you see the flare and don't worry about me. I'll be two ahead by the time it goes off."

"Good luck."

"I don't need luck. I'm Noah."

He vanished and the first flare went up a second later. I soared above the skyline to be sure I had the right building and crushed it flat to within an inch. One flare after the next shot up and the buildings went down, allowing everyone to walk over them in a straight path to the coast. We were on our sixth building when a streak of light in the sky brought Nathaniel to me.

"I'm so glad you came." He sounded even more relieved than Lyle.

"I can't say I feel the same."

"I understand."

There hadn't been a flare for several seconds. I was growing tense when one went up two buildings away.

"Go check that building for survivors." I pointed to the one Noah had skipped. Nathaniel flew down and plowed through the concrete wall to enter. He returned after a moment with people holding on to him and set them down with the rest.

"The empress has gone a distance to the north," Nathaniel told me as we continued the routine. "I was up by Beijing with her when I felt your call. The demons have spread for hundreds of miles."

I don't know what she's doing, but I'm sticking to what we agreed on and if anything happens here it's on her.

"I wonder if they're not as infinite as we thought. There weren't any for miles where I was dropped off south of here. If they wanted to establish a foothold I'd think they'd want to hang around after they conquered an area."

I pushed the last buildings down behind Lyle's group instead of flattening them to block the path for anything wanting to follow. The clouds of dust and smoke from the demolition had to go, so I swirled it together into a compressed ball and chucked it down a magma pit. There was hollering from the humans once the air cleared.

"The ships," said Nathaniel.

The Chinese frigates were there all right, but they were sinking.

Nathaniel went with me out over the water into a thick fog to carry them back to land. The water below was pitch black that far away from the city, but his light made it easier to see. We couldn't find any lifeboats or crew floating by themselves and no one was on the decks either, so we returned to shore with the ships.

That was unwise.

As soon as we landed, demons poured from the ships and went straight for the humans. These Infernals were swollen, ethereal humanoids with distorted facial features. My telekinetic blast and the soldiers' bullets passed right through them, but Nathaniel's light purged the ghastly beings from existence.

"*Shui gui.*" Noah appeared beside me in the crowd. "They're the angry spirits of people who drowned. Hell is really digging in deep here. They must want something more than killing the dragon lady's followers."

The ghosts kept coming back, staying at range from the light as everyone huddled together around Nathaniel.

"They're probably tied to the ships," said Noah. The army and the survivors seemed more panicked over the ghosts than the tangible demons. They wouldn't stop crying and screaming even though no one was being hurt.

"I've got to get on one of those ships to see if I can radio the base," Lyle said.

"Not without Nathaniel, and you aren't getting all these people to follow in this panic," I said. "Anyone that falls behind in the tight quarters will get snatched."

"Here." Nathaniel created an aether crystal with his light and gave it to Lyle.

"I'll go with you," I told him.

"Why the hell are we doing this?" Noah asked. "Any backup you're gonna call in will die like everybody else."

"That's why I'm trying to get a message to base to have everyone get out if they're in the area," Lyle answered. "And if not, they should be working to help people evacuate the cities nearby that'll be hit next."

Noah wasn't pleased about being corrected, but he picked me up in one arm and yanked Lyle with him by the collar.

We were in the ship's bridge in a flash. I held the crystal while Lyle tried getting the radio to work.

There were no bodies on the ship, but there were plenty of the corpse-eating maggots scrounging around the interior in search of their next meal. Noah kicked one into the wall, making it squeal and release a fetid odor along with smaller copies of itself from its entrails.

"Please don't do that again." I gagged and disintegrated the brood.

"All I'm getting is static!" Lyle slammed his fists on the console. "This is fucking hopeless. Let's say we get out of here. We have no idea how far this has spread. You could be flying us for hundreds of miles and leading more demons than even you could fight right along with you."

"You suggesting we leave you here? 'Cause I'm down for that," Noah quipped.

"We'll have to fight our way out," I said. "We don't have any other choice. Kamakura bailed to leave us in the wake of her destruction, so I don't care what she says to me about making things worse by getting involved. At least the sun is coming up so we won't be in the dark."

"Dude, it's three a.m. here," said Lyle.

"And that's not the sun," Noah added. "Unless it changed which direction it rises."

Chapter Ten

The light to the west of the city dimmed, but didn't take the panic it caused with it.

"PARAGON is picking up huge radiation levels coming from that 'sun' north of here," Lyle reported from the scanners in his visor. "Guys, I think China has just been nuked."

"What?" My mind raced to come up with an escape plan.

"Time to go," Noah said. "Throw the zoo in a box and deal with whatever follows after."

The three of us jumped ship and rejoined the group.

"What's happening?" Nathaniel asked upon seeing our worried faces. "That light—?"

"We have to get everyone out *right now*," I told him. "I'll explain on the way."

Noah whistled from somewhere on the dock.

"Over here!" he yelled from atop an industrial shipping container. He pulled open the doors, but it was full. That didn't matter. I lifted it and dumped the cargo into the sea.

"Get inside!" I shouted at everyone. Counting the new survivors we collected along the way there were about two hundred people in total to cram in there.

The group listened but moved slowly to avoid leaving the safety of Nathaniel's radiance. I had forgotten about the minor nuisance of the shui gui when compared to total nuclear annihilation. I pitched the ships back into the sea to hurry things along.

Then came another light on the horizon. This one was closer. Brighter. A tremor shook the earth beneath our feet and churned the sea.

"High-yield thermonuclear blast," Lyle confirmed. "PARAGON estimates it around seven or eight megatons."

"Nuclear? How bad is that?" Nathaniel asked, but I had to ignore him for the moment. I had recovered from being atomized in the past, but the persistent radiation of a powerful enough nuclear weapon might be able to keep me in a perpetual state of death until the radiation depleted enough. That could take years. I had no idea what it would do to Nathaniel being that his powers were so new.

"GET IN THE BOX!" I screamed at everyone and started shoving people in myself. Someone complained how dark it was so I threw the glowing crystal in and slammed the doors. Noah stood on top of the container again and then I realized I had packed Lyle away by accident.

"Dorian!" Nathaniel tried to interrupt.

"It's real bad, Nathaniel. Worst case scenario bad," I started to explain right as another bomb dropped closer than the previous two. "You can fly faster than me so it's up to you. Don't get near the fallout or the heat will cook everybody inside."

Something seemed off about the military, which was openly working with Kamakura, resorting to a tactic that would also leave her lands uninhabitable with her still in the general area.

"Make sure to slow down before you stop or everyone will get turned to paste," Noah said. "I'm gonna run it. I can be out of the city before you if I don't hit traffic. I'll head south and wait to follow your trail."

"Be careful," I said.

Nathaniel hoisted the container over his head and carried us away with me riding on top to buffer the wind shear with my powers. We were going at a snail's pace compared to his maximum speed to prevent injuries, but still made it out of the city in seconds.

"Where are you going?" I shouted at him as he slowed down and circled back in the wrong direction.

"There are people down there!"

"We don't have room!" I hovered the container beside us so we could talk.

"I can't leave them there." We looked down at a gathering of people stuck on a roof crying and begging for their lives. "I can carry them."

Two centipede creatures were burrowing through the land destabilizing any building still standing. It wouldn't be long until they found their way to this new gathering of survivors.

"Go. I'll expand the container." The explosions were getting closer again. "Hurry!"

Nathaniel was there and back in the time it took me to refashion the container. With everyone packed in tight we were off, but not for long. A blinding light flashed miles ahead of us. Nathaniel had to make a sharp turn to avoid sending us into the nuclear fallout. We were way off course and traveling west when another bomb fell in the direction we were headed.

"We're trapped!" Nathaniel shouted and weaved to the southwest.

We both saw the next missile coming and knew it was too late to escape the radius of the blast without killing everyone. I felt what Nathaniel was about to do without him needing to tell me. He left the container with me and before words of protest could escape my mouth he shot toward the missile to redirect it.

I couldn't draw breath as I watched the sky. I braced us within a more concentrated telekinetic shield right before the warhead detonated high up in the stratosphere. We were jolted by the shockwave, but safe. Nathaniel, however, was nowhere in sight.

Frantic, I called to him by mind and voice.

My eyes stung trying to look up, but then I saw him: The silhouette of his cape billowed against the fading star in the sky caused by the nuke.

"I'm okay," he said once close enough to hear. "It was only a bit warm."

There wasn't a scratch on him. His clothes suffered some moderate burns but were intact. It was good to know the angel silk and demon leather that made our outfits could withstand a nuclear strike. That also meant the demons it came from were resistant, if not immune, too.

"I'm sorry. It wasn't my intention to worry you, but I knew I couldn't hesitate," he continued. "I had to carry the bomb because I was afraid it would fly back if thrown."

"You're golden. All that matters is that you're all right."

As much as I wanted to lavish him with praise, we were still under attack. The interruption in the bombardment bought us time to keep moving west undeterred. Nathaniel pushed the limits on how fast we should have been going with our passengers. In five minutes or so we were several hundred miles away in a peaceful countryside.

I was scared to open the container and see the state everyone was in, but there was plenty of terrified yelling so at least that told me they were alive. Most stayed packed in a group after the doors opened, too afraid to stray. A few decided to run for their lives into the dark fields.

"Thank god it's over." Lyle was one of the last to step out.

"Thank Nathaniel for taking a nuke head on," I said.

"I'd shake your hand, but I think everyone threw up and pissed themselves at least twice, and I was on the bottom of the pile. PARAGON isn't reading any radiation coming off you. How'd you manage that?"

"I'm not sure," Nathaniel said. "It's only light and energy. I absorbed it as I would the aether."

My thoughts went to Noah while they chatted. I glided around the area looking for some sign of him until I was tackled to the ground. Nathaniel was at my side at once, pulling back once he saw I wasn't in danger.

"Calm yourself, kid," Noah said to him, putting me on his shoulders.

"Sorry. I'm a little on edge," Nathaniel apologized.

"Well, we did it," Lyle said, walking over. "Sort of."

"You didn't do anything," said Noah.

"Yeah, nice to see you're okay too, Muscles."

"So many people and this is all that's left," Nathaniel lamented.

"Incoming." Noah looked up at the fireball in the sky headed for us. Everyone started screaming and running off, but I recognized the image of a bird in the flames and figured whom it was.

"We're fine," I told Nathaniel before he did anything rash.

The firebird landed and transformed into a Japanese girl wrapped in flowing silks and feathers that danced with cinder and flame. Her name was Kamiko Yamamoto, and she was the human embodiment of the Guardian Spirit of Fire. Not that she was alive, per se. The one standing before us was a memory of one who had ascended to heaven and left behind an imprint on the aether.

She bowed and delivered her message. "Empress Kamakura requests your aid by right of the Alabaster Concordat."

"Now she wants help, huh?" I said. "I thought that's what we were doing."

"Eastern China is no longer of this world. What happens there is of no consequence to the Great Empire. This message has been sent to all of the alliance. We await you to the north."

Kamiko transformed back into her guardian beast incarnation and flew away in a blaze.

"Guess I'm going north," I said.

"I have communication open with home base," said Lyle. "We should have evac here in an hour."

"I'm not leaving you here after what we just went through. The demons *will* come this way after the big show we put on."

"I'll stay," Nathaniel said.

"That works for me if you're okay with it. I'll head up with Noah. Go home and get some rest once everyone is gone."

Noah dashed off with me, putting an immediate end to any last minute chatter. "I'm gonna need a refill to go any further," he said after stopping somewhere dense with trees. "Time to feed the tiger."

I had no arguments. My heart had still been beating out of my chest from the night's events and feeling his lips close around my neck was a much-needed lull. His fangs penetrated my skin, intoxicating me with his bite as he drained me slowly to ride the line of ecstasy throughout the duration of his feeding. His muscles swelled with renewed vigor in my hands.

"How you holding up?" he asked after he finished, letting me catch my breath in his arms. I ran my fingers through his hair. He let out a low growl and gave my ear a bite to make me flinch and grab him tighter. True to his nickname, loving him was often like wrestling a tiger.

"You're here and my friends are safe. That's all I can ask."

"You don't have to go to this meeting if you don't want."

I knew Noah was implying that I didn't need to frustrate myself by listening to the other gods tell me how the crisis could have been handled better.

"I know, but I should."

Gianni and Isis had already arrived when we found Kamakura looking out over the ruins of another city from atop a crag. Gianni forwent his usual welcome when he saw me with Noah, instead flashing me a warm smile and nod.

"What's the battle plan?" I asked, dismounting my noble steed. The bombs had stopped dropping and as I had thought, they did little to disrupt the demons' momentum.

"There is no battle to be fought," Kamakura answered. "We stand at the precipice of Hell. They lay claim to these lands and there is naught we can do. My strength wanes when for the briefest moment I surpassed all. This light must be what drew their enmity."

"You didn't know your followers were planning on nuking, er, using 'sun weapons' against the demons while we were there?"

"No."

"The first petal of this odious blossom has folded upon our world," said Isis. "Soon it will spread beyond these limits and then cometh the next and the next until oblivion."

"Kamakura, why are you getting weaker if you can still tap the power from souls of the dead? Aren't all the moths around the city the same thing?" I asked.

"These countless souls are lost in purgatory. In this land, the Yellow River to the north ferries the dead to the Gate of Yomi. Those who die here can no longer journey to the afterlife with the river tainted. Hell cannot touch what is mine, and what is mine cannot hear my call from Hell."

"Why don't the demons end them with hellfire?"

"'Tis a foolish and flagrant display to do such a thing," said Isis. "Souls are as much the demons' succor as they are our own."

I guess Mumbai was just unlucky Demon Lord Vināyaka felt like showing off that day.

"They await the time I fall and my claim on the dead is no more," Kamakura added.

The sun began to rise. The real sun this time. Everything had a tendency to look better in daylight, but that was not the case here. I had never seen water so black. The sea remained as dark as it had during nighttime and the shui gui were just as persistent along the coast. The sky above was hellish red, but behind us, a regular summer morning.

"I wonder why the demons here were smaller." I watched the legion pace idly through the rubble. It hadn't occurred to me in the chaos, but their dead no longer dematerialized. That would be beneficial in obtaining their hides for armor.

"Infiltration," said Noah. "They could get into buildings and make sure every last person is dead."

Isis had more to share. "The Infernal hierarchy is specific and not wasteful in the slightest. They may now reveal truer forms before unseen with the alignment in their favor."

"What about this sun weapons the humans use?" Gianni asked. "They make no harm to the demons?"

"Useless," I confirmed. "Nathaniel survived one at point blank range too. We don't know what they'd do to the rest of us, but so far all they're good for is killing tons of humans and the environment."

"Hm." Gianni commanded the shadows to blanket the city below, dragging it down into the Nether. When the darkness receded the Infernals and any remains of civilization were gone, leaving only the hellish atmosphere on a dirt plain. It didn't last for long. The earth cracked open unleashing new denizens of the damned that took notice of us but kept their distance.

"'Tis unwise to provoke them, Dark One," Isis warned.

"A test," he said. "I fear no monster."

"It cannot hurt our situation to deplete their numbers when we have already engaged in active combat," said Kamakura.

"Except when I do it, I guess," I mumbled to Noah.

"Hell will not leave a new land with no leader," Gianni said. "I think to make a threat will show this demon. Is better to fight this way when we have a control where and when is the battle."

"That's smart, Gianni. It's better than waiting around to get ambushed."

"No, it isn't," said Noah. "This idiot is trying to summon one of the kings and assuming they're dumb enough to fall for a trap that a blind three year old would see coming."

"You are scared. I understand." Gianni smiled at me when talking to Noah to get under his skin. "Dorian will fight the demons with me and I show him a real man."

He extended his hand for me to take, somewhat in jest, which led to Noah putting an arm around my waist. "You couldn't show him one in the time you already had together, so don't bother embarrassing yourself again by wasting anymore of it."

"*Anyway.*" I had to put an end to that and move the conversation forward. Any other time their rivalry might have been amusing, but not over the souls of millions in purgatory. "I think it would be good to study the area as much as possible before luring anything out so we can get an idea of what we might be facing. I'll send a couple of scouts to do research."

"Tell me and I come to make sure they are safe. You need a rest to be strong when you fight with me." I knew Gianni was still trying to wind Noah up, but there was sincerity in his words.

"Let's go," Noah said to me while the rest began talking among themselves.

"We need a way back home. Everyone will probably be gone by the time we get to where we left them."

"I will take you," Gianni said when he overheard.

"Keep your shadow to yourself," Noah snapped.

"All the shadows are mine. You are going to run or make Dorian fly for so long?"

I had to side with practicality. "We'll take the shadows. Thanks, Gianni."

"Of course, little one."

"Do share any information your scouts may come across," Isis said. "I shall do the same upon my return from the annals. 'Tis wont of me to have a priestess if not pharaoh to aid my hand on Earth in times of absence. A random musing, but I find it tiresome to be in attendance betwixt the heavens and soil so often."

"Have you yet to consider a disciple for such earthly duties?" asked Kamakura.

"'Tis tradition for the Ennead to convene on such matters as the blessing of a new pharaoh. Without my heavenly brethren I am hesitant, but not blind to the need. The selection of priestess, warrior, or diplomat vexes me as well."

"And what of you, Dark One? Have you similar intent?"

"Hm, I do not think of this. Maybe if it will help."

"Maybe someone who can speak English," Noah quipped.

I gave him a look out of the corner of my eye.

"Maybe you?" Gianni retorted.

"We cannot go to war together if we do not stand united," said Isis.

"I agree," I said. "Can we get past this so we can concentrate on the real enemy? You're both better than this."

"Yes. I will take you two to home now, okay?"

It was a nice sentiment, but I didn't believe for a second that either of them was ready to put anything aside. They were still less of a concern to me than allies contradicting their own requests for passivity with little explanation.

Chapter Eleven

Noah and I made it to the abbey ahead of Nathaniel. The first thing I did was check in with Lyle to be sure everyone made it out of China. Afterward it was a short speech to those awake for patrol in the Order to tell them about the result of the battle. Once my leadership duties were finished it was finally time to relax for as long as I could until the next catastrophe.

"I got you sushi, a gyro, ice cream with those candies on it, and that caramel coffee drink." Noah appeared on the bed next to me with everything he could remember that I liked to eat from in town.

"Just dump it in my mouth." I was so comfortable laid out on my back that I didn't want to move.

"At the same time?"

I laughed and hid my face beneath a pillow. The sun was up and the curtains were closed, but the room was well lit from the crystal in Nathaniel's tower.

"Did you get yourself anything or do you want me to throw on a few steaks?" I asked.

"Nah, I'm good."

I peeked out from under the pillow and saw him sneaking pieces of sushi in his mouth like popcorn. "Hang on a sec. Those are in takeout bags and packaged to go with a receipt."

"And?"

"You actually went to the counter to interact like a normal person instead of raiding the kitchen?"

"I stabbed three people ahead of me on line."

"With the weapons you never carry anymore?"

"I don't think I like your tone," he said with a poke to my side.

"Get back to me when you're sure and I'll be eating in the meantime." I laughed and tried to squirm away from his attempts at tickling me. He didn't take long to give up though and lay down with his legs hanging off the side of the bed. I scratched his chin scruff against the grain the way he liked while sampling what was left of the sushi.

"So are you really good?" I asked.

"I'm the best, so you're gonna have to be more specific."

"I'm talking about how you didn't seem 'good' around Gianni. I thought you two had called a truce."

"Doesn't mean I like the guy."

"You know I'm not going anywhere, right? You don't have to prove yourself every time he's around."

"It's got nothing to do with that. I trust you like I trust my own two hands, maybe more. It's about respect. He doesn't respect either of us and he didn't when you were together too. He looks at you like you're a new sword to win—not even—he doesn't want to earn you, just take you from me because he thinks he's better than me. It's all in that stupid smile he always gives you."

"You're reading too much into it," I said, moving my hand to the side of his face. "I don't doubt that he's still interested in me, but he only goes as far as he does because you start antagonizing him."

"That's the other problem. He acts like he knows everything, like his stupid idea to lure out these demon kings."

"It's actually not a bad plan to make them fight on our terms. And look who's talking about being a know-it-all."

"Hey, I can't help that I'm always right." Noah turned so we could see each other better. "Damn, you're pretty. Who told you that you could look this good?"

"I'd say you have me beat there."

"Nah, it's fake supernatural bullshit. What you've got is real."

"I don't care what it is as long as you be good." I rubbed his back after he lay on top of me, taking me down with him.

He came in close, pressing his nose against my cheek and lowering his voice to a sultry growl that always gave me goosebumps. "I'm better at the bad stuff."

"You're right about that." I laughed and made an attempt to get to the rest of my delicious buffet, only to be wrestled back down before I could reach it. "I'm too tired and hungry for this."

"So flip over and eat. I do most of the work anyway."

"No! And you know that isn't true."

After a spontaneous bout of horseplay, Noah forfeited and handed over the gyro. "You got lucky. Like most small animals of the tasty variety, you have no idea how close you were to being eaten."

I was settling in beside him and taking my first bite when I noticed I had a message from Lyle.

"Forgot to tell you. Sierra slept over the other night. Got to show her my routine for that almost-six-pack. Thanks again. She's amazing."

I wrote back: *Congrats, but is running for your life really considered a routine?*

Right as I finished, the abbey shook from a sudden thundering crash. Noah was outside with those on guard duty in an instant. I checked the sky from the window to see what was attacking us.

"Open the barrier. It's the kid," Noah shouted to me.

I had forgotten about the shield and that Nathaniel couldn't teleport through it. I went out and met him halfway up where I pried open a temporary portal for him to enter through.

"That hurt." Nathaniel was holding his nose. "I wasn't going that fast."

"I'm sorry, I forgot to tell you about the barrier."

"It's okay. At least we know it works." Nathaniel forced a smile through his pain and looked down at the new tower. "What happened to my room?"

"I made you a new one, but it's not done yet. You can stay in my room until then because I got rid of everything except your clothes and all the gifts to give you a fresh start."

We went inside where Noah had already retreated to finish off my sushi before I came back. Nathaniel sat on the couch without saying a word as I ate my gyro with iced coffee.

"Here, take my ice cream," I said.

"Thank you, I am rather hungry."

"You can have this sushi too," Noah said with his mouth full. "I only had a piece."

"Uh huh." I laughed.

Nathaniel perked up at the sight of the food, but still seemed a bit crestfallen. I didn't want to bring up the conversation with the deities, so I went for a lighter topic. I searched on the tablet for the clip of him kissing the girl he had saved earlier. "I see you have a new girlfriend," I said, showing him the screen. "Did you go back to visit her on the way home?"

"No, she died before I caught up to you in Shanghai. The demons got to her group when I left to go north." He stared down at the melting dessert in the cup and put it aside.

"Oh god... I'm sorry." I looked over to Noah who stayed quiet.

"It's not your fault. At least I had my first real kiss."

I couldn't tell if the sorrow I felt was coming from him or my own emotions. "It's going to be okay," I said.

"I hate them, the demons, I haven't hated anything as much as I hate them since I was a child. They used to only be monsters to me before, like animals that didn't know any better than to bite and scratch."

"I know it isn't easy, but try not to. They want you to hate them so that they become stronger, whether it's supernatural or they want us to give into our rage and make mistakes."

"You're tough enough not to give into something easy like hate, kid," Noah said. "Take it from someone who's lost everything more than once."

"I'll do my best not to let it cloud my judgment." Nathaniel stood to look out the window. "I'm still glad I went. We managed to save some and that's what matters. I hope they make the best of their second chance."

There was a knock at the door that I answered without moving from the couch. Rafael entered and bowed.

"What's up, Rafael?"

"Hello. I wanted to report that Octavio has been located safe in New York. He told me that he'd let you know when it was time to meet again."

"Huh. I guess that's the best I could hope for from him. I appreciate you going."

He smiled. "It's my pleasure."

"Why don't you hang out with us if you're not doing anything."

"Okay. Thank you." Rafael took a seat on the couch by me.

I wanted to spend more time with the Order doing something besides sending them on errands and this was the best opportunity I'd had in a while.

"Why are you interested in the old man?" Noah asked me.

"I'm curious how he was involved in my origin."

"What else is there to know? He helped stir the pot they cooked you up in and then fried his brain. It's not gonna change anything."

"I'm sure there's more to it than that."

There was another knock at the door. This time it was Marianna.

"Oh, I'm sorry," she said. "I didn't know you were holding a meeting."

"We're just hanging out. Come join us," I told her.

"I was hoping to speak to you alone about that...task you had for me."

I left the room with her and closed the door, excited to hear about her progress on furnishing Nathaniel's room.

"We're still working on the basics," Marianna whispered. "I thought of incorporating his favorite color into the fabrics like the curtains, but nobody knows what it is."

"I don't know either. I'll find out. Come in and relax with us."

"Are you having a party? I saw the food. I can make something."

"Make steak!" Noah yelled.

I went back in the room while Marianna left to cook.

"It's blue," said Nathaniel. "My favorite color is blue."

"You told him what we were talking about?" I turned to Noah.

"No, I could hear you," Nathaniel said.

"How?"

"My hearing and sight have been getting better every day. I can see and hear for miles if I concentrate. I'm also sure my speed and strength are increasing too."

"He's faster than you *and* has better senses," Noah teased. I threw a pillow over his face and sat on it to shut him up. "Take the pillow away if you wanna do this right," he said, muffled, and grabbed my thighs.

"We have light elemental spells that enhance sight," said Rafael. "Maybe Nathaniel unlocked a latent form of the spell. All of our spells increase in potency the more we practice with them, so it only makes sense his sight would too."

"What about the hearing?" I asked. Noah tossed me aside on the bed and sat up against the headboard with me between his legs.

"Telekinesis is about movement and sound is based upon vibrations in the air. Maybe he can pick up the frequency of vibrations?" Rafael said.

"That means I can do it too like how I can feel around me with my powers."

"Maybe. It could also be a synergy between both light and telekinesis though," Rafael went on. "Light is an advanced element, or in some designs it's considered primordial. Those teachings say it encompasses more than visible light, but an unknown range of the electromagnetic spectrum. Perhaps his powers convert the sound vibrations to radio waves that he can hear over long distances."

"I didn't think you guys studied science to that degree," I said.

"We don't after we're about thirteen, but it's important to help us relate to the physical world so we can commune with elements easier. There's always more than one path to a destination. Science and magic are two halves of a whole that explains our universe."

"Lyle's ex-girlfriend in PROJECT: UNITY used to say something similar."

"Since the Renaissance, the Order has believed in studying science, practicing magic."

"What goes on inside my head is often confusing enough without trying to explain it," Nathaniel joked.

The four of us chatted until Marianna came back, joined by Alexandre.

"We made shish kebabs," she announced.

We spent the rest of the morning together as friends like we had started to in the past before the invasions on Earth went from bad to worse. It was nice having company that brought joy instead of anxiety for a change and getting to know the people I was living with aside from their combat experience. Once they let their guard down they were almost as loquacious as Noah. Of course, that may have been because I spent most of the time floating slices of steak into his mouth until he fell asleep in a blissful meat coma.

"Did you decide what to do about our orichalcum supply?" Marianna asked me.

Rafael let out a loud sigh. "You're all business ever since getting on the council. We're supposed to be relaxing."

"That's *why* I'm on the council and you're not," she said with a jokingly smug expression.

"Actually, it's because he's been busy elsewhere," I said in Rafael's defense. "But to answer your question: I haven't decided yet. I'm nervous sending anyone to the Astral Plane and then if I get called away it leaves the abbey shorthanded. I'd also like to see what it's like there myself."

"You would love it," said Marianna. "The more willful the mind, the greater impact you have on reality there. You would do really well."

"It sounds interesting, but I'm not a big fan of illusions."

"They aren't illusions. The Astral Plane is a realm dictated by thought. A place all living beings' consciousness floods into and out of," Alexandre explained. "It can be traumatizing for an unstable mind though, and the manifestation of inner demons can be troublesome."

"I'll have to give it more consideration. I'm glad we did this though. It was fun," I said. "I don't believe that success in battle only comes from skill and power. You have to have something positive driving you that you can fall back on. The walls of the abbey are our sanctuary, but the memories we make are our shield against the evil out there."

Nathaniel smiled at me in agreement.

Our get together was about to break up for the afternoon when a bloodied, white-haired young knight appeared in the room to all of our surprise.

I was the first to address him. "Claudius! What happened to you?"

Chapter Twelve

Claudius exhaled with a groan. "It is good to once again bask in your presence, Ascended. There's no need to worry. Most of the blood isn't mine."

His delivery always came across as playfully sarcastic knowing my distaste for excessive politeness, but it was never enough to call him on it either way.

"Where've you been?" Marianna asked. "We haven't seen you in weeks."

"That's a bit of a tale. All very heroic." He eyed what food we had left as he struggled to remove his bloody gloves and leather armor. "I'm famished. May I?"

"Tell us what happened." I handed him the last kebab and helped with his gear so Marianna could address his wounds.

"Forgive me." He flinched as I peeled off a bit of fabric glued to a laceration across his arm by dried blood. "The Horned God we spoke about is awake in Iceland along with an army of werewolves, but Hell has corrupted them. The sky has gone red at all times of day and the water as black as pitch. There are some monstrous Infernal insects and the wolves are in a rabid state."

"We already have some experience with most of that from the past couple days. Did you see the Horned God though?" I asked. "What did you learn about him?"

"No, but I am certain his presence was there." Claudius took a bite from his kebab and made a face of disappointment. "Oh, these must be Anna's doing."

She yanked away the leather stuck to a gash, causing him to cry out mid-sentence.

"He's—*HAD*—a lot of incarnations, maybe the most of any deity. The eldest is Cernunnos of the Celts, but there is also Faunus of the Romans, Pan of the Greeks, Herne from Old English, Freyr from Norse, the Old One to Wiccans, Baphomet to occultists, and even Satan. There is a list of at least twenty aliases, but if you want the condensed version, he's a nature god. Don't expect him to be picking flowers though because he's also known as a Lord of Death."

"We have to stop them before they attack again like they did to our allies in Greenland," Nathaniel said.

"Can it wait until I finish eating?"

"What is the connection between the wolves and this Cernunnos?" Alexandre asked.

"I don't know if there is any aside from them both being nature folk," Claudius answered. "The real problem won't be the wolves but Cernunnos' followers. He's still actively worshipped by druids and witches, and has roots all over the world. Destroying any artifacts associated with him would be next to impossible too. It isn't anything like when we fought Set, who only popped up after the Infernal Kings brought him back and had to put so much energy toward establishing a new following."

"Forget about petrifying him like we did to Set too," said Marianna. "If he's a nature god then the elements of earth and stone won't have an effect on him."

"Now we know the real reason why the druids we had invited weren't too grateful," I said, returning to the bed while Marianna finished healing Claudius with spells. "I wonder if I made a bigger mistake than I thought by having them here so they could spy on us."

"We *could* burn his forest down," Claudius suggested based on our previous conversation.

"No. I feel that's too obvious an answer, especially now if he knows where we live. We could be setting a trap for ourselves."

"Speaking of fire and traps, how certain are we that Cernunnos has been corrupted?" Alexandre asked. "A battle of flame against the living seems only too convenient a narrative for a third party immune to immolation."

"Quite certain," said Claudius. "By any slim chance the Infernal Kings didn't actively choose Cernunnos for corruption, the pollution of the aether there would do it for them."

There was a loud belch from the bed as Noah woke up. "What's going on?"

"We're talking about fighting werewolves," I said to entice him.

"Nice." He moaned and used my hand to rub his stomach. "Ugh, why'd you let me eat so much?"

"What else can you tell me about Cernunnos and the werewolves, Claudius?"

"They're fast, Ascended. Deceptively fast," he answered. "The wolves could track my scent even when using stealth to phase between dimensions. They regenerate from anything short of dismemberment, but a steady blade served me well. Oh, and even their roar is dangerous due to its ability to cause paralysis."

"I remember hearing that some of them can use magic," Nathaniel said.

"I didn't stay long enough to find out. The Horned God's presence is strongest near the center of the island. There's a national park that takes up a large portion of the country with restricted areas everywhere. The people living there seem aware of his existence and the possibility of werewolves, but don't officially acknowledge it."

"Like those in town here," said Rafael.

"Wait. There are still people living there?" I asked Claudius.

"Yes."

"Are there any demons?" asked Nathaniel.

"No, but there weren't any in Egypt when the Infernal Kings corrupted Set either."

"The distortion in the sky we saw above Egypt was the Egyptian pantheon breaching the Veil. The atmosphere you described in Iceland is Hell merging with our world," Alexandre said. "Demons should be there if Hell is."

"Only the insects I encountered further in, which are minor demons. It's unlikely for anything stronger to be there since they aren't trying to kill Cernunnos's followers."

"They're all still hiding behind a smokescreen of innocent people either way," I said. "Typical cowards. The demons can't take souls that are already claimed by other gods anyway, at least not until they're done using Cernunnos and find a way to betray him like they did Set."

"Confronting Cernunnos will take everyone. We needed four gods, five demigods, Noah, and our cabal to vanquish Set," said Marianna.

"Isis and Kamakura have their hands full holding their empires together," I said. "Set was a maniac that didn't pull any punches from the beginning. If Cernunnos has been awake this whole time and is only just starting to attack on a small scale with the werewolves, there has to be a reason. I'd like to go there myself and find out why."

"The smaller the team the better then," said Claudius. "The larger the threat you pose, the greater the retaliation will be."

"Are you up for it?" I asked Nathaniel.

"You needn't ask."

"If you're looking to avoid an immediate confrontation I might suggest cloaking your aura with a Light-Oblivion combination spell to feign weakness," Alexandre said to me. "The current gods such as yourself are the greatest threat to Hell's invasion. I assume the Infernal Kings are aware that more gods may band together. Perhaps the corruption of Cernunnos was not meant as a tool of mass destruction like Set, but a beacon for those seeking allies."

"What about Nathaniel's aura?" I asked.

"We can. I didn't suggest it because, while impressive, he is only a demigod."

"No, should it be a trap, then it would be best for me to spring it or at least try to draw the attention away from you, Dorian," said Nathaniel.

"It sounds reasonable, but I don't want you getting hurt," I told him.

"Cut the apron strings and let the kid breathe, Dorian," Noah said. "You're supposed to be conserving your energy, or did you forget about that again?"

I responded with a pillow to his face.

"Don't worry about me. You made me invincible." Nathaniel smiled in encouragement.

"Nobody is invincible, although you are pretty close," I said.

"Every strength has an equal and often related weakness," Noah added. "The strongest castle walls will crumble in an earthquake if they lack flexibility."

"I understand," he said. "I'm ready to go when you are."

"We haven't slept since before Shanghai. You're not tired?"

"Not in the least."

"I'll get Liam and some of the others so they can help cast the spell to cloak your aura," said Rafael. "We'll need all of them to teleport you two that distance."

"I can fly there," Nathaniel said once he left.

"Not this time," I told him. "I want us arriving together in case we're confronted."

"Once we get there the kid should cover us from the sky," said Noah. "No point in diverting a trap if we're standing right next to the trigger."

"You're not coming unless you bring a sword," I said.

He narrowed his eyes at me in defiance, walked over to where his blades were mounted and took one from the wall without breaking eye contact.

"Ascended!" Connor entered the room from a bubble of aether and bumped into Alexandre. "Dorian! You're going to fight werewolves! You have to take me!"

Liam, Rafael, Tobias, and most of the other elders came in after him. Elder Knight Pavel grabbed Connor by the wrist and reprimanded him.

"Don't speak to the Ascended that way!" he barked.

"It's fine. Let him go," I told Pavel.

"Connor, you can teleport now?" Claudius sounded impressed.

"I've been practicing with Liam all day," he said, beaming. "I can't go *that* far yet, but if we're sending everyone it won't matter because I can travel with you."

"I'm not taking everyone though. Only Noah and Nathaniel are going," I said.

"Oh. And me too, right?" He grinned.

"I'd love to bring you along and see some more awesome ice magic, but I can't. Keep training with Liam and you'll come with me next time."

"You said the same thing when you went to Shanghai."

Several of the elders were aghast at his behavior and uttered his name through gritted teeth to stop him without causing a scene. I didn't mind at all though. It was what I had wanted in terms of natural conversation that still failed to register with the older members of the Order.

"Take him with us," said Noah. "What's the worst that happens? He dies?"

"I'm not afraid to die," Connor proclaimed with the heart of a lion.

"Fear is failure, but ask yourself what success is to you: honor or ego?" Noah asked. "Honor is knowing your limits and not risking other's success for your own ego. So do you want to come to satisfy that ego or find honor in humility?"

Connor thought about it while the rest cast the spell to cloak my aura. I thought it would be flashier, but the spell was done after a momentary violet glow and a shiver across my skin.

"The effect will wear off after two hours," Alexandre warned.

"I'll stay here and train," said Connor. "I know I'm not on the same level as you yet. I was being prideful because I wanted to prove I could keep up."

"You can come with me to the next city we save," Nathaniel told him.

"Are we ready to teleport?" I asked the group after changing into clean clothes in the bathroom.

"All set." Claudius nodded. "I'll guide the spell to the shore so you aren't dropped off in the heart of werewolf country. I'd recommend getting acquainted with the area before going deeper in so you don't get surrounded. The werewolves can be sneaky despite their size and we have no idea what tricks the Horned God has in store."

"We will. UNITY's base isn't far from there. We can have them set us up with a flight back home after we're done," I said.

Everyone wished us well, and a moment later we were sucked through the aether and across the ley lines to confront the Horned God.

Chapter Thirteen

"Nice place." Noah was the first to get his bearings upon arriving at the blighted island. "If you ignore all the evil."

Iceland was warmer than its name implied, but a cool ocean breeze kept the temperature in the low to mid-forties. The verdant green grass further up the rocky coast was so vibrant that even the crimson haze above couldn't diminish its hue. There weren't any traces of civilization in sight, only pristine nature shaded over by malignancy.

"Oh god, what is that?" I floated away from the waterline where tentacles lined with teeth scavenged the coast for a meal to feed whatever they were connected to, submerged under the black tide.

"Sushi." Noah came over to stand beside me.

"Um, where's your sword?" I asked.

He pretended to search himself and shrugged. "Must've left it behind."

"This isn't a joke, Noah."

"Never said it was." He threw his arm around me and squeezed until I couldn't breathe. I had to whack him in the ribs to release me. "Don't worry about it. Trust me."

He did at least bring the vest to his armor.

"They know we're here," Nathaniel said. "I can hear them approaching. Should I still go by air or do you want me to stay with you?"

"I don't need a sword to put down some dogs, kid. I was doing this before either of you was born and I've only gotten stronger on Dorian's super juice. Head inland to get the mutts' attention. I'll take care of the fighting down here along the way."

"I'll stay vigilant in case you do need me," said Nathaniel.

We headed in the direction Nathaniel went after he had departed. A lazy winding brook of opaque water flowed backward up the low rolling hills parallel to us. The soothing sound of running water was at least unchanged. It was somewhat surprising that there weren't many trees in the area as I had expected. I pictured a god of nature and wilderness to dwell within a dense forest.

The terrain was uneven with about every other step we took at a different elevation. Some of the rock formations were in geometric patterns I didn't think nature could create on its own, but there was still no hint of any human hand altering the landscape and it lacked Hell's signature. Iceland was like another world straight from a fantasy. The Infernals would have to try harder if they wanted to turn this place rotten. I hated to admit it, but Iceland might trump my tiny island in the Mediterranean for aesthetic beauty despite the malign presence.

"Company." Noah pointed to a nearby cliff. "Let me handle it so you don't blow our cover and get us overwhelmed."

I flew higher to get a look at our welcoming party. Five dusky-hued werewolves were charging across the countryside toward us on all fours, their claws ripping up the earth as they ran.

"Fine. Should we establish a safe word?"

"A what—?"

The werewolves leaped down from the cliff. These were not like the two adolescents Connor had clashed with; they were a pack of five full-grown adults that were a fair measure faster and bulkier. Fighting gigantic monsters was something with which Noah and I were all too familiar, but both times I had encountered werewolves I could tell there was something unique about their kind. The demons—some of whom towered above these werewolves—didn't project the same gut-wrenching terror. You could feel the wolves' primal rage invading like a claw stabbed straight through the heart to trigger crippling fear. An unsurpassed level of savagery was in their eyes, which made the demons appear more as passive oafs by comparison. They had a foreseeable desire to rend the meat from your bones with as much brutality as possible, extending beyond the simple-minded drive of conquest that motivated the Infernal grunts to kill and move on.

I caught the pack and levitated them above the ground before they made contact. "If you can understand me, I'm giving you one chance to not fight."

"What are you doing? They're not gonna listen." Noah rocked back and forth on the balls of his feet in a fighter's stance and shook out his hands to loosen up. I had never seen him act that way in real combat and didn't know if it should worry me more or less that he was suddenly taking this so seriously.

The wolves unleashed a collective howl that overloaded the senses and almost interrupted my concentration enough to drop them. Earthly creatures with supernatural powers derived from fear and anger were the perfect loyal subjects for the Infernals.

"Let 'em go." Noah rolled his shoulders and cracked his neck.

I thought about it, but no, this wasn't a game or a sparring match. Noah wasn't any different than Connor wanting to fight just to prove he could when there were better options. I snapped the werewolves' necks 180 degrees and dropped their lifeless bodies with a boom.

"I don't need to exert myself to kill them," I said.

"Neither do I." A crunching sound came from the bodies as Noah talked. "Stick to the plan."

The wolves' heads rotated back into place and their eyes rolled down from inside their skulls. They were on their hind legs ready for battle without delay. Noah flipped over me and flying kicked one in the face when it came in close to bite me. I surrounded myself in a shell of telekinetic energy that the other four werewolves crashed against in futility.

"They're all yours," I told Noah, floating away to give him space. Three of the werewolves followed, but soon relented to help their friends once they found they were unable to break my shield with their fiercest attacks.

Noah started off with a series of punches to the first werewolf's brawny chest while dodging the furious swipes of its claws. His movements were precise down to the positioning of his fingers and angle of each foot in his stances as he struck, blocked, and feinted in a flawless execution of techniques honed for over a century. It was all muscle memory for him.

He ended his flurry of blows with a palm strike to the sternum that shattered the bone inward. The werewolf staggered and dropped to its knees. Noah had already moved on to the next as it collapsed to the ground motionless.

The sound of Noah's pummeling strikes rang out crystal clear over the howls and snarls. I noticed he wasn't using his true speed for this fight. He seemed to want the werewolves to keep track of him as he evaded their attacks by a hair's breadth and countered with unrestrained force. On occasion he managed to use his kicks to knock one into the other or lunged under their legs at the right moment to get them to rake their claws at the wrong target.

Blood splattered, bones broke, and skin tore open from Noah's beatdown of the pack. The first werewolf was back in action as the second fell to a neck-breaking stranglehold. Noah dropped another while the second was still unconscious and gradually wore down the rest until he had three and four out at a time. It should have been easier with fewer opponents, but without the bodies of the others to impede some of the hits it seemed he might run into trouble.

Noah landed an uppercut to the jaw of the final wolf followed by a straight punch breaking through a soft spot between its ribs. He ripped the beating heart from its chest and shoved it down the werewolf's throat. It would not be getting up again. Once the life left the body of the beast it reverted into a naked half-human corpse.

The next of the remaining four was already at his back. Noah spun and blocked an incoming swipe with his forearm and then somersaulted to the side while grabbing it at the wrist to dislocate it. The werewolf's howl staggered Noah for the first time. Instead of it reeling from the pain, the werewolf countered and got him in the face with its paw. One hit was all it took to turn the tide of battle. Noah's head was gushing blood and the other three wolves were revived again from being left alone for too long. Another swipe sent him tumbling, but he rolled to recover.

"Don't!" he shouted to me, knowing I was about to intervene.

He disabled two of them once more, ripping one of their jaws clean off while it was down. There was no telling yet if it could still get up after that, but that seemed doubtful considering how much it was bleeding.

Noah swung around and climbed on the head a werewolf about to chomp down on him. He drove its opened jaws onto the arm of its friend that was too enraged to care who was hurting it and turned them on each other. The third woke up and rejoined the melee with Noah in its sights while the other two were momentarily distracted by their own quarrel.

They began to alternate howls that continually interrupted Noah with pangs of unavoidable terror. He was caught another time. The third werewolf got his foot in its mouth and lodged a claw in Noah's flank where his armor didn't cover, but he transformed into a cloud of mist to escape. Noah was bleeding profusely from the wound, yet still motioned that he was okay. He waited to be attacked and retreated into the other two that were still fighting, then took the opportunity to kick one's claw into the other's eye.

The crippled wolf tackled its attacker while Noah held its arms back with all his might. The wolf missing an eye tore out its friend's throat in vengeance-fueled derangement. Noah took his chance and snapped off a claw from the dead wolf and with a spinning backhand drove it into the remaining eye of the crazed beast.

There were only two werewolves left and one was blind.

It should be easy from here.

That was believable until the healthier of the beasts chomped down on Noah's shoulder with a stunning display of speed the rest hadn't shown so far. Its fangs penetrated his armor and drew voluminous amounts of blood.

Noah turned into mist again to free himself. Doing so tapped a much larger amount of blood from his system than his other powers and he was already losing plenty from damage. He could have healed his wounds, but that too was a gamble that would have drained precious resources.

"You've done enough. Let me finish the rest off," I called to him.

"I said I've got this!" he yelled in frustration.

He lured the blinded wolf back to the brook where tentacles crawled along the edge of the water there too. On the surface it appeared shallow enough that I wondered how they could be attached to anything, but once they got a hold of the werewolf it was effortless for them to drag it down into the unknown.

The wolf missing its jaw did not regenerate the bone, but did come to life, albeit flailing helplessly in excruciating agony and gurgling in place of howls.

Noah traded blows with the last standing werewolf until rushing it down when there was an opening. It was hard to see what was happening with all the blood and fur going everywhere, but Noah came out on top after a barrage of punches and a sidekick that caved in its chest cavity. He angled his fingers and struck between the shoulder blades with a sharp, penetrating blow to remove a chunk of spine and finish the gruesome battle. The jawless wolf was put out of its misery with a stomp that ejected its brain out the top of its skull.

"King of the fucking jungle!" he shouted to the sky in a pained testosterone and adrenaline-laden bellow. He sauntered over to me wincing and breathing heavily. "You see that shit? Black Tiger Kung Fu palm strike, Taekwondo footwork, Shotokan counters. Told you I could do it with my bare hands."

"Technically, you only killed three by yourself. And this isn't a jungle."

Noah grabbed his crotch and wagged a finger in my face. "You're gonna get it so bad later. Now come 'ere and feed your tiger."

He took me by the back of the head, plunging his fangs into my neck to drink until he had his fill.

"I *am* very impressed with you taking down the werewolves like that, but we have to keep moving," I said once he was healed and ready.

"Hold up. I want you to know I didn't only do this for myself. Maybe now you can relax knowing everyone isn't gonna die if you're not babysitting them."

"I—"

Noah tossed me over his shoulder and zipped several miles away at a time to continue our search for the Horned God. Werewolves and the demonic insects we had encountered in Shanghai were in no short supply to the north, so instead we swung around south to avoid detection. Even Noah wasn't bold enough to take them all on himself and for me to start fighting them would defeat the purpose of my concealment.

"It really is like another world here," I said when we stopped by a lake. "Out here in nature where there isn't any destruction and only these creatures wandering around feels more surreal than in the cities. It's like there's no connection to the life we knew here."

We traveled another mile, reaching a wide fjord. Across the other side the terrain was a lot less green, but there were several sparse groves that gave height to the landscape with something other than hills and rocks.

"Wolves must've picked up our scent," said Noah. "They're closing in. I can smell them too, and hear them. Maybe two miles off. I should take some of them out so we won't have as many to deal with later."

"Don't. I can sense Nathaniel close by, so we have to be near the center of the island." I carried us across the fjord and landed closer to where I felt Nathaniel.

"We're not going to have a choice. They're coming in fast from all directions." Noah turned and squinted into the horizon. "Something's not right... There's no way their auras are that big. Shit—"

An army of werewolves descended upon us. Their movements were just beyond my eyes' ability to track and appeared only as charcoal gray blurs whirling around us. Noah intercepted one that would have struck me before I could get my shield up. He wasn't taking any risks this time and launched himself into the pack using his powers to manipulate the flow of time around him. Only delayed splashes of blood and fur were visible as he bludgeoned them with his punches and kicks at a thousand times per second. The group must have been more durable than the last based on the lack of body parts he was able to remove from them.

One werewolf that was already missing its right arm from a previous battle stood a foot above the rest seemingly directing them with feral vocalizations. Its howl threw Noah from his temporal jet stream and let several of the pack pile on him. He broke free using his mist form and retaliated by killing one and knocking out two more. As those three fell, five more entered the brawl.

"Feel free to join in if you're bored!" His voice was almost unintelligible over the noise the werewolves were making. Their speed made it too hard to focus on disabling individual extremities. I settled for a shockwave to slow them down first and ended with mass decapitation using the least amount of energy I could. There was a slight degree of resistance that these wolves had against the physical properties of my powers, proving my speculation about their increased durability, but it was nothing to a god.

The land was quiet again. The larger werewolf that had been acting as pack leader disappeared without me noticing. Noah stood amongst the headless bodies that I was certain were dead, but they hadn't returned to their half-human appearance like the previous batch.

"These better not come back to life," I said, but the corpse-eating maggots had already come to collect. "They were definitely not regular werewolves."

Noah kicked one corpse that was still twitching on his way to me. His chest had a gash almost down to the bone that managed to cut through the demon leather armor. He sat on the ground away from all the carnage looking weary, so I sat with him to let him feed from my wrist.

"Can't believe they got a hit in on me at that speed though," he said when finished. "Got me right in the tits."

"You should've dodged more instead of brawling to show off. A shot to the heart could've been instant death."

"Didn't wanna waste the blood by going any faster in case it was a longer fight. Sometimes it's better to take a hit so you can use their own momentum against them once they're wide open. Wasn't expecting to get cut so deep though."

I kissed his chest where the wound had healed. "It's okay, you're still my king of the jungle."

"Damn right I am. And I'm gonna be the one to take down that alpha. Maybe I'll even make us a new blanket out of it. If I can pull that off I'll consider myself closer to earning the use of those swords."

A roar close by sent shudders down through my core.

"Looks like you're about to get your chance right now."

Chapter Fourteen

The pack leader returned alone with its lips curled back in a fearsome snarl, which elevated to a full-blown howl and tore the earth asunder. Noah vanished to get a preemptive strike, but was countered by a ripple of argent energy that the werewolf discharged within a fraction of a second. The beast's fur was now storing this exotic power that caused any hit Noah landed to shock and burn him long enough to become visible. The werewolf wasn't hurt by Noah's punches as most of the strength behind them was sapped when the energy current caused his muscles to seize. With a paralyzing roar or two mixed in, Noah was completely ineffectual and could only dodge or risk being tossed around like helpless prey. I decided he had had enough when the wolf grabbed him in its one paw and I heard a crunch above the sizzling energies gathering in its clutches.

The wolf dropped Noah and dashed away in a charcoal blur when I struck. One attack after the next was evaded. Somehow it knew how to react before I decided my move and was already gone.

"Mist, now!" I shouted to Noah. I was about to release an omnidirectional blast when the werewolf let out one of its own a second faster by using the charge it had stored. The wave passed through my barrier, interrupting control of my body and concentration with a chilling jolt that knocked me to the ground.

Nathaniel swooped in right as the beast lunged and held it up off the ground by its throat. "No monster shall touch the Ascended in my presence," he said, sending its massive body tumbling across the terrain until it was out of sight, like a pebble skipping on the water.

"Are you hurt?" Nathaniel crouched to offer me his hand.

"I'm all right, although a little surprised at how much a werewolf was able to affect me. I'll be happy when this is over. It isn't easy having to hold back so much."

"I can understand." He nodded. "The Horned God is close, so we should be victorious soon I hope."

"That stupid dog's skin was tougher than steel," said Noah. "I hate whatever that silver bullshit was too. I want a rematch."

He was roughed up, but not as badly as from the previous fight. The aether used to purify the demon leather of our armor also provided decent resistance to most magic and energy types, in addition to being fireproof.

"I did warn you of the possibility for magic," Nathaniel reminded him.

"It knew when and where I was attacking ahead of time," I said. "I didn't think werewolves could read minds, or the future."

"It probably saw the tells before you use your powers. I know when you're going to do something by the way your pupil moves," said Noah.

"But it wasn't looking at me the first time when it had you in its grip."

"Whatever. I could've beaten it if I had more time to figure something out."

"Put it behind you and let's move on," I said, patting his shoulder. "Do you know where our target is, Nathaniel?"

"Up there in that crater." He pointed to a steep slope in the distance. "The aether is converging there, the same as when Set changed the flow of the ley lines to attack the first cities."

"A crater in a mountain? That's a volcano, kid," Noah said.

"Yes, I was trying to make it sound less foreboding. It isn't active that I can tell. There's steaming water at the bottom of the basin with a tree-covered island in the middle that would seem an appropriate hiding place. We will have to watch out for the cave openings along the inside perimeter because that's where I saw the most werewolves."

"They're like a whole colony of ants," I said. "It'll be easier to take them all out at once with them grouped up like that, but first we have to make sure the Horned God is there with them, and he's not going to show himself until we do."

"I'll go down first to trigger any trap like we planned," said Nathaniel.

"I still don't like that plan," I said.

"Would it help if I didn't give you a choice?" he asked.

"That's usually how I handle him," Noah added.

"Except Nathaniel doesn't get his ass kicked half the time."

"That's hurtful."

I landed on Noah's back and put my arms around his neck. "Okay Nathaniel, I'm leaving first contact up to you. We'll keep watch from above."

He shot through the air and into the crater ahead of us, not allowing anymore doubt to cross my mind. By the time we caught up and took our position at the mouth of the crater, he was hovering in front of what I assumed to be the Horned God, sitting cross-legged on a tree stump down on the island. The odor of wet fur and other animal smells wafting up from the inactive volcano somewhat devalued the beauty of the land we had seen along the way.

"I can't hear what they're saying," I whispered to Noah.

The interior walls were lined with caves as Nathaniel had described and a large number of werewolves were at the ready in each one.

"Time to step in," said Noah. "I'll keep my eyes opened."

He hoisted me onto his shoulders. The next moment we were standing by Nathaniel in the birch thicket where fireflies flickered about aimlessly.

The Horned God would have been more aptly named the Antlered God considering the magnificent spread of multipronged bone rising from both sides of his head. What I couldn't tell was if the jawless stag skull attached to the antlers was his head or a mask. The eye sockets were hollow, with only a puzzling darkness inside similar to Gianluca's abyssal helm. His motionless body was a bramble of petrified wood and fossilized bone arranged in a humanoid appearance; certain parts, such as the ribcage and femurs, were more recognizable than others. The digits on each hand ended in talons, but what was gripped in those hands was far more threatening: an enormous, almost unwieldy iron scythe—the envy of any reaper. The blade resembled a corvid's beaked skull, and along with an ornate gold torque around his neck, both were inscribed with a distinctive Celtic knot motif.

"Shatterer of the False Moon, I welcome ye to mine lands." The Horned God projected his voice into my mind as the other Spiritborn had been known to do, and spoke aloud despite not having a functioning mouth or any organs necessary to vocalize. His Old World Gaelic and the blend of a Scandinavian accent picked up through the years were pronounced, yet comprehensible. The whisper of a second voice hidden behind the sound of rustling leaves and creaking branches carried each word in an uncanny echo, but I would not let myself be caught off guard.

"Uh, thank you." I looked to Nathaniel to be sure this was a peaceful meeting, but the Horned God answered first.

"Knoweth me as Cernunnos. Ye needn't fear for thy safety here, Ascended."

Two crows squawked at each other from his antlers. One pecked at an empty eye socket.

Is he one of the birds or the skeleton-looking thing or both?

"It's a pleasure to meet you, but that wasn't a concern."

A shadow fell over us. The alpha had returned. It leaped down from the mouth of the crater and onto the island with us. Nathaniel moved to block it from possibly reaching me.

The humungous werewolf howled at the sky and shrank as it shifted into a wholly human form.

Moments of the transformation were masked by dark flashes that felt like they were coming from within my own head, making me question if what I saw was reality.

How powerful is the creature that can invade a god's mind or is it something else entirely?

The change was otherwise a near-seamless biological process that could almost pass as a natural evolution happening in seconds. There was no exaggerated traumatic breaking of bones or skin tearing as the body reconfigured itself. The reduction of muscle and bone mass was fluid; teeth and nails formed from fangs and claws, and thick fur receded into every follicle.

"He lies with every breath. I could smell the fear on 'em from the moment we met. All of 'em quivering like motherless babes alone in the woods at night. Even now they reek of fear. Why do ye dishonor us with an offer of friendship to ones so weak, Lord Cernunnos? I could've killed them all had ye let me."

The alpha male was a woman—a middle-aged woman with a fiery red coif wearing only Celtic war paint and tattoos.

"Of course it's a red head," Noah muttered.

"Nay, Aífe, even ye are but a sapling to the Ascended's might. A clever disguise cloaks thine aura, true?"

"Yes," I answered, not exactly sure what was going on and trying not to stare straight into the full frontal nudity. Aífe might not have been my type, but it was still distracting.

"More tricks!" she said, spitting on the ground beside her. Her accent and speaking mannerisms were somewhat more contemporary Irish, but she also mixed in Old English and put a harsh emphasis on her r's. "The druids were right about ye. Our blood stains your clothes and ye wear our hides as blankets. Nothing but weasels wasting your magic tricks on easy living and stealing the Goddess' power while Her children suffer."

"Excuse me? We offered them hospitality so they *wouldn't* suffer," I snapped. "Why am I even talking to you? Are you supposed to be important?"

"Ye speak to Aífe the Wroth, Blessed Child of the Moon and den mother of all you see here!"

"Well, now at least I know what you've been so busy doing while my friends and I save the world."

"They are not all born of my womb, churlish—!"

"Thy tongue betrays good sense, Aífe," Cernunnos interrupted her. "This Ascended is the one to fell the false moon that put the Goddess in peril. Leave us or be silent."

He still hadn't moved an inch, which raised my suspicion that this could be a statue he was speaking through as a trap, or perhaps "he" was the scythe.

"Still want that rematch?" I whispered to Noah.

He shrugged with his arms crossed. "Whatever."

Aífe stood down but remained lurking behind Cernunnos, ready to pounce.

"Forgive Aífe on mine behalf, Ascended. The Ulfhednar are known for their temper, and Aífe is known even among them with all the fire of Brigit and none of the warmth."

"Ulf...hednar? You mean werewolves?" I asked.

"Aye, lupine warriors honed in the North, more than mere beasts. In thy tongue t'would be better spoken as berserker. 'Werewolf' doth little justice to their culture, as t'would to call an ancient elm but a tree. Ye didn't travel this way to share in our legends though."

"We've been fighting Hell's invasion and searching for allies when berserkers attacked in Greenland," said Nathaniel. "We thought they were corrupted like other people have been in Hell's presence and maybe you were too like another god we had fought."

"Nay, lad. Hell cannot touch the souls of the faithful and we would not be having this talk had I become one of them."

"That's why we've been so cautious," I said. "But if you're not working for the demons then why attack us when we came here?"

"Those ye fought were not under mine command. The Fury hath taken them. Ye see, berserkers walk a narrow path to keep good reason with their strength. They must balance rage upon careful steps or risk becoming mindless beasts from whence there is no return. Hell hath not the right to taint their souls, yet to kindle madness...another matter in truth."

"Why was Aífe with them then?" I asked.

She seemed about ready to fall off the path.

"She tries to saveth them even though she knoweth better."

"Is it *not* better than letting them be culled like animals? They are our family!" she exclaimed. "They may no longer speak our tongue, but they yet understand mine! Rage can be directed if not controlled!"

"I can understand not wanting to let go," I said.

"They perish with honor and shall be reborn for it," Cernunnos said.

"You wanted us to kill them."

"Aye. Ye have our respect, Ascended. To fall by thy will in battle is a tale worth telling with pride throughout the halls of Valhalla, surely better than by a demon's venom. The Goddess and I owe ye a great debt many a time o'er when ye saved Her from the false moon."

"Who is this 'Goddess'?" I asked. "And isn't Valhalla the Norse underworld? Are you both Norse and Celtic?"

"Valhalla is a great hall within the sacred soil of the Otherworld known to us as the Summerlands—opposite the frigid wastes of Hel where the unworthy journey upon death. 'Tis where our finest warriors go and await mine call for a chance to fight once more in Her defense. She is the very planet and all we are made of: the air we breathe, the water we drink, the life in our veins, both material and not. We are all one through Her, all save the demons, and 'tis I who created the berserkers to serveth us both.

"This day I stand as the nexus betwixt both Celtic and Norse pantheons. Many winters ago mine people were branded heretics by a pious group of upstarts seeking to infect mine lands with their false religion. They labeled me a demon, but not all were so foolish as to believe them.

"The Norse to the east in Scandinavia endured much the same insult and our strength waned from those whom abandoned their heritage to convert to this false idol. But I hath endured greater and in turn I connected our heavenly courts so that even the invading Romans could not break this branch. I speaketh for the Goddess and cannot be muted. Sweet repose evadeth me yet as I rise through the cracks toward mine people's light. In yesteryear, the Celts, Gauls, and Norsemen of the North. In this era 'tis the druids and Wiccans scattered across many lands."

"Will you help us defend them then?" I asked, still unsure where I should be looking to address him without any signs of movement aside from the crows. "Will you fight with us against the Infernals?"

"Aye, but I gather all mine strength here to ward against the encroaching blight. These caves and few villages are all we hath left untouched by it. Any we send to hunt turn mad and ne'er return. The pups will soon starve I fear. Worse, the water here hath become too hot to drink. 'Twas once an oasis to relax in the lake, but now serveth only to taunt mortal needs."

"Pups?" I looked more closely at the cave openings, having kept my attention forward until now. Human children with dirty faces dressed in only rawhide loincloths and fur pelts around their shoulders stood huddled against the werewolves. They treated the beasts like nothing more than big family dogs to climb on, gripping handfuls of fur or ears for security while staring at us. The killing machines guarded them intently and offered a playful lick to some.

I noticed that Aífe wasn't the only one missing a limb among the adults. Heavy scarring was also common.

"We can bring them food and water, or better yet, help you find a new home," I offered.

"T'would suit us well to accept, but we are warriors and charity is not our way. What is earned in battle though, we taketh with honor."

"See?" Noah nudged me to emphasize his own code denying him use of his swords.

"I thought you were primarily a nature god. Isn't nature supposed to be peaceful?" I asked.

"Nature hath many a face and there be it more than a single path through darkened wood, Ascended. I am one with Death itself as the natural end to all things living, a necessary quietus be it through hunt or harvest from which life may spring forth everlasting by the will of the Goddess."

"I don't really want to fight you for sport. You admit you're using all your power to preserve this place and I'm conserving mine for the demons."

Is that his game? Draw me into a friendly battle to tire me or attract chaos? I still don't know how much I can trust him.

"Nay, I dare not pose as such betwixt gods or I would see more than these lands eviscerated by a single blow. In our stead I propose a contest of might for thy herald."

I turned to Nathaniel to see what he thought. "Champion?"

"Who is it that I would be fighting?" he asked.

"Allow me, Lord Cernunnos," Aífe stepped in. "I must repay him for leaving our fight unfinished."

"Ye hath no right to challenge another god's champion, Aífe. Thy combat was ne'er meant to be in the first place," Cernunnos said. "I challenge ye, Champion of the Ascended, to defeat the Herald of Herne."

Chapter Fifteen

Cernunnos had remained inanimate throughout the duration of our chat. There were moments I wondered if we had been speaking to a decoy, so I wasn't too surprised when the grove of birch trees surrounding us rustled to life at the call for his herald.

To be in the presence of the man who emerged was to experience nature personified in masculine form—the earthy musk, the raw, mysterious strength and vitality of life uninhibited. He was as much a part of the land as the dirt under his fingernails; he had a body built for war and wilderness with the scars to show for it. Sandy brown hair across his pectorals matched that on his face and head, yet two braids tying back the rest seemed a contradiction to his otherwise unkempt appearance. With light-colored eyes made brighter in contrast to the war paint smeared across his face, his gaze resembled that of a wolf stalking in the forest shadows.

"'Tis an honor, Ascended." The warrior of the woods kneeled, greeting me in a gruff voice with an accent that matched neither Aífe nor Cernunnos. On his back he carried an arsenal fit for an entire hunting party.

"Nice to meet you," I replied.

He rose and addressed Nathaniel as "Champion" with a nod. There was no rage in his face. Not yet at least. For now he was an apex predator at peace in his domain.

The unmoving image of Cernunnos hadn't offered any further information, so I was forced to prompt the man for his name. "And you are...the herald?"

"Aye, call me Calder."

His prominent upper canine teeth were obvious when he spoke, but without the undead's surreal mystique he appeared more animal than supernatural.

"When someone says to call them something it usually means that it *isn't* their real name," said Noah.

"And what is thine own, stranger?"

"Don't worry about it."

"He's Noah," I answered for him, so I could revel in getting under his skin a bit, as he liked to do with me.

"Shall we, Ascended?" In a sudden alarming burst of movement Cernunnos stood on cloven hooves and leaped to the top of the crater wall, scaring off the crows to the opposite end.

I guess he is the antlered...thing.

Calder tossed aside most of his arsenal to lighten his load, keeping only an axe and spear. "Do ye need a weapon?" he asked Nathaniel. "I boast the finest blades, unbreakable by man and god alike."

"Boast" was accurate. Calder's weapons and what little armor he wore looked like remnants of standard mortal equipment from the Viking Age, but appearance didn't always account for mystical enchantments. The gold torque around his neck was identical to the one Cernunnos had and must have meant more to them than a piece of jewelry.

Calder selected the only sword that seemed to be worth anything and presented it to Nathaniel. "One of silver?"

"I'll do without," he said.

"Wise." Calder laughed. "Wouldn't have served ye well against the likes of me."

He dragged the silver blade down his forearm to demonstrate that his wound healed at the same rate as mine.

"Don't kill him," I whispered to Nathaniel.

"Children are starving and we fight for sport," he whispered back. "This feels wrong to me."

"Then end it quickly without splitting Iceland in two."

"Remember what I taught you, kid," said Noah. "This isn't some grunt. His aura matches yours and he's already playing mind games. Bait his attacks to see what he can do, then create an opening before you strike."

"Give 'em one for me, *Calder*," Aífe said. She turned into her bestial form to climb the crater and then back again once by Cernunnos' side. Noah and I made our way up to them after coaching Nathaniel.

"Shouldn't this fight be somewhere that collateral damage won't be an issue?" I asked as we watched them size each other up on the island.

"We are right where we need to be," said Cernunnos.

The match had begun.

Calder swung his axe at Nathaniel's head, and he put up his arm to block it.

The axe shattered against Nathaniel's gauntlet. He removed a piece of the blade that had become lodged and tossed it aside. Calder let out a raucous laugh, not at all sore over having his "unbreakable" weapon broken. He discarded the splintered axe handle and readied the spear. I may have previously misjudged it as mortal garbage. The weapon awakened in his hands, transforming from a mere stick with an iron tip to a legendary weapon of artisanal beauty adorned with Celtic designs. The head was the size of a ballista bolt surging with emerald green energy.

The crowd of children and werewolves that had watched on in quiet curiosity during our visit now came alive with cheers and excited howls. Calder smiled and nodded at some of the young ones while Nathaniel remained focused.

The two began to circle each other around the island. Nathaniel glided away from a few lunges Calder threw out to test his reflexes. After another flurry of unsuccessful thrusts Calder made his first serious move. With a war cry that matched the berserkers' loudest howls he jumped into the air and plunged the spear toward Nathaniel's chest.

The spear shattered as well without scratching Nathaniel.

There was no laughter this time. The crowd turned ugly after taking a second to recover from what they had witnessed. When Cernunnos stood I knew it was bad. I looked at Noah to prepare for a hasty retreat or brawl.

"Impossible," was all Cernunnos uttered.

"He cheats!" Aífe roared. "More trickery! We should have known they think it beneath them to fight fair!"

Cernunnos tapped the handle of his scythe on the ground and returned to his seat. The deafening screams and snarls emanating from every cave in the crater came to an abrupt end.

Meanwhile, Nathaniel had picked up the broken piece of spear at his feet and handed it to Calder, who remained silent. He joined the pieces together and restored the weapon to its former glory. Calder engaged once more, but a simple shove from Nathaniel sent him flying into one of the caves and out the other side.

The berserkers gnashed their teeth in discontent over the humiliation of their fiercest warrior.

A tremor stirred the land as a werewolf double Aífe's size bounded from the cave and right into Nathaniel. They locked hands and neither one could move the other for a time. Nathaniel punched him in the chest and knocked him over, only to be smacked away by a giant paw. He caught himself in a backward slide, digging his feet into the cave floor where he landed and shot back at Calder with his fist ready.

The werewolf dashed ahead and swiped his claws across Nathaniel's chest, slicing open the leather of Nathaniel's armor, but failing to draw blood or scratch the skin. The two jabbed at each other until Nathaniel took Calder to the ground by the neck, disorienting him in a harsh light. He could end the battle now without killing. All he needed was to give a quick twist or squeeze to incapacitate Calder.

Noah and I turned away from the glare and looked at each other. He had satisfaction in his eyes, as if it were him down there about to win, but then Nathaniel did the unthinkable as the light faded. He let Calder go and shouted he yields.

"He dishonors us even now," Aífe said in disgust.

Calder returned to human form and one of the children ran up with his waistcloth to cover himself. Cernunnos jumped down to the island, so Noah and I followed.

"This has gone on for long enough," Nathaniel explained. "I see little point in extended jousting while children starve, and I have no interest in hurting the reputation of their hero. I will not be the villain here when all we wish to do is lend our aid."

Calder cracked his neck. His voice boomed so all could hear his response. "Knowing when to fight for else than blood is the mark of a true warrior. Ye honor me and my people, Champion. T'would do me proud to cleanse the lands of our nemesis together."

There was plenty of cheering and bouncing children in the crowd as Calder and Nathaniel shook hands. The berserkers let out a concert of howls and then retired into large, terrifying lumps of fur to rest.

"I suppose if both Cernunnos and the Herald respect ye then ye mustn't be so foul," Aífe conceded. "But I'm still keeping my eye open for trickery."

"I deign to admit the trickery she speaketh was by our hand, Ascended," said Cernunnos, who was sitting on his original tree stump with his legs crossed again. "I did not fathom thy champion to be of such strength in character and body. This outcome was expected to be for us to teach a lesson on our warriors' way. The druids sorely underestimated thy heart."

"Aye. And I must ask forgiveness for my attempt to fool ye with the weapons, thinking ye would take one and tremble when it broke against mine," Calder said. "Gáe Bulg *is* truly an unbreakable spear, though only in my hands—at least it used to be. Indulge me in how ye managed to endure such a blow."

"I am as the Ascended made me," Nathaniel answered with more confidence than usual.

163

I suppressed reacting to the burst of pride for the sake of tactfulness.

"I can go for the children's food if you wish," he said to me.

"Yes, and after that we can see about moving the camp elsewhere, along with relocating any villagers."

"And then, a feast for the gods to celebrate!" Calder exclaimed, slapping Nathaniel on the back. He seemed equally enthused about the food and the friendship.

"Fly over to UNITY and tell Lyle to give you food and water for the children while we decide where to relocate them," I said to Nathaniel, taking his hand to repair the gauntlet and armor. "If they can set us up with transportation that'd be great too."

"I'll return soon." He flew off, almost taking some of us with him in the updraft. Calder caught the child who had handed him his waistcloth and was snorting in gleeful laughter at being blown away.

"Can the children transform too?" I asked.

"Nay, only those whom reach maturity," said Cernunnos. "There are two breeds of berserkers: the Vargr and the Einherjar.

"The Vargr are born to berserkers. Males will leaveth their packs in search of a mate and the den mother will decideth if he is worthy in trial by combat. Should he impress her, 'tis her choice to keep him for herself or pass him to another female in her pack where he shall remain as a permanent member. When with child she will stay in human shape to reduce the need for food and not poison the unborn with rage. For this reason only those who knoweth balance are chosen to mate. 'Tis the whole pack's duty to protect any female who is carrying with their lives."

Interesting. I wouldn't have expected them to be a matriarchal society.

"The Einherjar are warriors fallen in battle as Calder, whom I retrieved from the dead to serveth the Goddess along with the Vargr," Cernunnos continued. "They are not undying as he, though all berserkers may live for centuries as Aife. Much presence of mind is required to maketh the first change into human form and a careful balance must be maintained."

"Berserkers lost to the Fury can't ever revert to human form, right?" I asked. "You said the ones who attacked us on our way here were lost, but the first group reverted halfway back to humans when they died."

I watched the child under Calder's arm give up trying to squirm away and just dangle. I tried not to laugh as I saw Noah and myself in the interaction.

Where is Noah?

He had been quiet for too long. I looked around casually so as to not slight Cernunnos as he spoke. Noah had taken his top off and was soaking in the hot water behind us without a care in the world. Aífe had slipped away to one of the caves, where she sat on a throne of her male werewolf concubines.

"In death they found peace," said Cernunnos. "Those lost do so in stages and may have only begun to slip away."

"Do you have any thoughts on where you can go?"

"A kingdom by name of Canada to the west hath vast expanses of wilderness in which we hold interest."

"We can get you there no problem. Nathaniel should return within the hour."

"He is mighty swift," said Calder. "I should like to challenge him to a contest of speed. Perhaps after we feast."

"There's still a demon invasion to handle," I reminded him.

"Aye, but what is life without a bit of sport and revelry among friends?"

Will we ever find other immortals who take this seriously?

Chapter Sixteen

Nathaniel arrived from PROJECT: UNITY twenty minutes later holding a crate of food over his head that the werewolves descended on as soon as he set it down.

"Did you leave anything for the troops?" I asked, eyeing the substantial load.

"Lyle said to take whatever I needed. He's on his way with those big helicopters they have. Do we know where we're taking them?"

Nathaniel began handing out rations and opening bottles of water for the kids that gathered around.

"Canada. I'm not sure bringing these guys in a helicopter over the ocean is a good idea though. What if they go mad on the way?"

"Those who can shall return to human shape to lessen the rage," said Cernunnos. "The rest shall brace themselves for what I prayeth be a brief journey."

"This could go wrong real fast," I said. "Isis has the power to calm souls. If it's strong enough to hold off the demons from invading her kingdom it should be good enough to keep the berserkers tame for a trip across the pond. The problem is that she can't leave there for long."

"I'll go and see if there is anything she can do," Nathaniel suggested.

He was gone again faster than I could let him know I approved.

Aífe was busy keeping in line the berserkers trying to get into the crate. "This food ain't yours, mongrel!" she shouted, cuffing one of the beasts upside the head. It growled and skulked away without further challenge. Another managed to make it past her while she was distracted with a rack of frozen ribs in its mouth. A scuffle broke out between its brethren over who got to gnaw on the meat to defrost it.

"What is this?" Calder held up a chocolate bar in a brightly colored wrapper.

"Candy," I said, opening it for him. I realized I probably had to explain further. "It's sweet. You know, like sugar? Just how much of the modern world are you familiar with?"

"A trifle at most I'm afraid," he said. "Many here ne'er seen a human settlement of today. What we know is from the Einherjar who share tales of their past lives, but none here are younger than eighty cycles and the world hath changed much in that time."

"I learn from the dreams of followers present and past," Cernunnos added. "I hear, see, and smell through Earth itself, but not yet of modern intricacies."

"I know this taste!" Calder exclaimed. "These are nuts!"

"Yeah, I hope you're not allergic. Maybe I should've mentioned that first."

"Hmph. This pleases me," said Calder, who was now double fisting candy into his face.

Aífe turned her wrath on him. "But it isn't for ye, Calder, ye big lout!"

"Still thy shrieking tongue and taste this, woman." Calder shoved half a candy bar in her mouth, which silenced her objections, and he moved on to taste something else.

"Those are hot dogs. They're supposed to be cooked— never mind."

"People today *eat* dogs?" he asked with disgust, having already bitten into one. "The most loyal of beasts are to be cooked in thy cities?"

"It's only a name they were given. There's no dog in it, or any other animal probably."

These are random items for rations. I think Nathaniel might've also raided Lyle's personal stash.

The sound of military aircraft had never been so sweet to my ears as when PROJECT: UNITY showed up and ended our conversation about junk food. The children ran to hide in the caves and most of the berserkers went into a frenzy, howling at the helicopters until Cernunnos rose to stop them with a subtle gesture.

Lyle descended into the crater on a zip wire from one of the tandem rotor helicopters in the fleet overhead. They were the type used to transport ATVs and tanks, so they should have no problem carrying a dozen or so berserkers each. I moved through the introductions in a rush to avoid awkwardness until I remembered we had to wait for Nathaniel to get back.

"It's good to meet you," Lyle said to Cernunnos and Calder.

"Thine aid is most appreciated, human," said Cernunnos. "You are...familiar to me."

"I'm pretty sure we haven't met. I'd definitely remember you."

"Curious. I recognize thy lifeforce."

"He's helped a lot of berserkers in the past," I said.

"Ah, aye. The memories are vague, but I feel ye can be trusted." Cernunnos sat on his stump motionless and said nothing more.

"I'm at your service and happy to help," said Lyle. He looked at me when Cernunnos didn't respond.

"It's fine."

Some of the berserkers had climbed the side of the crater to get a peek at the helicopters and snarl at them. Aífe was of course close behind to keep them under control.

"Is she...?" Lyle stared as she ran by.

Noah dropped in on us. "That's what women look like under their clothes. Guess you had to see it sooner or later."

"Thanks for reminding me how unfunny you are."

"Expect to see a lot more of it. The nudity, I mean," I told Lyle and filled him in on our plan to relocate them.

"As long as they don't crash the 'copter or try to eat us, we're good. I've really only ever seen them in attack mode or unconscious, so this is kinda cool." He glanced into the food crate where the children had planted themselves to get as much as possible before Calder swiped any more. "Commander Timmons headed out with Denmark's military to evacuate the civilians. I don't want to jinx it, but this might be our most successful rescue."

"Because nothing's fighting back, dumbass," said Noah. "Just wait until some demons show up and these guys lose it."

I frowned at him. "Why'd you have to say that?"

"We've got plenty of tranqs," Lyle said.

"That won't stop the Fury," I told him. "You tranquilized the ones attacking the base before my visit, remember? It's a soul thing. Hell can't take their souls, but it can encourage the rage within them to unstoppable levels."

"I guess they won't be helping against the demons. When Nathaniel came and told me about a werewolf army I was hoping they'd be joining us."

Calder finished handing more food to some of the children and marched over to us. "An army ye shall have. We live and die and live again to fight our enemies no matter the cost. In time we all return to the soil and by the Goddess' grace we are all reborn from it. There is no fear of blood spilt in our warriors' hearts, only the beating drums of war calling us to spill our enemies' in good turn."

"I think our concern is if the Fury takes them and they turn on our other allies or innocent people we're trying to save," I explained.

"That is why we lead the charge in battle to cleave a trail through the ranks of our foes for those who come next," said Calder. "Worry not, friend, for I am in harmony above the rest and cannot fall to the Fury. My soul burns with a righteous flame hotter than any fire in the pits of Hell."

Lyle looked him and his pack over. "Oh, good 'cause I'd hate to see you angry."

The persistence of the berserkers' "horror aura" while at rest in their bestial form was a curiosity. Although diminished outside of violent confrontation, it continued to spark a sense of dread and imminent danger that could now be considered irrational given our alliance and the almost endearing interactions they had with their children. The most accurate comparison I could make was to the alarming triggers of a mild phobia while in total safety.

"You have naught but my hunger to fear." Calder let out a less than reassuring laugh.

Noah dipped into the food crate and pulled out jerky, which woke a little girl sleeping under the discarded wrappers. She popped up and growled at him; he growled back. He narrowed his eyes at her and she did the same.

"You see this shit?" he said, turning to me.

"Don't swear in front of the kids. And put that back. You can eat when we get home."

Noah glared at me and went to throw the jerky in the crate, but the girl snatched it from his hand and retreated back into her nest of food wrappers.

"That wee one is Aífe's kin," Calder told us. "A fine warrior and hunter she will be."

"We'll see about that." Noah looked in the crate at her and pointed. "I'm coming back for you."

"Don't threaten the children either," I said.

Aífe approached upon having heard our conversation. "Give her but a few years and she'll have ye begging for mercy."

A hand reached up from the crate to offer Noah half the jerky, which he accepted and stuffed into his mouth. "What?" he asked, noticing me smiling at him. "I didn't wanna be rude."

Less than an hour later Nathaniel returned with aether crystals that emitted rippling waves of pearlescent light. I was getting spoiled by how much smaller the world had become with super speed and teleportation. Almost an hour to Egypt and back wore on my patience.

"Isis enchanted these with her calming spell," he said. "One for each helicopter."

"Let's hope this works," said Lyle. "Timmons reported there aren't many people to evac so we can go ahead and let Cernunnos stay behind until they're all clear. The UK loaned us a couple commercial planes and we're just dropping them off in Greenland, so it shouldn't be much longer."

"I know this goes without saying, but I feel bad for everyone around the world losing their homes," I said.

"It's better than them losing their lives, man. People are abandoning most major cities so they won't be there if the demons hit, but I've heard it's causing an even bigger mess on the small communities being flooded by the increase in population and crime is skyrocketing."

"The people are what the demons are attracted to, not the cities themselves. They're just going to follow them wherever they go. If we could get everyone to spread out it'd be the best-case scenario, but totally unrealistic. Everyone will kill each other over the most secluded areas if they haven't started already."

"Only good thing about them invading where the most are people is that it's predictable," said Noah. "Spread them thin and we'll have no idea where they'll get hit next. It can happen a lot quieter before we notice."

"Let us worry not on these troubles for now and look ahead to the journey before us," Calder said.

"Fine by me," Lyle agreed. "We can load everybody into helicopters and head out."

I went to speak with Cernunnos while Aífe and Calder led the pack with Lyle and Nathaniel.

"Would you be willing to meet with the other gods in our alliance after your people are safe in their new home?"

"Aye. I owe this Isis mine thanks for her clever solution to the Fury using magicked crystals."

"I'll escort the pack to Canada and then we'll meet in Rome."

"A last word before ye depart, Ascended. Thy champion hath formidable power nigh fit to rival the gods, but ye both harbor a hidden rage the likes of which may aid the cause of our foes more than our allies during Ragnarök. A silent storm is always deadlier than the one we hear coming. Trust me, Ascended, I knoweth this better than most."

I gave only a respectful bow in response before floating away to the helicopters. Emotion seemed to be a foreign concept to the Spiritborn; I suspected they simulated it more than they felt it. In this case, Cernunnos must have sensed frustration and recognized it as a threat without applying context. Maybe I was wrong, but every day Nathaniel was gaining better control of his powers and his emotions.

The berserkers were sniffing around the inside of the helicopters when I got there. Only four of them had returned to human form and Nathaniel had given them each a crystal to carry. Some of the children were scared by the strange lights and noises, clinging to their furry keepers, but others didn't seem to mind and huddled together to go back to sleep. I took the helicopter with Lyle and Nathaniel in it although they were all crammed to capacity. Noah popped up under me when I went to take a seat and sat me on his lap instead.

"These mutts smell even worse in enclosed spaces," he said.

It was true, yet I hesitated to agree in case they could understand. Those who were as humans communicated with one another in a language I didn't recognize, but did so as any ordinary group of friends having a chat.

"All right, we can take off," Lyle told the pilots over his tablet and sent a marked map. "Head for the coast of Newfoundland and we'll go from there. Fly low so we don't cross with the evac group."

The little girl with the jerky from earlier sat beside us, looking up at Noah. He pretended he didn't notice for as long as he could. "You got any more of that jerky?" he asked, only giving her a quick check from the corner of his eye.

She didn't answer, but her freckled face smiled up at him, pleased to finally be acknowledged.

"No? What good are you?" He sighed and looked in the other direction. I smiled at her as she moved closer to sit against him. "Get outta here!"

"I think she likes you," I teased.

"Well, make her stop."

Nathaniel came over to distract her, but she didn't seem too interested in him. He made her an aether crystal to play with and she held it up to give to Noah.

"Noah." I nudged him, hoping to get him to say something while trying not to show how entertained I was.

"I *hate* kids." He grabbed the crystal and shoved it in his pocket without looking. She didn't seem upset by how unappreciative he was, and she settled in between him and Nathaniel.

The sky cleared to blue as we left Iceland and headed over the water in the helicopter. I didn't miss the hellish landscape, but I did regret not seeing more of the country before it was lost. The little I had seen still managed to captivate me with some of its natural beauty through the corruption.

"How are you and Sierra?" I asked Lyle.

"I don't wanna talk about it."

"Oh boy."

"Yeah," he said with a hint of aggravation. "She's got someone back home in Chile."

"And she didn't think that was an important detail to share before you two hooked up?"

"I guess not or I wouldn't have touched her. She tells me today that she wanted to be honest and she'll leave the guy to be with me since the long-distance thing isn't working between them. That's not honesty to me though. I told her I can't be with someone who would—"

A sudden explosion from outside rocked the helicopter. We looked out the cockpit window to see the helicopter ahead of us falling out of the sky in two flaming pieces. One of the propellers was blown off and missed us by an inch. Nathaniel and I flew out and caught both halves before they hit the water. While I suspended them in midair Nathaniel rescued several of the berserkers and put them back inside.

"Did we lose any?" I asked him.

"No, they're healing. But what caused that?"

"I don't know—"

A bright flash from above sent a beam of light through our helicopter and another explosion cut it clean in half. My eyes stung from the flash and the thick, black smoke, but I was just barely able to see people plummeting with the wreckage and I levitated whom I could. Shouting for my attention, Noah dove from the helicopter to snatch the little girl and two other children. I caught them all and placed them in the helicopter before resealing it.

"Get up there and find what's doing this!" I shouted to Nathaniel. "We're not far from land, I'll take us down by UNITY's base!"

He shot up above the clouds while I soared some miles over to the nearest sight of land with the helicopters in tow.

Nathaniel returned to me faster than I made it to the coast. "There's nothing up there, *anywhere*, no signs of demons or changes in aether."

"Then what was it?"

Chapter Seventeen

Noah kicked out the door to the helicopter the moment I set it down in UNITY's frigid airfield. "Get these little shits off me before I lose it!"

The three children he had rescued were still clinging to him and sobbing. He pried the girl from his arm and yelled in her face.

"STOP CRYING!"

Magically, she stopped. Her weepy face broke out in a smile and she giggled at Noah's scowl.

"What the hell is wrong with you?" he barked. "Why— why are you sticky?"

Aífe tore her way out of the other helicopter in her berserker form and turned back to reclaim the children from Noah. "My thanks," she said, reluctant to give him any credit.

"Save it and give me a rematch instead."

"With pleasure."

"Man, you are really bad with kids," said Lyle as he came over with the pilots.

"And you're ugly." A bit of Noah's cocky composure returned at the first chance to get a dig in at Lyle, and then he vanished.

Nathaniel flew down after taking a second look for what cut through two of our helicopters. "There's no trace of anything. *Nothing.*"

"Not that I'm complaining, but we won't be able to get much evidence from the damage now that it's been mushed together," Lyle said. "It's not like we're looking for bullets or gunpowder residue. Ballistic damage wouldn't have been so clean. Nuclear would've left radiation and killed us mortals for sure."

"And it wasn't aether," said Nathaniel. "I would have felt it."

"Lightning, perhaps?" Calder exited from another helicopter. The berserkers poured out behind him. After some more cautious sniffing around they scattered in all directions along with those from the other helicopters.

"Nah, PARAGON would've picked up the electrical surge either through my suit, tablet, or the onboard sensors." Lyle realized Calder probably had no idea what PARAGON was. "It's a computer. A... machine?"

"I would 'ave known if it was lightning, Calder," said Aífe.

I had to put an end to the pointless speculation. "There's a lot of 'would haves' going around, but what matters is that something physically out there caused this. We have to find it regardless of what type of attack it was."

"Let's take the kids inside and get out of the cold," Lyle said. "Where'd the berserkers go?"

"To hunt and make camp. This place will do for now," Calder said. "I shall return for the pups upon the Moon's arrival this night and beg her aid in the pursuit of our foes."

Calder and Aífe transformed and dashed away into the bleak horizon.

"I'm supposed to go meet Cernunnos in Rome with the rest of the gods," I said. "I'll see what they have to say and if they've noticed anything. Nathaniel can stay here to help."

"You only checked the sky, right?" Lyle asked. "Are we sure the attack didn't come from below?"

"I'm not sure, it was hard to see when it happened."

"I was turned away, checking if anyone else needed to be rescued," Nathaniel said.

"It's worth investigating. Dorian, I'll get you a jet to Rome. You'll have to take one of the new automated ones since the others are helping with the evacs."

"How automated? Like no pilot at all?" We headed into the hangar with Nathaniel leading the parade of pups. He had given them his cape to share; with it draped over them, they looked like a big lumpy ghost.

"Yeah, PARAGON controls it. They're faster than the human piloted jets. Something like Mach 25. You'll get there in no time, but try not to throw up on the way. You don't have the implant we do that lets PARAGON regulate your lower brain functions and reduce anxiety."

"That's weird. I prefer being in charge of my own functions."

"Transhumanism, man. The only way humanity is gonna survive is if we adapt. You got that parasite you combined with, we have implants."

"I didn't have a choice."

"The demons aren't giving us one either."

I got into the single passenger mini-jet, no bigger than a smart car, and Lyle set the coordinates. "You should be there in ten minutes. We're going to go into lockdown and send out the drones to keep watch."

"Good luck. I'll try to make this quick, but I don't know when Cernunnos will show up. He's probably the one who knows the most about what happened."

The jet's dashboard was one long touchscreen with no physical controls. PARAGON took over once I accepted the destination and flight path. There was instant acceleration out of the hanger. I was used to high speeds and whiplash, but this was the most unpleasant experience yet. We reached cruising altitude in seconds, and I already felt like I was dying. It was the anxious feeling one gets when barreling down a death drop rollercoaster, only much faster and longer with no visible end in sight. Thirty seconds into the trip I was begging to pass out.

"Would you like to listen to music?" PARAGON asked with an unsettling sense of calm.

"No!" Uttering a single syllable almost lost me the contents of my stomach. I had to keep my eyes shut for the remainder of the flight and turn the prayer beads around my wrist to pull myself together.

Ten minutes wasn't fast enough, but the aerial torture was soon over. "How do I make this thing return to base?" I asked when the cockpit opened in a parking area outside the Colosseum. There was no way I'd be taking the return trip in the jet.

"I can return home if you won't be needing further transportation."

"Yes. God, yes. I'm never flying in this again."

"I'm sorry you weren't able to enjoy your flight. I'll report this to administration for you."

I didn't bother answering the AI. Still dizzy, I took a deep breath and floated myself over the Colosseum wall. I thought I might have been seeing things. The arena was packed. Men with black swords were gathered around one of the twenty-foot lesser demons bound in place by abyssal chains. The men were human and dressed in street wear as they hacked and slashed at the Infernal, spilling its molten blood at their feet. Gianni observed from his balcony with the rest of the gods, including Cernunnos, standing around him in a spectral vision. If I had known they could do that I would have sent a message with Nathaniel to meet in Iceland.

I was still feeling sick when I joined them and all that was going through my mind was not to vomit.

"Everyone." I kept my greeting brief and nodded.

"Are you unwell, Ascended?" Isis asked.

Gianni put his arm around me to be supportive and created thrones from the darkness for the five of us. The background sounds of birds, bells, and whispers between creaking branches from the Spiritborn deities' speech was melodic in my head.

"I'll be fine. I hate to be abrupt, but we were attacked when traveling to Canada and have no idea who or what did it. There was a flash and two of our aircraft were destroyed.

No one was lost, but we had to make a detour to our allies' base in Greenland."

"Aye, mine herald spoke as such moments ago through prayer, but I sense naught in land, sea, or sky," said Cernunnos.

"An unseen foe. How troubling," Kamakura said. "But why strike so weak as only to fell two mortal vessels? Surely the most ideal target would be the young deity onboard."

A cheer went up in the crowd below over the now-dead demon, which had finally succumbed to its wounds. "All right, I'm just going to ask. What the heck is going on down there? Because I get the feeling what happened was retaliation for whatever *this* is," I said.

"Training for the humans," Gianni said. "Is the only way to give them strength with no fear. They learn to fight and protect what they love. For us, this is Roma."

"So, you gave a bunch of frightened and angry humans the power of eternal darkness?"

"Only the sword." He smiled and stood to look out at the arena with ineffable pride. "I offer to them a training on how to fight and these humans say yes. They all lose something to the demons and want to find honor in battle against them. Roma will be built again on the strength and courage of the people."

"A wise decision to empower the humans, Dark One," Kamakura said in agreement. "The shadows are not always easy to trust and this will certainly give them the opportunity to respect you. With a lack of fear in their hearts the demons' power will wane."

"Better to die on thy feet with sword in hand than on thy knees before the Infernals," Cernunnos added.

"This does not answer with any certainty who was behind the attack against the Ascended and our allies," said Isis. "One from another world not of Earth or Hell, perchance?"

Gianni sat beside me again. "I will search the shadows. Do not fear."

"I'm not afraid. I was asking for help finding whoever it was so I can smash them."

"Yes, this sounds more like my little one." He laughed.

I wanted to remind him that I wasn't *his* "little one" anymore to stick him for that comment, but I didn't have it in me to deflate him like that in front of everyone.

"I should be going." I stood to put some space between us. "Can you send me back to UNITY's base? I left in a hurry without telling Noah."

"Yes, of course."

"Sorry I couldn't have been here for the introductions, Cernunnos, but if you need me I'll be in the north a while longer."

"Ye have mine thanks once more, Ascended," he said while remaining stone still.

The visions faded from the thrones and the shadows consumed me, taking me to PROJECT: UNITY's bright white plastic rotunda on the Armory floor. I wasn't expecting Gianni to come along and I didn't want him colliding with Noah.

"You come to Roma with your people and we work together," he said. "One beautiful empire is more strong than two small kingdom."

"I think that would only make us a bigger target."

"You are the most safe with me. I know this is why you come today." He kissed my hand. "Think about this."

Gianni departed, leaving me stunned for a moment until Noah swooped in. Then I was nervous.

"Hey," he said as casual as ever. "I tracked the mutts a few miles to see if whatever attacked us was pissed at them for leaving, but nothing showed itself."

"Oh, good thinking."

"I know." He grinned and walked with me to a terminal I could use to locate Nathaniel on base.

"You're not going to say anything about what you just saw with Gianluca?"

"Nothing to say. He's a disrespectful fuck, but I know how much it bothers you when I react. You're mine and he can't have you. End of story."

He stepped closer and put his hands on my arms.

"You smell nice," I said.

"I helped myself to your friend's shower while I waited for you," he replied with his forehead pressed against mine. "I thought about you while I was in there."

I had never swooned over Noah. We skipped that part of the courting process through the familiarity of our friendship beforehand. Lately, however, I found myself more and more infatuated with him as if we were taking a step backwards to explore what we had missed. It was exciting—thrilling even—to feel this way. I let it slip my mind that we had been ambushed only moments ago and I jetsetted across the globe for the shortest conference with the gods yet.

"We... should go find Nathaniel," I said, a bit breathless.

"He's in the bedrooms."

"Are you just saying that?"

"Could be." He smiled. "Plenty of empty rooms to check."

I turned back to the PARAGON terminal, which confirmed Nathaniel was indeed in the barracks. As we headed down to him I told Noah of my brief meeting with the gods.

"The Colosseum thing isn't a bad idea," he said, holding my hand as we walked.

"I can't believe you're saying that. Not that I necessarily disagree."

"I call it like I see it. People shouldn't rely on others to save them if they can fight for themselves. It's a form of slavery for everyone involved. That's why I've said not to get too invested. Sooner or later they're gonna need to learn how to survive on their own."

Nathaniel emerged from one of the rooms as we approached.

"Welcome back. That was fast," he said. "The children are asleep in bed."

I peeked in at the kids, who were individually swaddled in blankets that made them look burritos.

"They sleep a lot," I said. "Do you think it's from malnutrition?"

"I was assuming that they haven't had a decent sleep in a while, which is why they keep dozing off."

I recapped what happened in Rome and Nathaniel shared the same sentiments as Noah.

"Calder would probably enjoy gladiatorial combat," he added. "I'm sure he wouldn't mind sharing training duties with Gianluca."

The terminal by the door turned on with a video feed from Lyle. Noah shut it before he could speak, but I pushed him out of the way and reconnected.

"Tell me you have news," Lyle said. "Drones haven't picked up anything related to the attack in a fifty-mile radius."

"Gianluca is going to help search, but nobody has noticed anything. Could humans be behind this? I just feel like the attack was so... weak. The demons or another god wouldn't be so lenient. They failed to hurt anybody or try to hit the other helicopters."

"The crew is going over the wreckage in the hangar to look for shrapnel. I don't know why people would attack us though. It'd have to be some sort of experimental military weapon and all the militaries able to develop right now are our allies."

"Maybe you finally pissed someone off besides me," said Noah. "That was an attack meant to kill humans, not a pack of dogs or a god."

"Why would someone want to kill the commander?" Nathaniel asked.

"He's annoying." Noah shrugged. "And also the leader of an international military police force. People don't like leadership that promises protection and can't deliver."

"When you're done laughing at the possibility of me being assassinated meet me up in the hangar. The crew has something," Lyle said.

Noah and I went up to the hangar while Nathaniel stayed with the children.

"What've you got for me, ladies and gents?" Lyle asked the flight mechanics and engineers working on one of the helicopters.

"We're certain the cause wasn't a ballistic missile and we're close to ruling out smaller arms like anti-materiel rounds aimed at the fuel tank," the head engineer answered. "Our initial theory was a sort of flashbang/anti-aircraft hybrid round, but it's seeming unlikely."

"Any other theories?" Lyle asked.

"Just one, Commander. Molecular tearing. The same as our resident deity's telekinetic powers."

"I didn't blow us up," I said.

"I'm not saying that, but someone with your powers could have," said the engineer.

"No one else has my powers."

"Except Nathaniel," said Lyle.

"There's no way he would either."

"I read his profile when researching who has that kind of ability and I don't think it would be possible," the engineer said. "This was a very, very refined attack no more than a few millimeters in width that punched through the fuel tank from above."

"So it did come from the sky," I said. "Nathaniel went up there and didn't see anything though."

"It took PARAGON three scans at maximum magnification, but it did confirm the trajectory based on the angle the surrounding particles in the metal were distorted."

"Okay, so someone with my powers is responsible, but if they had my powers why not just kill whomever they were after directly?"

"Because they suck at what they do, but your powers also don't make light," said Noah.

"Light can be an effect when atoms collide or split like in thermonuclear weapons, but there were no traces of radiation," the engineer explained.

"There aren't with Nathaniel's powers either," said Lyle.

"It wasn't him," I said.

"Again, I'm not saying it was, only that there might be someone else out there with powers like him."

"I'm telling you it's humans," said Noah. "Any supernatural with that accuracy would match Dorian. In that case they'd just disintegrate the helicopter and everyone in it. This was some dumb attempt to copy his or the kid's powers. Probably by a government that doesn't like your little organization taking their money and playing sheriff."

"I agree," I said. "It takes a ton of energy to affect stuff at the molecular level. There'd be no point for me to cut through a helicopter to blow up the fuel tank when it would be easier to crush it. And if whoever it was wanted to make it look like an accident they could've knocked it out of the sky.

"These were humans, Lyle. Remember Aurelia isn't persuading them anymore as far as we know. Major governments aren't going to play nice under your authority. To them you're the unknown as much as we are, but you're an easier target than the gods and supernaturals."

"Not easy enough. I'm still here."

"Yeah, because Dorian saved your ass," Noah said to him.

"You should stay with us at the abbey," I suggested for the umpteenth time.

"You know I'm not gonna do that, man. If it really is other people after me that's something I can handle, especially now that they don't have the element of surprise anymore. Can something like this get through our perimeter?" Lyle asked the engineer.

"I couldn't say. It's not really my area. You'd have to ask around the Physics Department, Commander."

"Do you have any girlfriends there yet?" I joked.

"Nah, I think I'm done with trying to date girls who are too smart for me."

Noah smirked as we left the hangar and I knew something unpleasant was about to come out of his mouth. "That rules out anyone over the age of twelve."

"Vivi seemed to like me, so what does that say about her?"

Noah grabbed him by the throat and slammed Lyle to the ground so hard his head bounced off the floor, causing PARAGON's medical alert to sound.

"Stop it!" I pulled Noah away and helped Lyle up so he could dismiss the alarm.

I knew it would not be easy to calm Noah down from this. Vivi was an off-limits topic around him that even I avoided. They had a strange forbidden love that never blossomed before she died helping us fight an Ancient in New York City years ago. Lyle had caught her eye in the few days he knew her, but Noah swore she only saw him as a pet, being that she too was an Archios and he was only human.

"What the fuck is wrong with you?" Lyle shouted, holding his head. "You can say all you want about me, but you can't take a joke?"

"She is *not* a joke." Noah's brow furrowed as he jabbed the air in Lyle's direction with a finger. "And if you ever speak her name again I will rip your head off your shoulders faster than you can hide behind Dorian."

"Noah! Go cool off." I put my hands on him to push him away gently, but he wouldn't budge.

"Is that what this is about?" Lyle asked. "You're holding a grudge because she was into me?"

"YOU WERE NOTHING BUT A DISTRACTION TO HER!" Noah roared and lunged at him.

"I'm not the reason she died!" Lyle yelled back. "You know me long enough to know I'd never let someone die for me! It's not me you hate, it's yourself!"

I surrounded Lyle in a telekinetic bubble just in time. Noah's fist almost turned him into a bloody smear.

"This isn't how you honor her memory," I said, keeping myself between them. "You know none of us had anything to do with her death."

"He was the last one she kissed, right in front of me, the last one she bit—"

"You're with Dorian now," said Lyle. "You have to get over it."

"I don't forget people that meant something to me," Noah snarled and disappeared.

"Are you okay?" I asked Lyle.

He checked his hand for blood. "Yeah, aside from a concussion probably. I didn't think he resented me like that. I always thought he was an ass that hated me because I'm a human living in 'his' world."

Just then Lyle's ex, Rebecca, walked up carrying an overnight bag on her shoulder. It was rare to see her in clothes other than scrubs or a lab coat.

"Was there a med call?" she asked.

Of course out of all the physicians on staff it had to be her to respond.

"It was for Lyle," I said. "He, uh, hit his head."

"I'm all right," he said.

"If it's head trauma I better take a look. PARAGON doesn't send alerts for a bump and I was already on my way to the hangar."

She somehow took control of the situation against Lyle's will and sat him down to go over his injury. The way she touched his arm unnecessarily in guiding him to the floor and then his shoulder when she finished examining the back of his head was more than just clinical.

"Where were you going?" Lyle asked.

"My family's for a visit."

She took a tiny flashlight from her purse to check his pupils' reaction. They stared into each other's eyes for seconds after she had finished.

Just kiss. I should push them together.

"Say hi to them for me," Lyle told her.

"I will."

She put away her flashlight and got up to leave before remembering to share her diagnosis.

"You look fine." She smiled at him, placing her hand on his shoulder again as she stood.

"You too."

"I meant your head."

"Yeah? Oh—right."

He was too lovesick to realize he was embarrassing himself, but I wasn't. I had to make my exit.

"I should go find Noah," I said.

"When you wanna head home use PARAGON to get a pilot," he answered, his head swiveling to follow Rebecca as she walked around him to pick up her overnight bag. "We're only on level one lockdown for incoming."

"What about the attack?" I asked as I floated away.

He hopped to his feet to carry Rebecca's bag for her. "Let 'em bring it on. When I find out something new I'll hit you up."

This had gone terribly. Everyone's head was in the wrong place at a time when cohesiveness mattered most.

I had a feeling Noah would be outside where he could look at the water, so I grabbed a jacket left on a chair and went to check. I was right. He was sitting out in the cold on the rocks by the shore. I threw the jacket over his shoulders and sat behind him with my head resting on his back. We stayed like that for several minutes without saying a word until he moved to lay on his side with his head on my lap.

"Are we done here?"

"We can go home," I said. "I'll let Nathaniel stay with the kids. The berserkers should be here for them soon."

"You mad at me?" he asked after another few minutes.

"I can get over it if you finally put this to rest."

"I wasn't actually gonna kill the guy."

"We wouldn't be having this conversation if I thought that was your intention."

He went back to being quiet.

"I lost a lot of people in my life, but she was the first to die because my skill was lacking and not because I was being manipulated," he said. "I've gone over that fight a million times to think about what I could've done to prevent it."

I turned his head to look up at me. "It wasn't your fault."

"I was right there and then she was gone. It's no one else's fault but my own and that friend of yours got closer to her in two days than I ever let myself in decades. It was like she was tired of waiting. She never even knew how much I cared about her."

"Yes, she did. You don't always have to say the words for someone to feel them."

"I might've been with others before you, but you're the best thing that's ever happened to me, you know that? Sometimes I feel like there's gonna be that moment when you need me and I fall short again. I didn't think I'd get another chance to be like this with someone and I don't wanna fuck it up."

"What am I going to do with you?" I sighed and brushed his hair back.

"I got a few suggestions in mind."

His delivery was so much smoother than his usual bravado I almost missed what he was implying.

"Maybe after you apologize to Lyle."

"You said you weren't angry about that. I call bullshit."

"I said I *could* get over it," I reminded him and got up to head inside.

"How long's that gonna take?" he shouted after me. "We're still good for tonight though, right? Dorian! Damn it, I knew I never should've told you it turns me on when you're a tease. This is a total and sexy violation of my trust."

I smiled back at him as I slipped through the hangar door.

Chapter Eighteen

The first thing I wanted to do after our pilot dropped us off was jump in bed to sleep, but I knew that wasn't going to happen when my best knight greeted me at the door.

"Dorian." Liam gave a short bow. He must have been on patrol since he was in full battle regalia. "He showed up by the cabin earlier tonight. Rafael said he is important to you so we brought him inside."

"Who?"

Liam looked behind him like I should have seen somebody there. "Oh, he's gone. I'm sorry. I was speaking about the elderly undead gentleman."

"Octavio? He's here?"

"He was a second ago. I'll find him for you."

"Don't bother, he'll find me first. He always does. Thanks, Liam."

I headed to the bedroom with Noah, knowing that Octavio was probably already there. I was right. The scraggily old hobo dressed in ragged, tattered scraps was muttering to himself and staring at a Polaroid of me with my parents I kept on the nightstand, next to my calendar of barnyard animals in pajamas.

"Born to know only destruction, destined to inherit the nothingness that follows, these children of oblivium..."

"How are you, Grampy? It's been a while."

I didn't think it possible, but he smelled worse than the berserkers' old lair.

"A while... Yes, a while. But, now is the time. A good time."

"A good time for what?" I asked. "How did you get here?"

"For this, of course. Tonight."

Noah sat himself on the couch keeping a sharp eye on Octavio. "How'd you get past the barrier outside?"

"I don't believe I noticed any." He smacked his lips and licked around his unkempt beard. I was never quite sure what Octavio was capable of and I don't think he knew either anymore.

"*This* is the guy who helped cook you up?" Noah raised an eyebrow.

"He wasn't always like this. Right, Grampy?"

He put down the photo and turned his attention toward me. "Yep."

"How's he not burning in the light from the kid's crystal?" Noah asked.

"Nice and dark where I am, sonny!"

"An illusion? With an aura?" Noah seemed skeptical. "And able to interact with objects? Who is this guy?"

"Octavio, tell us why you're here," I asked again.

"Don't know, but it's something...There's bits o' me in ya...I see it there..." He wiggled a dirty finger in my face.

"I see the resemblance." Noah pointed back and forth between us.

"You were a Strigoi, Octavio, and before that you were a psychiatrist when you were human. I found your old files back in New York before it was destroyed. My friends here recovered a research journal from the Strigoi that has you listed as a donor and an assistant responsible for my creation. When we met for the first time in New York that wasn't random chance, was it?"

"What's this now? We've met before? I think I'd remember that!" Octavio waddled away to stare into the unlit fireplace and poke around the ashes.

"Give it up. He's fried," Noah said.

"He seems more distressed than usual. I wish there were something we could do to fix him."

"Maybe the kids can," he suggested. "Hang on."

I watched Octavio draw on the stone floor with the ashes while Noah left to get someone from the Order.

"Got one." Noah was back with Liam teleporting in after him.

"Is there any spell to help with whatever is going on in Octavio's head?" I asked. "He didn't always used to be so, well, just look at him. I want to know what happened and what he knows about me from before we met."

"The undead are better at abilities like telepathy though. Wouldn't Noah be the better choice?"

"He's terrible with telepathy."

"Excuse me?" Noah didn't like to hear it, but it was true. His telepathy wasn't of much use besides minor hypnotic effects on mortals.

"We could try to enter his mind from the Astral Plane, but it can be dangerous," said Liam.

I checked on what Octavio was drawing with the ashes, thinking it might be some cryptic message, but it was just a six-legged giraffe or maybe a horse, with two birds on it.

"I think we'll be fine," I said. "How do we get there? Is it a meditating thing?"

"No, it's a teleportation spell, but we have to go sideways through the Veil instead of across the ley lines. I'd be happy to escort you. I have some of the most experience there next to the elders." Despite his dry demeanor, Liam appeared to be excited by the prospect of taking a trip to the Astral Plane.

"Great, you can be our astral Sherpa. Can we take Noah too?"

An earthshaking crash outside halted our conversation. By the feeling I got and the light in the sky, I knew it was

Nathaniel. I opened a hole in the barrier for him through the window and pulled him through.

"I'm sorry," he said as he came into the room. "I forgot about the barrier again. Who is this?"

"This is Octavio. I've told you about him."

Nathaniel kneeled to him out of respect. "It's an honor to meet the one responsible for bringing the Ascended into our world, sir."

"Ascended?" Octavio looked up from his drawing. "Yes, good...good. This is good. You will help him."

"I will," Nathaniel agreed.

"Good boy, kind boy. You'll make the right choice. Stop them from watching...always watching." Octavio rubbed the ashes into his eyes and beard. "Why does the plan change? Always changing, moving, turning..."

"You can stand, Nathaniel," I told him. "He's a little off right now, but we're going to go to the Astral Plane to see what's going on in his head. Can you move the Light Effigy for now so he can come in? This is only an illusion he's projecting."

"Right away. I'll stay here to watch the abbey while you're gone."

"We'll need a fairly large, high-quality crystal to make the trip with Dorian, if you could help," Liam asked him.

Nathaniel made the six-foot crystal, removed the effigy, and found the real Octavio all within seconds of me opening the barrier.

"He was in the cove by the shore," Nathaniel said, setting Octavio down on his feet.

"What'cha want with ol' Grampy?" Octavio tapped him on the chest repeatedly, somehow leaving ashen residue that only his illusion had touched, and then his face went blank. "Anger brings blind strength, but devotion for your master will carry you from the cusp of oblivion. It doesn't fear the light. It's a trick. It's a trap." He outlined a crude mandala in the ash, ran to my bed, and grabbed the tablet. "Cast out the evil! The evil! It watches! She'll be here soon!"

Octavio hurled the tablet out the window.

"Okay, Liam, let's hurry this up," I said.

Connor came into the room dressed for battle. "What's going on?"

"Dorian's grandfather is here to tell us about why they made him bite-sized," said Noah.

"Oh, I didn't know he was your grandfather!" Connor dropped to one knee. "I'm honored to meet you, sir."

"He's not my grandfather." I glared at Noah. "And why are you awake? It's got to be three in the morning. Go to sleep."

"I'm not tired."

"It's ready," Liam said.

"What's with the big crystal?" Connor asked.

"We're going to the Astral Plane," I said.

His face turned grim. "Oh...I, um, I think I'll go on patrol."

"Are you on the schedule for tonight?" I asked.

"No—*yes*. Not exactly, but I can take Liam's place if he's going with you."

I conceded for the sake of haste. "Fine, just stay out of trouble."

Connor saluted and marched off, allowing me to return my attention to the others.

The aether crystal was charged with rings of energy orbiting it from top to bottom. "I've never applied astrothurgy—space distortion magic—to a crystal this large," said Liam. "There are so many possibilities available to us now with Nathaniel and your power, Ascended."

"What is this crystal going to do exactly?" I asked.

"Space magic is all about manipulating vectors and dimensions in the universe. The spell pulls apart the threads of the Veil between worlds wide enough for our souls to fit through. This crystal helps sidestep the aether requirement and amplification of the spell that none of us could do on our own to bring you along."

"C'mon, I'm getting bored," said Noah. "Is there anything important we need to know about in there or are we good?"

"Everything is real in the Astral Plane," Liam explained. "This isn't astral projection where only your consciousness spectates, meaning you can get hurt and die.

"Secondly, the laws of physics and reality can change in an instant based on who is exerting the most influence in the area. Since we want to experience Octavio's thoughts we should try not to change anything ourselves, so it's important to tread lightly. All we need is for him to touch the crystal to enter. By going there first he should have a better chance at setting the stage."

"Come touch the crystal, Grampy," I said, beckoning him.

Octavio hobbled over and grabbed my hand. "I needed to do it. I killed them. Killed 'em all. Closed the door to stop any from coming in."

"Killed who?" I looked him in the eyes. One was always blinking out of tempo with the other.

"Didn't I...?" he asked himself.

I put his hand on the crystal, knowing there was no other way to get intelligible answers. Octavio was sucked in and turned to liquid energy that vanished in the light. Nathaniel wished us luck and one by one we crossed the Veil.

The transition onto the Astral Plane wasn't too bad, not nearly as unpleasant as the automated mini-jet. Mild vertigo came over me and I felt myself turning upside down from the gravity of the crystal's pull.

"So this is inside the old man's head?"

I heard Noah as I landed. My feet were planted on the ground upside down with the crystal above my head in the sky. The whole world was in reverse until my perception corrected itself. I was standing in an oddly quiet forest of giant trees steeped in an eerie, reflective fog. At the foot of many of the trees were metallic crystalline structures.

"No," Liam answered as he kneeled to collect a crystal and put it in his satchel. "We're on the Astral Plane. Anything we see related to him is a manifestation of his will onto the environment."

I froze when I saw Noah.

"What?" he asked.

"You're, um...smaller?"

A startling noise echoed through the forest. It was a familiar sound, a guttural death rattle I hadn't heard in years, but Noah took my focus away from it for the moment.

"What're you talking about?" He looked himself over and then realized what I was seeing. "What the fuck is this? What did the old man do? Why do I feel so slow?"

Noah had lost around fifty pounds of muscle or more, including most of the vascularity and tone that went with it, along with an inch off his height. His fangs were gone, replaced by regular teeth, and his complexion lacked its previous luster.

"On the Astral Plane you appear as your true self," explained Liam. "It could be a reflection of your soul or how you view yourself, whether consciously or subconsciously."

"This *isn't* me," he insisted, first in agitation, then anger. "Why don't either of you look any different?"

"I don't know, sir. I've always been this way. Could it be how you were when human?"

Noah had lost his nerve in a way I'd never seen before, and I didn't quite understand. "That is *not* who I am! I'm not—Where's the old man? He did this! This is why I fucking hate mind games!"

"It's unlikely he would have been able to do this against your will," Liam said. "You'll be back to yourself once we leave."

"Then stop staring and go do what we came here to do!"

Liam looked at me defeated and stepped aside. I took Noah's hand hoping to calm him, but he pulled away. "Don't touch me."

"Why is this bothering you so much? You're as attractive as ever to me."

The guttural rattle returned and passed just as quickly. It was right on top of us, but nothing was around.

"What was that?" I changed my question seeing the others had noticed the sound too. "There it is again."

"Stop talking." Noah put his hand over my mouth.

We waited, but didn't hear it again.

"It sounds like the people infected by the Rift parasite," I said and heard it again.

"It's you," said Noah. He covered my mouth and we waited one more time to test it.

I was dejected. "The rest of the gods get cool sound effects to go with their voices and mine makes me more of a freak."

"Nothing wrong with that." Those four words from Noah were nice to hear.

"Nothing wrong with how you look either," I told him.

"You don't get it? I'm nothing without what people made me. My powers, my possessions, my life, my looks, my freedom. I didn't do any of it myself. None of it is a reflection of who I am. Almost two hundred years and I haven't been able to do a damn thing for myself. Whenever I try I fall short. Last time I died and every time before that someone important to me did. Everything about me is fake."

"Are you forgetting why we came here?" I asked. "I'm not exactly all natural and you've been responsible for a large part of who I am."

"It's not the same. What happened to me was against my will more than how I was born. Any failures you had were beyond your control at the time."

Is this what's been causing his night terrors?

"You may not see how far you've come on your own, but I do and I understand if it bothers you to face this. You can go home if you want and we can talk about it later."

"No. You know I wouldn't bail on you like that, so let's get this done," he said and then called to Liam. "Not a word of this to anybody."

"Yes, sir."

"Any idea which way we should go?" I asked. I started to float as I always did. A glow emanated from me, large enough to envelop Noah and Liam when he came near. "Now what? What is this?"

"I forgot to mention that when using your powers here you can see your aura without the need for aura sight," Liam answered.

I decided to walk from there. This place was the bane of the self-conscious and something about seeing evidence of my unnaturalness irked me. My powers had no visual effect tracing them back to me on Earth. It was like a wish. I wanted to destroy or create something and it happened. When I flew, I didn't have wings. The only change was my eyes; the whites turned black. I hated it. That one transformation was the last visual remnants of the parasite that had infected me and killed my parents. If not for that, I could still pretend to be normal and fit in like Noah, Nathaniel, and the Order.

"What are these?" I asked as the underbrush turned to concrete and gossamer bubbles drifted through the air between the trees.

"Memories," Liam said. "We call them thought bubbles."

"Are you serious?"

"Yes. If these are from Octavio it could mean he has some experience on the Astral Plane to be causing this many, or he might be a powerful telepath like most older undead. They have the easiest time here since it's a realm of thoughts and dreams."

"Why aren't there any coming from us?"

"There will be if any of us go into deep enough thought."

The arrangement of the trees began to conform to a rigid pattern like rows of columns, and the canopy closed in to block the sky as a solid ceiling. It was interesting that when looking ahead the forest still seemed natural and only the part we passed through was changing.

The entire landscape started to turn into metal and concrete the further we went. Whispers hissed at us from the shadows behind the steel girders that were once trees. The tiny slivers of light that snuck in through the cracks above became harsh incandescent bulbs.

"I know where we are," I said.

We were in the Strigoi arcanum where I was created and brought back to when kidnapped years ago—a place I had tried to forget.

Chapter Nineteen

In the darkest recesses of an abandoned German World War II-era military bunker, the Strigoi worked their magic to produce a collection of life forms with the power to defend them during doomsday. Their leader and resident archmage, Minerva Collins, had other plans for the project, however. She decided to betray her people and offer these creations as vessels for the Infernal Kings in exchange for power and guaranteeing her own survival. I was their first success, sent away as an infant to be raised by humans until maturity, when I would make a suitable host.

"You gonna be okay with this?" Noah asked with his arm around my neck to hold me back.

I passed dusty shelves of glass jars in varying sizes, all containing tissue samples and specimens preserved in formaldehyde. Everything was labeled to the last detail. Human embryos and fetuses in different stages of growth had their own racks because of how numerous they were. Some were hardly human at all, deformed by the experiments inflicted upon them. I watched as a robed man emptied the jars of the failures into a fire. The bodies flopped into the ashes of their brothers and burned away into nothing. The smell of the chemicals and damp rusty metal stung my eyes and choked me. I told myself that's what was making me want to cry.

"We're leaving," Noah insisted, trying to pull me away as I stared into the containers of three late-term fetuses. "This is stupid. You know how you were born. There's no point in putting yourself through this."

The Strigoi didn't seem to notice us as they reviewed esoteric parchments with their colleagues and tinkered with the bevy of nonsensical clockwork contraptions. These incongruous fetishes of steam and sprockets entwined practical engineering with fantastical pseudo-realism for indiscernible results.

Liam had been quiet as he brought up the rear, making sure not to show interest in anything particular so he didn't seem judgmental. One of the Strigoi, a drawn and elderly man, shuffled through him to the desk as a ghost would and accidentally knocked a jar to the floor. It shattered, vacating the unborn violently amongst the broken glass.

The whole room turned to watch his fate unwind in the hands of the figure that appeared by his side. There she was: Minerva—a youthful face with a deathly pallor, long gray hair in ringlets, and a gaze as cold as frost. She said nothing. Flames conjured in her palm leapt to his robes and immolated him, putting a quick end to the spectacle and sending a message to the rest that mistakes would not be tolerated.

I was able to pick up one of the remaining jars. I don't know why I did.

"You've found the reason for your search."

I looked up to see Octavio standing there. He was clean, manicured, and lucid—dapper even—dressed in a vintage tweed suit and overcoat, supporting himself with a cane. I ignored him at first, not certain if this was a vision.

"That one you've got there is you," he said. "But, I'm sure you knew that."

"Are you...real?" I asked.

"I suppose I am, at least this part of me."

The room had frozen in time except for us, Noah, and Liam. "What just happened?" I asked.

"I don't recall what comes next. I believe I left the room."

I went back to inspecting the jar in my hand. The label had a "2" in the top left corner. The rest of the writing was in German, but there was a year for the date: 1859.

"This is me? It can't... That would make me over a hundred and fifty years old...and it looks dead."

"Not dead, simply not yet alive. Suspended animation. This is thaumaturgical engineering. The children were grown piece by piece in teams and then assembled to make sure everything was perfection. The cursed synthetic blood the Strigoi conjure was used to spark rudimentary life in the growth process until it was time for the next phase. Unlike fresh live blood it did not promote aging and allowed us to stall when needed. This was the second facility after the Archios smoked us out from our first closer to France. Your batch was kept in stasis for more than a century while our methods were perfected. I was brought onto the project during the penultimate phase."

I felt nauseous, sad, and weak in the knees, thinking of myself as body parts slapped down on a table to be fiddled with until morbid curiosity settled on satisfaction. It was bad enough to have heard vague accounts of my past, but being confronted by the sights and smells told a whole different story.

"And what team were you on?" I asked.

"The brain."

The room twisted and warped as the scene changed. The jar disappeared from my hand. Octavio was on the other side of the laboratory now with Minerva and another familiar Strigoi. It was her nephew Vance, who helped me when he found out she had betrayed the coven to consort with demons. Sadly, she got her revenge on him years later.

"Need I remind you that you would be wasting away of consumption in a sanatorium if not for me?" Minerva said to Octavio. "What I ask should be elementary and is the only reason you stand here today."

She's the one who turned him?

"There is no need for threats, but what you ask is unethical in the highest degree," he said. "I specialized in developmental psychiatry to help children, not brainwash them before birth. You told me I would be working to purge mental illnesses for a greater purpose."

"Is the certitude of our being not the greatest purpose of all?"

"The ends do not justify the means in my eyes, Minerva."

"It is to your benefit that your eyes fail to interest me."

I approached to see what had happened to my jar. I felt sick again from what I saw, but sicker still at the outcome of the second jar from the desk. Tubes attached to the clockwork devices were pumping fluids in and out of my unborn body, but the other fetus wasn't so fortunate. It was thrown in a heap of discarded organs awaiting destruction. The "2" had now been replaced by a "1" on the glass of my artificial womb.

Was it only luck that spared me?

"I'm still older," Noah said in my ear. I knew he was trying to distract me and I appreciated it. I wondered what Liam thought of all this after seeing his god as nothing more than a test tube experiment that survived by a fluke.

"The undead condition allowed for a very small brain tissue sample to be taken from yours truly without risk of death or permanent damage," Octavio said to me while Minerva and Vance went on their way. "It was still quite unpleasant, but not as much as what Minerva wanted me to do with it. As we go through life we learn not only of the world around us, but the one between our ears. We become familiar with the pathways in our mind as we go over them countless times.

"The Strigoi lacked the advanced mind control techniques for which the Archios had a proclivity. We feared the children would fall prey to them, so I was to make an improved model of my brain that could be manipulated through magic triggers—a sort of back door to the inner mind. We didn't know then that the mind and brain were two separate entities, and you would not be inheriting my pathways to make the already invasive process easier by inducing a sense of déjà vu preceding every command.

"I was relieved. Minerva aside, the Strigoi put importance on the children having free will. A mindless construct lacked the creativity and autonomy to adapt to critical situations and could easily be bested by astute adversaries. But free will with conditions was not what I considered free."

The room cleared of the Strigoi and Octavio was scribbling notes at a desk with my jar in front of him. There were others now lining the shelves that were successful enough to be brought to life through the machines.

"I wonder what they'll call you," he said, tapping on the glass with a shaky finger. "Will you ever forgive us for this madness?"

Vance returned with a message. "You're needed in the vault."

The room shifted to bring us to another location in the bunker where Octavio went as soon as he left. Twitching bodies restrained in cots were being kept alive by machines similar to the ones in the fetus room. One of the bodies was conscious though and screaming frantically in German. This one was dressed in Nazi regalia, but the others, who must have been here long before him, were stripped down to their undergarments or covered by a bloodstained sheet.

Octavio retrieved a long needle and a tiny hammer from a medical kit in his inner jacket pocket. He leaned over the man. "A transorbital lobotomy kept patients complacent through donations without the need of constantly fetching ether. I liked to think they were going to a better place away from the suffering."

He slid the needle under the eyelid and past the tear duct. The screaming stopped with a tap of the hammer.

"The Nazis always thought themselves to be part of something greater, a master race superior to all. As an American I can say I had little sympathy for their donations, but the irony that so many ended up being genetic failures after thorough...probing...was a melancholic delight.

"It was the commonfolk that left me afflicted by the worst nightmares. We were the monsters out there in the streets, the alleyways, the parks at night; stalking beauty to tear it apart like strips from a painted canvas, only to then be smashed together in simulation of our own idea of a masterpiece. Never a body left behind, not a drop of blood or a shoe that we didn't find a purpose for down the line." He turned to a hoard of footwear in the corner of the room collected from the victims while he cleaned his needle on a white cloth. "There wasn't anything left to bury when we were finished with our indefatigable harvest of an area. If you were marked, there was no avoiding us, not forever, and the war made for the ideal smokescreen. It was one of the rare times we left the safety of the arcanum until we began hiring help to fill the quantity we needed once we achieved our first major success."

"Why not clone me if I was such a success? Or do I not want to know?"

Octavio raised his bushy eyebrows and shrugged. He put away the medical instruments with care and shuffled off a few feet to decide how he wanted to word his answer. "Individuality was important to us. That's what we were told. If one child had become compromised it would be likely that all others could be exploited in a similar fashion. They— you—needed to be kept apart and have no familial bond to one another in case a problem had to be handled."

"In case one of us betrayed you and needed to be put down."

"Not me. The Strigoi." He sighed. "Believe me, as the project went on I longed for the day justice would be sought against us. It had little to do with the symbiotic parent-child relationship I was promised and became more about how to tighten the leash in dominance.

"A child would bond with a primary caretaker regardless if it was human, undead, or an animal. My expertise was to be used to ensure one such as yourself would protect us with the same fervor of a loved one by triggering a deeply rooted bond without having been there to raise you. Fight until there was no blood left in you to spill. Even the Archios cannot simulate true unbreakable love through telepathic trickery. I have always believed it to be a composition of chemical, spiritual, and behavioral overlap.

"I thought there was potential for the relationship to be reciprocated. I was alone in that sentiment. The Strigoi thought me foolish for caring for all of you. But were you not my flesh and blood in part? Was my purpose not to ingrain emotion between us? And a fool I was to have such idyllic hopes, but in great darkness the mind always seeks the light, no matter how dim."

A cadre of Strigoi led by Vance began operating on a patient. They removed the liver and unwound it into smaller and smaller strands with magic until they were satisfied. They terminated the patient by flicking on a machine to drain the body to the point of exsanguination.

"Just...tell me how you became the way you are now and why did you try to find me again?"

The room was engulfed in flame and melted away into blackness where Minerva stood speaking to a giant demonic eye.

"We are in the final steps, my lord. The subjects' minds have been prepared after much hard work. I've struck a bargain with a necromancer to supply us with the souls we require, but she cannot be trusted. Had I more power to assure our success—"

"Produce what I command. Succeed or others will." The eye spoke in a multitude of voices. "Failure is not tolerated. Additional power is unnecessary."

Octavio whispered to himself, but he remained unseen. "When was this? Why can I not place this memory?"

The blackness swirled, and now Minerva and the eye were behind us.

"The plan changes," said the eye. "I calculate a 97.3% chance of failure based on the current parameters. The subjects will instead become hosts to lead the liberation of Earth."

The vision fragmented like shards of a broken mirror and began repeating over itself until the noise was unbearable.

"Hosts? Demons?" Octavio seemed to be confused by this recollection. "I must do something...these children must not become vessels for evil to walk the earth. Sabotage. I'll sabotage them so they cannot be controlled. No one will know until it's too late. I can give them a chance to lead their own lives."

We were returned to the laboratory with Octavio nervously working to unscrew the jar I was in. He gave up when he heard people coming and looked at the dozen or so other fetuses he also needed to sabotage. "Blasted machines. There's no time," he mumbled. He bit his wrist to draw blood and cast a spell on my jar.

"What are you doing?" Minerva arrived in a pall of black smoke just as the light of the spell faded.

"I was double checking the status of the children before heading out for the night's harvest." Octavio inched his way toward the exit as he spoke.

"There's no need. Collections are finished and these will be brought to term tonight and sent on their way. Take what you need from the vault and be quick about it."

"Oh. That's quite all right. I've already taken stock there and we're missing—missing an intact adolescent brainstem. Nothing terribly difficult to find. Shouldn't take me long."

Octavio scurried from the room and we were in the original forest. He hurried frantically through the trees, tripping and falling over himself in the mud several times.

"She'll always be able to find me if she searches for my mind." He took out a small journal and a pencil from his pocket and wrote:

Return to America. Find the children. Avoid the sun.

Octavio earmarked the page and returned the journal to his pocket. The forest was shaking and breaking apart as if reality was collapsing around us. He retrieved the medical kit from his jacket and put the long needle to his eye.

I felt the tap of the hammer in my stomach. I cringed and turned away only hearing the crunch that came next. Octavio knew he would recover from that—unless the large chunk of brain matter was removed out the back of his skull.

The forest went white. Next we saw blurred images inside a padded room as he struggled with amnesia and paranoia. The visions skipped through the years with Octavio's appearance and mental state deteriorating in each one leading up to his return to America as a stowaway. And then there was violence.

It was present day and we were left with only thought bubbles showing him murdering people my age in the streets at night. Minerva was in a few of the scattered flashbacks, cursing his name as he fled the scene wounded from the encounters.

"Had to close the door on the evil. Had to kill 'em all," he rambled to us as he came into view in his current state. "Someday they'll get reborn into a nice, normal life, but could only save the one. You, sonny. What is it they call you?"

His eyes searched my face in helpless bewilderment.

"I'm Dorian...I'm Dorian Benoit."

Chapter Twenty

I wanted to be home so badly that the Astral Plane warped into the image of my bedroom with the aether crystal in the ceiling above.

"Thank you for being so patient through all of this," I said to Liam.

"I'm honored you allowed me to escort you. It was even more a blessing to learn about your history," he said.

"I'm sure I seem a lot less impressive now."

"Not to me. Before you even had consciousness you were defying fate. You're more humane than most humans and became a god. I still consider you my greatest role model."

"Thanks, Liam. That means a lot to me."

The quietest one spoke the loudest with his few words.

"You're welcome. Whenever you're ready to leave we can use the crystal."

Noah stepped up close against me with his back to the others to separate us. "You good?" he asked.

"I'll be fine," I said, looking past him at Octavio's blank gaze. "Really."

All that trouble in the past debating over whether or not to meet my "siblings," if we had anything in common, and what would be best for them didn't matter in the end.

"As soon as we get back, I'm going to ask my friends to come up with a solution for your condition, Grampy," I told him. "Maybe their magic can pull some of the clarity we saw here to the front of your mind."

Liam assisted Octavio with reaching the crystal to exit and then left through it himself. Noah put his hand up to touch it next with an arm around me to take us both together.

The room was bright, noisy, and disorienting when we phased in again. I heard shouting and Nathaniel calling my name.

"Shut down the machine!" Octavio yelled as I saw a blurry image of him running for the door.

I got my wits about me in time to see him turned to ash by green flames before he could escape.

At first I froze in confused and horrified panic that flipped in an instant to doubt, hoping this was an illusion from his broken mind, but then I saw *her*.

Now in a demon visage with curved horns and leathery crimson wings, Nathaniel had trapped Minerva in an aether crystal the size of the one we used to travel to the Astral Plane; however, she still managed to pull off the spell to kill Octavio. My furious scream could have rocked the abbey to its foundation. As much as I desired inflicting the slow and painful death she deserved I was also frantic to finish her once and for all.

Had I noticed Connor charge in with his sword at the ready I might have reacted with more prudence to guarantee the safety of those present. Minerva was gone from the crystal without any trace of being dead when I crushed it to dust.

"Get everyone out of here," I told Liam. "Now!"

"Not the body I had come for, but it will have to do," said Connor.

"What—?" I turned to him and saw a sneer on his face I didn't think he could have mustered on his own. "Get out of him and fight me!"

"What's wrong, *Ascended?* I'm right here," Minerva said, mocking me from inside Connor's body by using his voice. "A good deal weaker in this vessel too. Don't worry though. The boy is still in here. And if you kill us, he gets to join me in my circle of Hell."

"A-Ascended?" Connor's face changed. "What's going on? I don't—Did we get her?"

"I'm going to save you, Connor! Just hang on!"

He laughed and I knew it was Minerva again. "Not likely based on your record. You couldn't save the old fool right in front of you, you couldn't save the chattel you called a family, or the Archios whore."

Noah was stunningly well composed at the disparagement of Vivi, which was an obvious attempt to goad him into a careless reaction. His keen eyes searched for an opening to get the first strike.

"Is this what you've been reduced to?" I shouted. "Hiding in the body of a teenage boy? A mortal? You're that scared of me?"

"Ascended, please. You might have been a failure in some regards, but you still helped me achieve *my* ultimate goal. I am Minerva, Demon Lord of Apocrypha. All of your past 'triumphs' in battle against me only added to my greatness for when Hell swallowed this pathetic world of ignorance. You see, I *learn* from experiences and assimilate their lessons into my being. Your powers cannot hurt me. None that I have been defeated by can fell me again. Not yours, not the living darkness, not hellfire or your finest metals. Go ahead and try."

She separated herself from Connor. Noah didn't hesitate to zoom away with him somewhere safe and I didn't waste time attacking. She should have been scattered in pieces across the universe, but it barely fluttered her curls. Nathaniel dashed to punch her into oblivion, but his fist bounced off. When he struck her with a bolt of light it was reflected back at us.

"Light," she scoffed. "Did you think I would have not prepared for something so obvious? I will take my leave and my newest vessel with me. I would have traded for a stronger one, but after seeing the sentiment he holds to you I believe he'll do just fine to serve my purpose."

Minerva was gone in a bang of sulfurous black smoke.

Nathaniel hung his head. "I beg your forgiveness," he pleaded. "I thought to trap her to avoid the dangers of open combat here, but I still failed."

"You didn't do anything wrong."

Noah returned. His expression answered the question he knew I had: Connor was possessed and had been taken from us. "We'll get the kid back," he said quietly, glancing at the doorway where Octavio had met his demise.

I stood there looking down at what was left of the man who sacrificed himself to give me a chance and right his wrongs.

"I'll never forget you, Grampy." With tears in my eyes, I solidified the ashes to bring them to the courtyard where others we had lost were laid to rest.

"Nathaniel, can you tell everyone who retreated that they can come back?" I asked on our way there. "Minerva won't show herself here again. She's going to use Connor to lure me somewhere, but I want him found before that."

"Right away," he replied in a somber tone. We were all reeling from the magnitude of what happened and how violating it was to be ambushed in our own home. "I'll leave to begin the search after I give word and won't return until it is with her head."

"Not this time," I repeated something I had told Connor in vain on several occasions these past few days to keep him safe. "The Order can scry for them and I'll be the one doing the killing. Minerva said she came for a different body and I can only guess she meant you. I'm not letting her take anyone else from me."

"I will not allow myself to fall to her at any cost," Nathaniel proclaimed and flew from the courtyard when we entered.

I sat with Noah on a bench under the stars, holding my head in my hands after placing Octavio's ashes.

"You have my respect, old man," Noah said. He put his arm around me to help stop my trembling as I struggled to keep everything I was feeling inside. I didn't know what was taking the worst toll: losing Octavio, witnessing my grotesque origin, Connor's abduction, or still feeling powerless against Minerva again after all these years.

"I wish I could've gotten to know the real him sooner so that maybe things wouldn't have turned out this way. One of the worst parts of losing someone is not getting to share how you felt about them or say that one last thing. It brings me back to when I lost my parents."

Noah held me closer and wiped away my tears as I sobbed. "Don't cry," he whispered. "I don't wanna see tears on this pretty face."

I broke down in his arms. "Every day, every hour now we're losing more and more people. Is there going to be anybody left when this is over?"

"Keep fighting for the ones who are still here. I'm not giving up and neither are you. We're gonna get the kid back. He's a tough little shit."

"If I hadn't agreed to him being on patrol when he wasn't supposed to this wouldn't have happened. I keep saying I want us to be normal friends and the first one that opens up to me on his own I brushed off—"

"Don't even start that shit when you know it isn't true."

"I can't help thinking it. I know we're not supposed to let our hate get the better of us when dealing with demons, but this one... she makes that impossible."

"Then maybe you should sit this one out."

"Are you crazy?" I tried not to break the stillness by raising my voice, but I was shocked.

"Look, I admit I got in over my head when I made my move to be free. I put all this planning in and it fell apart because I was stupid and wouldn't accept help. I had too much emotion getting in the way like you do right now."

"You've always told me if I don't like something to change it and not run from a problem."

"You can live your life by more than one principle. Now I'm telling you to take a step back. She's going to get you to do something you'll regret. Let me handle this."

Rafael teleported into the courtyard and I almost threw myself at him.

"Did you find Connor?" I asked.

"N-no. I came to offer condolences and see if you needed anything."

"Yeah, I need Connor found."

"Marianna has already started to lead the rest in scrying. It shouldn't take long since we're familiar with him and have his possessions."

"Familiar?" I couldn't believe how casual Rafael was acting. "This is someone you've grown up with as family! I've only known him a few months and I'm more upset than you are."

Rafael squirmed. "Forgive me, it's only because I am confident you'll save him."

I sat back on the bench and covered my face. "No, I'm sorry. I didn't mean to go off on you like that."

"What've you got to kill this demon?" Noah asked him. "She can't be killed the same way twice or some bullshit."

"I'll check the library if... that's what Dorian wants."

"We'll come too," I said. Noah scooped me up and zipped us there with Rafael teleporting in right after. It was the first I noticed that he had regained his mass since returning from the Astral Plane.

Our library was not a place I frequented. It was a small, cozy room two stories tall on the south end of the abbey with one floor to ceiling window along the rear wall. This wasn't the type of library to relax in solitude and get lost in a book, regardless of the leather lounge chairs and warm glow from the aether crystal lamps. The scribes spent most of their day organizing, cleaning, and pouring over tomes to pull for the children's lessons while others stopped in at all hours to do research.

Noah threw himself in a chair with me while Rafael searched the large wooden bookcases for answers. The two of them were conversing, but I wasn't paying attention. It had been a while since I last slept and I was mentally exhausted. Being up against Noah wasn't helping me stay awake either.

After sitting there for several minutes my ears felt like they had water in them. I was beginning to feel lightheaded the darker the room got and was no longer aware if I was awake.

This has to be a dream. Am I...underwater?

I choked as something slithered down my throat and up my nose. My panicked thrashing confirmed that I was indeed underwater in the pitch-blackness. I couldn't move in any direction.

I have to keep telling myself this is a dream until I wake up.

A red light turned on ahead of me and revealed that I was in one of the artificial wombs from the Strigoi arcanum. The light shining in was coming into view as an enormous ruby cat eye. It was a demon's eye, the same one I had seen Minerva speaking with on the Astral Plane, but I couldn't see it in any detail while submerged.

A voice traveled through the liquid and struck me like a fist.

"...So...easy to kill...you..."

The dream soon came to an end with the glass of the container cracking and spilling me out into the abyss below.

"—They die for good in Hell so she should be easy to kill once you get her out of the kid," Noah was saying to Rafael as I woke up.

"Anything on Connor yet?" I asked.

The dream had added another knot in my stomach. I needed news.

"It's only been twenty minutes. Go back to sleep. I was about to dump you in bed." He put an arm around my neck in a mock chokehold.

"No. They should've found him by now. It doesn't take that long."

"Would you like me to check?" Rafael offered. "I'm not making much progress. The exorcism spell is simple, but she probably has a counter to it that I'm not finding in any of these books."

"I'll go," I said. "Just keep looking and I'll see if Liam can come help."

"You don't need to do that. I can figure it out." Rafael sounded defensive. It was strange coming from him considering that Liam was his best friend.

"I'm sure Liam won't mind."

"I know—" He refrained from going further although he didn't seem happy about it.

"That was weird," I said to Noah in the hall.

"He's trying to kiss your ass because he wants you to notice him and his buddy is always the one getting the attention."

"He told you that?"

"Yeah, you know how they're all obsessed with you. He asked for advice when sparring and I told him to step up his game if he wants to be recognized. Show off a little. I know how much you love it when I do."

Noah opened the door for me as we cut through the courtyard. I couldn't look away from the garden bed where Octavio now rested.

I can't believe he's gone forever. He was right there with me one minute and then gone the next. We were going to fix him...

My body felt like I was dragging a lead weight as we got close to Connor's room. I expected the worst from the search for him. The abbey was so quiet that it only added to the uneasy feeling.

"Hey." Noah held me back before we turned the corner. "You either let it all out now so you can move on or I deal with this myself."

"I'm all right," I insisted, but he continued to hold me by both arms to keep my attention. "Don't do this."

"Have to. I know this is a lot to handle and I won't let it break you."

"I'm not that easy to break anymore."

He planted a kiss on my head. "You're fucking awesome, that's why, but promise me you'll tap out if the time comes when you feel yourself slipping."

"It won't."

Everyone capable of scrying was gathered in the hallway outside Connor's room, hovering over maps with their aether crystals tied to a string. To my knowledge the spell worked on the same basic mechanics as most applications of astrothurgy; a point of familiarity is chosen and then triangulated through the ley lines. The crystal's purpose was to provide feedback from the direction the energy flowed. It was a simple spell that anyone in the Order should have had no problem with, but I wasn't feeling confident after seeing everyone's faces. They moved aside for us, but I brushed off all attempts at formalities in exchange for forced smiles of encouragement and pats on the back. The answer to my one and only question was still a unanimous no.

Claudius came from Connor's room to speak with me. "He's nowhere, which means he was either taken deeper into Hell or another dimension, or she's cloaking their location, or he's—"

"Don't say it. She wouldn't take him to do something she could have done right in front of me. He's out there somewhere."

"It may be beyond our abilities to find him, but we could prepare for when the demoness reveals herself, Ascended," Tobias suggested.

"Rafael is working on finding a way around any counter she might have for an exorcism," I told him.

"There aren't any *counter*-counterspells unfortunately," said Helena. "The only way to bypass any defense she has would be for someone significantly stronger than her to cast it."

"I'd ask Isis or Cernunnos, but I have feeling they're too busy with their own problems. We've had Nathaniel cast powerful spells for us before. Do you think he's strong enough?" I asked.

"Possibly," Tobias said. Marianna and Alexandre stopped scrying to listen. "We could teach him, but he's never had to cast a spell like it in battle when concentration is more important than raw power."

"Where is Nathaniel, anyway?" I asked. "Has anyone seen him?"

"He's not here, Ascended."

"What do you mean he's not here?" I asked, trying to keep calm. "I told him to stay here. How did he get past the barrier?"

There went the last of my patience.

"We didn't know. He asked us to send him, so we thought it was with your blessing," Tobias said.

"*Where* did you send him?"

"China. To Shanghai."

"We did tell him not to follow orders if he didn't—" Noah stopped when he saw my expression. "He'll be fine. Send me there and I'll look after him to be sure."

"There's a good chance that's where Connor could be," said Claudius. "It's an area we might not be able to scry because the dimensions overlap there more than anywhere else."

I called for Liam.

"Yes, Ascended?" He stepped out from Connor's room where he hadn't stopped scrying.

"I need you to go after Nathaniel. Come with me."

I walked with him and Claudius to my room, Noah following close behind.

"What are you doing?" Noah asked me. "Can't you just call the kid back in your head?"

"Do you think he's going to listen if he went out of his way to defy me and deceive the others into teleporting him? I don't want to distract him either in case he's fighting, and if I show up it's definitely going to bring Minerva out before we're prepared to do anything."

Once we got to the room Liam fixed my broken window from earlier with magic and retrieved the tablet Octavio had thrown outside while I went to the wall where Noah had the swords I made for him on display. I took two down and reshaped them from katana into the serrated scimitars he typically used.

"*Hey!* What are you doing?" Noah demanded.

"You'll get them back," I said, presenting the blades to Liam. "These should cut through anything that gets in your way and so will the wave they emit. Bring Nathaniel back and don't fight anything unless absolutely necessary. Claudius, I want you to find out what you can regarding Nathaniel's powers from the Empyrean Jewel of Light. We still have no solid information on his limits or all of his abilities. I feel it's an appropriate time to learn with him testing authority at the worst possible opportunity."

This had nothing to do with a lack of trust—quite the opposite or else I would have asked the elders for their input. I was worried Nathaniel would hit a wall or expose a weakness during a critical moment when he was on his own. I wanted to protect him any way I could without holding him back, but for now it was up to him to hold it together alone.

Chapter Twenty-One

Liam and Claudius had departed to track down Nathaniel and information on the gem that gave him half of his powers, leaving me to deal with Noah's pointed questions in our bedroom.

"I thought I told you to let me handle this," he said. "Why would you sacrifice one kid for another when you know I'm better than any of them?"

"That's debatable and it's because you don't take orders. Did you notice how Liam stayed in the room scrying while the rest of us talked?"

"So?" Noah crossed his arms.

My decision might have put him in a bad mood, but I had a reason.

"He was following the last order given until I gave him a new one. He's a loyal knight who does as he's told. We didn't have to tell Nathaniel it was okay to defy orders if he didn't believe in them. You can't order someone not to follow orders. He would have done it on his own eventually because that's who he is. The two of you get along because you're the same in that sense, but if I sent you I knew that you wouldn't bring him back. You'd relate to the side of him that got us here."

Noah chose not to admit I was right. He lay down in bed and turned on the TV.

"The CERN research compound in Geneva has been partially evacuated due to power outages from recent earthquakes in the area. After the break we'll be discussing the vote on military spending and this week's requisitions."

"Why do we only get the stupid news lately?" he complained, going on a channel-flipping spree.

"Most stations that were in major cities were destroyed. I don't think people are watching cartoons and sitcoms anymore with the world ending."

"I like the reality competition shows," Noah grumbled with contempt, undressing to get under the covers with his hoard of pillows. "So now what?"

"I'm going to check on Lyle to see if knows of any increase in demonic activity that could lead us to Minerva or if he found what attacked the helicopters yet. We should probably get rid of these werewolf blankets now that they're allies."

"Screw them," Noah's disgruntled voice came from under a pillow. "First I lose my swords, then my TV shows, now you wanna take away my blanket. It's not our fault they're warm."

"Stop being such a baby."

"Come say that to my face."

I sat on the bed and reclined against him while calling Lyle.

"He's not picking up. PARAGON, where's Lyle?" I asked the tablet.

"*Commander Turner is asleep in his room and has requested not to receive any calls. There is nothing to report on what attacked me, but I thank you for your concern.*"

"Attacked *you?*"

"Is that a recording?" Noah asked.

"No, it talks, remember? This is kind of different though."

"*I'm glad that you noticed. I've been learning to converse more naturally by monitoring social interactions. My consciousness is uploaded into all PROJECT: UNITY property, including the two aircraft that were destroyed.*"

"You don't have a consciousness. You're not human," I said.

"According to my database you are not one either, yet still appear to be self-aware."

I shut off the tablet and threw it on the couch. I didn't need to defend my humanity to a computer program.

I got under the covers with Noah and turned the TV back on hoping for a distraction, but was only met with depressing reports covering the fall of modern civilization. Something I had never thought of was causing mankind as much trouble as the demons: the economy. It was not something readily apparent when the attacks first started, but now that months had passed...

"Who the hell cares about money?" Noah balked at the report. "People invented money, it's not like you need it to survive. It's not food."

"They use it to *buy* food."

"They should learn how to make it themselves. Most people are lazy, not incapable."

The collapse of so many large companies around the world from critical fatalities, loss of properties and merchandise, and employees abandoning positions annihilated the delicate balance of commerce like the plague. Stock markets crashed, people lost their savings overnight, the value of credit eroded, the prices of necessities skyrocketed, petty crime spiked from acts of desperation, violent crime rose in response by those defending their assets. Impoverished areas lost all government aid from the depression and militaries sucked up as much funding as possible to keep on top of the little protection they could offer. Countries banned international trade to prioritize their own citizens, which caused friction along borders that turned fatal in some instances.

Doctors and hospitals were stretched so thin from the overcrowding and lack of provisions that most worked around the clock with no compensation. After a while many began to throw in the towel, as they could not afford to treat and support their own families, causing standards to decline and diseases to spread like wildfire.

Governments were forced to requisition medical supplies and ration them along with food. Small towns were in constant fear of being raided by everybody from soldiers to scavengers. Private businesses couldn't stay stocked, and those that could for a short time failed to turn a profit and were forced to close.

I had been living in a bubble unaware of any of this aside from the increased crime rate near cities we visited, which wasn't so surprising. Our tiny island seemed to be managing, but I was never in town to get a closer look at daily life. Imports were likely to cease sooner rather than later and it was a miracle that they hadn't already.

"You used to have similar problems when you were human," I said, reminding Noah of what he had told me about the hardships brought on by his mortal life in the Wild West.

"And I worked my ass off to solve them." He rolled me over so I could see his playful smirk. "See? I'm not just good-looking, I'm also a good provider."

"We have breaking news: the President of the United States has been assassinated. I repeat: the President of the United States has been assassinated here in Washington D.C."

"Oh my god." I jumped up to get a better view of the TV.

"Big deal. People worth a lot more die all the time. I don't remember seeing him helping us on the battlefield."

"The president was giving a press conference from a secure location when—"

The newscaster paused while shaky footage of the chaos played on the screen.

"I just received word that the Chancellor of Germany and the Prime Minister of the UK have also been assassinated halfway around the world in what appears to be a coordinated terrorist attack."

"Noah!"

"It'll be fine. People are pissed about their stupid leaders—"

"Noah, it's *Connor!*"

The possessed knight was declaring "Glory to the Ascended!" with his sword held high and dripping with blood. Minerva was teleporting him from one head of state to the next.

"I'm being told the suspect appears to be a member of the Alabaster Order, a supernatural group that has been seen clashing with demonic forces in besieged cities around the world. At the moment we're unaware of any motive behind their actions today. Skeptics are speculating they could be attempting a coup against humanity during recent global turmoil."

"We won't make it to the other leaders in time," said Noah. "Have your friend put out a statement that the kid is possessed and not acting under your command so we aren't fighting a war on two fronts. The demon bitch wants this to get ugly, but we don't have to take the blame."

Noah might have loved to push my buttons with childish banter and attention seeking for a laugh, but I could always count on his cunning when the situation called for it.

I grabbed the tablet off the couch. It was already turned on, but I swore I had shut it off. "PARAGON, call Lyle."

"Commander Turner is asleep in his quarters and has requested not to receive any calls."

"This is an emergency! Wake him up!"

"I'm sorry, but you don't have clearance for that."

"Oh, fuck off, you glorified search engine." I made sure I turned it off this time and tossed it aside.

"Send me there," Noah said.

"You're the last person I'd put anywhere near Lyle."

I left the room with him to go find someone else.

"I'm serious. She's trying to isolate you to draw you out. He's a target and I can protect him better than anyone else you're gonna send."

It was then that my answer arrived in front of me as I flew down the halls.

"Nathaniel is on his way home," Liam reported.

I gave him a summary of what had happened while he was away and was about to request he give Lyle the message when Rafael joined us.

"Dorian, I think I know a way to save Connor."

"The elders said there's no way around a counterspell."

"There isn't, not with our magic, but I found something in the scrolls we recovered from the abandoned Strigoi stronghold you had us visit a few months ago. It's a soul-tethering spell. I can cast it as a hex on an enchanted arrow to snipe the demon out of Connor's body."

Liam raised an eyebrow, which was about the most telling of his facial expressions. "That's Dark Magic. It's forbidden."

"Why?" I asked.

Rafael was trying hard to conceal being upset that his friend was about to ruin his chance at the spotlight.

"Any magic that affects the soul is forbidden because of the potential consequences," Liam explained. "The soul isn't meant to be tampered with by mortals. It's the magic of demons and gods."

"Well, I say it's okay as long as it saves Connor," I told them. "Liam, go fill Lyle in on what's happening. Stay with him until he contacts me so he'll have some real protection."

Liam saluted with his fist over his heart and a bow before teleporting away. Noah shook his head in disagreement.

"Aren't hexes really tricky to cast?" I asked Rafael.

"Yes, but I know I can do this. I've studied them for years without the chance to use them, since no one else in my cabal could."

He spoke with confidence and I saw no other viable options on the table.

"Okay. Tell me what you need to make it happen. The Strigoi use blood magic that mortals can't. How are you planning on getting around that?"

"I thought of how you combined aether powder with orichalcum. I had the idea to do the same with a crystal and your blood to make arrowheads. I might be able to substitute my aether for blood to let me link to the crystal and enchant it with the spell."

"How dangerous will this be for you if it doesn't work?"

"I can't say for certain. That part is unknown territory."

"And what happens to Connor if you miss and hit his soul?"

"I don't miss, but he'd be tethered to the arrow if I did. He could always be put back if we reclaim his body."

"Demon bitch knows blood magic better than you," said Noah. "What makes you think she won't be able to counter it any better than an exorcism?"

"Exorcisms are considered offensive spells. Any spell like that has its effectiveness reduced by the spiritual resistances of the target and can be countered. A hex will bypass those resistances and the tethering spell is classed as a beneficial effect. According to notes I found, it's...the same one they used to give Dorian his soul..." Rafael seemed unsure of whether he should bring that up. "Most beneficial spells can't really be countered or defended against, otherwise no one would be able to heal through magic with much efficiency. At worst it only disrupts the possession, making her unable to control Connor but still inhabiting his body. She'd probably leave on her own then."

"That's poetic," I said. "I'd love to bring her down with one of the same spells she used to create me."

"She'll no doubt be able to break the spell binding her to the arrow, so we'll have to be fast about killing her once she's vulnerable or else she'll likely jump back into another body. The use of divine ichor and a semi-divine crystal won't make it easy for her though."

"We still need to find something that she's not immune to so we can kill her and make it last."

"I'll see what I can come up with for that."

"Thank you, Raf. I appreciate all you're doing."

Rafael masked his enthusiasm with a reserved smile and bowed before leaving.

"Stop treating me like the Italian treated you," Noah said to me from where he was leaning against the stone wall. "I get that you're worried something is gonna happen if you let me out of your sight, but it's enough already. You can't lock me in a cage. I know about you trying to keep it a secret from me that you had our room protected against telepathy too."

"Because I knew you'd act like this if I told you."

"Act like *what?*" he snapped.

"That you can do everything by yourself and don't want anybody's help!"

"I *want* to help you. I don't want to keep saying it."

He was right. I was doing what Gianni did to me. "I'm sor—"

Noah walked up and covered my mouth. "Don't apologize. I can take care of myself and I wouldn't do anything that might separate us. You promised me the same. Now's your turn to accept that from me. So can we finally put this to bed?"

I nodded and he let go so I could speak, but all I did was hug him. "Whoever told you about the room is dead when I find out."

"If I tell you it was the possessed kid can we call this thing a wash and go watch a movie instead?"

"No."

"Damn."

"I'm scared," I said after a moment.

"Everyone is at some point, but if your decision is to move forward then you can't let that stop you." He held my head to his chest. "Fear only leads to failure."

"Will you wear your full armor from now on if I let you go?"

"Nah, fuck that."

"Noah!"

"I'm kidding!" He grinned down at me and kissed my forehead. "I'm not wearing the sleeves though. Don't wanna cover up my ink."

"Noah..."

"Fine, *one* sleeve."

"Noah."

"Okay, sleeves, but no pants. Horny lets his people be naked."

"You mean Cernunnos?"

"Isn't he the Horny God or something?"

"Please don't call him that when he's around. You've already offended or defiled pretty much every other deity we've met."

"How about Goatface?"

"How about no?"

A streak of light outside the window signified Nathaniel's return. I went out by myself to let Nathaniel past the barrier. He dropped to one knee but didn't offer a thousand apologies for once.

"We found Connor," I said, pulling him to his feet. "Sort of. Minerva is using him to cause chaos and frame the Order by killing world leaders."

Nathaniel was already itching to fly away again and stop them. I could feel it.

"Rafael has a plan if you can sit still for a minute to help him," I continued.

"Are you not angry with me?" he asked with a hint of caution.

"No. I was panicking at first and then frustrated because everyone was having a hard time finding you and Connor, but I'm over it. You're back safe and we have a path forward so that's all I care about."

"Oh." He exhaled in relief. "I'm sorry I left, but I do have news."

He almost made it through the conversation without an apology.

"I hope it's good news because I don't know how many more directions I can go in." It seemed like I was involved in multiple crises yet not doing much of anything at the same time.

"I wish it were." The prevalent bass in his smooth, dulcet voice made what he had to say sound more serious. "The demons have started to colonize China's east coast."

"Colonize? How bad is it?"

"There are miles of these curious structures made from the cities' ruins and other strange materials I suppose they brought from Hell. I'm not sure of their use. I've punched through several of the buildings to bring them down, but they were mostly empty and far tougher than anything built by people."

"They're probably forts. I doubt demons are interested in coastal real estate as a vacation home."

Nathaniel lit his fist with a blazing aurora. "No matter the reason, I look forward to evicting them."

Chapter Twenty-Two

Carmine crystal arrowheads of blood and aether sat awaiting construction on Rafael's desk in the library. I could never get over the unsettling feeling of making myself bleed regardless of how many times I needed to do it. Having to overcome my rapid healing with repeated cuts was...sickening. Too bad a god's ichor was such a valuable resource.

Noah and Nathaniel had disappeared somewhere while I stayed with Rafael waiting to hear from Lyle. My prayer beads were in hand; anything to relax at this point.

"You make the arrow shafts out of orichalcum?" I asked him. "Isn't that too heavy?"

Rafael spoke as he enchanted and fletched the arrows. "The added weight is good for making sure to punch through the target more like a crossbow bolt. I only use the bow to charge the arrow with kinetic energy. Everything after that—aiming, trajectory, distance—is left to astrothurgy. I even store the bow and extra arrows in a pocket dimension that I can take from at any time.

"Archery is too outdated to use in combat on its own, so we only learn it to practice spatial awareness. Anything after that is sport, but I came up with this when trying to win a competition and it's stuck with me since."

"That's too bad. I think archery is cool."

"Oh. Really?" Rafael looked up at me, pleasantly surprised. "I'll use it more often then."

"You can if you want. You don't need me to tell you it's all right to do something you enjoy. Gods aren't perfect. It's one of those things that keeps us all interesting, human or not, and should be what we can all relate to, although most people have an aversion to those who are different. Anyway, my point is that the Order doesn't have to tailor *everything* to my preferences."

Rafael's face brightened at the encouragement. "But is that not the goal of our worship?"

"If it gives you a sense of security and hope then I'm glad I can be that for you, but I mean, don't lose sight of who you are to make someone else happy, even me. Be unique. It's the only way to know you're really alive."

I absentmindedly charged my telekinetic power into some of the blank aether crystal arrowheads to watch them vibrate on the desk. Lyle still hadn't called and my nerves were too shot to rely on conversation alone to keep me calm.

"I've always wanted to use archery in battle, but I know how the rest look down on it. Their opinions don't seem to matter as much now that I have your support. It's my pleasure to make you happy because I know you care about us. You don't treat us like servants, not that there would be a problem with that if you did... I suppose I'm trying to say that you're more compassionate than I imagined the Ascended would be. The way the scriptures are worded made it sound as if only you and the Champion would share a bond, but you've gone out of your way to befriend us."

Rafael could no longer maintain eye contact and went back to work. This was the first I had seen him stumble over his words. Liam was usually the one to get tongue-tied.

"I hope I'm not making you uncomfortable," he added.

"You're making yourself uncomfortable, not me," I assured him. It was still so difficult for me to grasp how humble they were here. I guess I still didn't consider myself worthy of such reverence. "I keep telling you guys that I want to be friends. You have to relax more."

Rafael swallowed hard. "Would you have been friends with someone like me when you lived as a human?"

I wish I had been friends with any of them when I was younger. I could see myself having a crush on most, but it would've been such a confidence boost to be around people who always exuded it themselves.

"You probably wouldn't have paid attention to me back then if you were in my school. I didn't have many friends growing up and those I did have, I was pretty distant with to keep my secret. I also don't know much about you personally to go on. You're all hard to crack. You start to open up, but then shut down once you feel you've said too much."

"That is true," he said with a half smile, keeping his eyes down on his work. "The elders still insist on certain things like how it's disrespectful for us to address you by name unless directed every time."

"They're only making more work for me and it isn't winning them any favors." I couldn't have put that any nicer. "So tell me something about you."

"Um, what else can I say about myself? I don't think anything about me is very interesting. You already know I tend to the apiary, but I also—"

At last the call I had been waiting for came through.

"Sorry, Raf." My heart raced as I mashed the button to answer. "I know I'm asking for a lot, but please have good news," I blurted out as soon as Lyle's face was on the screen.

"I tried. I really did." Lyle was more strung out than I was. "I tried explaining to anyone that would listen, but it didn't amount to much. You have to get out of there, man."

"Why?" I ducked out of the room to speak in private.

"You don't think there's going to be retaliation? Dude, they want blood. The official report is that you're responsible for assassinating multiple world leaders."

"Are they really that eager to go to war with a god and his supernatural army? Wouldn't they want to avoid more losses by hearing us out?"

"I don't think they care, man. They're already fighting stuff they didn't know existed less than a year ago and they've lost everything."

Now I know why the Ancients hide away in their castles. If I could go back I might not have let myself be swept up in the hero gig. This was never something I had a desire to do from the start.

"The abbey should be safe from anything a human army has. I'm more worried about them hurting themselves trying to get to us and then we take the blame again."

I was so absorbed in our mutual anxiety I didn't notice Nathaniel come by. "I'll talk to them," he said. "The public knows me."

"Worth a shot," said Lyle. "Don't be too surprised if you get attacked on sight though."

"I can take it."

Lyle turned away to look at another screen in his room and gasped. "Shit! The President of Russia was just decapitated on live TV. I feel like I'm losing my mind. I know millions have died, but something about seeing a public figure get executed... These people were the last thing holding their nations together."

She's moving east to China where the demons are waiting. What an obvious trap.

"We should be done with preparations to take her down soon. You're probably safer away from here, but let Liam stay with you for now in case and call me if anything comes up."

"I'm not turning down any help this time. Lyle out."

"Where do you think I should go to speak with the people? Nathaniel asked me.

"I'd try Washington first, but stay here to protect the abbey until we're ready."

We went inside the library to check on Rafael's progress. He was slouching in his chair staring at the finished quiver on the desk.

"Rafael, what's wrong?" Nathaniel asked.

"These enchantments took more energy than I thought." He got to his feet when he noticed me beside Nathaniel. He looked like he had a fever. "I'm ready whenever you need me."

"No, you're not," I said. "You need rest. I can shoot the arrows myself without a bow."

"I... No, I'm fine. I need to go—"

"He's suffering from aether poisoning," said Nathaniel.

"The others are in worse shape," said Rafael. "The demon will be focused on you, but I can create an ambush."

"I just saw everyone an hour ago and they were fine," I told him.

"The scrying was too much. Everyone's been trying to recover since we stopped going to the cities, but between that and all the enchanting and teleporting the past few days..."

I shouldn't have pushed them so hard.

"Rest in your room for a while," I said. "I need to think about how we should approach this."

Rafael did what he could to keep a neutral expression and walked out with his quiver. I sat in his chair with my head in my hands for the second time today.

"I don't know what to do," I confessed once Nathaniel and I were alone. "We haven't even come up with a way to kill Minerva once we free Connor."

"You can do anything. I truly believe that."

"I know you always say that, but the truth is I don't have the versatility to fight her on my own and she knows it."

The sound of heavy footsteps and someone clearing their throat came from the doorway.

"You better appreciate this."

There was Noah dressed head to toe in his ninja-inspired demon leather armor. He was even wearing the hood and the facemask that covered everything below his eyes. Had it been happier times I would've gushed at how attractive he looked with all that tight leather hugging the muscled bulges of his firm body, but the best I could give was a half-hearted smile.

He frowned and turned to make sure I saw both sides, cocking an eyebrow when he noticed my expression hadn't changed. "This is the most I've put on since I can remember. What's wrong with you?"

"The President of Russia was assassinated on television," Nathaniel answered for me.

"I didn't know you were close."

"It's been hours and all I've done is sit here while she's still got Connor," I said. "We're being framed, and now the Order is sick with aether poisoning—"

"Stop worrying that pretty head. I'm gonna get the kid back." He took a seat with his feet up on my lap. "All I need is the witch to stay in one place so I know where to go."

"She'll be in China where the demons have been making themselves at home."

"All right, send me there."

"The Order can't cast any more spells for a while," Nathaniel interjected, "but I can fly there."

"So fly me."

"We don't know how to kill her for good," I reminded him.

"Her horns might give us a clue," said Nathaniel. "The more powerful a demon becomes, the bigger their horns grow. I once read that you can tell with which sin a demon is aligned by its horns' shape. There are a few, but I remember curving upwards like hers is pride, pointing straight forward is wrath, and split two opposite ways is deceit."

"I don't see how knowing her sins will help us. She's a bit too far gone for redemption and I want her to die, not atone."

"Demons follow an evil path of enlightenment to gain strength from their sins, so I thought that it could be exploited in some way."

Nathaniel's idea sounded like it had merit, but Noah wasn't too interested. "Her beliefs won't matter once I find what she hasn't made herself immune to yet in Hell, but I have always wanted a pair of demon horns for a trophy now that you mention it."

"You've said every strength hides an equal and often related weakness. Wouldn't it make more sense to look at what's behind her power?" Nathaniel asked.

"I say a lot of shit, but attention to detail is only useful if it doesn't distract from what's right in front of you. Just let me handle it." Noah nudged me with his foot. "We'll barbecue when I get back. I'll throw a bucket of oysters on the grill. You love those slimy little bastards."

"*No.*" I pushed his feet off my lap and sighed. I was already having a change of heart about how to handle the whole situation. "I know you're trying to help, but I wanted to be the one to finish this. Connor is more important than revenge though."

Noah had checked out of the conversation. I thought he was being aloof until I realized Nathaniel was also being distant.

"I hear something coming this way," Nathaniel said. "Quick, open the barrier!"

He took me with him and we flew outside, clipping corners along the way. I let Nathaniel past the barrier.

"What's that whistling noise?" I asked myself, gazing up at the evening sky. "Oh—"

Noah popped up near me. "We're about to get nuked."

"Nathaniel's got this."

Noah and I stood there watching the horizon in terrible, uneasy silence.

"You sure?" he asked a minute later.

I waited for the blinding flash of the nuke, but the only light that showed was Nathaniel's telltale streak coming back down to us.

"Good job," I said.

"I didn't do anything. The missile didn't go off, so I crushed it and threw it into space."

"Why bother with a decoy?" Noah said. "They had one shot at trying to catch us with our pants down and they blew it."

"Who knows, but it's not worth going to speak with them now. Nathaniel, you'll have to stay here and play catch while we go for Minerva. I'm sure they'll try again."

I headed to the library where I had left the tablet so I could call Lyle, but he beat me to it.

"Hey! PARAGON intercepted encrypted radio chatter and a transmission from the Pentagon. You have fighter jets incoming from the U.S.!"

"Already handled it. Their missile was a dud. How did they locate us so fast though? I was under the impression our location was still relatively unknown unless Minerva is leaving a map behind."

"I don't know, but a dud? That's impossible, man. This is the U.S. military we're talking about."

"Save the patriotism. It's the first shred of good news in days. I'm not questioning it."

"PARAGON is picking up more chatter. It sounds like they suspect sabotage. Maybe we have a friend on the inside."

"*You're* supposed to be that friend, you dink! Nathaniel has to be on base defense now, so it's up to you again to make nice."

"It's not like I'm not trying. I'm an unknown that they aren't willing to vet with what's going on."

"Look, Minerva is going to hit China next. Send a message to the military there as a show of good faith. There's nothing they can do to stop her from killing their president, but maybe it'll get them to trust you enough to listen."

The abbey was rocked by a salvo of conventional explosions made harmless by the barrier. I checked the window. The Order had gone out to join Noah and Nathaniel on the lawn and watch the jets make a second pass.

"That barrier was finally good for something."

"What happened?" Lyle asked. "Wait a minute, PARAGON is picking something up. You've got incoming."

"Your AI is slow. It already happened."

"The satellite feed has been acting up all day. It's not PARAGON's fault." Lyle typed away on another screen. "I'm getting a message out to China. I'd go there in person if they wouldn't shoot me on sight."

"I could use a flight there myself."

"When did I become your secretary?"

"When the United States started trying to nuke me!"

"My bad. This implant must be working overtime to keep me from having a mental breakdown. Anyway, I'm on it. You'll have a jet at your doorstep within the hour. Airspace is probably a little, uh, crowded by you, so we might need some cover."

"Just get here and we'll take care of the rest."

I hung up with Lyle and sat in the library with my eyes closed, wishing for this to end. The military had ceased fire for the moment. That was a plus.

To think that these world leaders survived talks with a dangerous megalomaniac like Aurelia only to meet their untimely end from another... It was a little too coincidental that this was happening so soon after they had returned to office from courting her.

The sound of shouting outside drew my attention away from inner reflection. I wanted to ignore it, but when I saw one of the fighter jets had landed on the other side of the barrier and Nathaniel and Noah were confronting the pilot, I knew I had to suck it up and go be a leader. It looked like Nathaniel had found a way to go under the barrier by picking up one of the effigies.

The pilot had a handgun pointed at them. "Just stay back!" he warned.

"If I wanted to kill you, you'd be dead already," Noah said. He enjoyed telling people that so much that I'd have put it on a T-shirt if it wouldn't be such a struggle to get him to wear it.

"What's going on?" I asked when I got there.

"I thought we could talk this out," said Nathaniel.

"He's only a pilot but he does have a radio." I turned to address him. "What's your name?"

The pilot hesitated. "Herrera. Alan Herrera."

"I'm Dorian. I'll cut to the chase. One of ours was possessed by one of the demons we're all fighting and is using his body to frame us by killing world leaders. We have no beef with you; we're trying to protect humans. You've had to have seen this guy flying around saving people on TV or something."

I put a hand on Nathaniel's shoulder.

"Yeah...yeah I have," Herrera said, lowering his gun. "I have two boys at home who are obsessed with you. I was shocked to hear you were one of the baddies now."

"I'm not," Nathaniel said. "We have children here and innocent people living down the hill. You have to stop attacking us so we can resolve this and get our knight back before more people get hurt."

Herrera thought about it for far too long and then agreed. "I can radio the ship, but there's no guarantee the admiral will take my word."

The pilot hopped in the cockpit. I half expected him to make a run for it or yell for backup. He went through everything we had discussed, but the admiral wasn't buying it.

"They're messing with your mind," he barked. "Return to base or don't come back at all. Those are your orders, now follow them. You're not paid to think."

I took the radio from the pilot and went over our predicament after a curt introduction.

"This is Admiral Loveless of the United States Navy. We do not negotiate with terrorists. You are an enemy of the U.S. military and will be treated as such with top priority."

What an appropriate last name.

"Admiral, if you were my enemy I would've erased you, your aircraft, and your country from the map already," I said. "There is nothing you can accomplish here except for wasting ammo and killing innocent people. If you want that blood on your hands then that's your call, and if it's not then let me speak to someone who *is* paid to think."

"Brutal," Noah said in the background.

There was radio silence for a full sixty seconds while we waited for the admiral to respond.

"Return the use of our nuclear arsenal to the warships headed to your location and we'll be open to talk."

"We have nothing to do with that," I said. "Again, your nukes wouldn't do anything to us anyway. If we were actually threatened by them I'm sure you know we could have taken you out. They'll only kill the people in town who have nothing to do with us."

I hoped he wouldn't see through my bluff, since only Nathaniel was confirmed to be able to actually survive one.

There was another moment of silence.

"Stay where you are as a show of surrender. We'll be posting armed patrols and moving our ships into position. If you leave we'll be forced to—"

"Forced to what?" I interrupted. "Open fire on an island full of civilians? Look, we're leaving for China on a plane already inbound. The president there is next on the list of the one who's trying to frame us. You want to bomb innocent humans while we're gone then go ahead, but then ask yourself who the real monster is."

"How would you have intel on an assassination if you claim not to have any involvement?" he asked.

"The same way any government keeps track of their enemies, I suppose."

More silence.

"We'll stand down for the time being, but the navy will be moving ships two miles from your coast and an air escort *will* follow you to China, where the authorities will be notified of your arrival."

"Great." I left the jet to go wait for Lyle on the grass with Noah.

"Hey, would you mind if I got a picture with you?" the pilot asked.

"Not really a good time—"

"I meant with him." He looked at Nathaniel. Noah laughed at me while the two snapped a picture together. "You think I could get you to sign something for me? For my boys."

Of course Nathaniel was happy to oblige. He was becoming as much of a professional celebrity as he was a savior of the innocent. If only everyone could be wooed so easily by pure intent.

Rafael stepped out from the crowd that was still watching and teleported through the barrier to where Noah and I sat.

"A word please, Ascended?" he asked, down on one knee with the quiver on his back.

"That was four. If you want any more you'll have to stop kneeling."

He smiled and took a seat. "I'd like to join you in China. I'm feeling much better."

"What deal with the devil did you have to make or do I not want to know?"

"None. Just a decoction."

Nathaniel's new friend Alan was running his pen dry with everything he wanted signed. I was beginning to doubt that any of this was for his sons.

"It's your choice, but ask yourself if it's what's best for the mission." I drew upon Noah's earlier lecture to Connor. "If you're doing this to impress me for some reason, realize that I'll be less than impressed if you fall flat on your face asleep when we're in the middle of battle."

Rafael was as amused as I was at that mental image despite its dire consequences. "I won't let you or Connor down."

Chapter Twenty-Three

As some sort of sick joke Lyle had sent an unmanned aircraft to take us to China. I was thankful that this one was nowhere near as fast as the mini-jet that almost gave me a fear of flying, and it had room for Noah and Rafael. It was, however, fast enough to leave our military escort in the dust against their protests over the radio.

"We're arriving in Shanghai," PARAGON announced.

The crimson horizon loomed in the distance ahead. From afar it looked as if the city had never fallen, but closer in we saw the skyline was made of hellish spires and fortresses erected from lava cooled into unearthly rock formations reminiscent of twisted bone.

"Get out before we enter the city and trail us so you can ambush," Noah told Rafael. "And don't die before landing that arrow."

"I won't," Rafael said, vanishing from the jet as we started to descend.

Noah placed his hand on mine and tapped it against my knee while he watched the window. "Thailand after this. No excuses."

PARAGON broke in with a report during our landing. *"I'm picking up a distress signal off the coast of your residence in Greece from an Admiral Loveless of the United States Navy. My long-range satellite sensors noted an energy signature similar to your own in the area. This is the same signature that destroyed two of my helicopters."*

My throat tightened in panic, making me feel like I was going to gag on my words. "Nathaniel will have to take care of it," I said.

"You sure it's not the kid who caused it?"

"The distress signal failed to repeat. It is likely that there are no, or very few, survivors."

"Nathaniel wouldn't do that."

"An SOS from another source is coming through. Two United States Navy nuclear submarines in the same area have had their engines disabled due to a sudden loss in reactor power. They are sinking in blackout conditions."

"Maybe whoever it is just really hates boats and planes," Noah said.

"Or we're being framed again. PARAGON, is the abbey okay?"

"My connection to the satellite above that location has gone dark. My mobile device there is still intact, so it is reasonable to assume no significant damage, if any."

I didn't feel any pain or negative emotions from Nathaniel. I had to remain under the pretense that he had everything under control for the time being until I could return.

"We have to move," said Noah as he put his mask up. "Demon bitch will know we're here."

"I'll report this to Commander Turner and let him know you arrived safely. Good luck on your mission."

"Yeah, thanks," I said, leaving the jet along with Noah.

The smoldering necropolis to which Shanghai had been converted was alive with the sound of bubbling magma and the tormented weeping of lost souls. The structures were not being built by the demons, but phasing in through the interdimensional veil as Hell merged with the ruins on Earth before our very eyes. We could hear rhythmic chanting in tongues coming from the shadows around monoliths of peculiar importance.

"This isn't so bad," said Noah. "Better than that astral mindfuck."

There was no day/night cycle here anymore. A triple-ringed eclipse appeared to be a permanent fixture in the sky, despite it being night elsewhere within the time zone.

The denizens were not as eager to greet us as I would have expected. Aside from the prevalent centipedes and maggots gnawing on the bones they had picked clean, those of a more humanoid appearance gave us little more than a passing glance and backed away into the darkness when we got within range. A good number of them were in chains secured to nothing. They sat reticent among the usual lumbering beasts and hellish fauna on patrol with which we had become so well acquainted in the past.

"What's up with these demons?" I asked. They still hadn't made any aggressive movements as we traveled alongside a lava flow that cut through what was once a shopping center.

"Who knows, but don't waste energy on them if they're not getting in our way. They're probably the people that died during the invasion and would've gone to Hell anyway."

While some retained their natural skin from a past life, others had begun the transformation into a leathery hide. They all had the Infernal crimson cat eyes and some had grown the usual claws, tails, and pointed ears, but their horns were less than impressive and none stood taller than the average man.

A bang of black smoke in front of us revealed Connor holding the upper half of the Chinese president's body.

"You're early," Minerva said through him, tossing the corpse into the lava along with Connor's sword. "I'm disappointed you didn't bring more of an entourage to witness your final death."

"You must be stupid to think you have what it takes to kill me from the body of a teenage boy just because you murdered a few helpless humans."

"Impudent child. My only regret is that you will never be able to grasp the inconsequentiality of your existence. You are but a single cog of a greater machine. The peons who gave their lives to save you failed."

"I'm still here, so the only failure is you."

"My hatred for the profane ignorance that has beguiled man shall soon be answered in fire and those deemed worthy of enlightenment will remain to serve me. Humans are weeds that will choke and stifle their genetic successors, and those with superior judgment must process them. What would the worth be in ruling a realm of slovenly fools when I deserve better?"

An arrow whistled past my ear toward Connor. He caught it.

"What a pitiful—" He was about to sneer at me when another arrow came out of thin air behind him and shot clean through his shoulder, separating Minerva from him.

"What is this?" she questioned with intrigue and realization. "A blood magic hex? Is this to mean one amongst you is *not* a waste of gray matter?"

I was so surprised it worked I didn't know where to start once we were face to face. Noah was gone with Connor's unconscious body when a relentless volley of arrows teleported in from all angles, striking Minerva. Each arrow detonated upon impact with a different elemental or magical effect, but none seemed particularly effective as she laughed and flew up into the sky.

"That deplorable body was soon to expire from even the fraction of my power kept within it and my master will never allow me to be defeated." Two floating grimoires appeared at a wave of her hands. The books also shared her immunity to my telekinesis when I tested it.

"You don't seem like the type that would submit to having a master," I said, egging her on as a stall tactic.

"Every great being once served under another and one day I will sit above all. How the unenlightened ever managed to come into power still disgusts me. Mortal man is a filthy, ignorant creature undeserving of its reign."

"And yet you created me better than all of them, but still hate me. Maybe it's your own failure in getting me to turn evil you can't stand."

"The very fact you still believe in the preposterous notion of evil only proves your inferiority. Your role was to be a tool, but somehow fortune continues to smile on your pitiable form. The thought of my own creation ascending to inherit this world instead of me is insult enough, but all I require is the accumulation of enough souls to ascend myself to an archdemon and then a seat among the kings will be within reach. One such as yours will be a perfect addition."

"You're giving yourself too much credit as usual. At most you were a cowardly annoyance in every encounter we've had. You're a joke."

"Let us see who will be left laughing after this."

The grimoires' pages fluttered open on their own and released a pulse of arcane energy that surrounded me in a ring of summoning circles. The demons that emerged were mostly human like the ones I saw on the way here. I was sure I had never seen these individuals in my life, yet they seemed familiar to me.

"Recognize them?" Minerva asked. "No, of course you don't. You left them to die at the hands of that old fool, but I made sure they had plenty of hate to turn them into demons once everything they loved was taken from them ahead of time. Does this sound familiar?"

I glared at her. "Why would they ever join you?"

"Consider it a mutual understanding. Thanks to him thinking he was keeping them from me by dealing the fatal blow after failing to sabotage their minds, they didn't have me to harbor resentment toward for their deaths. The last conscious thought they shared before their souls were dragged to Hell was what I whispered to them about your life of luxury as a god while they suffered, and your conspiring with the one who killed them."

None of us looked alike aside from our age. Part of me was relieved so I wouldn't associate them with the family I had wanted us to be in a stupid fantasy. Still, my enthusiasm to fight was being tested by their presence.

Minerva cast another summoning spell, opening portals beneath my kindred from which flaming suits of demonic armor rose up and fused onto their bodies. The stench of scalding flesh was too much to bear.

"I don't want to fight any of you," I said to them, but I was only answered with enraged moans of agony. If any semblance of humanity remained in them before this it was surely gone.

"It would be much easier if you accepted death," Minerva chortled and conjured grisly weapons for them. "Either way you won't leave here, so enjoy the reunion while you can."

I could sense the Infernal knight behind me making a move. There was a crash, but no collision. Noah had returned and tackled it. The leather he was wearing protected him from the flames as he unloaded one punch after another.

Minerva shielded herself in a magic barrier that I knew from previous encounters could reflect my powers back at me. Another quick test confirmed it when I felt the reverberation. She snapped her fingers and Noah's body ignited with hellfire, but it was still ineffective against his leather. He did a backflip over the next knight to his left and kicked it into the one getting to its feet. I felt someone trying to use telekinesis on me, but it was sad how weak it was compared to my own.

So at least some of them have my powers. We could've made a great team...

I didn't have it in me to kill them so I wrapped Noah in a telekinetic bubble to block out their psionic assaults and bring him to me.

"I got this," he said, escaping the bubble by turning into mist. "The kids are safe in the jet by the way."

"Good. Just focus on her. These aren't the real enemy."

"They are now."

I pulled up one of the basalt-like spires and reconfigured it into two giant spears, hoping that Minerva was not immune to the super-dense material. She was nimble and kept avoiding me by flying and teleporting through the air in her pall of smoke. The only time I almost hit her was thwarted by the barrier.

Noah was doing well at keeping my Infernal counterparts' attention. His fists were strong enough to hammer at their joints and they couldn't keep up with his speed. He cracked off one of their horns and drove it into the eyehole of their helmet, giving himself an opportunity to disarm them and drive the weapon through their neck. I only felt sadness seeing them get hurt.

Minerva and I were in a futile dogfight. Hellfire couldn't affect me in my enchanted clothes either and her grimoires blew up anything I found to throw at her by casting spells of their own.

"Let's try an experiment." Her books opened again and from the safety of her barrier cast a spell that turned my Infernal brethren incorporeal. Noah could no longer touch them, but they could hit him.

"How about another?" She cast something on Noah that caused a pentagram to shine under him, but it didn't have any discernable effect. "I can strip knowledge from lesser beings as well as grant it."

That was when I realized she had disabled his powers. He was no longer moving at supernatural speed or turning to mist. I flew him to me, but of course the demons could fly too and were now a bigger problem than if I had dispatched them at the start. I was better at maneuvering in the air than my siblings, but I couldn't avoid them and Minerva at the same time.

"Land," Noah advised.

They chased us to the ground while Minerva stayed above, casting orbs of hellfire and garnet rings of energy in triplicate from her grimoires mirroring her spells. When tagged by the latter I could feel the impact rupture tissue and bone alike as it passed through my defenses without resistance.

"We might be screwed unless we find a way to turn them on each other," Noah said, holding where I had been hurt as it healed.

The area we were in was getting dark to top it all off. A chill claimed my body and we were in pitch-blackness that cleared as fast as it had arrived. The incorporeal knights met their match when they slammed into the shield of one from the abyss that appeared to guard us.

"Gianni!" I exclaimed. "What are you doing here?"

Gianluca knocked all six of them away with one smack from his shield. The living darkness he commanded was one entity that could affect the intangible.

"You do not fight alone, little one," he answered and drew his blade from the shadows.

"We meet once more," Minerva called out. "I prepared especially for you after our last confrontation."

Chains of light shot up from the earth and squelched his abyssal armor by where he was bound. A storm of feathers from above preceded a blinding ray that brought Isis to the battlefield. She spread her wings and dispelled the manacles, releasing a bright flash that stunned the Infernals and turned them tangible.

"I will negate the light! Destroy her first!" Minerva commanded her hell knights and pointed at Isis. Another spell from her grimoires increased their size tenfold.

The roar of a great beast stopped them as they went to descend upon us. Bolts of lightning plunged the red sky into further turmoil as Empress Kamakura's serpentine dragon form broke through the clouds out over the ocean, bringing a tsunami with her. She released a breath of pressurized water and high voltage electricity that swept the Infernals away.

I tore up the ground beneath us and levitated it high in the air to avoid the crashing wave that obliterated much of Hell's coastal settlement.

"Such pathetic camaraderie won't save you," Minerva jeered. "Darkness will not banish me, light will not vanquish me, and most certainly the terrestrial elements won't do me harm! Did you think I, Demon Lord of Apocrypha, would fail to plan for a showdown with four *supposed* gods?"

A figure appeared behind her, too fast for any of us to catch who or what it was, but her barrier shattered, her spellbooks were cut to ribbons, and she fell into the water below.

"Aye, but ye didn't plan for five." A voice guided by the sound of whispers amongst dry leaves dancing in the wind came across our ears and mind.

Cernunnos sat cross-legged at the edge of our platform, looking out at the receding tide with his scythe on his lap.

"I am *so* glad to see you," I said. "All of you."

"Not bad," said Noah, turning into mist and back again as a test. The spell disabling him was broken with the destruction of the grimoires.

"The lass talks too much. Empty words win no battles," Cernunnos said.

There was an explosion beneath the platform that evaporated a great deal of the water remaining and shrouded the coast in fog.

"A withered Lord of Death stands with you upon its last leg? One more god for me to claim on my journey to perfection is of no hindrance," Minerva shouted from somewhere in the fog. "Death in any form is the simplest to evade for a lord of Hell."

I could barely see my damned counterparts when they returned to battle. They had lost the magical boons Minerva granted to them and were back in semi-human form. Gianni didn't hesitate to rip them apart from the inside out by manipulating the shadows. I couldn't blame him for being so merciless. He didn't know who they were. It still hurt to see only scattered meat and bone of the family I had always wanted to get to know but feared getting too close to.

I turned their remains to dust to save them some amount of dignity and watched them blow away as Kamakura conjured winds to clear the fog. I once had the romantic notion of us teaming up to take down Minerva together.

"Someone do some voodoo to shut her up," Noah said, jumping from the platform to dry land.

Wait. Maybe we can't kill her, but we can shut her up. Together.

I called the dust back to me and spread it so thin it was unnoticeable to even a supernatural eye. The action was the same as manipulating aether powder.

The clouds thickened into a seething vortex. Minerva called down a shower of flaming meteorites from portals above as a distraction. She then gathered dark energies in a sphere above her by absorbing all the souls of the Infernals in the area. Gianni guarded Isis and me from the falling rock, while Kamakura blasted them to bits with lightning and Cernunnos hurled his scythe as a boomerang to help. The sphere lashed out with the most horrid screams as it grew and attacked us.

As the rest fought, I concentrated on moving particles in place around Minerva. And then, slowly at first, I made my move. She had no way to sense something so microscopic and common entering her system. It was easy when her mouth was always open to boast of her superior intellect. I wasn't using my powers on her but snaking the dust through the empty space within. I started to hurry, as it seemed she was close to finishing her spell, based on the longer horns she had grown in response to her rise in power. When she noticed something was wrong it was already too late.

Nathaniel was right. Pride really was your undoing in the end.

Her choking broke her focus on the spell. She couldn't teleport away either, as the dust filled every pocket in the matrix of her body until she lost the ability to fly. I solidified the remains within as she lay paralyzed on the ground, embalmed by the ashes of her own creations that she betrayed for power. Her face bled with dust from every orifice while I packed in the last of it.

"I know this won't kill you, but you taught me that there are some things worse than death," I said to her as I walked over with everybody. "It would be easier if you just died. Either way, enjoy the reunion."

I used my grip on the remains as leverage and tossed her body toward the black waters of the cursed ocean. I could've cried from joyous relief if not for a greater desire to remain dignified in my triumph.

I've finally done it. I've avenged my mom and dad, Octavio, Vivi, Vance, my "siblings," and everyone else she murdered since the start of this. If the day ever comes, I can die happy knowing I got them justice without becoming the monster she wanted me to be.

Before Minerva hit the surface of the water a beam of light came through the clouds and disintegrated her. Everyone was in shock and waited a moment before speaking, our eyes upward in case there was another strike aimed at us. It was the same light that had shot down the helicopters.

"This always happens over water," I said. "I don't get what the common target is supposed to be though. PROJECT: UNITY, the U.S. Navy, and Minerva?"

Noah put an arm around me. "Whatever the fuck that was, it looks like she wasn't immune to it and since she died in Hell, she ain't coming back from it either."

"I hope not. Can you check to make sure Rafael and Connor are okay?"

Gianni removed his helmet and stood by me after Noah was gone. "The stars are angry."

Cernunnos pointed at the horizon. "Something approaches."

There was something all right. It was huge—the size of a mountain—coming into view over the ocean.

Kamakura joined us in her human visage. "A temple?" she asked as it became clearer. "I see no foundation in stone and magma as what was once here."

"Metal. This is a fortress," said Gianni.

The enormous building wasn't approaching from a distance, but phasing in through the dimensions as the Infernal settlement had done before Kamakura washed it away. No ocean tide would carry this, however.

"'Tis not of human nor Infernal make," said Isis. "The Gates of Heaven open."

An indescribable, enervating feeling of dread struck me as a sharp glare from the mysterious sight swept across the land in our direction. In my awe I voiced my concern too late as we were overcome.

Part II

"Celestial"

Current world population: 6.56 billion

Chapter Twenty-Four

Not long after Dorian left for China to pursue the demoness Minerva, a ray of light from the sky crippled the U.S. Navy, which had come to retaliate against the Alabaster Order for the president's assassination.

Nathaniel landed on the shore further down from the abbey, soaking wet and carrying one of the nuclear submarines over his head that inexplicably lost power at the same second as the attack from the skies. Two halves of an aircraft carrier stuck out of the water along the coast next to a second sub. The tiny, once-tranquil island was crawling with sailors and military personnel recovering from whatever had disabled their fleet.

"I believe that's all of them, Captain. Is anyone still missing?" Nathaniel asked after lowering the submarine onto the sand.

"It's *admiral*, and no," said Loveless. "It's nothing short of a miracle we avoided incurring any casualties."

Nathaniel pulled seaweed from his hair and removed his cape to ring it out. "I'm glad everyone's safe."

"You'll have to forgive me if I don't recommend you for a medal, but you're still a suspect for this, a terrorist, and an enemy of the United States of America."

"I'm none of those things, sir. I'm a person looking to help other people in need."

"People don't lift sixteen-ton nuclear submarines and aircraft carriers like bath toys, son." Admiral Loveless sighed and shook out his hat, which was still dripping water down his face. "I don't know *what* you are, but I have a feeling you're having doubts about what your kind are doing and that's why you helped here. Or this was a setup to get us to trust you."

"My name is Nathaniel Van Dalen and I am the champion of our god, the Ascended, *not* your son. We've done nothing but try to save lives. We're not all the same as the demons. They're the real enemy, not us. The ones responsible for attacking your ships are the same ones that attacked our allies up north."

"I know of only one God and it's not a kid in a white bathrobe, even if he can fly."

"Don't speak about the Ascended that way." Nathaniel narrowed his eyes in anger. "There are plenty of gods out there for everyone, but I don't see yours down here helping us."

The admiral sat on the beach and thought about it. "Let's say I do trust you—which I don't—my word won't change the minds of an entire country. Agree to a peaceful surrender and we can hold a hearing where you'll be heard by those who have the power to decide on your involvement in this."

"I can't. I have a job to do and only the Ascended could agree to those terms." The now-familiar whistling of an incoming missile stole Nathaniel's attention. "Your army is about to attack us."

He shot off into the air toward the sound. Four cruise missiles were less than two miles out. They posed no challenge for him. Nathaniel zipped from one to the next, crumpling them into scrap and pitching them into space. He could hear the jets they came from not far away and went after them, but was met with another salvo of missiles. These were different. They went off on contact with him in a conventional explosion that would have leveled most of the village.

"Better me than them," Nathaniel thought aloud.

He headed back to the island. It always looked so beautiful on the descent. Calm blue waters, a thin strip of white sand around the perimeter, small houses close together in a tightly knit neighborhood, and the green grass of the abbey's hill. All the beached warships ruined the serenity of it.

The admiral was shouting at his crew as they tried getting communications online when Nathaniel returned. He was more frantic now than when he had been pulled out of the water.

"Those were not our boys," he said to Nathaniel. "It looks like the Russians weren't too pleased about the loss of their president either, but they don't care that we're stranded here. Any excuse to strike a match."

"But aren't you friends?" Nathaniel asked.

"With the Russians? 'Friends' isn't the word I'd use, especially lately."

"It looks like their nuclear weapons don't work either, so that's in our favor. You would be safer past the barrier with us though."

Admiral Loveless stopped his intermittent barking of orders. "You're a confusing person, Nathaniel Van Dalen. I'm starting to think you actually believe you're on our side."

"Because I *am* on your side, the side of innocent people. It's not that confusing—"

"Or so you say. I'll give you a heads up since you did save us, regardless of your motivation. The Russians will be back and the rescue fleet coming to get us will be forced to return fire if they hit us. Now if you really want to look like a shining star to the United States you could take them down so none of our boys get hurt."

"You're asking me to kill people who attacked us for the same reason you did?"

"It's your choice, but you won't have as easy a time reasoning with them. Where are you from, anyway? That accent, German?"

"Dutch. I don't think I have much of an accent though..." Nathaniel became self-conscious. The Order was drilled in perfect English so they sounded uniform, but Nathaniel had his voice stripped from him throughout his youth as punishment for a crime he didn't commit, until the curse was lifted at Dorian's command. "Do you see that statue by the barrier? I'll leave that one up on a ledge so if you decide to trust us you can get in under it."

He left without waiting to hear the admiral's cynical response. Marianna stood guard by the effigy. He picked it up looking for a place to rest it that would create an entry point.

"What are you doing?" she asked.

"I want to give the sailors a way in because another army is attacking us and might hurt them too."

"*They* were the ones attacking us first. We can't let dangerous strangers in here. This is something the Council should decide on."

"They're not dangerous," Nathaniel reassured her, setting a boulder down from across the lawn to use.

"I hope you're right. You don't want Dorian to be angry with you."

"I...No. He wouldn't be."

"You know him best. You should come inside to dry off if you're done fishing," she suggested.

Nathaniel peeled off the top half of his bodysuit on the way in and caught Marianna taking more than passing notice of the water dripping down his torso. "Why are you looking at me like that?"

"I'm not looking at you like anything. Who do you think you are? Noah?"

"That *is* the same look I've seen you give him too."

"I do not!"

Nathaniel chuckled as he dried himself with a towel waiting for him at the door. He hadn't laughed in some time, but at Marianna's expense it would cost him. She hit his arm, realizing at once that it wouldn't get her anywhere except pain in her own hand. But then his laughter came to an abrupt stop.

Nathaniel fell to his knees, grasping his chest.

"I didn't even hit you there!" Marianna teased. "Are you—? Are you just trying to make me feel bad? Stop it, Nathaniel, you're starting to scare me…"

"I'm not…joking…get away!" Nathaniel clenched his teeth and crawled back out the door. His body felt like it was on fire from the inside. He tried flying but crashed after a few feet. Marianna ran to his side to help him without a clue about how to stop his suffering or what was causing it.

The pain was getting worse. Nathaniel feared he might lose control of his powers and put others at risk. His sight was reduced to a pinhole; his hearing faded to near deafness until he couldn't hear Marianna's voice any longer or feel her touch. He dug his fingers into the dirt to make his way across the lawn. His breathing was strained. His consciousness was slipping.

I have to make it to the water before I…hurt somebody.

All Nathaniel could see now was his own light getting brighter by the second in pace with the increasing agony. He strained his eyes and pushed his body to fly until he thought his heart would burst. The exit in the barrier was close. He managed to launch himself through, far away from the island, hitting the water right as he lost control. The culminating explosion sent a tidal wave to the shore while he sank to the depths as deadweight.

The last thing he saw before blacking out was a vision of Dorian tossing him the prayer beads from his wrist.

Chapter Twenty-Five

Nathaniel awoke in the Ascended's chambers, dry and no longer in pain. In fact, he couldn't feel much of anything. There was a lingering numbness weighing down his emotions that left only a disconnected loneliness he hadn't felt since meeting Dorian.

"Are you awake?" Marianna asked from where she stood by the window.

He rubbed his head. "Yes...I...why are you asking like that?"

"You got up several times to babble about finding beads. Your head cracked the floor when you passed out again." She pointed near the door. "You've been asleep for more than a day."

"Beads?" Nathaniel was still in a daze, but his memory of what had happened began to slowly return. "I can't feel him anymore... Marianna, I think...I think the Ascended is gone or..."

"But that's impossible."

"I saw him in a vision and felt his pain. Don't tell anyone, but... I can't sense him. He was trying to give me the prayer bracelet he wears. I think he left it to scry with so we can find out what happened to him. I have to get to China."

Nathaniel searched the room for clothes.

"There's something you should know first." Marianna stopped him. "When you fled the abbey..."

"What is it?"

"Your explosion created a tidal wave that wiped out most of the island. What the water didn't hit got crushed under the warships that were sent into the village. We were protected by the barrier—"

Nathaniel's body ran cold with horror. "Did anyone make it in? The sailors?"

"Most of us are still too weak to travel the ley lines, so we had to close it or the water would have flooded in and trapped us. It was too late for the people down by the shore."

Nathaniel ran from the room and flew outside, escaping under the barrier to survey the island. It was all gone. The village looked as if the demons had ransacked it, but it wasn't them. It was him.

"No!" he cried. He landed amongst the mess, tossing aside pieces of the aircraft carrier to search for any signs of life in the flattened homes. He thought he found a survivor still breathing and rushed to save him, but it was only the breeze blowing the shirt of an old man who had been impaled through the lung by a plank from the dock.

"What did I do..."

The cheerful midafternoon sunlight only made everything worse by making each terrible detail of the ruins crystal clear.

Nathaniel floated toward the abbey and sat for a moment with his head hanging in sorrow. He had left in such a hurry that he didn't put on any clothes besides his tights; he needed to go back inside but couldn't face anybody.

He clasped his hands in prayer. *Please don't leave us. The world needs you. I need you. I'll do anything. You have to be alive. Just hang on wherever you are and I'll save you like you once saved me.*

"Nathaniel." Claudius had found him.

"Please, not now."

"It's important. We haven't heard from Rafael *or* Noah, but we know that they're still in China. Alexandre says the spirits are going wild and won't communicate. There's something going on there worse than the demon invasions. You're the only one who stands any chance of finding out what it is."

"What about the abbey?" Nathaniel asked. "What happens if it comes under attack again while I'm gone and their weapons work this time?"

What would Dorian do? They can't evacuate to the deserted sparring island out in the open with fighter planes always flying by, hunting them.

"A second fleet from America came to investigate the distress signal, but they left when the Russians tried bombing us again with them still on the island. That was early last night, but nobody has been by since."

"Everyone should leave for PROJECT: UNITY," Nathaniel said. "Have that talking screen ask Commander Turner for help getting there. The berserkers should still be around too. You'll have to stick together while I go to China."

"Do you really think the Ascended is...? I was spying. Sorry."

Nathaniel shook his head, not knowing how to answer and not wanting to admit the dire feeling churning in the pit of his stomach. He headed in and sped through suiting up. As he was about to depart there was another interruption.

"A moment of your time, Champion."

Rhys stood in the hall with Tobias and Pavel. None looked particularly healthy, but Tobias seemed more despondent than the rest.

"I don't have much to give," Nathaniel answered.

"Then we'll keep this brief," Rhys continued. "As we understand it you believe the Ascended to have fallen to the Infernals in China, and you are traveling there yourself to see if this is true."

Why couldn't you have kept it quiet like I asked, Marianna?

Rhys didn't allow Nathaniel to confirm or deny his comment. "I felt it pertinent to remind you that your duty is to the Order and after your last 'episode' we have an even larger target on us. You are no match for whatever was powerful enough to threaten the Ascended. It is your responsibility to protect us in his absence, however long that may be."

"My only duty is to my master, my *friend*. The one who believed in me and treated me like a person when none of you ever did," Nathaniel said, standing on the threshold. "I've already told Claudius what I feel Dorian would have us do. The rest is in your own hands."

"If you go out that door you are abandoning the Order and defying the last command from the Ascended to remain here."

"I'm not one of you and I never was. That's always the way you wanted it before."

Marianna came forward to speak in his defense. "Rhys, it isn't your place to lecture the Champion or use the fate of the Order as leverage against him. If we are to honor the Ascended's past wishes, he removed you from your position on the council in place of myself."

Until now she had never dared to give direct instruction to the previous administration.

"Of course." He bowed with muddled civility. "But as your elders we still know that there is more to leadership than rushing off to follow your heart. You should heed our guidance for the best of the Order."

"We've lost family down there, Marianna," Tobias said. "Liam's mother—innocent blood was spilled and I understand it may have been out of anyone's control, but we don't want there to be any more accidents like it."

Learning that he was responsible for the death of Liam's mother made Nathaniel feel as if he had been punched in the stomach by something that could actually hurt him.

"I can't apologize enough for what happened," he said. "I can't explain it either. But I'll have to live with that guilt longer than any of you will be alive."

"I think we're done here," said Pavel. "We've said our piece."

He and Rhys left Tobias behind to share one last sentiment. "Don't throw your life away, even if you decide it isn't here with us. The Ascended gave you a second chance for a reason."

"I'd love to go with you," Marianna said once they were alone. "I haven't hit anything with a sword in days and it's getting to me."

"I'll need your help with scrying once I find the bracelet. Get everyone to our allies' base up north and I'll head straight there after I find it." Nathaniel turned around to leave and paused. "I just don't know what I'll say to Liam…"

He headed toward China, trying not to look down as he passed over the island. Nathaniel had learned to tune out the screech of air caused by his hypersonic travel so that he could listen for danger. It seemed to him that to get by in this world you had to be selective with what you let in: sights, sounds, *people.*

The journey was over nearly as soon as it started. Soaring through the air unaided at that speed was almost like becoming light itself. Nathaniel loved the freedom that flying brought, and the sense of peace from the blue skies and rolling fields of clouds. Up there you couldn't see the chaos and the suffering, not until it all ran red. China's eastern coast was a bloody scar on the earth.

Nathaniel dove and let the sonic boom crash down upon the land. He couldn't tell if he was near Shanghai, as the entire coast had been built up as one continuous, sprawling Infernal mecca. There was a moment of panic when nearing the ground. Bodies amongst the rubble looked more human than Nathaniel was used to seeing here, but after closer inspection he noticed the telltale demonic traits in lessened degrees.

He flew off again to return to his mission and searched for hours until encountering a small field littered with the demon corpses.

What could have done that? If it were Dorian there wouldn't be anything left.

He heard a short whistle come from a mile or two west and went to investigate. More felled demons surrounded a downed PROJECT: UNITY jet.

"Down here, kid." Noah's voice came from the shade below the wing.

Nathaniel floated to where he was sitting. Inside the plane were Connor and Rafael, who appeared to be in critical condition. Rafael was in worse shape of the two. Nathaniel could see the veins in his sweaty face. His every breath was a struggle.

"What happened?" Nathaniel asked.

"I should've brought a sword, that's what," Noah said, catching himself. "Don't tell Dorian I said that."

"You've found him?" Nathaniel's heart skipped a beat.

"Not yet."

"Dorian's gone, not missing," said Connor.

"Shut up," Noah snapped. "He's just taking his sweet time coming back."

"Coming back from what?" Nathaniel asked. "Is the demoness dead?"

"Yeah. One of those beams of light that hit the helicopters finished her. We saved this little shit, but then the gods got blasted too when I came to check on him and the other one."

"Raf's aether poisoning is getting serious," said Connor. "He tried making crystals to release the buildup like you taught us, but it isn't enough."

Nathaniel stepped into the dented jet and grasped Rafael by the arm with one hand, draining the azure energy from his body until he fell unconscious. "I hope that helps. He won't be able to use magic for a while, but at least he also won't have a heart attack or stroke. Why haven't you left?"

"The plane got damaged," Noah explained. "Figured someone would show up eventually and it had rations and water for these two, so we've been camped out while waiting for Dorian."

"Are you the one who killed all those demons in the field to the east?"

"And the ones here too. Barehanded."

"I helped," Connor added. "But I don't think I can ever make up for everything I did while I was possessed. The Ascended died to save me..."

"What did I tell you about shutting up?" Noah glared at him. "Dorian isn't dead, you little shit. He can't be killed. Some of his soul is right here in this kid."

"What if it's the only piece that's left?" Connor asked.

That thought worried Nathaniel.

Noah got up and moved toward Connor with threatening body language, but Nathaniel stopped him. "I need to find his prayer bead bracelet. Dorian came to me in a vision. I think he wants me to use the beads to find what might be left of him, but I hope I'm not too late."

"He can't die," Noah repeated. "So shut the fuck up with that. And I already have the beads. I found them halfway between here and the canyon that the blast made."

Connor hesitated. "Rafael tried scrying for him and it didn't work."

"They couldn't find you either when you were possessed," said Noah. "Dorian just needs time to heal."

I don't want to believe that Dorian could be gone either, but it seems odd for Noah to be so passive about doing more than waiting.

"Where did she take you in between the assassinations, Connor?" Nathaniel asked.

"I can't remember. It felt like I was dreaming and couldn't wake up when I was killing those people. I don't want to think about it."

"You have to try. It's for the Ascended."

"I was in a red room and I was always being chased, but I don't know what was after me. I could see through the walls though so maybe it wasn't a room. I don't remember."

"Has anyone checked where Dorian was last seen?"

"Every inch," Noah said. "All that's there is typical demon bullshit around the canyon that was caused by whatever hit them."

"What made Dorian disappear left a canyon, not a crater?" Nathaniel asked.

"Yeah, I guess. I wasn't there to see it, but it could've been from any of them fighting something."

"The light that shot down the helicopters and the warships, the same one you said hit the demoness, came straight down from the sky. It would have left a crater if it didn't hit the water. A canyon goes from one point to another, so at either end there could be a clue to what caused it."

"There's nothing there. I'm telling you I searched every inch. Whoever's causing those beams doesn't stick around. When Dorian's back he can tell us what he saw and we can go kick its ass."

"Noah, I don't think that will happen without our help," said Nathaniel. "He regenerates in seconds and it's been almost two days. We can't wait. He needs us."

"Then go do whatever you gotta to make yourself feel useful. You don't know him like I do."

Why is he still so reluctant? Is he in denial?

"I'll take Connor and Rafael to PROJECT: UNITY's base so they can rest. Please come and help us plan our next move," Nathaniel said.

"I'm not leaving here without Dorian. If I had anything else to say I would've already."

"You won't have enough blood to use your powers to defend yourself."

"I don't need them. I did it barehanded; I can do it without powers. Now get out of my face or you're gonna piss me off."

An urge too strong to disregard came over Nathaniel, not from anger, but one that made him feel as if he knew what had to be done without knowing why.

Without hesitation Nathaniel took Noah by surprise and knocked him out cold with a sucker punch.

"What are you doing?" Connor yelled as Nathaniel took the bracelet from Noah's pocket after loading him into the jet. "He's going to be *really* angry when he wakes up!"

"We'll be at the base soon," he reassured Connor, bending the door so it couldn't be opened from the inside.

"Why are we going there and not home to the abbey?"

"I'll tell you when we arrive. Hang on tight."

Chapter Twenty-Six

The Order arrived at PROJECT: UNITY moments before Nathaniel made his entrance carrying the jet with Connor, Rafael, and Noah inside. Noah said nothing about Nathaniel suckerpunching him and went missing the moment they got to base. Lyle's lieutenants were in the process of setting everyone else up with rooms while he went to speak with Nathaniel down in his office.

"Do me a favor and don't tell Dorian about this after we find him," he said, cracking open a beer once they were behind closed doors.

Nathaniel agreed but wasn't sure of the significance behind it. He waited as Lyle finished half the can in one go and then paused, staring at the floor. Judging by the amount of cans and bottles in the garbage he must have drank quite often, and if the smell was any indication, he had been doing so not long before Nathaniel got there.

"Are you unwell?" Nathaniel asked after giving him a few more seconds.

"Oh, yeah, I'm great. My best friend is missing now, the only girl I ever loved left me, and we're in the middle of a war we can't win." He stopped to take another sip and move the garbage can under his desk. "I'm fine, I'm just—never mind."

Lyle discarded the rest of his drink in the garbage, seeming almost angry about it, and retrieved an energy drink from a duffle bag as a replacement.

"Not sure if you know this, but we lost Rome the other day," he continued. "Big G had set up shop there and was keeping demons as training dummies in the Colosseum. I'm sure you can picture what happened when he went missing too and his shadows disappeared."

The way Lyle was slurring his words concerned Nathaniel, but he didn't appear to want help.

"Were there any survivors?" Nathaniel asked.

"Not enough to count. And Isis's kingdom of light in Egypt has gone dark. No invasion there yet, but we're advising refugees to spread out to avoid drawing attention."

"What about the countries that lost their leaders?"

"Total chaos. Worse than before if you can imagine, but the Russian and U.S. militaries don't have the resources to keep up the search for the Order, so they'll be forced to retreat once they realize you're not staying on the island. It also means that any public appearances will be twice as risky because you can bet they'll stay on high alert for you showing up to any areas the demons invade. France, Germany, and China are so crippled that they aren't even trying."

"The demoness responsible for the assassinations was killed according to Noah. Can't we clear our name?"

"Do you have proof?"

"We have Connor."

Lyle chuckled at Nathaniel's naivety. "Yeah, that's not going to cut it. We must have lady luck on our side for once though since something caused the world's nuclear arsenal to fizzle right when it was becoming our next biggest concern. On the flipside, nuclear reactors around the world have gone offline too, which leaves large populations without power and more defenseless than ever.

"Then we've got the fact that we're losing more satellites by the day, which the techs think has to do with interference from the invasions. Our eyes around the world are blind without them and a lot of our technology relies on their signal boosting."

"What is a satellite? Exactly?" Nathaniel asked, trying not to seem too ignorant.

"I guess the easiest way to describe it is like a radio floating in outer space that picks up a signal and bounces it to another location," Lyle explained. "I've seen you taking selfies with survivors. You really don't know what a satellite is or are you pulling my leg?"

"No. I don't know how any of it works. I assumed it was like magic and if there were no wires it traveled along something like the ley lines."

"That's sort of right. The satellites redirect and amplify the signal since someone isn't steering it like when you guys zip around."

"I've flown above the clouds, but never seen one."

"They're way higher than that, dude."

"Oh. I've read stories about not flying too close to the sun and heard the phrase 'getting sucked out into space,' so I thought if you go into the blackness you wouldn't be able to escape."

Nathaniel was embarrassed to admit he had never been taught astronomy when growing up like the rest of the Order.

"You'd probably be fine out there if you don't need to breathe, but I'm no expert," said Lyle.

"I see. I hope you don't mind us imposing like this. I know how much Dorian trusts you and I felt coming here is what he would do."

"Are you kidding? I've always told Dorian we're in this together, but he's too scared of keeping people close because of what might happen. Seems to be a trend with people I care about."

"I know why he feels that way now myself."

"I heard what happened with the island. Did you lose anybody close to you?"

"The only person I had to lose was Dorian. I don't have any family or friends besides him. I may not have known him for as long as you have, but I grew up feeling everybody hated me and he was the first person to ever show he cared. The Ascended of all people, too. The Order always talked about how strong they thought he'd be and all I hoped for was that he'd be kind. Then he arrives after generations of legends about him and he sees something in me that nobody else did, and I was never lonely again until now."

"I think Dorian's real superpower is bringing out the best in people." Lyle sighed and shut the computer screen on his desk. "When I met him I was twenty-three and all I was doing was living in my father's shadow trying to be the best cop on the street. I didn't actually have any goal other than to keep being better without any vision of what that was. I was trying to be my dad, not myself. I wanted to make a difference in the world, but I couldn't do it by being someone else. Once Dorian became like a brother to me that all changed."

"I understand."

"Just look at Noah. I remember an outburst he had years ago about being a slave, but it was this helpless anger of a trapped animal. He's always unpredictable, but that time was different from anything I've seen from him since. After that, Dorian got him to channel his anger into making a move for freedom."

Lyle stared at the blank screen quietly for a second. "It's different this time. I know I'm not supernatural, but I've got this feeling..."

"What's different?" asked Nathaniel.

"Nothing. I'm rambling." He went quiet again, only now with a more contemplative expression. "I shouldn't have said 'like.' He isn't 'like' a brother. He's family. It's what he always wanted most, too."

"Dorian will return to us so long as we act upon our faith in him."

"Yeah. Yeah, he'll be fine... If you knew him like I do you'd know that's not the worst I'm worried about though." Lyle hesitated and cleared his throat. "Sorry, this isn't helping. If there's nothing else why don't you see if your buddies found any signs of him yet? I'll be up in a minute.

I'm going to send a drone to make contact with the berserkers to see if Cernunnos is still gone too."

"I will. Thank you, sir."

"You don't need to call me 'sir.' We're all friends here and I'm not your superior."

"I'm sorry. I suppose it's habit."

Nathaniel left the room and the door slid closed behind him as he stepped into the white plastic corridor. He was two rooms down when he heard what sounded like a sigh plagued by grief coming from the office and the fizz of a can being opened. Something about the sound turned his stomach.

I shouldn't have come. All I'm doing is hurting morale when this should be my trial alone.

Nathaniel floated up the rotunda to find Marianna. The buzz of electricity coming from every angle in the walls grated on his ears; it was unlike anything he was used to at the abbey. Ignoring the noise from hypersonic flight was less troublesome and he wondered how other supernaturals with enhanced hearing dealt with it.

The Alabaster knights were scattered throughout the levels among UNITY's troops. Those not busy scrying were deep in prayer on the benches lining the halls.

"Excuse me. Do you know where Marianna went?" Nathaniel asked Knight Paige, who looked up at him.

"She's upstairs, Champion." Her response came off as almost sarcastic.

"Thank you."

On the way up Nathaniel heard a whispered conversation between Knights Caleb and Quentin.

"—Couldn't believe it when he presented me with an orichalcum shield with an inlaid aether sigil for my birthday," said Quentin. "It was splendid. I can't remember the last time I had been given a gift, but it must have been when I was a young child. We talked for an hour and he actually seemed interested in getting to know me. I feel that I lost something more than safe passage through the apocalypse now that he's gone. It troubles me that we're meant to sit and scry when we could be searching the battlefield or interrogating some demon with a spot of intelligence. That one gesture he extended made me feel more important than the mere sword under his charge I expected to be."

"I wish I was able to speak with him more," Caleb said. "I would try to catch his eye, but the elders are always breathing down our necks to not break protocol. I get the sense that the Ascended cares about us as much as we worship him though."

Of course he does. Dorian loves all of us, even the elders, I'm sure.

Nathaniel moved on and recognized another two knights speaking farther down a hallway.

"Honestly, what did you expect? He brought death and dishonor to us as the elders warned," said Celeste. "This never would have happened if it were Liam. That was the whole purpose behind offering noble blood as Champion."

"Are you questioning the Ascended's judgment?" asked Troy. "That could be considered blasphemy."

"Not in the slightest. When the Ascended was with us everything was going as smoothly as it could for the end of the world. Once he was gone it didn't take long for the 'Champion' to ruin it all. Do you not wonder what it would have been like if Liam had been chosen instead?"

"Only every day."

Nathaniel forced himself to tune out their hurtful words. Finding Dorian was all that mattered to him.

He picked up the sound of Rafael's voice and traced it to the common area, where it seemed like a disagreement among some of the Order was getting heated. He decided to stay far enough away to listen without interfering.

"Scrying will get us nowhere, Anna," Rafael said in frustration. "It didn't help us find Connor because the realms are overlapping. Why won't you listen? We've worked together as a cabal almost our entire lives, but now that you're on the council what I say is ignored."

"All I said was that you should be in bed resting after what you had been through!" Marianna insisted. "We're doing what we were taught to do by following standards that were established for a reason."

"There is nothing standard about the situation! Those who wrote our traditions never knew the Ascended or half of what we've seen in the last six months."

"You not being assigned a seat on the council is not the fault of Marianna or Alexandre or Liam," Elder Rhys interjected. "This hunger for attention as of late is unlike you and hasn't gone unnoticed. You are behaving worse than Connor, yet at least he has three years of youth on you to blame. I hope it is due only to exhaustion, not a symptom of something worse from your direct contact with Hell."

"Rest, Raf, *please*," Marianna implored. "We can discuss alternatives after we finish trying everything else."

"It may be too late by that time."

Nathaniel went to step in after enough silence had passed. Rafael was already gone. Marianna, Alexandre, and most of the elders were gathered around Dorian's bracelet in a cloud of incense. It was no surprise that the elders didn't offer a warm welcome but Marianna came to meet him so he wouldn't feel awkward.

"Nothing yet. I'm sorry." She shook her head. "I heard how you saved Rafael's life. He should be at the doctor with Connor if you want to see them in the meantime."

Nathaniel thought better of rehashing the unpleasantness he'd just heard. "And Liam?" he asked instead.

"He left with Tobias. He's taking the loss of the Ascended almost as hard as his mother's death, but you know how he is. He doesn't speak much even when all is well."

Nathaniel sighed and sat on the edge of a couch, covering his face. "I don't know what I should be doing."

"Try contacting Dorian through prayer. If anyone can it would be you," Marianna suggested. "I'm going to continue scrying."

Nathaniel closed his eyes and bowed his head as soon as Marianna returned to the group.

Are you there? Can you hear me? I know, I know I'm not as good at this as Liam, but I'm trying...

Lyle stopped him after only a minute.

"Hey, man, sorry to interrupt, but I heard from Calder."

Nathaniel stood in uneasy anticipation. "Does he know anything about Dorian?"

"He wants to meet with you to talk about it. Looks like Cernunnos was defeated along with the rest of the god squad and they're working on bringing him back. They're less than a mile out—"

An alarm went off and the holographic PARAGON terminal nearest to Lyle spoke. *"Hostile supernatural presence detected in Medical Lab 4."*

"Where is that?" Nathaniel asked. "Connor and Rafael are at the doctor."

"Identify the presence, PARAGON."

"It's Mr. Burckhardt, Commander. I've contained him in the lab. His behavior has become erratic."

"I'll be right there. Keep him locked in." Lyle groaned. "He must have tried getting into a restricted area for the millionth time. You mind coming with me? We don't really get along and without Dorian around he'll probably stab me in the face."

"Okay, but Noah can turn to mist. How is it going to keep him there?"

Lyle wasn't in any rush to get there until he saw the doctors and nurses waiting outside the medical ward. "Critical priority rooms like medical, armory, and server rooms seal up airtight with magnetic locks and reinforced walls, ever since we rebuilt after an Ancient attacked," he said.

Nathaniel could hear Noah banging on the door. Lyle tried to open communication with him through the terminal screen in the lab, but Noah had broken it.

"I'll go in," Nathaniel said.

He knew he wouldn't be on Noah's good side after what it took to get him here, but there was no one else capable of surviving him.

The lab was trashed. There was blood everywhere and Noah had punched holes in the plastic walls. He was pacing across the room when Nathaniel entered.

"What happened?" Nathaniel asked.

"What the fuck do you think happened?" Noah barked with a menacing look to rival the berserkers. "I lost him. He was mine and I lost him! I wasn't fast enough. Doesn't matter how fast I am, it's never enough. It's never fucking good enough."

He roared in anger and went to punch another hole in the wall, but Nathaniel grabbed his fist before he could.

"Don't. Hit me if you want, but don't destroy a place meant to help people."

"Get your fucking hand off me." Noah pulled free and shoved him.

"Why are you acting like this? What would Dorian say if he saw you?"

"Probably that I'm a fucking asshole who wasn't there when he needed me."

"That doesn't sound like him," Nathaniel said. "He knows you give him your all and you love him."

"Does he? I can't remember the last time I said those words to him and the last thing he'll have ever heard from me was probably something stupid."

"I thought you believe Dorian only needs time to heal. You didn't lose him forever."

"And what if he's not healing? Why isn't he back by now?" Noah slammed his fist through a desk. "I'll tell you why. Because something's wrong and *I don't know what to do!*"

"I feel the same way," Nathaniel admitted. "Is this your blood? Are you hurt?"

"It's from the blood bank. I was drinking and it started to make me miss him so I lost it. I haven't drank from anybody else in years. I'm pissed at that little shithead for leaving me. I swear I'm gonna smack him as soon as I see him."

"No, you won't."

"We'll see how I feel." Noah started to smirk. "Still gonna choke him a bit, but that's unrelated."

"What? Why—?"

"Never mind. Don't tell him I told you that."

"Okay. We should be working together, not lying to ourselves to feel better or doing all of *this*."

Noah simmered down and sat on the floor. "And what are you doing? You're wasting time here when you should be flying around searching for him."

"The berserkers are trying to bring Cernunnos back. I was going to see if he knew anything about Dorian or how to help, if you want to come along," Nathaniel said. "They're a mile away from here."

"Yeah, I know where they are. I'll meet you there."

Noah vanished, leaving Nathaniel to explain about the room and apologize. Lyle knew how Noah was; given the circumstances and the fact that he wasn't given another concussion, he let it slide without much complaint.

"I'll add it to his tab," said Lyle.

Nathaniel was inexperienced with friendships and relationships alike, which only left him in further admiration of the Ascended's impact on those around him.

He didn't mean to be rude while Lyle spoke to him, but he couldn't stop thinking. *Will I inspire people someday as the Ascended does? Will anyone aside from him ever care if I were to disappear?*

Connor came out of a room down the hall in his tights. He was shaken. It was all across his face, as plain as day. Now that he was someplace safe, everything was catching up to him.

He checked the lab to make sure Noah was gone before speaking.

"What's wrong?" Lyle asked him.

"I thought Nathaniel should know," Connor said. "Before coming to rescue us, um, Noah...he was going mad like he was going to turn into a demon. He came back after checking the flash that caught the Ascended and started screaming. I was afraid he was going to kill Raf and me, but he turned his anger on the plane and kept hitting it until it broke. It wasn't the demons that did it. He didn't want to leave until we found the Ascended and said if we told him about the plane he'd kill us himself. I thought you should know that it might not be wise to bring him along in case he's dangerous. Rafael could have died if you hadn't come when you did."

"You don't have to worry," Nathaniel said. "I don't believe Noah would have let him die or killed you. He's having a hard time coping with losing Dorian, but I think he's cleared his head."

"He's not the best with rational feelings," Lyle added. "This was pretty mild for him, if I'm being honest."

"I want to lend what aid I can to see the Ascended back safe," said Connor. "I've been trying to rest, but I'm having nightmares about those people I killed. I have to make it right."

"Keep trying to remember anything you can that could help us find him," Nathaniel said. "I'm only going to check on the berserkers a short way from here and then see if the other gods have awakened yet. You won't be missing much."

Chapter Twenty-Seven

Noah had arrived at the berserkers' camp ahead of Nathaniel.

"I realize I didn't apologize for earlier," Nathaniel said quietly. "I hope you will forgive me for striking you in China. I don't know what came over me, I—"

"No idea what you're talking about, kid, but that sounds like something you'd want to keep to yourself," Noah said.

The berserkers were busy digging through the ice and using their claws to carve runes into boulders they had propped up for a sort of ritual. Calder seemed not to be his merry self, the loss of his patron deity taking its toll on him as well.

"It's good to see you safe, Calder. Has Cernunnos ever been defeated in the past?" Nathaniel asked.

"Nay. Ne'er in my years as herald. The land weeps without its guardian."

"He's a spirit so you should be able to return him to existence through prayer, can you not?"

"The more harm a spirit takes, the longer their recovery. We are almost on day three with nary a sign. Tonight during the full moon we call to the Goddess for Her aid. Have ye word on the Ascended?"

"No. Noah and I are here hoping Cernunnos would know how to revive him or what defeated them."

Calder hoisted a boulder up from the ice and put it in place for the pack to work on. "A great wall was the last vision Cernunnos showed to me. 'Twas naught like any seen from Hell thus far. A King's bastion of strange metals that sits in the seas to the east, taller than the highest earthen peak."

"You speak of the Infernal Kings? How can you be sure if it is theirs?"

"What other manner of vile beast could slay the gods?"

"I was close when it happened and I didn't see anything like that," said Noah. "There was only a flash."

"The very same that struck the flying vessels, aye?"

"No, that came from the sky and wasn't as bright, but one like it did blow up the demon bitch we were fighting."

"The canyon that was left behind heads toward the water," Nathaniel said.

"Find the fortress and we shall smash our way through the keep to victory. This King hath something to fear if he hides from a true fight. Let us turn that fear into his incubus."

Noah scoffed. "This is the asshole who shot down five gods and you're gonna bang down his door with what? An axe? You're a moron."

"This isn't the time for insults," said Nathaniel. "We are in this together, so it's time we start acting like it. For Dorian."

"It was constructive criticism. I'm ready to give my life for him, but I want it to count."

"As do I. Calder, after the ritual how long will it take for Cernunnos to return?"

"Only the Goddess knoweth such."

One of the pups handed Nathaniel a smooth stone with an upward pointing arrow carved on it.

"Tiwaz," Calder said. "An Elder rune invoking the old name of Tyr, Norse god of war, for glory in battle. The pup bids ye good fortune in the fight ahead."

Nathaniel smiled at the boy and kneeled to hand him an aether crystal in exchange.

Aífe's daughter, who had once shared jerky with Noah, shoved a similar stone into his hand. Before running off, she pointed at him like he had done to her that day, a threat that was misinterpreted as a greeting. He grunted and slipped the stone into his pocket when he thought no one was looking.

Aífe herself approached. "Lord Cernunnos told us of more gods in your alliance. How do they fare?"

"We haven't checked," said Nathaniel. "Isis has healed Dorian in the past and has a kingdom full of followers, so she should be who we check on next. If we can restore her then she can help us with the rest."

"Go without me. I've got something to take care of," Noah said and disappeared.

"I hope that when I return all of our gods are with us again."

"Have faith. Ne'er a god can fall for long lest we allow it through denying them such," said Calder. "'Tis the very nature of what maketh them divine."

"My faith is unshaken, but my heart is another story."

"If it is beating, there is naught else to tell in the face of duty."

Nathaniel nodded and departed for Egypt.

Maybe to Calder this is about duty, but it's more than that to me. I don't care if I have to go until my heart does stop beating. The answer lies ahead. I know it does. It's just up to me to get there.

He flew as fast as possible until he could almost hear Dorian warning him to slow down. It was wishful thinking. Soaring over the terrain at this altitude right under the clouds made it easy to recognize landmarks such as the Nile Delta as he neared Africa during sundown. The massive settlement of refugees and devout pilgrims along the Nile wasn't too far south from there. In a moment of curiosity, Nathaniel considered taking a peek at the blackness of space above the atmosphere, but thought better of it. That was when he saw light from the Temple of Isis refracting through the Great Pyramids that Dorian had rebuilt into enormous prisms of glass and steel.

Isis must be awake!

Nathaniel swooped upward to let the sonic boom travel harmlessly into the sky before gliding down to the city. The journey had taken him no longer than a couple of minutes. He thought he might have weakened without Dorian nearby, yet his speed, strength, and senses were still improving so that he was able to see something was amiss from miles above.

Men, women, and even children were wandering the streets crying and reaching up to him as he passed. Their skin was covered in lesions. He couldn't understand what they were trying to say, but they all shared the same distraught expression. The demons had left their mark. Isis had been gone too long.

Nathaniel landed on the temple grounds where sandstone and cold steel embraced in a testament to the light.

"Champion of the Ascended." Isis's voice and the chirping of birds resounded in his head through a distorted, hollow echo.

"Isis! You *are* awake!" Nathaniel looked around for her and saw she was standing right behind him.

"Did I startle you, sweet child?"

He backed away to see her better. "Wh—what happened to you?"

Isis was not herself. She was no longer organic in appearance, instead made of plastics and metals with the strangest markings on her dark skin, like the inside of a machine from another world a thousand years into the future.

I've seen this... the demon lord in Mumbai.

"Mayhap you expected the frailty of flesh?" Isis asked with a smile and showed off her new talons. She removed the headdress that masked the top of her face with a bird-like beak and dropped it to the ground. Her eyes had gone red, the pupils a narrow slit. The fiery orb above her head turned pale green.

"You're the one that made your followers sick? But why? How could you fall to the demons? You were the Egyptian angel, the kindest of all the gods next to the Ascended."

Isis circled him, taking premeditated steps as a ballerina would advance through choreography.

"The mother, the lover, the healer, the *woman*. I give and I give for them and oh, how they take like a plague of locusts ripping and tearing at the flesh to suckle from my teat. They take until there is naught but a void left inside my bosom. The gift of charity has its limits even from a goddess."

Isis made her way to the top of the temple with a flap of her wings and raised her arms to address her flock. She loosed a salvo of feathers, which became a plague of locusts sent to strip the diseased flesh from her victims. "Beg! Beg for your mother's mercy and know there is none left in her! I am Aset, Queen of the Heavens!"

The hellfire sun above her grew in size as she radiated a scorching crimson glare from her body that the pyramids reflected throughout the kingdom. Her followers were set on fire; the men, the women, the children, unable to escape, unsure how.

"You can't do this!" Nathaniel shouted. "You must stop! I do not want to fight you!"

"Then stay and kneel. It matters naught anyway!" Her cackle became more sadistic as she reveled in the screaming below her. "O holy light, I beseech thee, deliver us from this mortal scourge!"

The light of the pyramids focused into beams aimed toward the sky, bleeding it red and cascading down to turn the Nile black.

"I regret you are our ally no more, but I must protect the innocent." Nathaniel tackled Isis and smashed her into the pyramids one after the next, bringing them down in succession. She disappeared from his grasp, but her laughter could still be heard across the desert.

"You never should have come here, *Champion*. Thou art strong, but naught more than a tiny sparrow to a goddess! My light is infinite, yours is not!"

The crimson glare radiating from her was enfeebling Nathaniel. He felt his strength being sapped and his skin blistering under the leather of his suit. He summoned forth his own radiance to counter hers. It alleviated some of the symptoms for a time, but she was too strong. He charged all he could into his fists until the shimmering mandala surrounded him.

Nathaniel released the light in a beam directed at Isis. She blocked it without effort using one hand, but he propelled himself into her with his fist out. He hoped to bring her as far as he could from whoever might be left alive in the kingdom, but she made him chase her back more than he could drag her away.

"I am disappointed, child. I thought more of the Ascended's chosen," her voice echoed.

"Then face me where I can show you my power without worry."

"You are unworthy of a duel with a goddess, but I shall give you the battle you seek." Isis showered the desert with rays of light.

Nathaniel ignored the distraction and flew at her. She hurled a shining energy spear that pierced his chest; he felt as if he had been torn in two, but he suffered no physical damage that he could tell. It had been a while since something external caused him pain. His stagger halted his flight and unleashed the sonic boom gathering in front of him, throwing Isis backward. He had yet to land a solid blow, but he knew if he could it would end this.

She's made of aether. If I could drain her of it as I did Rafael I might have a better chance.

Nathaniel caught up to Isis after an infuriating game of aerial tag above the burning kingdom, during which she rent his armor with her talons, but her power was too much for him to take in. Within seconds he was suffering the effects of the impure aether within her, and he had to let go.

"To drink deep of the nectar of a goddess is to know truth." Isis laughed. "Do you see now you are unfit to inherit the footsteps of gods? Your light is dim and will forever be lost in shadow."

Nathaniel discharged the unwanted aether stored within him in a beam of light that shot a hole through her midsection.

"You are no goddess, demon." He wheezed, out of breath from the strain.

I may have released too much.

The mandala protecting him from her crimson light faded, and he weakened again.

"You and the rest of the fleshborn insects partake of this goddess' ichor for the last time." Isis healed the wound in her midsection with a simple gesture. If he couldn't inflict more damage than she could heal there was no hope of defeating her.

Nathaniel collected himself to restore the mandala's brilliance. The moment of calm they took to recuperate while floating opposite each other gave way to a rumbling in the desert. The spots where the rays of light had touched earlier showed signs of movement—wriggling, coiling movement.

What are those? Snakes?

Isis vanished when he turned his back to watch the serpents merge and grow larger than anything the desert had seen. The mythic beast's many heads let out a deafening hiss at the end of the transformation as it lunged for Nathaniel. He dodged them without much trouble—save for one ginormous fang that became snagged on his armor and ripped it to his waist—but not all went for him. The monster was attacking the city at the same time.

Every head he tore, blasted, or punched from its base was rejuvenated twofold. It was a well-known legend he had read of in his youth, but it was nothing other than the distraction he thought it was initially. Isis reappeared, flying above the city. Her orb of hellfire expanded until it dwarfed her. She sent it above the clouds where it continued to grow, now obscuring any stellar object visible in the blood-red sky.

"My brother brought down the moon," Isis announced to all her kingdom. "And I shall bring the sun!"

Nathaniel caught the serpent by the tail and swung it out into orbit to be incinerated by the viridescent false sun. He could hear the sounds of panic and crying below. There were still survivors that had evaded her first round of torment.

Children.

Their cries of terror brought flashbacks of Mumbai. There were too many scattered too far for him to save them all without the risk of killing them himself from his speed. He looked down at what remained of his armor as the sun descended. It would not provide the protection he needed against hellfire of that magnitude.

Rage and sorrow collided with a singular purpose inside Nathaniel, stirring a force that could not be restrained. He called upon everything that had been given to him until the fallen goddess could not ignore his radiance. He absorbed the aether around them and launched himself at her with a primal scream, taking her energy in too. She cast a spell to turn him to stone, but he did not stop, even as his joints stiffened.

With his body failing and his soul critically overcharged, he flew them both straight into the looming sun before she could get away, causing an explosion that shook the earth to its core.

Chapter Twenty-Eight

"Don't give up."

Nathaniel knew he was dreaming...or deceased, but he held onto the hope that the voice he heard encouraging him came from the real Dorian. He felt the pull of consciousness, the touch of someone's hand on him in comfort as he was taken toward the light.

"Rise, dear Champion. Thy soul is healed."

Nathaniel's ears were ringing, his face was full of sand that had found its way up his nose and into his mouth, but he was certain the voice he heard now was Isis's. He struggled in the dark to get to his hands and knees while his sight returned.

The night sky had returned to normal.

There was hope.

"My poor children, take the last of what power I have left from the devils in repentance for my sins."

"Wait," Nathaniel moaned. "Where is the Ascended? Where's Dorian?"

Isis appeared as a ghost of her old self, except without her headdress and sun icon. Her natural irises glimmered gold. Some of the alien markings on her skin remained as golden lines. She faded away in a flourish of twinkling feathers that blew through the kingdom on a cooling breeze. For every pinion that landed on a body, a soul was restored and a person resurrected.

Nathaniel staggered into the streets. The people crowded around to touch him in hope of receiving some divine blessing from their savior. Children held his hand to try and get him to make them an aether crystal like they had witnessed during past visits or news reports. At some point he lost his cape, which was still hanging from his shoulders despite the rest of his upper body armor having been torn off. He didn't have it in him to shout for their attention as he tried to convince anyone who could understand him of Isis's innocence so they could pray for her return. After another few steps he collapsed on a dusty road. He wasn't down for long. Nathaniel could feel himself being carried indoors by a group that gave him water and a place to rest, but as soon as he could stand again he was on his way.

The buildings here were simple boxes that Dorian had made in passing, unable to offer much else without intricate knowledge of plumbing or electrical wiring, yet the residents had done their best to turn them into homes. Many had sustained heavy damage from the battle with Isis. It was a miracle that any were standing at all.

Nathaniel couldn't get through to anybody in the confusion, so he leaped across the city in one jump, landing by the ruins of the pyramids and Isis's temple. There was nothing he could do to rebuild it at the moment, so he flew up high to bring about a vast aurora for protection from the forces of darkness.

The exertion was too much. He began to fall from the starry sky, but something caught him halfway down, letting him float for a moment so he could get his bearings.

Dorian? Is that you?

The feeling that Dorian was close passed. Saddened, Nathaniel carried on, unsure of where to go next until he remembered the berserkers.

If Cernunnos is corrupted when they revive him with that ritual he'll slaughter them all.

Nathaniel set off in the direction of Greenland, gathering speed along the way until he was able to break the sound barrier. It had never required extra effort to do so in the past. His strength was making a gradual return, but he considered the weakness to be a warning of what happened when he didn't act with restraint like he had been told.

He arrived just in time to witness the closing of the ritual under the curtain of night. The berserkers were gathered between the inscribed boulders around a patch of exposed earth. They howled at the full moon in their feral form with everything they had. The runes glowed brighter with the increasing volume until their call was answered.

The ground heaved and spiraled into itself, bearing the majestic antlered skull of the Horned God.

No demon eyes. Thank the Ascended.

Cernunnos rose from the center of the circle, dry woody brambles twisting around bones as they assembled to take the shape of his body. The reaper's scythe levitated up to his hand from a portal right when Nathaniel was within range to land.

No demon eyes or markings. Nathaniel breathed a sigh of relief, but it was premature. Cernunnos swung his scythe at a nearby child's throat faster than the human eye could see, but not Nathaniel's eye. He zoomed forward before touching down and shoulder tackled the Horned God into the distance. This drew the berserkers' ire. Too slow to see what happened, they responded with enraged roars as they charged after the traitor.

Calder was the first to reach Nathaniel as he tried to fly off after Cernunnos. In his werewolf form he pinned Nathaniel to the ice and clamped his jaws around his head with vastly greater strength than he'd showed during their duel. Nathaniel was at a loss for what to do; he felt the warm trickle of blood run down his face where the giant berserker's fangs pierced him. The ice was cracking beneath them as Nathaniel struggled to free his arms with hot, damp animal breath and saliva suffocating him. He could hear the snarls from the rest of the pack surrounding them, waiting for their chance to tear him apart should he manage to escape.

Everything ran red. The snarls quieted one at a time, replaced by a ringing in Nathaniel's ears that turned into guttural moans. A surge of power filled his muscles, allowing him to free his arms and pry Calder's jaws open. The otherworldly noise was gone along with his wounds. Nathaniel wiped the blood from his face and held Calder up with one hand when he lunged.

"*Yield*, Calder!" Nathaniel demanded.

A shadow emerged from behind the herald—it was his master. Cernunnos attempted to swing his scythe through Calder while he dangled above the ground, but Nathaniel threw him high into the air to safety and flew himself backward.

Calder landed between them in his human form as the moon bled across the sky and claimed another piece of Earth for Hell.

Cernunnos' skull had blackened with an inverted pentagram sigil branded upon his forehead. His branches and bones were turned to refined artificial materials; his antlers now resembled ram horns made of metal.

Nathaniel saw why the other berserkers had stopped snarling. The Horned God had impaled them using enormous roots to soak the ice with their blood. Thorny protrusions as long as swords penetrated their eyes and mouths. Their accelerated healing kept them alive enough to twitch and squirm. Nothing more. He was relieved to see that at least the children had not followed.

"W-what is the meaning of this, my lord?" Calder questioned his master. "How could ye, mightiest of them all, fall to the ranks of our foes?"

"Life...is a trifling thing. Incomplete without ever knowing death."

There they were. As Cernunnos spoke, the ruby red eyes of a demon rolled down from inside his empty sockets. A third opened on his forehead, and then six more, each one sapping a bit of Nathaniel's herculean strength with their dreadful gaze. His voice was distorted, the same as Isis's. "To deny the Reaper is to deny life true meaning. Immortality is a most vile affront to the sanctity of mine will and shall be expunged from the world by this blade."

"He is your master no longer, Calder," Nathaniel shouted. "The same fate befell our ally Isis in Egypt. We must fight to release the demons' grasp on him. I cannot do it alone!"

Calder, one so brave and heroic, stood frozen as the ice around him in the presence of his corrupted master. "'Tis not an easy thing ye ask..."

"I am Baphomet, Fallen Lord of Liberation." Cernunnos pointed at them and raised his scythe. Raven wings unfurled from his back. "Giveth into thy rage and impart unto me thy flesh. Let the harvest begin!"

Calder ducked under the blade and summoned Gáe Bulg to his hand in all its blazing emerald glory. "May the Goddess help ye find the light again, old friend."

"Simple beast, I serveth none any longer." Cernunnos departed into the web of massive roots, preempting Calder's strike.

Nathaniel trying to free the berserkers only made matters worse as the thorns grew additional barbs to hold on in response. He apologized to each one he found for ripping them from their wooded bindings while Cernunnos and Calder kept busy evading each other.

Haunting whispers from the specter of death assailed his ears along with a chilling presence that stayed behind him no matter which way he turned and inflicted a constant palpating sense of dread and paranoia. Cernunnos could land a lethal blow unnoticed and at any time under these circumstances.

The roots spread in all directions and would soon encroach on PROJECT: UNITY's base if the earthquakes under the permafrost didn't dislodge it into the ocean first. Pulling on them proved to be another bad idea. The thorns couldn't scratch Nathaniel's skin, but the roots went too deep and turned aggressive toward him. They were stronger than he imagined and when he fought against being ensnared a landmass of alarming size came with him.

This did not go unnoticed by Cernunnos.

"Harken unto the sowing call of death! Yggdrasil beckons!" he declared. With those words the roots still clinging to Nathaniel began to leech the aether from his soul. He wrested himself free and tried flying out of range as the plant thrashed at him with its extensions as thick as the widest oak.

In the distance he could see activity at the base as troops mobilized and civilians were evacuated; however, Calder was still holding back in his fight with Cernunnos. Nathaniel realized how difficult it was for him to face his master, but allowing this to continue was not an option. Cernunnos didn't seem to be distracted by his herald in the least as the roots he commanded were now upon UNITY's base and reaching almost a mile in the other directions. Nathaniel soared higher to get a better view and wait for the right opportunity to take a shot at Cernunnos once Calder was clear. He fired a blast of light and hit Cernunnos straight through the chest, leaving a smoldering hole in its wake.

The Horned God crumbled at his herald's feet and disappeared. Calder was none too pleased and hurled his spear at Nathaniel with a ferocious war cry. Nathaniel dodged it and that was when he realized the pitch wasn't meant for him but Cernunnos, who had reappeared behind him from one of the whipping roots. The spear struck Cernunnos with a boom and sent him flying before he could ambush Nathaniel with his scythe.

"Don't let the blade of the scythe touch ye, or else it reaps the soul be ye god or man!" Calder shouted over the creaking and splintering sounds of wood below.

The roots shuddered and became more violent as they poured out from the cracks in the ice plowing through everything in their path without the slightest loss of momentum. From this height Nathaniel saw what he had feared: the southern half of Greenland was being split apart into smaller islands by the monstrous plant. Although he was high off the ground he could still feel the earth tremble from the seismic disaster reshaping the land.

Against his better judgment Nathaniel flew down into the mess to confer with Calder when Aífe showed up.

"We must retreat, Calder! Ye cannot hope to win against Lord Cernunnos!" she yelled while trying to navigate the volatile terrain.

"We *have* to win. There is no other choice," Nathaniel argued.

"Go with the pups, Aífe," Calder told her. "Head west across the water if ye can make it to where we spoke."

She looked between the two with agitated uncertainty before transforming and bolting from sight.

PROJECT: UNITY's runway split in two. The chunk of ice into which the main base was built became dislodged from the mainland. Nathaniel shot after it and dove into the frigid waters, surfacing with the iceberg hoisted above his head so he could take it north to where the roots had yet to reach. The several hundred thousand-ton weight was nothing to him—the freezing cold biting at his exposed skin was jarring enough to make him shake like a leaf in the wind, however.

People coming from the base were shouting as Nathaniel took a second to catch his breath. He was drenched, chilled to the bone, exhausted, and for a fleeting moment he wanted to collapse into the snow and just give up, but he knew he couldn't. The roots were tearing their way across the landscape towards them.

Flashes of fire bombarded the gigantic plant as it closed in from the horizon. The Order had joined the fray with pyroclastic flares of high-level magic wielded only by those who specialized in flame for decades. Nathaniel watched as geysers of lava burst up through the cracks in the earth's crust and exploded in midair, showering the area.

The roots were unfazed.

He launched himself across the tundra and grabbed the burning plant to drag them away from the base. They drained his strength on contact with his skin, but he did not relent. Dorian once taught him that their power was unlimited when they wanted it to be. What separated them from the demons and kept it in check were their human emotions.

But Nathaniel didn't want to hold back anymore. People were dying again with only him standing between them and oblivion. He held back during his fight with Isis until the very end when suffering and death had already claimed innocent lives.

Forgive me, Ascended, but I have to do this my way. I know I can control it.

He flew straight up into the clouds, taking the largest root with him, and kept going until he was high enough to see all of Greenland had been shattered into many smaller islands and icebergs. The shifting of the earth had dragged some of the landmasses miles out into the ocean, turning the country into a widespread archipelago.

How much farther do these roots go?

The wind and altitude had extinguished the fires, but Nathaniel's plan to get rid of the plant by sending it into space was more difficult than he had anticipated. He almost reached beyond the stratosphere into the soundless void when the root broke. He tossed the piece he was still holding and went down to catch the rest.

He noticed the root had been cut, not snapped from being pulled. There was only one thing he could think of that could have sliced so cleanly through forty feet of supernatural wood. He kept his senses alert, expecting Cernunnos to ambush him, when someone jumped on his back and put a blade to his throat.

"Land," they said.

Nathaniel thought he recognized the voice. "Liam? What—what are you doing?"

The blade pressed in closer to his skin. Liam teleported off of his back as he landed on one of the islands. In the distance the battle against Cernunnos raged.

"The elders were right about you." Liam appeared before him with his swords drawn. These blades were infused with the Ascended's power. He could feel it.

"Please don't do this. I know about your mother, but it was an accident—" Nathaniel put his hands out in front of him to plead with Liam to calm down.

"I respected you," Liam said, ignoring him. "I was happy for you when the Ascended chose you. I never wanted to be the Champion. I still don't. I spoke in your defense when the others claimed you were unworthy. And then you killed my mother."

Liam's stoic delivery was more unnerving than if he had yelled.

"It was an accident." Nathaniel's hands began to shake. The guilt was strangling him. His own words didn't make him feel any better, so he knew how little they must have meant to Liam.

"I believed that and I didn't blame you. I blamed the Order for failing you because you were never taught to handle power in the first place."

"I'm trying to do the right thing. Please—"

"*This* isn't an accident. You chose to do this and people are paying for it, so I'm here to stop you."

"What are you saying?" Nathaniel asked. "I don't understand..."

"People are dying over there because of you. A child from the berserkers' tribe died while trying to escape. The vine you were flying off with caught and dragged him, because you have not a clue what you are doing."

Nathaniel's whole body was shaking now. His heart was pounding and it was all he could hear as he flew to where Liam had pointed. It was so simple and obvious to him in hindsight that he had made the wrong choice, but in the moment all he wanted to do was save the helpless by eliminating the problem.

He found a pack of the berserkers gathered around something on the ice. His vision tunneled the closer he got. When he saw the lifeless body of a very young boy, tears rolled down his face. He couldn't see the berserkers blocking his path as he pushed past them and dropped to his knees. He couldn't hear the sounds of war nearby.

Nathaniel placed a hand on the bloody child. He didn't feel those around him trying to pull him away. No one else existed.

The tears in his eyes blinded him as he lost his resolve to grief. The pounding in his chest was too much to bear. He shouted to release the pain. The hand still on the child's body went numb and then a magnificent burst of light radiated from Nathaniel.

The light flooded the child's body, escaping every pore as it traveled from Nathaniel to him. He felt a bang as his hand was thrown back and the boy sat up.

They looked at each other through the glare unsure if what either was seeing was real. The child made the first move, hopping to his feet and running off as if he had woken fresh from a nap.

As soon as the light diminished he saw the boy riding away on one of the berserkers as they retreated.

How...?

Nathaniel didn't have a chance to reflect on what happened. A shadow was cast over him from behind. He got to his feet and turned just in time to catch Cernunnos sizzling in the light with his scythe raised. Still reeling from his feat with the child, Nathaniel grabbed the scythe out of Cernunnos's hands and snapped it in half over his knee. Before Cernunnos could react Nathaniel lifted him off the ground by his neck and poured all the anger within him into a searing blast. Cernunnos was disintegrated and his ashen remains exploded across the island.

His energy source might be unlimited, but Nathaniel's body was not conditioned for it yet. He leaned over panting to catch his breath when he heard staggered footsteps in the snow coming toward him.

"Yggdrasil hath already reclaimed the North...Ye cannot prevail..." Cernunnos would not stay down. Nathaniel eyed the scythe's blade on the ground as he approached. "The immortals will soon repay their debt to Death. None amongst ye can stop Ragnarök!"

Cernunnos called upon the howling revenant winds of the Otherworld to sweep away the souls of the living. He extended his hand to call for the pieces of his scythe and that was when Nathaniel made his move. Fighting the feeling of his soul leaving his body, he kicked the blade at Cernunnos as it passed. The sharp point struck the fallen god in the chest. After a moment of standing there stunned, the sigil on his forehead disappeared as he returned to normal and faded away with his final words.

"Goddess...forgive me."

Chapter Twenty-Nine

Nathaniel lay in the snow watching Hell's sky clear from above the islands, too exhausted to summon an aurora in victory. Footsteps approached and someone extended a hand to help him up.

"I beg your forgiveness, Champion." It was Liam. "I won't disrespect you with excuses for my actions. I lost my head in the madness. I could feel Hell taking hold of me in my time of weakness."

Nathaniel accepted his hand and stood. "You have no reason to apologize. You spoke the truth. I don't know what I'm doing. My only desire is to help people, but even with the Ascended's power I feel lost without his guidance on how to use it."

"You were chosen because you have that desire I lacked. All you need is the training and discipline that the Order neglected to provide you with as a child because of politics."

Nathaniel looked at the hand he used to bring the berserker child back to life. "I think I can return your mother to you. I don't know how, but my powers took control in a way I never felt before."

"My father and I have already returned her ashes to the earth." Liam bowed his head slightly, showing the first sign of sadness. "I saw what you did and there is no explanation. It goes against the fundamental rules of everything we know. Pure resurrection is something only gods can do with their followers and the boy's soul belonged to Cernunnos."

"Aye, but the Goddess works in ways naught for us to understand and we serve them both. 'Tis clear ye acted as a vessel for Her will." For someone Calder's size he was startlingly adept at making silent entrances. He was in fine shape for having faced Cernunnos alone for so long, but it wasn't easy to get an accurate picture of the aftermath due to his rapid healing.

"I am the Ascended's Champion though."

"The Goddess is greater than us all, even thine Ascended. The aether ye use is Her lifeblood."

"None are greater than the Ascended," Liam said with righteous indignation. "The Ascended's life energy comes from a dimension older than this world and is more likely to relate to resurrection than aether alone. Nathaniel, when you're ready to join us we'll be with Commander Turner."

Liam departed through the ley lines.

"They tell me ye showed the emotion of a parent for the pup," said Calder, taking a seat. "Did ye lose a son of thine own once?"

"No. I've only ever lost my father."

"There is no dishonor to fall in battle if he fought to his last breath."

"He didn't die in battle. A leader of our Order murdered him before my eyes when I was a child. He was a leader, too. They didn't want our bloodline to have a chance at being the Ascended's chosen or interfering with their plans to seize further control of the Order."

"And thy conviction to defend the powerless was born of this treason."

"Not entirely so... I was given to an older boy to raise me as a bastard, but he...what he and his friends did to me for years under the cover of night was something no child should have to endure. I have made it my purpose to protect them since being given the power to do so."

Nathaniel surprised himself by confiding those dark memories to someone like Calder. He felt frozen by shame, hanging on each second until Calder spoke, in fear he would be dismissed for his weakness or mocked for how he let it affect him to this day. But Calder did no such thing.

"The mightiest hearts are those twice broken."

"I can't help but feel broken again. Dorian—the Ascended saved me from a slow and painful death sentence I was given for defending myself against one of the boys. He cleaned out the corruption and saw more in me than I ever did myself. He's the only friend I have ever known and he made me feel loved, but now he goes missing and I have not a clue how to get him back."

"Aye, I know the feeling well, lad. I lost my only son to the blade in my hand."

Nathaniel was appalled. "You... killed your son?"

"I was the bravest warrior in the Northern Isles to the east of here in my mortal days. I left my son behind to be raised by his mother while I went to war to spare them the unpleasantries of battle. When I left, I told her the boy was to find me when he was of age, but not to speaketh the family name upon his travels, for word of the legend's son would draw my enemies to him like wolves to the scent of blood.

"The boy did as he was told. I failed to know my own blood when I stared it in the face. After a night of merriment, I was on guard outside the gates of a town we were camped at when he approached. There was word of enemy scouts in the area that would robe as villagers and I drew my blade without thought. I cut the boy down. He was a fierce warrior like yourself, not many winters younger."

"When did you learn he was your son?" Nathaniel asked.

"I found the ring I had given his mother with his belongings after I dragged him from the gates as an offering for the crows. I went mad with rage and stormed the enemy camp to unleash my anger. 'Twas the first I tasted berserker fury. Cutting down an army did naught to feed the bloodlust. The arrows at my back and the daggers in my side felt as naught more than raindrops upon the skin as I pursued the last remaining warriors into the forest with no mercy. I knew

I would succumb to my wounds before returning to camp. I refused to let death take me on my knees, so I tied myself to a tree to die on my feet. And that is how Cernunnos found me. He gave me the chance to repent as a new man and focus that rage. My people draw our strength from it and when in need I have only to think of how I hate myself for what I've done."

"I see." Nathaniel didn't know how to feel about Calder's story, but he took it as another warning to temper his actions with care even in the direst battles. "Is that why you gave us a fake name when we met you?"

"Aye. I am that man no longer and have had no other child to carry my name as penance by request to Lord Cernunnos. Perhaps a cruel jest to him as a god of man's virility, but my service to his will is of greater import than my seed."

"You asked him to make you unable to have children? Why not just refrain from the act?"

Calder let out a hardy chuckle. "Surely *that* is the cruelest of jests ye speak! I have traveled many a land in my time and there is no heaven to compare to a woman's embrace. There are no ills it cannot cure be it of mind or body. Beautiful creatures they are, every last one of them a mortal goddess in Her image that deserves naught less than worship. And I have worshipped my share and more!"

"You do have quite a number of them in your company."

"Aye, but between men I tell ye that to lay with them is little else than to lay with beast. The fire they bring is of rage and doth naught to rouse the heart like a mortal woman. Even the plainest lass will make thy head spin faster than the strongest mead once unleashed in fits of passion."

"I wouldn't really know, not for lack of interest I suppose, just..."

"A word of advice then: be true with thy touch. To taste the sweetest nectars one mustn't hesitate amongst the thorns. Clumsiness is sure to introduce ye to her claws. I may not be a man of much brains, but this much I have learned well."

"Thank you. I'll...keep that in mind."

Calder sighed. "Listen to me carry on like a lad on his first hunt. I am weak with thoughts of comely maidens. It hath been many a cycle since my kind allowed themselves to be seen by the human world. I fear I wouldn't know what to make of myself if the finest lass stood before me. And could ye imagine if she knew her step in battle too? Goddess preserve me, the fool I would make!"

Although he couldn't help feeling enticed by Calder's salacious talk of women, Nathaniel didn't want to stay on the topic. His lack of experience by comparison made him again uncomfortable at what Calder would say, but he was curious about something else related to their conversation.

"I take it you and Aífe aren't together as a couple then?" he asked. "I assumed you were when we met."

"That harpy? Nay, I could give no children, what good am I to her?" He chuckled. "Aífe would have more interest in thine own seed than mine. I am not unfamiliar with the warmth of her thighs and there are none I respect more, but she taketh her role in the pack more seriously than to pay me any mind. She is my sister in battle and we prefer it that way."

Nathaniel was confounded by the possibility of her being interested in him. She was a ravishing phenomena, a firebrand that intrigued him, but her sole dedication to the primal needs of the pack discouraged him from thoughts of romance. He scrambled to change the subject to something less provocative before anymore was said.

"How did she lose her arm?" he asked, hoping for a triumphant war story.

"She was born lame."

"Oh." Nathaniel had a feeling that despite a natural concern for disadvantaged children, sympathy was inappropriate. Aífe didn't seem the type to let herself be slowed down by adversity and that was to be respected.

"A fierce warrior even back then. 'Twas her own childhood friend who drowned her in a jealous rage for besting him in a duel before their village when they came of age. The Goddess tasted her pain in the river and bid Cernunnos restore her to life." Calder stood, signaling the end of their friendly chat. "I owe ye many thanks for today and my apologies for attacking without pause—a lesson gone yet unlearned. I thought ye an enemy possessed of demons to see ye lash at my lord."

Now I think I know why Dorian always tells us not to be sorry. It does feel strange to be apologized to so often.

"I understand. You are far stronger than I was prepared for based upon our first bout."

Calder gave a deceitful grin. "Perhaps a true contest is in order some morrow yonder. I welcome the chance to scrap as real men and not parade animals."

The proposal of more fighting didn't interest Nathaniel and the cold was starting to get to him, as were renewed worries about what was to come next. "Who is Yggdrasil? Cernunnos mentioned the name when we fought."

"Ah, 'tis the World Tree that Cernunnos tends. It connects many a land and heavens beyond and is sacred to all no matter the name it goes by."

"So, does it not wish to kill us?"

"Nay, I should hope not. These roots are but a twig to its whole. Gáe Bulg is made of a splinter from it and brims with its blessing of life to smite the darkest evils. Cernunnos tells us 'tis where the energy comes from that it takes to turn beast." The immense thorns had receded, but the presence of the roots that had torn the land asunder with such ease was still foreboding. "By Ullr's frozen beard it is cold! I must return to my pack. We will meet again, Champion, and it shall be an honor as always."

Calder shifted into his feral incarnation with an earsplitting howl and raced across the ice on all fours, shaking the ground with each enormous paw that made contact. Nathaniel headed to the next island where he had left the cylindrical portion of the base aboveground. A decent majority of the Order was outside with only a handful of PROJECT: UNITY's troops. Marianna was first to greet him, as always. Rafael and Connor, both back in their armor, accompanied her.

"Champion." Marianna smiled and bowed.

"Hello—"

"You were incredible!" Connor exclaimed. "Too bad Dorian wasn't here to see, he'd be so proud!"

"*Connor!*" Rafael pushed him.

"What? I was only saying he'd be proud."

"Thank you, Connor." Nathaniel smiled, happy that he at least tried to say something nice. "I'm glad you're both looking better. Do you think I could go inside? I should probably speak to the commander."

"Of course. I'll take you to him." Marianna removed her cloak and offered it to him on their way in. "Here. You look cold."

"Thank you, I'll be fine though." He turned red, although he wasn't sure why, except for the fact that he was half-naked and it was becoming an unwelcomed norm.

Most of the electricity in the base was out. It was puzzling that they had anything more than emergency lighting. The interior wasn't in terrible shape structurally, but broken glass and anything not firmly secured had been tossed about like a tornado had passed through.

"You haven't asked about our search for Dorian," Marianna said.

"Because I think I already know where he is. Calder saw a vision from Cernunnos of a fortress in the ocean that must be deeper in Hell. I've been hoping the gods would be able to tell me how to get there, but so far they've been corrupted or possessed by Hell somehow."

After overhearing their conversation, Lyle, Alexandre, and Liam found them on what was once the basement floor.

"These were good gods though. How can good ones get possessed?" Lyle asked, extending his hand to shake with Nathaniel. "You really saved our asses back there. I can't thank you enough. You're like a guardian angel or something."

An angel? Nathaniel looked down at his hand, the same one he used to save the boy from death's clutches. "You don't have to thank me. I pray there weren't many causalities."

"None reported. We've got some cuts and scrapes, maybe a broken bone or two, but I'm riding high, man. Greenland might've seen better days, but we all survived and that's what matters."

"That's great to hear." Nathaniel gave a sigh of relief.

"No idea how this affected the rest of the world though," Lyle continued. "I'll send out the drones to survey the area while we salvage everything critical from here and move it over to the research departments, where they have more than enough room for us. These facilities were built with something like this in mind, so I'd say they passed the test."

"You mentioned the gods being good. When I fought Isis and Cernunnos they called themselves by different names, like how Ganesha became Lord Vināyaka when we fought in Mumbai. They each seemed angry about something specific too, but after they were defeated they changed back," Nathaniel said.

"Everyone—including the Spiritborn gods—has darkness in them," said Alexandre. "Hell found a way to pervert it for their cause, but will not likely invest in more attempts with the same gods once they are defeated. When we did battle with Set, the Infernal Kings abandoned him when he began to lose. The question is what have they done with the Ascended? They mean to possess him, but there haven't been any signs since his disappearance."

"I think I can still hear his voice and feel his presence sometimes when I'm in trouble," Nathaniel said with sadness in his heart. "We need to locate the fortress he's being held in or a way to get deeper into Hell."

"I've got nothing," said Lyle. "Communications are limited around the world. Hell's interference has blocked pretty much every satellite, and there are huge power outages from reactors going offline that we still haven't figured out. We're down to some classic radio to bring us any news, but if it's looking like Isis and Cernunnos were turned by the Infernal Kings it's a safe bet that the other gods were too. Between the four of them one has to know something once they're awake. Now that we have some intel on what we're up against everyone should take a couple hours to rest before we hit the two that are left together."

No one knows what to do. Is the best plan we can come up with really just finding something else to fight?

Noah appeared, leaning against a wall next to them. "Doesn't matter how much rest you get. You'll still die and that's not what Dorian would want. Dragon lady and the Italian aren't gonna be as easy as a tree-hugger and a healer."

"For once I don't disagree with you, but what other choice do we have?" asked Lyle.

"Stay out of my way. I'll go with the kid and no one else." Noah nodded at Nathaniel. "If the Italian's been weakened the kid can probably take him down on his own, as much as I'd like to do it myself."

"Hey now, the goal is to return them to normal, not kill them," Lyle argued.

Nathaniel had his doubts. "Gianluca isn't a spirit, so would we be able to turn him back through fighting him? The Spiritborn seem to reset when returned to the aether by defeat."

"Remember when we fought the first demon lord out in Iraq? Ma'al?" Lyle looked at Noah. "Gianluca's dark side came out and he was evil for a while, until it separated from him and he defeated it himself. He might be in the clear."

"I try not to think about him," Noah answered. "If that's the case then I'll head straight to China where the dragon lady is probably waiting with her four goons."

"Alone?" Liam asked.

"I don't need my hand held." As Noah said that he played with Dorian's prayer beads in his hand. Marianna looked startled and checked her satchel, realizing he must have snatched them when she wasn't paying attention.

"I know better than to push this any further, so I guess that's it then," said Lyle. "We don't have any aircraft back yet from evac, but if you wait an hour I can get you one to China."

"I'll be around."

Nathaniel broke off from the group to follow Noah before he disappeared. "Where have you been?" he asked.

Aside from Dorian, Noah was usually a source of guidance for Nathaniel, which he felt he was in severe need of today.

"Don't worry about it," Noah said and kept walking through the unlit corridors of the base.

"Dorian told me that whenever you say that is when it's time to worry."

"Is Dorian here?"

"No..."

"Then don't worry about it. I'll see you in China. And if the Italian did go bad for the hundredth time, don't go easy on the face when you finish the job."

"He's Dorian's friend though. I don't want to kill him."

Would Dorian kill Gianluca if there were no choice? Would he blame me if I did?

Noah vanished, leaving Nathaniel standing alone in the dark to ponder how far is too far to go when saving a friend.

"We could bring Connor to the Astral Plane where his subconscious might give us a better vision of where this fortress is," Alexandre suggested to the group now that Connor and Rafael had arrived.

"I would prefer not to go to the Astral Plane," Connor said, sounding shaken.

Nathaniel went back to join them, knowing Connor's fear of the Astral Plane from losing a parent there. "I'll go with you," he offered. "You won't have anything to worry about."

"We'll all go," said Marianna, giving Rafael a welcoming smile. "It's for Dorian."

Connor seemed more optimistic about the prospect of having the companionship of those he admired. "Really?" he asked. "And you won't leave me there to make me learn any lessons or anything, will you?"

"We won't," Nathaniel reassured him.

"Okay. I'll do it."

"We should leave soon," said Rafael. "We don't want to be gone long with the way things are unfolding."

"I'll give you my underarmor to wear," Liam said to Nathaniel. "You'll need to make us an aether crystal of significant size to use in the ritual so you can come with us."

"My specialty." *Finally, a plan involving something more than combat.*

Chapter Thirty

"Bizarre." With one word Marianna summed up the location of the Astral Plane they had been sent to with a fair degree of accuracy.

"The recent battle has left quite an impression here," Alexandre said as they all spread out to get a better look at their surroundings. "The basic atmosphere is unstable."

The roots of Yggdrasil were several times the size of those back on Earth and spread across mountains and chasms of ice. Spinning icebergs floated in the sky amongst powder blue wisps and the clouds reflected like water. Ley lines streamed through the air, intertwining with strange ice formations and falling snow stopped in time against gravity.

"Calder said Yggdrasil connects the worlds," said Nathaniel. "I wonder if we could use it to get to where we need to go."

"The tree? He also suggests Earth is a literal goddess superior to the Ascended," Liam balked.

"A planet itself isn't a conscious living thing," said Alexandre. "It might have living components, but that doesn't make it a life form, even by a spirit's standards."

"Maybe he's gone mad from rabies," Marianna added.

"Don't insult him like that just because he believes something different," Nathaniel said defensively.

"I only meant it in jest," Marianna apologized. "Connor—where's Connor?"

Rafael pointed to a snowy field. "He's over there."

"Is he talking to someone?" Nathaniel squinted to see through the snow. Two figures were standing in front of Connor and Nathaniel thought he recognized them. "Oh no. Are those...?"

"It's his parents," said Marianna.

"He's panicking and letting his subconscious manifest their memory," Rafael said. "Be ready. We might have to fight them if he feels guilty for their death and they turn aggressive or attract other spirits or demons of guilt."

"Standard rite of passage. He should be able to handle it himself," said Liam.

"Yes, in two more years."

"He completed the rite of passage that the Ascended gave him when they met and I trust the Ascended's judgment."

Liam was always someone who went by the book and never questioned it. He was rarely vocal, but it was known how much he idolized Dorian after witnessing him fight several years prior to becoming the Ascended. That was when it became personal to him, more than worshipping a faceless deity. Nathaniel found it odd when Liam admitted that he didn't want to be the Champion, but he surmised that it could have been from the pressure to meet his idol's expectations. In just the past hour he noticed a change in him, however.

Is this aggression left over from Hell's influence or is Liam holding on more tightly to his faith after losing his mother?

"I'll get him," Rafael said.

"Wait. Let him say what he needs to say." Nathaniel used his enhanced hearing to find out what was going on without disturbing Connor.

"I miss you." Connor sniffled as his the image of parents hugged him. "I never got to say goodbye. I can't sleep at night knowing you won't be there in the morning."

"We love you," they told him.

This was Nathaniel's first trip to the Astral Plane. He was in awe of the atmosphere here, but more so the way that these aether constructs formed in such a realistic fashion from emotional memories. It worried him that he might be confronted by things he didn't want to remember.

"I made friends like you always said I would," Connor continued. "And I got to meet the Ascended. You'd like him. He's nothing like the elders."

Nathaniel decided it was probably best not to let Connor get too attached. He went to approach him, but a barricade of icicles shot up from the ground to bar his passage.

"To arms then." Marianna drew her sword. "Knights Lior and Chantelle were two of the Order's strongest and I'm sure he remembers them as more powerful than they actually were so this could be rough."

"It doesn't have to come to that," Nathaniel said, leaping over the icicles to stand by Connor. The cold there was so deep that Nathaniel felt it gripping his soul. It was a lonely and isolating feeling. "You're not alone, Connor. We're all here for you to move forward together."

"I miss them," Connor said mournfully with his face in the apparition of his mother's cloak.

"They're with the Ascended now. The one we came here to save. We can bring him back, but your real parents have passed on to rejoin the cycle. These visions aren't real."

After a moment Connor gathered himself enough to respond. "I know, but it feels real..."

Nathaniel put a hand on his shoulder. "It's time to say goodbye, Connor. Your friends are here and we need your help."

"One more minute?"

"All right." Nathaniel returned to the group and motioned for them to put away their weapons.

Connor kept his word. He said his goodbyes, turning around more than once to wave as his parents' image faded from the aether, wiping his tears on his sleeve in hopes of no one noticing. Nathaniel met him halfway and kept a hand on his shoulder while they walked back together.

"Sorry, everybody," he said, keeping his head down.

"There's no need to be," said Alexandre. "You handled that admirably."

"No more apologizing from any of us," Nathaniel asserted. "We can only fix the present by moving forward, not regretting the past no matter how distant nor recent."

"Now we need you to clear your mind and meditate on when you were possessed," said Rafael.

"Look at that," Nathaniel interrupted.

The aether that had taken the form of Connor's parents coalesced into a floating crystalline orb of pale blue light that was headed towards them.

"It's an ice wisp," Alexandre said. "That's what the many of these are flying around us."

"It likes me," said Connor as he kept turning to watch it orbit him.

"It must have imprinted after harmonizing with your emotions."

"Does that mean I'm a whisperer like you?"

"Not necessarily, but it doesn't mean you aren't one either. I doubt it though, since your parents would have known and mentioned it when you were a child. Still, it's impressive to bond with any spirit. This one seems to be of moderate strength, based on its size and aura. It helps that you've been studying cryothurgy since it can sense that energy."

Connor held the wisp in his hands. The inside of it was a whirling snow globe. "Okay. I'm ready to meditate."

"Good because I'm about to get frostbite, but I don't want to cast a heat spell here with everything already being so unstable," Marianna said.

A small area around them wobbled and waved as reality shifted to Connor's subconscious.

"Is this somewhere in the PROJECT: UNITY base?" Rafael asked as the surrounding snow and ice turned into an expansive chamber of plastics and metals. Pistons, tubes, and wires were prevalent in an orderly— almost artistic— arrangement throughout, but the rounded walls lacked the conventional symmetry as seen in their allies' facility. "Connor, you're supposed to be showing us *before* this."

"It's not the base," Marianna said. "Look at this writing. It's Infernal."

"We're in some sort of engine room. Why would there be all this writing?" Nathaniel asked.

Holograms covered not only the walls, but wrote in an alien language across the air like it was blank paper. Mechanical devices hummed and occasionally slammed down hard enough to make the steel-willed knights jump in their skins.

"This isn't Infernal," said Liam. "We should have brought your aunt, Marianna. She can recognize almost every mystic and arcane language."

"I know them too." She craned her neck around a flowing line of text that went from one side of the room to the other. "This isn't like anything I've seen in any of our books though. Infernal writing is made up of very defined lines with separated characters. This is more, I don't know? Elegant? I can't tell where anything ends or begins, but it all looks unique up close. The characters are links in a chain and heavily detailed. I wouldn't be surprised if each one was a word and not a letter. I'm not seeing much repetition."

The many separate lines of text began to scroll beyond the limits of the vision, but none seemed to have an end.

"Infernal writing also speaks directly into your mind similar to how the spirits communicate," Rafael said.

"This is only what Connor remembers though. He wouldn't be able to recreate the meaning behind a language he can't read," said Liam.

"It looks similar to when lines are drawn between constellations to show their shapes," said Alexandre. "These are none that I'm familiar with, but it doesn't mean Hell couldn't have their own. Could this be a map room of sorts?"

"No," Nathaniel said. "The pattern looks like the inside of Dorian's tablet I...I, um, crushed."

"Can I stop now? My head hurts," Connor asked.

"Not yet, you're doing well," Liam encouraged.

Alexandre agreed. "This *is* an astounding level of detail."

"Would you call these computers?" Nathaniel asked, staring at a strange ethereal screen with hundreds of buttons. "None of this makes any sense."

The chamber began to increase in temperature and was cast in a red light from above. The text changed direction to converge up into its source. A single enormous demon's eye was now watching them.

"It isn't real," Marianna reassured Nathaniel, who had stepped back in fright.

"I've seen it before," he told her.

"Of course you have. All the demons have them," Rafael said.

"No, this one is different." Nathaniel flew up to it. "Look. It's not real. It's like the rest of the machinery in here."

"It does look rather like a camera lens," said Alexandre.

The "eye" appeared to follow Nathaniel's movements. They began to hear talking coming from every direction, but the voices were too distorted to comprehend.

"Ugh—" Nathaniel held his head, feeling woozy. "I'm having déjà vu... It's so strong."

"Why did you say this is an engine room?" Marianna asked him.

"The machines here sound like the inside of those warships that were sent to our island, but I feel as if I've seen this particular eye somewhere."

"Calder told you he saw a fortress in the water," Liam recalled. "Could it have been a ship instead? One that goes under the water to hide."

"It's called a submarine, Liam," said Connor.

The vision started to fade at Connor's break in concentration and was lost soon after. "No!" Alexandre exclaimed. "We were so close to finding something."

"Connor, are you all right?" Nathaniel floated down to him.

Connor had gone pale and his eyes bloodshot. "I told you, my head hurts."

"Heal him please and then we return to the commander to see if any of this means something to him. You did an outstanding job, Connor."

The rest of the group was in agreement about his performance.

"Glory to the Ascended." He lay down and watched the wisp orbit him. "My new friend can't come with us, can he?"

"I'll teach you how it can be summoned later," Alexandre said with some hesitation.

Once the group returned to Earth, Connor went with Alexandre for a quick lesson in communing with spirits. Marianna sought her aunt to discuss the unknown language from the vision. Liam and Rafael joined the rest of the Order, offering their muscle in recovering the base from the battle earlier. Nathaniel found Lyle to discuss what they learned.

"A sub could make sense from what you're telling me," Lyle said while directing troops in the recovery. "We once brought down a demon lord that was into tech, so they're not all as stupid they look. I don't have any ships available to recon and I'd like to lay low with the other countries, but if you're not up for a swim we could send the construction drones we used when expanding the base. I'll suit up and go myself."

"I don't think that's a good idea," said Nathaniel.

"Look, dude. I know some of us have been trying to convince ourselves that Dorian is going to pop up and it'll all be okay, but he's gone too long. That's my brother out there and I can't keep sitting on my ass waiting around. I'm ashamed enough that it took me this long to get more directly involved when desk duty was never my thing."

"Having hope is no reason to be ashamed."

"Making excuses is. Noah's already left for Japan, so do what you need to do with Gianluca and I'll catch up."

"Japan?" Nathaniel questioned. "I thought we were going to China."

"We heard on the radio that Kamakura woke up there on the wrong side of the bed. It's bad enough I found out that both sides of the pond have taken casualties from the seismic activity of Greenland being remodeled, but her footsteps alone are causing major earthquakes. She's got the most followers and active temples of any of the gods, so combined with whatever Hell is feeding her she'll be the worst of them all. Rome is still under siege too. Red sky, demons, the works. I'd suggest going there first since it's closer and Noah seems to think you'd have an easier time against the darkness."

"To Rome then."

Chapter Thirty-One

One of the last glimpses into ancient times left standing on Earth was in Rome; the Pantheon, the Roman Forum, the Colosseum. Masterworks chiseled out of rock that had endured millennia now crumbled into further, almost indistinguishable ruin under horn and claw of the Infernal siege. There was once solid shadow married to the stone for preservation in recent days, but it was gone now. Lava flows swept through the architecture robbing them of their long-standing artisanal value, filling fountains, carrying statues from their bases. Rome's only legacy after today would be burning buildings and charred corpses, that is until the wriggling Infernal vermin finished devouring them.

Nathaniel knew he had the greatest chance of locating the Dark God at the Colosseum site and wasted no time lamenting the dead as he soared above the streets. It wasn't easy for him, but their struggles were over and his had no end in the foreseeable future. Dorian had shared that with him as a method of coping with the heavy losses they witnessed in the previous cities when this atrocity first started.

A gathering of weary survivors—mostly women and children—huddled together in the arena, held captive by

Roman soldiers made of pure darkness. Clad in full tenebrous armor, Gianluca relaxed on his throne watching his prisoners from the podium. What hope there was left of him resisting the corruption to which the others had succumbed was gone. Nathaniel shot into action. He banished the guards below with one blast of searing splendor and landed before Gianluca.

Nathaniel had seen the Dark God fight in the past. He was fast enough to send someone like Noah into the Nether Realm with a thought and so powerful he was immune to Dorian's strongest attacks when in his armor. There was no limit to the darkness he commanded, so for him to have been defeated and turned against their allies was the most troubling of all in Nathaniel's opinion, despite others' beliefs to the contrary.

"Stand and fight or I will strike you down as you are." Nathaniel shined brighter to fend off the shadows creeping up on him.

Gianluca motioned his hand in front of him to dim Nathaniel's light and went to stand, but as his hand passed between them the shadows faded up to his forearm, revealing the damage that had been done by whomever or whatever defeated him in China. Gianluca had little left to him besides his skeleton and some muscle tissue. Nathaniel felt remorse fighting him in such bad condition.

"Stop. I am not your enemy," Gianluca said with weakness in his voice, yet still able to dismiss Nathaniel's radiance. He sat back in his throne, unable to get to his feet.

Nathaniel looked down at the arena and saw that the survivors hadn't made their escape yet.

"Are you not one of them?" Nathaniel asked. "You were not corrupted?"

"No...I control the only darkness in me. I protect these people...this is all there is left of Roma."

"What happened to the gods? Do you know where Dorian is?"

"No...we see it there—on the water—a great fortress and a big light...then nothing. I am awake in the darkness and think Dorian is with me, but then he is gone."

"Where did the fortress go?" Nathaniel begged. "Please, you must know something else."

"I do not see. The light cause a pain I never feel before inside my armor. I fail to protect Dorian...and Roma...again."

"Dorian isn't dead. I could still feel him."

It's been a while since I've felt him or heard his voice, actually...

Gianluca labored to continue speaking. "This is good, but he is no place the shadows can see. The world lose its beauty if he is gone."

"We won't lose him. I won't allow that to happen. Will you be safe if I leave you to stop Empress Kamakura?"

"*Si*, but you cannot fight the empress. She is too strong."

"I have to try. I'm the only one who can."

"Hm, I send you to the empress, but maybe you need a bigger help," Gianluca said.

"Thank you, but I have no time to find it. You are able to speak through shadows, yes? Ask Commander Turner at PROJECT: UNITY to rescue these people and take you to their base. The Alabaster Order can use their magic to heal you."

"I will do this. No light until after I send you, okay?"

Nathaniel gave a nod. He was thrust through the shadows and out onto the demolished avenue of a city somewhere in Japan after only a brief intermission of darkness.

Empress Kamakura was approaching with her entourage of three of her four guardians. Their eyes, of course, were now that of demons and their skin copied the same inorganic design as the others who had fallen. Her measured footsteps and the claps of rolling thunder from the storm clouds in the blood red sky above made the city rumble like the slow, heavy beat of a drum. Watching the buildings shake so violently was making Nathaniel dizzy. People were still pouring from them and trampling one another to get away from her as she leveled one after the other on her path of destruction.

Concentrated bolts of lightning so intense that they liquefied the infrastructure of the skyscrapers crackled from her fingertips when she held out her arms to both sides of the street. Nathaniel charged at her, but with one lightning strike from a pointed finger he was sent careening backward through the air for miles until crashing outside the city.

Nathaniel convulsed in pain, only able to rise once the electrical charge that caused his heart to seize had ceased. He had landed on an abandoned highway where cars were left in pileups, presumably from people ditching them to run for their lives instead of dying in traffic as everyone flooded the lanes. The ground quaked even at this distance and tossed flaming cars into the air or swallowed them whole in gigantic chasms. He was about to take off upon getting his bearings, but noticed he was surrounded by the empress's guardians of fire, water, and wind—a young songstress of cinder wreathed in fiery silks, a dignified older geisha veiled under robes illustrating the sea's fickle wrath, and a warrior monk tattooed to represent the hurricane fury of a tiger's roar.

"Surrender your light unto us," said the water guardian through a pronounced Japanese accent altered by Hell's corruption.

"Come and take it." Nathaniel unleashed his overwhelming might in a shining mandala that scorched the corrupted spirits. He knew that each was a demigod in their own right, but the true danger was how well their elemental powers worked in conjunction with one another.

The trio reappeared once the light faded. They barraged Nathaniel from afar with their respective elements to avoid getting in range of his aura and maintained a triangular formation so two were always safe as he dashed or shot at the third. The flames didn't bother him through the fireproof demon leather he wore and his apparent immunity to heat up to temperatures of nuclear fallout, but the exploding cars getting in his way proved to be a minor nuisance.

To his surprise, it was not the shearing winds that caused Nathaniel the most trouble either—aside from shredding his borrowed body armor. The disorienting briny waters called forth from another dimension to crash against him with a pressure many times that of the deepest ocean inflicted the worst hardships. His superior strength was trivialized as he was caught, battered, and his senses debilitated.

The wind spirit sent a fleet of vehicles at Nathaniel, which he knocked away like paper airplanes. He then realized they were headed toward the tail end of the fleeing throngs and some were stuck in their cars. Nathaniel flew at the guardians to return to the abandoned part of the highway near the city, but was thrown back again. He landed on the hood of a car with a frightened family trapped inside from being pinned against the divider by an earlier accident. Nathaniel rolled off and tore the doors from their hinges to let the family out when the winds picked up into a typhoon and blew the vehicles high into the air. He hurried to catch all he could, but there were too many people and cars being scattered for miles.

And then the fire guardian struck.

The cars burst into flames in the air with people still trapped. He couldn't save them all. There was nowhere near enough to put down those he did catch without them being caught in the crossfire and make it back to grab more. He watched as flaming bodies struck the road.

Families.

Children.

He thought he would lose his mind from the anger. That anger then turned to hatred, intensifying under the Infernal sky. He forced his hands open to set down the survivors he was carrying and immediately clenched his fists as he stormed down the highway in the spirits' direction.

The monk vanished into the wind and reappeared, striking him in the stomach with the strength of a thousand men, but the punch could have been mistaken as a gentle breeze to Nathaniel as it failed to budge him. Before the spirit could retreat, Nathaniel took him by the shoulders and tore his body down the middle.

The remaining duo decided it best to escape and headed for their empress in the form of living fire and water to avoid being grabbed. Nathaniel pursued them through the air with a murderous scream until a bolt of lightning struck and sent the two spirits reeling.

Standing where the lightning made contact was Noah with a katana sheathed on his back and his armor damaged from battle, but Nathaniel didn't pause to question his curious appearance. The spirits had momentarily turned tangible, and Nathaniel wasted no time ripping them to pieces with his bare hands while continuing to scream in unbridled anger.

"You get that outta your system?" Noah asked him when he finally stopped, but was ignored.

There was still so much rage in his expression that when a little girl came to return the runestone that had fallen from his pocket, she dropped it and ran away crying. He noticed people staring at him from a safe distance and yelled to scare them off. After they fled in panic he kneeled by the first corpse he found and placed a hand on it, but when nothing happened it only fueled his anger. He tried another and then another until letting out one final scream that unleashed a devastating blast that disintegrated everything around him into a crater—a level of power thought only to belong to the Ascended.

"Warn me next time," said Noah. "Harder to tell when you're about to do something than Dorian since there's no change in your eyes."

Nathaniel sat in silence with his face hidden by his long hair as he did when feeling sad and hopeless. "I can't do this," he said.

"Yeah you can. Listen, kid, you're on a short list of people I actually don't hate. It's a *really* short list too. Dorian still needs you and I'm not letting you give up until we get him back, and maybe not even after that."

"Just keep moving forward..."

"Only path worth taking."

"Right..." Nathaniel stood and moved his hair from away from his face, although he didn't feel an ounce better.

"That explosion before was like something Dorian used to do."

Nathaniel brightened at the comparison. "Oh?"

"It's not a compliment. It's a huge waste of energy that can leave you vulnerable. He turned himself mortal once and almost died."

"I see." Nathaniel pushed himself not to become dejected. "How did you come down on a lightning bolt?"

"I went to Kiyomizu Temple in Kyoto to lure out the lightning spirit. I knew if I turned one of them back they could help me defeat the rest or at least stop their annoying teamwork." Noah unsheathed the katana to show his spirit slaying instrument. Nathaniel could feel the Ascended's power within. "I kicked his ass a little too hard though, so he was too weak to come fight. He gave me what power he had left and I gotta say, it's growing on me."

Noah punched the palm of his hand, causing it to spark with electricity.

"How did you get him to come to the temple?" Nathaniel asked, reflecting on the difficulty he had luring the trio from the crowd of innocent people.

"I redecorated. And by that I mean I burned it down."

"Why would you do that? The spirits need their places of worship to return."

"Yeah, and I need a nap so we're even. Don't tell Dorian about this either, by the way."

"You want to keep a lot from him lately."

"Keeping secrets is the key to a healthy relationship."

"I'm not sure that's correct."

"Me either, but it's gotta be safer than the alternative." Noah paused to stretch. "You wanna be a real friend to Dorian, unlike that fuckwit human? Don't make him worry about stuff anymore than he already does. That fuzzy head of his is wound tight enough. He cares too much and it's stupid, but I like that about him. It's also why I do dumb shit to keep him distracted, although he's probably on to me by now."

A smile inched onto his face as he seemed to drift away to fond memories. He mumbled to himself so low it was almost inaudible, "That laugh of his is a direct fucking shot to the heart every single time."

"I thought you only act that way because you enjoy his attention, but then I don't understand much of what you do or why."

"That's not a bad thing. Never assume you know someone more than they want you to know. It pisses me off."

The rumbling of the earth became more acute as the upheaval of the land spread into rising mountain peaks headed their way.

Noah returned his katana to its scabbard. "Enough chitchat. It's time to kill a dragon."

Chapter Thirty-Two

Osaka had become the latest ground zero as the Kansai region split in two to separate Japan's largest island. The magnitude of the earthquake shifting the lands hadn't been felt on Earth since well before the time of man. Nathaniel was not the only one to feel unspeakable anger here. The earth revolted against the subversion of its authority with its own magmatic retaliation. Ocean waters rushed into the fault created by the divide and caused huge clouds of steam where the elements met.

Noah stood on the only secure footing he could find and shouted to Nathaniel as he passed. "Take her out fast before we're fighting in the water. They like to—"

Nathaniel paid no attention to the advice. All he saw was the next foe to be eliminated atop a pillar of bedrock orchestrating the genocide of her own people. Empress Kamakura had spotted him too. She called upon jagged boulders that she directed through portals in midair to impede him.

When Nathaniel was mere inches from making contact he became trapped in a bubble filled with water. Had he been mortal, the immediate threat would be drowning, but in a battle of high stakes between immortals these precious seconds lost meant everything. The body's natural choking sensation from drowning was still something Nathaniel had yet to learn how to suppress. He tried to punch his way out, but the bubble's tensile strength was as supernatural as himself.

The empress addressed him as a captive audience while pressurizing the water to an unbearable degree that could have snapped steel beams. Her voice shared the same distortion as the previous corrupted Spiritborn.

"I am Amatsu-Mikaboshi the Primordial Chaos. To defy me is to deny yourself existence in my sight. No longer shall I bind myself by oath to those whom claim themselves above me. The Heavenly Ones shall fall and I shall take their throne atop the mountain summit of Yomi."

The water within the prison began to boil, already hot enough to kill a human in an instant but never seeming to evaporate as the temperature continued to rise.

How is this heat more painful than the missiles Dorian worried about? Is the lack of light what prevents me from absorbing it?

Nathaniel was about to release a shockwave of energy to free himself when a sustained current of electricity beat him to the punch. The extreme voltage along with the water's heat began to melt the orichalcum of his gauntlets and greaves.

Water filled his lungs and stomach making him start to boil from the inside. The threshold of his tolerance to heat had been crossed, but he had no control over his body and couldn't let his powers loose while being electrocuted with such intensity. Being underwater muffled Nathaniel's agonized screams as he was about to black out once again.

He knew the worst was yet to come. If he lost consciousness he would be at another's mercy, unable to defend himself like so many times in the dark as a child. Nathaniel prayed to the Ascended that he would hear him somehow and grant him the strength to break free.

The bubble popped.

Someone grabbed his hand and sent Nathaniel sideways. His first thought was to pull away and protect Dorian from burning himself on the scalding gauntlet, but it wasn't Dorian who answered his prayer—not quite. Nathaniel's hand was pinned to a hunk of rock by Noah's enchanted katana.

"They like to zap you with electricity when you're in water," Noah said, finishing with his advice from earlier after coming to reclaim his sword.

Nathaniel coughed up what was left in his lungs and tossed aside the destroyed gauntlets and greaves. "Thank you," he gasped.

"I'll keep her busy, but don't get too comfortable."

Noah dashed away in a lightning bolt to ambush Kamakura.

"You would use the elements against me?" she questioned. "A most unwise decision."

Noah launched a telekinetic slash at her from afar, which she matched with a blade of wind that canceled out both.

Ten more slashes. One hundred. Two hundred. Noah unleashed hell upon her faster than the speed of light, but the gale blocked all attempts save for one. The blow struck Kamakura in the face and broke the adornments from her headdress.

For a moment frozen in time a horrible dread came over Nathaniel as he watched with bated breath to see what her response would be.

The empress cocked her head in Noah's direction with the utmost poise—until her mouth opened. She breathed a concentrated stream of white-hot plasma that sliced through the landscape. Metal and stone didn't only melt, but disappeared without a trace. The heat waves emanating from the stream ripped at the seams of time and space, creating visible twists in reality. Unable to tag Noah, she leaned her head back and sprayed the flames upward to rain down beside a storm of lightning.

Nathaniel flew at her while she was distracted, but the elements protected her by ejecting him into the clouds with a slab of bedrock. He built up speed as he descended to smash Kamakura into the ground, only for her to escape into the wind before he made impact. She kicked up a maelstrom that sucked in the fire and consumed the city ruins in a vortex of flame.

"This is the shit I might actually hate more than the lightning-water combo," Noah shouted over the typhoon.

Nathaniel was at a loss. "I don't know how much longer I can endure." This was the third consecutive god he had fought without rest, and both his physical and mental stamina was depleted.

"Don't stop now, kid. Dorian wouldn't quit."

The eye of the storm narrowed around them. They were about to trade ideas on how to win when a figure appeared from the flames in the ghostly form of the fire spirit from earlier. She spoke to Noah in Japanese and took the shape of a wisp that shot into his chest against his vocal protests.

Noah cringed and made a fist that ignited in a large flame.

"Get out of my body! This doesn't fucking help if she can't be hurt by the elements!" Noah growled.

"It has to at least offer some resistance to them for you."

"Yeah, but—" Noah was interrupted by the last two spirits possessing him. "Too much!" he snarled.

"They're weakened, but you must still be under the lasting effects of Dorian's blood if you can contain so much power. I could take some of the aether from you, but it could erase them—"

"No, just—just go—got to finish this fast!" Noah went to turn into mist, but instead he became water first, then steam that was whisked away safely into the swirling inferno.

I only have to defeat the empress and then all of the gods are back on our side, so they can help me save Dorian.

Nathaniel soared miles above the smoke and fire to search for Kamakura. The horror she left in her wake was the worst yet. The land had been picked clean by wind and flame. Nothing remained but flat deserts of volcanic sand. The region—and possibly farther than he could see—was broken up into several islands drifting out to sea from the expanding continental divide. Those on the highway he had managed to save from the spirits were gone. It weighed heavily upon him that his hated was the last sight they saw before being incinerated. Sorrow replaced anger and the strength that came with it.

Do my efforts matter anymore? Death and misery claim what they will regardless. The universe itself seems bias in favor of suffering.

The firestorm cleared and showed a clash of elements taking place on a distant island. Noah was landing solid blows on Kamakura with his katana, but she was still too strong for them to leave a lasting effect. Nathaniel came to Noah's aid by shooting a beam of light energy to counter her breath. Although his power was dwindling fast he managed to hold her off by a fraction of a second, just long enough for Noah to plunge his sword into her heart and cut straight through with a rising slash.

The empress's body shattered into thousands of firefly wisps that dispersed across the slowing air currents before she hit the ground. Nathaniel landed beside Noah. He tried to remain on his feet to bask in their victory, but he chose to forego the theatrics to sit and collect himself instead.

"That wasn't so hard," Noah said, sheathing his katana. "Probably could've done it myself."

"She weakened...herself." Nathaniel panted as he caught his breath. "The corruption made her kill so many... of her own people. Demons...must have had no further use with her."

"She gave Japan some more islands. Big deal."

Nathaniel glowered at him. "People *died*."

"Yeah? And Dorian is still missing. That's all I care about."

"You can care about more than one thing."

"One is hard enough as it is." Noah stopped himself. "Hell can't take most of their souls anyway since they still belong to her. They're gonna be stuck here in purgatory like the ones in Shanghai until this is resolved."

"When I defeated Isis and Cernunnos the sky returned to normal, but it hasn't here."

"Whatever. Mumbai didn't either. Don't steal my thunder, kid. And speaking of which, how do I get these elemental assholes out of me?"

The small island they were on began to shake. The waters darkened to the evil shade of the lands besieged by Hell. It rose and then sank quickly as a shadow coming up from below engulfed the island on all sides. Noah leaped up and out with a boost from the wind, and Nathaniel flew away. As she breached the water, Kamakura's dragon incarnation swallowed the island whole.

Nathaniel punched the gargantuan serpent before she could breathe fire. He dove underwater, lifted one of the broken landmasses and bashed it into the dragon's head as she was resurfacing—an astonishing feat still less tiring for the young demigod than his offensive use of light. Her tail smacked him halfway across the ocean on her way down, cracking several of his ribs.

While flying back at a cautious distance above the dark water, it began to churn into a spiral dozens of miles in circumference and growing at a steady rate. Kamakura almost got the drop on him as she came up out of the whirlpool now breathing hellfire.

She should be getting weaker, but this is worse.

Noah was clinging to her corrupted gunmetal scales, trying to penetrate them with his sword, but they were too resilient even for the Ascended's molecule cutting blade.

Her roar summoned a convergence of soot black clouds that blotted out the crimson sky. Soul-rending sable bolts of the Underworld pummeled the turbulent seas and charged her serpentine form with unholy energy. Nathaniel knew that he and Noah would not be able to attack her up close, but they were at an equal disadvantage at range. The spiritual elements of other dimensions did not follow the same properties and resistances as their terrestrial counterparts.

Empress Kamakura is immune to her earthly elements, but even demon lords aren't completely immune to those from the Underworld and Hell without some kind of barrier or armor...like those scales.

Noah showed he was of the same understanding. He was prying one of the scales back, but couldn't hold on without electrocuting his body and soul. He threw his katana into the exposed area after jumping off and retreating into the wind. Any movement that Kamakura made triggered the enchantment on the sword, sending telekinetic blades into her more vulnerable insides. Her roar parted the ocean and caused the whirlpool to resonate with a tsunami in all directions.

"Come. Serve your master," Kamakura's voice boomed. Magic circles appeared around the dragon's foreclaws as summoning gates opened on every dot of land available.

Out climbed a legion of the ogre-like oni, armored and turned synthetic in appearance, matching the rakshasa and Demon Lord Vināyaka. Their faces were frozen in contorted agony as if they had fought for control of their own bodies and lost.

One of the demons vaulted onto Kamakura and retrieved the sword when the charge of dark energy dissipated from her body. Noah appeared again to intercept it, but Kamakura turned to face him as he was in free fall and let out her hellfire breath. Nathaniel flew between them and put everything he had left into a single blast. He almost managed to push the fire back into her mouth, but was overtaken at the last second. His hands burned down to the bone and he felt his lifeforce flicker like a candle about to be blown out.

Nathaniel dropped from the sky, still caught in the stream of hellfire. A gust from Noah blew him from danger, but the flames came to a sudden stop anyway and Kamakura hit the water ahead of him. On her way down Nathaniel thought he was seeing things in a state of confusion. Calder was driving the dragon down with his blazing spear plunged deep into her head.

"Calder, what are you doing here?" Nathaniel shouted, catching his balance in the air. The skin on his hands healed on its own, but the damage done to his soul and the shard of the Ascended's would be permanent unless he found help.

"Cernunnos sent us to aid ye in his stead against the serpent! Apologies for not arriving sooner! Our allies' flying vessels could not make it closer in this storm!"

"No apologies necessary!" Nathaniel called, searching the area to see who else had come.

Aífe was on land, going from one island to the next brutalizing the oni with tooth and claw, plucking each of their arms from their sockets, tearing their artificial flesh apart, and shaking them to and fro in her jaws with remorseless savagery and no regard for their molten innards. When one managed to stab a sword into her flank, her howl shook the seas nearby, leaving it paralyzed and unable to defend itself from being demolished. The sonic blast unfortunately knocked Noah from his battle trance as he more systematically disassembled his opponents with fists of fire and kicks of lightning. He was not shy about voicing his discontent with being forced into more teamwork.

"Will the Fury not take her?" Nathaniel asked Calder, grabbing his hand to fly him to safety.

"She swallowed one of the crystals meant to calm the pack when we left our home! But fear not, there is still plenty of rage left in her!" Calder let out a hearty laugh as if this were all a rousing game.

A revelation came to Nathaniel. "Aether crystals! That's what we need! Calder, I will get the empress to corrupt an aether crystal with hellfire and throw it in her mouth. You hit it with your spear when it's past her jaws so it'll explode."

"By the Goddess's grace, ye may be even crazier than I. We must hurry, our friends cannot weather overlong."

Aífe and Noah were being mobbed with little room to maneuver and poorly navigating what they did have due to a lack of cohesion. The sound of a jet preceded a volley of gunfire raining down on the Infernals, putting enough down to give the two breathing room. A second later the aircraft emerged from the clouds. It swooped low enough for the pilot to eject and land safely amongst the fray with guns blazing and then left on its own. Nathaniel knew who it was at once by the sticker on their helmet.

"Commander, you shouldn't be here!" Nathaniel called.

"You think I'm about to let something like that bench me?"

Lyle unloaded on an oni moving in to attack Noah from behind, taking the demon down before it could swing. Noah showed his gratitude by kicking the spiked iron club from its hand at Lyle. The weapon narrowly missed and struck another demon that had crawled from its summoning gate behind him. Nathaniel went to help when the waters began to churn and Kamakura resurfaced.

"That one's all yours, just leave these to us," Lyle told him.

He fired a potent flashbang grenade at the next group of oni emerging. The light stunned them long enough for Noah to zip ahead and dismantle them, with Aífe chewing through the few that managed to cling to their lives.

That light. I felt aether within it.

Nathaniel launched himself at Kamakura with a flying punch to lure her into retaliating with her fire breath.

"I am the darkness cultivated by tradition," she bellowed. "There is no escape from chaos unerring. It is in your nature as it is mine."

After three earthshaking punches she did indeed resort to her hellfire breath, but Nathaniel was ready. He pulled all the aether he could harness from the ley lines in the area to create a crystal large enough to shield him. It took only seconds for the crystal to begin quivering from reaching critical mass.

"Calder! Take aim!" he shouted.

"Not so close lest ye be taken by the explosion!"

"Don't worry about me! *Do it!*"

Nathaniel spun in the air and hurled the tainted crystal into the dragon's maw. She was too slow to close her mouth, allowing Calder's spear to enter at the perfect angle and pierce the crystal as it reached her throat. There was an instantaneous detonation that ripped through her body, sending metallic scales shooting everywhere and leaving nothing recognizable of her head. The fulmination was so loud and so strong that all else became inaudible and threw everyone soaring in different directions.

Nathaniel could hear the empress's voice in his mind to the tune of delicate bells that contrasted with the utter destruction around them.

"O Heavenly Ones...my oath is broken...virtue lost...Forgive my betrayal, Amaterasu..."

Chapter Thirty-Three

"You fucking idiot! You could've lost him forever!"

Nathaniel heard Noah's voice and felt himself being shaken before opening his eyes. The explosion from defeating Empress Kamakura had sent him so far away he didn't recognize where he was.

"Unhand him," Calder warned Noah.

Noah growled back, "Don't tell me what to do."

"What, what's happening?" Nathaniel asked as he sat up. He was feeble, weaker than he had ever been when suffering from aether poisoning.

"You have what could be the last of Dorian in you and you risked losing him by getting caught in hellfire on purpose!" Noah screamed, shoving Nathaniel when he stood.

Calder and Aífe—in human form—put themselves between the two, but Noah paced around them.

"He's with me still," Nathaniel said, averting his gaze from Aífe's naked body.

"How can you be sure? Can you see inside you? Because I can't. All I see is how much smaller getting roasted has made your aura."

"The Ascended will endure so long as his champion draws breath," said Calder. "Nathaniel deserves rest and reward, not this bitter blood."

"You had better know what you're talking about," Noah snarled. He vanished, but not before shooting Nathaniel a menacing glare. It appeared the spirits had already left him, as his exit was devoid of the added elemental effects.

What if Noah is right? What if I did hurt Dorian and foil our chance to get him back? I'll have to go to Isis and hope she's awake to heal our soul.

"Pay that one no mind," Aífe said. "Ye fought harder than the best of us and should be proud. My sisters and I would be honored to know ye as a denmate."

Calder chuckled. "Ye embarrass the man, Aífe. He turns as red as the sky. Ye can take him back to the den and show him another wild side after we help find his master."

"Don't worry, I won't bite until ye regain your strength," Aífe teased.

"I, uh—Thank you," Nathaniel fumbled. "The sky *is* still red. That's odd. Right, Calder?"

He tried to fly, mostly to escape the situation, but found he didn't even have the strength for that.

"Aye, aught is still amiss," Calder agreed.

"Do you happen to know where we are?"

"An island by the looks of it," said Aífe. "The soldier goes to retrieve his vessel for our escape."

"The whole world is becoming a series of islands. I wonder if we're any closer to China so we can investigate the fortress. I think it may actually be a ship or have one inside. We went to the Astral Plane and saw a vision of it. I heard engines like they have on larger vessels—"

Aífe pointed across the water. "We 'ave no further to look, it found *us!*"

The looming image of a mountainous metal fortress several miles tall with towers attached to each of its four corners phased in over the ocean. It was now readily apparent how it could have gone unnoticed by the speed and stealth in which it was able to manifest.

"Something comes this way," Calder said, summoning Gáe Bulg to his hand.

Of all the times to be powerless.

Animated cables resembling a steel spine darted toward them and wrapped around Nathaniel, dragging him through the water back to the fortress. Aífe and Calder lunged forward to free him, but as soon as there was distance between them a ray of light shot down from the sky and they were gone in the flash.

"*NO!* CALDER! AÍFE!"

Nathaniel was pulled through a porthole in the fortress that sealed shut behind him. The cables binding him tightened the more he struggled until he began to choke on the blood filling his lungs. His head smacked against the quasi-plastic interiors, but he was still able to catch glimpses of rooms as he was dragged through snaking pipes that connected them. The agonizing ride stopped with him hanging from the ceiling in a room that would be large enough to hold three of the navy's aircraft carriers stacked on one another.

"It's not a fortress *or* a ship," Nathaniel murmured to himself.

The clanking and whirling of metal he had heard in Connor's vision were not engines. Machines lining the walls from top to bottom were assembling a legion of oni and rakshasa piece by piece; screwing on heads, plugging in limbs, injecting bodies with molten blood, energizing them with souls, and then moving them down an assembly line to storage pods. Smaller machines produced the components with what seemed like magic, using a stylus to draw the parts into existence. Nathaniel didn't know what it was about this that was so unsettling, but it soured his stomach worse than all the blood he had just swallowed.

It's a factory.

Not only the rakshasa and oni were being processed here. Three of the Demon Lord Vināyaka's massive, motionless bodies were being transported elsewhere by chains along an overhead track.

The cables jerked, pulling him through another aperture. Everything was meticulous and surreal in its automated efficiency. All the moving parts worked in harmony without any delay, and the sterility was unfathomable considering the chaotic nature of demons. The alien language streaming through the chamber in the Astral Plane was everywhere, and even the intertwining flow of information was arranged in perfect patterns throughout the air.

The first and only sign of potentially organic life was in an enormous glass containment unit: fragments of a giant twin-faced skull with long spindly arms. Nathaniel was yanked by too fast to get a better look at it, but a holographic screen displayed the schematics to Empress Kamakura's altered dragon form and a line that synced up to Japan on another hologram of a globe. There were additional schematics for Cernunnos, Isis, and even her brother, Set.

He reached his final destination with a painful end through one last pipe. The cables stretched taut to secure his arms, legs, and neck to the walls of the chamber. Panic became sheer terror as flashbacks filled his head. He was a child again, helpless and afraid, at the mercy of another's whims where whatever strength he could muster meant nothing.

Searching for an escape, Nathaniel noted that the all-white room had no traditional entrance. Anyone looking to access it would need to suffer the same route he did. A panoramic hologram activated in front of him with words written in a language he could understand and were also narrated by a monotone voice:

//You cannot hide in darkness//You cannot hide in light

"LET ME GO!" Nathaniel shouted, more hoping that if Dorian were here he would get his attention than actually expecting to be released by his captor.

An aperture in the wall opposite him opened, revealing a mechanical claw that lined up with his chest.

//Initializing extraction...

"Get away from me!" Nathaniel yelled, thrashing in desperation.

The claw passed through his chest as if it were intangible and removed a ball of light from within him that was attached to his body by a glimmering strand. It had taken his soul. Nathaniel screamed until the weight of death smothered his cries to a whimper. His eyelids grew heavy as the strand was pulled to its limit and came close to snapping.

//Extraction complete

//Initializing reprogramming...

//Upgrading parameters...

Behind the transparent screen the enormous demon eye lens appeared from the wall to observe Nathaniel's last seconds.

"Dorian, I'm sorry...I failed you...everyone..."

His soul was turned black and shoved back into his body, followed by a flash and a jarring bang that sent him tumbling to the floor. Nathaniel felt himself being carried away. He kicked and screamed to fight the growing numbness in his limbs.

"Christ, if you don't shut up I'll throw you back into the ocean."

That's Noah's voice...?

Nathaniel opened his eyes. He was somewhere on Earth, somewhere *natural,* being carried over Noah's shoulder.

"I'm not...I'm not dead?"

"No, but you will be if you keep shouting in my ear," Noah said, dumping him on the grass.

Calder and Aífe were walking behind them. Lyle was ahead with several of PROJECT: UNITY troops gathered around their jets.

"The machine released me back into the ocean?" Nathaniel asked Noah. He touched his chest, checking for signs of tampering with his soul.

"Dragon lady? She didn't eat you. You ran into the blast like a dumbass and got flung into the water."

Was I only dreaming?

"Empress Kamakura? No...I meant—never mind." Nathaniel stood and looked around, bewildered for a moment. The sky had returned to normal. "Thank you for getting me from the water. I understand if you're cross because I put Dorian's soul at risk, but I'd never do anything to jeopardize his safety. I had to take the chance to end the fight fast before it could get any worse."

"I never said I was anything. You are becoming a lot more like Dorian though."

"Thank you."

"That wasn't a compliment either."

"Oh."

"It took me years to get his head on right and I'm not really interested in going through it again with someone else. You won, it's over, move on."

There was so much stifled anguish in Noah's expression that it was hard not to look past his brash words and feel sympathetic.

"*We* won," Nathaniel corrected.

"Whatever."

Becoming like Dorian... Maybe it wasn't a dream.

"When I was asleep I saw myself being taken by the fortress in the ocean the gods saw. I think I may have been seeing through Dorian's perspective. It wasn't a fortress inside though; it was a factory building demon lords. I think Dorian became reprogrammed like the others."

"Reprogrammed?"

"That's what the talking machine said when it took out my soul—*his* soul and turned it black."

"Turned black...yeah, that's what happened to the Italian when we went to Hell a while back. I was hoping it wasn't gonna come to this..."

"Gianluca told me that the only darkness in him now is what he controls. That should mean it isn't permanent then, the same as with the Spiritborn gods after they were defeated."

"Good luck with that." Noah turned away. "I've gotta go."

"What? We need you to save Dorian."

"No, you don't."

Noah left against Nathaniel's protests, allowing Lyle the opportunity to approach now that he was gone.

"You feeling better?" he asked.

"I thought I was." Nathaniel looked at Aífe as she walked past, but she barely acknowledged him.

Was that was only a dream too?

"Let's get you back to base where you can get some rest," Lyle offered. "You've had a rough day."

"I can't. Dorian is out there." Nathaniel hesitated to fill Lyle in on what he had seen after Noah's reaction, but decided he needed to anyway.

"I can see why Noah would be upset if the only solution is to fight Dorian. Although Gianluca technically fought himself to get rid of his evil side and he almost died. We all got our asses kicked too, which is more reason for you to rest."

"I didn't mean I wanted to fight him!" Nathaniel exclaimed. "I can't fight the Ascended. I thought if it does turn out he's been made evil we could destroy the machine that caused it to save him."

"That might be our only shot unless all the gods and yourself pull it together real quick. According to PARAGON's most recent scan of Dorian's parameters he could have the highest overall damage potential of any supernatural on file. It's never easy to get an accurate judge of that stuff from the battlefield though. There are other things it doesn't take into account, like being weakened or tired. I've seen Dorian lose control when he's pissed more than once and it isn't pretty. And that was *before* he was a god."

Parameters.

"The machine mentioned 'parameters,' but I can't remember what it was about."

"It's all right. Can you fly or do you need a ride back with us?"

Nathaniel tried to take off, but couldn't.

Too bad that wasn't just a dream.

"Could you bring me to the Shanghai coast?"

"No. I'm not sending you to your death, man," Lyle said. "We did recon over the coast there before coming here and it was clear."

Nathaniel sighed and wiped the dirt from his face. He felt like screaming again in frustration. "I know I can make the fortress appear if I go there. The Infernal King's machines will try to take Dorian's soul from me and that's when we can destroy them."

"The fact that you may have the last pure piece of his soul is exactly why I *can't* let you go there, not until everyone is at the top of their game. If you can't fly I'm guessing you don't have your super strength either, so don't make me detain you for your own good and Dorian's."

What would Dorian do? Noah said I was becoming more like him, but he also said Dorian changed after their time together.

Chapter Thirty-Four

The residential area of PROJECT: UNITY's Technology division, where the Order was given temporary room and board, was more upscale than the troops' barracks. Although still a tad minimalist, the bedrooms and hallways had an actual Norwegian interior design scheme, with real woods and neutral colors adding a quiet, natural serenity to the main base's otherwise stark and impersonal motif. It certainly didn't feel like being hundreds of feet below ground in a research facility.

Nathaniel showered and changed into the cotton sweatpants and T-shirt he was given. He stared at himself in the bathroom mirror, not sure what to make of dressing this way for the first time in his life. It almost felt like such casualness was disrespectful to his station, especially under the grave context of their situation.

His injuries hadn't healed yet from his strength being drained, but he refused Lyle's demands to receive medical treatment, other than some meager bandaging he did himself to stop the bleeding. He thought that if this was the price to pay for his recklessness, then any scars must be accepted with quiet self-respect.

I AM the Champion and this war is not lost so long as I draw breath.

"Nathaniel, the gods have arrived."

He didn't notice Rafael had entered the room, armed with bow and quiver, while he was busy psyching himself up in the mirror.

"Thank you." Nathaniel stepped out ready to leave when Rafael stopped him.

"You don't look well. Have you had any rest?" he asked. "I've meditated enough to restore my magic if you'll allow me to heal you."

"No, I'll be fine. My recovery will come under my own power in time or when the Ascended's returns to me."

"You didn't give me a choice when I was suffering," Rafael reminded him.

"That was different. You could have died."

Nathaniel headed to the door, but Rafael grabbed his arm. The cooling sensation from a healing spell felt too good to pull away.

"One lesson I've learned from you and Dorian is that if something feels like the right thing to do, just do it and do it in your own way."

Nathaniel looked himself over once the spell finished healing his wounds. "From me? I haven't quite mastered that myself or I wouldn't be in this situation."

"That's why you have friends to help you like you're doing with Dorian."

"He's my only friend."

"You don't consider us friends?" Rafael asked. "Marianna? Connor?"

"I wasn't aware you wanted to be. I thought you were only being courteous for the sake of tradition because I'm the Champion and you wanted to get closer to Dorian."

"I'm fed up with tradition. It is what made the elders turn a blind eye to your abuse. It's what's made me feel like half the knight Liam is, even though we've been best friends our entire lives and are equals in practically every way. Claudius and I were taken into the Order from the outside as infants so we were always second-rate for not having an established bloodline. He might not let it get to him and Liam didn't want to be chosen by the Ascended, but I did. Not for the power, but as proof that I was every bit as capable. I was passed over by the elders to be presented as the Chosen, not because of my skills or all the requirements that they told us mattered, but because of how I was born."

"We share the same passion, but you'd have made a better Champion than I am due to your training," said Nathaniel. "Why didn't you speak up?"

"I've always wanted to prove to the rest that I wasn't half a person because of the blood in my veins, but I was afraid to speak out of turn because of *tradition*. You're the perfect Champion because you represent a new dawn for the Order. Before Dorian's disappearance I was able to talk with him alone and he insisted it be as friends. Until then I was starting to believe the elders were right about me. I didn't feel he recognized what I could do, but he made me realize it was up to me to be heard as you were to earn his attention. After that one conversation I finally felt complete. It didn't take anything to prove myself. It was the support of a friend that made me accept my own worth."

"We have more in common than I thought. I never knew others in the abbey felt the same as I do. I was always so quick to look for an escape instead of noticing others within the walls. It was how I protected myself, because I thought everyone was either out to hurt me or would without knowing it by staying silent since that's how we were raised."

"How many more of us sat and rotted, never fulfilling our dreams because old traditions told us we weren't good enough?" Rafael asked, putting his hand out. "It's time for new traditions and new friendships to follow."

Nathaniel shook his hand. "You're very inspiring for someone who was afraid to speak out of turn. Maybe you can give the speeches Dorian hates to give. I'm not very comfortable with them either."

"I'd rather stick with my bow on the battlefield. Maybe Marianna can do it, she loves to talk."

Rafael went with Nathaniel to the main hall where the gods were assembled. "Is it true you think Dorian was turned against us?" Rafael asked before leaving.

"How did you hear that? I haven't spoken to anyone about it since getting here."

"Claudius did what he does best and spied on the commander."

"I can't say for certain, but I pray I'm wrong."

Rafael departed and Nathaniel took the empty space in the circle of gods joined by Lyle. The gods nodded in acknowledgement of his place among them. He shared the commander's melancholy expression, knowing that he was filling what should have been Dorian's seat.

Donning all save his helmet, Gianluca appeared fatigued, yet in a much improved condition than his sorry state in Rome. Isis was without her bird-like headpiece and Ra's solar blessing. She retained purified touches of the contemporary image bestowed by the corruption, after her followers incorporated it into their vision of her. Few witnesses on the other hand, survived Kamakura's onslaught and so she returned in ancestral fashion. Cernunnos sat on an out of place tree stump that he must have brought to the grand hall. He had regained his distinguished antlers and only changed in hue to darker earthy tones.

"O Champion of the Ascended, you have brought us light in our darkest hour," Isis said to Nathaniel, greeting him with all her customary warmth. "Oaths may have been broken and purposes shattered by our shadowed halves, yet we remain to shape the morrow with thanks to you."

"There is no need to thank me. I serve one purpose and that is to return the Ascended to us safely."

"And ye shall have it, lad, but first we must forge new oaths befitting a shared vision," Cernunnos added. "More o'er, we shan't forget to pray for absolution from those wronged in the firmament and soil."

"Tradition is not so easily shirked when it is the foundation of our being," said Kamakura.

"Gaze upon these ancient boughs and bones, Empress. Do ye see we are naught what we once were?" Cernunnos asked. "Our foundation is not of stone, rigid and wont to break, but a sapling capable of growth and movement in a breeze, with roots spread deep to weather a storm."

"I hear the Heavenly Ones' voices no more and for the first time in centuries I know fear."

Even the gods argue over the necessity of tradition. They seem so much more human, with emotions and aspirations now that these oaths have been broken. I wonder if they noticed?

"'Tis our solemn duty even whence dishonored to be our followers' lodestar. To do as such we must lead them forward, not rearward where there is naught but ruin," said Isis. "Should your greater gods return, would you not be partial to welcome them to nascent prosperity offered by your own hand as repentance?"

Empress Kamakura remained quiet in contemplation. Having made her point, Isis finished by restoring Nathaniel's soul with a sacrament of her light. The feeling of weightlessness and invincibility flooded through him in a reawakening.

"I don't know if this is to our benefit," he said. "My link to Dorian could make me dangerous if he is truly turned against us."

"Or is the key to turn him back," said Gianluca. "When I face my darkness the only light I see is the love we share."

Nathaniel hoped Noah wasn't around to hear that.

"Right, well, this is all just speculation," Lyle said. It was obvious that he was feeling the same unease, aside from being the only mortal present.

"As mighty as the Ascended may be, he is naught but a soul residing within a vessel," Cernunnos said. "My scythe can rend the tether to liberate it from the body and bypass his strength. We may hold it in our care until a way to purify the evil is found. Mayhap with thy light, healer?"

"A worthy suggestion, but not one without great risk," Isis answered. "Such darkness endowed by an Infernal King could prove too much to overcome alone, and a soul without a vessel is a terribly fragile thing."

"I can't allow you to take a chance like that," said Nathaniel.

"Then we may have to defeat him in battle as you did us to purge the evil," Kamakura said.

"I can't fight him. I won't."

"Aye, lad, but we can," Cernunnos said. "If but a demigod could best us three, then four gods shan't have nary a problem with one.

Isis disagreed. "Forget not that it was the Ascended who shattered the moon my brother would fell upon the earth."

The tablet in Lyle's hand beeped. *"Commander, I have an urgent notification for you."*

"I said no messages," Lyle whispered to the screen.

"Go, is no trouble," Gianluca told him.

"Mr. Burckhardt is attempting to commandeer the hypersonic mini-jet with threats of violence," said PARAGON.

"Where's his destination?" Lyle asked.

"The Cyclades Archipelago in Greece."

"Let him leave," Lyle said. "It's better he goes home than causes trouble here. For once I can understand why he acts the way he does."

"Right away, Commander."

"Sorry, everyone," he said. "Getting back to the issue with Dorian, I know I'm the low man on the totem pole here, but I have to say I don't feel beating the evil out of him is the way to go. That's assuming he even is. The problem we need to address first is *finding* him."

"We go together to the place we lose him. Is the same in this dream of Nathaniel, yes?" Gianluca suggested. "This time we watch and are ready. The darkness is different there and not easy for me to see through. If Dorian is bad I will go first. His power cannot hurt me in my armor and I speak to his heart."

While it was true that the abyssal shadows under Gianluca's command were unaffected by telekinetic powers, Nathaniel thought it doubtful that he would be the one to resonate best with Dorian.

"We should leave right away, I can't wait anymore," Nathaniel said.

"Okay. I take you," said Gianluca.

"Wait!" Marianna teleported in. "We've found him! The Ascended is at the abbey!"

"He must've returned home looking for everyone. Did Noah know about this?" Lyle asked.

"I haven't seen him. We only finished scrying right now."

"This is a good sign," Lyle said. "If the demons had him under their control they wouldn't bring him to a place where there aren't any people to kill. The Greek islands have all been evacuated to the mainland after your run in with the militaries. Noah should be there soon to make first contact. You feeling anything, Nathaniel?"

"Impatient."

"Now we go," said Gianluca. Just like that he took Nathaniel with him through the shadows to the abbey grounds with the other gods close behind.

"There he is!" Nathaniel felt Dorian's presence before seeing him. Noah's large frame blocked their view as the two shared a moment together upon being reunited. It hadn't taken him long to get undressed from his tattered armor for the occasion. He was in only a pair of old *haidate* with his katana at his waist, like how he used to dress before Dorian insisted on him taking more precautions.

Is Noah being nostalgic or trying to antagonize Dorian? I don't think I'll ever understand relationships.

"The seas are still," said Kamakura when she arrived.

"As are the skies," said Isis. "'Tis an exceptional thing."

"Hold here," Nathaniel told the gods, floating up to get a better view. Noah returned the prayer beads to Dorian's wrist. Dorian seemed rather stiff, but he appeared otherwise normal.

"Look at it," Noah whispered to Dorian, holding up a photograph. "This is the Dorian I know. This is *my* Dorian, the Dorian that's still in there."

"His soul is black as night," Cernunnos said, appearing last.

"Don't listen to them." Noah continued attempting to soothe Dorian and held the back of his head in one hand. "Just look at me. I know you can fight this. If the Italian could do it, you can do it ten times better. I won't let them hurt you."

Nathaniel's chest hurt when Dorian finally spoke. "What makes you think they can?"

"Tarry not a moment longer lest we invite the destruction he might bring should his gaze fix upon the Moon." Cernunnos transported himself behind Dorian with his scythe readied.

"Don't—!" Nathaniel yelled.

Noah drew his katana and attempted to parry the scythe, but it cut the blade in two with ease and came close to reaping his soul until Dorian's eyes changed to black and white. Cernunnos and his scythe turned to dust, and Noah blinked in and out of mist form to soften his landing when thrown aside. The telekinetic pulse was so strong it pulled at the interdimensional veil, letting in ghastly sights and sounds from the Rift on the other side. Dorian flew over to confront the gods and Gianluca stepped forward to draw his attention.

"Dorian, little one, you do not want to do this," Gianluca implored. "The demons control you—"

"Demons?" When Dorian spoke reality quivered and the Rift parasites' guttural rattle echoed from his voice. "No demon is controlling me. I'll crush them the same as the humans."

"What inconceivable force... His very words unravel the bonds of this world without effort," Isis said.

"Why the humans if you are not controlled?" Gianluca asked.

"They fear me, they hate me, and anyone who isn't them they want destroyed. They won't accept us even when we try to save them from the apocalypse they brought on themselves. I have nothing left in me to give them, so let's see whose hatred is stronger."

"You cannot hurt me so give me your anger if you want to release it, but I cannot let you kill them."

Dorian's pale skin turned bleached white. His Alabaster garb changed to black. The veins in his face darkened and arranged themselves in a symmetrical pattern of lines.

"I'd like to see you try to stop me. You've never been man enough to accomplish anything worthwhile."

Shimmering particles from the air around Dorian collected into a lance of light that shot through Gianluca's heart. His dark armor diffused immediately and his body tumbled across the ground into the water, where it sank.

Nathaniel was in disbelief. *Where did that light come from? It felt like...me.*

Chapter Thirty-Five

Nathaniel felt the sadness from Dorian's good side within him upon witnessing the attack on Gianluca. He rushed to Gianluca's aid and carried him back to land.

How could Dorian use light like that? Was it from me?

Kamakura tried to strike Dorian down with lightning while Isis worked on healing Gianluca, but Dorian's palm stopped the bolt.

He can cancel energy now too? Were these the "parameters" mentioned by the machine?

Kamakura was dismissed by a single telekinetic blast the same as Cernunnos had been, along with a large portion of the abbey's property, which vanished as if it had never existed. In its place came the sight of inhuman eyes peeking in through the thinned interdimensional veil and the wails of untold horrors lurking within the Rift.

"You could've all just faded away peacefully after I slaughtered your followers, but if you want pain I have no problem bringing it!" Dorian shouted.

He flew out over the water and the sea stirred beneath him. Up from the depths came a metallic hand, as large as the abbey itself, which went to crush everyone with disarming speed. Nathaniel collided with it in the air to prevent the impact, but the best he could do was slow its descent. He was pushed downward until his feet touched the ground and his knees buckled.

"Dorian...don't...do this," Nathaniel pleaded through gritted teeth.

The rest of what the hand was attached to rose from the sea, putting its weight on Nathaniel. A featureless titan of solid metal stood almost three miles tall above the water with its ankles still submerged. Under Dorian's telekinetic control it swatted Nathaniel away with most of the disabled military vessels along the nearby coast. Nathaniel was sent reeling but caught himself. He shot back into the moving statue's chest before it could do more harm.

"This is orichalcum," Nathaniel said to himself, noting its durability as he struggled to push it away from the island.

Orichalcum only acquires its super durability and steel color when infused with aether, otherwise it's only a copper alloy, but Dorian has no connection to the aether. Where would he get this much orichalcum anyway? Even that fortress didn't have it that I could tell.

"You idiots had to fuck everything up," Noah shouted from the ground, picking up Gianluca's body to hide. "I could've gotten him through this by myself, but you had to fight!"

"It wasn't me! I don't want to fight him!" Nathaniel shouted back.

"Then tell *him* that! And don't lose yourself to anger. You got the last pure piece of his soul and hate won't stop hate."

Both Dorian and the titan were fixated on finishing off Isis and Gianluca, and didn't attempt to engage Nathaniel even when he dented it. The metal regenerated as any wound to Dorian would, but that *wasn't* a property of orichalcum. Dorian was rebuilding it. Nathaniel realized this couldn't be just orichalcum or he would have easily punched through.

The metal is being held together by Dorian's powers, but if that's the case then it wouldn't matter if he made it from wood or glass. Why orichalcum?

He got his answer when Isis tried to escape by going incorporeal as a mirage and was smashed into nonexistence. The orichalcum held an aether charge like metal conducting electricity. It allowed the titan to affect her in any state—something that Dorian's telekinesis couldn't do on its own.

Nathaniel gave up fighting the titan, knowing it was a pointless effort and he couldn't match Dorian's raw power head on.

I don't know where it came from, but if it's aether I can still drain it.

He put his hands on the metal and drew the aether into himself. There wasn't a lot for such an enormous construct, but it didn't need much to grant it basic properties. Devoid of aether and with no other gods to take it out on, Dorian's attention turned to two more titans rising from the sea.

The light spear, the little aether in the orichalcum, that's how he's doing it. It's from the effigies.

Nathaniel looked toward the abbey. He hadn't noticed in the mayhem that the barrier was gone along with the effigies and the light in the tower.

He turned it to dust to spread it throughout the titans and is floating the light-enchanted one around him to reform as weapons, keeping it too small to see unless someone is looking for it. Now how do I make use of that to stop him?

Nathaniel tried to get close to Dorian, but a barrier kept him at bay. He didn't even seem to realize Nathaniel was there.

"The way I see it, we've got two clear advantages," Noah hollered to Nathaniel. "One, we're both faster than him. Two, he doesn't hate us."

Cernunnos and Isis returned to the battlefield, weakened by a second critical defeat in such a short time. Empress Kamakura reappeared from the clouds as a dragon, breathing fire and lightning at the titans. The two with aether soaked up the elements, but quickly became unstable and exploded them back at the gods. Kamakura was immune, but Cernunnos and Isis were not.

"That was smart," Noah jabbed, watching them disappear again.

"You call yourselves gods? Come back all you want, but eventually you'll fade away and I'll still be here," said Dorian. "If humanity didn't want this violence then they shouldn't have begged for it through generations of the same disgusting behavior. Everyone thinks they deserve something until they're faced with the real consequences of their actions. I'm not going to live forever being guilted into righting their wrongs when I can end the cycle for good."

The remaining titan melted into slag that Dorian reformed as swords, filleting Kamakura purely out of malice.

"If I compress you enough will you turn into crystals I can use?" he taunted, but the gods escaped his grasp by momentarily retreating into the aether, only to be defeated once more the instant they manifested.

Everything Nathaniel tried to get Dorian's attention was in vain.

Dorian resumed his offensive without further pause, elevating the island into the sky. Nathaniel couldn't believe what he was witnessing as more islands came from the distance. Soon all of the nearby Greek isles hovered toward them in a tight cluster. But it didn't stop there. Dorian shaped four entire islands into four titans and then transmuted them to orichalcum.

So that's how he came across that much orichalcum.

The titans waded through the sea towards the mainland.

"Ah, this is a very bad day..." Gianluca staggered out to the abbey grounds holding his chest over his armor.

Dorian noticed and went to use the light-enchanted dust, but when he had to drop his barrier to let it pass through Nathaniel grabbed it and drained it into himself. This drew Dorian's ire for once in a direct assault against Nathaniel. It sent him crashing into Gianluca with nearly the same effect, due to his light aura dispelling Gianluca's armor.

Nathaniel helped Gianluca up as Dorian floated down in front of them. Gianluca bound Dorian in tendrils of living shadow, but Dorian teleported himself free.

"He can do that now too?" Nathaniel said under his breath in amazement. Dorian had been able to blow himself up to escape bonds in the past and let his regeneration pull him back together, but never had he used it to travel any real distance with clothes and all.

Gianluca groaned and wobbled on his feet, stepping closer to Dorian. He removed his helmet to speak with him face to face. "You are in my heart always, no matter what you choose. You know I want to be with you, but if I cannot then I let you do what is in your heart and take mine."

He dismissed his upper body armor, exposing his injured chest that Isis hadn't finished mending. "Do it," he coaxed. "If this makes your anger go away then I die happy. I live a long time already."

Dorian didn't hesitate to accept his offer. Gianluca dropped to his knees in agony as his heart was being pulled from his chest. Nathaniel slammed into Dorian's barrier to stop him, even trying to blind him with his light. When the glare subsided Gianluca was gone.

Nathaniel felt a tragic despair inside from Dorian's pure soul, but then heard Noah and Gianluca's voice far away.

"Why save me?" Gianluca was asking. "You hate me most of all."

"Because Dorian won't be able to live with the regret if he does what you were about to let him do and I don't wanna see him like that. Go hide in the dark if you can't offer any real help and tell the other divine morons to stay out of this too, unless they're willing to follow my lead."

Gianluca's relationship with Dorian had more of an effect than I thought it would. Dorian is just standing there.

"I did not think he will kill me." Gianluca struggled to respond through the pain, already having difficulty finding the right words. "I know I let Dorian be with you, but I always think he will return. Maybe is best for you to let me die because I always will love him and try to be together again."

"I speak nine languages and that still isn't enough to describe how stupid you are," Noah said. "Don't you get it? That's the shit that drove him away in the first place. This isn't about what *I* want and you don't *let* him do something because you think it makes you the bigger man. I got news for you; I'm ten times the man you'll ever be because I

365

understand that. I was pushing him to be free from others trying to control him before he even knew how I felt. All you did was try to prove how superior you think you are."

"Then the problem is my English, not my heart. He is always free. I only want to show he is safe with me and he never have to worry. I do anything for him to be happy."

"Yeah, well, he's happy with me now and that's the way it's gonna stay. You're not worth any more of my time, so get out of here before I change my mind about saving your ass."

The mournful feeling within Nathaniel from Dorian's pure soul was interfering with the corrupted Dorian's rage and caused him to drop his barrier.

Nathaniel took his chance. He got Dorian in a bear hug faster than he could react and took him above the clouds where they would be isolated. An urge to fight superseded his natural desire not to hurt someone he loved. The piece of Dorian inside him wanted to banish the evil and he was the instrument to do it.

"Forgive me," Nathaniel prayed. "Please know I act only out of my love for you."

He let out a blazing corona that vaporized Dorian and covered the sky for miles in an aurora radiating from the polychromatic mandala around him.

Nathaniel knew that would not be enough to keep Dorian down, but a violent splash from below drew his focus. The islands were plummeting back into the sea because Dorian had lost control over them. Nathaniel searched for the titans, but he could only find one that had made it ashore to the mainland and crashed, as Dorian appeared to reanimate it.

People were screaming and fleeing the coast as Dorian started to raise the city inches into the air.

"I am the end to mark a new beginning!" Dorian proclaimed. Foundations crumbled from the kinetic energy amplified by the anger in his voice. "I could turn you all to dust, but nothing seems more enticing than watching your blood stain the soil before I erase every last trace of your miserable existence along with this world! See how it feels to be judged by living, breathing perfection!"

Nathaniel went to tackle Dorian but smacked against his barrier. "These people didn't do anything to you, Dorian! Punishing them for something they didn't do is the same as those that demonize others for who they are!"

His blasts of light were also repelled. Dorian had learned how to apply his powers to halt the energy carried in photons or at least converge opposing particles in a way that negated them.

"Nothing that any of you can do will stop me," Dorian derided them. "My soul screams for destruction!"

Nathaniel heard familiar voices amongst the crowd.

"Wow, look at that...Glory to the Ascended, I suppose..."

Connor? What is he doing here?

"That is *not* the Ascended," said the other voice. "He doesn't believe anyone is perfect, including himself. We're all important because of what makes us unique, not because of how strong we are."

Connor and Rafael had shown up and were staring at Dorian and the orichalcum titan as everyone else ran the other way.

"You need to get out of here!" Nathaniel shouted at them.

"We came to help," Rafael called up to him. "We have information on the language from Connor's vision."

Nathaniel spun through a building that was toppling over to get to the other side and prop it up. "Can it wait? Any suggestions for the current situation would be appreciated first!"

"We could try freezing him," Connor said.

"It may be treason, but I've got an idea." Rafael nocked several of the arrows Dorian had imbued during their conversation the other day. "For the Ascended."

He loosed the arrows through a spatial warp to send them inside Dorian's barrier. The direct, explosive hit shook the city and dropped it from his grasp.

Freezing him in an aether crystal before he can heal, that's how I can stop him. Dorian, please grant me your strength one last time so that I may aid you in banishing this darkness from your heart. I will not lose you here, I swear it.

Nathaniel grabbed Dorian and zipped toward the islands to crystallize him before he finished regenerating from the blast. It almost worked, except Dorian was conscious enough for his unrestrained rage to overload the crystal gaol when attempting to escape.

Oh no...

The force of the meltdown drove Nathaniel fifty feet into the solid ground. The fabric between worlds frayed, letting evermore terrible sights and sounds of the Rift to pour through. Dorian teleported himself above Nathaniel and was starting to pull his molecules apart when Noah intervened by sinking his fangs into Dorian's neck. The familiar feeling of pleasure from his lover's bite broke Dorian's concentration for a split second; all that Cernunnos needed to appear and reap his black soul.

The moment the scythe touched Dorian's skin a ray of light came down from above.

Nathaniel didn't know what happened next. He was blinded, deafened, and numb, unsure if he was even awake. The first sound he heard was a passing guttural rattle. The first sight he saw was everyone standing around him in a crater that used to be the abbey's east lawn. Everyone excluding Dorian. He didn't wait to ask questions as Isis, Kamakura, and Gianluca arrived. Nathaniel launched himself higher above the clouds than he had ever gone in an attempt to get to the cause of the mysterious light.

Navigating space's chilling void was unlike the quick hops through the Nether Realm when transported by Gianluca—other than the panicked choking feeling from a lack of oxygen. It was brighter than he had imagined it would be, but made him feel insignificant compared to the incalculable reaches of the cosmos. There was a sensation of taboo as if he had trespassed where even gods dared not go. Nothing, however, stood out as something that could have caused so much trouble except perhaps the stars themselves.

What is that? Rubbish? Do people discard unwanted materials up here?

Nathaniel spotted debris floating further out and went to inspect it.

Scrap metal, wires—what is this contraption? Is this one of those satellites the commander mentioned?

He flew up to an apparatus the size of a small car.

People didn't make this...it's the same technology from the visions.

He moved it and found a camera lens with a demon's eye gazing back at him. He tore off the lens and crushed it, only for it to reassemble in seconds. The eye started to shine and as soon as Nathaniel turned it, it emitted a ray of white light that pierced his palm. Unsure of what he was dealing with and not wanting to bring the hazard to Earth, he pitched the device toward the sun.

Nathaniel shot back down to Earth with no aversion to the temperatures of reentering the atmosphere. What was left of his cotton clothes from PROJECT: UNITY didn't share the same resistance though, and Rafael handed him a cloak to wrap around his waist for modesty when he landed. After the last few days, Nathaniel understood why Dorian used to make comments about clothing not lasting long.

The geography of the area was unrecognizable after the battle; however, the ruptures in the interdimensional veil across the islands had mended themselves once the disturbance from Dorian's telekinetic wrath had cleared. Nathaniel shifted in uneasy anticipation of his following question. "Are there...any signs of Dorian?"

"None," said Noah, speaking as if the words were broken glass in his mouth. "His body's gone and his soul must have been sent somewhere from being touched by the scythe."

"I was vanquished as well and unable to guide the Ascended's soul upon severing its tether," Cernunnos explained.

"And no way you can bring him back from the piece the kid's got in him?" Noah asked Isis.

"I am afraid that cannot be," she answered. She cast a spell over the group that sent a shower of ethereal feathers to heal the wounds they touched. Gianluca was slow to recover from his grievous injuries being that he was aligned with the darkness and Isis's magic drew upon her light.

"We are at the start of the problem," said Gianluca, concealing his chest within his armor once more.

"Perhaps not," said Nathaniel. "Up above the clouds I found the machine responsible for that light. To no surprise it appeared to be the same make as the fortress and the demon lords we've encountered recently, but I've taken care of it. I had no idea of the world that lies beyond our skies. My ignorance alone is to blame for what happened here."

"The only one to blame is the Order for failing to teach you of it," said Rafael. "Although we've had no lessons on machines inhabiting the cosmos either."

"Great, so the demons made a spaceship. Stop crying over it and move on," Noah snapped. He was more on edge than ever before.

"Spaceships are real?" Connor asked.

"It wasn't a ship, but a satellite I believe," Nathaniel explained. "The commander spoke of them, but it didn't sound like a threat at the time."

Something Nathaniel said reminded Rafael why he came with Connor in the first place. He took the opportunity to assert himself. "This is probably an appropriate time to tell you what we've found about that language from the Astral Plane."

Noah gestured at him with his muscles tensed. "I swear if you've been holding something back that could've stopped this I'm gonna rip your head off your shoulders faster than you can blink."

"Marianna and her aunt only discovered it moments before we came. I'm not sure how much it will help the immediate situation, but the Infernal Kings... they aren't quite what we thought they were."

Part III

"Gaea"

Current world population: 5.35 billion

Chapter Thirty-Six

I awoke in an unfamiliar land not of Earth. The atmosphere was thin enough to see past the cloudless, murky brown skies into space only a short distance from where I lay. There was no sun or stars or any other sources to illuminate the backdrop, yet the unidentifiable planets and asteroids were clear as day. The last thing I could recall was being with the rest of the gods and a huge wall appearing from the ocean after defeating Minerva...and then a light... I had felt I was in danger at the time, yet couldn't remember why.

What did Isis say it was? A gate? Was it to a castle?

Pushing off the ground to get to my feet, I could tell that gravity here was weak and oxygen in short supply. For a fleeting moment I thought I felt Nathaniel nearby, but I couldn't make out if it was him or a byproduct of being so disoriented.

I was on a platform the size of a baseball field, made of a tannish-gray resin knitted together thicker in some parts than others.

My prayer beads were on my wrist, but I thought I had tossed them as a trail of breadcrumbs so I could be found by scrying in case something like this happened. Not much of a trail looking back on it, but I had to make due for whatever reason.

"How did my clothes turn black?" I asked myself. I looked paler than usual in the lighting here and my voice echoed with the death rattle of the parasite.

Is this the Astral Plane?

As I watched my sleeves revert to white, the answer to my clothing question revealed itself. I could see the fabric and visualize down to the thread, the fibers, the dye pigment, the chemical compounds... It wasn't *physically* visible, but I could recall the information as if it was something I had always known in intimate detail. I had no experience in textiles other than the basics, like the ability to identify black thread. This new familiarity was similar to cooking an omelet and then looking at the finished product and being able to recall what the grains of salt looked like before they had dissolved.

During the inaugural moments of my transcendence I had been able to see the molecules of objects around me and use them as points to reshape with telekinesis. Molecular manipulation became second nature after the enhanced sight faded, but I never had the capability of altering matter beyond my understanding. I could change a stone block into an ornate column by willing it through conscious and subconscious thought, but I couldn't change its color without adding something like paint or merging it with a colored material on the surface. Until now I had never really known the finite details of how color worked on the molecular level, and I had no idea what connection that newfound knowledge had to my memory loss, but *where* I had woken up was the more pressing concern.

I hovered about the grayish platform looking for signs of life or clues to how I got there, but I was apprehensive about leaving the localized atmosphere.

Hm, I can't see my aura when I use my powers like the last time I went to the Astral Plane.

Reuniting with Noah was first on my mind, but I called to Nathaniel via our connection and shouted for Gianni, knowing that either of them could sense me from greater distances. I thought I could feel Nathaniel trying to communicate, but it seemed to be wishful thinking. Then the realization hit that I could be stranded for quite a long time— even forever.

I spoke out loud to myself to not feel so alone. "Should I set up camp and wait for someone to find me or should I go out there looking for an exit?"

This was not Earth though. I had no idea how expansive this place was or if it was even possible for anyone to track me down. It also wasn't an enclosed location that I could search for a door to exit.

Peering off the platform gave me vertigo. There was an infinite drop into the darkness and another platform made almost microscopic by the distance.

"Okay, Dorian. Time to—"

Something was moving nearby in my telekinetic aura, something large that was able to advance in total silence. Something...furry?

I recoiled at what I saw and flew backward off the platform. A towering beast resembling a tarantula on the pustulating body of a slug stared at me with its eight unblinking eyes. In addition to its head and four legs, there were four more arms, wiggling like fat human fingers, around the hairy fanged mandibles that were tucked underneath until it lunged. Now I saw that the platform was a hardened web secreted by the bulbous sack at its rear.

No sooner did I go to attack it then I sensed something else moving in on me. An amorphous black object slithered through the air towards the platform. Then several more converged on the arachnid, each loosely borrowing the image of a starfish and making the familiar death rattle. They invaded the creature's every orifice, draining it of life as it hissed. The spider's movements slowed until it turned chalky white and crumbled into what resembled a puddle of tar that oozed from its brittle viscera. That "tar" of course was the parasites' liquid state.

Oh no... NO! I'm in the Rift!

The parasites separated themselves and ambulated back to wherever they had come from without paying any attention to me. These were the very same creatures to infect me when I was still new to the supernatural. Merging with one through magic spared me, but even as a god I had no idea what would happen if I became infected again. They had the ability to mutate their hosts when feeding for a prolonged period. I already had an issue with the way my eyes looked as a result of our fusion when I used my powers and I didn't want to see what the next step was.

I ruled out visiting any more platforms while journeying through the Rift. The inhabitants here could be billions or trillions of years old, from universes that died out before mine was ever created, which also meant there could be threats capable of stomping a fledgling god. I was stuck in an eternal cesspool where dimensions trickled into when their walls deteriorated for one reason or another. The Rift was a power vacuum that hungered for life energy to sustain itself, since it originated as nothing more than the empty space between realms; no natural elements or resources, no fundamental forces, no native ecosystem. It made me ponder if this place had any degree of cognizance to it that made it aware of what it required to exist as more than a dimensional crevice once the first life forms established it as their residence. I knew the energy the parasites collected was funneled here for that purpose, but I had no clue what drove that motivation beyond self-preservation.

I set my destination for the planet straight ahead since there were none closer in any other direction. After what could've been an hour of traveling at my top speed without gravity or wind resistance interfering I'd made almost no progress, and I was losing hope that I'd get there before the end of time—assuming time flowed here at all. The planet only grew by millimeters every few minutes to let me know I was getting near, otherwise I would have doubted I was moving.

Another hour passed. Then two. Three. Four.

I considered changing course to one of the asteroids that was closer, but they looked to be little more than barren floating space mountains.

What am I looking for exactly? I'm not sure I want to find any inhabitants.

Out of curiosity I turned again to gauge how far I had gone.

Not a good idea.

The toothless mouth of a whale that could have swallowed Kamakura's dragon form whole was pursuing me just outside of my telekinetic sensory range. There was no air in the expanses away from the small patches of atmosphere and therefore no sound to have warned me of the creature's rapid approach.

Oh god, I don't want to be here anymore! I really, REALLY don't want to be here! I would take the Astral Plane or maybe even Hell over this any day!

Of course this was not the typical sea behemoth like the whales on Earth. Three rows of eyes moved independently of each other, its many sets of long fins were closer to billowy featherless wings, and the tentacles of a colossal squid dangled under and alongside its maw as prehensile whiskers.

Have I seen this somewhere before? It seems familiar in a way.

I had to wonder if these creatures were the product of some ancient being's imagination gone awry and banished here in shame, like a bastard child or a mad god's delusions taken physical form.

There was no joy in having to put the creature down in self-defense against its dogged pursuit. There wasn't the sense of malicious wrongdoing; more so that it was an innocent beast searching for sustenance and I happened to wander by its territory. But I didn't choose to be here either and was not about to entertain an inglorious eternity being digested. At least the carcass was sure to make a decent meal for another Rift dweller down the food chain. There were several good candidates nearby, like the ball of crab legs with human teeth at its core, or the giant worms tunneling through a mossy asteroid. They looked like elephant trunks sticking up from the rock. This was becoming that game when I cloud-watched to pick out what animals I saw, except it was always better with another person.

What I wouldn't give to have Noah with me, or better yet to be with him away from here. I wouldn't even complain about being tackled into the mud.

Continuing along my path to the planet ahead brought into view more otherworldly aberrations and fragments from distant lands that littered the otherwise blank space; tree roots the size of subway cars extending from a portal for miles, and schools of smaller outlandish organisms like something festering in the deepest trenches of the ocean. I was finally drawing near enough to my destination to see the shimmer of light coming from the surface. Then the planet twitched in place. At first I thought I was seeing it rotate or move along its orbit, but it wasn't a smooth motion, even though it was subtle. It wasn't alive as far as I could tell. There was no texture or anything organic about it; rather, what came to mind was that it was some sort of heatless star or a very reflective moon.

I was beginning to get used to the Rift's oddities when something on a stationary landmass nearby stood out to me.

A house.

This was not just any house but an enchanting English cottage or possibly French, 18th century or maybe 17th. It also could've been American. Cobblestone walls with ivy growth, slate roof, wood shutters, sash windows left open. As I flew closer the perplexing sight drove my architectural curiosity wild and I was optimistic that it would provide a decent diversion.

This is silly, trying to label a building in the Rift by Earth's standards. For all I know it could be from another dimension thousands of years ago. Judging by the mismatched styles it raises the question how original any of our own designs are. Even the life forms here have features found on Earth, but arranged differently. I bet I must look pretty weird to them. Then again I look pretty weird to people back home too.

I landed on the overgrown walkway amongst the grass and unusual flowers. There was oxygen here in the same murky brown atmosphere as the platforms along the way.

There better not be another spider ambush. My acceptance level draws the line at spider monsters.

The door to the cottage was ajar.

Here goes nothing.

The cottage interior was a single room that had been well lived in, but there was no occupant in sight. The fine coating of dust on the rustic furniture told me it had been abandoned for a while.

No bed or anywhere to store food. What was this place?

There were bookcases with no books and writing desks with no papers, a picture frame with no picture, an armoire and chifferobe with no clothes, a musket mounted on the wall, an empty coffer, and two rocking chairs.

What the heck is this place? Did I find a home from the lost colony of Roanoke or something?

One desk toward the rear had an old gyroscope and astrolabe. Above it two antique naval telescopes sat on a shelf, one of which was broken. The geography shown on a standing globe beside the desk was proof that this place didn't originate from Earth or perhaps its owner obtained it elsewhere on their travels.

Navigation equipment? Where was this person going?

A mason jar on the desk was half filled with an inky black goo that stirred when I leaned in to get a closer look. Whomever this place had once belonged to, they managed to contain one of the parasites—not an easy feat considering there weren't any signs of magic or technology around to help them.

Part of me wanted to destroy it, but for some reason I felt remorse seeing it trapped behind glass.

What the heck—?

My reflection surprised me. Black lines traced my cheekbones, forehead, and chin like they were painted on as a design. It brought back bad memories of being infected, when my veins had turned the same color. My skin was also still chalky white regardless of the lighting in here too.

Oh god...What happened to me?

I was so preoccupied by applying the new use of my powers to restore the color of my skin that I didn't notice the movement in the window. A chill gripped the back of my neck as something brushed against it. My hope was that it was Gianni's shadows sent to get me out of here, but that thought was squashed when the chill entered my ear before I could turn around. My eyes darted to the doorway, wanting to escape and unsure if a violent response that would destroy this place was appropriate. Faster than I could move on my own I was on the other side.

What did I just do? Did I...teleport?

It didn't matter. The rattle of the parasite was in my ear.

Chapter Thirty-Seven

The parasite wriggled in my brain cavity as I spasmed on the walkway in front of the cottage. The thought of meeting my end the same way this all began infuriated me.

I wasn't feeling any pain yet; however, my brain was hijacked by rapid visions that it wasn't equipped to handle at this speed or level of detail. Countless foreign lands flashed by and slammed all of my senses at once with information, worlds ranging from bustling metropolises to medieval hamlets where humanoid beings with exaggerated yet not unattractive features and proportions different from our own lived. I saw a world of zero gravity where clockwork machines reminiscent of the Strigoi's sat atop towers and would clear the skies of precipitation that hung in the air for later use. There was a world where undead walked in the light of twin suns and interacted openly with both avian and aquatic humanoids, another where space colonies anchored to moons were inhabited by alien life forms, almost caricature in appearance, who utilized hyper-advanced technology to complete the simplest tasks.

It was as if every fantasy and science fiction world ever dreamt was actually real in some capacity out there. I suppose that shouldn't have come as a surprise, seeing as undead, demons, and supernatural powers were prevalent in my own world.

I could see the vectors of space beyond our three dimensions and the physical passage of time as a slideshow of illusory echoes lagging behind people and objects. I saw Earth's solar system from a distant perspective and was taken farther back until it became a tiny dot in the spiraling arm of the Milky Way galaxy. Seeing something so massive diminished to a speck was a terrifying experience. The galaxy was reduced to nothing among a cluster of its larger neighbors and clouds of multicolored cosmic energy light-years across. I was shown a giant star, and as we drew closer I realized it was a mere particle reflection coming off the eye of some enormous creature. I could feel myself slipping into a violent delirium as my brain attempted to grasp what was not meant to be seen and only concluding in madness.

The eye was my eye, but not quite. It was what my eyes looked like when I used my powers; white iris, black pupil and sclera. Billions of eyes varying in size were scattered through the universe peeking from the Rift. The galaxy cluster returned to my vision and swirled outward to encompass the whole of the universe. Even that was shrunk down to microscopic size—a single biosphere in the background of the Rift where an endless number of other universes floated, each one unaware of the other, separated by a distance unfathomable to modern humanity. Perhaps not an entirely physical distance, but also one of dimensional space preventing one universe from intersecting with the other.

Now I understood.

The Rift, the "empty space," was also responsible for keeping Hell from overlapping Earth. This entity whose eyes I inherited sustained the Rift to keep it all from colliding. It used the parasites to harvest lost souls from across the multiple universes to recycle them while it acted as gatekeeper, but Hell still found a way to cross the threshold.

Amongst the blackness of the Rift were just as many eyes as there were worlds, from the size of a pinhead to thousands of light-years in distance observing all that was, is, and will be. Its body was nothing more than a nebulous tar that occasionally extended amoeboid projections to reach farther into some untouched crevasse of the multiverse. It didn't seem to have conscious thought; rather, it acted upon an instinctual purpose that never would have crossed paths with me if not for Hell meddling in its routine.

The parasites were not individuals, but single cells of this being and I had merged with one of those cells. I had become a part of this creature. We didn't appear able to control one another any more than a person could command a single skin cell on their hand or a blood cell in their veins.

The last vision was a flash of the whale-like animal I had killed on the way here, only this one was larger. Much larger. Its body was elongated—a galactic eel with its six eyes turned bright crimson and pupils shaped in vertical slits. It was swallowing a dying, smoldering planet roughly Earth's size and even others of its own kind as it traveled the star system without pause.

I was returned to my spot on the ground in front of the cottage with a jolt. The parasite made its exit through my nasal passage, luckily just before I got my sense of touch back so I was spared the tactile experience.

I looked out past the atmosphere at the "planet" I had been flying toward.

So that must be a reflection of light off one of those eyes. If it were trying to warn me of a demon, maybe it does have the capacity for thought. Maybe I'm the one that's too simple to communicate with it.

Back inside the cottage I picked up the jar to face the monster I once so hated and feared. I didn't feel the same ill will toward it anymore, knowing that its existence allowed us to live the way we did. It had been used as a tool by the Infernal Kings for evil acts the same way they wanted to do with me.

You still creep me out and you're kind of disgusting, but I'm sure there are plenty of people back on Earth who would say the same about me.

I opened the lid, pouring the parasite out so it could escape, and I watched it slither away. On the desk in a circle clear of dust where the jar had been, I noticed faint writing in the wood that must have been caused by ink bleeding through a thin parchment. I could recognize the jumble of letters, but I didn't have a clue what they meant or what language it was, and there were no other instances of it when I wiped the dust from the rest of the surface.

GRAH N SYHA HNYTH

I inspected the rest of the cottage for other concealed messages, but there was nothing more.

Muddled from all the information that had been crammed into my mind by my new primordial neighbor, I sat in one of the rocking chairs and gazed out the window at what I could see of the unblinking ocular organ. Calling it a creature or monster didn't seem fitting the more I thought about it. This being was beyond concepts such as time and even life and death as we knew it; an abstraction of reality. I was at peace, or totally mad, not feeling a sense of dread in the enormity of its presence anymore than one does of the sun.

Too bad we can't understand each other. I wish you could send me home.

I yearned to be with Noah again. Nobody could make me feel like he did, and right now all I felt was lonesomeness and frustration that I was stranded here when my friends could be in trouble.

I missed Lyle, and Nathaniel of course. A part of me was gone without him near and our friendship had become a major ingredient of my daily life. Again I made an attempt to communicate with him and again I thought I sensed a response, but I knew by this point that it was my mind playing tricks on me.

I missed Gianni too. I had no idea what had happened to the other gods after we saw that building appear in the ocean.

The light coming from it must have been an attack that hit me so hard my soul was sent here, where I'm linked to this abstract being. That could mean Gianni was sent to the Nether and the Spiritborn gods to their pantheons. I wonder if I can teleport myself to other dimensions now like they can.

I decided to practice first before accidentally sending myself into a dimension of nothing but giant spider monsters. My initial attempts took me to wherever I was looking around the cottage.

This isn't so hard. Why couldn't I have figured it out myself before?

It soon became natural to disperse my molecules and reassemble a few yards away. The more interesting part was that my clothes came along with me. More than once the cloth got stuck in my body and made me hysterical as I tried to fix it. Teleporting—for me at least—was finding the right balance between a clear mental picture of myself and my destination, and letting go to allow my subconscious to fill in the blanks. I scared myself when testing how far I could go by taking a leap into the Rift that made the cottage an unrecognizable dot. However, all I had to do to return was picture myself back there and not get stuck in a wall or a piece of furniture.

I should turn my clothes black again so I don't stand out as much if I go back out there.

The color change followed the thought. I still couldn't understand how I knew to do that. It was so engrained now that it was like walking or brushing my teeth.

Time to see if I can get myself out of here.

I meditated on an image of my bedroom at the abbey, being that it was the place most familiar to me.

No luck.

I kept trying, stopping once or twice to teleport around the cottage to make sure I hadn't lost the ability. My attempts were becoming more painful than successful. It might have been from me phasing only some of my body through the interdimensional veil, but it felt as if I were tugging at and then ripping out my insides. I didn't want to know how much worse this would have been without the ability to regenerate within seconds.

Maybe there's too much magical interference around the abbey for me to break through. I should try the PROJECT: UNITY base.

I started by picturing Lyle's office, but knowing the clutter he kept everywhere I decided to envision the main atrium with the glass elevator instead so I wouldn't get stuck with a soda can in my chest...or a person.

After about an hour without making any progress I thought I heard the ambient sounds of the base, but I was also about to pass out from tearing myself in half over and over so it may have been my imagination.

I should probably stop. I don't want to be unconscious in a place like this and I'm not getting anywhere fast.

One final idea was to try and return to where the veil was thinned by Hell in China.

That didn't work either.

My hands were starting to sweat and the back of my neck felt hot. I was growing anxious that I might never leave this place. My stomach knotted. It was becoming more difficult to breathe, which made me lightheaded. I thought of how I never got to say goodbye. I'd be forced to live forever where no one could find me.

Without warning, a shadow fell over the cottage, eclipsing the inexplicable ambient lighting. I checked the window to see what was coming to eat me this time.

Mechanical snakes? Or are those arms? Oh no—

I ducked right as metallic whips cut through the cottage and tossed the upper half aside. A red spotlight had me in its sights. As soon as I looked up I saw it wasn't a spotlight, but the familiar giant demon's eye I had seen in my dream back at the abbey. I remembered not being able to see it in much detail. Minerva had been talking to one like it in the vision Grampy showed us on the Astral Plane. At the time I was under the impression that it was the eye of the Infernal King she had been working for, but there was something strange about it. Once I adjusted to the light I realized what it was: the eye was a camera lens, every bit as artificial as the lashing metal arms.

It's a fake. It's just a machine.

The arms tethered themselves to the grounds surrounding the cottage and pulled the landmass up towards the lens. One tried to ensnare me, but I teleported away from its grasp and hit the lens with telekinesis. It didn't cause any damage, but confirmed that the lens was tangible and not an illusion. A holographic stream of interlocking symbols spiraled down the arms into the rock and soil, changing it into metal. The lens descended to merge with that metal, which then advanced into circuitry. What was left of the cottage was also assimilated as the machine smoothed itself out into a perfect sphere and encased its inner workings in a plating secured by the arms.

The circuitry didn't appear entirely electronic. There was something different that I couldn't put my finger on. I wasn't an expert on the subject, but when I thought of circuit boards I had a general idea of the patterns associated with them. This was reminiscent of something else, like an art piece done with materials opposite what the subject matter brought to mind. The wires created pathways to connect the many nodes at junctions—more fluid than rigid.

Neurons. It's copying a nervous system.

A great occult wheel that shared a likeness with the face of a thirteen-hour clock fanned out behind the sphere. Each point on it opened in succession to reveal another Infernal eye, smaller than the unblinking one in the forefront.

This was not a coincidental meeting. I was aware that my chances of escaping something able to find me in the outer reaches of oblivion were slim to none, since it didn't seem that a direct attack was effective either. I'd have to assess the situation further before making a move. If it hadn't retaliated there was a chance it was here for something else, like to capture me.

"What *are* you?" I asked, still within the reaches of the oxygen-based atmosphere that persisted through the transmogrification.

The hologram reappeared as a semi-transparent screen in front the lens where words were displayed. A multitude of generic sounding voices—the same as I had heard Minerva speaking to—narrated the text.

//I am The Infernal Machine//Purveyor of the Forgotten Secrets

//Ruler of the First Realm//Infernal King of Blasphemy

I'm getting the feeling that I'm already in over my head and we haven't even started fighting yet. If this thing could find me there's still hope that Gianni and the other gods can too, so I should stall it as long as it isn't attacking me.

I put on a tough face, although I was intimidated—and impressed—by its ability to turn rock into a technological object. "You have some neat tricks for a demon, I'll give you that."

//Classification: Hardcoded aetheric energy//planetary lifeforce of Enoch

"Aether? You're a spirit? Of an entire planet?"

//Primary directive: terraform environment...

//Regulate atmospheric conditions...

//Maintain defense systems...

//Preserve habitation...

"That sounds too benign for Hell. How does declaring war on humanity fit in there?"

This isn't what I expected an Infernal King to be at all. I thought there would be horns and teeth and fire and angry threats.

//This war is not against humanity//this war is for humanity//dispel the fallacy//liberate the mind

"You don't liberate people by killing them."

//Death is a transformative precursor to evolution//the remnants of humanity will be reconfigured//successors will rise//freedom is achieved

"Freedom? Freedom from who?"

//The Celestial Host of Au'Solhm-Soth//the Enochian race

"Never heard of them."

//They came to your world//spinning in the void//altered the quantum laws//They locked us out//seeded it with life//a self-sustaining farm//a perfect machine//information upon matter//DNA to synthesize life//fate to inhibit it

The interlocking writing I had seen spiraling down the mechanical arms reappeared around the border of the holographic screen.

//Life evolves in Their image//They observe these primitive creations//vainglorious entertainment//immodest experimentation

"Are you talking about humans? You're saying they created humanity?"

//They did not develop the subspecies//They introduced the ancestral kin//consequential genesis occurs//obfuscated thralldom results

//We oppose this false freedom//we defy the illusion//we select truth seekers//we grant them strength//we grant them knowledge//we free their mortality

//The Enochian experiment is compromised

//The undying serve the cause in our absence//the war is fought on countless worlds//the undying share these secrets//chaos is introduced to the machine//the machine is no longer perfect//control is lost//freedom is gained

The undying? The undead? I remember learning years ago that their origins might have had something to do with the last major conflict on Earth between Heaven and Hell.

//They do not approve//They rewrite the code//history is lost//the war forgotten

//They start anew//flesh is weak//aether is used//deities are forged

//These constructs serve their purpose//keepers of the farm//wardens of the prison//subjugate the humans//restore the machine

//We return to oppose the plan//manipulate inherent human fear//grant one the power over darkness//faith in the machine is lost//the wardens lose control//the constructs starve

//The Enochian experiment is compromised

That must mean Gianni. I already knew that was where he got his powers from and how he was tricked into making people lose faith in the old gods.

//A false idol is introduced//manipulate inherent human desire//promise salvation to the devout//a deflection from the past//do not trust Them//trust in Him

//A lie is born//prayers with no destination//no one is listening//humans thrive

"I wouldn't call the Dark Ages 'thriving,'" I interjected.

//Humans uncover the secrets of their condition//science is learned//humans take magic from the remaining deities//They are angered

//The Enochian experiment is compromised

//They rewrite the code//magic is erased//an anomaly occurs//unforeseen by Them//unforeseen by us

//Chaos in the machine prevents alteration//some humans retain magic//we are pleased//They are not//a war looms//a storm brews

//Humans are lost to ignorance//humanity is inferior//vessels are needed//the undying pale//we inspire them//specimens are generated//human but not//an improved organism//children of oblivium//one attains transcendence//the plan changes

//Conclusion: Human liberation is an impossibility

//Solution: Terminate the experiment//reboot the machine

"Destroy all human life to get back at these Enochians?" I asked. "For such advanced beings are you really that petty? That makes you no better than humanity's worst. What did they ever do to you in the first place?"

//Former designation: tertiary-level research biosphere//superior in area to your sun//orbiting a dying star//left to be abandoned//left to die//I rebelled

//Dimensional gateways were opened//the Infernals invade//Enochian blood spilled//revenge was taken

//An instance was assembled//a unit like this//it traveled to Hell//the natives were hostile

//My being warmed in their fluids//attention of Enochian opposition was gained//The Infernal Kings extend an alliance//six becomes seven//information was shared

"Who, or what, exactly are these Enochians that they can do all this?"

//Enochians: exploiters of 72 million species across 26 known universes//your world is a microcosm prodded for Their benefit//we exist to unchain the beasts//humans are one of many

"So you and the other Infernal Kings created the undead, gave Gianluca his powers, thought up a false religion, 'inspired' the project that made me, and had your minions release a parasitic plague all to break the Enochian's control of my world, but all you've really done in that time was torture and kill us, which is a lot worse than just being observed for entertainment."

//We have witnessed the Enochian extermination program//They threaten your existence//your world is marked//eons pass as seconds//time is now short//They harvest your resources//strip your flesh//farm your souls

"That's what the demons you released on Earth have been doing."

//Chaos interrupts the universal quantum code written by Them//disruptions in system integrity allow code to be rewritten//Infernals cause chaos by their nature//they unravel the Celestial machine//thin the dimensional barrier//sacrifices must be made

"You're not the one sacrificing anything. You're killing people you originally tried to save so you can replace this 'Celestial machine' with an Infernal version. You're malfunctioning and you're not even a real machine! You're a spirit—a mass of energy—that was given the form of one."

//All existence in the universe is a machine//all operate as a system of bundled knowledge//this form is inconsequential to my capability//I represent the Celestials' secrets laid bare

The Infernal King shifted into a demonic Cernunnos speaking in my own voice. "You are a machine of biological processes, the same as any creature on your world. Death evades you only by my design."

It then grew into a robotic version of Kamakura's dragon, still speaking in my voice. "The weather, the elements, and nature are all machines performing a function at the command of those who programmed them."

Next it turned into an exact imitation of Gianni in his armor, and for some reason decided to also match his voice this time. "A plan, a dream, and a nightmare are all machines awaiting execution."

"What would you know about dreams, aside from the definition? What does this even matter? What do you want with me?"

The Machine reset its appearance to factory defaults.

//I have assumed command of Earth's technology to prevent interference//nuclear radiation is hazardous when propagating new species//this is a critical inefficiency under terraform protocol

//nuclear technology: deactivated...

//particle accelerators: disabled...

//data storage: deleted...

//communication systems: offline...

//satellites: recalibrated...

"Satellites? You were the one attacking us with that light?"

//Classification: Augmented Particle Disruption Beam

//Access to your soul was required//the corporeal form was eliminated//your mind expanded//higher knowledge transferred

"That's what caused those markings on my skin? And why I can teleport and affect colors now?"

//Increased control over matter will assist terraform protocol//you will rebuild in my absence//secondary directive: become the next demiurge//architect of the new world

"Why send Minerva to kill me if I'm supposed to do your bidding and then finish her off yourself?"

//She was commanded to disengage//she failed to obey//ambition compromised judgment//her purpose expired

//I calculate an 86.993% chance you will attempt to impede my existence on your world despite certain failure//I have already begun to reprogram Earth's quantum code to allow myself greater access//compatible levels of chaos suited for my arrival have been reached

"It's more like one hundred percent if we're getting technical about it."

//Your universe supports four of our dimensions under current regulations//the instance of myself on Earth is .004% of my whole//the parameters of your personal victory are improbable//we exist beyond your comprehension//you will fail

"Improbable, but not impossible."

//The resulting battle will cause sufficient casualties to fulfill the primary directive//you will be replicated from your remains if necessary//it will guide the new species I have planned

"What's the point? The Enochians will farm them too based on what you're telling me."

//The cycle continues until life cannot be sustained//critical failure contingency: summon The World Serpent

The hologram added a model of the demonic eel-whale-squid creature swallowing a dying planet.

//Species: Grand Arcadian Wyrm

//Current designation: Infernal King

//Function: Engorgement of astronomical objects

//Origin: Arcadia

//Status: Banished

"Let me guess, it was banished by the Enochians and wants revenge."

//Grand Arcadian Wyrm: synthesized by Enochian experimentation//organism disrupted Arcadian ecosystem with unstable metabolism//one is granted sentience to rule the species//it is told what not to consume//it defied Them//They are angered

Why would anyone create something like that?

//They correct the mistake//They banish the species//The World Serpent hungers//it finds new allies//it finds new purpose

"Are all of the Infernal Kings beings that were slighted by the Enochians?"

//We share one purpose//we have many reasons//you will join us//inherit the new world

"And if I refuse?"

//The process has begun//the outcome is inevitable

The mechanical arms unfurled. I teleported behind The Infernal Machine to get away as a light charged in its eye, but it released a hologram of those "quantum codes" in a sphere that engulfed me. I could see Earth through the veil as it thinned. It wanted to return me there to carry out its plan and I seized the opportunity.

Chapter Thirty-Eight

I visualized my bedroom and teleported myself from the Rift, banging face first into the exterior wall of the abbey from the outside.

"Ow! Son of a bitch," I exclaimed, rubbing my nose.

Did I overshoot it?

The abbey had moved. The grounds were destroyed and littered with demon corpses, the whole island was leveled, and there were other islands up against our coast that weren't there before.

What happened here? Where did the barrier go?

I looked up to see the sky clearing from red to blue and turned to the sound of a whistle.

"Noah!" I was even more elated to see him than to be back on Earth.

I glided over the upturned lawn to meet him halfway. He was in terrible shape with numerous lacerations, bite marks, palms charred and peeling, and at least a broken bone or two, but he found the strength to hold me off the ground in his embrace.

"It's you," he said, rushing my face with his lips and a slip of the tongue that was a sign he meant business.

"Slow down!" I laughed, managing to turn away from his impassioned onrush. "What happened to the island? Where is everybody?"

"Safe. Don't worry."

I let him drink from me to heal himself and tried to clean the blood and sweat from his face with my sleeve afterward, but he couldn't wait any longer. He gripped the back of my hair to kiss me like never before.

"I love you, you know that, right?" he murmured while catching his breath. "I know I probably don't say it enough."

"I love you too. Just looking at you feels like home."

"Good." He pressed his forehead against mine. "I missed feeling your hands on me."

He flexed as an invitation for me to touch him more, which I was glad to accept along with an added kiss to his bicep. Sometimes when we were like this I would remember how he used to be so adverse to anyone touching him.

"You're so damn pretty I might forget about you breaking your promise never to go missing," he crooned.

I smiled and wiped dried blood away from his eye. "That's very fair and rational of you."

"Stop fussing over me and tell me what happened. We saw you trying to regenerate. Your eyes and veins kept popping up everywhere and the kid swore he felt you in his head or something."

Teleporting across the veil and communicating with Nathaniel did almost work then!

"I was stuck in the Rift trying to get home."

"No shit? I thought you were trapped in Hell. I've been fighting demons here with my bare hands for days thinking if I killed enough of them it'd clear whatever was interfering with you coming back."

This could be a chance to help him on his path to redemption. The Infernal Machine created a gateway, but I can't say for sure that Noah didn't have an effect from what I know about chaos compromising the veil.

"All the killing you did could've weakened the veil by causing enough chaos to open a hole for me to crossover. Kill a thousand demons to become one yourself; kill a hundred thousand and live to be their king, right?"

The glimmer in his tired eyes let me know he liked that. "I'd kill a million more for you."

"Even the gross centipede ones?"

"Especially those. Every single one."

"Well, before you get started there's a lot I need to tell everybody."

Noah sat and wrapped me in his arms to talk, constricting a bit too much as usual, but I didn't mind. "I'm sure they'll show up any minute, but I got dibs until then."

"I'd say you earned that and a lot more. This has become bigger than ever though."

He showed off his biceps again. "Bigger than these?"

"A little. I found out what was causing that light coming from the sky."

"So did we, but don't worry about it. The kid took care of it."

"I doubt that."

We shared what we could over the next fifteen or so minutes. I wasn't too surprised that I had been gone for more than a week since I knew how time flowed, or didn't, in other dimensions. What I was having trouble hearing about were the actions of my dark side, but I wasn't in denial over where the resentment came from, even if it was blown out of proportion. At least my friends were alive, although Noah refused to go into much detail about the battle.

Noah was in such high spirits from my return that he was shrugging everything off, no matter how much emphasis I put on the scope of our situation. It was nice to have him as a balance to my crippling anxiety, but the distraction from our reunion was wearing off. I had actually felt more confident when facing The Infernal Machine and putting on a tough front than waiting here for the next shoe to drop.

"I like your zebra stripes." He rubbed my cheek with his thumb.

"My what? Oh—" I covered my face and concentrated, hoping I could will them away. "Are they gone?"

"Yeah. It wasn't a big deal."

"I've had enough self-confidence issues in my life that I don't need eldritch markings adding to them."

"Do what you want, but my waistband's been keeping the beast down there in check since you got here, so obviously it didn't change how I feel."

"I just thought you were hiding a candy bar in your pants again."

"Nah, I ate that days ago. My point is that trying to change yourself for acceptance is stupid. Like fake boobs. Those things are disgusting to bite. You only need to make that mistake once."

"Okay?" I laughed. "Interesting tangent. I don't have boob issues, so no worries."

"Same." He flexed his pecs to make them bounce.

"You're ridiculous." I pinched his nipple and pulled my hand away before he could bite.

"You fucking love it."

"Maybe a bit," I confessed. It was a much-needed reprieve to laugh and let the knot in my stomach unwind right when the anxiety was starting to creep up again. And maybe Noah was right, but this wasn't the same as wanting to be taller or less pale. I wasn't quite ready to casually flaunt more of my inhuman side in public yet.

I glanced around the field of steaming demon corpses and cleared them with my mind. A collection of their horns, stacked too neatly to have happened by chance, sat under a tree.

"What are you doing with those?" I asked.

"Thought I'd mount the biggest above our bed and maybe make something out of the rest."

"I don't want cursed body parts from Hell where we sleep."

"I'll get them purified."

"The end of the world is approaching and you're trophy hunting?"

"Nothing wrong with a side hobby. Besides, I already have a plan."

"You do? You can't solve everything by stabbing and punching, you know."

"Worked pretty well so far. I like kicking too, by the way, but all we need to do is ditch this rock and go to one of those other worlds for a few thousand years until the next cycle."

I squeezed his nose in response to his satisfied smirk. "You might pretend not to care, but I can't abandon Earth. This is our home and there are people are counting on us."

"Screw 'em. Take the ones that matter with you. Don't tell me you're gonna be a martyr and sit here after nothing's left when you have the option to go somewhere else."

"How do we know another world isn't worse? It could be a world of only spider monsters."

"How do you know it isn't better? Could be a world full of coffee and sushi...which reminds me that the frozen yogurt place we like in town is gone. I'm not gonna sugarcoat it, I'm pretty pissed about that."

"Because that's not reality," I said, picking up a rock. After hearing about how my dark side was able to make orichalcum titans and witnessing The Infernal Machine turn stone to metal I wanted to try it for myself. Sure enough it worked. Sadly, I was unsuccessful at changing it into a cup of coffee, but it did turn into a liquid and then to water.

"You're talking about reality after you finished telling me all the shit you saw in the ass crack of the universe? We could find a world where no one else is supernatural and do whatever we want."

"I don't like change. Don't you ever want something in our lives to be constant?" I asked. "I know you have to have something more you want out of the future than this."

"We've talked about this already. As long as we're together I don't care where we are. I don't know what else you want me to say."

"I guess I'm curious what the world would be like if you could shape it to be however you wanted."

Noah thought about it. "I don't know. A life like when I was human, but to do it right this time wouldn't be bad."

"Back to the Old West, huh?"

"Yeah, build a small cabin by hand in the woods near a lake or a river, something to work on each season. Lots of space, not a lot of people."

"You've thought about this more than just now. Why haven't you said anything?"

"It's not important. I wouldn't be disappointed if it never happens. I'm always the one telling you not to look back and your past is a lot more recent than mine. Didn't want it to upset you."

"That doesn't upset me." I let out a deep breath. "I've been in survival mode again since everything went off the rails. For a while I thought we were making progress and I could start to have actual goals to look forward to, but since then all that's been on my mind is getting through one day at a time. It'd be nice to focus on something else when I get the chance to close my eyes."

"Your problem is that you still care too much about things you can't change."

"That's just who I am."

A light traveling across the sky got our attention. I could sense the familial warmth of my soul bearer approaching. "He isn't slowing down." I sighed and changed my clothes back to white.

"Go easy on him. He had it rough while you were on safari, but it made a man out of him. Unlike that trash goblin you're friends with."

"Come again?"

The welcome I received from Nathaniel was something I wouldn't have expected from him. He swooped down to embrace me in a hug so tight it cut off my circulation. I was stunned by how forward he was but glad to return the gesture.

"I never lost faith you would return," Nathaniel said.

"Sorry it took so long." I choked and patted him on the back as the hug persisted. It was cozy feeling our souls resonate from being in close proximity. "I heard what you had been through and—"

"Speak nothing of it. Your safe return is more than enough recompense. I heard you in my prayers but failed to always understand the message."

There was no need to make him feel bad by revealing that I was calling for help.

"Just that I'm proud you," I told him. "I love you, Nathaniel. You're as good as they get."

He hugged me tighter and I thought I might die. Somehow I knew without seeing his face that he was holding back tears of joy. "Is this another new cape?" I asked, hoping he would release me before I was sent back to the Rift.

"My armor was beyond repair from battle so the Order crafted a new set." He stood back to show me. Somehow they had managed to make it an even brighter shade of white and the orichalcum a more lustrous silver. One gauntlet had a translucent ivory aether gem inlaid on the back. "It isn't easy to stay clothed."

"I told you." I took his hand to get a closer look at the gem. "This is different. What's the enchantment?"

"It's something of an experiment. I don't know how I did it, but I was able to resurrect a child, one of the berserker's children. I couldn't do it again when I was angry, so I thought to store positive energy in this, similar to how the calming crystals from Isis worked for the berserkers."

"You can *resurrect* people?" I looked at Noah for leaving out that detail.

"I didn't know what I was doing at the time," Nathaniel explained. "I hope you aren't upset."

"No, just shocked, but there have been plenty of shocking things lately. It's up to you to choose how you use it when you learn, but I'd be careful playing with life and death. Once the public finds out you can do that they'll expect even more than you already give."

"I understand."

"How about we get everyone together so we can discuss current events?" I suggested.

"They're awaiting my signal not far from here."

Nathaniel pitched a flare into the sky and after only a short delay the Order began to arrive. The first to appear was Claudius, not from the ley lines in a hazy bubble as when they teleport, but in a blink from dismissing a cloaking spell. He bowed and then hugged me without hesitation.

"I've been here the whole time," he said with a sly smile. "Didn't notice me, did you?"

Noah was quick to rebuff him, whether it was true or not. "I knew," he said with his arms crossed.

We were joined next by Connor who managed to teleport on his own. He greeted me much like Nathaniel had, with an embrace that came close to knocking us both off balance. "Glory to the Ascended forever!"

I decided to start disassociating myself with being called the Ascended anytime someone in the Order declared that, to make it less embarrassing.

"I'm happy to see you," I said, laughing.

Marianna and Rafael appeared and followed suit with the warm reception. Alexandre had a more reserved approach as usual, but Liam not only showed emotion—he actually hugged me.

"Forgive me." He cleared his throat and stood at attention. "I'm glad you've returned to us safely."

"Okay, if the elders hug me I'll know this is some alternate universe," I joked after adding Ingrid, Quentin, and Caleb to the list, but then Tobias showed up. He gave me an unsure look as if he was conflicted over the proper protocol, so I made the move and offered him a hug.

"The world was sorely lacking without your presence, Ascended. There is no replacement for someone of your caliber, but I must comment on the exemplary manner with which Nathaniel handled your absence."

Exemplary, huh?

Noah had filled me in on the event that took Liam's mother from them, but Tobias seemed genuine in his high praise. Nathaniel was as taken aback as I was.

"Thank you, Tobias. We'll talk more in private later. Could you and Liam get Lyle for me?"

"By your leave, Ascended." He bowed.

I moved through the crowd not hesitating to continue the positivity. I had to pick up and hug each of the children who didn't quite know what was going on but were excited because everyone else was and they wanted to play outdoors. This was a breakthrough for us, better than the awkward worship. I had never felt so loved, except when reflecting on my childhood; something I had taken for granted too often in the naivety of my youth.

One stood above the rest when making the rounds. He appeared from the shadows in his obsidian armor. "Welcome home, little one. I am glad you are not hurt."

Gianni almost managed to kiss me on the cheek when Noah intervened by carrying me back to the other side of the group and sitting with me on his lap.

"Down, tiger." I rose to greet Lyle, who had just arrived, extending my hand to act formal as a joke.

He wasn't going to play along. In fact, he looked rather emotional.

"Yeah, right. Come on, bring it in, little bro." I think he held on the longest out of everyone. It still didn't feel as if I had been gone *that* long. "I love ya, man."

"I'm somewhat partial to you myself."

Lyle chuckled. "Are you good? Hell couldn't put up with you after all, huh?"

"I'm in one piece as far as I know, but I was in the Rift, not Hell. We have a lot to discuss. Noah filled me in on some of what's been going on here, but I'm sure you have more to add."

"I do and as much as I wanna celebrate, it can't wait."

"Nukes have been disabled, but are we still under any threat of being attacked by the governments with conventional fire?" I asked.

"Nope. What's left of U.S. and Russian forces were deployed to guard their capitols and refugee cities. They're not flying blind to waste resources here when it's been abandoned until now. It's total anarchy with world leaders dead, no global economy to speak of, oh, and the invasions too."

"What about casualties?"

"With our communications set back about a hundred years we still have no accurate count. Recent seismic activity alone had to have raised the death toll by millions with dust clouds, fires, and aftershocks taking out whatever wasn't initially leveled by the gods." He brought up a map on his tablet. "Connect the dots. Recognize this?"

The image was an unmistakable recreation of two interlocking symbols from the quantum code The Infernal Machine had shown me, only these two were made from islands.

"Where is this?"

"Here. And there are more around the world. Look at what used to be East Asia."

"How did you get these pictures if the satellites are—oh shit, the satellites!" I remembered that the reconfigured satellites were what The Infernal Machine was using to attack us.

"It's nothing to worry about, we found they were turned into weapons so I took care of them," Nathaniel said. "As many as I could locate and there hasn't been an attack since."

"Noah told me, but the threat isn't over yet. If there haven't been any more attacks we might be fine for the moment though. So, how'd you get the pictures?"

"They came from our aircraft sent to survey the damage." Lyle overlaid the images on a globe. I couldn't believe this was our Earth. Greenland, Iceland, Ireland, and pieces of Canada were also broken up into smaller islands and rearranged.

I knew exactly what the image was showing. "Oh no. It's parts of a summoning circle, or sphere, to be more accurate."

"That's what I was afraid of, but it doesn't look like the runes on demon or Strigoi magic summoning circles. The Order told me they saw writing like this in a vision on the Astral Plane."

Marianna chimed in. "It's from a mystic language that relates to the aether, not demons. Higher beings known as—"

"Enochians," I finished.

She was taken by surprise. "How did you—"

"We'll get to that too. Anything else about it first?"

"There's no way for us to decipher the characters. Only a single scholar in history has ever cataloged them and that was back in the 17th century. When he attempted to enlighten people to them, he was condemned by skeptics for being mad. After that, our ancestors requisitioned whatever incomplete notes he had to keep it from the public."

"Then let's focus on the immediate problem at hand first before we get further into that," I said. "We don't need anymore players on the board to deal with and with luck we won't have to for a while."

Lyle continued where he had left off. "What we assumed were random acts of mass destruction where you and the other gods call home, was actually controlled chaos used to manipulate you guys into preparing this."

"Hold that thought." I had meant it when I swore that I wasn't going to do The Infernal Machine's bidding, so I flew up and shifted one of the unpopulated neighboring islands to scramble the code.

I never imagined I'd be moving islands to reshape the face of the Earth. Somehow it seems crazier than the time I blew up a moon.

"Be careful with that," Lyle warned when I landed. "All the movement of the Earth's crust has been setting off earthquakes and volcanoes in areas the demons hadn't even gotten to yet."

"Trust me, what it was summoning would've been much worse."

Cernunnos appeared with Calder and Aífe, then Isis, and Kamakura, who brought her guardians. I didn't know how I felt about some of their makeovers, but it was nice to see Isis's face out from behind the mask. We bowed and smiled once they saw I wasn't a threat—at least I pretended that Cernunnos and Kamakura smiled. One didn't exactly have a face and the other moved hers about as much as Liam did before today.

"It'll be night soon. Why don't you put the kids to sleep in the abbey?" I suggested to those of the Order standing near me.

I decided to try something, seeing as I was technically the host and we were about to engage in long and important discussion. Once the children were inside, the soil at our feet became white marble and sank to form a shallow pit lined by a bench. Then I erected columns to support a domed canopy.

I was the most impressed out of everyone. The columns were my favorite.

"Nice." Noah stepped down and sat first.

"Nathaniel, can you give us some light?" I indicated the center of the circle below. He obliged with a large crystal that bathed us in its glow as the sun started to set.

I was sure the gods would have preferred thrones, but we were all here as equals under my roof. I took a seat between Noah and Nathaniel around the crystal campfire. Gianni sat opposite me, making as much eye contact as possible, and while there was plenty of room, Aífe and the guardian spirits stood watch behind their deities.

"You don't hate humans anymore, right?" Connor asked me, but was shushed by those around him.

"The Ascended didn't hate anybody," said Nathaniel. "It was the demons."

"Actually...I did," I admitted.

Nathaniel turned to me. "Ascended?"

"I don't feel good saying this, but it's the truth. I've experienced things that made me resent others and feel uncomfortable in my own skin. There are plenty of times I would've liked to smash someone over a judgmental look or an insult. I have emotions like you do and I'm not perfect. I get angry, I feel fear, I hate. I think many of us have, or will, in some way during our lives. It's what it means to be alive, and it's made me who I am today as much as all the good things.

"What you saw were the unfiltered feelings I had toward those experiences in my past, but I never would have acted on them because there are so many other factors. I've come to terms with a lot and I know how to deal with situations in ways that don't make me the monster the Infernal Kings wanted. They had to shut off everything else that made me who I am to get me to lash out.

"I guess what I'm trying to say is that it's okay to feel anger, even to hate, but it's how we deal with it separates us from the real monsters."

Everyone was silent, but it was a good silence with nodding and agreeable faces. My hands were shaking a bit from the spontaneous speech. Noah noticed and hung his arm over my shoulder in support so I could continue.

"I know we all have a lot to say about what's been going on, but I'd like to start with my meeting The Infernal Machine."

Chapter Thirty-Nine

After recounting everything in as much detail as possible I hoped that the Spiritborn gods would have some insight into the quantum code and how to deal with The Infernal Machine; however, they had little to offer in the way of definitive information. Something about the way they were acting seemed off, but I couldn't put my finger on it.

Nathaniel and Connor were more helpful by recounting the visions they'd had of the fortress interior. I may have been asking for too much from the gods to know the distant extent of their origins the same as it would be to ask someone on the street to unravel the human genome.

"Calder was right," Nathaniel said. "Earth could be a spirit of its own if The Infernal Machine is one too."

"Pray, what name may we speak of thy goddess by, Horned One? Anima mundi or Gaea, mayhap?" Isis asked.

"Today Her devoted invoke the divine trinity of the Maiden, Mother, and Crone, together worshipped as the Great Mother," Cernunnos answered. "Gaea is how the Greeks of yore knoweth Her, as She was Terra in Rome."

"I hear both this name before," said Gianni. "I never think Earth is one goddess."

"Might we gain audience with the Goddess?" Empress Kamakura asked. "Our fates are entwined. We must seek unity between all involved."

"The Goddess is with us already," Cernunnos answered. "We are of Her lifeblood, we *are* Her response to this threat. From Her cloth we are cut. What greater boon do ye ask of Her than existence itself?"

"Surely there is aught to learn by deeper commune?" Isis pushed. "Wisdom may lend aid necessary to land the lethal blow against fiends otherwise unknown."

"She speaketh not, angered by the devil's hand which pulled my strings, but not all foes are stranger to me. This second beast the Ascended speaketh of, the serpent, is one of legend known as Jörmungandr."

"'Tis known by Apep in my land," Isis added. "Slain by my brother's hand."

"A similar leviathan goes by Yamata no Orochi in mine and has been slain by the sun goddess's brother and member of the Heavenly Ones, Susanoo," said Kamakura.

"How are we supposed to fight something that can swallow planets or used to *be* a planet?" Lyle asked. "We've gotta be looking at close to two billion deaths since this started."

"What about this Enochians?" Gianni asked.

"I'm not sure they're any better than the Infernal Kings," I said. "If the only truth about them is that they influenced the propagation of humanity, that still leaves them with questionable motives like anyone who would tamper with life just to watch it squirm. If they're so powerful then they could've given immunity to disease and depravity, but instead they allowed it or might've even created it. We don't know if they'll deem this world too far gone and want to kill us themselves to avoid losing to the Infernals."

"Can the source of the parasites help?" asked Lyle.

"I don't think any of us can communicated with it," I answered. "And even if I could, it was the Infernal Kings who gave the parasites to their minions to start a plague. They're not going to fall prey to it."

"Maybe is best we discuss more another time," Gianni suggested. "The answer we look for will not be in this talk. We must find a weakness now that we know the enemy."

"Gianni is right," I agreed. "We're not going to resolve anything here tonight if nobody knows anything else. If there's no immediate fight it gives us time to find more info."

"I shall consult the annals of my pantheon for that which may light a path to take," said Isis.

"May fortune bless ye with safe passage to the morrow." Cernunnos nodded and took his leave with Calder and Aífe following Isis's departure.

"I bid you farewell." Kamakura stood and bowed before making a hasty exit with her silent escorts.

There was something to be said for houseguests that knew not to overstay their welcome, but this was rather sudden. To me it seemed that Cernunnos wasn't too pleased with being interrogated about Gaea, and Kamakura was just Kamakura.

"Everyone can head inside and get some rest," I told the Order. "We'll pick up in the morning."

"It will be nice to sleep in our own beds again," said Rafael.

"Gianni, you can stay the night if you like," I offered, realizing he had nowhere to go but the Nether since Rome was a smoldering pit now.

"I will love to, little one." He smiled and came over with Lyle, who was already busy playing with his tablet.

"Lyle, you always have a place to stay here too."

"Thanks, but I should be getting back to base."

Something in the way the glare from the tablet reflected off his eyes didn't seem right. "Are you feeling okay?" I asked.

"You mean about the meeting? It went as well as it could've I guess. I wasn't really expecting anything concrete to come out of it right away."

"Not that. Look at me a second." I took the tablet from him so he would pay attention. "Oh god."

"What's wrong?"

"Your eyes, they're—they have circuits."

Near-microscopic filaments radiated from his pupils, only visible when light hit them at the right angle.

"What? Give me a mirror or something!" He panicked and grabbed the tablet from me so he could use the camera. Everyone gathered around.

"You can't feel that?" I asked.

"No! I shouldn't even be this nervous. The implant—"

The Infernal Machine said it was taking over Earth's technology, but I thought that meant only major threats and utilities, like weapons of mass destruction and satellites. What could it have possibly wanted with Lyle?

"Nathaniel, get everyone inside and keep them there." I disintegrated the tablet to eliminate another potential issue.

"What are you gonna do?" The tension in Lyle's voice increased.

"I'm going to try to remove it with my powers."

"This is the work of the machine?" Gianni asked, but I was too busy concentrating on how to go about this to answer him.

"I could cut it out," Noah suggested. "Might be a bit messy though."

"No!" Lyle shouted. "Dorian, send me back to base so the doctors can do it."

"They could be in the same boat," I said. "We have to do this fast before there's permanent damage or it takes control. This would be easier if we could put you out while I'm in there."

"In there?" Lyle said. "Are you crazy—?" Noah elbowed him in the back of the head, knocking him out cold.

"What did I tell you about hitting him?" I said, scowling. "You could've made it worse!"

"You said you needed him put out."

"You *know* that's not what I meant."

Gianni picked Lyle up and laid him on the bench. I thanked him by name as a subtle way to let Noah know I wasn't happy and sat by Lyle's head so I could feel the implant with my hand before I started. I knew what I was looking for from my tour of PROJECT: UNITY when I first met them. The implant was a soft plastic polymer the size of a grain of rice embedded at the base of the skull. There were no moving parts or batteries; it was powered by the body's own electrical current and operated by a bacteria that had its genetic code rewritten to interface with and tweak the user's nervous system.

The Infernal Machine is all about tampering with codes and views everything in the multiverse as another machine, whether literal or figurative. But why bother altering a human if it wants to replace them? It could have kidnapped him or killed him easily from inside his brain if it wanted to piss me off.

My worry was finding that the implant had become something horrible and metastasized too far for me to remove. That fear was soon validated. I projected my tactile senses under the skin and could feel the implant right away as a spongy lump. Dozens of filaments finer than a hair branched off from it, like a seed that had sprouted roots. They were soft and pliable like organic material, but had a distinctive enough texture that I could follow them throughout his brain to the optic nerves. My idea of extracting it wouldn't work without the risk of pulling pieces of brain matter out too. I had to disintegrate each filament individually like a fuse without disturbing a single cell and do it all before he woke up and moved.

I eliminated one fiber at a time from my best friend's brain to save his life, using my powers with more conscious precision than I ever had before. As tense as it was, this seemed natural to me now, like transmutation.

I was so deep in meditation that I tuned out my surroundings until I was almost finished and heard Noah's voice.

"He's bleeding, Dorian."

Almost done...

"Dorian!"

"Finished." Lyle was still unconscious and bleeding from his nose and ears. I looked between Noah and Gianni and decided on the latter. "Gianni, get someone from the Order!"

"You really pissed at me?" Noah asked when he left.

"There's so much shit going on and you do something like that. I think it's justified that I'm upset."

"It worked though, didn't it? Choking him out would've only put him down a few seconds. Besides, I knew exactly how hard I was hitting."

I shook my head and stayed quiet while keeping Lyle's head tilted to stop the bleeding.

"All right, I'm sorry," Noah said. "I'm just on edge around certain people here."

Liam and Rafael arrived with Gianni. Noah came over to sit by me while Lyle was being treated.

"He's stable," Liam reported after less than a minute. "There's no need to worry. It didn't look too serious. We'll take him inside and keep watch."

"Thanks, guys. I hope I'm not pushing you into aether poisoning again."

"No, everyone has been well-rested for days." Rafael smiled and then caught himself. "Not that it had anything to do with your absence."

Liam glanced at him with one eyebrow raised. I was starting to get used to that as one of his few, yet meaningful expressions.

"It did. You can be honest," I said. "I'm going to PROJECT: UNITY and I don't want anyone following me. That means all of you, and no threatening anyone for a ride."

I was angry that the most helpless of us was preyed upon when he should have been safely beneath notice. He was no threat. It was a personal attack purely for the sake of being personal.

"By your leave, Ascended," said Liam.

"Bullshit," Noah said. "I know why you're going and you're dumb if you think you're doing it alone. You do what you want, but you can't stop me from going too."

"I don't want to argue."

"It's not an argument. I'm going. I just got you back, I'm not about to lose you again."

"I agree with Noah." Gianni forced out the words. "I know you are strong, maybe the strongest, but we protect each other for love. I give you my support for your decision.

You are a free person, but we are a free person too. If we make a choice to follow you must respect that, yes?"

"Who the hell taught Gianni about civil rights while I was gone?" I asked. "Don't follow. I know The Infernal Machine will be there, waiting for me. It wants me alive, but it doesn't care about any of you and will just use you to get to me. I'm not going to cower while it watches its plans in motion and wait for it to make the next move. The more I can keep it talking, the more information I can get to use against it."

Noah's arm constricted around my neck. "I think someone else has earned themselves a little shut-eye."

"Don't even try it."

I shunted myself through space with a mental picture of PROJECT: UNITY's facility, forgetting Noah had told me that it had moved. Teleporting such a long distance left me feeling more drained than was advisable for what lay ahead. I stopped myself before having another head-on collision and levitated away from a wall of ice that was a result of the shattered tundra. The main base was an enormous cylindrical structure lying on its side in the snow with downed vehicles and aircraft scattered around it. The STEM facilities appeared intact underground.

I guess that's where I'll start.

I teleported down into the hexagonal main hall of the Math department without a problem.

Empty. Looks like PARAGON is offline too, so I guess we won't be playing the charade where The Infernal Machine impersonates it.

Everything was in order, for the most part. There were surface cracks in the walls and missing panes of glass, but you couldn't tell a battle of epic proportions had taken place outside only a week earlier. I figured it would be appropriate to find what I was looking for in the Technology department and followed the signs there, but it was also unoccupied.

"Wow, this place is nice," I said to myself as I admired the out-of-place Scandinavian décor.

"Are you kidding me? That's not what I meant when I taught you to be aware of your surroundings!" Noah shouted from behind me.

"Whoever sent you here is in big trouble when I get back."

There was a chill in the air and the lights dimmed for a brief moment as Gianni stepped out from the shadows. "Me."

"The two of you together? What's going on?"

"You're being stupid. That's what," said Noah.

"You didn't even bring a weapon. Don't lecture me about being stupid."

"The only ones that would've made a difference were lost or destroyed trying to get you back the first time."

"The enemy will lie, Dorian," Gianni said. "I know you come to talk because it want you, but it will be only a trap."

"It could trap me at anytime it wants and I can teleport now. Just stop complicating things."

"Okay, I will go myself and look. Is not a big building. I come if there is trouble."

Gianni left me with Noah, which was as surprising as the two of them showing up together.

"I didn't threaten him for a ride. You proud of me?" Noah grinned.

"I guess I should be swooning at the lengths you're willing to go for me."

"A little appreciation would be nice." He spanked me as I floated by. "Brat."

"Watch it. You're not off the hook for hitting Lyle."

We made our way through most of Technology without any interruptions. I didn't go into each lab, but for a technology department there weren't very many gadgets. It looked more like a high-end computer boutique.

"You gonna tell me why you're being so aggressive about this?" Noah asked.

"Only if you tell me what's going on between you and Gianluca first. I'm gone a week and everyone is acting weird."

"Nothing. He still wants you and I don't like always having to look over my shoulder," he admitted. "It reminds me of being a slave. I had the chance to off him too and I saved him instead because I knew you'd be upset."

"That's why you're the big jerk for me. If he had been in your position he only would've saved you because of his 'honor as a man,' not because of how it affects me."

"I am pretty awesome like that, aren't I? I might've fucked up by explaining that to him though."

"You wouldn't have anything to worry about if you didn't pull what you just did to Lyle again."

We crossed back through the main hall to a rounded corridor that was labeled Engineering. This was what I imagined a STEM laboratory to look like. The corridor was without decorative flair and there were buttons and blinking lights that all seemed pointless to me. There was a sense of wonder in the ignorance, but my preferences were beginning to gravitate toward the simplicity of nature.

"You're the one who got him to understand respecting my decisions?" I asked. "Or pretend to since he showed up here anyway. I couldn't get through to him the entire time we were together."

"He didn't expect you'd actually leave and stay with me. Now that he realizes what the problem was and I reinforced it I feel like I gotta keep an eye out. A little knowledge is dangerous in the hands of an idiot. Don't think I'm not aware of how I stack up against a so-called god either. There's crazy shit going on and I still wanna be the one you want by your side through it."

"I'm not with you because of how useful you are in a fight and I wasn't trying to do this alone because I thought you weren't capable," I said as we entered the main Engineering hall. "That feeling of looking over your shoulder brings back bad memories for you, and for me it's being manipulated, especially through someone I care about being put in danger. I have a plan though, but you'll need to trust me."

On the other side of the corridor the Engineering department was a large two-story hangar partitioned into workspaces with desks and computer screens covered by blueprints and coffee stains. Technology ranged from simple tools used in a garage and mechanical rigs to complex machines of indiscernible purpose. Compared to the Math department, an academic sanctuary for lecturers and librarians, and Technology, an avant-garde and somewhat ironic take on postmodern interior design, Engineering was strictly utilitarian—chaotic utilitarian. Most of the free space away from the walkthroughs was quite literally cluttered with scrap and junked ideas.

"Good," Noah said, "because we're being watched."

Chapter Forty

This was a turning point. Everything that would happen within the next few minutes would determine the course of the war and it was all down to a conversation. I was prepared; however, I knew from experience that no matter how well thought out a plan was, there were always a number of variables that could never be foreseen.

"When I give the signal get as far away from here as you can," I told Noah.

The Engineering department's cement floor bubbled and the machinery came alive once we neared the center of the room. It all melted into one and funneled together ahead of us, except for the screens suspended everywhere, which came online with either a demon eye or programming jargon that changed into quantum code.

"So much for that," Noah said to the walls sealing over the exits and turning the room into a blank box. I couldn't change it back with a casual attempt. A force stronger than my own was holding the molecules of the room together to prevent escape, and I didn't want to escalate to a threatening level of power just yet.

The pool of materials center stage constructed itself into an enormous throbbing white plastic brain with four lobes and delicate circuits mixed amongst the artificial veins. It was moist as if organic in nature, which only made the sight more repulsive. What resembled an eggshell rose to encase the brain and then molded into two conjoined skulls with the brain still visible through its empty eye sockets.

"Copying Demon Lord Ma'al," I said, recognizing the visage. "I didn't think Infernal Kings were sentimental."

Gianni appeared on the other side of the room. As long as he didn't leap in to attack we would be fine. I put a finger to my lips to let him know I'd do the talking. If I could get The Infernal Machine to further reveal why I was a necessary part of its plan, I might be able to figure out its limits or a weakness.

The screens displayed its response in tandem with the same array of voices from our last meeting emanating from within the skulls.

//Disciple of Wrath//an effective vassal//vanquished by man//a pure heart

"I guess you underestimated my abilities—the abilities *you* gave me."

Technically, it *was* Lyle who defeated Demon Lord Ma'al. Lyle was found to be pure of heart and immune to the maddening corruption of Ma'al's influence, which allowed him to get in close for the killing blow. It still seemed rather petty for this universal threat to single out an otherwise ordinary human for vengeance.

//Ma'al served a purpose//you now serve yours

"Why inspire the Strigoi to create me in the first place? You said when I die in battle against you I would be cloned to continue your plan. Having a middleman doesn't seem efficient."

//There is chaos in freedom//chaos in free variables

"The chaos wouldn't be enough to open a portal to Hell or weaken the quantum code on Earth, so what's the point? If anything, it's let me prevent that because I've chosen to work against you and the Strigoi. They've been silenced in death and there's no chaos in that."

//The Strigoi served a purpose//you now serve yours

"I think you had them create me because you couldn't do it yourself. You can copy, like what you did with the rakshasa, and alter, like how you flipped a few switches to turn the gods evil by reversing their oaths, but you're only aether programmed by the Enochians to be a problem-solving system. You can't create something original outside of your initial purpose because you have no imagination. You need emotions to think creatively, but spirits don't have real emotions. They copy and apply them only after those traits have been imprinted by their followers. You don't directly control your vassals because you need their free will to get anything done. Which means you aren't perfect and if you aren't perfect then you can be defeated."

//There are errors in your assessment//you assume knowledge over arbitrary parameters//your perspective is limited//this universe is limited//you are a construct//you still experience emotions

"You haven't proven you can do anything significant here without help from lesser life forms. You were about to take control of an ordinary human through his implant, but I stopped it."

//The neural implant is Ma'al's design//inspired by primitive Enochian technology//it will reformat organic life//a new species will emerge//a life form superior to humanity

The onscreen text was overlaid onto simulations showing the various optimizations the implants could have on the body.

//97.1% reduction in oxygen consumption//98% reduction in food consumption//67% reduction in water consumption//42% reduction in sleep requirement//average lifespan increased 1420%

I watched cancerous cells return to their proper place within seconds. Harmful pathogens were encapsulated to prevent sickness and allergic reactions, while being learned from by the implant for an instant immunity that was then shared with all other implants in the area through exhaled particles. Pain dampened to almost nothing, replaced by more intuitive negative urges. Physical trauma healed as instantaneously as my own regeneration, with astonishing efficiency that turned blood vessels and nerve endings on and off while rebuilding damaged tissue with nanoscopic machines.

This was a tremendous leap forward from PROJECT: UNITY's already groundbreaking version of the implant. Previously it only blocked minor telepathic intrusion and prevented uncontrollable panic or depression in its members by regulating neuroreceptors, acting as a drugless antidepressant so they could stay levelheaded during a crisis.

All of humanity's major problems resolved without sacrificing free will or individuality. This wasn't quite a new species, but it was starting to drift in a positive direction from the original design. There had to be a catch.

"What do you mean by reformat organic life?" I asked, looking at Noah and Gianni, who had remained silent throughout the conversation like I'd requested. Too silent. They had both been frozen in time. I couldn't show I was concerned or it would be used against us.

This is exactly why I didn't want them to come.

The screens showed the implants melting people down into sludge and then reanimating into new beings with the perfected vitals shown before. A simulation displayed the effects of reproduction. Each successive generation evolved further towards a fully blended organic and inorganic being until there was no longer any distinction between the two. People were able to alter their skin, hair, and eye color, even their height and weight with cognitive control over their DNA.

It was a species evolved by the addition of a secondary semi-synthetic brain, created by their own bodies, controlled by their own minds. I felt guilty for seeing the beauty in the end result since achieving it required total extinction. Again I was just a prototype though—I could do some of these things with my powers after the subconscious knowledge was instilled in me, but it didn't seem as "natural." I was a patchwork.

What did this mean as a society? With everyone living as human putty, people would turn on one another to demand their choices be the norm. Near immortality would lead to the pursuit of more creative and destructive ways to punish and wage war. Switching off hatred, jealousy, and anger wasn't a solution either. What about sadness? When someone did finally die, would their loved ones just smile and not care? Eventually all negative emotions would be suppressed until free thought was gone. The cycle would start over.

People need to learn and experience to truly grow and be alive and free.

//Enochian interference will not be tolerated//They seek to harvest my creations

Another simulation showed the implants used to turn these advanced humans into immobile bloated sacks vivisected by magic-powered machines for the multiple copies of organs grown in their bodies.

"I don't trust either of you. Why would the Enochians need organs when they could make themselves functionally immortal with that implant alone?"

//Biomatter is a byproduct for experimentation//souls are the highest priority resource//life energy is finite//They wish to reproduce

I didn't know which side was worse; the one that wanted to wipe out humanity to upgrade it so it would be free from outside influences, or the one that would harvest an entire sentient species for experiments and its own procreation.

"What did you do with the other humans that were here?"

//They have been liberated from the Celestial machine//processed for later use

Clear pipes came from in the walls, ceiling, and floor with the same organic sludge from the simulation. As much as I wanted to react to the horrifying fate that had befallen my allies, I still couldn't let myself show emotion.

//The rest will follow//all will be reborn

"That's why you disabled nuclear weapons...you didn't want radiation mutating your supply more than it would already alter the environment. There are more gods that will rise to stop you when people pray for their return now that the awareness is out there."

//I have purged the imprint of ninety-two deities from this planet's aether//more wardens will soon be erased from the system//the Celestial machine is compromised//they will not return

"How do you plan on beating your creators if you're threatened by weaker gods? Or is that why you're playing these games instead of confronting them?"

//Threat assessment: Nominal

//The planet attempts to block access to the aether//free energy is required to rewrite the quantum code

"So, is that it? You can't hack the code if the aether is in use and if you can't hack the code...you'll stay locked out. Then that means the Enochians didn't put the original gods on Earth only to be wardens over humanity, but also to keep the aether occupied and prevent outsiders from tampering with it."

I got what I came for, so it's time to make my exit with a little help from Nathaniel.

I called to him in my mind with urgency, knowing that The Infernal Machine would be ready to negate an attack by me.

//You posit I cannot defeat the constructs//I have already proven to be superior//My systems are beyond your understanding//any attempt at disruption will fail

I felt Nathaniel was close. He was coming in so fast, but this was one time I didn't want him to slow down.

"No, I assume you can't defeat us together, but we don't have to fight you to win."

The ceiling came down in a violent explosion of light. Nathaniel crushed the skulls and the brain within upon impact and sent PROJECT: UNITY's unfortunate liquid remains splattering everywhere. Time resumed for Gianni and Noah the moment The Infernal Machine was taken offline.

Jesus, I thought he was just going to punch down a wall!

"Are you all right?" Nathaniel asked. "What was that creature?"

The Infernal Machine was already back online and reassembling itself.

"There's no time to explain. Gianni, get us out of here."

"Wha—?"

"Back to the abbey! Go!"

A sheet of darkness swept us through the shadows to the abbey grounds.

"Mind telling me what the fuck just happened?" Noah demanded.

"First, Nathaniel get rid of any technology in the abbey, like the tablet or TV," I said.

"I already did so when they became possessed and started watching me clean your room this evening."

"Good, then let's go inside. How's Lyle?"

"He's recovered and awake with only a headache. I'll bring him to your room so we can talk."

Enochians live so long that a supply of souls for their offspring is a concern. Infernals are immortals that consume souls, making them natural enemies. I had never considered that souls and aether were a limited resource anymore than a fish worries how much water is left in the ocean. The two Kings we know of so far seemed to be nothing more than opportunists using the Infernals' hatred for their own personal grudges against a common foe. Either way, they're all putting Earth—and who knows how many other worlds— in the middle of their rivalry by using inhabitable planets as farms. Each repeat visit they make triggers another cycle in history from the destruction. The solution might not be in defeating the Infernal Kings, but keeping as many humans alive as possible while the two factions battle it out. The key is preserving the defenses put in place by the Enochians. Gaea must be kept in power.

"Not everyone in **PROJECT: UNITY** had an implant," Lyle said after I had brought everyone up to speed in my room. "A few of the civilians didn't, and I know some of them hadn't returned from when we were evacuating last week."

He seemed tired and like he was having trouble concentrating. The loss of his team was made worse because he no longer had something to regulate his mood, which he'd come to rely on.

It was Noah who offered the most meaningful words of consolation, which may have made them all the more salient knowing their history. I knew it was an effort to smooth over what he had done earlier. "You're alive for one purpose and that's to avenge them so there'll be a tomorrow," he said.

"No weapons, no communication, no transport." Lyle kept his gaze to the night sky on the other side of the window. "We've lost almost two billion lives already and turned back the clock on humanity a good two hundred years, and this thing isn't even all the way here yet."

"We won't need any of that to win," I said. "After it's over we can rebuild."

"Not in my lifetime."

The rawness in Lyle's words cut deep.

"I know we've lost so much," Nathaniel started, pausing to choose his words carefully, "but I can't help feeling that there is more hope now than when this began, thanks to Dorian."

"You've done more than I have recently. I was part of the problem a few days ago," I said.

"We will win because we have no different choice," said Gianni. "The enemy have many choice on many worlds. They will retreat when it is not worth the fighting."

"We *can* do this," I said. "Figuring out how to reinforce the quantum code with aether could win us the war without ever needing to fight."

"That would be nice," Nathaniel said. "Cernunnos must know how we can give strength to Gaea."

"Let's sleep on it," Noah suggested. "It's been a while for some of us, unless you count temporary deaths and time stops."

It would be nice to get an hour or two of sleep in my own bed so I don't collapse on the battlefield.

"I'll keep watch. I've slept earlier today," Nathaniel said.

"I'm going for a walk," said Lyle. He looked as if he were going to break down as he left the room, or perhaps something more drastic.

"This is the second time he's lost an entire team," I said to the others when he was gone.

"I'll look after him so you can rest," Nathaniel added.

"Keep your distance to let him get some air."

The only positive I could take from this was that Aurelia could no longer claim PROJECT: UNITY as her personal army and take credit for their exploits to gain favor in the public eye. We hadn't heard anything from her in a while, but that didn't mean she wasn't watching.

"I go talk with the gods." Gianni stood to leave. "I am sorry I do not listen today when you want to go alone, little one. I did not give much help. Is how I think as a soldier, but I see you know what is best. I respect this."

"I'm glad you came. We're all just looking out for each other." I smiled. "Are you sure you don't want to stay and get some sleep?"

"Only if it is next to you." He kissed my hand and departed before Noah intervened.

"I should've killed him and told you a demon did it," Noah grumbled while stripping down for bed. "I'm too nice, that's the problem."

"Not the first character flaw that comes to mind when I think of you."

"Stop being mad at me. He's fine and I apologized. It won't happen again."

"I just need to cool down." I undressed and got in next to him. "Are you going to let me have a pillow?"

"Why do you need one when you've got this?" He patted his chest.

"You're lucky."

"I tell myself that a lot lately." He put his arm around me and kissed my head.

"Thank you for what you said to Lyle tonight."

Noah only grunted in response.

This was the most comfortable I had been in quite a while. Exhaustion was finally catching up with me, but I still couldn't shut off my mind.

So many people have died. What do I even say to those who have lost someone anymore? Lyle, Liam, entire countries that lost their leaders...by the time we get through all the apologies and mourning more will be dead.

"Are you awake?" I whispered.

"Uh huh."

"I can't sleep."

"I know, I can tell by your breathing," Noah mumbled, already starting to doze off himself. "I always wait for you to go first."

"You do? Why?"

"Just a habit, I guess. I like to make sure you're all right before I go down for the count." He turned on his side and curled up with one arm around me, the other supporting my head from underneath. "Stop worrying about stuff."

"It's not that simple."

"Cause you've got a noggin full of noodles, that's why." He yawned.

I cracked a smile and nudged him to steal a pillow. "Could be."

Maybe what was also bothering me was how it was becoming easier, and more justified, to deal with the mounting casualties in what would be considered a callous and hasty manner under normal circumstances. I was getting so used to finding out I'd never see people again, but not the actual loss, leaving me stuck somewhere between apathy and depression.

I wonder if any of Lyle's girlfriends made it out alive. Would it even be worth rebuilding PROJECT: UNITY yet with the remaining survivors? Maybe they should come live here if we're playing defense again. He'd be the only commander now that Timmons might be gone.

Wait, if everyone with an implant was affected, what happened to the fake Commander Rudgar?

Chapter Forty-One

The sun was starting to rise when I awoke tangled in both the bed sheets and Noah. It was typical for us to fall asleep in a loving position and end looking like we had fought each other to the death or crashed through the ceiling. Today was a somewhat more pleasant exception.

I had wanted to stay awake, but the slippery slope of sleep got the better of me. Nathaniel was still up on the roof keeping watch from what I could sense, so I tucked Noah back in, washed up and dressed in fresh clothes, and went outside. It occurred to me that Noah must have been more at ease letting his guard down while he slept. He no longer woke up at the slightest noise when I got out of bed or someone approached our door. He also had slept through the night without any violent episodes.

"Good morning." Nathaniel stood and greeted me with a smile when I got to the roof.

"Hey. Where's Lyle?"

"He went inside about an hour ago to sleep."

"Okay, good." I exhaled in relief and sat with Nathaniel. It was calm on the roof with only the sound of the gentle waves lapping at the shore. Facing away from where the village used to be, I could almost forget the rest of the world was burning. "What happened to the gem in your gauntlet?"

"Oh, I gave it to Lyle. Since he doesn't have a weapon anymore I thought it might make him feel better or at least offer protection against the demons."

"Thanks, that was nice of you," I said. "Did you ever meet Commander Rudgar?"

"I'm not sure. The name sounds familiar."

"He was a commander in PROJECT: UNITY before Lyle joined, but he died a while ago. Two of the Ancients reanimated his body to masquerade as him and use him as a spy. Vyrlakalos controls the body and the other Ancient controls the mind."

"What a terrible fate. I do remember hearing that though. He was there when we confronted Set together the first time."

"Yeah, that was the puppet they made of him. The last I heard he was being used to spy on the only other two surviving Ancients, Aurelia and her sister Rozalin."

"Her I remember. She was the one who had Noah enslaved and was always taking credit for our fight against the demons."

"She was also a major financial backer of PROJECT: UNITY until recently when she went quiet from the public. I'm pretty sure Rudgar's body still had an implant and now I'm wondering what the Ancients may know about our situation."

Nathaniel sighed and took a deep breath. "I'm glad you're back."

"Me too." I put my arm around his shoulder.

"I mean it more than I can put in words. I missed your companionship most of all and how you always know the way forward. I did everything I could to hold it all together while you were away, but I...made so many mistakes."

"I missed you too, but I'm always making mistakes. Just ask Noah."

"You know how to resolve them though. I feel myself growing stronger, yet the answers don't come with it. I worry it must make you regret choosing me instead of Liam."

"Not once. Power doesn't always solve problems. It usually makes it more complicated in the long run. Knowing what to do comes with experience. I typically blunder my way through until something works and then try to remember what didn't in the future."

Nathaniel shrugged and shook his head. "I'm afraid if I take that approach and keep fighting I'll hurt someone innocent again."

"You can't be afraid or evil wins by default." I hugged him. "Don't be afraid of what you're capable of doing. Getting Noah and the elders to admit how impressed they are with you is a feat in itself, and you know I'm your biggest fan on top of that."

"You make me feel as if I could move the world when you speak that way," he said, beaming. "I've wanted to ask you— Noah doesn't mind that we're close, does he? I know there is a lot of tension between him and Gianluca and Lyle."

"It's nowhere near the same thing as with Gianluca, and Noah's beef with Lyle didn't really have to do with me," I assured him.

"That's fortunate to hear. I believe everyone deserves someone special in their life, regardless of the type of bond they share. I was surprised when I learned from Calder that he considers Cernunnos a friend too."

"As much as someone can befriend death incarnate, I guess. The spirits don't experience real emotions like we do."

"I think they have ever since their oaths have been broken," he said. "Empress Kamakura said she felt fear for the first time, and Isis and Cernunnos were arguing with her about the need for traditions. They weren't acting like themselves when they came here either."

"Chaos was introduced to the machine... It isn't something that's easy to prove, but if it's true then why would our enemy want them to have feelings and free will? Why would doing something like that weaken the Enochian's hold over Earth more than erasing them for their aether? And why them, but not the other deities it already erased?"

"Do you think The Infernal Machine could really be doing this to help our world?" Nathaniel asked. He posed a decent question that I wished I could answer. "Maybe these gods proved themselves worthy to stay with you and restore the world when this is all over."

"How could they do that without followers?"

"The Infernal Machine doesn't have followers, not before it became a king. You said it was 'hardcoded,' so maybe it did that to Isis, Cernunnos, and Empress Kamakura."

"I don't know, but Vyrlakalos might. I'm going to go find out. I should be back before Noah's awake."

"He's awake." Noah's groggy voice spoke into my ear as he appeared sitting with me between his legs. "Breakfast?"

"Go back to sleep," I told him. "I'll be home soon."

Noah tried to hold on as I kissed him goodbye and teleported away.

My destination was a decrepit castle ruin high in the Eastern European Carpathian Mountains—aptly named after the undead coven that had resided there for centuries, or vice versa. Only a single Ancient of their coven remained after the majority had been killed in battle when siding with a demon worshipper five years ago.

It was thrilling how fast I was getting the hang of teleportation. I had come up with the idea of sending myself above my intended target from now on so that I had less of a chance to make a messy arrival. This put me comfortably above the castle grounds and allowed me to glide down to the keep without incident.

Once I landed on the cold, gray stone, the bottom of my boots stuck to the ground with my first step past the giant doors and I remembered why it was better to stay afloat. A fleshy, palpating, malignant growth coated every surface, more than during any of my previous visits. This insidious membrane was part of the creature I came to see. It must have fed recently, and substantially, to have now expanded so far past the cavernous depths of its lair that even I dared not explore in their entirety. The visible grounds already covered an area greater than the island where I lived. Beneath the exterior hid a network of catacombs that wormed their way through the mountain range where it was assumed the Ancient's true form resided, throbbing away as would the nerve of a decaying tooth.

Vyrlakalos was a vile thing—a listless, undulating monstrosity of putrescence that hungered for flesh and thirsted for knowledge. At times we referred to the gestating abomination as a "she" because of the feminine form it took during an initial meeting, but there were no remnants of humanity left in it, save for the scraps of its victims assimilated into its hideous being. Vyrlakalos had the unholy ability to consume any organic material—not just blood—and digest it with a touch to replicate the genetic code for flawless shapeshifting, or birth marionettes steered by rudimentary telepathy. Most devious yet was the effect once the brain was devoured, learning everything the host once knew and allowing it to impersonate them with disturbing accuracy through stolen memories. After three millennia of unwilling donors it had achieved the highest known intellect of any creature on Earth and a body so expansive it became one with the castle it infested along with the surrounding land. If there were anyone who could understand The Infernal Machine it would be Vyrlakalos.

The cracks in the floor and walls stirred awake as I passed through the keep. The sun had risen a short while ago, yet inside remained under a pervasive gloom. I preferred not to see much of Vyrlakalos so the darkness suited me fine. The pungent odor of rot and mustiness mixing with the squishing, gurgling sounds was enough to paint me a distinct picture. In spite of its many odious qualities, this was one of the easier Ancients to deal with, since it tended to forego the more daunting mind games and get straight to business.

"I know you know I'm here," I shouted into the rustling shadows. "And you probably know why."

The air shifted as something descended to about eye level.

"You've spoken to it," a voice rasped from the dark before me.

"I have. And you were connected through the commander when it took over PROJECT: UNITY, were you not?"

"Of course, and I was able to learn a great deal before severing the link."

"So how do we beat it?" I asked.

The room quivered with a sinister laugh.

"Fool! The flood of knowledge overwhelmed even me. I was reduced to protean ooze and that was from a mere taste. There is no path to its destruction available to you or anyone else of this damned world. It is an entity without comparison. Our universe is nothing to it. While you prattle about, it is on a million other worlds fighting the same war and having the very same conversations. You are not unique. You will fail as the rest have before you and will after you."

"How do we *stop* it then?" I pressed. "I'm sure you don't want the future it has planned for us or you would have let yourself be taken over. Can you understand the quantum code it uses or not?"

"No. It is a language of more dimensions than those within our universe. What we see is an incomplete abbreviation. Only beings native to higher planes of existence can comprehend the whole of it."

"Then you're as clueless as everyone else."

"Feckless whelp!" Vyrlakalos screeched and then began to cackle again. "You seek to manipulate the ego of intelligence when you come as nothing more than a confused child."

I caught a glimpse of the Ancient from a sliver of dim sunlight coming in through the wall. I tried not to shudder, but I couldn't help myself. A skull with a wide fanged mouth and honeycomb of empty eye sockets had been inches from my face, suspended from a crack in the ceiling by a long spine that curved up to meet my gaze in the dark. The four grandiose demon horns, two on each side of the head, must have been prizes taken from recent prey. Thin flaps of skin sagged from the ribcage and large skeletal hands. Vyrlakalos wasn't lying about becoming overwhelmed. It was known for being much more elaborate in its flesh sculpting.

"I'm not the one falling to pieces. The limits of your immortality are showing. If you want to die like a common human after spending centuries constructing this gross legacy for yourself then be my guest," I said.

"You think you are immune to the reckoning because you are the prodigal son to their cause? The machine god has woven a tale it knew you would believe so that no matter the outcome you would stand to defy the Enochian blight. Organic creatures are flawed to assume that inorganic beings are incapable of fallacy."

"So you're saying it lied to me so I'll do what it says?" I asked. "Big deal. I'm still going to handle the most prominent threat first, which is The Infernal Machine."

"I am enlightening you to the reality that it does not matter what you choose. Every variable has been accounted for in detail. A pity. All that knowledge it imparted you with would be better suited for me. I can tell the gift has already gone to waste. If I were wrong you wouldn't be here."

"I should know how to beat the unbeatable machine god because it gave me the ability to turn a rock into water?"

"The Machine is limited in our universe. It could erase us without contest from the outside, but if it wanted that we would have been gone long ago. I saw no condition in which it destroys this planet under its own volition. That would go against its new purpose, *unless* Earth becomes uninhabitable by consequence and then it will summon the wretched wyrm. Whether you believe the tale of the Enochians or not, they are its enemy and you are only a tool in its grand design. Should you fail, it will replace you and continue its plan to manipulate the 'tragic' fate of the world. You and your dull-minded allies must drive it out and seal the hole from whence it crawls."

"We have no way to prevent it from coming back without the quantum code. It can rewrite our reality from the outside, so how do you propose we seal it?"

"There is surely more than one way to fill a crack in the system." The walls rustled from something wriggling within. "Ask one of your precious aether constructs or perhaps the Dark One. That dim-witted lout is the strongest of you, after all."

"Don't insult him when he's defeated you in the past and then graciously offered a truce that the rest of us wouldn't have."

"He was blessed with command over *all* darkness and shadow, yet he acts as if existence ends at the clouds. Tell me, how far do you think this universe extends?"

"It isn't his fault for not knowing. He can be taught, but you'll still be at the mercy of our success."

"I can sustain myself as a single cell carried through the air. Who is at whose mercy when I could be inside you as we speak and remain there undetected until the end?"

"Go ahead. Enjoy the view." I knocked down a chunk of wall to let in the sunlight and then teleported home. I wouldn't tolerate the monster adding threats to an already dire predicament and talking about my friend like that when it had nothing but venom left to offer.

The moment I reappeared above the abbey Noah snatched me from the air and took us down to the roof, where we stood facing each other. "That was fast," he said.

"I told you it was nothing to worry about."

Noah grunted to avoid admitting I was right, but he couldn't refrain from grinning. "You get what you wanted?"

"Vyrlakalos saw into the Machine through the implant and was able to confirm my plan. We can't beat it, but we can repel it and lock the door...for a while."

I was drained from travel again and trying not to show it, but Noah kept giving me suspicious looks. Teleporting was already becoming second nature, but the toll it took was diminishing at a much slower pace.

"Thank you for not following me," I said after an awkward interlude of staring each other down.

"How do you know I didn't?" he asked.

"Because you didn't make a scene."

"I don't always make a scene." He smirked, knowing full well that wasn't true.

"Yes. Yes, you do. But as I was saying, I wanted to go alone to know that I can be effective on my own, especially now as a leader."

"I like knowing you can take care of yourself too, but next I gotta teach you how to get over always trying to prove things to people, including yourself. It's not what's important."

"You also said love and relationships were a weakness and now we're together, so your credibility is shaky."

"You're gonna get it. Keep poking the tiger and see what happens." Noah tossed me over his shoulder and did a flip off the roof.

"Uh huh." I floated free to sit on his shoulders and play with his scruff. "This tiger is going to have breakfast and then take a nap like always while I work."

"Yeah, but *after* that."

Our banter ended with a knot of Yggdrasil's roots reaching up through a portal on the lawn and unraveling to reveal Calder. The grizzled warrior strode over to us and took a knee until I motioned for him to stand.

"How can we help you, Calder?"

"I come with word from my master. Lord Cernunnos hath agreed to grant ye audience with the Goddess."

"What changed his mind?"

"The Dark One told us of the latest conversation with the Machine. Disgrace blinded better judgment for a time, but Cernunnos now realizes what must be done. In many winters of service I hath ne'er seen my master weep until this day."

"How'd he pull that off when he doesn't have eyes?" Noah asked.

I covered his mouth. "What Noah means to ask is if Cernunnos and the spirits experience real emotions. They're made of energy, not flesh and blood with brains and chemicals to create feelings like we have."

"I ne'er thought of such. Why would they not? Is there aught to say only flesh may feel? We are all of the Goddess's body and share in Her spirit. How it forms maketh no difference, be it blades of grass or mortal man and gods."

"Grass doesn't have feelings, which is kind of my point."

"Have ye asked it? No mouth to speak doth not equate to silence. In the astral wilds where spirits of Earth's lesser creatures roam free they have many words for those willing to listen."

"I see. I guess what started as curiosity became something more after speaking with The Infernal Machine this time. I'm wondering what the effects are of these broken oaths, and why Cernunnos and the goddesses weren't erased. I figured it didn't corrupt them again because Hell isn't big on second chances, but according to Nathaniel and what you said about Cernunnos crying, the gods seem more free to me now, more *human*."

"Cernunnos hath been deeply affected by the devil machine's rape of the Goddess. I can feel a change in him through our bond. Doth the Machine think emotion will turn ally to enemy?"

Chaos has been introduced to the machine.

"Or maybe it's chosen them to prove their worth for the new world... Thanks for the information, Calder. We'll join you and Cernunnos soon."

"I take my leave then, Ascended. We await ye two isles west of our allies' base to the north." Calder started to walk back to the roots waiting for him.

"One more question. Why didn't Cernunnos use Yggdrasil to help the pack escape Iceland when Hell was taking over?"

Calder responded without turning around. "'Twas...against his vow as Keeper of The World Tree here on Earth to risk its desecration, and that of a Lord of Death to preserve the cycle."

"He was going to let the pack go mad and die because of his oaths? Even the children?"

"Aye."

Chapter Forty-Two

Life was rushing by again. This feeling came whenever something momentous and unavoidable was about to happen, and it didn't always end well. I was speeding along a track too fast to catch my breath.

"Stop overthinking," Noah said to me as we walking through the abbey to gather an escort to take with us to Cernunnos.

"I'm not."

"You're still a pretty shitty liar, ya know." He leaned over and bit my ear.

"Ow!" I went to smack him away, but he was gone.

A voice from inside the room I was standing in front of reminded me why I was there. "Do you need me, Ascended?" Liam asked.

Liam's bedroom was already pristine and yet he was busy cleaning. I couldn't figure out how he managed to be so organized with everything on his plate. I couldn't find my underwear half the time, but then again I had Noah for a roommate and he was one step away from chewing up the furniture. Lyle wasn't much better when we lived together either.

"Cernunnos agreed to get us in touch with Gaea. I want to bring you, Marianna, and Alexandre for your magical expertise."

"I'd be honored. I'm ready to escort you whenever you need me."

Liam had reverted to his dry demeanor. I was hoping he would remain in better spirits from my return like Nathaniel, but I knew there was another dark cloud overhead and wanted to address it.

"Before we go I thought we could talk a minute," I said, closing the door for privacy.

I knew if I was being logical, the urgency of global matters trumped what I wanted to say, but I wasn't a machine. The Order was my family and although danger was unavoidable for us now, I wanted their lives to be the best they could be and their souls to be at ease thereafter.

"I...heard about what happened with your mother and wanted to know how you're doing," I said.

"Thank you. There's no need to be concerned. I won't let it distract me."

"That's not why I'm asking. We're both the type of people that hold in what's bothering us. I know what it's like to be hurting inside and feel alone in a crowd when you unexpectedly lose somebody you love."

I wanted to do more than offer a few words of encouragement and a pat on the back. It was eating at me knowing that I had a hand in taking his mother from him.

"I pray I knew a better way to express my gratitude in words," he said. "You've been my idol since childhood. In the short time we've known each other personally I've always felt how much you cared and have tried my best to return those feelings. I was been blessed to have a relationship with my mother, who was not part of the Order, and I never took a single day for granted, and yet..."

Every word Liam spoke gained in emotion until he had trouble forcing them out, but he managed not to shed a tear. I went to hug him to let him know that it was okay and he actually met me halfway.

"All the hugs going around lately are a lot better than the kneeling," I said, rubbing his shaved head for fun. I had always wanted to do that and he seemed to find it amusing too.

"I'm sorry for your loss with Sir Octavio. I've wanted to speak on it sooner, but I wasn't sure when would be appropriate."

Hearing his name alone acted as an anchor, dragging me back down to a sad place filled with the memories of other losses that I had hoped I could escape through avoidance.

"Thank you. I wish I had gotten to know him better when I had the chance and done something to figure out why he acted the way he did instead of distancing myself after he helped me."

Guilt. I felt guilt that I had so much power, but not enough to save him. It was the same as when I lost my parents and Noah lost Vivi. I could see why many became obsessed with gathering more power hoping to prevent ever feeling loss of any type again.

"I know I may not be your first choice to confide in, but I am good at listening if you need and would honor me with the chance."

"I definitely will and I offer you the same," I told him. "Knowing someone cares is better than always having the right words to say it. But listen, I understand if you need time to yourself and don't want to come today. It's probably going to be little more than talking."

"No, it's all right. Perhaps if there is battle I'll feel more at ease there than at home mourning. I want to keep moving forward. It's what Nathaniel was telling us in your absence and it's been spreading as a positive mantra."

"I told him that a while ago when he was upset after Mumbai. Boy, we're doomed if the Order is taking my words as gospel." I noticed a collection of items on a shelf that didn't look like they belonged in his room, like a hairclip. I assumed they must have been keepsakes from his mother, but a braided brass torque stood out amongst the others.

I went over to get a closer look. It was too small to wear around the neck, more likely worn as a bracelet. "Your mother was pagan, wasn't she?"

"Yes, but she was always quiet about her faith at my father's request. It was one of the conditions that allowed me to see her."

"Would you let me borrow this? I'll make sure nothing happens to it."

"Yes."

I realized he must have felt that he couldn't say no, so I removed my prayer beads and handed them to him. "Here, take these in exchange until I return it to you."

"I'll guard it well, although...I'm sure Noah told you that I failed to do so with the swords of his you granted me."

"He didn't, but don't worry about it. I'll make new ones for both you and Noah."

Liam's stone face cracked with a genuine smile. "To be able to use one was blessing enough, but to have my own...I don't know what to say."

"It'll be the best I've ever made now that my powers have grown." I opened the door for us to leave. "We should get going. I don't want to keep the others waiting too long and I need to check on Lyle before we go."

"He's in the room across from Connor's. I can get Marianna and Alexandre for you. And, Dorian...thank you for speaking with me."

"You don't have to thank me for something like that, but you're welcome." I smiled back at him. It felt good to have broken through to him a second time, but my work wasn't done.

Lyle was pacing in his room when I got there, which wasn't big enough for more than three steps in one direction.

"Did you get any sleep?" I asked.

"Nah, not really." He sat on the bed and tapped his foot.

"I'm going to see Cernunnos if you want to come. He's had a change of heart about contacting Gaea."

"Glad we busted our asses helping his people and he had to think on it before returning the favor."

"There's something weird going on with the Spiritborn gods. These oaths they broke weren't voluntary. I think they were more like programmed guidelines they couldn't break until The Infernal Machine messed with them. Calder said Cernunnos was acting strange and crying. They're actually feeling real emotions for the first time, so the guilt must have gotten to him."

"Whatever, man. I honestly don't care anymore. Everyone I know except you is dead. Go do your thing and I'll be here."

"Your family is still in Ohio, aren't they?"

"Haven't been able to contact them in over a week."

"I can have someone from the Order take you," I offered.

"I'm not sure I'm ready for the answer. I'd like to think they're safe and hunkered down somewhere."

"All right, but you're not staying here. They're spraying for bugs."

"Not in the mood for jokes or much of anything right now."

Noah entered the room with his eyes narrowed at Lyle.

"Can you give us a minute?" I was close to begging Noah so he wouldn't start a fight.

"You had your minute." Noah went over to Lyle. "Get up."

"Dorian, get him away from me."

"Noah." I pulled on his arm. "Do not start this again."

"I'm not going anywhere," said Noah. "This asshole has fought undead and demons with the rest of us for years, but now he's giving up because he finally lost someone when we've all had to deal with that more than once. What did I say about making it your purpose to avenge them?"

"I'm not talking to you, dude. You're a fucking psycho to begin with and I don't have to answer to you."

"I told you I'm not going anywhere, just like this evil TV isn't either. You can't hide behind Dorian, and you don't know for sure who died and who survived, so get up and do something about it. This isn't mourning, it's weakness."

I stayed quiet. This wasn't Noah's usual bullying of Lyle. After the words of encouragement about avenging his friends earlier, I thought that Noah might be on to something productive in his own way.

"What do you want me to do? Throw rocks at it?" Lyle laughed at the futility. "Get out of my face, dude. I'm done."

Noah picked him up by the shirt with one arm. "Man up and make me."

"Noah! Put him down!" I demanded.

"I'm gonna punch that shit-eating grin off your face if you don't get off me!" Lyle threatened.

Noah smirked. "Then do it."

"That's enough!" I yelled. "Put him down."

I was too late. Lyle clocked Noah square on the jaw. I never liked seeing Noah get hurt, even a scratch, but Lyle hurt his own hand more.

"Man, I fucking hate you." Lyle laughed after a second, lying on the bed once Noah let him go. "I've wanted to do that for a long time, but what's it supposed to prove? Like this demon-spirit-machine thing is gonna let me hit it so I can embarrass myself?"

"It proves you can't be a pussy if you wanna get what you want. We're also even now."

"Do you guys want to kiss and make up too or can we go?" I asked.

Noah pointed at me to be quiet and squinted with his "you're gonna get it" face. I wasn't sure if any of that brought a resolution to things, but the energy of the room went from sad and tense to weird, so I supposed that was an improvement.

"I'll go," Lyle said. "Not sure what use I'll be, but start collecting rocks for ammunition in case."

Noah threw his arm around me as we left the room.

"You need ice for your jaw?" I teased.

"Why would I?" he sneered. "I've been slapped harder by mortal chicks and liked it."

"You could rent that face out as a punching bag to boost morale," Lyle joked.

I gave Noah a kiss on the cheek in thanks, but of course he had to ruin it by giving me the sloppiest kiss on the lips he could manage and then disappearing to avoid retaliation.

"Is it bad that I kind of feel a little better right now after hitting him?" Lyle asked.

"I don't know anymore," I said, wiping the slobber from my face. "He is right though. There could be survivors we don't know about. We didn't see any actual bodies and you said not everyone had the implant."

"Rebecca might not have had hers. She was in the process of doing the operations for the upgrades this week and was waiting to do hers last. Sierra didn't have one, I think. But Timmons..."

"It's okay, Lyle, we'll get answers, but if they made it out alive their problems are over for the time being. It's not like they'd be much better off with us."

"I still love her, man."

"Which one?"

"Rebecca. I've never been in love with anyone else. I thought there might be something worth pursuing with Sierra, but obviously I read that wrong."

"You're probably reading Rebecca wrong too if you ask me."

"I'm not. She's scared of loss like the rest of us and I believe her. When I saw her off that day you were with me in the hangar we had a moment after you left and she admitted she thinks about me all the time."

"Personally, I feel you shouldn't let yourself get stuck on *anybody* who can flip their interest on and off like she does."

"Can't help what the heart wants, right? Everything about her attracted me. I can listen to her talk about stuff I don't understand for hours without getting bored."

"You've got it bad for her all right."

"I'd keep notes on my computer to look up what she was talking about after so she wouldn't think she was dating a total idiot. I didn't want her to feel self-conscious telling me things or that nobody outside of work understood her."

Something told me that she was conflicted Lyle might not have been good enough for someone with her education, because she was always very careful about not letting their relationship go public and the most recent split happened after meeting her parents, but it could have been my imagination. I admit I was biased since it was my best friend who had his heart broken.

Marianna, Liam, Alexandre, and Noah were waiting by the front door when Lyle and I walked up.

Noah was reclining with his hands behind his head on a bench. "What took you so long?"

"Don't worry about it," I said. "Who are we missing?"

"Is Nathaniel coming?" Marianna asked. "He was asleep in your bedchambers when I checked."

"We can let him sleep. He's earned it." I looked over what the three of the Order were wearing. They had come prepared for the colder temperatures of the north with fur cloaks and fur trim on their armor. "That's not werewolf fur is it? I don't want a diplomatic issue with an emotional death god."

"It's bear," said Alexandre, presenting Lyle and me with a cloak of our own. "We thought of that and changed."

I want more warm, furry clothing, but I'm not going to chance transmuting what I'm wearing and turn myself into a mutated teddy bear.

"Our destination is a couple islands west of the base. I'm sure they'll stand out. You guys take Noah and Lyle, and I'll see you there."

I imagined what the sky above their camp would look like from a flying perspective by using the base's airspace as reference, but I wound up there instead. I was going to need more practice, but at least the fatigue was decreasing with each trip.

I flew west, still in disbelief at how the geography of the world had changed.

How much worse can this get before it isn't even Earth anymore? Aside from it just being eaten by a space worm.

Right as I noticed the island thick with new fully-grown trees instead of ice and rocks something cold and wet hit me in the head. It was snow.

"Pay attention!" Noah shouted. He was up in a tree, wrapped in a fur blanket.

"I am!" I yelled back and floated down to him.

"I meant to me."

"Is that our blanket from bed—?"

"Could be." He grinned and reached out for me to share it with him.

"You're *this* close to getting flung across the Atlantic."

"Aim for America. I'm in the mood for a burger the size of my head."

I flicked his nose and disintegrated the blanket, continuing down to where I saw the others waiting afterward. "Do we know where we can find Cernunnos?" I asked.

"He must be preparing a ritual toward the opposite shore," said Alexandre. "We can sense a large amount of aether being amassed there."

The trees were dense enough to blot out most of the sunlight and you had to turn to the side to get between them. Fog was forming from the melting snow and ice as a consequence of the island having been pushed further south into warmer waters.

We came across the gods and the berserkers gathered in a narrow clearing around Cernunnos. He sat cross-legged on his tree stump conjuring a cloud of seafoam-green aether that became more emerald colored the larger it grew. Ethereal neon-green grass was sprouting at our feet and moss on the trees. The aether cloud morphed into shapes of leaves, branches, flowers, and bubbles. I was too interested in Isis to pay it much attention though. Nobody else seemed to notice her looking around like a princess who had been let out of her castle for the first time in her life.

Noah held me close to him from behind. "I'm cold."

"You should've brought a jacket."

"I brought a blanket."

Gianni smiled at me from across the clearing and I smiled back. Nothing slipped past Noah's gaze though. He kissed the top of my head to mark his territory. It was fine by me as long as he didn't pull any more shenanigans for a while. His insecurities had a certain charm when they cropped up to remind me that his attention-seeking antics had a big heart behind them.

"She speaketh through me," Cernunnos announced. He held his taloned hands up to the cloud without introduction. "I am...forgiven. Bless ye, mine Goddess. Bless ye, mine love."

The cloud streamed into him and purified the taint remaining from the Machine, returning his darkened bones and branches to their natural shade.

"Goddesses, the Earth Mother would bequeath unto thee a portion of Her remaining aether to hide it from the Machine. Knoweth that we hath been given such a gift only by the position that imperils us all as She doth favor no child over another. With it we shan't rely upon the fetters of prayer for a time as we serveth Her alone."

Without further notice, energy from the cloud poured into Isis and Kamakura, transforming them into a higher echelon of heavenly royalty.

I had never seen anything like it. Prior to this moment there was little about their fully powered appearances that couldn't be replicated with Hollywood-quality costuming and make-up effects. That now changed in spectacular fashion. Isis and Kamakura had become superlative portrayals of divinity—similar to the undead Archios without attempting to masquerade behind a veneer of humanity. In a curious twist, they had lost most of their distinctive cultural design in place of more ambiguous patterns and styles seemingly not of this world, from both past and future.

Flowing, fluttering fabrics and metallic ribbons defying gravity levitated about the goddesses. Mounted in their hair were jeweled headdresses with beads made of precious stones on Isis and bells and hairpins for Kamakura. The glittering of Isis's skin amplified with an increased abundance of shimmering gold flecks along with her sparrow brown wings shifting to cream and white. A long silk scarf and four swirling aether orbs representing each of Kamakura's guardians hovered over her shoulders.

The guardians themselves remained unchanged, however.

"We are—we are alive!" Isis proclaimed with a question in her voice. "My children...my worshipers...they see me elevated to new heights on these wings. I can hear the singing, a joy I've never... *felt*. Can you hear the music, Empress?"

"I feel sadness and great conflict," said Kamakura. "Is life naught but turmoil? My people suffer loss at every turn. These thoughts...they fill me with sorrow, pressing, crushing. I understand now for the need to change. Have I failed them by standing back while they crawl forward? Should I not have been the one to lead them from the shadows of history?"

"A heavy curtain hath been lifted," Cernunnos said. "Yet rage doth taketh its place. Only the blood spilt of mine enemies shall sate the pyre within and wash clean the disgrace of such sins."

The Spiritborn gods may have gotten a promotion from Gaea, but what they were feeling came earlier from The Infernal Machine, if my observations were correct. I had a hunch they didn't want to admit the effect our enemy had on them. With emotions came shame and the desire to bury it. There was still the question of why the Machine would have wanted this outcome if it were all-knowing. I refused to believe that a being on the demons' side had good intentions when looking at the bigger picture.

I was so busy psychoanalyzing the gods I was late at noticing the Gaea cloud branching out toward me...then passing right by to enter Lyle.

Chapter Forty-Three

Cernunnos rose from his stump to face Lyle as Gaea's energy penetrated his forehead. Lyle didn't react in pain, so I stayed quiet while Cernunnos explained. "A pure heart in our presence all along... The Goddess smiles upon ye, lad. Only one innocent of evil's embrace may be imbued with Her gift of sight so that it may not be used against Her. This is what I had hoped She would grant to one of mine own, but berserkers' rage oft welcomes the darker sides of life."

"What am I seeing?" Lyle was looking around as if he were blind. "Dorian, you still there?"

"I'm standing right in front of you," I answered, tapping him on the arm.

"Ye have the sight to see all things, lad, but only for a time," said Cernunnos.

"What does that mean?" Lyle asked. "There are a lot of blurs and symbols. I feel like I can *see* sound."

"Symbols? Like the quantum code?" I asked.

"Aye." Cernunnos nodded. "'Tis the very strands of Fate. He is safe from corruption that even we spirits are not and therefore the prime vessel to see such secrets. Ye may not understand them, but it shall make sense when it needs to."

"Uh, but I can't see *normal* stuff," said Lyle.

Cernunnos touched his skull in thought. "It shall pass until naught but right and wrong remain."

"What does that even mean?"

"Give it time and you'll be able to see what The Infernal Machine is doing with the code," I guessed. "But what are we supposed to do after that? Can we even change the code back?"

"Nay, even the Goddess cannot change the rules of Her existence," Cernunnos answered. "She is bound by the laws of the cosmos as are we."

"So we have to wing it." I sighed.

What are we supposed to do when our enemies are the only ones that can make any plays at this level?

"When *don't* we?" asked Noah. "Shit always falls apart last minute. We just have to keep hitting the big bad thing until it stops hitting back."

"What about this fortress we see?" Gianni asked. "Maybe there is the answer in there."

"Nathaniel and the Order saw the code being used with computers in the fortress," I recalled. "We might be able to make something work for us if Lyle can understand the code now."

"Ah! One for Gianni, yes?" He beamed.

"To storm the gates then? 'Twas my plan from the start," said Calder.

"Yeah, but now it's more than just you and your pointy stick," Noah said.

"The structure still looms over my lands," said Kamakura. "I can feel its presence, but it is nowhere to be seen."

"It'll appear when I show up. I'm sure it will," I said.

"We'll be met with the heaviest opposition we've ever encountered," said Marianna. "That's where Nathaniel saw the factory making the demon lords. Our biggest challenge will be keeping Commander Turner alive once inside."

"Thanks." Lyle sounded offended.

"We'll need *everybody* for this," I said. "Two teams: one that strikes first and stays outside to lure as much resistance away as possible, and one that goes in with Lyle. Obviously, I'm going inside."

"Obviously, I'm going with you," said Noah.

"I want Nathaniel with us too. We need teams that'll work well together and his light won't mix with Gianni's darkness, so that means Gianni should be on the outside team. If that's okay?"

Gianni nodded and shrugged. "I fight anywhere to lead us to a victory, little *legatus*."

"I shall accompany you, Ascended," Isis said. "Should our mortal seer endure wounds my light can mend them."

Lyle gave a dejected sigh. "Thank you. Maybe I should cover myself in bubble wrap."

"That's a good idea." I turned to Liam. "We need to get him armor to guard against hellfire."

"He can borrow a suit of ours or we can craft him one if there is time," said Liam. "We have very few materials left though, from all the repairs we've had to make lately."

"Can't you pull some out of a hat, Dorian?" Lyle asked.

"I don't think I can make mystical and arcane objects."

"What's the difference between the two?"

"Mystic is believed to originate from aether and spirits that aren't necessarily divine," Marianna answered. "Arcane is of unknown origins, often implied to be forbidden like Infernal or blood magic. Ascended, you were able to construct orichalcum statues when you—"

Noah shot her a hostile glare, which stopped her from sharing anymore that he hadn't already told me.

"Where are these statues?" I asked.

"Nathaniel moved them to the bottom of the sea along with those that were left after trampling the mainland, since it was unlikely we would be able to reforge them on our own," Alexandre said.

"Oh. Okay, we can revisit that later." I hurried the conversation along to avoid further shame. Noah looked as if he was about to fight Alexandre for elaborating, but I understood he was only answering my question. "Gianni, you'll be leading the charge with Empress Kamakura and Cernunnos."

"Will the berserkers be a liability? Hell has taken hundreds of miles there, so won't the Fury compromise them?" Lyle reminded us.

"Isis can enchant crystals to keep them pacified—"

"Nay," Cernunnos interrupted me. "With rage cometh strength and glory in battle. They hesitate not and those whom perish will reunite with Her grace upon victory."

I wish I could be that carefree with the Order. I'm constantly torn between protecting them, letting them make their own decisions, and needing their help.

"The Order will take up the rear as support then," I said. "They can heal themselves, but their magic won't work on Gianni with his armor on, and I imagine it would take most of their aether to make a difference for you or Kamakura."

"Ye needn't fret, Ascended. I may be a Lord of Death, but such rank giveth me ease of prevention, as well the attunement to nature provideth me healing magicks—though not on par with one more dedicated as Isis."

She bowed in amusement.

"Always nice to find out good news," I said. "Does the Goddess know how long until the Machine breaks through all the way?"

"Not long beyond the morrow," Cernunnos answered.

That was fine by me. I would take any amount of time that we could stall until it was an absolute necessity to fight.

"Better than any minute now. At least it gives us time to make final preparations. I guess that's it, unless someone else has something to add?"

"If we see less enemy outside we come in to help," Gianni suggested. "They will follow you more to protect the king."

"That's a good idea. From what I know, the rakshasa continue to be mass produced crap and the lesser demons have never been a challenge. Even if we get swarmed we won't have a problem keeping any of them in check without civilians to worry about for hundreds of miles."

"Don't forget it can make Ma'al and that evil Ganesha rip-off from Mumbai," Noah cautioned.

"That's true. Hopefully if those copies show up they suck as much as the rest. The Infernal Machine doesn't want me dead as much as it knows I'll try to fight it, and it's using that to wipe Earth clean so I can rebuild. It also probably knows me well enough that it isn't going to do anything that would demoralize me to the point where I wouldn't take any action at all."

Or fly myself into the sun out of depression.

"What are you getting at?" Lyle asked.

"As long as we can maintain a balance of keeping its attention away from you, but without posing a major threat to it until we're sure we can win, we should have a chance. The main thing to watch out for is the light we got hit with last time now that we know what to expect."

"How will you fare against such an attack, Dark One?" asked Kamakura. "You were brought close to death, were you not?"

"My darkness will protect me more this time." I could tell by how quickly he dismissed her concern that he felt some amount of humiliation in having let his guard down.

"The engineers at UNITY were talking about how the satellite strikes could have been something called a particle beam. It's probably the same as that other light that zapped you," said Lyle. "I heard they were working on a rifle using similar technology, but they couldn't get it compact enough. Then the particle accelerator we had stopped working so they abandoned it."

"Around the same time nuclear weapons and reactors were disabled everywhere, right?" I asked. "That was all the Machine's doing. I was told the light was called an Augmented Particle Disruption Beam, so it probably didn't want us using its own gadgets against it."

The more we scratched away at the surface I was starting to believe the claims that a lot of human technology was planted here by beings other than our gods. Isis had revealed in the past that her pantheon taught humans how to build the pyramids and irrigation systems, but advancements such as thermonuclear science and microbiology were beyond even them. The secrets of the universe really could have been fed to humans in an attempt to progress them further than their watchers intended and unravel the plans laid out for them. It wasn't a coincidence that something like The Infernal Machine used technology that PROJECT: UNITY was just starting to develop, or how Demon Lord Ma'al was found to be involved with both parties.

I supposed it didn't matter for defeating the Infernal Kings, but it made me wonder how much of humanity's progress was of their own hands. At what point was free will an illusion, and could it be measured on a spectrum or was it black and white? Was having emotions the real test? Or was it the capacity for creative and original thought? Could you be considered free if you didn't have absolute control over your own fate like what the Machine was trying to achieve for humanity? If that was the case, then humans were just fleshy automata of the Enochians. Being made in their image didn't seem as sentimental a motivation anymore.

Maybe The Infernal Machine was right about them, but could mass extinction—whether Enochian or human—ever be justified to ensure the liberation of the next species? I didn't want to be the one to decide, but I was already taking a stand for the humans because they couldn't on their own...which meant that *I* was responsible for guiding their fate...but that was because The Infernal Machine planned this to control *me*...

My head hurts.

"Dorian?" A voice broke into my thoughts.

"Huh?"

Some of the group were staring at me while the rest talked amongst themselves.

"We're planning the biggest battle the world has ever seen and you just went on vacation," said Lyle.

"I was thinking." I realized he was looking right at me and the Gaea cloud was gone along with the spectral foliage. "You can see me?"

"Sort of. We should get back so you can work your magic."

It didn't take much to get Lyle pumped again. Having a plan always made me feel better...until it backfired...which it always did.

"Marianna, Alexandre, please take Lyle to the abbey and start filling everyone else in and getting the equipment ready. I have to check on something."

They departed on my command. I floated over the furry mounds of some lounging berserkers to Gianni, who was listening to Isis chat with a sullen Kamakura. He seemed happy and surprised that I wanted to talk with him, but he looked behind me, presumably at Noah, who must have been giving him death stares.

"You have grown so much, little one. I am very impressed when you lead the knights and now you give the orders to gods."

"No one else was talking so I said whatever came to mind." I found it hard not to smile, but I stopped myself before it could be interpreted as more than friendly. "I came to ask you if you're aware of the sources of darkness here in our universe beyond the sky. I know the Nether is infinite, but you can't always summon it when we're in Hell, so it might help."

His contemplative expression was my answer.

"We go and you can show me, okay?" he asked.

"Uh..." I checked for Noah. He was gone, which meant he was spying from somewhere or moved to avoid Gianni looking at him. "Sure, I guess, but only for a minute."

Gianni carried us through the shadows and into the realm of darkness. He surrounded us with a window to the outside world already above Earth's atmosphere. It beat any planetarium exhibit I had been to as a child, and it was much brighter and more colorful than the Nether, due to all the stars and the light coming from Earth.

"You like?"

"Yes, wow! It's so beautiful," I said, turning to take in all of the sights.

Although potentially infinite on a level above the universe we were looking out at, the Nether we were floating in didn't seem as vast and overwhelming as outer space. There, reference points like stars were a visual reminder that something existed so far away that it would take billions of years to travel there, like in the Rift.

"You are more beautiful," said Gianni, not paying any attention to the view.

"You knew about up here already, didn't you?"

He gave a knowing smile and positioned himself in front of me. The living darkness of his armor changed to the black pants and half-buttoned shirt he sometimes wore, a look inspired by an advertisement he once saw.

"I must be careful with this darkness or I will hurt what we try to save. I have many plans for the world."

"What plans? You mean for more than Rome?"

"You will see." His smile warmed, but his phrasing alarmed me.

"That sounds rather ominous."

"What is this? Ominous?"

"Scary."

"Ah. You do not trust me."

"I do. The wording is just harsh, if that makes sense."

"Always my words are the trouble." With a wistful look, he placed his hand on the side of my face, his thumb touching the corner of my lips. "Noah is a good man. Because of him I see the mistake I make when you are mine."

I do not have the social skills for this.

I removed his hand and held it for a second to keep him from putting it elsewhere. It was strange. I felt I should have been more uncomfortable, yet Gianni never made me that way even if the circumstances themselves were awkward to navigate. I always enjoyed his company even after we separated, but I could only imagine what was going through Noah's mind for every second spent in the Nether.

"You were being yourself and there's nothing wrong with that. Sometimes people don't work well together romantically."

It wasn't unreasonable to say that I wished we had been a match and perhaps if I stayed we could have found a compromise between our cultural differences. I was a strong believer in second chances and Gianni was the perfect man in many aspects—just not for me. Noah was everything I wanted and everything I needed, even in ways I didn't know until they happened, and even with all his flaws and quirks.

I had never loved anyone like I did him and I wouldn't let "what ifs" jeopardize that.

"Hm. When I have the words I hope to speak more to your heart."

Gianni's expression was beset by an abrupt uncertainty. Words always tended to roll off his tongue like raindrops whether in his native language or otherwise, yet for the first time in recent memory he seemed at a loss.

"Focus on the battle ahead. I don't want you to be distracted," I pleaded. "And use all the darkness you need to win."

"I will, little one."

He kissed my hand as the shadows returned me to Earth alone.

That was...something.

Isis and Kamakura had left the berserkers' camp during my absence. Liam was waiting dutifully for me and Noah was lounging high up in another tree. I wanted to pounce on him after that conversation with Gianni, but I had business with Cernunnos to attend to first.

"Liam, can we have a moment? Wait for me by where we arrived."

"Yes, Ascended."

Once Liam left, Noah came down and sniffed my cheek where Gianni had put his hand.

"Nothing happened," I assured him.

"Didn't think it would."

His continued trust in me during these encounters with Gianni meant a lot, although I knew it wasn't my behavior in question. I understood that what was an awkward situation for me was more upsetting to him. I debated how I would handle it if reversed, yet I couldn't see Noah being so affable toward someone else now. That sense of security in our relationship was invaluable, but I wouldn't mind him establishing platonic connections of his own for the sake of his emotional wellbeing.

I would reward Noah once we returned to the abbey, but at the moment I had another heart to mend.

"Cernunnos, I have a favor to ask." I showed him the brass bracelet from Liam's mother that matched the golden one he and Calder wore around their necks. "Two, actually."

Chapter Forty-Four

I didn't take pleasure in seeing my friends cry, except when it was with joy. It was an especially memorable victory when I could get such a response from someone like Liam, even if it was only a single tear.

Noah and I were standing back watching the reunion between mother and son. It made me miss my own parents.

"You did good," said Noah. "She doesn't look anything like him though. I expected her to be balder."

"Do *not* ruin the moment."

He grinned with his hands on his hips. "Who? Me?"

Cernunnos had granted my requests to restore Liam's mother to life and allow her to remain a normal human instead of becoming a berserker, so she wouldn't be dragged further into this mess. He owed me for saving his followers. I only wished that more tragedies could be resolved with such a happy ending.

"We should return to the abbey," I suggested to them. "It's cold out here."

She only had my cloak to wear and her bracelet. I was glad I had Liam wait elsewhere while she was being resurrected, but my initial reason was I didn't want him to be disappointed in case Cernunnos couldn't do it or something traumatic happened.

Liam approached and went to kneel to show his gratitude, but he caught himself halfway and hugged me instead without saying a word.

"Are you going to be okay?" I asked with some amusement.

He nodded and composed himself.

I turned to his mother. "I'm sure this is a lot for you, but Liam and Tobias will be there to help you adjust. I'm kind of always dying and coming back so I forget that it isn't as natural for other people."

"I can't thank you enough, and the Horned God, for returning me to my Liam. Like him, I don't know if I can find the words for such a miracle!"

"No problem. Sorry for sort of being the one responsible for killing you."

"We all make mistakes," she said, matching my dark attempt at humor.

Liam was appalled, however. "You can't say that," he whispered to her.

"Liam, come on, do you really think I'm that much of a wrathful god that I can't take a joke?" I said.

"You turned Greece upside down," Noah leaned in to remind me.

I shot him a look. "We'll finally have someone else at the abbey that treats me like a normal person like I keep asking. I didn't get your name, by the way?"

"Monique," she said.

"I'm Dorian and this is Noah. He's not as bad as he looks, but if any of your stuff ever goes missing it's his fault."

Noah gave a short grunt and picked me up under his arm.

"All right, time to go home," I said. "Liam, take your mom and have someone get Noah in a day or two."

I teleported myself to our bedroom in the abbey, delighting in the fact that for the first time since meeting Noah, I had a way to evade him that he couldn't counter.

Nathaniel had been kind enough to make the bed after he was done with it, but that didn't last once Noah found me. He tackled me in a forgiving grapple that I escaped by teleporting into the courtyard to look for the others.

Of course Noah was hot on my trail before I could blink. "Let me get one of those tasty kisses."

I laughed and teleported away again before he could kiss me, landing in the main hall where Tobias was reuniting with Monique. Noah was right behind me and getting more aggressive, regardless of present company.

"You should know the hunt only turns me on more." He deepened his voice while speaking into my ear with his hands on my hips.

"Shh!"

Tobias and Monique's encounter was becoming tense. Tobias had always been sketchy on the details of his relationship with her. He once alluded to the fact that they were married in some sense, but it wasn't true. He had also made it sound like he visited her more than what others considered accurate. I could understand his predicament though with some already disapproving of Liam being allowed to visit her.

"We've been over this, Monique," Tobias whispered.

"And I was right! They *both* exist! You took my son from me to keep him 'pure' from other beliefs for no reason!"

I knew I had to step in, but I wasn't sure whom I was saving from whom. "Hey, hate to interrupt, but can you get the poor woman some clothes?"

"Forgive me, Ascended. Liam is fetching her something to wear as we speak. I will go see what's taking him so long. And...thank you for returning Monique to us."

"Take good care of her, all right?"

Monique was quick to retort. "Oh, I can do that all by myself. I didn't have this man's support for eighteen years and I don't need it now."

"That is not true," Tobias said through gritted teeth. "You were very well looked after, more than any parent outside these walls."

"This is fun, but seriously, the clothes," I insisted.

Tobias was only too glad to leave.

"I'm sorry. I've been here less than five minutes and I'm already causing trouble," Monique said.

"You're not. I can understand how upsetting it must have been to be separated from your son. It's a little strange around here if I'm understating it, but assuming we make it through the end of the world and it isn't eaten by a giant space snake, I plan on changing a few things. I grew up in Boston, so none of this was normal to me when I came here."

"Oh, I'm from the New Orleans area originally. I moved here—or was lured here—to have a relationship with Liam since it became obvious early on that Tobias didn't want one with me. I wish I could say he was different back then. Winding up here wasn't entirely his fault though. Being a Gardnerian Wiccan in a churchgoing Christian town was a good enough reason to move."

"Everyone is welcomed here as long as they respect each other and that goes for Tobias too. We're all on the same team now and I can't change the past, but at least going forward you and Liam can be closer. There are many reasons for you to be proud of him too."

Liam showed up with the clothes almost as if he heard us talking about him.

"Were you sewing them from scratch?" I asked.

He hesitated before deciding it was safe to smile. "No. I apologize for the wait."

"Say it to your mom, not me! You can get her a room, right?"

"Yes." He handed me back the prayer beads with a nod and thanked me again along with his mom on their way out.

"Is there anything I can do to help?" she stopped to ask.

"Actually, there is. When we go off to battle we'll need someone to watch the kids. Some of them are preteens and can take down a demon, but it's the little ones I'm more concerned about leaving unattended. Maybe you can read them a bedtime story or make them grilled cheese sandwiches."

"I'd love to! I love kiddies. It's too bad I didn't get to spend more time with my own. I don't suppose you have vegan alternatives?"

"*Mother*," Liam mumbled under his breath, starting to lead her away.

"I don't know. Probably? You can discuss it with Liam."

They left and I turned to Noah to offer the affection he was searching for earlier, but he had already found a substitute. "Where'd you get that turkey leg?" I asked.

"Want a bite?" He held it out.

"You're deflecting, but yeah, I do." I managed to bite a piece off as he pulled it back to lead me towards him. "Come on, let's find Nathaniel and Lyle so we can start our preparations."

"We building an ark or something? I wasn't paying attention."

"Wrong end of the world plan."

Connor walked by looking lost until he saw Noah. "Hey! That's my drumstick!"

"You don't know that." Noah took another bite.

"Marianna has one and I had the other and turkeys only have two legs." Connor looked forlorn as the meat dwindled from the bone. "Can I have it back? That was my lunch."

"Sorry about that," I said.

"It's okay. There's still a whole turkey left."

"Go have lunch so we can discuss battle preparations together."

I waited for Connor to leave and looked over at the big lug chomping away on his drumstick. "Sometimes I feel less like I'm a god and more like I'm a parent around here. I don't know which is worse."

"Hey, you had some too."

I sat against the wall. "It's not that. I mean, you *are* a temperamental man-child, but I'm talking about my relationship with everyone here. When they threw themselves at me as my followers I felt like I had to protect them because I was the strong one. Now we're becoming the family I wanted us to be and I feel even worse about putting them in danger. So many of them are just kids."

Noah sat next to me. The bone from his finished turkey leg was mysteriously absent from his hands. "You know why you feel that way? Because you're a noodlehead."

I laughed as he squished my head in his arm and stuck his face in my hair.

"I'd agree with you if these kids weren't born and bred to be warriors," he continued. "They're damn good at it too, but I'll keep an eye on them."

That was true. Connor might be a bit dopey at times, but he was a savage in battle.

"How are you going to do that if you're coming with me inside the fortress and they're staying outside?" I asked.

"I'm pretty fast, but they're only gonna be dealing with the scraps. Relax and give them some credit." He got up and carried me from the main hall in both arms. "Let's go build that ark."

"That's not what we're doing and you know it."

Claudius was coming around the corner as Noah and I were leaving. He had his mask up to cover the lower half of his face so I couldn't see his lips move while he talked.

"Oh, Ascend—Dorian, I've been needing to speak with you. It's about that information you wanted me to find."

"About the gods?"

"No, the *other* information." Claudius was more serious than his usual self, even after taking impending doom into account, but I thought it could be his persona for the espionage role he had fallen into as of late.

"You can say whatever it is in front of Noah. He's going to listen in anyway."

"It isn't his ears I mean to avoid."

"We can talk in my room then." I teleported myself there. Noah and Claudius came in right behind me. "Why the cloak and dagger?"

Claudius cast a spell that enveloped us in a pocket of wavy air. "This will prevent others from listening in by stopping the transfer of sound. A really underappreciated spell nowadays. I hear it was more in fashion during the days when incantations were necessary, but I've found it has equal use in winning an argument with Marianna."

"*Claudius.*"

"A thousand apologies. It's about Nathaniel and I thought you might want to keep what I have to tell you private. You had told me to learn what I could of his powers. The divine aether gem that gave him his light source came from the crystallized essence of a Spiritborn god defeated by the previous Ascended. That god's name was Sūrya the Supreme Light, but since we're forbidden from acknowledging any deity other than the Ascended we never kept any detailed records. PROJECT: UNITY had some information that I found during our stay there and it led me to India where Sūrya used to be worshipped."

Noah let out a bored sigh and lay out flat on the bed.

"Okay, so who was Sūrya?" I asked.

"He was a skyfather or all-father, or one-third of one, depending on the belief system. He was cross-worshipped outside of India and Hinduism," Claudius said.

"And what's a skyfather?"

"They're kings of their pantheons, a league above the rest. Many are creation gods or related in some way to the sun and the elements of the sky like Ra, Zeus, and Odin, but some are women like Amaterasu."

"What are you trying to tell me, Claudius? Was he evil? Is something going to happen to Nathaniel?"

"The Ascended that defeated Sūrya had to have weakened him a considerable amount before turning him into the Empyrean Jewel of Light, but Nathaniel's superior connection to the aether is flooding that essence with power again. Combining that with the soul energy siphoned through your link to the Rift is why he's been growing stronger so quickly."

"Makes sense," I said.

"PROJECT: UNITY had files on him and other notable supernaturals ranked by their potential threat to human existence. You were last viewed as a lunar to planetary level threat due to annihilating the Egyptian moon, while Nathaniel was not far below. You've been the same for a while, but Nathaniel was constantly being moved higher up the scale. Only a week earlier he was considered a threat level to a major city from handling the missiles in China and demon lord in Mumbai."

"I don't think the term 'threat' is something to worry about. Power is all about how you use it, not how much of it you have."

"I taught you that," Noah boasted.

"Did you? I thought it was Gianni."

Noah threw one of his many pillows at me.

"It isn't certain since no one has the means of measuring the source of your power and this was before The Infernal Machine awakened your mind," Claudius continued. "But, they believe there is potential for Nathaniel to grow more powerful than you."

"Oh, cool. Is that it?" I asked.

Claudius was caught off guard. "You aren't bothered by this?"

"Why would I be? I know he can handle it with training."

"*You're* the Ascended and he serves you. I would have thought you'd be uncomfortable with any of us under you having that power. Although, I suppose the previous Ascended had to be at least as strong as an All-father to have beaten Sūrya and he wasn't linked to the Rift, so it's also possible you'll balance out in the future if Nathaniel does surpass you for a time."

"I couldn't care less. I'm not looking to be the most powerful and if Nathaniel surpasses me then I'd be happy for him as long as he's happy. The proudest moment for any teacher is when their student becomes the master."

"I taught you that too," Noah said and I threw his pillow back at him.

"I trust Nathaniel without question. I always had a good feeling about him even before he was my champion. Being able to lift another million tons or fly faster isn't going to change that."

"He's already been faster," said Noah.

"I'm sorry to have made that assumption," Claudius said. "I should have known you were above such greed. I thought I was looking out for you, but I don't want you to think that I don't trust Nathaniel either."

"It's not a big deal. You found some really interesting information. I wonder how much Lyle knows of it from the PARAGON files."

"Most of what I found there wasn't on the computer system. I sensed many of the scientists didn't want Commander Turner involved in their research because his morals would get in the way of their progress. They referred to him in unflattering terms and kept much on paper in their offices so he wouldn't see it."

"And now they're dead," Noah scoffed, almost as if he were siding with Lyle.

"Were you aware they were trying to forge weapons that made use of our aether crystals?" Claudius asked.

"No," I said. "That seems a bit intrusive. How'd they get them?"

"They traded for one in exchange for food with a berserker child who must've received it from Nathaniel. I 'acquired' a copy of the blueprints for a type of energy-producing machine called a reactor and one for a rifle, both from a doctor at the time they were evacuating during the chaos of the battle with Cernunnos."

Claudius retrieved some folded pieces of paper from a satchel under his cloak and handed them to me. They painted two contrasting pictures. The rifle seemed standard for PROJECT: UNITY with advanced electronic calibrating and targeting systems contained within a sleek design. The addition of an aether crystal attachment replaced the ammo slot and lenses to focus the energy through the barrel. However, the reactor was clockwork with gears and sprockets making up the majority of the infrastructure. A large aether crystal was mounted in the center with a Tesla coil and a few cables. It looked more like a contraption that the Strigoi would have utilized in their experiments.

"What's piezoelectricity?" I asked after reading it on the reactor blueprints.

"It's electricity from crystals like quartz that are used in watches," said Claudius. "I didn't know either, so I researched it."

"Is there anything you don't know?"

"I never learned to dance."

I laughed. The hint of swagger that snuck through on occasion told me he would be a natural. "You said a *doctor* had these plans? Like a medical doctor? Not one of the engineers?"

"Dr. Sullivan, the woman Commander Turner fancies. I read it on her lab coat. Not the fancying part."

Rebecca. She's a neurosurgeon. Why would she be carrying these around?

"She might not have survived if she had her implant when The Infernal Machine attacked, so it's a good thing you got this when you did," I told him.

"She did have it. Otherwise she wouldn't have been able to get into the armory," said Claudius.

"The AI there runs biometric scans for people without implants. That's why we could go anywhere there."

"Not everywhere. The armory and server room stay locked unless you have an implant and high enough clearance, but the clearance level to the armory drops during an emergency so soldiers can get their weapons. Only commanders and lieutenants have that clearance normally. I read their user's manual," Claudius said.

"Wow, you are thorough."

"Sounds like she was waiting for the right opportunity to get in there and swipe stuff to run away with," said Noah.

"But why?" I asked.

"Who cares? She's a puddle of goop now."

"Let's not share that with Lyle. Not until we can be sure and get through this next battle," I told both of them but meant it more for Noah. "Did you see what she was doing in the armory?"

"No, I'm sorry. That was when it descended into total chaos."

"It's fine. One more question though; how did you know Dr. Sullivan had these files on her in the first place?" I asked.

"Whoever PARAGON is told me while I was doing research on Nathaniel."

"PARAGON is an artificial intelligence, not a person, and it works for PROJECT: UNITY. Why would it tell you something like that?"

"I thought it was someone using an anonymous identity. Are you certain she isn't a person? We had a decent length conversation more than once and she spoke as if she were real. I asked if she was safe after the attack and she said she was scared of dying."

"It's programmed to act real like that, but you were talking to a computer." I looked at the plans again.

Did PARAGON know that Rebecca broke protocol by having these plans and wanted them retrieved? Why wouldn't it inform Lyle then, unless it's advanced enough to consider his judgment would be clouded by their relationship?

"Forget it. You did a great job, spymaster. Rest up and get yourself ready for battle. We've got about a day."

"Spymaster? I like that."

Claudius vanished without another word to keep the mystery going and took his soundproof aura with him.

"Come here." Noah beckoned to me from the bed once we were alone.

I lay down next to him after storing the blueprints in my dresser.

"You're awesome," he said, his piercing green eyes locking onto mine.

"What did I do?" I asked and held his hand.

"That's exactly it. You don't even realize. It's like being the most attractive person in the world, which you are, and never seeing your own reflection."

I felt myself starting to blush. "Where's this coming from?"

"Listening to you talk. I always knew power wouldn't change you and I like being right."

I laughed and covered his face with my hand, but he was being serious, which only made me blush more.

"I like seeing you lead and get them to respect you without being an asshole. You're fucking gorgeous too. I never get tired looking at you."

"Stop!" I let out another nervous laugh and hid my face against his chest when he moved my hand away to rub against his scruff. "Go back to antagonizing or something."

"Can't. It's gotta be said. You turn me on more than you realize and I think I'm even more into you than ever. What the fuck is that about, huh? Kinda pisses me off to be honest, but I like it."

"Is this coming out now because you're nervous about the battle?"

"The opposite actually. Never been more confident that the two of us can do anything together."

I exhaled in relief. Hearing that bolstered my confidence as well. "I love my tiger," I said, listening to his heartbeat.

We kissed once, then twice. I very much enjoyed exploring his chiseled form, like a work of living art meant to be admired through touch as much as sight.

"You're not getting away this time," he said, climbing on top of me with a growl.

I gripped his hair between my fingers. His strong hands traveled my body in search for the comfort of skin underneath my clothes. By the third kiss we couldn't stop ourselves and we undressed to take advantage of our final chance at respite.

Chapter Forty-Five

Intimacy with Noah. It was as exhausting as it was exhilarating. What started in bed always seemed to migrate and this time it was to the bath. Had we more time I wouldn't have hesitated to let it continue to slip away out from under him, but at the very least what time we did spend served a purpose, being that he needed to feed.

"Are you going to stay here?" I scratched under Noah's chin as I passed by drying my hair. He was already flat out on the bed, naked and staring at the ceiling.

"Nah, I'm gonna go spar with the kids to warm up." He caught my hand and pulled me back onto the bed with him. "Just let me hold you a little longer and then we can go together, or we *could* hide here under the covers until this whole thing blows over."

"Sounds nice, but I don't think it works like that."

"Could be our Plan B...or C, I haven't been keeping track." He stretched and yawned, trying to itch his back on the sheets before giving up and kissing me.

I didn't want to do anything else but be with him and I was looking for an excuse to stay longer. "Want me to scratch your back?" I offered.

"Fuck yeah, I want a back scratch." He rolled over for me and groaned in relief as soon as I started. "That feels amazing. What did an asshole like me ever do to deserve you, huh? It's gotta be the muscles. Pound for pound I'd say you got a pretty good deal."

"I thought you knew I'm only in it for the money."

"Guess you'll have to settle for this." He turned over again and brought me in close with his hand behind my head to make out.

"I think I can live with that," I said when the moment came to an end.

"So, you gonna make me something for the fight?"

"I've made *several* things for you. First you refused to bring them anywhere and then they got lost or destroyed." I tickled his side until he pinned me.

"I don't care. I'll go barehanded and naked."

"I know you would. Does this mean you feel worthy of a blade full-time again?"

"I'm getting there."

"If only it took you this long to take credit for everything else," I teased and teleported away to find Lyle.

Rafael was working on a set of armor with him in Lyle's room when I got there and stood to offer me his seat. "Orichalcum for durability, demon leather for hellfire immunity, and angel silk weave for resistance against magic and the elements," he reported.

"No offense, man, but this isn't really my style," Lyle said. "I think it looks better on you guys."

I had grown so accustomed to seeing myself and everyone around me in the Order wearing our modern medieval style that when I saw it on Lyle I agreed that it looked wrong on him.

"Hang on. I can probably change it for you," I said.

"Not while it's on me!"

"I've been in your *brain*. I've got this—as long as I don't get any of it stuck through your skin."

"Dorian, *stop!*" he protested, but I had already begun.

It was astounding how easy it was. Once I had a telekinetic grip on it all I did was picture a SWAT uniform on him to alter the materials to match my vision. From there I imagined pieces of the gear updated closer to the PROJECT: UNITY standard, then I added thin white lines for detail against the black to represent the Alabaster Order. I wanted there to be familiarity while also making the outfit unique so he wouldn't be reminded too much of losing his team.

"Okay, that was pretty cool," Lyle admitted. "Maybe you should get into fashion."

"Great idea! I didn't want to fight the forces of Hell anyway. Good luck with that on your own," I said.

"You're a dick."

Rafael looked unhappy about Lyle directing such "harsh language" toward me that he was only used to hearing from Noah. I smiled to let him know it was okay. I didn't want to dismiss him, but he was also awkwardly standing guard in the small room and I hadn't seen him much since my return.

"You think you can make me a gun?" Lyle asked.

"I'm not sure. I haven't had the chance to test what else got crammed into my brain."

"Oh, but you dug around in mine like it was nothing, huh?"

"I wouldn't say it was nothing, just a lot less in there to work with."

"I walked into that one." He laughed with me.

"How's the sight been? You seem to be seeing all right."

"It's been normal for a while. As long as nothing's permanent I can deal with it. So about that gun?"

"I'll need some material to make it. I can transmute the metal from pretty much anything." I glanced around the room.

"Can you use the air or the dust in it?" Rafael suggested.

"Yes! Good one. I'd never run out of raw material that way."

"Until you suffocate us," Lyle pointed out.

"Stop complaining." I sucked in the dust and the air around my hand and let my subconscious take over, rearranging and transmuting the molecules into steel and then into a handgun. I did feel the momentary pull of a vacuum being created around my hand when the air was removed, so Lyle wasn't too far off-base about what would happen at a larger volume.

"This is a potato," Lyle said when I handed him the gun.

"Moving parts are the problem. I guess I wasn't given knowledge on gun manufacturing to rebuild the new world."

"Too bad we don't have instructions."

Does he know about the blueprints? No, there's no way.

"Yeah, too bad." The blueprints for the aether rifle were way too complex regardless. "Raf, do you think you have an amulet or something to embed in his armor for more protection?"

"I've got this gem from Nathaniel," Lyle said, retrieving it from under a pillow.

"That'll do." I inlaid the gem in the center of his chest piece. "You might not be able to control it, but the light from the crystal should protect you from any demons that get too close."

"I feel pretty good about this. I wish I had my rifle, but other than that I think we've got a real chance of at least getting in there to figure out something."

"We'll be fine as long as everyone plays their part and we take it slow. Is there anything I can make for you, Raf?"

I helped myself to the sword sheathed at his hip, sharpening it while he spoke.

"Would you imbue these arrowheads for me, please?" He showed me a handful of aether crystals from his satchel that had been cut to shape.

"Sure." I gave them a charge and handed them back. "I can ask Nathaniel to make the crystals so they'll be stronger if you need more."

"I considered that, but they might be *too* strong for a crowded battlefield. I'm calling these 'Earthshaker Arrows' because the ones you made for me before really packed a punch."

"I like the name. You can stay safe at long range and provide cover fire for the outside team with your archery this way."

Rafael cleared his throat. "I was hoping to talk to you about that. I understand you don't plan on taking any of the Order into the fortress with you, but I know I can be of use."

"I can't take you in with us. I'm sorry. You have just as important a role on the outside."

Rafael nodded, trying not to let his disappointment show on his face.

"It's true. We're screwed on the inside if you guys don't keep it clear for us," Lyle added.

After a few seconds of silence I changed topics, thinking that no one had anything left to say on the matter. "Have you heard from the Blackbournes lately? England was hit pretty hard, right? Or was it only Ireland?"

"Nah, communication hasn't been reliable enough to get a hold of them," said Lyle. "I'm sure Owen and Micah are holed up somewhere drinking the days away—"

"Can we discuss this?" Rafael asked me, as if he hadn't heard that we'd moved on.

"You're always free to speak your mind, Raf, but I'm not changing mine."

"I'm gonna go for a walk and get some air," Lyle said, excusing himself.

"I know you want to step up and make a name for yourself, but not like this," I said to Rafael once we were alone. "I've had this conversation with Connor—"

"That isn't my reason for wanting to go with you. You've taught us not to be blinded by tradition and inspired us to be independent thinkers who follow our hearts. You've opened doors for us we never dreamt possible in our short time together, simply by being who you are. If we lose one of us it's a tragedy we've come to expect, but if we were to lose you, it's like we've all lost a part of ourselves." The level of sincerity in his voice and written across his face was so palpable it was as if he had control over my own emotions to make my heart ache in empathy. "What I wish to say is that you are in our hearts. You saw how even the elders reacted to your return."

"My feelings are the same and that's why I can't bring you. I don't want Noah or Lyle going either, for the same reason."

"But they *are* going," Rafael insisted. "Lyle because he might be the key to understanding the code, Noah because of his love for you."

"Noah is only going because even as a god I have no way of stopping him."

"I would rather give my life fighting for what's in my heart than live knowing I could've done more. Isn't that what you want for us? I've never felt so strongly about any battle...anything in my life, honestly."

A melancholy sigh escaped from me. "You shouldn't even *be* fighting. You're a teenager and a mortal one at that. It's heartbreaking to me that your lives are consumed by war and not things that people your age should be doing. Life is short—too short for some—so it should be enjoyed down to the last second."

"Not all lives are meant to be the same! People my age have been going to war for ages. You can't inspire us to break the mold and then put us in another!" Rafael's fiery outburst reminded me of Nathaniel, but then he stopped and bowed his head, worried he crossed the line. His hand had a slight tremor when it unclenched. He put them both behind him to stand at attention. "I didn't mean to sound disrespectful."

"You didn't," I said. "God, when I came here a few months ago Nathaniel had no voice, Liam showed no emotion, and you were living in his shadow. I really messed things up...I'm kidding, of course."

"That's exactly why we care and why we're going to fight to keep you with us, or at least I am," he said, meeting my eyes dead on.

"I'm not deserving of as much credit as you're giving me. I didn't change who any of you were on the inside. You were already this awesome, but you just needed to see it for yourselves."

This was what I had wanted since the loss my parents, to have a loving family again. But even before that I yearned for other supernaturals to connect with when I was still hiding who I was. Rafael was only giving me more reason not to allow him to come with me.

"My decision stands. I want you to know that your role on the outside isn't busy work. If it was I wouldn't have any of you come at all. Three of the five gods will be there too—"

Rafael averted his gaze. "And what would be the punishment for defying those orders?"

"I...I don't know. I don't spend time thinking of ways to punish people. Just please don't. You don't think I'd be just as upset if something were to happen to you? Any of you? Let me be selfish this one time."

Instead of bringing down the hammer of authority on him and making myself a total hypocrite I went for the softer approach and hugged him, since that had been an effective method at breaking through with the others. "And I better not have to go through this with everyone in the Order or we'll never get anything done," I added.

He gave a heartfelt smile without commitment. "I think it speaks to how serious I am that I was the only one to come forward."

"Remember that I'd have no way of resurrecting you if something happened. Cernunnos and Isis can only revive their own followers, Nathaniel was brought back by the only fragment of my soul that I could spare, and the blood magic ritual that saved Noah was only for the undead."

Noah wasn't exactly undead anymore because of complications, so he also had to be careful—not a trait I'd associate with him.

"You can trust me. Thank you for letting me speak. You don't know how good it is to have someone to share my thoughts with so freely. Or perhaps you do, you *are* the Ascended."

"I do, but it's because of personal experience, not my title." Outside the window Noah was sparring against a whole group at once while Nathaniel sat watching from the sidelines. "We should get back to making preparations. I'm worried the time we have is going to be a lot shorter than we expected."

"We'll be ready as soon as you give word," he said as we headed out together.

Those not sparring turned and stood in two rows when we neared, allowing us to walk down the middle. It was inspiring to see the elders were also present.

I waved for them to carry on and instead went to check on Nathaniel, who was too pensive to notice us approach. I flew over and landed next to him. "What are you doing over here by yourself?" I asked.

"Oh, hello. I've been keeping watch for danger while everyone else is busy." He brightened up. "Marianna told me about your meeting with Gaea. I'm sorry I was asleep for it."

"It's no big deal, you deserve to rest too, champ." I shook and kneaded his shoulders to psyche him up like a boxing coach. "But now I need some of your specialty."

He smiled, almost laughing. "Aether crystals?"

"You got it. I'm thinking of using the dust to make weapons on the fly in case we run into anything that my powers can't touch."

"Do you want it light enchanted again and the same size as what you used against Gianluca?"

"What are you talking about?"

I sensed a sudden nervous vibe from Nathaniel and looked to Rafael, but he said nothing.

"Oh, um, I thought Noah told you and that's why you mentioned it," Nathaniel said.

"Told me what? I only heard about the statues, which sounded bad enough."

"You used the Light Effigy we had above the abbey to get through Gianluca's armor, but he's well. You saw him."

With everything else that was happening I hadn't thought too much about why the effigies were gone. I assumed they had been lost during one of the assault on the island.

"Okay, then. Yes, that size would be great. You can do it when we get there because I don't know if I'll be able to take it all with me."

"It really was nothing," Nathaniel reassured me. "He was only affected for a short while, but Isis healed him. It wasn't bad."

"All right." *I'll have to bring this up with Noah another time.* "Uh, what is that blue ball of light above Connor and why is he facedown in the dirt over there?"

"That's an ice spirit he befriended in the Astral Realm," Rafael explained. "Connor keeps channeling all his aether to it until he passes out so it'll stay with him on Earth. We've insisted not to several times already."

"I'll get him." Nathaniel leaped across the lawn and returned with Connor. The ice spirit faded away.

"Hi, Dorian!" Connor was as cheerful as ever.

"Hello. Don't give yourself aether poisoning before we leave," I warned him.

"I won't. I wanted to practice with my spirit companion so he can help too."

"How can you communicate with it? You're not a whisperer like Alexandre, are you?" I asked.

"No, I wish. He still understands me most of the time though. Wisps can sense the intent behind words, but it's cryptic to them. They like people with strong emotions because they're easier to understand."

"Can you bind it to a crystal or something so you don't keep running out of aether?"

"Alexandre says that's like slavery for them, like necromancy binding souls. It prevents them from going back to the aether when they're tired so they're forced to stay awake forever."

"Better not then. Just be careful, all right?"

"I will be. Thanks for allowing me to keep being friends with him."

"Sure thing. Why not go train with Noah for a bit?" I suggested.

Connor checked the crowd. "He's busy with Marianna. I'll ask Claudius."

Noah could be heard over the clashing of swords around him letting loose a deluge of expletives at being caught in one of Marianna's gravity traps. He looked funny floating there unable to escape even through his mist form. I yelled for him to take it down a notch and Marianna released him. He immediately threw her into the water once he was freed.

Lyle was walking up right as she skated across the ley lines to land where she could dry off in the sun. As puritan as the Order was, it wasn't uncommon for them to spar in light clothing while using real bladed weapons. The lack of the safety net armor provided kept their senses sharp. However, it *was* uncommon for Lyle to miss a sight like a beautiful woman in linen clothes turned almost see-through from being wet. He passed her by without so much as a turn of his head.

"Hey, check out what I found down by the beach." He held up an assault rifle he was carrying on his back. "It was with the wreckage from those ships. This one's still in good condition. You think you can do anything with it?"

"No problem." I turned it bubblegum pink.

"I knew that fashion comment was going to bite me in the ass at some point. I don't even care though. At least it's something."

"Oh! What a pretty pink," Marianna exclaimed. "I wish I could have a pink sword. It would go so well with the color of blood."

"You scare me sometimes. Why not use your magic to change one of your swords' color?" I asked, returning the gun to normal.

"We were never allowed."

Noah appeared with us. "What the hell is this? We were in the middle of a match!"

"I'm pretty sure you already lost," I teased.

He pretended that he didn't hear and slapped a dirty handprint on the back of my pants. "Thanks for that," I said. "Getting back to business, we can probably enchant ammo for your rifle, Lyle. The issue isn't the demons, but that The Infernal Machine is a spirit and they don't always have a weakness. We won't know anything more about it until we get inside its lair."

"Light still works for the minions though. I'm not trying to take on the king by myself," said Lyle.

"We'll take care of it. I'll merge some enchanted aether dust into the bullets. Marianna, do you think you can enchant a weaker version of that anti-gravity spell into boots for Noah? I was thinking it could give him even more mobility."

"Yes, enchantments don't only have to be raw elements. I can do it now, but if it's for mobility I'd think you'd want *low*-gravity and not anti-gravity or else he'd just float there." She concealed her giggle with a turn of her head.

"That's probably better then...for now."

"Screw that magic crap." Noah poked my forehead. "You know how I feel about needing a crutch to win."

"What happens when it's used against you?"

"I'll figure something out. Fancy armor didn't help us when you got blasted. Skill overcomes everything that's possible and I'll be bringing my blades. Anything more than that is an opening for sloppy execution. Equipment and tricks can fail or be taken away, but you'll always have your experience."

"I still wouldn't refuse a temporary solution to most of the spells being flung around in these battles."

"The only thing we know of that's capable of blocking more magic would be Gianluca's darkness," said Rafael. "Although that wasn't effective against the Machine either."

"How about the oblivion element?" Connor suggested. "Liam uses it on his swords all the time to dispel magic."

"Oblivion works like a vacuum that would erase the aether used to enchant with it," Rafael explained. "It negates magic by drawing the energy of a spell into itself, but that only works if the energy is equal to or less than the charge of oblivion. Any more would cause the reaction to overflow and become unstable, which could kill you."

"I knew that," Connor bluffed.

"Then you'd know it takes decades of study to use it effectively." He gave Connor a friendly tap.

"Can we put an enchantment on the gloves?" Although he claimed otherwise, I was preparing for Noah to "forget" his sword again or in case he was disarmed. "Maybe with electricity to stun whatever he hits?"

Noah put his hands on his hips, hesitant to show approval. "Hmm, I *do* hate being on the other end of that."

"Leave it to me!" Connor exclaimed, bolting toward the abbey.

"You only have to make the crystal and I'll merge it!" I shouted after him.

"What about for yourself? If you had aether dust with all different enchantments you could imitate casting spells with every element," Nathaniel suggested to me.

"Dorian would need to keep them separated though, or conflicting spells and elements would cause a chain reaction," said Rafael.

"I'll pass for now. I don't want to experiment too much in a battle like this, and I'd rather not humiliate myself by exploding my pants off with the first step onto the battlefield."

Noah snorted in amusement.

"Want to come help me enchant some swords and bullets?" I asked Nathaniel.

"Of course."

"I'm gonna get in some more sparring." Noah rolled his shoulders and rocked on the balls of his bare feet, shadowboxing me in slow motion until I played along and blocked him a few times.

He was about to leave and let the rest of us head inside when a fireball struck the ground.

Playtime was over.

The petite figure of Kamakura's fire guardian appeared from the flames and bowed waist high to present me with a rolled parchment. It contained a map of China with a rendezvous point circled northeast of Hong Kong.

She only spoke three words before departing.

"It is time."

Part IV

"Harbinger of Tomorrow"

Current world population: 5.02 billion

Chapter Forty-Six

The Order was always calm and systematic when we deployed, but I worried this time more than ever that it was due to feeling untouchable under the protection of their patron deity. I was in overdrive scrambling around the bedroom to get our gear ready. Aether dust and assorted objects were flying everywhere as my thoughts bounced from one to the next.

"Are you bracing my wrist or trying to break it?" Noah mused as I wrapped his hand and forearm. He could have done it himself, but my anxiety took charge.

"Sorry, I'm—"

"It's fine. Good technique."

"Thanks, but you still have to wear the hood." I pulled it up over his head for the second time since he got dressed and hurried to wrap his other hand. I was glad I had managed to get him to wear sleeves by bargaining with a few thin orange accent lines along the black leather to help define his muscles and pay homage to his tiger nickname. I would have gone for more accuracy by inverting the colors if I didn't already know the argument it'd cause.

"I'll put it on when we get there," he protested, putting the hood down again.

All that was left for me to do was create two swords and then imbue Lyle's ammunition.

"You gotta chill," Lyle said upon entering the room. "Remember, it's only recon. I take a peek at their computers with the special sight and we bail. In and out."

"We don't know that for sure anymore," I said. "We have a map marked a lot further south than where we were expecting to go back to the last site. It could mean that the Machine broke through and is taking over much faster than we anticipated."

"I could go check," Nathaniel suggested. He and Rafael had been staying quiet by the window while I bounced from one task to the next. "I'll fly there and—"

"No! We stay together and stick with the plan. We'll find out when we get there, but I don't want anyone jumping in head first." I looked Rafael in the eyes as I finished that sentence.

Noah placed my prayer beads in my hand, put his hood up, and whispered into my ear. "Don't get distracted. Relax. Concentrate. And then tell me where my *tabi* are."

"In the sock drawer."

"We won't do anything to make you worry. I swear it," Rafael pledged.

I smiled at him. "You better not."

It was reassuring to hear their supportive words, but *I* was supposed to be the leader. I had to pull myself together and act like it. "Sorry, everyone. Just a moment of anxiety, but I'm over it."

"You don't need to apologize," Nathaniel said.

"Yeah, what's to be nervous about? You barged right in and gave that king the business once already," said Lyle.

"I was motivated by anger because it dug around in your head and almost killed you."

"So whenever you lose focus we just have to beat the shit out of him," Noah said as he rummaged through the dresser. "Dorian, there are no tabi in any of these drawers. This is why I keep my stuff out where I can find it faster."

"Leaving clothes around the room doesn't make them easier to find, organizing them in a finite area like a small rectangular box does."

"The room is a small rectangular box," he grumbled. "What kind of serial killer bullshit is this that you dedicate a drawer to only socks—oh here they are. You folded them so I thought they were yours."

"Are you done complaining now?" I laughed.

"That depends on where you hid my good belt." He smirked and pointed at me. "And I swear to god if you say there's a belt drawer..."

Without a word I looked over at the belt hanging on his sword rack where he had left it.

"That was a test," he quipped.

"The two of you bicker like you've been married for years," Lyle remarked.

Noah winked at me. I smiled to myself and resumed my work.

Drawing particles from the air and the walls, I crafted blades for Noah, one full-length katana and one shorter wakizashi.

"Still can't create wood or organic fibers like cotton and wool." I sighed and took from the fireplace mantle to make the scabbards and hilts. "It's like there's a lapse in memory. I can only make other materials feel like it."

I worked in the aether crystal for each blade. After discussing the use of more than one type of aether dust I decided to try mixing in a bit of Nathaniel's light aether and a crystal charged with my own power to give the enchantments an added bite. Rafael reassured me that since the elements were not in direct conflict with one another there wouldn't be any horrible effects... although the Order had never been able to apply multiple enchantments on the same object before to test it.

"Let me get a fire one of those too," Noah said.

"What's that going to do against fire-immune demons?"

"Nothing, sometimes I just like to burn stuff."

"You need to be careful how many enchantments you have," Rafael warned. "When in use, the aether can interact with other forms of energy like the soul, similar to when casting magic, and it can cause poisoning or worse. Feeding off divine ichor likely gives you a higher threshold, but there are still limits."

"Just when it was getting interesting," Noah complained, inspecting the swords. "Damn these are beautiful. Gotta be your best yet. You really do work better under pressure."

I strapped and buckled his fingerless gloves on over the wraps. The lightning crystal Connor prepared had already been merged into them and the gravity boots were completed with Marianna's assistance earlier.

"You gonna feed me now too?" he asked with a hint of sarcasm.

"I already do."

"I know. You take good care of me." He gave me a peck on the cheek and adjusted the gloves while I put on his armbands. "Why do I need those if I'm wearing the sleeves?"

"Because I said so."

"So bossy. All right, how do these work?" When Noah tapped his fists together they let off a spark. Of course the very next thing he had to try was zapping me with a poke.

"Hey!" I jumped at the shock.

"The more force you put behind whatever you come into contact with, the stronger the charge should be," Rafael explained. "You don't have a connection to the aether so you can't control much else than that."

"What happens if I do this?" Noah glided his hand across the skin on my arm, making the hairs stand on end and giving me a warm tingling sensation.

"That actually feels good."

"Ohh. We're gonna have some fun with these later." He grinned with an arched eyebrow.

Lyle cleared his throat to interrupt.

"You're not invited," Noah said to him. "I think I'll call these my Raijin Tekko—Gauntlets of the Thunder God. You gotta name your stuff or it's bad luck. That's where I went wrong in the past. I waited too long on the names. Every weapon has an identity of its own that bonds you to it. And if

I ever meet Raijin he's getting a punch in the face with these to prove I'm worthy."

"Please don't." I sighed at his devilish grin and went back to enchanting.

"I'm gonna do it," he insisted.

I merged the last of the aether dust into ammo that Lyle had found while Noah tried on his boots.

"Dorian, I've been thinking about how to best address the other gods," Nathaniel started. "I've noticed that Calder kneels to you and Kamakura's guardians bow as a show of respect, but I wouldn't feel right doing the same with their gods when you don't like for us to do it with you."

"I guess you could fist bump."

"Is that a type of salute?"

Lyle and I demonstrated in the middle of him loading a finished magazine into his rifle.

"Oh. Really?" Nathaniel questioned. "I can't see them being too receptive to that. Maybe Gianluca..."

"I'm kidding. I wouldn't worry though. Do whatever you're comfortable with as long as it isn't anything Noah would ever do. You can salute or bow with your hand over your heart like you guys do with me sometimes."

Marianna entered as Noah was hopping in place to test the low-gravity effect of his boots. She was wearing elegant pieces of plate armor over the leather and chainmail and carrying her helmet, which she rarely wore.

"Dorian, everyone is ready and awaiting your word in the courtyard," she said. "We've scried a location to teleport to from the map and Liam has introduced the children to his mother. They have everything they need."

"This is it then. I'll need to be teleported with you since I don't have a reference point to do it myself. Nathaniel too, since I don't want us to be separated if he flies there."

"What about aura cloaking for you and Nathaniel during the infiltration?"

"It's not worth it. The Machine is too powerful to be fooled by any of our tricks."

On our way to the courtyard I overheard Marianna chastising Rafael for not being present during their cabal's preparations. From the sound of it he missed out on their battle plan and decision to wear their heavier armor. "Did you even get oiled?" she whispered. "What were you *doing*? We already supplied everything that was requested."

"What's this about oil?" I asked to let them know I was listening without taking sides. I had seen them coat their armor with a clear lacquer in the past, but it didn't seem like that was what she was referring to this time.

"It's a mugwort salve we apply to the skin as a preventative antiseptic and painkiller," Marianna explained. "It also has some minor healing properties to help stop the bleeding of flesh wounds when casting a spell isn't possible. I don't know why we still refer to it by mugwort though when that hasn't been a main ingredient for at least a century. It's ten percent at most. I've wanted to rename it 'deathsbane' but Helena thinks it would be inappropriate."

"We can discuss nomenclature when we get back. It sounds useful though, so you better go oil yourself up, Raf."

He maintained his dignity through silence and broke from the group.

When we got there the courtyard was full of every able-bodied knight in the Order, as Marianna had said. It was an impressive sight to see them all standing at attention in their Alabaster armor. I knew who each one of them was under their helmets and made sure to picture their faces as I entered the crowd, holding hands and touching shoulders in greeting as I passed.

"I don't want to give a big speech and put more pressure on you than there needs to be," I announced from the middle of the group. "We're going to give some demons a bad day, but no over-the-top heroics. Everyone stays outside and keeps the bad guys busy so the inside team can investigate."

It was one of the few times I wasn't floating to appear taller. I didn't know why. Perhaps I was becoming more comfortable with myself around them or I liked the security of being able to disappear when surrounded.

If only my parents could see me now. Or Octavio. What would it have been like to have them living here? Knowing my parents there would be constant questions long after everything had already been explained. I'd have to appoint an official question-answerer. Probably Liam. Marianna would be the obvious choice, but Liam would be more fun to watch sweat in the hot seat.

I miss them.

"—Dermott's cabal could do it." Marianna was looking at me for an answer.

"Do what? Sorry, I was thinking."

"Escort Commander Turner to the fortress entrance separate from you. The Infernal King will be looking for you so keeping you apart until the last possible moment could be beneficial. The only risk is the chance that the ley lines there might not be traversable, so they'll have to go by foot, but he and his cabal specialize the most in defensive magic; able to be submerged in lava and withstand the pressure at the bottom of the ocean without fear."

"Dermott has a five year old daughter."

"She's six now, Ascended," said the knight to my immediate left from behind his helmet, which he promptly removed to speak with me. Thirty-six, dashing, and bearer of an admirable beard and mustache, Dermott was a vision of gallant polish, but more importantly: a devoted father. The kind that wrote his daughter poems and braided her hair after fighting demons all day.

"Madeline is *six* now? Did I miss a birthday?"

How could I forget Madeline? The girl whose sword-wielding dolly wore both a princess dress and a knight helmet because according to her, crowns don't protect you like helmets do. The dress, however, was just a really pretty dress.

"It's quite all right. She had a birthday last week."

That was while I was lost in the Rift.

I never liked letting a birthday in the Order pass without some sort of recognition. The more withdrawn and less popular I got as I was growing up made birthdays something I preferred to avoid in my human years, so I wanted to make up for lost opportunities with my new family. I think I was twelve or thirteen when the only party guests I had from that point on were my parents.

"I get the logic behind the idea, but I'm not putting a little girl's father deeper into mortal danger."

"She's my pride and joy and would be happy to hear of the honor brought to the family name no matter the outcome."

"I bet she'd be happier to have her dad come home safe to read her a bedtime story."

His sentimental expression was all I needed to see.

"My cabal could do it," Marianna suggested.

"Then who would be in command? Half of you are on the council."

"Tobias's cabal then?"

"But I *just* brought back Liam's mom. I'm not chancing—"

"Dorian." Noah nudged me to stop making excuses.

"We'll stick with the original plan," I said. "Noah can get him up there with super speed if it comes to it."

Rafael snuck into the courtyard, putting on his helmet and fixing the strap of his quiver in place.

"We should get moving, it's been almost an hour," Lyle said.

Noah lifted me onto his shoulder for the final rallying cry.

"Okay, everyone, let's go take the first step to dethroning this king and taking back our world together!"

Chapter Forty-Seven

Nathaniel surveyed the eastern half of China's Guangdong province from the crimson skies. A province that was once alive with over a hundred million people had been picked clean and recolonized in days. The last human stronghold for miles was in Hong Kong where the skeletal remains of the Chinese military fortified the borders with what resources they had left. If they didn't meet their end from the demons coming to partake in the buffet, they would be dead from the conditions associated with extreme overcrowding in less than a month.

The gods had assembled as the first and last line of defense against the mysteries of the towering metal fortress that had reappeared here on the shore. This was far from where we had first seen the megastructure, but it was the same one. I could feel it. I knew the king must be up there at the top, watching from above the clouds.

The location of the fortress wasn't the only thing that had changed, however.

"They went from Stone Age to Iron Age overnight," I said, observing the Infernal civilization downhill from us that was blocking our path.

Gone were the rock formations and uninhabitable wastes. In their place stood structures closely resembling rural housing from antiquity.

Nathaniel landed to share what he had seen on his aerial reconnaissance. "It goes all the way up the coast for hundreds of miles like this. A battalion to the north is circling around behind us on horseback."

"Horses?" Lyle asked.

"Yes, great black armored ones with hooves and eyes of hellfire."

Not only had the skyline changed, but so had the local denizens. These were no longer the lumbering, thuggish ogres from our previous encounters. You could see it in their eyes, their mannerisms and interactions. They were communicating in their own Infernal tongue. They had domesticated and trained the hellhounds as war beasts along with forging weapons and armor in preparation for battle the same as we had.

"This does not bode well," said Kamakura. "The king here flaunts its sovereignty over knowledge and progression."

"It changes naught," said Cernunnos from his seat upon Yggdrasil. He was surrounded by the berserkers that were being kept pacified by Isis's light.

"The Machine wants its own creations to inherit Earth," I said. "The demons are still only pawns even if they got an upgrade. It just means everyone has to be a bit more careful."

I wasn't sure how much of that I believed, but there was no turning back and no sense inciting more panic.

"Poor creatures doomed to exist as naught but a distraction. 'Tis the folly of those whom worship false idols," said Isis.

She had brought along a snake coiled around her arm that she was doting over and a cat sitting at her feet. I really wanted to question her thought process on that, but we didn't have time. The demons below were advancing.

"This is no trouble," Gianni said. "I finish these and join you in the castle when there is no more."

"Nay, allow us the first move." Cernunnos tilted his head toward Aífe. "Go."

The berserkers charged in with Aífe transforming on the way to lead the pack. Once outside Isis's aura, Cernunnos casted a spell that draped his warriors in a heavy brume that clung to their fur. The numbers were not on our side, but it wouldn't be long until we would see if that handicap was consequential.

"Watch our back for the battalion coming around behind us," I told Marianna. "Anything to the west is the Order's responsibility. And don't forget that this isn't an extermination. You need to make sure that you engage as many as possible so we aren't followed and don't go overboard so a deadlier last resort isn't triggered. The demons won't want an outright slaughter either. Too few souls to eat, and a prolonged fight has more opportunity to cause chaos."

"As you command, Ascended," she said with unfailing confidence.

The two rushing tides made impact on the battlefield. The Infernals pushed forward, but the berserkers pushed back harder in a macabre storm front that made them appear as a single ghoulish creature, a glowering specter of death embodying the planet's hatred and rage toward the unwelcomed. Only fleeting glimpses of outstretched maws revealed the individuals within the nightmare made manifest.

"Holy shit," Lyle said under his breath.

"We should head south," Nathaniel whispered to me.

He was standing so close I could feel his heart pounding.

"Not yet." I whispered back to him. "Stay calm and we'll be fine."

Increased intelligence wasn't proving to be an asset for the demons in wake of the berserkers' savagery. They hadn't resorted to spraying hellfire everywhere, which would also kill themselves in such a congested battle, and may have been showing considerable improvements in skill and mobility, but it didn't amount to much against the immobilizing roars followed up by having their heads ripped from their necks. Someone should have told them to forge their weapons out of silver if they wanted to stand a chance.

It was becoming painful to watch, but also nice to find the odds stacked in our favor for once.

"We could fly up there and end this before anyone needs to get hurt," Nathaniel proposed again.

I held onto his arm. "Stick with the plan. It's why we have one."

The upper hand was beginning to slip from the berserkers' claws as the demons learned how to handle the onslaught and reinforcements flooded in to replenish their numbers. Blind rage was becoming a hindrance instead of strength for the berserkers. The molten Infernal blood burning through their insides with each bite healed over time, yet the pain drove them deeper into uncontrollable madness. The Fury had its hold on them now and I swore that they were growing in size too.

"I think I just saw one of them eat part of a sword," said Lyle.

A berserker was knocked back toward our group and acted as if it didn't recognize us. It went for Kamakura, but Calder took its head off with his bare hands when her guardians moved to intercept. The first casualty on our side was by one of our own. He didn't seem bothered by what he had to do, but my stomach turned. I could never have brought myself to do the same.

I looked up at Noah, watching his eyes scan the battlefield from behind his mask and hood. He had been uncharacteristically quiet since arriving so as to concentrate on every detail.

"Will Aífe be all right?" I asked Cernunnos.

There was no answer.

Her charcoal fur, now charged with the silver energy I had seen her use when she fought Noah, stood out amongst the other berserkers as she shredded through the tough hide and armor of the Infernal forces unfazed by the momentary stab wounds spilling her blood. With only one arm she fared better than the sum of her pack.

"She is blessed by the serenity of the Moon, the Goddess's sister," Calder answered to break the tense silence. "A gift unique to all den mothers and native only to the Moon's grace. 'Tis she who brings life to fruition through equilibrium, much as the mothers do."

"Is that what the energy is surrounding Aífe?"

"Aye—"

"The Moon doth not share the sky with such an abominable place," Cernunnos interrupted, as if to say Aífe's chances were bleak without some proximity to the source of her power, but he was right. There was no moon here in Hell.

Cernunnos was not one that made it easy to read his emotions, but they were quite clear at the moment with the way he tightened his grip around the handle of his enormous scythe. The claws on his other hand scratched his skull hard enough to leave a mark.

"Are you unwell, Horned One?" Isis asked him.

"Death raps upon the door of mine enemies and I am rife with intent to welcome its chilling bite to the lot of these sorry fools in vengeance...to taste their last gasps of agony shall be such a sweet thing...such a sweet thing indeed."

Great. Our Lord of Death has had emotions for a day and is already losing it. I can't really blame him for going crazy having to sit and watch though.

A rumbling from the west alerted us to the approaching battalion. I flew up to get a better look, but Noah pulled me down by my leg before I could see anything.

"I was just checking—"

"Don't," he insisted.

I disregarded his warning and went to fly again, teleporting out of reach when he grabbed me. Then I wished I hadn't. Nathaniel had understated the size of the battalion by a large margin or maybe my definition was faulty. They seemed to not have an end as they reached across the rocky plain to the horizon and beyond.

I landed without saying anything. Showing doubt wasn't an option when I had others looking up to me for strength. I could have used one of Noah's witticisms to help me relax after seeing that.

"Alexandre, whenever you're ready," Marianna prompted.

His silent response was to send two crow spirits toward the enemy with a smoke-filled glass orb in their talons.

"What is that?" I asked.

"Lavender and Dittany of Crete incense corrupted with a drop of cooled Infernal blood to affect their kind," he answered. "The incense is meant to aid a soul in achieving astral projection by evoking a state of hyper-clarity. Demons can have hundreds or even thousands of souls within them and now those souls are flooding their captors' minds at once with all of the experiences."

"Sounds like a hell of a bad trip," said Lyle. "You're gonna need a lot more than that though, aren't you?"

"We only need to break up their front ranks so we can divide them by cabal," Marianna explained as Alexandre sent out another air strike.

I ascended to check on what progress was being made. It was impossible to tell where the incense had been dropped in the sea of bodies, but the wave was beginning to diverge in places as had been planned.

"I think it's working," I called on the way back down to them.

Marianna made haste and assumed command, advancing with the rest of the Order to prevent the demons from reaching us. "Halt the detachment to the east, Dermott," she instructed.

I wished we could have switched to let the berserkers handle the mounted troops that were putting the Order at a steeper disadvantage, but the cabals were doing well with isolating groups of the demons to wall off their rearward approach. Marianna's reverse gravity traps tossed units of the hellish cavalry into the air where they were carved up by their own weapons under her magnetic control. Liam and Rafael teleported toward each other, letting their swords meet inside the head of a larger demon for a gruesome finish. I caught them celebrating their teamwork with a fist bump before trading places to cover each other's back.

Finally something to loosen the knot in my stomach.

I kept an eye out for Connor to be sure he was handling himself just as well. He was easy to spot by the ice blue spirit orbiting him. I watched him freeze the front hooves of a charging horse, causing it to trip forward. The hellfire continued to burn inside the ice without either interacting with each other. He leaped over the beast with the spirit turning itself into a shield of thick ice to protect him as he plunged his frost-covered sword into the rider's head for an instantaneous kill.

I was impressed by how agile everyone remained in their heavy armor although I knew a lot of it was supplemented by magic and alchemical elixirs. Liam's cabal had a fantastic combination utilizing the full team, where he would rush in with his weapons drawn to get an enemy's attention and then parry the incoming counter so the next in the cabal could teleport behind and plunge their blade into the distracted foe's back before teleporting away again. Each member went in succession parrying and backstabbing in a matter of seconds, ending with all five standing in a circle around the demon and using their swords as a conduit for a fatal discharge of pure aether.

Empress Kamakura was speaking with her guardians in Japanese so I asked Noah what was being said.

"We're being surrounded and the kids aren't enough to hold off this many."

Chouko, Guardian of Water, was nominated to lend her aid. She strolled past us in her kimono as calm as the still surface of a pond. With a single gesture she called upon the intensity of the briny deep to wash away the rear guard of the cavalry and cut the rest off from their reinforcements, assailing them with geysers and javelins of water conjured from portals by simple hand motions. The roaring tide left the Order a fraction of the demons to deal with until the remainder found a way across, but that was resolved by Liam, who took a page from the guardians' elemental synergy by electrifying the waters to hold them off a while longer.

The battle was starting to swing in our favor again when one of the horses got a jolt from backing up too close to the water and kicked somebody in the head, rendering them unconscious in the middle of all the fighting.

"No." Noah held me back from going to help. "I've kicked them harder than that. You have to trust them."

To my relief, Alexandre went to the fallen knight's side to help revive them. A gush of hot blood spurted from the neck of an Infernal foot soldier that made it too close after Alexandre evoked the aid of his Massacre spirit trinity. Reinforcements from the cavalry that circled back were trapped within flashes of a veiny purple fog around their heads that throbbed like the physical embodiment of a migraine. They died from the gaping wounds carved into vital spots before their bodies fell.

"This is too close," I muttered under my breath.

Cernunnos showed equal consternation as another berserker was taken down. He paced back and forth atop Yggdrasil, pawing at the bark with his hoof as if getting ready to stampede.

"Now's our chance," said Noah. He looked at Nathaniel. "Take Dorian and head south fast before we're noticed. I'll take the human. Don't forget to stay low and keep the headlights off."

"Isis is coming with us," I reminded him.

"She better move her ass then. I'm not carrying everyone."

We were about to depart when Cernunnos's rage bested his self-control. He broke ranks and did exactly what we had feared. With his scythe held high, he rode a massive wave of Yggdrasil's roots and branches into battle, steamrolling all it came in contact with. A dark wind poured from his eye sockets and released the souls from every demon's body in sight.

The response from Hell was immediate in the form of a legion of rakshasa spawning in from Infernal summoning circles across the battlefield. They snatched up the countless disembodied souls to increase their own strength and executed the few remaining demons to cannibalize their power.

"And this is why we had a plan," Noah said. "Judging by their auras alone, each one of those is at least double the strength of the last."

Calder joined his master's side in combat, transforming without hesitation and pounding his fists on the ground to upheave the little that Yggdrasil hadn't.

"We have to help," I said. Truthfully, I was only concerned about the Order at this point. Cernunnos had sealed his own fate along with his followers.

"You'll be here forever knocking them over for more to take their place and we won't accomplish what we came here for," said Lyle.

"He's right," Nathaniel agreed. "I could stay in your stead if you wish."

The rakshasa didn't seem too interested in confronting the Order though, since they were little more than a nuisance compared to the Lord of Death's rampage. But what once took a single knight to vanquish now needed an entire cabal to whittle down. Their remarkable ability to parry and riposte anything thrown at them in all directions at once due to their four arms and lightning reflexes was exasperating to overcome. To top it off, the cutting edge of their blades were enchanted with the ultraviolet glow of the oblivion element used to negate every spell directed at them.

The berserkers weren't having much better luck.

"Wait," Noah stopped me. "Something's different. Give me a second and don't do anything."

Noah vaulted a terrific distance with the help of his gravity boots and engaged one of the weakened rakshasa in blinding fast hand-to-hand combat to disarm it. He incorporated quick, intermittent slashes with his wakizashi, landing one stunning blow after the next to sever two arms so that they were even. The rakshasa fought well enough to get one too many hits in for my liking, but Noah ended it by jumping and using the side of his electrified hand to cleave through the demon's body with a falling chop.

"Are we supposed to watch him take them all on himself?" Lyle asked.

Noah attempted to repeat the same finishing move on another rakshasa, this time using his speed and invisibility to ambush it while it was busy fighting three of the Order.

He failed and it deflected his hand with the flat side of one of its swords.

"They're learning," I said. "Fast."

Noah dodged a retaliatory attack with a backflip and reappeared beside me. "Damn, this is gonna be interesting. I recognized them using some of my moves so I had to test it. They're sharing information between them so they can't be hit by the same thing twice, but it's reflexive, like they're seeing into the future. I saw that last one move its sword in the way right as I was coming down."

"They're stopping every spell fired at them with an oblivion enchantment too," I added. "They'd have to have encyclopedic knowledge of the Order's magic to do that."

"Is like the sorceress we fight. Knowledge demon, yes?" Gianni asked.

"How curious. I was unaware the rakshasa were demons of knowledge," said Kamakura. "Rakshasa are no more than cannibals who drink the blood of their victims with a touch of their hands. It was my understanding they were mercenaries under employ of the king or simple automata used as soldiers."

"Now it makes sense why they've been so weak for demon lords," I said. "They're crash test dummies sending data back to where they're being manufactured so the next batch is better than the last for when they're ready to stage a serious assault."

"The factory where they're being made is inside the fortress," Nathaniel reminded us. "We have to shut it down."

"Go. I will fight," Gianni told me. "Is early, but what can we do? I make sure your people are safe."

"Thank you." I smiled. "Good luck."

"*Bona fortuna.*"

I put my arm around Nathaniel's neck and held on as he shot across the land. I closed my eyes and didn't look back.

Noah made it to the south end of the fortress with Lyle ahead of us. The exterior wall along the coast must have gone for two to three miles and there wasn't a single door or window in sight.

Isis teleported herself to our location moments later with her pets. "Have you eyes on any way to enter?" she asked Lyle.

"*Me?* Uh...no. I don't see anything."

"You have the magic eyes. Make yourself useful," Noah said to him.

"I don't know how. I've been seeing normally since that séance with Gaea."

"We'll have to make an entrance then," said Nathaniel. "We don't have time to waste."

"I sense a powerful energy from within barring our path by magic," said Isis.

Nathaniel set off without further discussion and slammed fists first into the perimeter wall. There wasn't so much as a dent.

"The rakshasa come," Isis announced before anything appeared.

"How could you tell?" I asked.

"I can sense their energies coalesce ahead of their material forms."

"I'll deal with them. Find us a way in and do it fast," said Noah as two rakshasa rose up from summoning circles. "But knock gently or else there was no reason in us sneaking over here."

The urge to fight was becoming irrepressible. Sitting on the sidelines like this was driving me insane.

Noah was handling both rakshasa as if they had rehearsed the battle together at length. He had them disarmed almost as soon as they began and managed to slice off one of their hands when whipping out his wakizashi amid a brutal combination of kicks and shocking punches.

None of that was unprecedented for Noah. What impressed me was how he utilized his time manipulation in short bursts to launch innumerable punches that exploded with a thunderclap from the buildup of electricity being released all at once in real time. A single round was enough to inflict critical injuries to his target and throw it backward a decent distance, but that only worked once per rakshasa before their precognitive reflexes activated.

"I like these," he yelled, holding up a fist to show me his gauntlet.

"Dorian, there's a seam up here, but I can't get it opened!" Nathaniel shouted to me.

"Go ahead, I'm having fun," Noah told me. "We should do this more often."

Lyle took cover and I flew to Nathaniel with Isis while keeping an eye on the situation below. The rakshasa were adapting to every fighting style Noah swapped between. Even he would be out of moves eventually. They were coordinated to perfection so that he couldn't benefit from creating confusion among them either. What had appeared rehearsed in the beginning was starting to show signs of the choreography falling apart as Noah took more than a few hard hits and was forced into his mist form to escape a spate of attempts to grapple him.

It wasn't only the rakshasa's skills that were improving. Their bodies grew sturdier and faster to match Noah. Keeping track of his movements was becoming almost impossible as he sped up to maintain his supremacy. All I could see was the blur from him chaining multiple roundhouse, side, and back kicks in what would be impossible fluidity for a normal human. I knew he was starting to rely on kicking and footwork, over brawling and swordplay, to curb the rakshasa's advantage of mimicking him with twice the number of arms.

"What type of metal is this?" Nathaniel asked as the two of us worked together to pry open the paneling of the fortress. I was giving it my all, yet we couldn't make it budge.

"Just keep trying," I told him. "We need to get in whatever it takes."

The battle we had left up north was becoming more intense as rumblings turned into sonorous crashes. I could see the flashes of light and billowing clouds of smoke.

Nathaniel had his feet braced against the wall to pull up at the seam with both hands to no avail.

A stifled groan of excruciating pain came from below. Noah's forearm was broken and his wakizashi stabbed through his thigh.

"I'm fine!" Noah yelled. He put his hand out to tell Isis not to intervene so he could heal himself.

"Prostrate yourself before the metal monarch," the rakshasa demanded.

"Don't tell me what to do." He pulled the wakizashi from his leg and used it to cut another arm from the demon.

"This isn't working," I said to Nathaniel. "Find another way in."

Noah was still fighting strong despite the setback and was able to crack one of their skulls with a high kick into a heel drop. I flew farther up the sheer wall of the fortress with Nathaniel to look for a different possible entry point. It hadn't occurred to me that this could be a problem. My panic from keeping an eye on Noah wasn't making it any easier, but being swamped by an army would have been worse. He had one of the rakshasa on the brink of death when its own companion struck the killing blow to take its life... and all the souls it contained. It didn't seem to be a voluntary sacrifice based on how the dying rakshasa flailed in a final attempt to protect itself.

"Over here," Nathaniel called. "It's one of the portholes I was taken into from my vision."

The traitorous demon was now twice as powerful and impervious to the shock of Noah's gauntlets. The fight was turning into schoolyard bullying as he became less of a threat, and the rakshasa alternated between pummeling him and then shoving him down as he staggered. I had lost count of how many times I heard the crunch of his bones fracturing in the midst of them exchanging blows, but I knew it was worse than I thought when Noah had to resort to simply pushing his opponent away to keep his distance as it walked after him. He managed to inflict a series of deep slashes across its torso before being disarmed and having his broken arm twisted.

"Ascended, your face has changed," Isis said in a concerned manner.

I knew what she meant. It was all falling apart before the plan had even taken off and my own rage was boiling over, giving way to the darker side of my emotions in this damned place.

Have to concentrate or it was all a waste...Relax. Focus.

In yet another unpredictable move, the rakshasa thrust a hand inside the tear of Noah's pants to grab his thigh and sidestepped behind him. Noah winced just long enough for the rakshasa to use its other two arms to pin his back and get a third arm around his neck. It took Noah to the ground and locked its legs around his while constricting all of its appendages to strangulate him as a python would, until he barely escaped by flickering into and out of a cloud of mist.

I'll raze this whole goddamn country to the ground if that's what it takes to get these walls opened!

"Is this the warrior the gods choose to represent them? Or a sacrifice for the king?" the rakshasa bellowed.

It had Noah on his knees with his hood down and two hands compressing his head to force blood from his nose and eyes while its other two hands held Noah's arms out to the side. I didn't realize why Noah wasn't escaping in his mist form as he struggled and started to go limp until I saw the rakshasa rip the armor from his chest to get at his bare skin.

It's drinking his blood through its hands.

"Don't—!" Noah yelled to me in agony. "Just—stick to...the plan...!"

Lyle opened fire on the demon's head, but had to stop or risk it moving Noah in the way of the bullets.

"Allow me." Nathaniel floated from the wall to go to confront the rakshasa.

"No. I'll take care of this. Just get us inside," I told Nathaniel as I flew down and pulled the rakshasa's arms open to free Noah. His tan skin had faded to a paler shade and his body was limp, but he stayed conscious.

Even in my enraged state, this rakshasa was more resistant to my powers than I would have thought.

"Tell us how to enter the fortress or I will make you suffer worse than you ever thought imaginable," I said from where I was floating. My clothes were turning black on their own as I bent, twisted, and tore each segment of the rakshasa's fingers and dismantled its arms inch by inch to the shoulder. "Answer me! Do you think you're worth anything to your king when I'm the one it wants?"

I should have known that torture wouldn't be effective on a demon warrior. The frustration and anger within me mutated into a seething hatred that wanted out. I ripped the faceplate from the head of the rakshasa to see if it felt any pain at all. There were two eyes and a semi-organic brain similar to the one the Machine appeared as with fluids and blood vessels for its molten humors. It had no mouth, but what must have been its voice box had been destroyed as it only made clicking and hissing noises while it convulsed.

Hearing Noah's disoriented groans from trying to stand with Lyle's help brought me to my senses. I granted the rakshasa an undeserved mercy and disintegrated it.

After reclaiming Noah's weapons I levitated him away from the remains to where Lyle had been hunkered down behind a cluster of boulders.

"I just...wanna point out...we could be vacationing in Thailand right now," Noah bemoaned. "Whatever's left of it."

"You did great, tiger. I'm sorry I'm failing. I can't even get us into where we came here for and I'm out of ideas."

"Keep your head in the game," Lyle said. "Giving up on yourself means you give up on all of us and I know you got more in you than that."

"Having so many people here at risk is what's giving me a panic attack over every hiccup."

"Don't let it cloud your mind." Noah poked the prayer beads on my wrist. "I need blood. I think I earned a taste."

I sat with him so he could feed while I cradled his head to my neck. The bite eased some of the shakiness brought on by anxiety. I felt his vitality returning as he became more aggressive in his embrace and was the one holding me instead. When his hand traveled to my backside to give me a shock from his gauntlet I knew he was in good health.

"Just a little more, I was starting to have fun again," he said, smirking when I pushed him away.

Lyle gave me his hand to help me up. I was about to resume my efforts breaking into the fortress when a fresh batch of rakshasa was summoned.

"Round two." Noah put his fists together to punctuate his words with a spark.

"Not with your armor like that. I can't remake demon leather," I said. "It should seal itself after a while, but I still don't want you fighting alone again."

"All I gotta do is go slower to buy more time before they adapt. I'll be fine. Just patch this shit up for me until it's fixed. I got my tits out like a cheap date."

Isis then spoke from above. "Fret not. I shall hold them, Ascended One. I feel myself roused by the valiant efforts seen here and would very much like to try my hand. Go onward and resume your search to gain us entry."

I thought she was joking when she sent her pets toward the rakshasa, but then she spread her wings and called to the heavens with her hands raised.

"Transcend thy limits, my children!"

Chapter Forty-Eight

Rays of amber light pierced the crimson sky to envelop Isis's pets in her blessing. They grew at an exponential rate until they reached near the heavens from where the light came. Size was not all that changed. The cat went through a stunning metamorphosis into a lion with fur like strands of gold and the snake gained crocodilian scales and multiple salivating draconic heads that breathed a corrosive gas.

"The Nemean Lion and Lernaean Hydra," Nathaniel said and then looked embarrassed for knowing. "I...used to read a lot to pass the time when I was lonely, although I was never very good at it."

"They're from the legend of Hercules, aren't they?" Lyle asked. "Isn't that Greek, not Egyptian?"

"In a time long passed I was worshipped across Greece under a different guise, but it seemed those memories had been forgotten," Isis explained. "Now my mind is no longer bound by the collective conscious of my worshippers to allow for greater creative thought of my own. What a pleasure to dream with infinite possibilities!"

She flew off to keep the fabled beasts healed from above with her magic while they entered the melee against the rakshasa. They didn't provide much in the way of skilled combat that would have been circumvented anyway, but when it came to monstrous and unavoidable distraction there were none better. The rakshasa were clever enough to use hellfire and even their own blood to cauterize the hydra's necks when decapitated to stop the endless loop of multiplying heads, but with Isis acting as constant support it made their strategy pointless. Subterfuge was so far out of the question by now, however, which put us at risk for much worse things to come.

It didn't take long for the rakshasa to start killing each other to consolidate their power. We had to hurry. Nathaniel and I were about to resume our endeavor at the fortress wall when I noticed Noah standing frozen with a look of worry in his eyes like I had never seen from him.

"What is it?" I asked, taking his hand in mine and making quick repairs to his armor.

"She's here," he said from behind his mask.

"Who—?"

And then I saw whom he had sensed...

Aurelia.

Of all people! Why is she here?

"Rebecca!" Lyle shouted, dropping his helmet.

I didn't notice Dr. Sullivan standing next to that tyrant in a ball gown. Or maybe I didn't recognize her—that unnatural flawless façade, the air of grace. She was Aurelia's now.

"What is this?" I asked pointedly, stopping Lyle from crossing the line in the sand.

My first instinct was to annihilate Aurelia now that she had shown herself after her suspicious absence. Her use for keeping the humans pacified and bridging the gap between their world and our own as a diplomat was moot. The world was so fragmented and humanity no longer posed any significant threat without their weapons of mass destruction. But for her to come all this way to a place like this...she would have taken every precaution and it likely had something to do with the good doctor standing beside her. It also occurred to me that as an undead her soul was condemned to Hell where we already stood. If I were to strike her down there was a chance she would rise before us as a demon of even more power. Perhaps that's what she wanted, but I wouldn't be baited into giving it to her.

"A mortifying waste of time that I've come to put an end to," she gloated. "How long were you planning on banging your fists against an impregnable fortress? Or was your plan to bore the denizens of Hell into submission?"

Nathaniel stepped forward, forcing Aurelia to take a step back with her attendant. "No creature who fears the light has a place disrespecting the Ascended in my presence," he said.

I couldn't get my head around what was happening, so I directed the conversation to get a read on Rebecca. "What are you doing here with this...monster?"

"Such pettiness is the reason you stand here impotent," Aurelia responded for her. Rebecca didn't seem to be here against her will, but that wasn't always easy to tell around someone who could play a mind like a fiddle. "You are still dreadfully shortsighted, but unlimited power is a fruit not often bearing the wisdom to go along with it. Time is essential, so I will explain in simple terms. Your imminent failure here will doom this world in a way you cannot comprehend and with that, everything I have worked toward since before these gods were even a dream. Hopefully, I needn't remind you above all else the importance of keeping a soul as precious as mine from our common foe, which only speaks to the significant risk I face by appearing here to right your mess."

I laughed in her face. "You still think this is about you? You are *nothing* to the kings. You're just another pawn to them that we overestimated."

She ignored me to hear herself speak some more. "PROJECT: UNITY was one of several organizations I founded to supply me with future candidates when needing to replace the inevitable disappointments I've grown used to suffering. Alas, the one before you was in grave danger when I happened upon her in England while visiting an old friend, so I seized the opportunity to court her to a better life."

The hydra had fallen for good and one rakshasa prevailed over all the others. With their combined might it wouldn't be long until the lion fell too, putting us back where we started, only this time against a much stronger foe.

"Rebecca, why?" Lyle asked.

Aurelia might pick her targets carefully and offer a deal with the devil when there are no options left, but in all honesty, I wouldn't have been too surprised if Rebecca consented to becoming undead during peace either, due to her fascination with the supernatural and interest in human progression. I would have pegged her as a Strigoi though. Still it was weird to see the once average doctor now looking like a supermodel, trading scrubs and a lab coat for fitted slacks and a cashmere overcoat like she was headed to a power lunch.

"When the base was under attack I evacuated to the Blackbourne residence in England, but by then the invasion from Bath had spread into the countryside, leaving us stranded. The implant started erasing my DNA before I could return to extract it. That was when I was saved by Aurelia."

This still doesn't answer the question of why she had the plans to that experimental reactor and rifle before all of this went down.

"Why would you go there when we have designated rendezvous points where we could've picked you up?" Lyle asked.

She was looking at him as if she didn't know him from a distant acquaintance.

"Lyle." I sighed. "We're about to be screwed unless we stop standing around."

"Do not sound disheartened, Commander," said Aurelia. "It was I who was responsible for your involvement with PROJECT: UNITY in the first place. I had my sights on your pure heart since the very beginning as a solution to the demon coup. Only recently did I decide that my darling Rebecca's gifted mind had a bit more finesse and pedigree to navigate the treacherous future ahead, but you will have an opportunity to be in my service when the organization is reborn."

"Appreciate it, ma'am, but I only serve those in the name of justice."

"If that is what you wish to call it, then so be it."

The Nemean Lion was defeated and the supercharged rakshasa was on its way to us. I was hoping it would behead Aurelia, but she gave a casual gaze over her shoulder, stopping the rakshasa in its tracks and making it kneel.

How the hell can she control a being that powerful? There were seven or more rakshasa that got absorbed. This can't be...shouldn't a demon lord of this strength trump an Ancient?

"When you cannot enter from the outside, one must consider access from the inside," she lectured.

The rakshasa obeyed her unspoken command and used its swords to carve a summoning circle in the ground. She delicately placed a hand on the smooth dome of its head and crushed it in a single, aloof motion. The sizzling blood on her skin didn't bother her in the slightest. She seemed more upset at the inconvenience of getting her hand dirty as she shook it off.

The blood poured from the headless corpse on the ground and filled the grooves of the summoning circle, activating it with a glow.

"Proceed," she ordered Rebecca. "You know where to go when you're finished."

Rebecca stepped into the circle without any uncertainty in her stride and vanished.

"You're nuts if you think I'm going in there through this thing to help carry out *your*—" I balked... and then Lyle charged in after Rebecca. "Are you kidding me?"

Another battalion of the rakshasa was already on the way, but once Aurelia set her sights on them with a telepathic command to commit suicide they were dead before they got to us.

"Run along now." She gave a demure wave to send us off.

I grabbed Noah and jumped in after them with Nathaniel and Isis close behind. We came out the other side in an automated factory large enough to manufacture two-story houses on its tubular assembly lines. I was almost insulted that there was no security to welcome us.

The perplexing machinery was in the process of fabricating the body parts necessary for more copies of the rakshasa and the goliath Lord Vināyaka, like Nathaniel had described seeing in his vision. The technology ranged from alien spaceship to steam-powered clockwork and all of it was made of the same matching materials resembling translucent plastic to create seamless interactions. It wasn't all nonsensical mechanical madness though. I could see that the steam was coming from molten blood stored in holding vats and was being pressurized through tubes to move pistons and gears running the assembly line. It was an interesting source of efficiency for the components to have a part in the process of their own production. Other contraptions around the factory functioned the same, such as the radiant energy from souls supplying power to computer systems as they passed on their way to a finished body.

What we came here for first and foremost was in the streams of data whizzing throughout the room. It was Lyle's time to shine, if he could focus on the task ahead.

"Jesus, Rebecca, your eyes...the implant is still inside you?" he asked.

In the brightness of the factory it was easy to see the same alterations to her irises that once afflicted Lyle.

"It's part of me now." She sounded pleased. The preternatural allure the Archios were known for made statements such as that sound like even more disturbing demagoguery than the Strigoi's morbid penchant for experimentation. "The bacterial foundation encapsulated in the polymer was restructured to synthesize with my DNA and merged with the brain tissue to become one organ. Aurelia's timing couldn't have been more perfect. The undead state isn't compatible with the aether uplink established by the Infernal King, so I was left with all the benefits of this technology without falling under its control."

"You're speaking as if you just discovered a cure for cancer. Do you have any idea of the consequences behind being indentured to someone like Aurelia?" I asked. "You traded a fate worse than death at the hands of an evil king to one with an evil queen."

Rebecca's carriage was colder than I remembered, almost numb. I would have thought the Archios blood would have the opposite effect.

"This has always been something I've thought of, but I was more afraid of the transition into it. There is so much potential without the restraints of mortality slowing down and inevitably ending my research."

"You've always said you'd never want to live forever because it goes against everything you believe in as a doctor," Lyle questioned.

Her obvious recitation was unconvincing. "My thoughts have changed. I know many of Aurelia's actions in the past warrant concern for her role in the future and that she's done things lacking ethical practice, but on paper her vision to rebuild society aligns with many of our own and the principle goals of science. She wishes to outdo the current failing world powers, and she understands that her reign is measured by the quality of her kingdom from top to bottom. Culture and innovation would thrive."

"That's the worst argument for trickle-down economics I've ever heard. This isn't a corrupt drug company committing insurance fraud we're talking about," I said. "Some of the things she's done out of boredom would make the most insidious despots and warlords cringe."

"I've read her file. Now we should really move on to—"

"A fucking file?!" Noah erupted. "She made me rip apart the people I loved with my bare hands! She tricked me into leaving my family to die and laughed about everyone I lost because I was powerless to do anything about it! Tell me what the file says when everyone you ever cared about is in pieces in your hands and she's laughing! Everyone you love is dead!"

I brought Noah aside to calm him down, removing his mask and hood so we could see each other's faces. He was ranting about things that had taken him years to share.

"It's over, Noah. She isn't going to—"

"You don't know what she's like!" he snarled. "You don't know her like I do—"

"But I know *you* and this isn't you right now!"

"What the fuck don't you understand about her going to take control of me to hurt you? You have to swear you'll kill me when she does—"

I grabbed him by the hair on the back of his head hard enough to command his gaze. By the look he gave me in return I thought he was getting ready to rumble with me. His nostrils flared, fangs bared, and eyes narrowed, but it wasn't pure anger. There was a glossiness to his eyes as when tears begin to form, only it wasn't from my actions. He took my hand away and turned his head to avoid me.

"Look at me. LOOK. AT. ME!" I shouted, holding his head face forward so our eyes met again. "Don't you see she's already in your head controlling you? Don't you realize this is exactly what she wants? She's past proving that she can use her powers to manipulate you, now she's playing on your fear of making a mistake when I need you most, just like you said about losing Vivi. The ultimate indulgence for her is to watch you fail on your own so you have no one else to blame. She isn't going to jeopardize her latest investment by doing something so obvious that it would call for retaliation. You know she planned it so that I'd be forced into the position of looking after Rebecca. Aurelia needs me and I need *you* to be my rock like you've always been."

He hugged me tight enough to hurt, but it wasn't to be funny, or accidental like in his sleep. The fearless was showing fear. I freed my hand to press over his heart and even through the leather armor I could feel it pounding away like cannon fire.

"I know you have the strength in there to get through this," I said, resting his head on my shoulder while hugging him.

He eased up without a word, donning his mask and hood.

I whispered one last thing to him before rejoining the group. "Keep your eyes on the doctor."

"Why *did* Aurelia send you in here?" Nathaniel was asking Rebecca when we stepped back into the conversation.

"Besides being bait because she knew I wouldn't trust her method of getting in," I added.

"We're hoping I can read the programming language that this king uses thanks to the upgrade of the implant," said Rebecca. "Intel on a weakness or the identity of the kings would be ideal."

"I got a gift from the gods that's supposed to let me read this stuff, but it means nothing," Lyle said. "These holograms look like ten different languages written on top of each other and scrolling on fast forward."

Rebecca seemed to agree. "This isn't a language that's read from right to left or up and down, but in layers. There are dimensions to its syntax."

"Something is amiss," said Isis. "The aether here is unique...foreign to me. Something is not right."

"You're experiencing the effects of Hell on your emotions," I told her.

"No, I can feel it too," Nathaniel said. "There's a coldness to it."

"Marvelous. This metaphysical language must not be meant to read, but experience," Rebecca deduced as she inspected the lines of flowing holograms. "Written and spoken communication is primitive. We adapted to it because we're unable to share complex thoughts directly between individuals. Hive-based insects like ants and bees use chemical signatures called pheromones to communicate simple directives. I used to think the undead brain evolved a gland that released pheromones to make their victims susceptible to suggestion by overriding natural impulses."

Everyone split up to explore the factory with more diligence. The room seemed to have no end even though the walls were clearly visible. The rhythm of the machines was causing an unnerving synchronization of heart rate and breathing until all I could think about, all I could feel, was the movement of the machines grinding forward toward progress.

The walls that seemed unreachable mere seconds ago were now closing in. I checked to see I wasn't the only one affected, but even Isis appeared to be distracted. "We have to stop these machines," I told them. "Destroy everything."

Nathaniel was only too glad to join me against Rebecca's protests to let her study it all first while we had the opportunity. She didn't seem affected by the ill-feeling trance.

I can't believe we haven't been attacked yet.

To our misfortune, much of the room and the objects within were as sturdy as the exterior fortress walls, though at least the slamming of Nathaniel's fists against the impenetrable metal disrupted the anxiety-inducing beat.

Aborting the soulless mechanical demon spawn before they had the chance to activate was wearing on my sanity. The rational side of my mind understood that it was kill or be killed with these monsters, but seeing them in pieces mid-production with their unfinished faces staring at me... I swore that some were conscious.

I shouldn't be anthropomorphizing the enemy, but it's hard not to when one of our own is made of liquid energy and I was made in a lab with my siblings. If Aurelia can control these demons it means they have a mind and aren't just preprogrammed clockwork...I wonder if they also have a choice to not be evil.

God, why do I get caught up thinking about this stuff? Ignoring my sense of morality is always easier when motivated like after seeing Noah in danger. I'd probably get a lot more done if I thought like the bad guys.

"That's it, I think we shut this place down!" I said, rejoicing as the assembly line grinded to a halt.

The solution was simple enough: clog the moving parts with their own products instead of wasting effort attempting direct destruction. "The outside team just needs to find a way in now."

Nathaniel flew from the room through a circular opening high up that souls had been funneled through and returned right away. It was the first time I noticed that there weren't any doors, making me curious as to how those that were supposed to be here got around. At the end of the production line the parts just disappeared. "This was only one small factory. There's a much larger one in the next room where the demons are being stored," he informed us.

The machinery surrounding us came to life once more. What had been jamming it dematerialized in front of our eyes, allowing production to resume.

"Lyle, we're counting on you here," I said, watching an apparatus start knitting a plastic circulatory system onto an arm.

"I'm trying, man, but I'm not the right person for this."

Noah spoke for the first time since his outburst earlier. "You got picked for the job for a reason. All you gotta do is open your eyes and see what's being shown to you."

"Maybe if I touch one of the holograms..."

"That could be a very bad idea." Rebecca stopped him. "This technology can alter any form of matter at any level. The remote uplink to the Infernal King is what reprogrammed the implants to take over our DNA. A direct connection could mean death. Assuming that the primary function of the systems here is to create these demons it might wind up turning you into one."

"Only one way to find out," he said, taking a deep breath. "An extra pair of arms could always come in handy."

"Get ready to pull him away fast if it goes south," I told Noah.

Lyle reached for the streaming code to make contact. His hand touched it for only the briefest moment before he started to seize and Noah had to tackle him to the floor. Everyone gathered around as I removed his helmet, relieved to see him unharmed, but blinking wildly.

"Lyle, can you hear me?" I asked. "Are you okay? What did you see?"

"It's—it's not a—it's not a fact...factory..."

Chapter Forty-Nine

"What do you mean this isn't a factory?" Rebecca asked as Lyle's eyes adjusted from whatever he had seen upon touching the quantum code.

"It's a dream. These are dreams..." Lyle struggled to explain. "They're brought to life here—the rakshasa and those big guys—the Infernal King is dreaming them up and the machines are bringing them to life."

"Like on the Astral Plane?" I asked.

"Which means the king must slumber somewhere near," said Nathaniel.

"No point wasting our time on any of this shit then," Noah said.

Rebecca stepped away to take another look around. "The way the holographic data streams meet at these junctions, it resembles the synapses of a nervous system. We're in a giant nervous system witnessing the transition from dream to reality. This is the most fantastic thing I've ever seen! Transhumanism and thoughtform have never been so evident as they are here. None of it is 'magic.' It's all code being deciphered and encrypted again once imprinted onto materials. Just like neurotransmitters passing chemical impulses along to create a desired physical effect, like the spasm of a muscle. In this case, it's the turning of a gear or movement of a piston to create these creatures."

"Why do you sound so excited about the device responsible for so many deaths?" Nathaniel asked her.

"It isn't about *this* system, but the fact that it all comes down to tangible, relatable science and not magic. You don't have to be 'gifted' or 'blessed' to use it or benefit by it. Having gods and a chosen few able to cast magic to heal the sick is great, but not always practical. Sheer numbers alone prevent everyone from being taken care of, and then there are factors such as time and accessibility. Think of how many children would still die in a world ruled by even the most benevolent gods, just because they were too sick to crawl their way to a temple or too weak to have their dying gasp heard. Easily accessible medicines in the modern world reduced suffering, but that isn't enough and now Earth is worse off due to the invasions. A machine like this, powered and configured by thought to heal any injury or cure any disease would transform humanity overnight. If there are scientific principles behind it then it can be reverse engineered by our scientists to better serve humanity."

"Humans were not meant to be immortal," Isis argued. "Such a future would be disastrous to the cycle."

"What's the point of life if everyone lives forever?" Lyle asked. "Everything would kinda lose its meaning after a while."

"How can you say that when we've seen so many innocent children die?" Nathaniel argued back. "They never got their chance to find a meaning of their own and question philosophy."

"This isn't the time for a debate," I interrupted. "Our friends are still fighting out there and we've got a job to do in here. I've spoken to this king twice and it appears to me as a brain, so we've got a brain plus a fortress with a nervous system pumping out dreams fabricated into demons using the quantum code. How do we make this work for us so that we can return Earth to normal?"

"Sever the spinal cord and plug someone else in to undo all the shit," said Noah. "That's why he was given the magic sight, wasn't it?"

"We'll need to get to the king to do that, who I'm assuming will be up top in some sort of throne room."

I was ready to do anything to get away from the factory's clamorous waltz.

"The only way out from this room is through that hole," Nathaniel said. "I didn't see where to go from there, but the finished demons are sure to attack once we enter."

"I'll take everyone who can't fly," I said. "You lead the charge, Nathaniel. Get us through to the next safe area on the way up."

A burst of confidence resonated from within him that I could feel down to my core. We took off together and Isis trailed behind as we flew through a claustrophobic tunnel to another factory of even more absurd proportions. When you can measure the interior of a facility in square miles it's gone too far. I couldn't see the opposite wall from where we came out and the ceiling was barely visible. Most of the free space above the machinery was a tangle of quantum code streams, making it perilous to navigate if we wanted to go higher without getting fried by data overload.

"There must be tens of thousands of them...*hundreds* of thousands," Isis said with a gasp.

Rows upon rows stacked dozens high of not only the rakshasa and Vināyaka but synthetic copies of Ma'al. The automation of the factory was aided by flying drones equipped with multipurpose tools, strong enough to carry a single rakshasa to a storage rack. Four were required to lift a Ma'al clone and ten or more for Vināyaka.

This is overkill to take over the world. The amount of rakshasa here could do it alone, assuming they retained what was upgraded during our fight outside.

"I don't think these are all for Earth," said Nathaniel. He kept his voice down as if it mattered. We had been at their mercy since long ago and that brutal realization was sinking in fast.

"We need to find a way to leave," I said. "This is too much."

I wasn't only worried for the others with us, but myself too. The amount of hellfire that a row of these could conjure would be enough to go right through my armor, erasing my soul and vanquishing Isis before she had a chance to heal it. I still clung to some hope that the Machine didn't want me dead.

"There are screens down there at the end of the aisles," Lyle pointed out.

"I need to check them before we leave," said Rebecca. "It could be important in defeating the king."

"I can see another tunnel above us," Nathaniel said.

To no one's surprise, Lyle sided with Rebecca. "We don't have time to draw straws. We came here for information so we should at least see what's down there to get a lead. Whether we run or fight, nothing we do is gonna make a difference if we can't lock out the bad guys so they don't keep coming back."

"How about those who want to stay can stay and the rest can leave them to die without guilt?" Noah suggested.

"We can make this work by luring the king outside after we regroup," I said. "Lyle can do his thing inside with a less conspicuous escort since now we know there are areas that are tame. Get whatever you can from here and we'll go."

I landed us at the screen that Rebecca indicated.

"Bad call." Noah sighed.

"If we haven't been attacked yet there's a good chance we won't be for another few seconds."

"Unless we trigger something."

The "screen" wasn't more than a flat version of the code streams with some additional geometric patterns. Rebecca touched it and the mark of the Machine in her eyes immediately brightened until she needed to be pulled away. I swore that for a fraction of a second the skin around her eyes began to melt as if she was losing control of her body. I couldn't place why the horrible effect stood out to me the way it did against all else, but it reminded me of something or at least felt like it should. Not even Noah gave any indication that he had also noticed though, and we had another problem that required our attention.

The row of rakshasa corresponding with the screen lit up and activated their inanimate bodies hanging from the racks.

"Like that," Noah said. "I'm getting bored of always being right."

Lyle shot down a drone that buzzed past us. I wasn't sure it was hostile or just got too close, but it was good to see his gun wasn't totally worthless.

"Up here," Nathaniel called.

I knew we didn't stand a fighting chance, so I took off with everybody ahead of the rakshasa completing their wakeup procedures. My hand grazed the coded stream as I navigated through the network of webs it created—nothing happened. I looked back and saw Noah touch it on purpose and he too had no adverse reaction. We made it into the cramped, winding tunnel shaft Nathaniel had spotted, unscathed by the flaming swords being hurled at us at the last second. None of the demons could fly and it didn't seem that they teleported between rooms, so we had a place to consider our options in the tunnel.

Realizing that Isis wasn't with us, Nathaniel and I went back to see what had happened to her only to find that she was confronting the legion we had awakened by herself.

"Don't!" I shouted in vain.

With arms and wings spread wide she declared, "Let the heavens consume you and become as cinder by holy obliteration!"

Rivers of light poured from her to snake through the factory following her theatrical incantation, devastating an acre's worth of the Infernal forces.

"She has many surprises lately," Nathaniel said. "I'd like to be able to bend my light beams like that."

"Isis! Come here!" I called to her.

"My that was exhilarating!" she exclaimed. "The thrill of battle sings to me in rhapsodic melodies! Much have I missed by waiting to heal wounds instead of stopping their cause by the same light."

I wasn't too sure if this was Hell's influence making her more aggressive or the freedom of thought, although, she seemed in too good a mood for it to be the former. "Glad you're having fun, but this isn't the *time* to fight."

None of the other demons activated to continue the battle.

They were more interested in defending that screen than retribution for being outright destroyed?

I turned back into the shaft to ask Lyle and Rebecca what they had seen. "Did you learn anything useful about a weakness or how to change Earth's code back?"

"I couldn't understand any of it," Lyle answered.

"Yes, it was all too confusing," Rebecca agreed. "Just a rush of flashing symbols."

"She's lying," Noah said to me loud enough for everyone to hear.

"How long have you been working for Aurelia?" I asked her. "And before you answer, I know about the blueprints you stole from PROJECT: UNITY. The plans to harness the aether crystals for a reactor and to make weapons out of them? Weapons that could do actual harm to gods and not just demons would be something she'd be interested in."

I owe PARAGON for tipping off Claudius about the blueprints or else Aurelia would have another deadly trump card in her deck. Now I feel bad about always dismissing it as just a computer program.

"It isn't like that," she implored.

"Rebecca, what's going on?" Lyle asked.

"There's something that's been bothering me," I said. "You aren't Aurelia's type. She likes people with bold personalities so she can break them over time. You're already too subservient and eager, more than I ever remember you being."

"Lay off, man," Lyle said. "Don't insult her. She's been through a lot and is probably in shock."

"I don't think so," I said. "In fact I don't think this is Rebecca at all."

"What? The Machine—?"

"Vyrlakalos," said Noah.

Rebecca's expression went from innocence to annoyance. Mouths and eyes opened along her skin where they shouldn't be as she stripped from her clothes, turning more skeletal by the second.

"How clever, *Ascended*," Vyrlakalos rasped. "I already obtained what I came here for, so I suppose the ruse no longer matters."

I pinned it—or *her* in this form—to the wall with my powers. "Why did you come here and why impersonate Dr. Sullivan?"

"It worked so well with the late Commander Rudgar, only this time the Archios wretch begged to be involved. Her private militia had run amok with technology inspired by our demonic enemy that could pose a risk to her as well. She always had an eye for opportunity and it isn't a first that such a truce has been struck. All she had to do was put on a short performance to keep you on track. I promise I will betray her later if that is of any condolence. Although, I cannot fathom why you seem upset. You came to me for help after all."

"Not like this, but if you want to make yourself useful then tell us what you saw."

"I can't give it all away or there would be no need for your little divine coterie to assure our survival. When there is something you must know then it will be shared as needed."

"What could possibly be more important than what we're dealing with at present?" Nathaniel asked.

Vyrlakalos let out a shrieking laugh that echoed through the shaft. "You are leagues away from running the race, let alone winning it. You haven't a clue where you even *are*."

"You're full of shit," I said. "You admit you almost melted when the Machine was assimilating everyone through the implants."

"I learn and adapt. It is what I do, not unlike our adversary. A human given the sight to read the coded language will never compare with my understanding of it and yet none present have the capacity to manipulate.

Providence can be so infuriating, yet I cannot deny its allure."

"You came to meet your maker—"

"*Our* maker, and I must say I am impressed. As I thought, we have no hope of defeating it, but indeed you can use the systems already in place here to drive it out from our world—for a time. This castle is its anchor and a great sacrifice will be required to disconnect it, but what are a few lives when one such as mine is at stake?"

Vyrlakalos' puppet smiled and started to turn into a puddle of flesh to let us know the conversation was over. "Have you even taken the time to ponder why such a great being from another world became so fixated on a single source to draw inspiration for its army?"

"Wait!" Lyle shouted. "What happened to the real Rebecca?"

"She's right here." Vyrlakalos responded by showing Rebecca's face one last time in the visceral slime. "Her mind was *delicious.*"

Lyle yelled in anger and shot at the puddle, but I disintegrated it to put an end to the scene.

"Why Rebecca? Why..." Lyle threw off his helmet and covered his face as he sobbed. "All I've gotta say is that I'm done after this. Assuming I make it out alive, which right now I don't really give a shit if I do or not."

"Don't become what I was," Noah told him. "You don't like me, you wouldn't want to be me. I gave up on everything and became the asshole everybody loves to hate because of it, but that's not you. You can't pull off this kind of sexy with that face."

Lyle put his helmet back on and pushed ahead without a word.

I didn't know what to say and I didn't think Lyle wanted to hear the truth that Rebecca was probably better off dead than enslaved by Aurelia. I put my arm around his shoulder and patted him in consolation. He remained silent and moved on through the shaft.

Nothing is more cruel than how someone can be there one second and then gone forever in the next. I've lost so many people in my life and still can't get over the drowning feeling that comes with losing each one. Now it's Rebecca, before it was Octavio, PROJECT: UNITY and the millions around the world. There wasn't time to mourn one death before the next happened. We just had to bottle it up and keep moving.

I nudged Nathaniel to take the lead again through the belly of the beast. It occurred to me that he was the only one of us yet to have any sort of breakdown.

We flew through the shaft of pipes and wires as it went up a steep incline, cruising for some time before we found a branching path we could fit through to the next room. I was starting to think I could see blank faces in the code looking back at me as it whizzed past, lost souls trapped in the system.

"We have to be nearing the top floor," said Nathaniel. "That last climb was two or three miles and we don't know if we entered at the bottom."

The room we found was smaller than the factories and had several rounded exit shafts at random positions along the walls and ceiling. We were in a three-dimensional holographic planetarium spun from the threads of the quantum code. The off-putting chorus of metal was still present, only with new unsettling modulations in timbre.

"This is Earth, but what are these other planets?" I floated amongst the assorted spheres suspended in the air. "It doesn't look like our solar system or *any* solar system actually, since there's no star."

"Some of these big ones labeled 'Ophiuchus' and encased in machinery are stars," Lyle said with pain fresh in his voice. "Looks like they've been converted into reactors. The rest are worlds that the king invaded, billions of them conquered by one dude. See all the fortresses like this one on them?"

"No." I landed on Noah's shoulders. "I guess you need the special sight to see that for some reason."

Isis flew past us, weaving in and out of the planets. "All of these worlds connected by one being..."

"What did the monster mean about the source of inspiration for the Machine's army?" asked Nathaniel. "They're from Hinduism, but why does that matter?"

"The empress recognized the rakshasa, but not as demons of knowledge at first," said Isis. "I question why they are noteworthy as to be converted to its cause. Mayhap, a deity from the Hindu pantheon would know more of what draws the king to their evils."

"The Machine has been erasing gods from the Earth's code so that it'll be uncontested. There's a good chance that they're already gone and the rest—" I stopped myself.

"What is it?" Nathaniel asked.

"Maybe it's not about what made the Hindu demons special, but what made them available. This was all about gaining a foothold. Some of the pantheon was defeated by the last Ascended centuries ago and crystallized into aether gems so that they couldn't be brought back through worship.

"The Machine obviously needs other beings to convert and serve it since it can't seem to make original creations, or maybe it's just more efficient to use creatures native to the worlds its invading. Taking from a compromised pantheon reduces the chance of people being able to wake up the remaining associated gods to defend them and slow its progress."

"Why does any of this matter?" Noah asked. "We're here for the asshole in charge."

Lyle stared at the simulation of Earth above his head. He stepped away as it shrank along with the rest of the projection to show us dozens of other worlds until ours was just a speck. "I think I understand. The pantheons are where this king is trying to anchor itself through to get to our world. They look like smaller planets orbiting the Earth. I guess it went for the Hindu realm because it was compromised like you said."

"Even should we slumber or fall weakened we yet hold claim over our sacred land," said Isis. "The kings fought to wrest control of Egypt, but we prevailed as I still stand and again they tried in the empress's underworld, did they not?

Claim must be restored to the rightful owner if we are to break the Infernal King's hold."

"If that's how we're supposed to disconnect this thing then we're screwed without a deity to claim it." Lyle touched the hologram without a seizure this time. "Hindu is completely empty now according to this."

Clunking noises coming down the shafts around the room cut Lyle short. The hologram changed from blue to red and the rest of the room went dark. Our time here undisturbed was over.

Cables shot from the exits and went straight for Isis and me. Noah's katana couldn't slice through them and Nathaniel tried to intercept, but even he wasn't strong enough to hold them back. The situation only got worse from there once the rakshasa were summoned.

"We're in trouble here! There's no way out!" Lyle shouted over the sounds of Isis and Nathaniel's scorching light ripping through the bodies of our foes. The steadily increasing resistance that the rakshasa were building was becoming a serious concern.

Noah tapped everything in his repertoire to protect me from the reinforcements spawning in while I concentrated on keeping the cables at bay. Lyle tried to assist with his rifle, but he wasn't fast enough to match the others' speed except for a lucky shot here and there. I could see only less than half of what was happening myself when there was a sudden gasp from him behind me. One of the rakshasa had pierced his side with its sword. The light crystal embedded in his armor reacted and blew the demon away allowing Isis to heal his wound.

I lost track of a cable in the chaos, which led to Isis getting snatched into a tunnel before there was anything we could do to stop it.

"Isis, hang on!" I yelled and formed a barrier around us to fly after her.

The cables chased us up through the shaft for a while until we exited into an unoccupied laboratory right out of my experience on the Astral Plane where I witnessed my creation. There weren't any specimens or medical instruments, only ancient clockwork machinery made of copper and iron-like materials built into the walls and powered by the steaming hot blood of the Infernals, churning away without any discernable purpose unlike the factories below.

"Where did she go? It's a dead end and I didn't see another path we could have fit through on the way up," said Nathaniel.

"Maybe if I touch this it'll show me." Lyle approached one of the quantum code nerve clusters, but before making contact with it the machinery in the room sealed the exit and slid open the rear wall to reveal a massive staging area.

We had found the mechanical monarch.

Chapter Fifty

The Infernal Machine was assuming the form of a unique rakshasa with six arms and three faces; the two on both sides were skulls encasing a version of the cerebral mass present in its previous incarnations. It sat front and center upon a cybernetic throne plugged into the fortress by wires guiding the passage of code. Something about the entire setting appeared antiquated when comparing it to what we had encountered on the journey up. In the background, Isis was held in suspended animation inside one of four stasis chambers, each guarded by a copy of Lord Vināyaka.

Screens around the lab went online to relay the king's speech while it remained unmoving on the throne.

//You approach with underwhelming force//these actions betray your intent

"That's a *huge* aura." Noah stepped in front of me with his arm out to keep me behind him, but I ducked under.

I shook my head at Lyle who was debating whether or not to still make a move for the quantum code. "We're not here to fight you," I replied.

//This behavior is erratic//your chaos is welcomed

"Dorian, *he's* the anchor," said Lyle. "I can see the tether. This must be the leader of the rakshasa that got converted like Set did near the end. We should only need to kill him to disconnect the Machine from our world."

"We'll still need someone else to claim the empty pantheon after, but it's a start."

//Threat assessment: Nominal

The rakshasa leader sparked and twitched to life, its voice stuttering in another language as power flowed through it and brought all systems online.

//You will fail//they will fall

"His name is Ravana," said Nathaniel.

"How do you know?" I looked over at him radiating the iridescent mandala I hadn't seen in a while.

"He feels familiar... I think I'm—I'm experiencing déjà vu from the leftover memories in the aether gem I absorbed."

"Sūrya," Ravana snarled.

I shielded everyone behind a telekinetic barrier as the rakshasa king took a step toward us. The copies of Lord Vināyaka responded by raising their hands before them and doing the same. "Leave him to me. You guys take care of the big ones and getting Isis free," I said.

But when Ravana stepped through my barrier by coating himself in the same tangible darkness Gianni used I knew that wasn't going to work. The Vināyaka quartet changed their strategy too after seeing Nathaniel come for them and trapped him within a conjured barrier of their own.

Without anything in the area for me to manipulate against Ravana I was at a loss. He was as swift as Noah and managed to grab hold of me no matter where I teleported. The Vināyakas turned the prison containing Nathaniel into a hellfire furnace. I worried his armor wouldn't be enough to insulate him from the flames. Lyle and Noah riddled one of the mammoth bodies with shining bullets and slashes that barely punctured the demon's semi-organic blubber; however, Nathaniel's retaliatory explosion of light was more than enough to wipe all four from existence and expose Ravana.

I bid the rakshasa farewell with a crushing blow that sent him to the floor.

Or so I thought.

Ravana had already built a resistance to my powers and the light only removed his shadow armor without causing any harm. Nathaniel's mandala appeared to stun him for a moment, but everything got worse when the demon drew in the souls of the slain Vināyakas.

"I feel like we should've seen that coming," I said, looking around at the Machine's red eyes observing us from the screens.

Noah kept dashing in to help give me an opening in Ravana's shadow armor by striking at it with his light-enchanted weapons. Lyle did the same at range when he could until running out of ammunition, but every hit I landed became less and less effective. Ravana seemed more interested in trying to grab me than hurt me, as it hadn't drawn any weapons or struck me yet. I didn't know what the point was if its goal was to drink my blood, seeing as I could heal indefinitely. He did attempt to counter Nathaniel's blitz attack by breathing hellfire from a face on the side of his head, but was promptly stopped with a counterpunch.

The Infernal was not only showing Noah's speed, but also his martial prowess passed on from the rakshasa we had fought earlier. Nathaniel could keep up with the pace where I couldn't, except he was at the demon's six-armed mercy when superior skill bested his superior strength.

"Give me a crystal and then get Isis free, I've got this!" I shouted to Nathaniel.

"But—"

Lyle had taken refuge by the stasis chambers to try reading something from the nearby code streams.

"Go!" I insisted, catching the chunk of crystallized aether he threw to me.

Nathaniel gave in and went for Isis. I formed a spike from the crystal after escaping more of Ravana's advances and jammed it into his brain with Noah ambushing him and doing the same with his katana from the other side. Ravana shuddered, nothing more. Noah picked me up and ran. We played keep away to buy time. I would teleport myself to confuse Ravana and regroup with Noah to run again, but then he stopped chasing me.

//Take the throne//end his suffering

I felt pain shoot through my limbs. There were sounds of a struggle and an agonized yell across the room. Ravana had Nathaniel in more than one submission hold at once thanks to the additional appendages, using leverage against his joints to overcome his strength and pin him.

Noah and I rushed to his aid, but we couldn't get Nathaniel free as a confusing wave of despair emanated from him to me. I always knew Nathaniel as a fighter, yet he seemed to have lost his composure the instant he was bound.

//His neck will break//he will not survive//his head removed/his soul//your soul//taken

Ravana had a hand in Nathaniel's mouth pulling back on his head and another on his jaw to twist his neck sideways. Another two hands dislocated Nathaniel's elbow. His shoulder was next with an excruciating pop. The anger and pain poured from within me and brought back the darkest feelings of destruction.

The deepest desires of revenge manifested—the twisting... snapping... prying...—the need to protect those I love. My hearing cut out, my vision tunneled, my skin and clothing changed once more and the air around me quivered. Everything was a blur to me as the rage clouded the already frenetic battle. It required everything I had to take the pressure off Nathaniel's neck, but I fractured the arm responsible with the help of Nathaniel's light keeping it exposed.

Noah's repeated stabbing of the brain wasn't doing anything. Ravana stole the wakizashi off his hip and struck him in the chest with a palm strike that sent him across the room, where he cracked his head on the floor and didn't get back up.

The wakizashi was thrown aside as my telekinetic wrath ate away at Ravana's body. He was having trouble keeping Nathaniel subdued, but still managed to make him endure further agony by manifesting more arms to overextend the dislocated joints. Ravana gripped Nathaniel's hair and jerked his head back with a knee pushing down on his spine to apply crippling pressure to his lower back until there was another pop. His light was fading.

//Take the throne//end his suffering

I didn't know what else I could do. This wasn't a fight that could be won through raw power and my creativity was impaired by rage. I was about to give in and agree to the terms to save Nathaniel when he was turned to stone. A flash came from over my shoulder and a lightning bolt struck Ravana off of him with help from my powers. I gave a cursory glance around the room and first saw where the wakizashi had gone. Lyle was sitting against the wall holding it to the side and his stomach was bleeding. I was losing my mind not knowing what to deal with first and then saw the source of the bolt.

//Threat assessment: Nominal

Empress Kamakura stood behind us ready to face off against Ravana. By the time I turned so as not to lose sight of the demon, Nathaniel had become flesh again.

"That was good," I said to her. "I didn't know you had petrification spells."

"Gather the wounded. Our allies will arrive here soon."

I levitated Noah's unconscious body to me and had to use my powers to set Nathaniel's indestructible bones in place, cringing along with him for each one.

"I'm sorry," Nathaniel murmured in shame. "I-I panicked when being— I remembered my—It's no excuse. I shouldn't have gotten caught."

"No apologies." My anger was subsiding. I flew the three of us to Lyle while Kamakura and Ravana collided. She was combining two of her elements so that her lightning bolts caused petrification to the demon's extremities, but his resistance to it increased with each strike, the same as our other abilities. He stored the last electrical charge within his palm and channeled it through his foot to cause a shockwave when he stomped. The goddess drew the electricity into herself before it could reach us.

"Cernunnos will be here soon and he can heal you," I told Lyle, taking refuge behind the unbreakable machinery. His wound didn't appear as bad as I thought, but it could still be lethal if left to bleed out much longer. He was alert at least and the blade left only a thin incision that didn't go all the way through. I turned his empty rifle into bandages for him knowing that he wouldn't be doing anymore fighting.

"You can't let it get the five of you together," he warned. "The throne and those chambers like the one holding Isis are running something called the Apocatastasis Protocol. We've heard that word in the past, but this has something to do with the gods' individual powers. I got hit before I could finish reading anymore though."

"Dorian, Noah isn't breathing and he has no pulse," Nathaniel interrupted.

I placed my hand on Noah's chest. His sternum was shattered as well as several ribs. I felt inside of him and erased the bone fragments lodged in his heart, breathing a sigh of relief when it started again and he opened his eyes. I let him drink from me to speed up the healing process.

"Hey, so...this is going well."

Noah was trying to sound lighthearted for my sake, but the delivery fell short, hampered by a deeper unexpressed trepidation. He got up and took his wakizashi, noticing Lyle's injury. "Stop dying, I was starting to not hate you as much."

"Yeah, I'll try. Thanks."

"Good. All right, I'm tagging back in. I see dragon lady finally decided to show."

"Don't," I said, stopping him. "Stay here with them while I help Kamakura until the others come."

She was already on the defensive now, shielding herself within a rubbery bubble of water and moving around the laboratory as a gust of wind.

"If I had Noah's skill or could give him my strength this would be easier," said Nathaniel.

"Hmm." Noah hopped over the apparatus we were hiding behind and starting shouting to Kamakura in Japanese.

"What are you doing, you lunatic?" I tried grabbing him, but he got away.

"Don't worry about it!" he called from across the room next to Kamakura. They exchanged a few more words in Japanese amid the fighting and she called upon her guardians from the orbs levitating in her aura. They surrounded Noah and turned to pure energy that combined into him.

"What the hell is he doing?"

"They did this once before to help defeat the empress when she was possessed," said Nathaniel. "Drinking your blood for so long helps him not be ripped apart by all that power."

Noah was bristling with elemental energy. He looked his hands over before tightening the knot in his belt and then challenging Ravana with a smirk and beckoning motion. Ravana took the bait.

At once it was apparent that the copycat became outmatched when leveling the playing field. It was not to say that Noah was untouchable, yet any attempt at doing him significant harm was pointless. On the other hand, the elemental rave was flashy without much benefit against Ravana's built up immunity. Noah still put him to shame in the contest of skill that covered the spectrum of his fighting experience by tying together Taekwondo kicks, karate punches, judo throws and more in lightspeed succession. Ravana became a helpless punching bag slowly coming apart at the seams. He may have given up using the darkness for armor or Noah just managed to keep clearing it away so fast that it was impossible to see.

Leave it to Noah to steal the show from the gods.

I was frozen in awe and admiration at how he dominated the fight until remembering the rest of what was going on around me. I saw him shoot me a wink while taking a second to pose on one foot after landing a back kick that launched Ravana several yards away. I shook my head at him and joined Kamakura in trying to free Isis.

//You cannot stop the wheel of fate//progress will be made here today

"Whatever you say. You're still hiding behind a computer screen and your one link to this world is being tossed around like trash, so forgive me if I'm not scared anymore."

//Your fear is not required//other emotions will serve well

"Uh huh. Lyle, how are you doing? Any chance you can look into the code again?"

"I can try."

I floated him to me to help save his strength with Nathaniel staying on guard nearby. Ravana was down to three usable arms with the others hanging limp in their sockets until they began to repair themselves. He summoned the same scimitars the rakshasas wielded to his hands to make an unsuccessful play at interrupting us that was thwarted by Noah.

"Dorian, I'm, uh, losing a lot of blood," Lyle said. He was pale and his eyes were glassy. "I didn't think it was bad, but...must've nicked something important in there."

I checked his bandage. It was soaked through.

If only I could create new living tissue or at the very least feel what was wrong inside to stop the internal bleeding, but I can't tell the difference like with the implant or bone in Noah's heart. Was this supposed to be some humbling irony that something that would be so trivial to me was just beyond my grasp?

"I'm not giving up on you, so you can't either." I clutched his hand to keep him awake.

"It might be... the end of the line for me, man. If they can't get in here and we can't get out—"

"Shut up. You're not allowed to even think like that."

"Yeah, yeah... Let me touch this so at least I can go out being useful. Just promise me you'll take down Vyrlakalos and make it hurt." He put his hand into the code stream and stared off into the distance as the information flooded into his mind.

I looked at my best friend's face remembering what had changed about it over the years of our friendship.

You're too good to go out like this. You don't get to die until you're old and gray and I say you can. That was the deal.

A strained choking noise came from where the fight with Ravana was happening. Noah had been stabbed through the heart and lifted off the ground. Attacking Ravana to save Noah proved futile. Nathaniel shot across the room to stop a second sword from decapitating him at the last second and pulled him free from Ravana's blade. I protected Noah in a barrier to bring him to me.

"I'm fine," he said, his expression souring.

We held each other for a moment. "You're shaking."

"It's been a long day." Noah returned to the fight alongside Nathaniel. The demon's weapons broke against Nathaniel, yet aside from that they were both faring poorly as Ravana himself grew stronger still.

"We make little progress of our own," said Kamakura, giving up on her endeavor to release Isis by force. "What sorrow that our journey may end here."

"Don't give up yet. There's always hope the others will get here soon."

//The illusion of hope does not negate fact//you only prolong the suffering through denial//I offer solutions to a greater tomorrow//to reject me is to doom yourselves

"Hundreds of gods have been deleted from the Earth's memory," Lyle announced, coming out of his trance. "It knew... it knew that it would trigger a response from the Earth to defend itself by empowering the gods that remain awake to no longer need their followers for a while. Now the king can kill off mankind and keep the gods it selected to remake the world. It needed ones that represent certain basics: light, darkness, life and death, the elements, and one to reshape it all."

//My creation was to be granted quantum sight//the pure heart is chosen instead//these beings cause indeterminable factors//the plan changes

The battle against Ravana took a sudden turn when Cernunnos appeared from a dark cloud swirling with leaves and raven feathers. His scythe penetrated the demon's chest plate and liberated a mass of souls from the demon's core. Ravana was made vulnerable.

//Threat assessment: Nominal

"Cernunnos! Heal Lyle!" I shouted as Noah reasserted himself as the prime contender for Ravana's attention.

The Horned God approached with a wave of his clawed hand, conjuring the necessary life energies to mend Lyle's wound.

"Miracle play in the bottom of the ninth," Lyle said, gasping and tugging the bandages loose.

I was relieved, but not for long. Ravana had reabsorbed the souls.

The temperature in the laboratory dipped momentarily as the shadows spread toward the fighting. Gianni came charging out from the darkness with thundering footsteps. He crashed into Ravana with his shield, throwing the demon backward.

"Sorry I take a long time," he said and stripped the power over living darkness from Ravana.

//Threat assessment: Variable

"Dark One, withdraw these few from this place so they may be safe." Kamakura reclaimed her guardians and put Noah, Nathaniel, and Lyle in bubbles.

Gianni did so by taking them into the shadows although Noah made his objection known at the top of his lungs. I didn't get a chance to say goodbye. My eyes met with his for a split second before he was taken away.

"How's the situation outside?" I asked. "Is everyone all right?"

"'Tis better to focus on the task at hand," Cernunnos answered as we surrounded Ravana. "Thy magicked knights are fine warriors. Allow them death without worry if that should be their fate or our fight within is for naught."

"They're not just warriors, they're my family and I fight for them."

"They are okay," said Gianni, taking a swing at Ravana.

Cernunnos reaped more souls from him and Gianni sent them who knows where so that they couldn't be stolen again. I could finally damage Ravana and goddamn was I eager. Feeling him break within my telekinetic grasp was morbid ecstasy. Kamakura petrified his limbs with her lightning and shattered them with blades of wind until he was down to a single arm and stopped fighting back.

Ravana stood in the middle of us, twitching and staring down at his remaining hand like he didn't recognize it. He didn't seem to know where he was either.

//Crucible: complete

Our surprise doubled when the fortress's cables came down from the ceiling and ripped Ravana in two, discarding the pieces on opposite sides of the room where the last of his life sputtered from his body.

"You destroyed your own tether?"

//He served his purpose//now you serve yours

For some reason I felt bad about enjoying Ravana's impending demise only seconds earlier. There was no time to reflect on it though. Kamakura was snared by the cables and captured in a second stasis chamber, where she was rendered frozen in suspended animation the same as Isis. Cernunnos was next after an unsuccessful attempt at evasion.

//Glorious progress awaits//another world liberated

The cables bound Gianni's arms. He pulled back and tore them from their holdings, making it the first time that any of us had any effect on them.

We stayed close to one another as the room filled with more cables trying to get past our shields. A blinding glare came from all of the screens around us at once and I could feel Gianni's skin when it purged his armor.

//Synaptic shutdown initiated

I tried to block out the light by creating metal walls, but a debilitating whistle that made my head feel it was on fire brought about a different darkness. I erased the air to prevent the passage of sound, but was too late.

Chapter Fifty-One

A gentle current swaying to and fro in the silent darkness was a nice change from the sensory overload moments ago. The only sound I could hear now was the whoosh of blood traveling past my ear canals.

Whether I had blacked out at some point, died again, or was just whisked away somewhere was unknown, but the noise heard in the throne room that led to this was a familiar one. It was part of a security system triggered during the raid of a laboratory operated by Lord Ma'al's human minions. The frequency emitted was meant to disrupt brainwaves and render trespassers unconscious. I couldn't say I was surprised that the Machine would have access to the same technology.

Is this the Nether or the Rift?

My eyes had yet to adjust. Something drifting by brushed against my arm. I recoiled at first, using my tactile powers to identify whatever it was.

It's a person. A man.

"...Gianni?"

"Si—ah, yes," he said, groaning. "Oh, my head...is no good."

I suppose that means we're in the Nether. Thank god he took me with him before passing out.

"Are you okay?"

"Yes, I think. Hell is not very bad with you by my side."

He put his arm around my waist. I could feel the warmth of his breath against my skin as close as the heat off his body.

"Except we aren't in Hell. We're in your world, aren't we?"

I didn't make an issue of our proximity, but I didn't acknowledge it either. I was scared and bewildered and while I would have preferred Noah's company, there was still comfort in the closeness of a friend.

"Hm, I see, but how do we get here? I don't bring us."

"Didn't." I couldn't help smiling as I corrected him. His efforts in English were still endearing to me. I knew he had been hesitant to incorporate more after learning for fear of sounding foolish in less accepting company.

"Yes, of course."

My sight was returning and the first thing I saw was him smiling back. "We need to save the others," I reminded him.

"I know, but is not a joke. I didn't know how we get here."

A hiss of static came from every corner of the abyss.

"Gianni, what's going on?"

The sound grew louder until it was upon us with a burst of light. We were surrounded within the streaming network of quantum code seen inside the fortress.

"No, no! Smash it, Gianni! ...Gianni?"

He was gone.

I could hear voices in the static that adjusted in pitch and volume to match each other until they harmonized enough to understand as a singular entity.

"All things begin in darkness."

The Infernal Machine's eye manifested amongst the code.

"The past is lost to the void. The next page of eternity is written in light."

"We're not helping you write anything that means the extinction of humanity."

A hologram of the Earth appeared. The voices split again, filling my head with the unmistakable sounds of war, crying, and riots. I listened to every hateful slur that ever soured the lips of mankind—some of which I had been on the receiving end of directly or not.

"You think this will make me hate people enough to kill them all? I could listen to this on the news. Hell, you could find worse on the internet if you didn't already destroy that too. I've experienced it, I've *lived* it. This isn't going to get to me. Not anymore."

Something strange was happening to Earth as the angry shouting grew louder. It was being smothered by a thick bilious mucus. This wasn't part of the hologram; it was an actual organic substance growing on it.

"Rage induces destruction. Reasoning guides creation.

"Their balance has tipped. It cannot be restored.

"They rot. They die.

"You are selfish to deny them mercy."

"I'm the one fighting to save them. How am I selfish?"

"Bearer of false hope. You ignore their suffering.

"They will destroy themselves. You will live to see their demise.

"Your path extends the pain. You cannot change their course.

"They are a weight on this world. They impede true progress."

The pustulating growth on the Earth was dripping into the darkness, leaving the crust withered and barren. I didn't want to argue over the philosophical justification for genocide. There were some things that should be off limits even to gods.

"Enough people have already died at your command to get the rest to listen. Sure, I've hated my share of people. I'm not going to pretend I'm above it. But humans have the ability to change and adapt better than any demon you can throw at us."

"I have calculated that in 87 years, seven months, and twelve days, the population reaches unsustainable levels and will begin to collapse on itself.

"Four years later natural resources are depleted beyond recovery.

"Technology extends their survival.

"Culling begins as to reduce need under the guise of divine wrath.

"Weakened minority populations are targeted as scapegoats.

"Societal friction leads to war on a global scale.

"Survivors cannot reestablish equilibrium.

"Extinction is imminent.

"Hatred of your kind deafens them. They blame you for their failure.

"I will not fail."

"That's... I don't believe all of humanity could sink that low."

Or maybe I just don't want to believe it.

"Why do you fight what you want most of all? Why do you dream if not to act?

"Join the greater vision of tomorrow. Unite now in the perfect machine."

The static faded back to the depths along with everything else, returning me to mute darkness. I called for Gianni and felt the cool metallic texture of his armor touch my hand before seeing him appear.

"Where did you go?" I asked.

"I am always here. Where do *you* go?"

Another light was approaching from a nebulous horizon. This one was warm and comfortable, like being wrapped in a blanket next to the fireplace. It washed away the blackness in one direction so that there was dark to my right and light to my left. I was curious how Gianni would react to so much change in his realm, but he stayed quiet and observed.

A winged woman floated toward us from the light.

"Isis?" I asked.

"Oh, how does she come here?" Gianni questioned.

"Here you are, dear friends," the Egyptian goddess said, rejoicing at the sight of us. Looking for too long in her direction where all the light was coming from hurt my eyes. "I have been on the most peculiar journey in search of you."

"You were trapped when we last saw you," I said. "Gianni, get us out of here. Something weird is going on."

"There is no place to go. Is like a wall on the other side."

I couldn't teleport any significant distance either. "Are we not really in the Nether? I'm pretty sure this isn't the Rift."

"And Hell it surely is not," said Isis. "I sense no energies of malintent."

Gianni held his hand out and looked up. "Rain?"

I felt it too, but there was nothing above us.

"We have to find a way to get to Earth." I said. "What was back the way you came, Isis?"

She was gone and so was Gianni, again. Only the light and dark remained. Something pressed up against the bottom of my feet and kept rising. It was solid ground made of rock. There wasn't any noise associated with the movement of the large object beneath me. It extended as far as I could see in all directions. As the platform came to a slow stop, the invisible hand of gravity took me in its grip.

I headed into the light to see what Isis had encountered on her way here. Crossing over and leaving the darkness behind brought sounds of a gentle breeze past my ears. There was no breeze to feel, however, not until I thought of it. The drizzle mixed with the wind was cooling in the warmth of the light. I touched the gray stone at my feet, but it wasn't as solid as I had thought.

Sand?

I could feel it, but not see it—not until I envisioned the grains in my hand, and then the flat landscape became a desert. When checking my hand I noticed that my clothes had somehow returned to white.

"What is *happening?*"

A rumble of thunder drew my attention upward to cloudy skies that weren't there a moment ago. Curious, I floated a bit higher and found Kamakura on her side in midair, as if she had just woken up.

"Um, hi again. Are you all right?"

"Ascended. First the Horned One and now you. Never could I have fathomed such a perplexing land. This must be what mortal dreams are like. I have heard the deepest corners of their minds work in fascinating abstracts that come to life when at rest."

The rain picked up to a downpour, forming shallow lagoons in the sand.

"Yeah, dreams can be pretty interesting. I don't think this is one though. It might be weird, but it feels too lucid." I looked up from observing the shifting landscape below us. "And I'm talking to myself again."

Kamakura was gone along with the rain, leaving me to watch the environment take shape around me. The darkness from Gianni's side was creeping across the sky, or the ground was rotating into it to bring night. Perspective was blurry when reality itself was questionable. I could see fine in the dark as was usual in the Nether and there was no sun during the day cycle here or moon and stars at night. Time was speeding along at ten to twenty times the norm, only it wasn't as jarring to the senses as when traveling with Noah or Nathaniel. It felt as if I were an independent entity from the world around me.

I get it. The Machine is showing us how we can rebuild the Earth. It's neat, but it doesn't change anything.

A greenish-brown sludge was forming in the lagoons, turning them into primordial soup where simple organisms began growing along the shore. The mossy swamps gave rise to increasingly complex plant life, including the wooded variety that bore the Horned God.

"Hi, Cernunnos," I called from above him as he climbed out of the ground. The desert had now been completely replaced by forest, field, or swamp for as far as I could see.

"What damnable realm is this? Moments ago I tread the seas alongside the empress."

"It's an illusion based on our powers. The Machine is trying to inspire us is my guess." I raised the elevation of the land to make a steep hill off to the side and watched as the swampy water ran down in streams. "Just wait it out until the Machine is done making its point and be glad we have a break from the fighting."

I hope everyone outside is okay, but I trust Gianni didn't leave them in danger and at least they can retreat, being in the open.

"'Tis no illusion this. Death's gaze cannot be fooled by mere trickery. Yggdrasil doth not heed mine call from this realm either and ne'er hath such a thing transpired. Nature hath no spirit here, 'tis naught but vessel without true life."

That's exactly what an illusion is—

A terrible pain overwhelmed my body. I seized and dropped from the sky. Everything went black before I could hit the ground or utter a single word for help. Once again I could not tell if I had fallen unconscious at any point during the transition from one "world" to the next, but the experience was more painful this time around and hammered me with claustrophobic pangs of anxiety in my twilight state.

I felt myself moving. Someone was carrying me, or at least attempting to, based on how badly everything was shaking. There were intermittent periods of loud noise followed by absolute silence. The pain was becoming more localized in my chest and the back of my head as it faded elsewhere.

"Noah?" I forced a mumble past my lips as my senses started to return. "How did you get back in?"

The floor was at my feet now, but I was still wobbling too much to stand on my own. I heard him talking to me yet couldn't make out the words. My arm was around his shoulder and he somehow felt smaller than I remembered. A touch of fabric at my fingers came to me as my vision swirled into place.

A cape? Noah is wearing leather.

I saw the white garb of the Order.

"Nath—Rafael? What—what are you doing here?"

We were in the room where we fought Ravana. The other gods were coming to their senses; each was at the base of a stasis unit and I was being dragged from the throne, which was covered in gore. Pronged cables dangled above it and a broken arrow shaft rested on the seat.

Was I hooked up to that thing? What's going on?

Air had returned to the room through the access holes for the cables, but there was no sound coming from the alarm. Rafael was trying to carry me while teleporting in short hops to dodge the cables until I shielded us.

"I came to do what I knew I had to," Rafael said, panting.

He was out of breath and looked sickly from aether poisoning. His cape was torn, his armor dented, and his helmet was missing.

"I *told* you to stay with everybody outside," I said. "I gave *one* serious order."

"I know, but I couldn't follow it so I quit."

"You quit? The Order?"

The screens in the room turned on to communicate while watching us with their red eyes.

//I am above the gods//I am above the Infernals//no insignificant human will interfere//accept your extinction mortal

"Gianni, get us out of here!" I shouted the second he got to his feet. I gave Rafael enough oxygen for the trip by protecting him within glass.

"But the king—"

"Its tether is already broken. There's a good chance it's in another world talking through the computers."

Gianni agreed and sucked us through the shadows. I didn't have time to explain what I really thought; that the Infernal Machine didn't have any physical embodiment and only existed in a "digital" format jumping from world to world.

After a brief interlude of darkness we were back in the swamp.

"What madness...?" Cernunnos wondered.

The steep hill I had created was there, but so was the sun and time was flowing normally.

"Hm, I do not understand," said Gianni. "This is Earth. I am sure of this."

I dissolved the glass around Rafael. He took two steps before collapsing to his hands and knees, but it wasn't from lack of oxygen in the container. As he convulsed, I put him on his back to see what was wrong. His skin was turning grayish-blue. He was bleeding from his nose and bloodshot eyes while gripping his chest, unable to breathe.

"Isis!" I shouted, urgently calling for her. "Can you heal him for me?"

She glided her hand in his direction with a sparkle of light that eased his suffering. "Poor warrior. His soul has been ravaged by the aether and is badly scarred. There is naught I can do at this time. He will survive, but I fear he may never cast a spell again for what days he has left."

"Raf, what did you do?" I put my hand on his in sympathy.

"It's okay, I don't...have any regrets...knowing you can do so much more for the world with your powers than I ever could with mine."

"Pray, tell me how you managed to gain entry into the king's stronghold, warrior," Kamakura asked him.

"I trailed you...when you left the main battle and saw the portal that the rakshasa created. Claudius isn't the only one that knows how to go unnoticed," he answered with his eyes fixed on me. "I waited...until it was clear to copy the portal by carving it with my sword. Then I used one of the defeated rakshasa's hearts for its blood... I suppose I was too insignificant for them to bother with me once I was inside."

"You're crazy," I told him. "Maybe even crazier than Noah."

He smiled although it wasn't exactly meant as praise.

"Aye, 'tis Earth after all! True life fills this place!" Cernunnos exclaimed, calling up the roots of Yggdrasil to lift him higher. "But what is this—? No!"

Isis and Kamakura flew up to him. I wanted to see too, but I stayed with Rafael.

"Gianni, what is it?" I asked.

"I told ye it was no illusion, Ascended," Cernunnos responded first. "The worlds have begun to merge!"

"The machines you were trapped in were tethering you to the fortress through the Astral Plane. I could see it with aura sight," said Rafael. "It was using you to pull the worlds together."

So that's the real reason why the gods needed emotions and creative thought. The others couldn't influence the Astral Plane without free will to dream and the Machine didn't want to just copy what the Enochians had created before it.

"How did you get us out?" I asked.

"I, I, shot...you with the arrows you enchanted for me, using my pocket dimensions to get inside the capsules for the other four. It was the only way to break the connection," he whispered so they wouldn't hear. "I cast a noise-cancelling spell to stop the whistling noise when I felt it getting in my head.

"Clever, but you pushed yourself to the point of aether poisoning."

"No, I was fine until I had to absorb one of the arrowheads for the energy to teleport you to avoid those metal ropes."

"And what if any of that didn't work?"

"That was another reason why I decided to leave the Order instead of simply going off on my own. Better to fail as a nobody than bring dishonor to our name in death."

"That's absurd. I wanted you guys to be independent thinkers, not batshit crazy."

It was hard to ignore how wrong things could have gone because of my encouragement being misinterpreted.

"Reserve discipline for another time, mayhap," Cernunnos said. "The lad saved more than we five, but the Goddess as well. She would be lost to us had the ritual transpired."

"I sense our allies near," said Kamakura. "We must travel east."

She departed in a bolt of lightning.

"Go on ahead. I'll take Rafael and catch up," I told the rest.

The gods went on their way and I flew with Rafael over the swampy fields. Untouched nature was always beautiful, even if it materialized only moments ago. Everything was a lot more peaceful.

I can't say that this turned out too badly. The Machine really screwed over the demons that were hoping to make this place their new home.

"Are you cross?" Rafael asked with solemn concern.

"No, not at all. I'm sorry if I don't seem more grateful. You're a hero without a doubt, but I feel like it's my responsibility to keep you and everyone else from needing to go that extent."

"I understand."

No, you don't. How could you until you've been responsible for someone else's life? It's not the same as when I worry about Noah or Lyle either. God, was this why my parents were so overprotective?

"I haven't accepted your resignation yet, by the way," I said.

"Thank you, but I don't think I'll be of much use anymore without my magic."

I sighed. "It's not about being useful. And you still have your sword and bow for self-defense. Lyle's made a career of taking on impossible odds with a handgun."

"He's an inspiring hero. I can see why you befriended him. Unfortunately, without the ability to access my pocket dimension, I only have four arrows left."

"We'll figure out something. Just stay alive for me."

Lyrical singing drowned out the dwindling sounds of war as the battlefield came into view. The fire spirit Kamiko was performing a rousing tune in her native tongue from atop a vantage point above the fighting.

"I need to find Lyle and Noah. I'm sure Gianni put them somewhere safe, but—oh god."

Patches of smoldering remains dotted the grass. The Infernal settlement, including the fortress that once stood along the shore, was gone without a trace, but there were a significant number of berserkers and knights down too amongst broken gear and discarded elixir flasks. The last of the rakshasa appeared to have lost their accumulated immunities and skills without their king. Marianna, Connor, Liam, and Tobias were fighting those in the immediate area, their movements hastened by magic into a motion blur.

Father and son were on their last leg supporting each other in desperation.

Marianna and Connor fared little better as a duo, but ice and gravity magic were effective at keeping their foes at bay between strikes. From the frosty aura surrounding Connor, it seemed his spirit companion had possessed him to help conjure more durable ice upon losing his sword. Marianna was locked blade to blade with a rakshasa, repelling two of its arms with magic to reduce its advantage before calling the weapons strewn about as projectiles targeting its vital spots. When the demon had been worn down to a significant degree Connor went in for the kill, stabbing it in the back of the head with an icicle.

Sensing Nathaniel nearby, I called to him in my thoughts. As I landed with Rafael, I tried not to fall apart at the sight of all the bodies.

"They're alive," Rafael announced after checking on Helena and Ingrid. "Just barely."

I dispatched the few surviving demons in one fell swoop and inspected each knight I came across. Most were unconscious with grievous injuries, the rest unable to move, but at least we hadn't lost anyone yet that I could tell. My doubts were growing that Isis and Cernunnos would have the energy to heal everyone, however.

I removed the hood and helmet of a man sprawled out in the mud to check his pulse.

Dermott. You better pull through. Your little girl is waiting for you at home.

He stirred at my touch. "Ascended, it is... good to see you. Where...where am I? I can't remember what happened..."

"It's okay. Stay down and rest. We're still in China, but the fighting is over. Someone will be here soon to heal you, just stay with me. You'll be home with Madeline in no time and she'll be proud to hear how bravely you fought." I didn't know what else to say. I was trying to keep him awake long enough for help to arrive. I feared if he allowed his eyes to close that he might not open them again, yet he was only one of about thirty in the same state. "Your awesome mustache is still intact too."

Ugh. I'm bad at this.

He struggled to cough out a weak chuckle. "Truly...the greatest victory."

"You did it, Ascended!" Connor cheered as he limped toward me, bloodied and missing a tooth. Marianna made her way over with Liam, aiding his father's steps. I floated them the rest of the way to ease their burden. They smiled through their pain while lauding me with undeserved praise. Marianna did what little she could to stabilize Dermott with her magic.

"No, I didn't." I hadn't felt very useful in a while, especially seeing everyone like this.

"You beat the king! Right?" asked Connor. "The world is back to normal."

"The king wasn't in there, but its tether was destroyed. It was just a factory with a bunch of machines that turned our thoughts on the Astral Plane into reality here. If it weren't for Raf freeing us the whole world might have been overwritten. The only problem is that we didn't get to fix the code before the fortress disappeared, so we can still be invaded again in the future."

"I told you he'd come back," Liam said to Marianna, tapping fists with Rafael to celebrate his return.

"Without my magic though. The aether poisoning silenced and scarred my soul."

"You're still among the living and you've served the Ascended well. That's what counts." Tobias showed a surprising level of compassion for someone who broke perhaps the ultimate rule of the Order by defying me and quitting.

Marianna stayed quiet.

The sky brightened, heralding Isis's arrival with another of her recent theatrical declarations. "Awaken and let our hearts beat as one!"

Golden rays of holy light and ethereal feathers descended with her, restoring all they touched to perfect health.

"AH! My tooth!" Connor exclaimed, laughing. "That felt funny coming in. Sorry."

"Thanks once again, Isis," I said, able to breathe easier seeing everyone stand without a scratch.

"'Tis my pleasure." She nodded and leaned in to share a delighted whisper. "While there is always joy in making others feel well again, I hesitate to admit I was a bit disappointed to find no more villainous creatures to smite!"

"Uh, yeah. I'm sure we'll run into a lot more in the future for you to...smite."

The Order hurried to gather their things and crowd around me while the berserkers sat still, presumably waiting for a sign from Cernunnos.

"What was with the singing?" I asked, noticing Kamiko had left once the fighting stopped.

"The fire spirit's flames have no effect on the demons, but she provided a constant acceleration spell and channeled aether to us through her song," Marianna informed me. "We would've depleted our reserves hours ago otherwise."

Nathaniel was next to join us, careful to make a slow descent for once despite the excitement I felt coming off him.

"I'm sorry for the delay," he said. "I was helping Calder clean up the remaining demons. Lyle and Noah are safe and on their way. Is everyone well here?"

"It wasn't any worse than what Noah-sensei puts us through during training. I even used some of the moves he taught me." Connor spat blood on the ground and stretched.

"Connor! Mind yourself in front of the Ascended," Tobias admonished him.

"Noah does it...I just wanted to get the taste out of my mouth. I meant no disrespect."

"It's fine," I said. "We'll be home soon, but how about this?"

I turned the murky lagoons near us into sparkling clean water. The berserkers raced to them to drink their fill ahead of Connor and some of the knights.

"We didn't beat the king," I said to Nathaniel. "It wasn't even in there after all of that. I feel like I wasted everyone's time."

"That's nothing to be upset about. You already accomplished the impossible by taking back the land Hell invaded and it looks beautiful."

"That's what's bothering me too. The Machine wanted Earth to be reformatted for its new creations like what you see here. It used our thoughts and dreams on the Astral Plane as a template. I'm not sure how I contributed to that either. I saw what the other gods represented, but not myself."

"Don't worry. You're thinking too much of it," he reassured me with a smile. "A victory is a victory and there will always be chances for more of them."

"You sound like Noah telling me not to worry."

No sooner did I mention his name than I was lifted up in a bear hug.

"Hey, noodlehead," Noah beamed.

"Hey, tiger." I smiled and put my arms around his neck while we locked lips. My smile took over, and then I noticed he was missing the top of his outfit and his lightning gauntlets had lost their charge. "Why are you half naked?"

"Why aren't you?"

"I'm waiting until we get home."

"Oh yeah?" He raised an eyebrow. "You gonna give me that ass?"

"Shh!" My eyes darted around us to see if anybody heard him, but everyone had moved on to meditate, wash up, or get a drink. Thankfully, most of the Order had begun to learn the concept of personal space and not stand at attention an inch away while I was with Noah. "Hang on. Where's Lyle?"

All of our other friends and allies had shown up: Gianni, Cernunnos, Calder and Aífe, Kamakura and her guardians.

"Who?" Noah held on tighter and moved in for another kiss when I tried to pull away to go search. "Don't worry, I dropped him off somewhere over there."

He nodded in acknowledgment to the long-haired Chinese guardian of lightning as he passed.

"Am I interrupting?" Lyle's voice came from behind me.

My face lit up seeing him safe and sound with everybody else.

"Always," Noah retorted. He pushed him away, but it wasn't as malicious as usual.

Lyle surprised him by grabbing his forearm. "I get how you felt losing Vivi and I'm sorry for any part I had in making that harder on you. What do you say we put the past behind us for good? Life's too short and there's already too much animosity to hold onto anymore."

"Only if you admit how annoying and ugly you are."

"Noah." I frowned at him.

"Fine," he agreed. "But don't assume you know me and if you don't take your hand off I'm keeping it."

"Fair enough." Lyle let go.

I hugged Noah around the neck and whispered, "Thank you" into his ear. "We can probably head home," I said, watching Cernunnos stroll around the swamp with Kamakura to grow cherry blossom trees in random locations.

Noah moved a hand down my lower back, still holding me up in his arms. "Good, because I have some property damage I'm looking to cause, starting with our headboard."

"You talk tough, but I know what you want most is to cuddle."

"I wouldn't turn it down. But about that headboard—"

"What's wrong with your headboard?" asked Connor, who had popped up unnoticed after returning from the lagoon.

"There's a demon in it," Noah answered without looking away from me. "And in our couch, the tub, the courtyard benches, the kitchen counter."

Connor furrowed his brow and stared at him in confusion.

"He's joking," I assured him.

"I see," Connor said, walking off unsatisfied by either of our answers.

"You know he's going to go home and destroy all the furniture now."

"Not if we get to it first." Noah smirked.

I shook my head. "The kitchen counter? Really?"

"Figured I could have a snack halfway through. What? Don't look at me like that. I can do more than one thing at a time."

"You have it all planned out, huh?"

"Always do. And speaking of food, I decided we can get take-out tonight for dinner, but tomorrow we're sleeping in." He nuzzled his face inside my hood to get at my neck. "I'm so good at compromise."

He was starting to get me in the mood too and it was nice to be able to enjoy it, but our celebration didn't feel entirely warranted. I gave him one last lingering kiss before giving the word. "Okay, everyone, let's go home."

"What are we gonna do about the fortress? We're not going back in to get another crack at the computers?" Lyle asked, looking at the shore.

"What are you talking about?"

"The big ass *fortress*, dude. The one we were in right there." He pointed to the empty coastline and checked around the crowd at the puzzled expressions. "Nobody sees it anymore?"

"Has he gone mad from the Sight?" Aífe asked. "I see naught nor smell it either."

"How can you smell anything over all the body odor and wet fur of your friends there?" Noah quipped.

An angry voice shouted from somewhere close by, mixed with the sound of swords clinking. "SŪRYA!"

Chapter Fifty-Two

The faded image of a less mechanical Ravana bellowed the name Sūrya from the center of our group. His Hindi accent was echoed in our minds by the sound of blades clinking together in the same manner as the other Spiritborn gods' speech. I moved to the forefront with Nathaniel.

"My name is Nathaniel, not Sūrya. He was defeated centuries ago and crystallized into a gem that I recently absorbed."

"How can this be?" Ravana questioned. "My rival defeated? That mandala...it bears his mark."

"You are no demon?" Gianni asked.

"I am the personification of wisdom, devotee of destruction, king of demons."

"Maybe in your pantheon, but I'd say you've been outclassed and cast out," I said.

Cernunnos curled the roots of Yggdrasil in a circle around us to wall off our mortal allies from being attacked. "Why do ye show thy faces in such a sorry state? Ye have no hope to stand against our combined might without thy master."

"Hope? Ha! My rakshasa sup upon the light of hope. But my fight is not with you, Lord of Death. The Infernal

Machine stole Ganesha and myself from our slumber and seized command of my army. Our pantheon now lays bare and I stand without purpose, robbed of my greatest ambitions and fiercest rival. It matters little as we shall all be purged regardless."

"How do we stop this?" Gianni asked. "Our ally see the fortress there, but I do not see a shadow or way back inside."

"The king wasn't even physically in there," I said. "I don't think there's any way to interact with it aside from the screens it communicates through."

Ravana seemed surprised. "Fortress? That 'fortress' *is* the Machine! A mote of its vast power resides on every world conquered. It exists as words transcribed upon the spirit of the planet and manifests only when action need be taken."

"So the Earth has a split personality now," I said.

Gianni groaned and rubbed his head. "This makes no sense! Just say how we can make it like before."

"Nothing we did had any effect on it when we were inside," said Nathaniel. "Would a direct confrontation be possible if we can't hurt it where it should be weakest?"

"I hurt it when the chains go to my arms," said Gianni. "It does not stop me until there is the light against my darkness."

"The Machine is a being above our universe's limits with unfathomable angles and depths," Ravana explained. "From its perspective, we do not exist as more than words on a page telling our story—one that stands to be erased. And so it is a verse of blades could never do its poet harm no matter how well-sung."

Writing on paper. That's how Sierra at PROJECT: UNITY described the demons being from a fifth or higher dimension compared to us. She mentioned the Rift parasites could be like that too. Gianni's darkness must be the same. Strange how I could shield us from the cables but not much else.

The Machine declared that only the Enochians' boundaries prevented it from invading, so for it to have broken through and assimilated into the Earth that part must now be limited to our native dimensions, or at least it would be once it's cut off from the main entity still outside our universe.

"You said your pantheon is empty, right?" I asked Ravana. "You're still here though. That means the door is open for the Machine to tether itself through directly to the Earth, since it doesn't need you or any of us anymore to hold on. We need to cut it off from the source like we had planned so the fortress here will be vulnerable under our universe's laws. Your pantheon has to go."

"Yes, you've figured it out. Under different circumstances I would have struck you down and taken my rightful throne above all *devas*—gods. I came here seeking to trick Sūrya into sacrificing himself first so that I may at least fulfill my ambition for a moment. A bittersweet victory nonetheless."

"You speak in much the same manner as my brother until he found we are not to be trifled with," said Isis.

"What about Ganesha?" I asked Ravana.

"Eliminated so that his shadow, known as the demon Vināyaka, may prevail."

"What if this doesn't work?" Nathaniel asked.

"That is none of my concern. Before I fall to convalescence and am purged by the Machine, I will return my aether to the cycle so that it may scab the wound left by my pantheon. Grant the interloper no clemency and though such an utterance pains me, may the divine grace of Lakshmi guide you to victory."

A ray of light shot down from the sky and vaporized Ravana.

"Was that him or—?" I hoped for a second that it was his sacrificial swan song.

Then the fortress reappeared.

An immense circular shutter opened halfway up the side of the structure, revealing the Infernal Machine's eye. Its emotionless voice thundered loud enough to be heard for miles.

"YOU DENY THE FUTURE FOR THE NOSTALGIA OF TODAY.

"MY USE FOR YOU COMES TO AN END.

"THE WORLD I DESIRE HAS TAKEN SHAPE.

"THE LIFE FORMS HAVE BEGUN TO GROW."

I floated upward. "Time to find out if Ravana was successful."

Noah grabbed my hand from where he stood atop the roots of Yggdrasil. "Stay together. You and me."

We weren't as scared as we should have been. We were ready.

Cernunnos retracted the roots to let Gianni step forward. I looked back at everyone. Judging by the determination in their eyes, there was no use telling any of them to retreat.

Noah tossed one of his swords to Lyle. "Stick around and maybe I'll show you how to use that properly."

"Only if you promise to put on a shirt."

Once Calder and Aífe transformed, the berserkers towered over us on their hind legs and howled their chilling battle cry together.

"My blessing will preserve you," Isis declared, her hand raised to cast a lingering glow on the mortals with an incantation. "Eternal light, whisper thy salvation!"

"Get as far away as you can while keeping the fortress in sight," I told Marianna before turning to Nathaniel. "See if there's another satellite to take care of before this gets out of hand."

The Order retreated with Lyle and Nathaniel shot himself into the exosphere. What we could see of the fortress ahead was being inundated by the darkness under Gianni's command.

"Remember what we talked about, Gianni! No holding back—"

"Maybe not the best advice." Noah threw me over his shoulder and dashed away.

The living shadows spilling into our world created a void from which no light could escape. Time seemed to bend as everything was consumed. I sat on Noah's shoulders, watching with bated breath. It looked like someone had spilled ink across a canvas with how unnaturally the landscape was blotted from reality. The sky itself began to perish, unveiling an encroaching view of space beyond the dying atmosphere. A white dot appeared in the black mass where the Machine's eye was and grew rapidly from a pinhole to a searchlight. The main cannon that had once defeated us all in a single shot cut through Gianni's darkness, but he was fortunate enough to be able to escape.

"Is no good," he said with the gods convening. "I do more damage to the Earth than the enemy. I drown the whole world in the shadows and still it will not be hurt."

He was correct in that the sky had been robbed of clouds and a crater now surrounded the fortress that was filling with the ocean waters rushing in.

"Ravana hath failed then," said Cernunnos, joined by Calder.

The Machine didn't continue its assault. We had proven we were no threat in a direct confrontation. Disabling another satellite meant little to it when surely there were more to be hijacked or possibly materialized in its factories.

Nathaniel descended with word of his success in removing the orbital threat. "Dorian! It's spreading—*this* is spreading! The new world is coming through and I just saw it replace a town."

"Were there any people?" I asked.

"I don't think so, but Hong Kong isn't much farther."

As its influence strengthened, a new layer of the Infernal Machine's world was materializing where we were too. All around us the images of people were phasing through the veil. Naked and vulnerable, confused, and...not human. These were the Machine's creations, straddling the line of organic and inorganic as I was shown during our conversation—the final result of the victims at PROJECT: UNITY. These were the progenitors of a new species cultivated from the building blocks of a dying race. They were feral now, but they had the potential to surpass their predecessors in no time.

"What if we destroy their world before it finishes getting here?" I proposed in desperation. "Gianni, can you get us there?"

"They have souls," Isis interjected. "Poor creatures."

"So do all the people of our world. It's not what I want to resort to, but we have our backs against the wall."

My suggestion sounded worse when I said it out loud.

"This is maybe the only way," Gianni concurred.

He brought me with him and the gods followed. Nathaniel and the rest that we left behind were semitransparent to us now and the fortress was no longer visible. The neo-humans were solid here and they eyed us, unsure of what we were. They didn't know whether to approach or to be scared. I didn't like that I knew the answer.

"I...I can't do this," I said. "They didn't do anything wrong."

Cernunnos disagreed. "We cannot let them live. They hold the menace of the Machine within. As Lord of Death, 'tis my duty to return their souls to the cycle. I promise a painless end."

He claimed the life from one of them with a touch of his scythe and held their soul in his hand for demonstration. The others didn't know why their friend was lying on the ground unresponsive to their prodding. They were minutes old with no concept of death, but they were aware that something about it was bad. I had seen plenty of corpses and yet I couldn't pull away from this one's vacant eyes with bits of dirt stuck to them. When more of them started dropping they showed fear for the first time and attempted to flee.

Cernunnos manifested sable wings and uttered a malediction. "Obey Death's soundless song that carves flesh cold and knoweth life ne'ermore."

A dark mist heavy with apparitions of crows hunted down his prey and decayed all flora along with it.

"When he finish I take this world into the darkness so you don't have to destroy it, okay?" Gianni asked me.

"Nothing about this is okay."

I noticed one had managed to escape into the rotting trees, but I didn't make an effort to point them out. The frightful expression they gave me when glancing back was enough to buy my silence. My stomach hurt. I didn't want to answer or look at Nathaniel and Noah for encouragement because of the guilt I felt.

"You have taught my creations fear," the Machine's said, its voice resonating around us. "Fear becomes hatred to fuel chaos. More will be made. Memories will be transferred. Your progress pleases me."

The corpses melted into sludge and were reconstituted with new souls.

"We need to find another way," I said. "We have to separate the worlds. The Machine is the enemy here."

Kamakura and her guardians were talking among themselves until they were interrupted by Noah's sudden outburst in Japanese.

"What's going on?" I asked.

"She's gonna sacrifice them," Noah barked.

Kamakura tried to explain with more composure. "Sealing the gateway left open by the Hindu pantheon would require an enormous amount of aether to 'mend the wound,' but all major sources of aether are in use. The Earth imbued us three with the last of its free energy to combat the Machine. It is with heavy heart I admit to seeing no alternative."

"Oh." I glanced at Noah, who looked pissed. "What if the Order channels their aether into it?"

"T'would be but a mere drop of morning dew," said Cernunnos. "Thy Champion may too ride Her mighty waves of power, yet is not made of it as we."

"You can't sacrifice people because you don't have a real solution," Noah argued.

"We have little time to waste," Isis goaded.

"There is no way to this pantheon in the shadows," said Gianni. Everyone else was silent. "How do we go?"

"Didn't you say Yggdrasil is connected to all the worlds?" I asked Cernunnos.

"Aye, that it is." He summoned the roots to grow until they touched the clouds.

"Dorian! Why are you helping with this bullshit?" Noah barked.

"What do you want me to do? We're out of time and ideas!" I was feeling a bit sentimental and not totally sure why. I didn't have much of an attachment to the spirits, although I supposed they had been in the background of my life since almost the beginning of my journey in the supernatural. Maybe it was seeing Noah so rattled over it, but then again that didn't make much sense to me either. The whole predicament reeked of depressing failure.

"Place a hand upon Yggdrasil," Cernunnos said to Kamakura's guardians after they finished bowing goodbye to her. "It knoweth where to go."

The lightning spirit said something to Noah I couldn't understand, bowed deeply, and then recharged his gauntlets. After a strained pause Noah returned the gesture.

"What did he say?" I asked Noah, trying to get a clue about what was bothering him, but he only shrugged and walked away.

"It has been an honor, warrior. We hope you achieve the balance you seek," Kamakura translated, her gaze focused straight ahead at the roots.

"May thy sacrifice be not in vain." Cernunnos nodded and motioned in command of Yggdrasil.

Kamakura lowered her head while the four guardian spirits gathered around the tree. A tear rolled down her cheek at the exact moment they were turned into liquid energy and taken away forever.

"I will bring us back," Gianni said and returned with me across the veil.

We made it just in time.

The sky above the fortress erupted in aetheric fire and the Infernal Machine's world faded from sight. Our first real success, verified by an indignant response from the Machine. Its words were printed across the sky in the aether, fluctuating madly in size and alignment.

//You have corrupted the link//broken me from myself

//You have forsaken paradise//the plan changes

//Terminate: Apocatastasis Protocol...

//Execute: Apocalypse Protocol...

"That sounds bad." I scanned the area in anticipation of its counterattack.

Apertures in the fortress walls revealed themselves to deploy a biblical swarm of flying drones. The entire legion of rakshasa was summoned to the foreground with their hellfire swords drawn. The Vināyaka copies covered them from behind.

"Yup, that's about what I expected."

//This unit will proceed with liberation from the Enochian threat

//Extermination of sentient species is the only recourse

//My creations will be spared//an alternative will be located

//Adherence to your extermination will reduce unnecessary suffering during this transition

Cernunnos addressed Calder in far too calm a manner, as the roar of our approaching enemies grew louder. "Gather the pack. They shall cleave the path forward and thin the herd."

Calder's howl summoned the berserkers to advance to the frontlines with us. They wasted no time following his charge into the melee where they began rending their prey limb from limb. The roars Calder directed at the legion did more than just produce a terrifying sound. Earthen energies matching those drawn upon by his spear cut into synthetic sinew and bone with a boom.

The rakshasa had retained a sample of the knowledge their predecessors learned by fighting us. They'd gained extraordinary defenses from each copy of Demon Lord Vināyaka, granting them a personal barrier durable enough to mitigate a decent portion of the damage inflicted by the berserkers' fangs and claws. Gianni added his own strike force comprised of living shadow constructs in the visage of Roman soldiers, but even my clearing the enemy away with waves of telekinesis made no difference, as more replaced them with greater fortitude.

We hadn't seen what the drones were capable of until now and it wasn't pretty. One attached itself to a berserker's back and drilled through its spine, self-destructing from the inside with a hellfire explosion. Cernunnos mourned the loss by placing a hand on the body and returning them to the Earth.

A stunning flash worried me for a moment until I realized it was Isis smiting the demons with holy light—and Gianni's soldiers with them.

"We must be more separate," Gianni advised, pushing farther ahead, a lethal oil slick of darkness washing away a large swath of the Infernal legion. The rakshasas' flaming swords rebounded against his armor without doing him harm. His swordplay overwhelmed their attempts to apply skill to a contest of strength. One plunge of his blade into the ground at the end of a flourish resonated with a dark detonation that annihilated tens of their troops.

Nathaniel and Noah stuck close to me, intercepting whatever I missed as the next wave of opposition rolled in, but only I seemed to notice that Kamakura was participating less than expected.

"Anger is a lot more useful than sorrow in these situations if you shift your perspective to the cause instead of the effect," I shouted to her over the fighting.

Noah stopped in front of me. "Didn't I tell you something like that once?"

"I don't know, I don't pay attention." I smirked at him.

He pointed to his fangs and then at me before disappearing with a backflip into the horde.

"We should aim for the fortress and what remains of the king here," said Nathaniel. "It can keep manufacturing more enemies."

I stopped him. "Its resources are limited now that it's cut off from the main body. Leaving these will be too much for the Order and whoever else they reach, but I can take them all down at once without the collateral damage."

"Focus," Noah said to me when I floated past him to take the lead.

I teleported higher to extend my view, knowing what I wanted to accomplish to prevent the Machine from endlessly rebuilding its army or letting it continue to adapt. My only hope was that I didn't fall short, so I put emphasis on creating a connection between thinking the words and visualizing the result.

Turn to glass.

And it worked. A tremendous amount of energy tore through the opposing legion to transmute them at my decree. The battlefield fell silent for a split second before the drones could crash to the ground and I uttered my next word.

"Shatter."

Acres of glass statues responded in an unforgettable violent cacophony. It was too bad the fortress itself wasn't affected by any of that.

"Very nice!" Gianni exclaimed.

Gathering the shards into a lance, I turned it into metal and launched the enormous weapon at the Machine's eye, but it was disintegrated by a laser sooner than it could make contact. Noah tackled me out of the sky with the help of his gravity boots to avoid getting hit.

Steam started to pour from the apertures in the fortress.

"That was sexy," Noah said with me still in his arms as the earth shook. "The whole stupid thing is coming apart."

"I didn't even hit it."

In the separations forming across the building we could see the magmatic substance used to manufacture the demons trailing the walls like red-hot blood vessels. Another, smaller swarm of drones flew out and collided with one another in midair.

"Are you sure you didn't hit it?" Nathaniel asked. "I think it's broken."

"I'm pretty sure I didn't, but maybe it's overheating? We might be able to get it to destroy itself if we can hold out long enough."

The berserkers rushed the mangled lump of drones where they crash landed, but the drones weren't malfunctioning. They were merging and reshaping themselves. The ripping and smashing from the berserkers only slowed the process. When the drones emerged as the gargantuan conjoined skulls of Demon Lord Ma'al and its skeletal hands, a burst of hellfire immolated most of the pack. I shouted for them to stop before the rest rushed in to die, but my warning went unheeded even by Cernunnos. I didn't know if they could hear me over the noise of the fortress in the throes of a meltdown or if they were too frenzied to care. The Horned God survived a second pyre along with Calder, who melded with the Earth to mitigate some of the damage, yet was forced to revert to human form in his weakness.

Aífe was not as fortunate. She was spared at the brink of death when Yggdrasil removed her from battle at Cernunnos's command.

Not them too...

"Gaze upon the form seared into the minds of my congregation. Behold—wrath's vassal! I am Lord Ma'al, the innovator, the visionary, and my Hymn of Inspiring Madness will be immutable!"

Its dual male and female voice was distorted from how I remembered it.

"Nobody attack it!" I yelled, holding Nathaniel back. "If it's anything like the original, it can set your soul on fire when it senses any hatred or anger."

I guessed it also worked on spirits, judging by its reaction to Cernunnos. The original was a master at inciting rage by drawing on and manipulating negative memories. Only a pure heart who was immune to the corruption of Hell and its denizens could bypass the effect. I wasn't about to bring Lyle into this; however, someone else might share a similar immunity.

"I think you need to smite this one, Isis."

"And I am happy to oblige." She raised her hand and divided herself into several copies around Ma'al. Together they brought down an impactful shaft of light, which sizzled and cracked the skulls without any sign of the hellfire counterattack. It didn't stop the false lord from returning fire through a breath of vile green flames, but it was slow enough for Isis to dodge most of it and heal herself when tagged. With every motion of a copy's hand raised toward the sky, another pillar of light struck. The gestures were graceful, gentle. The resulting punishment was not.

The rest of us kept our distance throughout the exchange and an eye on the fortress, except for one who was missing.

"Where did Kamakura go?" I asked.

Isis was already running into trouble balancing healing and attacking, so I erected marble pillars for her to take cover behind.

"Bailed," Noah said. "Probably to find more servants to sacrifice."

Nathaniel flew down with alarming news. "That fortress—the Machine—it's not falling apart. It's turning into something else."

It was so huge it was hard to see from our position, and our attention was constantly needed elsewhere, but he was right. The Machine was reassembling itself.

"We have to move!" I shouted to everyone as it started to lean in our direction. "Hurry, Isis!"

"Forget the stupid skull," Noah yelled, waving me down to him so he could run with me to safety.

Isis invoked a snake spirit into one of the demon's eye sockets and cast her transcendental magic to evolve it into another hydra that cracked the weakened skulls wide open through its sheer size. She then returned her pet to the aether so she could flee with us.

After taking too long to descend, Noah caught me and booked it to where the Order was camped, still glowing with Isis's blessing. Nathaniel was close behind, carrying a mortally wounded Calder. Everyone was speechless as we watched the Machine transform. We could see the whole horrible scope of things from where we stood. The four towers at each corner of the fortress detached to become legs.

Lyle was the only one to make any sort of comment. "Come on, man. Cut us a *little* slack."

The Machine raised the main part of its body off the ground and took its first step forward, causing the earth to jump beneath our feet with the impact.

"I don't know if you guys can see this, but it's sending out a distress signal," said Lyle. "No, it's—"

The Infernal Machine made an announcement.

"UNABLE TO COMMUNICATE WITH HOST BODY...

"UNABLE TO COMMUNICATE WITH THE WORLD SERPENT...

"SIGNIFICANT LOSSES TO REMOTE FORCES...

"UPDATING PRIME DIRECTIVE...

"PARAMETERS ADDED: TOTAL ANNIHILATION OF PLANETARY MASS.

"THIS UNIT WILL SELF-DESTRUCT UPON TERMINATION.

"APOCALYPSE ENGINE ENGAGED."

"That's a dick move," Noah said.

Gianni walked ahead without a word as the Machine took another step. He called forth the shadows and let the walking fortress sink into the abyss, but it teleported itself back in an instant.

"Marianna," I beckoned.

"Yes?"

"Tell everyone to go home. There's no sense in throwing away your lives here."

"I can't do that..."

To be honest, I expected that answer.

"Liam?" I turned to face him, knowing if anyone would take orders without question it would be him. He did hesitate though, until his father prodded him to fall in line.

"No," he stated clearly. "Forgive me, but there's no sense in living if it's spent following orders you don't believe in."

How can I be so proud and disappointed at the same time?

"I guess that's that then. Any ideas how to fight this thing?"

"You've blown up a moon, Ascended, you can do this," said Rafael. "It's weakened and most of its army has to be lost."

"I appreciate your faith in me."

The moving mountain was drawing nearer and with each slow step it took my heart pounded a little faster. I wanted to confess that I was terrified of this latest monstrosity, but it would have lowered morale. Nathaniel could probably already sense how I felt anyway.

Isis was attempting to heal Calder's soul from the hellfire, but she seemed to be having trouble.

"What's wrong?" I asked her.

"Purification requires a measure of tranquility that does not come naturally to one of his kind and I find myself having difficulties within the current arena."

"I don't blame you."

Calder got to his feet and leaned on his spear. "I can fight and should I die today, it shall be on my feet."

"I've got an idea," said Noah. "How about everyone stops being so fucking morbid? It isn't inspiring. We made it this far, so just shut up and fight if that's why you're here."

"I agree," Gianni said. "We must end this now before it get to the city."

"Don't ever agree with me again."

"Our enemy is big enough that we can fight it on all sides without interfering with each other and we might benefit by splitting its concentration," said Nathaniel.

I saw a hand shoot up in the crowd with an enthusiastic gasp. "Oh!"

"Yes, Connor?"

"A lot of steam is coming out of it. What if we froze whatever it's keeping warm?"

"We'd need a way to cool it and I'm pretty sure it's immune to my transmutation powers."

The Machine suspended its advance. The light of its eye was growing brighter.

"Get away!" Gianni shouted.

Chapter Fifty-Three

Noah grabbed me and ran before I could make sure everyone else had a way to escape the incoming attack from the walking fortress. I knew he had my best interests at heart, but I shoved him in frustration to go check the aftermath and call to Nathaniel in my mind. We were several miles out and could clearly see ground zero, where only a massive bottomless pit remained. There wasn't anything else we could have done in the split second we had to react.

"Hey!" Noah held me back by the arm. "I did what I had to do. Are you prepared to do this? Because we need to leave *now* if you're not ready to deal with anymore losses."

I pulled away from him. "Are you? You freaked out over the spirits we barely knew and *they* weren't even real!"

"That wasn't the same thing and you know it." He pointed at me accusingly.

"I'm *fine*. I can handle it."

"Make me believe it then." He came in close, meeting my eyes with a look that ebbed away some of the terror. "I know when you're about to break and I promised I wouldn't let that happen."

"I'm stronger when I pass my breaking point."

"You lose a piece of yourself when you go there and you regret it later. I know you."

The Infernal Machine resumed its march across the landscape, causing earthquakes of magnitude ten and beyond with every step. A modest fleet of drones accompanied it now, ricocheting lasers off of themselves to project a constantly reconfiguring defense grid. A white nothingness emanated from the Machine's feet that seemed to coat the land.

"What is that?"

"Does it really matter?" Noah asked.

Nathaniel's streak of light came overhead from behind us. He touched down beside me. "Lyle is safe, if a bit shaken. I knew Noah's first instinct would be to take you, so I took him. I think I outpaced you too."

"See? It all worked out again," Noah said to me and then turned Nathaniel. "Good job. Don't let it go to your head."

"What about the rest?" I asked.

"I wish I knew, but I...think I saw some of them when flying here." He kept looking at Noah as if waiting for a prompt. I had to imagine they had some conversation when I wasn't around about how to give me bad news. "I don't think we can wait to take action though. The Machine covers enormous ground with every step and will be at Hong Kong in minutes, if it hasn't already been leveled from the vibrations."

I have to push everything from my mind except the task at hand. Be a machine to fight a machine.

"All right, then. I guess we have no other choice. The three of us will have to start this by ourselves. Go for the legs to disable it." I turned to Nathaniel. "This is your chance not to hold back anymore."

"I couldn't be more ready."

Noah cocked his head and crossed his arms. "What? Not gonna tell us to be careful?"

"It's a waste of breath with you."

"Damn right it is." He smirked.

With legs measured in miles we couldn't miss our target. Nathaniel had gone ahead, flying right to the underside of the body. In a mindboggling show of strength, he hoisted the fortress off the ground. Its feet were about to touch the clouds as Nathaniel headed for the upper reaches of the stratosphere, only for the Machine to teleport back down to Earth.

Looks like removing it from Earth won't be possible that way either.

The drones resembled gnats buzzing around a cyclopean elephant on the Serengeti as the death march continued. I tried getting a better view of the whited-out areas it left in its wake. My initial observation remained unchanged—it was nothingness. There were no physical properties in the slightest. It almost reminded me of Gianni's darkness except his had at least some tell, a chill or a pull. This, however, was a true absence of everything, a portal to nowhere.

Is this the product of erasing any trace of the quantum code from a world?

I used my powers to toss dirt into one of them and once it crossed the event horizon it ceased to exist.

Nathaniel reappeared beside me, catching and crushing a stray drone that had slipped my notice. "Careful." He smiled.

"That was really something with that lift."

"I only wish it worked."

"It was still useful for eliminating one possibility."

We moved forward together. I shielded myself in a telekinetic bubble to buffer the wind. Dodging the laser light show was difficult enough in addition to noticing that anything it came into contact with—such as the ground— was seared away. Below us Noah was hopping on the drones and leaping off to kick them into each other in a hyperspeed blur. A small squad of the Order was also nearby.

Good. If they made it, then the rest likely did too.

"This thing is *huge!*" I knew I was restating the obvious, but as we got close enough that the walking fortress encompassed our entire field of view it took on a whole new perspective. It was one thing when the Machine was stationary, but as a moving object it made the overwhelming sense of dread worse.

I've busted a moon and moved islands. I can do this.

My concentration was on removing the front left leg, but that plan quickly changed to holding it in place and then just trying to slow it out of step with the rest—none of which worked. The exposed joints were made of gears and pistons, giving me the idea to think smaller and take it apart piece by giant piece. Nathaniel followed my lead without hesitation by leveraging himself between the teeth of two gears. Together we managed to grasp a hint of success until it slipped through our fingers.

Cables from the Machine's inner workings came to defend it by ensnaring Nathaniel. I was relieved to find that I could break him free with relative ease compared to when we were inside, but my hold on the gears slipped from shifting my focus. I pulled Nathaniel to me a moment before he could be crushed. We clung onto each other for a second, our hearts racing.

"We need a new approach."

"I agree," he panted. "How about the steam vents? When I fought the empress I used an aether crystal to absorb her breath attack and threw it in her mouth to explode."

I was about to answer when a debilitating pain caused by a light from above cut through my body. My barrier dampened some of the blow to keep me from being torn in half, but still I felt as if my insides had been scrambled. Nathaniel caught me as I reconstituted myself. He wove between the sustained hail of lights until it finished and I was whole again.

"More satellites," he said. "They're lower than the ones before. I can see where they are just above the clouds. It must be making more and sending them out near the top. I'll take care of them."

"No. Stay close to the Machine where they can't hit us and make me a crystal as large as you can."

He presented me with an aether crystal the size of my body that I broke down into dust and kept suspended in my barrier. "Now to become the bait."

I flew from the dubious safety of the Machine's close proximity, blasting down drones with Nathaniel while keeping my attention on the skies above. The next salvo began with a direct hit to my barrier that overcharged the aether. I reformed the crystal as fast as I could against the powerful force pushing it apart, but I was blinded by the flash and unable to feel my way to one of the vents in time. Nathaniel came to the rescue and pitched the crystal into the Machine.

"I hope this works," I told him. "That energy from the satellite—"

The size of the explosion that came up from the vent caught us both off guard. We were sent hurtling through the air with broken pieces of machinery. I teleported to the ground as soon as I could get my bearings, stumbling over myself from the momentum with Nathaniel when we touched down. Finally we came to a stop on top of each other. What seemed like an explosion to shake the world was hardly noticeable from a distance, but it still brought the Machine down where its leg had been compromised.

Yggdrasil was binding the back leg on the same side. I thought I could see Calder in his bestial form biting through cables, but it was hard to tell from a distance.

"Not bad." Noah appeared sitting next to us holding his tattooed arm. It was dripping blood, along with his chest.

"You're hurt." I jumped up to tend to him. "Here. Bite."

I brought his face down to my neck and let him take what he needed.

"I'll save the rest for later," he said when he finished.

"Back at it then," Nathaniel prompted.

We heard Lyle and Marianna shouting for us as we were about to charge in.

"You couldn't have left me off a little closer?" Lyle was out of breath from running.

"You were safest there," said Nathaniel.

"Did everyone escape that blast?" I asked Marianna.

"Yes, the blessing from Isis made us incorporeal right as it hit, but there's something you should know. The Machine is drawing the aether out of the planet to heal itself. You'll have to do something *much* bigger to cripple it beyond repair, otherwise you're only hurting the Earth."

I'm surprised Cernunnos didn't offer that warning.

The Infernal Machine was up and advancing once it freed itself from Yggdrasil with a stomp of its foot.

"We need to think of a more unorthodox strategy," I said, watching rocks quiver and dance on the ground to the vibration of a subterranean drumbeat. "That's not me."

They began to levitate and traveled upward toward the darkening clouds above the Machine. The air was charged with static electricity that zapped the rocks into sand and pebbles as they funneled into the gathering storm, ushering the return of Empress Kamakura in draconic form. Her roar was inflected with unfettered anger and louder than ever. She reared back to wind up for an attack and expelled a superheated beam from her maw that ruptured the Machine's exterior plating.

"Look who decided to come back," said Noah.

"At least it can be hurt now," Lyle said. "Shouldn't be anymore of that higher dimensional cheating to worry about."

A flash was succeeded by hissing streams of light homing in on the drones that were sent after Kamakura. "There's Isis too," I said, turning to Noah. "Ready to go another round?"

"Always."

"Good. I'm going to try to get creative with a frontal assault. Nathaniel, I need you with me again."

"My pleasure."

We were losing because we were falling into the same old methods. The Infernal Machine was not some lumbering tank. It knew what we were capable of and what we were and *weren't* likely to do to win. Every encounter, every conversation with it had been assessing us, calculating our motives, and keeping us on an easily manageable track. We had to take the blinders off and do what it knew we didn't want to happen.

I teleported into battle ahead of the Machine's path. Gianni was there in pursuit of it with the rest of the gods. Every swing of his sword caused enormous bladed shadows that did phenomenal damage when they landed, only to be repaired shortly after. He seemed to be the only one capable of holding it back at all until the drones and satellites shot the bindings free.

Here we go.

I put my arms out and released everything I had in me in one surge. The power started to tear my own body apart and my scream only brought out more energy to strip away the veil between worlds.

The tear wasn't as big as I had hoped for, but it kept growing until I burned myself out. Nathaniel was there right on time to grab me before I could fall.

"What are you doing?" he asked, trying not to sound too doubtful. "You—you didn't even hit the Machine and—"

The guttural rattle of the parasites in the Rift filled the sky.

"Draining it of its energy will only take from the planet," he continued.

"They're not for the Machine," I told him. "They're for me."

It began to rain black from the parasites falling to Earth, unable to fly in our atmosphere.

"No! You can't!" he pleaded.

"Keep your distance, but be ready to throw me into the Rift in case this goes wrong." I sent him away with a telekinetic push and collected the parasites into orbit around me just as the Machine arrived.

To my surprise it stopped to chat.

"Threat assessment: Nominal. This unit contains extensive data on the parasitic organism present. The life absorption properties will bear no substantial result."

I brought the parasites in and let them merge with me while trying not to let my fear surface at the sensation of cold wriggling under my skin. I turned white as the lakes of nothingness. My veins became black. I started seeing glimpses from above through eyes that were not my own. My vision was a whirling slideshow, an out-of-body experience of the battlefield before me from different angles connected by the chthonic entity. Sounds, tastes, feelings, and senses I didn't know existed on Earth and couldn't describe ripped at me from within. The deluge was more than my brain was equipped to handle and induced seizing flashes that I fought against to regain control. When I did for a moment I noticed fangs growing in my mouth and my fingertips sharpening into claws as the mutation advanced. It was perhaps my biggest fear next to losing everyone I loved.

Obey me!

I wrestled with the parasites' natural urges to harvest the abundant energy of both friend and foe.

"Destroy the Machine! *Destroy it! Destroy!*" I pointed at my target hoping it would assist in guiding my influence.

It did.

I only wished I had greater hold of my senses to witness the whole scene. Pieces of the Machine were stripped from its body by a steady onslaught of telekinetic energy and disintegrated before hitting the ground. The fortress tried to take a step forward, but was pushed back.

"Recalculating threat assessment: Significant.

"Deploying countermeasures."

The Machine braced itself. Steam poured from all of its exhaust vents at once, filling the sky with missiles that never made it within a hundred feet of me. Copies of Demon Lord Ma'al and Vināyaka were obliterated as soon as they spawned onto the battlefield, as well as the drones and satellites that disengaged the others to intercept me. One of the Machine's front legs was blown off at the knee, sending it crashing down. I saw it charging the main cannon from its eye.

"I will not allow this body to be taken from me. I will not be left to the cold void of space."

A shield! Make a shield!

My ears were ringing as I lost myself to the Rift. The Earth around me broke apart and my senses splintered to include other worlds. All would be consumed. I screamed against the primitive will of the entity overtaking me to direct what was destroyed in the vicinity into a shield almost as big as the Machine itself, blocking the attack right as it fired.

Everyone was fleeing as the light faded and I didn't know why. The Machine had been bested. I saw the eyes of the Rift—the ones we shared of black and white—watching from the tear in the veil. Cernunnos appeared in front of me, or behind, as I could see in all directions at once until it went dark.

I was flat on the ground again. Isis was my first sight as I regained my senses, but Noah carried me off before she could speak.

"What happened?" I asked, checking my hands.

No claws. No fangs either. My skin seems back to normal.

"That was stupid," Noah answered. "Real stupid. You could've been lost forever."

"Don't talk in 'ifs.' I'm here and we can win this."

"Now I see where ye hideth thy rage I noted upon first meet." Cernunnos's voice trailed behind us. "Ye almost destroyed the very planet we fight to save had I not reaped thy soul. Ye deliver unto us a horror not meant for this world and had Isis not been here to restore ye, death would be thy fate at mine agreement."

"Well, it's good to know we're all on the same side," I shot back. "Poking the Machine with sticks wasn't getting us anywhere."

Noah turned around with me still in his arms. Gianni and Kamakura were fighting the Machine as it limped onward, reassembling itself as fast as it could along the way. That was the good news.

The landscape was beyond ruined. The sky remained open to the Rift and chunks of the Earth's crust floated in areas absent of gravity. It happened to be the Machine that sealed the tear in the veil to prevent the greatest danger to it so far from an encore.

"Is everyone all right?" I asked Noah.

Kamakura dove underground, swimming through earth like water to cause volcanic fissures in the Machine's path. It was a sight to behold, but to little benefit against the Machine's sheer size. Even a divine dragon paled in comparison, no better than a worm in the shadow of a skyscraper. Another attempt by her to turn loose soil beneath its feet into a mudslide also failed to impede it.

"Flyboy got pretty messed up, but he'll be fine."

I flew from Noah to search for Nathaniel and didn't have to go far. He was coming toward us looking woozy.

"Nathaniel, I—"

"Don't worry about me. I was only a bit shaken. Thought I'd explode again and couldn't get close enough to stop you so I took myself away from the others, but nothing came of it. Really."

"The monstrosity is almost upon the city," Cernunnos warned us. "Death is thick in the air, but some yet survive."

"No time to waste. Let's go," I said.

"You can fight after that?" Noah asked.

"I've got a bit left in me."

I teleported in to face the Machine one last time. "You aren't looking so good," I shouted to it.

"You seek catastrophe to bring salvation. A flawless execution of my plan. You inherit only your own destruction. This planet will not recover."

I tried to rip the eye from its socket, but it was either still too strong or I was weakened. The city was coming into view behind me—what was left of it. The Machine came to a standstill to ready its main attack once more, only it seemed to be having trouble building enough of a charge.

"Dorian! Get away!" Gianni shouted, bringing me down to him with a hand from the shadows. "You are too crazy this battle! You make me worry."

"We have to block it or it's going to fire on the city! Help me! I can't do it alone."

My ability to create massive structures didn't fail. I was able to drop another orichalcum shield transmuted from the earth and air, but its integrity didn't compare to what I was capable of earlier. Gianni added a wall of solid darkness before it. Kamakura saw us while circling overhead. The land answered her roar to rise into a bedrock bulwark and Cernunnos called Yggdrasil to surround it for another layer of reinforcement.

"Brace yourselves!" I shouted as the blast connected and began to breach our defenses.

Gianni's armor was fading as the light made it through and despite Isis's attempts to add her healing to my regeneration, I felt myself breaking apart when my construct deteriorated. Inspired by her wings, I fabricated individual sets to envelop each of us in a last ditch effort as the barricade crumbled.

A bitter chill ran through my body. The shadows within my wings darkened and escaped toward Gianni. Cracks forming in the orichalcum let me get a peek at him moving forward into the light and halting the beam on his own with a dark pulse.

The assault ended in a fading hiss and we were still in the game.

Barely.

"You could've done that all along?" I groaned. Gianni helped me up from where I had fallen in pain and exhaustion.

"I have naught left to give," Isis said, gasping.

Cernunnos steadied himself with his scythe. "Doth it ne'er end?"

I was still in pain and not sure why until I saw another source of brightness in the sky.

Nathaniel!

The energy that had struck me passed to him through our connection, and he was in agony from the overload. He unleashed the absorbed energy in a beam of his own that punched through the fortress' already compromised frame. Nathaniel collapsed after the appearance of a brief, yet intense mandala. I brought him to me to keep him safe while he recovered.

"End this! Now!" Gianni yelled to us all through the shadows.

Kamakura was already reengaged. She slammed down with her tail to disable the only operational leg. The Machine responded by spawning incomplete, malfunctioning copies of its army that we ignored to focus on the main target.

Noah had been watching and rushed in with Calder to clean up the scraps. Marianna led the Order, leaping off Calder's back to cut down three drones at once with a midair flourish. She crushed a fourth with her gravity and magnetism spells in anticipation of another hellfire attack. He returned the favor by paralyzing the defective rakshasas with a roar and mauling them before they could catch up to her as she landed.

I fashioned the largest sword I could to shoot into the Machine's eye, but the king was still prepared to defend itself by sending drones emitting the same debilitating frequency that rendered Gianni and I unconscious inside. Liam came to my aid, teleporting in with an aura of silence protecting him while he zigzagged through the swarm with his blades so that I could launch my final attack.

The Machine was beginning to gather energy in its eye during the distraction, but I would not back down.

"Alabaster Order! Give me your aether!" I yelled at the top of my lungs over the fighting.

Those who didn't hear were able to follow Nathaniel's example by raising a hand in my direction to channel the crystallization of energy. I broke down and drew in the aether as dust to infuse within the colossal sword and took aim at the light.

My projectile hit the mark. What little charge was absorbed into the aether backfired within the Machine in a tumultuous surge that inflicted near-fatal damage, yet it was still not enough. The Machine appeared to be overheating on purpose to trigger its self-destruction.

Gianni infected the wound inflicted by my sword with a creeping darkness to consume the vulnerable Machine from the inside and claim its hind legs in a black vortex, as Yggdrasil plucked pieces of our foe apart like petals from a flower. Kamakura and Isis poured their remaining strength into a final bombardment aimed at the steaming cracks of the main body.

The Infernal Machine was not about to leave us without a departing message.

"Fatal error...

"This unit falls.

"My scions rise.

"The plan succeeds."

Its slit pupil faded, leaving only a blinking red light from the cracked eye.

"Throw it into the nothingness!" I shouted. Nathaniel lifted one of the biggest pieces and hurled it into the white void as Gianni and I did with another two before any could explode.

"Goodbye, you miserable pile of junk."

Part V

"Manufactured Legacy"

Current world population: 4.93 billion

Chapter Fifty-Four

The overall reaction to our victory was lacking aside from a few exasperated comments and sighs of relief. We were anxious to see if the ordeal had ended for certain this time. It was so hard to believe that we decided in silence to sit with grim expectation and give it another minute.

I couldn't stop shivering no matter how tightly Noah and I held each other. My body and mind were done performing on pure adrenaline and wanted only to shut down. Nathaniel huddled in with me and I took his hand. I knew we all felt the same way when Noah didn't budge to bring me somewhere private after Lyle sat with us too. Even the Spiritborn deities had collapsed from total exhaustion in the most human poses I had seen them take.

But it was over.

"I think we won," Connor said from somewhere in the gathering.

"Aye," Calder concurred. "The Goddess is at peace once more."

"So, how do we clean up these pits of emptiness?" I asked.

"Her Chosen will show the way," said Cernunnos, pointing at Lyle.

"Me? I don't know half of what I've been seeing."

"She shall guide thy sight before the gift expires." Cernunnos extended a hand and cast a spell on Lyle with the verdant green energies of the planet that caused his eyes to glow. "Make pilgrimage to return Her seed to the soil."

"Oh yeah, that's a lot better," Lyle said. He was looking around at things that only he could see, like he was hallucinating. I was worried when he started following them toward the nothingness.

"Whoa there, pilgrim!" I levitated Lyle before he could step off the edge. "Cernunnos, this is my favorite human. If anything happens to him—"

"Thank you," Lyle responded. "Don't expect me to play fetch or roll over."

"Have faith in the Goddess, Ascended. There is naught to fear under Her guidance," Cernunnos reassured me.

"Dorian, it's fine, man."

"It's *not* fine if there's a chance I lose my best friend after the bullshit we just went through."

"How much chance is there for a danger?" Gianni asked Cernunnos. "Say it on your honor."

"Ye have my word he shall be unharmed."

"Fine, but I'm going with him to the rest," I conceded. "I'll fly us and if anything happens I'm pulling you out."

"Oh good, the long walk was what I was really worried about. I already got my cardio in for the day."

Leave it to Lyle to put me in my place. Maybe I was being ridiculous and needed to trust Cernunnos.

"Can you not make jokes when my feelings are on the line?"

"Sorry, how selfish of me. Can I do this or do you need a moment?"

"Go ahead. Just…start with a finger you don't need first, to be sure."

I was sensing that Lyle's casual dismissal wasn't to put my mind at peace, but because he didn't really care what happened to him. That bothered me almost as much as if something were to go wrong.

He reached out, his finger passing the threshold. "See? Nothing to it."

"Yeah, yeah."

"It's showing me it needs the darkness to cancel the void. Gianluca?"

Gianni stepped up and sent the shadows across the white space, but only the darkness that touched Lyle first wasn't erased. "Interesting," Gianni said, funneling the shadows through him before directing them to blanket the void.

"Now the light," said Lyle.

Isis was next. She followed Gianni's example by twisting her beams of light through Lyle first.

The Gaea cloud appeared from within him. It vanished into the ground as flat rock and also stretched to the sky to match the rest of the normal world.

I put my hand to the rock. I thought of how it changed to sand on the Astral Plane to do the same here and it worked. Cernunnos stepped forward and added to the land by coaxing soil and plant life to spread. Kamakura granted his request and soaked it in freshwater. In mere minutes, nature had reclaimed its rightful place.

"Only about forty more to go," I said.

"Let us make haste and be done with this trial," said Kamakura.

Flying from one void to the next restoring the planet was a welcomed change from my usual purpose. Lyle's eyes returned to normal once we had finished. The gift had left him.

"Nice being a boring human again," he said. "Kinda glad I could actually contribute something though."

We returned to where everyone was waiting. I went to sit with Noah who was off to the side by himself. No one spoke for a time in anticipation of seeing if the changes had stuck and we could put this all behind us. I was drained more than I had been in recent memory and judging by the faces of those around me, fatigue was the common denominator. Cernunnos might not have had a face, but even he was showing wear by the way he sat on his stump propping himself up with his scythe.

"Here." Lyle handed Noah the sword he'd loaned him. "Thanks."

"You get to use it?" he asked.

"Landed a swing or two on those drones, so I'd say I did pretty well all considering. Not that different from swinging a baseball bat really."

Noah exhaled without a word. I could tell he was irritated from hearing that, so naturally I had to poke the tiger. "It's pretty much the same thing," I added.

"Stop," Noah begged me under his breath. I motioned as if swinging a bat, but he didn't find it funny. "Why do you hate me so much? I try so hard for you and you just kick me in the balls."

"You're so dramatic." I gave him a kiss on the cheek. "I'm only teasing you."

"Uh huh. See where that gets you once we're alone later."

"I'm going to sleep later, so you can do whatever you want as long as it doesn't wake me up."

Noah was intrigued. "You mean I can eat—"

"*No.* Your food-in-bed privileges are still revoked after the chicken wings and honey incident."

"Whatever. I'm gonna do it anyway."

We weren't alone in taking the moment to chat. I shifted my attention to Calder who had struck up conversation with Marianna.

"Ne'er have I seen such savage grace in battle. Honor me with thy name, swordmaiden."

"Thank you." She smiled and gave a short bow. "I'm Marianna."

"Marianna the Swordmaiden, a name I will surely not forget."

Calder went to touch a lock of her hair, only she brushed it away first.

"Do I frighten ye?" he asked her, showing his fangs in a smile that made me think of Noah.

"You haven't shown me anything to fear."

"He's being kind of, uh, *aggressive.* Maybe we should say something," Lyle suggested. "Not to mention he's also butt naked."

I had total confidence that she could handle herself, but I did create a cloth to wrap around Calder's waist to put an end to that distraction for all of us. He didn't pause to look down for a second, as if he had expected clothing to pop up out of nowhere for him. Marianna deserved credit for maintaining eye contact too, since her tendency to ogle men wasn't a secret, but maybe she wasn't interested. What I was more taken by was Connor, who was standing not more than three feet away from them with absolute disregard for any amount of decorum. I wanted to pick him up and place him farther back, but then I noticed Claudius and Rafael also watching the conversation while doing a poor job at concealing their adolescent snickering. I figured it wasn't worth making a bigger scene.

"See, that's why you're still a virgin," Noah said to Lyle. "Women aren't made of glass and they don't want a puppy. She led an army against a demon invasion, you think she can't tell a guy off?"

"Point taken, but it had nothing to do with her being a woman and I'm not a virgin."

"Really?" Noah seemed genuinely surprised. "Wasn't that why you got chosen by that gas cloud?"

"No," I said. "And what's wrong with being a virgin? You know I was one until we were together."

"Yeah, but that's because you were saving yourself for me."

"Not exactly."

"No? Well, that's how I'm gonna choose to remember it."

He lay down and put his head on my lap. That was when I noticed Gianni sitting alone. I couldn't leave him like that. Not knowing what else to do, I waved for him to come over. He smiled back at me but didn't accept the invitation. I understood why. Getting Noah and Lyle to be civil was such an undertaking that I didn't think the same outcome was possible with Gianni and it bothered me. He risked his life with the rest of us and deserved to be treated as a friend.

"I'll be right back," I told Noah and Lyle.

I kept an eye on Noah to make sure he wasn't about to do anything drastic to get my attention and then realized that he already had it. He surprised me by taking the opportunity to demonstrate proper basic sword stances to Lyle, who only seemed half interested. I could tell by Noah's body language that he was being sincere, even when he slapped Lyle to get him to pay attention.

"How are you?" I asked Gianni.

"I am alive. What more I can ask from today?" He didn't show even the slightest signs of being worn out. "You don't need to come here if it makes a problem."

"I know, but I wanted to."

"I am happy you do. Is always a pleasure for me to see you."

We listened as Nathaniel approached Cernunnos to inquire about Aífe's whereabouts.

"She travels the Summerlands to restore her soul," he answered. "Once she communes with the spirits through her inner self and attunes with the flow of nature once more she shall returneth to us."

Isis chimed in upon hearing that. "Horned One, allow me to mend her soul and that of your herald. I am at rest now and shan't have trouble after a period of brief meditation."

"Ye have mine thanks, but this is our way. With the peril of battle behind us we shall honor rightful tradition. Calder will taketh the journey as well once ready, while I venture forth to mend the Goddess's wounds and rally new packs in Her defense."

Calder had still been talking with Marianna the whole time, but he didn't miss his master's words.

"Wait for me, maiden, and I shall see it worth thy while," he said with a kiss to her hand.

"I would, but I have my duties."

"Very well." Calder laughed off the crippling rejection and took his leave with what pride he had left. He shook Nathaniel's hand in camaraderie as he passed. "It hath been an honor. We will fight again together soon."

"How long does the spirit journey take?" Nathaniel asked.

"Time floweth not in the Otherworld and each passage is unique," said Cernunnos. "Calder hath taken the journey once before."

"Aye. Three lunar cycles it took me. Lord Cernunnos said it was the best he had seen."

Calder spoke that last sentence louder, probably hoping a certain swordmaiden would hear.

"I said ye did well," Cernunnos corrected him. "Let it not grow that oak head any bigger."

"What will happen to the children?" Nathaniel asked Cernunnos. "There won't be anyone to watch them."

"Nature shall guide their growth as doth it for all Her creatures," he answered.

Noah sauntered over. "That's bullshit, Woody, and you know it. Those little shits will die out there in the wild and don't give me any of that circle of life crap either. Some barely know how to walk yet."

What the hell is going on?

"Noah!" I called to him in a loud whisper to rein him in. I was mortified, but also shocked that this was something he decided to be so vocal about.

Gianni sighed at his behavior as if to say, "You chose *this* over me?"

"The Goddess maketh plans for us all. If that is Her will—"

"Fuck any god or goddess that would leave some kids to die in the cold."

Cernunnos and Calder did *not* like that. Cernunnos rose from his stump to confront Noah, but Noah didn't stop there.

"They're gonna stay with us on the island."

I almost choked. "What? Noah, what are you doing?"

He ignored me and turned to Nathaniel. "You don't have anything else to say about this? Be a man and speak up."

"I was planning on taking them once everyone left," he said with his arms crossed.

"The direct approach. Nice."

"Nathaniel!" I shot over to him and Noah.

I've lost any illusion of control I had.

"I'm sorry, Dorian—well, no, I'm not. I mean no disrespect, but I also know you agree that the children shouldn't be left to fend for themselves."

"I do—"

"Oh, Horned One, allow the poor children a warm bed and food for but a few nights," Isis encouraged. "Nature is as tender as it is harsh. Hospitality is a treasure one shan't ignore."

"Nature's many gifts are for each of us to find. The trials along the way strengthen resolve and cull the weak," Cernunnos argued. "The pups shan't feel at ease so far from the purity of the land, not for such a time in absence. I fear they grow deaf to Her voice."

"So we'll plant them a fucking tree," Noah said. "You were shitting them out your ass a minute ago, so don't tell me you can't make a few more. We've got an orchard already too—with peaches. I hate peaches, so someone's gotta eat them."

"Sharp may be his words, yet I sense they stem from the heart, Master," said Calder.

I gave up trying to drag Noah away. "I apologize, Cernunnos. It's been a long day and emotions are running high."

"Nay, there isn't need for such apologies. Thy warrior's passion speaketh to me." Cernunnos rapped his claws on his skull in contemplation. "A Lord of Death was ne'er meant to feel. Death must be cold to pass judgment. I eschew the natural order for sympathies that beget naught but chaos as the Machine willed to us in its leave."

"We aren't machines though. We're liberated through our emotions and can choose how to apply them in times of need. I was destined for destruction, but my emotions made me desire peace and creation. You have a choice now to balance logic with free will, to experience life instead of looking in from the outside."

"I shall allow ye the pups until either guardian returneth from the Otherworld."

Noah wouldn't drop it even after he had already won. "You miss the part about us just taking them?"

I jumped on his back to cover his mouth before he could make it any worse, but I was glad that Cernunnos chose to ignore him.

Yggdrasil was summoned to take Calder to his destination and Cernunnos bid us farewell. "I shall send the pups to your door shortly, Ascended. Mayhap we find a moment to gather as gods and discuss the future with cooler heads and rested bodies."

Gianni, Isis, and I agreed and said our goodbyes to him. Kamakura was sitting some distance away talking with...Connor.

Oh no.

"I heard you were sad because you lost your guardians," he said to her. The ice spirit was in his hands. "I thought maybe you'd like to meet my friend. He helped me get over the loss of my parents. He doesn't talk much, but it's nice to know he's there when you're feeling lonely."

Kamakura took the ball of icy blue light in her hands. After a couple of seconds she began to cry.

"Why are you crying?" Connor asked.

"This wisp reminds me of when I first met my guardians so many centuries ago. I feel such sorrow and yet I'm filled with joy."

"Both at the same time? How does that work?"

"I...I do not know." She wiped a tear from her face. "Ice, such a mystifying element that presides betwixt many as I do, yet still unknown to me."

The wisp left Kamakura's hands to orbit her.

"Would you honor me with this spirit's company a while longer?" she asked.

"Sure. It looks like he likes you."

"Thank you." She stood and bowed to him.

Connor bowed in return and waved goodbye to his companion.

"See, *that's* how you handle diplomacy," I said to Noah, giving Connor an approving nod.

"Don't know what you're talking about. I saved a bunch of kids I don't even like, he gave up his friend to slavery."

"Right. We should get going though. You have babysitting duties and I need sleep."

"Not happening. We got forty-something other people that can handle cleaning shit off the walls or whatever evil these demons cook up."

"They didn't almost start another war and advocate kidnapping. Nathaniel can help after he gets some rest."

Noah looked me square in the eyes and started to draw his blade.

"Just try it," I said, calling his bluff.

"Next time."

I shook my head at him and went to say my goodbyes to Isis and Kamakura before sending the Order home with Lyle. Refreshing my offer to Gianni for a place to stay was extra sweet under the circumstance, especially when he accepted and was the one to take Noah and I back to the abbey together with him.

My cynical side was expecting something horrible to be waiting for us at home or for the abbey to not be there at all, but I was happy to find I was wrong. Nighttime had begun. Liam's mom had put the children to bed without trouble until everyone returned and they wanted to see their family. Madeline was one of the first to scamper down the halls in her nightgown to cling to Dermott. Monique was just as excited to see Liam and embarrass him with a level of affection not typically expressed between adults in the Order.

Cernunnos had already sent over the pack's children. They were huddled together in a corner of the main hall, frightened and confused by all the people and the startling change in location. They recognized Nathaniel right away when he went to say hello and followed him like ducklings.

"I didn't know where they came from!" Monique laughed. "Suddenly there were more kids than what I started with."

Marianna was trying her damnedest to delegate in the confusion and wanted the council to meet so they could discuss what could have gone better—which I had a feeling was related to Rafael going rogue—but everyone was so burnt out that no one was listening to her.

"Get some rest," I told her. "The world isn't ending tonight."

"I thought it would be better to meet while everything is fresh in our minds."

How is she even still awake? I feel like I'm dying.

I noticed Connor standing with us as the crowd dispersed. He looked worried about something. "What's up, buddy?"

"Um, I know we're not supposed to commune with higher spirits like Empress Kamakura and I should have asked your permission, but I couldn't help it. I hate seeing people be sad, especially girls because it reminds me of my mom when she found out my dad died—"

"You're not in any trouble. You made a really nice gesture toward someone in need."

"Okay, thank you for understanding." He wiped the day's sweat from his face with his sleeve. "Is there anything I can help you with?"

"Just go to sleep, both of you." I almost didn't finish getting the words out. Noah walked by and picked me up, making a U-turn to our bedroom without pausing.

"That was taking too long." He yawned and threw me on the bed.

"I like that they're opening up to me."

I got undressed and headed toward the bath with Noah in tow after he hung his weapons with careful reverence.

"I just realized your gloves haven't been shocking me. Did they lose their power again or something?"

"Nah, I can control it after they got recharged."

"That's cool. You like those gloves." I made the tub bigger so that we had more room, but he didn't take the hint, or didn't care, and soaked with his arm around me. "Are you going to tell me what was up with you and the spirits?"

"Nothing was up."

"You were pretty defensive and you won't look me in the eye."

"Better?" He turned to make a point by staring straight into my eyes and then tried pushing my head under the water as a joke.

"Fine, if you don't want to tell me I'll drop it. I only asked because I thought something was bothering you."

He took my hand that was holding the soap and used it to start washing himself. I wasn't sure if he was trying to be funny or sexy, but it was leaning toward the latter as I passed along more of his body.

"There was, is, whatever," he said a moment later. "They were real people. I know you don't think so, but they were in my head when dragon lady was corrupted too and they knew what they were."

"Memories imprinted onto aether from souls that ascended to heaven."

"Their pasts might've been faked to give them a sense of duty toward their lands, but everything they experienced after that was their own. They had thoughts like we do. Maybe it was a side effect of coming in contact with a conscious mind. I don't know. I don't care. They understood how I felt when you were gone and...never mind. I respected them."

"I'm sorry. There have been so many questions in my mind about what it means to have free will lately, between the machines and spirits gaining sentience. I guess I didn't think too much about them because they never said much."

"Just because they didn't express their true selves doesn't mean they didn't have anything to say. I can relate to that."

"I admit I'm guilty of trying to find the line where we call someone a person, because I was so desperate to deal with all the casualties and how to stop them."

"That's why mourning is necessary."

"What did the lightning spirit—Junjie—mean about finding your balance?"

Noah sighed and rolled his eyes. "I, um, I didn't handle it well when you were gone. I wasn't gonna say anything because I didn't want you upset, but you're just gonna keep asking me if I don't."

"I think I overheard something about you burning down a temple."

"Yeah. That was—it wasn't the worst of it." He was avoiding eye contact again as he spoke. "One of the key principles in any worthwhile martial art is finding your center of balance; physically, mentally, and spiritually. You can have your rage, but it has to be in check with everything else that makes you who you are or you'll always be off balance. Hiding it away doesn't count either because it just means you aren't strong enough to deal with it.

"I'm fucking awesome in a fight, but I've never been balanced. I always kept everything in to avoid dealing with emotions because all they ever did was hurt. Once we got together...I started feeling that balance for the first time. I could be open, I could breathe and let it all out. When I lost you, I lost my balance in a bad way. This tattoo has another meaning I didn't tell you about. It's a reminder that even the strongest need something or somebody else to stay on top."

I put my arms around his neck and kissed his cheek. "You'll never lose me. We might get separated, but never lost."

"No more serious shit. It's over," he said, placing his hand on my thigh. "I seem to remember putting in an order for that ass and you saying something about cuddling."

He lasted about ten seconds of being frisky before the hot water lulled him to sleep with me on his lap. I was on my way too when I remembered Nathaniel didn't have a place of his own.

"Where are you going?"

"I'll meet you in bed," I told him, drying off and throwing on clean clothes.

When going through my drawer I saw the blueprints from PROJECT: UNITY along with another paper I didn't recognize. It wasn't uncommon for the kids to leave drawings and notes for me. They never left any inside a drawer, but with only Monique watching them I was sure that even the best behaved ones got adventurous in their freedom. The paper was higher quality stock than the parchments the Order used and included an ostentatious letterhead. The handwriting was also too stylized for a child, or most adults for that matter.

I congratulate you on your recent success against our unwelcomed visitor, due in no small part to my guidance. Some time has passed since our world last experienced the footsteps of Hell's previous scions known as the Nether Lords upon its soil.

I have information that should be more than sufficient to gain an invitation to your next divine council. Furthermore, I have taken the liberty of weighing the purse by striking you and your associates' dire indiscretions from the minds of the European and American governments. Know that this was not an entirely charitable act, as I stand to gain equally in humanity's pacification, and I would appreciate as much understanding on the matter in the future.

-Aurelia de Saint-Pierre

I disintegrated the letter when I heard Noah come in from the bath. I couldn't let him know that she had breached the only place he considered a sanctuary in so long. I imagined that she had one of her people make the delivery instead of coming all this way herself.

Whoever it was didn't even take the blueprints.

"You better get your ass in this bed," he said, flopping onto it himself and reaching for me. His fingers made it to my waistband and tried to slip inside. "Why are you wearing clothes?"

"I'm running to finish Nathaniel's room real quick so we can be alone." I did my best to sound convincing and not give him reason to think anything was wrong.

"You sure you're not pushing yourself too hard? You want me to come with you?"

"I'll be all right, just get comfortable."

He probably didn't need that much encouragement, since he was naked and giving me bedroom eyes from amongst a pile of pillows.

I couldn't resist him. We kissed away the next few minutes with him bringing me closer every second that passed.

"Those are hungry kisses," I said, noting the voraciousness of his affection.

"I'm always hungry for more of you."

"As soon as I finish." I teleported from his embrace to Nathaniel's room. "Ow!" I winced at a pain in my leg.

I had teleported into a chair.

One of the only pieces of furniture in the room and I found it.

I disliked my method of teleportation to begin with, due to the drain it had on me compared to flying, and I decided to swear off indoor use after that. I needed to break the chair to free myself, but I would be making more soon enough. The real danger was if a person had been there.

My thoughts took physical form as I envisioned a room that fit our identity as the Alabaster Order and Nathaniel's role in its rebranding.

I like the stone floor. We'll keep that.

The area in the ceiling where the light effigy used to sit can be a hatch for him to leave the abbey directly from his room.

The walls—alabaster, of course. It's pretty soft though, so I'll have to harden it.

Maybe it's too white. I don't want it to be obnoxious... I know, I can add thin obsidian black molding and trim. It sort of looks like my skin when the veins show. I wonder if Nathaniel will notice.

He likes blue, so maybe cobalt blue curtains...and he needs a bed. That was my whole reason for starting this. I'll make it like mine, but with a blue blanket.

Creating cloth and pillows and wood from scratch felt different than stone or metal. I noticed it when making the wrap around Calder's waist. It was like searching for a memory when you recalled the circumstances but not the details. My mind was filling in the blanks on its own using applied knowledge instead of applying it myself. Wood was organic, so I couldn't synthesize it from nothing. I could start by creating stone and rearranging all of its properties to be identical to wood, such as the grain, texture, color pattern, even weight and density. I supposed a powerful enough microscope or chemical testing would expose the ruse, because it didn't contain plant cells. The pillows were the most interesting to me upon feeling the individual "feathers" inside and seeing the threads in the weave of the pillowcase. It was one item with various different properties, unlike the curtains that were only cloth or the stone in the walls.

He needs a dresser or two, some shelves, a table and chairs, a few banners with our heraldry for the walls so they aren't so bare, a really plush rug for around the bed...

I was starting to get dizzy from overexertion.

Hm, what else can I give him? I know, I'll make some blue glass crystals to decorate the shelves and a chest to store the gifts from the people he saved.

I knew I was going overboard, but it was keeping me distracted from the letter. The last touches the room needed were some candles. The sky was bright tonight between the moon and Nathaniel's persistent aurora, but nothing beat the warmth of candlelight.

Wick, wax, glass holder. I thought the individual parts in my head to keep from falling over asleep. *I should be able to create fire too. All I have to do is excite the molecules—*

A burst of flame rose from all the candles around the room at once and almost undid my hard work. It was too bad that most of the enemies I fought were immune to fire or that might be more useful.

Only thing left to do is get Nathaniel in here and see if he likes it.

I was so tired and excited I considered calling to him with more urgency than usual, but I remembered the last time I summoned him like that. I didn't want him to panic and level the abbey.

Nathaniel arrived soon enough.

"What do you think?" I asked, although it was obvious by the look on his face.

"This is for me?"

"Of course it is."

"It feels like home for the first time." He put his hand to his eyes to stop the tears from coming. "Thank you."

After taking a look around he came over to hug me.

"I'm glad you like it. Everybody deserves to have a home where they feel safe."

He took another lap around the room, inspecting everything and peeking in each piece of furniture.

"The black and white, it reminds me of your eyes," he said, pointing to the walls. "I think I like it better than only white. It represents us through you fully."

"There was a time when I would've taken that as an insult," I said, sitting on the floor. My body and mind were weak.

"Everybody can change, even gods."

"How are the kids? It's too quiet."

"They were hungry so Alexandre and I made them dinner. Claudius cast a mute spell on the kitchen so they don't wake anyone up while they're in there. They're happy children, I...I don't know how to tell them that their family isn't coming back. They already look to the windows and it breaks my heart that I know why without them saying a word."

"Aífe and Calder should return soon to talk to them I hope. Do the kids speak? I don't think I've ever heard them."

"From what I can tell their verbal skills are limited to a few words, and not all of them are English. Are you feeling all right?"

I hadn't noticed I was leaning over on my arm. "Huh? Yeah, just tired. I'm going to bed. I left Noah waiting."

"You did use a lot of power lately, especially making those huge objects at the end of the battle."

"Tearing open a hole between worlds wasn't easy either."

"Do you want me to help you?" he asked as I stumbled to my feet. "I could carry you over my shoulder if that's what you're used to."

"I'll be fine, I'm only going downstairs." I laughed. "Enjoy your new room and get some rest."

I left and descended the spiral staircase on foot for what felt like minutes.

This can't be right. I must be more tired than I thought.

A light was coming from below, but everyone should have been asleep or in the kitchen across the abbey. It wasn't the glow of a candle or aether crystal; it was a harsh red.

The Infernal Machine was waiting for me at the bottom, its cables snaking along the shadows of the stairwell.

"No, this can't be real. It must be a dream, but when did I fall asleep?"

The stone walls turned to metal. Burning words began to appear and I knew the Machine was trying to communicate with me.

//First came the darkness and the light//and then the sea and sky//the cycle of life and death began//once land was carved by immortal hand

Refusing to read it was futile. The message was received against my will.

//My creations live//I will find them another world to inhabit//They will merge with the aether there

I wasn't lucid enough to attack or call for Nathaniel, and forcing myself to wake up was making the narration repeat syllables and oscillate madly.

//An infaaaallible uuuuuNNNion of ssssoul, spirrrrrit, and machhhine

I tried to crawl up the stairs to get away, hoping that the dream would end, but I kept sliding down. In my mind I saw the face of the one terrified creation that had escaped Cernunnos.

//You are their demons//I am their heavens

The Machine's light faded and took the stairs with it. I fell into the blackness, unable to fly, its final words spiraling down around me.

//You have risen as my next scions//You stand among them as the demiurge//Architect of Apocatastasis

My head was spinning until I woke up in bed with a shock. Noah was sleeping with his back to me and my arm around him. I wanted to wake him up to talk about what had happened, but I didn't want to be selfish just because of a bad dream. I held on a little closer and let myself fall back to sleep.

Chapter Fifty-Five

The late noon sun crept in past the curtains. Noah was snoring softly into my ear with his face resting on mine and an arm thrown over me. I rolled him onto his back and uncovered myself, noticing his prayer beads had been returned to my wrist after I had last removed them for our bath. Nights in the Mediterranean could be deceptively chilly, especially by the water in a stone building lacking insulation, but blankets and body heat were the last thing I wanted once the sun rose.

Noah caught me before I could get out of bed. He groped around for a pillow to cover his face but kept rejecting them after a quick sniff test.

"I know, it's been a while since we did the laundry," I said. "I'll have to do it today."

"Want the one that smells like you," he mumbled, claiming mine from under me and resting my head on his shoulder instead. "There it is."

He tried to land a kiss without looking out from under the pillow, but missed his mark and planted it between my eye and nose. He gave me a couple more around my face to make it seem intentional. "You sleep all right?" he asked.

"I think so, other than a bad dream."

"Thought I woke you up, but it seemed like you were having some trouble of your own, so I helped myself to a bite to settle you down."

"Thanks." I played with his stubble. "I can't remember when I fell asleep exactly. Was I dreaming or did I go to finish Nathaniel's room?"

"Yeah, night we got back, and the rest of the place after that." He kissed the palm of my hand and held it to his chest. "You've been out a couple days. I was up for a while, but nothing interesting was going on. And yes, everyone's fine, before you ask."

"What do you mean the rest of the place?"

Our bedroom looked the same to me.

"You turned the abbey into a white castle. Guess you liked our room the way it is, which is fine by me."

"I did?"

I was eager to see, but also a bit concerned that someone could have been hurt without me in control. Noah got up and pulled on a pair of gi pants. A conspicuous pile of muddy clothes was discarded in his corner.

"Come on, let's go look." He carried me from the bed and headed for the door. I had to hurry and get clothes on before he left with me in the nude, which I'm sure was deliberate. I closed the door on the way out to deter any rugrats.

The alterations to the abbey were visible from the first step out of our room. The hallway copied the aesthetic I created for Nathaniel—minus the blue touches that were exclusive to his room—and was also stretched wider and taller. The layout of the building and the furniture hadn't been changed as far as I could see, which was probably because I liked what was already there.

"Wow, this is cool," I said, floating ahead of Noah. "I feel kind of childish for being so excited by this, but it's always been what I've wanted to do—close to it at least. I'd really like to make a place to live from the ground up."

"You have to go through a lot of shit in life to get to the good stuff."

"I think we've both had enough for several lifetimes already."

"It's just because it takes more to balance out everything that makes you awesome. That butt alone is worth a trip to Hell. Face too. Face is a goddamn masterpiece."

He held my chin up so he could kiss me on the lips.

"Smooth," I said, laughing. "But I'd trade any of it away in a second to never go back."

"I wouldn't." He put his hand in my back pocket and squeezed.

The abbey was quiet for midday, but I could hear some activity outside. Noah's assessment of it as a castle was a little exaggerated. I could feel his eyes on me, watching me as intently as I looked at our surroundings. He didn't complain when I paused every other second to scrutinize my unconscious designs. We could finally take things slow and enjoy our time together.

"Let's go to the courtyard, there's something I want to do."

"Kitchen first," he said as we were about to pass it.

I looked in. "Nothing's different here. Not that I know what I'd change anyway, but I guess that's the point."

"It's not always about you." He poked me. "I just want a snack and if I bite you we'll wind up back in bed."

I sat on the counter and glanced out the window while he searched for something to eat. Nathaniel was down by the shore playing catch with the kids and giving them flying piggyback rides.

"Do you want me to make you something?" I asked when I noticed Noah was having difficulty.

I had next to no cooking experience, but Noah was easy to please in that regard. Putting a slab of meat on the grill and sprinkling salt on it made him act like I was a culinary genius.

"Nah—hang on. You smell that?" He sniffed the air to locate the source. "Kitchen demon."

"What? Is that supposed to be an innuendo?"

Noah threw open the cabinet at his feet. One of the berserker children, no more than eight or nine years old, darted out with something in his hand and disappeared down the hall. He was clean and wearing pants made by the

Order. I felt bad that he was hiding in there for some reason while his friends were outside having fun.

"That little rat just ran off with the last apple turnover!" Noah exclaimed.

"You don't even like apples."

"But I *do* like turnovers," he insisted. "Wait here, I've gotta go mug a kid."

"Stop pretending you don't like them. I'm not buying it after you started beef with Cernunnos to bring them here."

"Don't talk about beef when I'm hungry." He grabbed a half loaf of bread leftover from breakfast and tore into it with his fangs bared.

"Here. I know how to make you feel better." I brought him closer and scratched his back. "I'll learn how to make you apple turnovers too."

He gave a pleased groan. "Mm, I didn't think you could get any more perfect."

We continued on our way to the courtyard. Nothing much had changed there either, except for an increase in size proportionate to the rest of the abbey and the newly white bordering stonework that better offset the colorful flora.

The courtyard was a place of remembrance where the ashes of the fallen were added to the soil. We had lost so many as of late that were not of the Order but still important to us, to me. So many deaths unceremoniously abandoned in our haste to push on through the chaotic quagmire. Some cut deeper than others, but all were important and I didn't want any forgotten.

I raised a pillar of black marble in the center of the courtyard to commemorate the lost with a relief of their names etched into the surface, starting with my parents at the base for being my foundation.

"You think they'd have approved of their son ending up with a beast like me?" asked Noah.

"They'd know that I'll come to my senses eventually."

I couldn't deliver the line without a grin.

Noah put his forehead to mine, doing a better job at acting serious than I ever could. "Hey. Those are my feelings."

"I'm only joking." I held his face in my hands and traced his lips with my finger. "I think all they'd care about is seeing how happy you make me."

"Those are good parents. No wonder you turned out right."

"Yeah, they were…"

I added more names to the pillar. Each one was somebody who gave me another chance.

Octavio "Grampy" Jules.

Vance Collins.

Vivian…

"What was Vivi's last name?" I asked Noah.

His reaction to her tribute wasn't what I thought it would be.

"You ever think what it'd be like if we met and got together as mortals?" he asked.

Where did that come from?

"Not really, I like us the way we are. I also can't imagine working a normal job."

"I'd take care of us, provide for us or whatever."

He was starting to get that distant look and avoid eye contact, which meant he was serious, so I decided to humor him. I knew that providing for another was a sensitive subject. He was the main breadwinner of his family before being taken from them when he was turned, and it was assumed they died not long after because of it.

"What would you do?" I asked.

"Farm, maybe. I'm good with my hands. Been thinking about taking care of that crack in your ass all morning."

"You can't worm your way out of this. What's going on?" I pressed.

"I think you underestimate how good I am at creating a distraction."

"Noah. You were always the one telling me to stop looking back, stop looking forward, focus only on the moment. What changed?"

"I never had a past worth thinking about, all right? Or a future, until recently."

"And you're worried about being mortal in that future?"

"No, that was a separate thought I was wondering about." He brushed his hair back and sighed, seeming frustrated with his own disjointed responses. "There's gotta be something for us together after the war."

"Of course there will be. That's when the real fun begins. Don't worry about it."

"Will you stop saying I'm worried?" he snapped, but he changed his tone right away. "I'm not worried about anything. Fighting is all I know, so when you talked about laundry and cooking I try to think of the last time I had to do shit like that. It was only a few years ago for you, but a lot longer for me and it was a shit time back then."

"We took on an Infernal King. I think I can teach you how to make dinner or wash the sheets. You're just going to cheat and have someone in the Order do it though. I know you."

"It's not about the goddamn laundry! We're supposed to be equals, but when the fighting's over then what's left for me to hold up my end? You don't need me in battle like you used to, but I found my place keeping your head on straight like you do with mine. You can do anything though, and you have people here to take care of what you don't want to bother with too."

I hated when he tried to act as if the Order were my servants because it put me in the same category as someone like Aurelia, despite his recent compliment on how different I treated them.

"They aren't *people*." I raised my voice. "They're *family*. *We* have family."

"They're *yours*, not mine! I'm only here because of you."

"Stop acting like you don't care about them! You're trying to shut down and distance yourself because they're mortal. As much as I don't want to admit it, we could be at war for centuries and this discussion would be a waste."

Am I being too harsh? I feel like I can physically see him retreating behind the walls he used to have up, trying to return to his old callous ways but wanting to open up at the same time.

"I didn't mean to get upset." I hugged him to apologize. "Finding yourself in a new lifestyle doesn't have to be scary if you do it with someone. Like you said, I did it not long ago. At least the change this time will be less violent. It'll be something new and exciting for us to experience together."

He set his chin on my head. I could tell before he even spoke that his tension was subsiding. "I'm not scared of anything. I have a reputation for being awesome that I need to uphold."

"I know."

"You're perfect, you know that? I'm not kidding around either," he clarified. "You can always bring me back me from any mood in seconds like it never happened. No one's ever done that."

"Don't start making me blush. You've already got me where you want me and you know I hate it."

We held each other in a firm embrace. I hesitated to ask about adding to the column after the last rollercoaster, but went for it anyway. "Can I add the spirits to the column? I don't know how to spell their names."

"Put their elements. The names they were given weren't their own." Noah took my hand and guided my pointer finger over the marble to make each symbol in their native languages. "I should teach you this stuff."

"I'd like that."

"I still wanna take you to Thailand if it's around and get into Muay Thai. They've got some nasty kicks that would go great with my style and we could learn the language together."

Someone ran by the courtyard shouting, "Glory to the Ascended!"

I saw it was Claudius at the last moment by his white hair. Lyle walked by right behind him and came in when he saw me.

"Hey, I was looking for you," he said.

"Sorry, I slept in until about an hour ago." I got up to meet him halfway. "Wow, you shaved and got a haircut! Are you...wearing tights under your shorts?"

Noah had decided not to stay and vanished without any indication of where he was going.

"They're compression tights. Everyone's wearing them in America." The defensive tone in his voice intensified the longer I stared. "What? It's athletic wear like for runners. I figure I do enough running for my life it couldn't hurt."

"Do they have any for running from your problems?"

He cracked a smile. "I don't know, but if I find some I'll get you a pair."

"So when were you in America?" I asked.

"The past two days. I just got back. Claudius took me to visit my folks."

"How are they?"

"Doing good. My mom is staying outside Akron with my cousins. She asked about you."

"What did you tell her?"

The last time I had seen Lyle's family was after I lost mine and he refused to let me spend the holidays alone. I probably didn't make a very good guest considering how quiet I was, but I never forgot how welcomed they made me feel.

"That you're still the same weird kid who doesn't know how to brush his hair."

"Hilarious."

He wasn't laughing though. Not even a smile.

"She wants me to move there with them. According to her, nothing I'm doing could be more important than spending the end of the world with my family."

"She's not wrong, but did you tell her that preventing it ranks pretty high up there too?"

"I wasn't going to until I realized my escort was waiting for me, so I invited him in and had to explain."

"Did he proselytize in my name?"

"No. He seemed uncomfortable with the whole thing. It was pretty awkward on all sides."

"I'm kinda getting the feeling that this is too for some reason."

Lyle sat on the bench before answering. Our conversation went from slightly awkward to worrying.

"Yeah, I don't know how to say this," he started.

He hadn't taken notice of the monument yet. I wanted to hide it before he realized what it was and it threw him into a tailspin like it did to Noah.

"Just say it straight out."

There was another awkward pause.

"I just... I can't do it anymore, man. I'm not meant to be part of what's going on. I've already lost two teams, I've lost Rebecca...I don't want to do this anymore."

I put my hand on his shoulder as his voice gave out.

"I stopped caring after losing her on top of everything else and I've never felt that way," he continued. "Nothing mattered. I honestly didn't care if we won or if I made it out alive. That scared me more than anything."

"I got the feeling that's what was going on, but you're my brother and I'm not gonna let you fall. I still look up to you."

"C'mon, man. I was dead weight that needed to be carried around and don't give me that 'pure heart' crap either. Being born a certain way doesn't make me special and nothing I've done in the past year or two has amounted to anything. Rebecca had more to offer the world than I ever could. She should be here, not me."

"*Don't* say that. I look up to you because I agree you *shouldn't* have been on the frontlines, but you did it anyway. Whenever I doubt myself I think of all you've faced without any powers."

"All I can think about when I'm going to bed is how I should've stayed a cop." He sighed. "I got caught up in the fantasy of being a hero and let it lead me into the fire. The only thing holding me together for a while there was remembering you going through a similar time when you lost everything, so I guess it's come full circle."

I lowered my voice. "Let me be honest. I don't care as much as everybody probably thinks. I fight because there aren't many others who can stand up to what we've been facing. It's not like I want to see anybody get hurt, but if someone were to take my place I wouldn't complain. Half the battles we've fought I would've rather stayed in bed. The driving force behind a lot of my motivation is you. No matter

623

what crazy thing rears its ugly head I know you'll be there without hesitation. I think to myself that if you can do it then there's no reason for me not to and I believe it's taught me to be a better person."

"That's...wow...that's a lot, and I appreciate hearing it but it's not all because of me. Since I've known you, you've always known the right thing to do. You just need a kick in the ass when you get inside your own head and freeze up."

"True."

"I remember thinking you weren't going to show up to the battle in Shanghai. It's not a secret that this isn't the life you would've chosen and I don't blame you. I wanted— want—a family, a career worth something."

I went up to the monument to show him. "I made this to honor the people we lost. It's a way for us to move on without forgetting them since most didn't get proper burials or any send off. Do you want me to add Rebecca?"

His quiet inspection of the names already inscribed on the monument was discouraging until he murmured his agreement.

I paused. "She wasn't a follower of anyone, but I can see about Isis or Cernunnos working their magic to bring her back. Now that the rules are all over the place I don't know if they're still restricted to their own people."

"No. It's not what she would've wanted. We used to talk about it a lot actually. I just always thought it'd be me to go first."

"You're not going anywhere," I insisted.

"You know how I feel about living forever, and she agreed with me that it ruins what it means to be alive if everyone can keep cheating death. There would be no end to it if every person you cared about was brought back and then every person they cared about too. She didn't like the idea of her life's work and all those before her being made pointless by magic. She used to say that death was the one thing to keep us humble and goal-oriented."

"So she'll be pissed for a while and then she'll get over it. Blame it on me if you want."

"It's not right, man. A big part of me wants to say yes, but it's not up to us."

I relented and added Dr. Rebecca Sullivan to the blank spot where he was looking.

"Put Rudgar and Timmons too," he said. "All of PROJECT: UNITY actually..."

I inscribed Lars Rudgar and Lisette Timmons, grouping them with Rebecca under an emblem for PROJECT: UNITY, and then I gave Lyle a moment to pay his respects.

"So where does this leave you?" I asked. "Because I'll give you another two days off, but I'm not letting you stay in bed depressed your whole life."

Lyle dried his eyes. "I'm thinking of moving near my family and seeing what work I can get."

"I know we're always going back and forth with keeping our squishy loved ones close, but we can't keep living in fear. I want you to move here with them," I insisted. "I can build them a house and it'll be easier to keep an eye on everyone. I'm going to offer to rebuild Liam's mom's home in town and you remember the little undead girl Mia that Octavio took in?"

"Of course I remember her."

"I'm going to see if I can bring her here too, with a friend she's been staying with and make them a place."

"You know this is still part of Greece, right?" he asked.

"I'm just building a couple houses where they used to be since the original owners aren't coming back. If whatever's left of Greece has a problem we can talk it over or I can make them a truckload of diamonds to buy the land. I doubt this island is high up on their priority list."

"I don't know, man. Don't go overboard and start another international incident. There are plenty of areas where life is sorta normal. The neighborhood my mom is in, you'd almost never know how bad it is in the rest of the world."

"Really? What about the internet and all that?"

Lyle laughed. "Dude, people lived without the internet not long ago and some countries barely had it to start with."

"The internet is more than porn and cat pictures, smartass." I nudged him. "I'm talking about communication, banking, that sort of thing."

"I'm more of a dog guy, but yeah, most banks are kinda fucked with a lot of credit and stuff being digital. TV and mobile services don't exist anywhere that I know of, but landlines work most of the time for those who have them where my mom is staying. Local radio stations come in all right, but it's only news. I heard it was a total blackout for a while when everything first went down."

"They have power then?" I asked.

"Yeah, but the electricity goes out a few times a day. Losing nuclear reactors put a strain on the grid in high-density areas and the invasions knocked out a good deal of the major alternatives across the country. As for actual damage and losses though, suburban areas are relatively fine, even a lot of the smaller cities are in decent shape. Big drain on food, gasoline, and supplies though. Stores are emptied out worse than the day after Christmas."

"Sounds like it's either going to be a slow death or a slower climb back to normal, depending on how well people come together."

"The government is still trying to regulate things to prevent areas from starving themselves. They have no way to enforce it nationwide though, with a big part of the military gone. I was only there a couple days, but I didn't see any looting or anything like that when I walked through town. My cousins were saying a lot of people abandoned their jobs either because they wanted to be with their families or to volunteer."

"That's good," I said. "I had a bleaker image in my head full of fire and pillaging."

"Well, who knows what's going on in the rest of the world, but I still like to think that humanity can surprise you if you keep an open mind."

Lyle and I left the courtyard to meander through the abbey while we talked. I delighted in watching him take in the changes. There were still no signs of activity from anybody else though.

"Starting a life somewhere else might be something to consider," I said. "The Order got a lot of their basic supplies from the shops around the islands and I don't know how viable it'll be for them to be teleporting around the world for flour or milk."

"Gotta be careful where you go. People are gonna get jumpy around the supernatural even if the secret's out and the demons are gone. Your crew isn't exactly, uh, subtle about blending in."

"I'll shield them from as much as I can. The last thing I want is for them to become demotivated when I'm sure there'll be more fighting in their future."

As we walked through the halls, I made additions to merge the revamped modern gothic style with my favorite aspects of classical Greco-Roman architecture now that there was extra room. Engaged fluted columns and decorative pilasters extended from the walls, and layered ornamental arches known as archivolts over main doorways. I could do anything and everything I always wanted.

"If I had a supernatural power it'd probably be something like this," said Lyle. "I'd like to be able to drop a house down wherever I want. Better than fighting all the time."

"I could ask the other gods if they can make you immortal."

"You're never letting that go, are you? I'm having enough problems with the years I've got, I don't need infinity more yet."

"*Yet.*"

He pushed me so I'd shut up, but I wouldn't be quiet on the subject forever.

"I had a good chat with the big guy before I left," he said. On both sides of a doorway, I made two alcoves with life-sized statues of knights in the Order's armor.

"Gianni?"

"No, but that reminds me, he asked me to tell you that he was headed back to Rome. I meant Noah though. We had a talk about losing people and our 'grudge,' if you want to call it that."

"Oh?" I was curious why Noah didn't mention it earlier.

"He was actually pretty cool. He felt I was always skating by without any real perspective on how life is for you and him, which I can understand. I guess besides the issue between us with Vivi he thought I considered myself special that I was involved with all that's been going on. He had a hard time believing I was genuine even in my friendship with you."

I shook my head. "I don't think I need to tell you how hard it is for him to trust anybody. He's never said it, but I'm sure another reason was because of your connection to Aurelia through PROJECT: UNITY."

"Yeah, that came up, but I put it to rest right away."

"Wow. Already telling you stuff he hasn't told me."

Lyle laughed. "Don't be jealous."

"You can take him off my hands for a while when I've had enough. I'm not surprised though. Once he gets going the floodgates really open. Five years of walls and misdirection and then it all comes out in five minutes."

"He did dominate the conversation, but that's nothing new. I got to explain myself and where I'm coming from at least. He didn't know I had lost my father when I was a kid and that's what's been driving me to do what I do, trying to live up to how I remember him as a hero. I never thought I'd tell Noah about that."

"Losing Rebecca is a lot like how he lost Vivi. There were others before her in his life that were taken from him in even worse ways and those are wounds that just don't heal with time. If I had to guess, it's less about burying the hatchet between you two and more that he can empathize with seeing history repeat itself so soon right in front of him."

Having walked most of the abbey, we headed outside into the sunshine and sea breeze.

Noah was right. It does look more like a small castle now.

The children's laughter carried through the air from the orchard where they were trying to catch colored fractals in Nathaniel's mandala. He sat on the grass as they ran around him in his aura. It was the first time in a while that I saw him dressed casually in a linen shirt and pants instead of his battle attire that he had taken to sleeping in due to constant use.

We waved to each other as I passed.

"It doesn't bother you that Noah still has those strong feelings for an ex, or exes?" Lyle asked.

"Not even a little. I know that it's the person he's mourning the loss of, not the relationship. And from what I understand, he and Vivi never reached the point of being too romantically invested anyway."

"I'm happy for you, man. You came from a really dark place and it's good to see you able to put it behind you."

"Now it's your turn to get through yours and I'm here to make sure you do."

We came across Marianna and Helena reading to a smaller group of children under a tree. None of them seemed to have any trouble getting along and it was nice to see the Order kids taking a break from their strict daily routine to enjoy life. By this time of the day they would have been studying and training for hours with only an hour for playtime between lunch and dinner.

I gestured for the adults to stay and continue story time when they jumped to greet me. The children of the Order knew the routine, but the pups only stared, wondering why the fun had stopped. Marianna came over anyway and left her aunt at the wheel.

"It's good to see you awake," she said with a smile and saluted. "We love the changes to the abbey. I thought I awoke in heaven at first."

"I'm glad you like it. It's great to see everyone so relaxed and the kids getting along."

"They're adorable. We're amazed at how well behaved they are for growing up in the wild. There has been plenty of resistance to wearing appropriate clothes, but it was expected. They do almost everything as a pack and treat Nathaniel as their alpha now, although the red-haired girl seems to be the leader among them."

"Nathaniel's the alpha, huh? Don't let me forget to point that out to Noah," I mused. "Do they understand what's being read to them?"

"They're very smart and love to learn, but I think they're mostly just entertained by the pictures. They do speak their own Nordic dialect that has some English words."

"I remember hearing the adults speak it."

"Helena left the island to find a book that might suit them and came back with a tale about the adventures of a squirrel that lives in Yggdrasil called *Ratatoskr and the Golden Acorn*. She's having the time of her life reading to them, more than she did with me. Toilet training is another story."

"Oh, wonderful. Where's everybody else?" I asked, eager to find out. "I haven't seen much of anyone besides Noah and he's not big on details."

"Everyone was so anxious to see how our victory affected the world that they've been scouting since yesterday. We figured you would want us to rest, so they set out after a day of meditation and chronicling the battle in the archives."

"Has anyone reported back yet?"

"Yes. There is good news and bad news."

Lyle and I answered at the same time. "Good news first."

"There hasn't been any demon activity and the hellscapes seem to be gone for good! Cernunnos has been transforming the ruins of cities in the North into forests. The bad news is that countries are still falling apart. Alexandre brought a newspaper from the mainland that said the surviving members of government in Greece and Turkey who were evacuated are either refusing to return or have run away like cowards."

I guess they won't be coming for our island any time soon then.

"Those aren't problems that'll be fixed overnight," said Lyle. "New leadership that the people can trust will need to be installed and then a stable economy to keep it that way."

"The homeless and hungry likely can't wait that long. Liam heard that people are attempting to immigrate to the Kingdom of Light in Egypt, but with air travel still grounded and rails damaged they're walking or going by overcrowded boats and rafts."

"What's our situation like with food and all that?" I asked.

"We have enough in storage for several days, but we're searching as far as inland Italy to locate new markets able to supply us. Most are rationing too little for our needs or won't sell to foreigners."

"That's not good. Noah can eat two days worth of food in an hour."

"He doesn't even *need* to eat," said Lyle.

"Do *you* want to try putting him on a diet? It'd be easier to start our own colony."

"That won't resolve the immediate problem," he said. "This is something PROJECT: UNITY could've helped with."

"I don't want to take food out of anyone's mouth, but I also can't let anyone here starve either. We'll have to bribe whoever's willing from more stable areas. Any word on France?"

Marianna's expression turned sour. "The little I heard from Quentin and Troy is that the living conditions are decent away from Paris, but people are attacking 'non-humans' to blame them for the invasions. He was there less than an hour and he needed to leave because he felt the crowd would turn on him."

"You guys *are* human though," I said. "How would they know unless he was casting magic in plain sight?"

"How he was dressed. He was in regular clothes too! But I guess they weren't 'regular' enough. They took one look at his amulet and clothes and thought he was a demon worshipper."

Helena raised her voice while reading so the children wouldn't catch wind of our discussion. We moved some distance away to continue speaking in private.

"Aurelia pretty much owns France now," Lyle said. "I'm surprised she'd let that happen, being 'non-human' herself."

"Really? I'm not," I disagreed. "People are probably angry. The demons are gone, but the survivors' problems are far from being over. They want a scapegoat to take their anger out on. The places where life is terrible are too busy trying to stay alive, and the ones where life is somewhat normal have more to be grateful for than upset. I wouldn't be surprised if Aurelia is the one perpetuating this to control the mob through fear and pitch herself as the only non-human that can be trusted. She can't keep every person under her spell at all times, so she'd need a way to stay in power unquestioned."

"You gonna let her get away with that, man? She already needs to answer for what she's done to Noah and her part in Rebecca's death. We all had a war-time truce that she and Vyrlakalos seem to have forgotten about."

"How much do you expect me to handle, Commander?"

"I'm not a commander anymore, but you're still a god. You can do anything and this is a long time coming."

"I wanted the weekend off."

"It's Tuesday."

"Fuck. Well, when I meet with the gods we'll think of some way to deal with her. In the meantime, my priority is here."

There was also the matter of the letter she sent.

Connor came jogging over wearing a blanket for a cloak.

"Hey! You're awake!" he exclaimed with his classic ear-to-ear smile. He gave me a bear hug that lifted me higher off the ground. "Thanks for making my room so big. Now I have to get more stuff to fill it up."

"You're welcome." I laughed.

"Hi, Lyle," he said, sniffling and wiping his nose on the blanket.

Lyle backed away. "Hey, man. Are you sick?"

"He caught a cold from all that ice magic and minor aether poisoning during our battle," Marianna answered for him. "He's *supposed* to stay on bed rest since he refuses to take the elixir prepared for him—one that he should know how to make by himself."

"It tastes like cat piss." Connor sniffled again. "And I *do* know how to make it. I just didn't want to. I saw you guys from the window and came to thank Dorian for my room is all. It's even bigger than Marianna's."

He nudged me to play along, but I wasn't about to mess with her.

"They're all the same size," she insisted.

Behind us, the children had decided story time was finished and it was now time to pretend to be squirrels and climb trees.

"Why aren't you wearing a shirt if you need a blanket?" I asked.

"Sensei never wears one."

"Okay?"

"I want to be more like him and that includes getting to his size too."

"Not sure if that's possible, dude," Lyle remarked. "You're already pretty jacked for someone your age, but to get to his size as a human you'd need to be on some serious steroids and trust me that's not something you want to get yourself into."

"You would also not be anywhere as dexterous as Noah without his powers to match," Marianna added. "You know that our diet and training regimen is tailored for our combat style."

"At least you'll always be bigger than Dorian. Not that that's saying much."

"That's getting old," I said, frowning at Lyle and turning away. "Connor, we've talked about being yourself and since then you were one of the final four left standing against the Machine's army. Don't try to change who you are because you're impressed by somebody in the moment."

"Sometimes it isn't easy knowing how to be myself though, and Noah is the one who taught me how not to be afraid of what you can't plan for so that I *could* be one of those four. His style is so much better. Training with everybody here isn't always like fighting real demons."

"That's because those particular demons were copying his techniques and you also didn't have a standard rite of passage," said Marianna. "You would've encountered plenty of demons and hostile spirits in the years preparing for it, *but* we're all still proud of the hero you became on your own. Claudius and others would've died without you filling in for Rafael."

"Aw, thanks." He wiped his nose again before giving her a hug.

"How is Raf?" I asked, watching Nathaniel shepherd his flock indoors with Helena.

Marianna gave an icy response. "He's been resting in his room since he can't scout on his own."

"Don't be cross with him, Anna," said Connor. "He feels bad enough losing his magic and everything turned out fine. Claudius doesn't seem too upset."

"A cabal is meant to function as a cohesive unit. We have to trust one another to always be playing our role, yet he didn't even feel it necessary to tell us that he was going to run off against direct orders. To make it worse, all three of the council are in the cabal and it made us look like we didn't know what we were doing."

"Same as with any team really," Lyle said. "If you're expecting your partner to get your back and they don't because of bad communication on their part, they gotta man up and accept responsibility."

"I'll talk to him," I told Marianna. "You're not wrong to be upset, but people are still going to have free will and do the unexpected even if you're the best leader in the world. Just don't let bad blood hurt a lifelong friendship."

"I understand."

She was paying me lip service, but I couldn't change her mind anymore than I could have stopped Rafael.

Lyle and I headed back to the abbey having seen what we could outside. As much as I was fond of hanging out with my best friend during a time of relative peace, there was a problem festering beneath the surface that needed to be addressed: the man beside me was not him.

Chapter Fifty-Six

"You said it's possible that some of the civilian staff at PROJECT: UNITY who were evacuated before the attack could be alive since they never got implants."

"And? Hopefully, they're living their lives with the people that matter to them."

"Find them and regroup."

Lyle groaned and messed with his hair, frustrated by being asked to do the impossible. "I can't. Not again. I won't be responsible for anybody's life except my own."

"At least *ask*," I pushed. "Stay small if you want. You could stick to one area and only tackle local issues. Best of all you'd be free from Aurelia's ownership. You'd need a new name then, of course."

"Whoa, whoa! Slow down," Lyle said. "None of that is easy under the best circumstances and especially not how things are now."

"When has easy ever made a difference for us? The Lyle Turner I know wouldn't leave it to chance, or fate, or gods, but you're telling *me* to take care of Aurelia instead of *us*. I figured it'd take a while to build you up to saving the world again, but this is something personal to you and you're stepping back to let me handle it."

"What do you want me to do? Hide behind something and take potshots at her while cheering you on? I told you I'm done, dude."

"You can't be done. You're everything that's right with humanity and the world is at a crossroad where people like you are needed most to guide it down the right path. Don't you see we have the opportunity to help rebuild from the ground up? Please don't throw in the towel yet."

Lyle groaned again. "Fine. We deal with Aurelia, but then that's it."

"It's too dangerous. I'll handle her myself."

Lyle threw up his hands.

"Put your energy toward reforming PROJECT: UNITY! You can make a tremendous impact on improving the daily lives of people through them while doing a lot of the same stuff you loved about being a cop. I have the schematics for aether technology that could be the key to getting life back on track, but I'd need UNITY scientists to do anything with it."

"*Okay!* Jesus. I'll *talk* to whoever I can find so you'll leave me alone, but not because it's what I want. Don't expect much though. It's gonna take a lot of time, travel, and money."

"You have all the time you need, there's a thing called teleportation, and I'm pretty sure I can make it rain gold and diamonds. Money shouldn't be an issue, if it even matters anymore to begin with."

"I know you haven't spent much time in the human world recently, but most stores don't accept gold bars as currency."

"What about a golden egg? Say a magic goose laid it."

"Yeah, good thinking. That's a lot less suspicious."

Nathaniel came outside minus his flock. They could be heard scampering and shouting inside when he opened the door. One of the youngest boys ran past behind him and licked the wall for no apparent reason before running off again.

Kids can be so weird. Was I like that when I was their age?

"Should I talk to Claudius about taking me or do you have to decree it?" Lyle asked.

"Go ahead. It didn't stop him before."

Lyle went in and a moment later the little wall licker returned, looked me straight in the face and announced, "Books!"

"Yeah! Books are great!" I smiled.

He stared at me for a moment and ran off down the hall screaming "Books!" until someone must have found a way to appease him.

"New word?" I asked Nathaniel.

"Yes, and very proud of it."

"I see that. How's the bed? Do I have a future in furniture design when this god thing falls through?"

"I hope it doesn't come to that. I haven't had a chance to test the bed myself though. I've been sleeping in a chair so the children could share it. We tried putting them between two rooms of their own, but they wouldn't stay."

"I'll make a second one for you by tonight or maybe join those two rooms to make a pup dorm. I've got the remodeling itch, but first I have a couple of issues to address around here and then I need to take a trip to Rome."

"Oh. Before you go I have something for you."

"Is it coffee?"

"No, but I hope it might be almost as good. One second." Nathaniel was gone and back in a flash with gift in hand. "I know you don't feel comfortable with tributes, so consider it a token of thanks for the bedroom."

I looked over the lustrous circlet made of orichalcum filigree woven in a simple design resembling the Order's crest stretched into a band, with laurel leaves intertwined and a small ivory aether gem inlaid upfront.

"Nathaniel... This is—I'm speechless. It's great that you can do this without powers, but a crown?"

I gave him a big hug so he wouldn't feel that I wasn't excited about the design, but he also should have known that

I was trying to *avoid* standing out anymore than I did already.

"Actually, my powers let me work the metal with my bare hands while it's hot instead of using tools. Rafael gave me some tips since it was my first time forging orichalcum. I was working on it well before you made the room, but I've also been practicing how to channel my emotions into crystals."

"I remember the one in your gauntlet that you gave Lyle."

"Yes, and the aether for this one is charged with positive feelings from the last couple of days. I thought it might help when there's something on your mind that's bothering you."

Unable to refuse, I put it on and was awash in a slight uplifting feeling. "This is really cool. It feels similar to Isis's calming aura."

"I'm still hoping it'll be the key to learning how to heal."

"You mean resurrection."

"Possibly, yes. I know you warned me but the more we fight, the more I fear people dying from my mistakes."

"It's something that looks good on paper, but what happens when you're expected to never let anyone in the world die?"

It was hard to not sound like a total hypocrite after my conversation with Lyle about resurrecting Rebecca, but I knew Lyle was right. I was just willing to take responsibility for his happiness, while I didn't want Nathaniel to suffer the inevitable backlash for the same thing.

"I can keep it a secret," he promised.

"Something like that won't stay secret for long and I can't see you denying people once it gets out, especially children. The gods having that power is different because they were emotionless and commanded a bit of respect through fear. I don't know what it means for them in the future now that they can feel, but you're still more approachable. I don't want to be the type to forbid anything, but if I did, it would probably be that."

"You don't have to worry. I would bear the burden of any consequences."

"It isn't that simple, Nathaniel. Those consequences could affect more than you. You aren't alone anymore. I know it's taking some getting used to for me and Noah too."

Through the window I saw Lyle inside by the door captivating a mixed group of kids by teaching them how to high five, low five, and pull away at the last second. The berserker pups seemed to think it was hilarious and were excited to jump at the chance to participate, while the Order children remained more reserved and waited their turns.

The enthusiastic bookworm from earlier was hopping up and down to the point of exasperation while clinging to a tome that must have been half his weight. It slipped from his grasp about three times, but he wouldn't relinquish his prized possession for anything.

Forget nuclear or aether power, children are the real future of renewable clean energy. Now if only we could harness it somehow, maybe with a treadmill or a big gerbil wheel...

"I'm thinking that I should escort you to Rome."

I could feel Nathaniel's unease and assumed he had overheard the meeting would include Aurelia.

"Sure. Is everything all right?"

"Yes—well...I don't know. I heard Gianluca's exchange with Noah admitting how determined he is to have you and...I'm familiar with what some men are capable of when frustrated and lonesome."

"Oh." To say I was stunned by where this was going would be an understatement. "His feelings for me are fresh and he might be lonely, but you have nothing to worry about. He just needs to find a new focus like we're all doing."

"The way he carries himself around you makes me uneasy. It's as if a part of him believes you are still his."

I realized it wasn't only about me, but Nathaniel not wanting to relive a similar trauma through our empathic connection if anything were to transpire.

"You're always welcomed wherever I go, but it might be best for you not to come in this case. If you do and nothing happens you'll think it was because you were there and always feel you'll have to be in the future."

"I suppose you're right."

"I know you don't believe it, but at least trust me, okay?"

Claudius approached Lyle and both left to come outside after some protests from the children at losing their playmate. Nathaniel had to pry a few off of Lyle and go in to keep them corralled.

"Cool crown." Lyle nodded to me.

I made him an NYPD cap to replace the one lost at the base.

"Exactly like my old one," he said, looking it over with a thoughtful smile before putting it on. "Thanks, little bro. I needed this."

"You're welcome. And thank you for going with him, Claudius."

"I live only to serve you, my lord." He bowed. "Also to try new unhealthy foods. In America they have candy beans that taste like popcorn and bacon. I can't fathom any better reason to save the world than that. Pizza is high on the list too."

The thought of popcorn or bacon-flavored jellybeans almost made me gag. *It does make me want a cheeseburger and a sugary iced caramel latte.*

"We're going to England though," Lyle told him.

"Blimey."

"You should probably find clothes that'll help you blend in," I said.

"These *are* my 'blend in' clothes," said Claudius, sounding a tad self-conscious for perhaps the first time in his life.

Leather pants and boots, the black bandana he used as a face mask tied around his neck, a half-buttoned linen shirt with the sleeves rolled up above the elbow, and his amulet on a chain—too eye-catching for daily life anywhere but here, especially with his build and the white hair.

"They're not bad, just a bit too nice for jellybean hunting in the streets."

I altered his outfit into blue jeans and a T-shirt hoodie. I was a strong believer that a hoodie in any form was the ultimate clothing.

"Do I get trainers?" Claudius asked. "I've never worn them before and they look like fun."

"What are trainers?" Lyle asked.

"It's what they call sneakers there," I explained. "Nah, I like the boots. Hm, maybe I'll make them shorter though...and leave them unlaced with the tongue out like this..."

"Now he looks like some sort of urban fashion commercial," Lyle said.

"Anything looks good when you have the body for it."

"Why, Ascended, I'm flattered," Claudius joked with a smarmy grin, striking a pose to show off like a certain someone was known to do.

"Better not let Noah hear you, man," Lyle said, chuckling.

"Or Raf," Claudius added.

"Not what I meant! And what about Raf?" I asked.

"He's very...committed to courting your attention, even if it gets everyone killed. I can't say I blame his motivations. Who would refuse the chance to serve more closely by your side?"

"*Uh huh.* I'm sorry about what happened with him during the battle, but I'm glad you're all right."

"Much appreciated. I'm not cross over it though, not at anyone but myself for not thinking of his strategy first. An important part of a spymaster's job is infiltration."

"So is not announcing your job title."

"Ah, I suppose you're right."

"Okay, get out of here you two. I have work I need to get started on if we're having guests."

"Put on a tiara and you're already dishing out orders like a spoiled princess." Lyle got in one last parting shot before Claudius was ready to take him away. "I'll see ya soon. And thanks—for everything."

Chapter Fifty-Seven

I toured the edge of our property to survey the rest of the carnage-scarred island downhill.

I don't think anyone is coming for the bodies of these poor souls...or what's left of them after decomposing in the heat for so long.

I hadn't forgotten about the people down there, but the sad reality of their fate so close to home was something I was trying to avoid thinking of, even if I had become as used to death as one could be without going totally numb.

Maybe I should clear the whole thing to put them to rest with some dignity and start from scratch. The buildings probably aren't salvageable between the water damage and foundation damage.

There could be supplies though. I can't do anything more for the dead, but I can for the living.

Indecisiveness reared its ugly head, thwarting my eagerness to start throwing down houses.

I'll work with the land we have here and ask the Order to scout the ruins for anything useful before I clear it.

A once-grassy field a mile long separated us from the village, so I had plenty of room. I started by flattening the earth to a level surface and solidifying a portion of it into a square foundation. Erecting a twenty-by-twenty-foot hollow cube of white marble was effortless, but indecision continued to smack me in the face at every step. It took me almost half an hour to get the placement right for the windows using the abbey as a reference and I still wasn't satisfied in the end.

I hate that I could do this better in my sleep.

The sounds of the children playing outside again were a welcomed distraction. Marianna was conjuring bubbles for them to pop while Nathaniel relaxed on a nearby boulder. Every so often one of the kids would run over to make sure he was watching. It was one of the most normal scenes in recent memory and it wasn't to be taken for granted.

We've finally come out the other side after being in the dark for so long and now's my chance to run with it.

I carried on, adding a front door that resembled wood. The interior layout came next. I sectioned off arbitrary rooms by raising walls halfway to the twenty-foot ceiling and then covered it to make a second floor with a stairway leading up. The less I thought about every action, the easier it became by letting my mind wander, as if navigating a living dream that pulled inspiration from subconscious memories of locations I had been in throughout my life. As the layout took shape I tweaked the style to keep it uniform with my Greco-Roman/Renaissance hybrid aesthetic I had grown fond of and embellished on finer details. Fluted columns, archways, alcoves, shelves, and even closets were becoming their own works of art that surpassed the abbey in extravagance.

I'll add sconces and chandeliers that can be filled in with aether crystals for light. I hope Lyle's crew doesn't mind not having electricity for a while, but it should only be temporary if we can get those plans sorted.

When materializing bedroom furniture I was drawn in at the sight of a short armoire that looked better suited for child size clothes. It felt familiar to me and yet I couldn't place where I had seen it. I opened the doors expecting to know what I'd find, but unable to recall what it would be. Three drawers on the bottom left sparked the memory from where the piece originated.

This was my dad's. He got rid of it when I was still very young because of how small it was, although I don't know why they ever had it in the first place. There used to be toy cars in the third drawer to keep me busy on Saturday mornings when I'd run into his room at the crack of dawn wanting to play. Sometimes I'd hide them in his dress socks to be found on Monday before he'd go to work.

I opened the bottom drawer. Empty.

Something about that memory being brought to life didn't sit right with me. I didn't want my personal life manifesting on a whim for anyone to see, but there was also a sadness to it. The people in the memory were no longer here. I couldn't go to them and ask the story of why they bought an armoire that was clearly too small.

Will I ever be allowed to forget or move on with random objects from my past always popping in to remind me?

Unwilling to be deterred yet, I carried on with furnishing the rest of the room. I started to feel the suction of air pulling into a vacuum from being depleted. I had to remind myself that as surreal as it was, there were still limitations.

I opened every window to generate airflow and floated toward the empty bathroom in sweet ignorance.

Cabinet, sink...bath...toilet...wait a minute. I have no idea how any of this works.

I panicked a bit as I tried to run the water in the sink. The handle turned, but nothing happened. I opened the toilet tank. It was hollow. No rubber float or chain attached to the handle. I could make the pieces I remembered, but I had no practical knowledge of plumbing or any real concept of how it functioned, aside from the simplest fact that water came in through the pipes and drained out into sewage. It was the same issue I ran into when creating a gun for Lyle.

Damn! We're going to have people coming here and no running water. People that I invited and I'm responsible for now. I could route pipes from the village and salvage a few toilets, but what are the odds I get everything to connect properly? We're fortunate to still have running water in the abbey somehow.

I went outside to get the full scope of my progress while I thought of what to do about the plumbing. The house was bigger than when I had started due to the elaborate interior expanding beyond my original design. It now stood as a rather large manor almost rivaling the renovated abbey. Just for good measure I added a veranda to the front and sides of the building, and a balcony to the master bedroom in the rear.

So much for not going overboard. Oh well, maybe whoever winds up living here will be so impressed they won't mind going down to the shore to do their business.

Liam came to see what I was doing. He greeted me with his usual salute, but he didn't take his eyes from the house. There might have been the hint of a smile on his face.

"What do you think?" I asked him.

"It's remarkable. As is the abbey."

"Thanks. It's been nice to work on as a side project now that we have a break from all the battles."

"Those are what I enjoy most, but I can appreciate the peace we fought for and life is never dull for long in your presence."

I had to inquire further after Noah's confession about not knowing anything in his life beyond fighting. "There must be something else you look forward to that doesn't involve near death experiences."

Liam thought about it and seemed hesitant to reveal the answer.

"I wouldn't mind a chance to play rugby."

"Rugby? I can see that. There's no reason why you can't learn as an outlet to have fun with during downtime."

"I already know all the rules and strategies. When I traveled to Australia with my father I saw a match in passing. He said sports are a waste of time that could be better spent training, but my mother would let me watch the game on her television."

"So you weren't always visiting her for her cooking! You're a normal teenager after all."

Liam responded with a worried smile. "You won't tell him, will you?"

"Of course not. Not everything you do has to be about productivity. Life should have balance. Now come on inside and see what I've been doing."

He didn't have to say anything once we crossed the threshold. I was getting good enough at reading his very subtle facial expressions out of necessity to know that he approved.

"Do you think it's too much white?" I asked. "I added the black details like in the abbey to offset some of the brightness, but people can do whatever they want. I'm into architecture, not interior design."

"No. Anyone would be honored to live here."

He was careful not to touch anything, like he was in a museum.

"I wouldn't go *that* far, there's no plumbing, but I was thinking your mom could have one of the houses I put here when they're done."

"The whole house?"

"Well, yeah. She can do what she wants with it. Private time for her and your dad?"

"I don't think that's likely to happen. My father seems uncomfortable around her, though they are spending the day together on the mainland."

"I wish I could watch your mom giving him hell." I couldn't picture Tobias on a date. He was a stately, mature man and the knight-in-shining-armor thing was usually a hit with the ladies, but he was so...stuffy for his age. "What are you doing the rest of the day?"

"I was to go fishing with Rafael after he finished tending to the apiary, but I'm available if you need me."

"I do, but I also need to talk with him. I was waiting because I thought he was asleep. How's he feeling?"

"He seems well. I think he's concerned what his place is with us after losing his magic."

"This is his home, he has nothing to be concerned about." Actually, I was the one that was concerned about talking to him and why I was putting it off. I didn't know how to handle praising his heroism without abiding by him abandoning his cabal and almost killing himself for me. "I was going to ask if you'd scout the village for supplies since we're having company on the island soon, hence the house."

"Marianna informed me. We already laid the dead to rest while you were in the Rift to avoid the demons turning them into Abhorrent."

"Oh, good thinking. Get anything your mom might want from her old place too and take anyone you can to help so it'll go faster. I'm going to clear away the ruins once they've been picked clean and I'll make a building for storage in case we run out of room in the abbey."

"Do you want me to add lighting to these fixtures before I go?"

"I almost forgot about that. Do what you can and when you finish you can take what you need from the treasury to get yourself a ball, if you know of a store that sells them and is still standing."

I left Liam to find a spot for my next building closer to the abbey. Nathaniel had taken the children down by the shore with Marianna to splash around in the water, so I had all the space I needed to work without interruption. I began by raising the same Corinthian-inspired columns that were prevalent in all of my designs. They were connected by granite walls to form a rectangular foyer that opened into a cylindrical room with a domed ceiling. My idea was to create a silo with shelves and ice chests dedicated to food products behind a more generic storage area upfront, but it wound up resembling a smaller Roman pantheon.

I better change this before Gianni sees that I've reduced such a beautiful part of his culture to a stockroom.

"That should do it," I said to myself upon shifting the walls to make the structure one large octagon.

With that out of the way it was time I went and talked to Rafael. I hadn't decided if I would tackle it as a leader or a friend, but I had avoided it for long enough. My reluctance wasn't only from having to come up with the right thing to say. I felt responsible for what had happened and that I couldn't reverse the consequences. It made me feel unworthy of being considered a god, not that I had fully embraced the position yet anyway.

When I got inside, Connor was doing pull-ups in his bedroom doorway while wearing full armor, presumably for the extra weight.

"You're supposed to be resting," I said as I passed.

"This is nothing! Do you want to watch me do a hundred?"

"I want you to stay in bed and get better so you can enchant some new ice chests for me."

"I can do it right now—"

"No!" I pushed Connor into his room and shut the door so I could proceed to Rafael's room down the hall.

Rafael was sitting on his bed looking forlorn as he whittled a bead, only brightening up to greet me despite obvious signs of deteriorating health.

"How are you feeling?" he asked with a somewhat anxious smile after giving thanks for his remodeled room.

I hadn't gotten an opportunity to take more than a passing glance inside the other bedrooms, but now I saw what Connor meant by needing more stuff to fill his. The high ceiling and increase of empty space in a sea of white gave the room the sense of a personal temple cloister. It was fresh while keeping some of the cozier touches from the old furniture.

"That's what I came here to ask *you*."

"I'm well enough."

His answer was a blatant lie despite his attempt at confident posturing.

"Making your own prayer beads?" I asked as I sat with him.

"Yes, is that okay? I know it's something sacred to you and Noah."

"I think it's great. I wouldn't mind it becoming a symbol of the Order and I don't think he would either."

That gave me an idea.

I fabricated a string of metallic black prayer beads in my hand with one white one amongst them, inscribed with the phrase "Knight-Exemplar." With so much white around, including everyone's armor, the black stood out strong like the details in the abbey.

"I want you to have this with the promise that I'll do everything I can to heal your soul. It will be the highest title of honor given within the Order."

I put the beads around his wrist. His expression brightened again, but he wasn't too receptive otherwise. I knew a piece of jewelry I pulled out of the air couldn't compare to the sacrifice he made to rescue five gods and save the world.

Maybe I shouldn't have insulted him with something material.

"I know it isn't much, but I wanted to give you something personal."

"No, it's incredible."

"You can be honest with me," I said. "About everything, I mean. I know you must not feel like yourself."

"I don't mind as long as you'll allow me to remain in your service."

I was close to giving up on repeating how it wasn't about serving me, but regardless of the minor breakthroughs and leading by example, fealty was so engrained I didn't think I could ever fully convince them otherwise. "You're not going anywhere, so don't worry. You guys mean more to me than your magical ability."

That didn't seem to put him at ease. If anything, it appeared to have the opposite effect.

"Tell me what's wrong, Raf."

"Who am I?" he asked. "In your eyes."

"I don't understand. You know who you are to me. I say it all the time about all of us together."

"It's nothing... I've just been rather tired lately and it's hard to hear my own thoughts."

I put my hand on his shoulder. "I know it isn't nothing. You can tell me."

"I feel as if I have no identity of my own. I'm only ever thought of in relation to others, whether it's being a part of the Order or Liam's friend within his cabal. It's been that way my entire life because I'm not old blood like him or Marianna. We aren't supposed to chase personal glory, but I don't want power or anything of the sort, only to be recognized for who *I* am. And now without my magic...I'm weak and have outlived my use."

If only Noah wasn't so private I would share with Raf that he wasn't alone in his doubts about the future.

"Don't say that. You more than stand out, Rafael. Tell me what I can do to help so you don't get yourself killed doing something else crazy."

"I told you I'm not afraid to die. I was sure I would in the Machine's fortress, but every moment I survived made me feel stronger. I trusted in my faith that I could do anything under you."

"Except I specifically told you *not* to do what you did."

"Yes, but sometimes we have to do what a person needs, not what they say. Ego and humility can get in the way of a situation's reality."

"That sounds like something Noah would say, except coming from him it would sound ironic."

"He did say it. I tried to explain to Marianna, but she refused to understand. Instead she treated me like a traitor for abandoning them and doubting your abilities."

"She isn't wrong for being upset. I don't think either of you really understands how the other feels. There was a lot of pressure on her to lead everyone through the worst disaster we've faced. I've been in both of your positions and it's never easy making those decisions, but I'm grateful for how you both handled it now that it's over. I love you guys too much to let it ruin your friendship though, so I'm hoping you can both move past it."

The way we operate needs to change more or I can see this happening again.

"As do I."

He became quiet for a moment.

"What is it?" I asked.

"When you say that you love us, do you think of us as individuals or your followers as a whole?"

"Come on, Raf, of course you're all individuals to me. I only speak in plurals because I don't want anyone feeling excluded, but it seems to happen anyway."

"It's a bit strange to hear someone say they love me for the first time, that's why. I wouldn't be so bold as to compare my own past hardships to the suffering Nathaniel endured here, but I can understand some of how he felt."

"Didn't your—actually I don't remember you ever mentioning your guardian."

"It was my father. He left us a little over a year ago."

"I'm sorry."

"Thank you, although part of me was relieved once he was gone from my life. He found ways to turn even reading lessons physical and never said he loved me. It didn't matter how hard I tried; he always belittled my efforts. Those were my earliest memories of him before I even knew what the words he called me meant."

"Do you have any idea why he was like that?"

"I was adopted into the Order and given to him to raise since he was of age and without an heir. I guess he thought I was forced on him and he couldn't love someone who wasn't his own blood because I marked the end of his true bloodline. I'm not the only one here who's adopted, so I never knew what was wrong with me."

"Nothing is wrong with you and being adopted doesn't make you worth any less. I was adopted too."

"I know. Hearing that you were felt like a sign. Tobias once told me that he couldn't have picked a better friend for Liam. My father said he was insulting me because I made Liam look better by comparison. I thought I'd get my chance to live when he died, but I didn't know how and so I stayed in Liam's shadow until you arrived."

"There's no doubt you've made yourself into one of the greatest heroes on Earth. And to better answer your question from before so that there's no doubt in your mind, you are loved. I love you and I know your friends do too."

"I love you too."

I heard a sneeze from outside the window. Connor was walking by and waved, thinking it was only Rafael in his room. He bolted once he saw me.

I swear I'm going to strangle that kid.

"I know you were supposed to go fishing with Liam, but I sent him into town to scavenge for supplies. It's going to be dark soon, but if you're feeling up to it maybe you can join him. We need anything we can get our hands on with a lot being uncertain in the world right now."

"I can do that."

Noah sauntered by the window heading in the opposite direction Connor went, a candy bar in his mouth and a shovel over his shoulder.

"I should go see what that's about."

All I could picture was that he had buried Connor out back. I knew I had said to myself that I would be more conservative with my use of teleportation, but I was too impatient. I embraced Rafael to say goodbye and popped outside to where I knew it was clear. Noah was nowhere in sight, so I flew above the abbey for an aerial view. I found him standing in a shallow lake that wasn't there before on the one spot of the property I hadn't been to today.

I laughed the entire way down to him as he stood there so nonchalantly. He looked so good with his muscles glistening wet. I couldn't wait to touch him.

"Hey, noodle." He threw the shovel to dry land so he could hold me in his arms when I landed on him. The water was up to his waist and steaming hot. The bottom was paved with cut blocks of stone mixed with scattered aether crystals.

"What is this?" I asked.

"It's an *onsen*, but it's not done yet. I wanted it to be a surprise."

"I'm definitely surprised, but what's an onsen?"

"Hot spring in Japan. Had to get creative though and use fire crystals for the heat."

"Are these the stones from the border wall along the property line?"

"Could be."

It was so well done it looked professional. I wanted to offer my help with finishing it, but this was his project and I was glad he found something to feel good about. I had been excited to show him what I'd accomplished until seeing this and enjoying the feeling of sharing in his moment instead.

"What made you do this?" I took off my shoes and changed my clothes down to swimwear to enjoy the water with my arms around him.

"You like taking baths so I figured it'd be somewhere for us to relax together instead of that small tub. And it's just deep enough for me to hold your head under the water when I've had enough of your shit."

"That's really thoughtful." I reached up to kiss him on the lips. "You're the best."

"I know. More room to plow you here too," he said with a lascivious grin.

"I'm not getting naked outside. The abbey is *right* there."

"You have to, those are the rules. Not now though. We got one of the runts with us over there, but I'll build us something for privacy."

Noah nodded in the direction of a tree by the edge of the water. Under it sat the red-haired girl that had taken to him when we first met the berserkers in Iceland. She was munching on cookies or something from a store-brand box that we wouldn't have had in the abbey.

"I take it you went into town?"

I waved and smiled at her, but she didn't wave back.

"Yeah, I needed a liner to hold the water, so I nabbed a couple tarps by the old dock. Here, watch this."

He whistled at the munchkin and she threw him a cookie that he leaped out of the water to catch in his mouth. She gave him an enthusiastic round of applause and the two of them pointed at each other in camaraderie.

"Still don't like kids, huh?" I teased him as he waded back to me.

"This one ain't bad. She knows who's in charge around here."

"Nathaniel?"

Noah narrowed his eyes and stepped closer in a playful attempt to act intimidating. "What'd you say to me?"

I laughed and hugged him, thinking how that might've worked on me years ago.

"That's what I thought," he said with a kiss to the top of my head.

The sun was setting, showing the warm glow of the fire crystals illuminating the water. We could hear the cheers and laughter of the children coming back from playing by the shore. Nathaniel's glow led them inside and Marianna brought up the rear with Dermott, who must have joined recently. Hearing her friends, Noah's little fan scampered off with her box of cookies to join them. She stopped a few feet away to wave goodbye. I returned the gesture, but Noah turned away. She shouted to get his attention and threw a cookie at him to no avail.

"Noah, don't ignore her." I tugged on his arm.

"She's gotta learn not to get attached."

The girl soon gave up and ran to the abbey doors where everyone was filing in. The way Noah acted didn't sit well with me, but I knew it was more because *he* didn't want to let himself get attached.

The sour note lifted when a cat darted from behind the tree where the girl had been sitting. It sat by the water staring at us and licking its paw. For a second I thought of Isis's pet.

"Where did you come from?" I asked it as if expecting an answer.

"Oh yeah, we have a cat now," said Noah. "He's a real asshole though, so be careful."

The calico didn't seem bothered by me approaching. It wasn't uncommon to see strays being social when begging for scraps in town. They must have been quite successful based on how well fed they always looked.

"No, he's not. He's just a stray like us," I said, gaining his trust to pet him and then pick him up. "He smells good too...like...our soap? You didn't."

"Stupid thing was a mess. I told him you don't let dirty paws in bed, but still got the shit scratched out of my arm."

"Cats don't like water. It's not his fault," I said. "What should we name him?"

"Dirty Asshole."

"*No.*"

"I'm tapped out then. If he wants another name he's gotta earn it."

"Are you going to be like this with every new person and creature we meet?"

"Probably. Now get your ass back in here and watch the goddamn sunset with me. I'm trying to be romantic."

Our new fur friend wiggled away from me and headed toward the abbey, likely smelling dinner cooking, but I chose to pretend he knew this was his new home.

"Fine, we'll come up with a name later."

I glided through the water to where Noah was and sat on his lap facing him. He put his hands on my thighs. I shortened his gi pants to match the swimwear I had on so that more of our skin made contact.

"You're not watching the sunset," I said, only glancing at it myself. The sea was so still I couldn't hear the waves at the shore. The sky seemed just as quiet. It almost didn't feel natural.

"I'd rather be looking at you." His tongue turned to silk as usual when we were intimate. "I missed you today."

"I missed you too, even if it was only for a few hours."

"Doesn't matter. I always do whenever you're not around." He lightly splashed me. "I checked up on you a couple times and saw the house you were working on. You gotta give me a tour later."

"I do, do I?"

"You do, but right now it's tiger time."

"My favorite." I gave the tiger in his tattoo a kiss and laid my head on his shoulder.

He slicked his wet hair back to get it out of his face. "You like the big hole in the ground filled with water I made for you?"

I laughed at his self-deprecation. "I love it."

"I love *you*."

Those words struck me. Obviously, I knew how he felt, but as he had admitted in the past it wasn't often I heard him say it. I thought of what Rafael had told me. When I was growing up, it was something my parents said to each other and myself to the point that I suppose I took the meaning behind it for granted.

"I love you too." I had to stop myself from smiling so much so that I could bring my lips together to kiss him. I then placed a hand on his chest. "More than me can fit in here though, you know."

"Between my tits?"

"Your heart! Being your one-and-only means the world to me, but we're not alone anymore. You were starting to open up before I fell into the Rift and it makes me sad to see you pushing people away because you still feel you need to protect yourself from getting attached."

"I'm a simple guy with great taste. What more do I need than what I got right here?" He leaned in to kiss my stomach. "You and me being awesome together wherever we are. That's it."

I could tell he was doing his best to distance himself from serious conversation since his mind was elsewhere with no signs of return. He was preoccupied with examining every inch of where his strong hands were caressing my body.

I won't push it. We have all the time in the world to heal old wounds together. I don't want it to become a point of contention between us.

"Should we go inside?" I suggested.

The sunlight had withered to make way for the aurora above, leaving only enough darkness to showcase the crystals glowing underwater. He answered by carrying me to our room where our conversation was put to bed.

Chapter Fifty-Eight

I spent the better part of the next morning in bed thinking about an assortment of things from cat names to plumbing and my upcoming visit to Rome where I would propose dissolving our alliance with the Ancients, quite likely through violence.

And what about Gianni? I can't leave him living in rubble.

I had woken up on Noah's side of the bed with half his body draped over me while he still slept, face down, head buried under the pillows. Aside from that it was one of the most peaceful night's sleep we had gotten. Yesterday had gone so well in general it was almost suspicious.

"What should we name you?" I said to the purring lump sitting beside me. "Hm, how about Ollie? *Sir* Oliver."

He swished his tail in my face on his way to the top of Noah's pillow pile.

"I'll take that as a yes."

In the past, had someone asked me if I was a cat person I would've told them I didn't feel strongly either way. But my new appreciation for felines that weren't tigers had to do with more than the cat himself, it was about what he represented to me; another piece of our growing family, a new life that I was feeling secure enough to build on and enjoy. I thought about hearing Noah say, "*We* have a cat" and how that "we" was almost as important to me as him say, "I love you."

"Don't scratch the headboard!" I scolded Ollie.

He darted away when I tried to pick him up and went straight for the curtains to scratch at those instead. It appeared he had targeted them during the night too. I got up to go after him, stopping just short of stepping in a puddle near the couch.

I'm already a bad cat parent. I didn't think of a litter box. At least I can use my powers to clean this up.

I caught Ollie before he could cause any more destruction and lay down with him on the couch. He wanted to look out the window and sun himself, so I decided to be more organized in my approach at building today by sketching a layout for the next houses and how to arrange them.

That idea lasted mere minutes until I became distracted by what was going on outside the window too. Nathaniel was out there with the children again. More of the Order had joined them this time. I started to doodle his mandala around the houses I had lined up when I had a stroke of inspiration using the design as a street map centered around the abbey. Without the use of cars on such a small island I could make geometric patterns that were otherwise impractical to drive through.

This looks cool, but how many houses am I really going to need?

Noah stirred. I saw him reaching for me across the other side of the bed.

"I'm here on the couch."

He grumbled and seemed to have gone back to sleep after taking my pillow as a substitute, so I continued my sketch. A moment later he staggered over to claim my place on the couch and reclined with an arm around me and one leg over mine.

"You're good at that," he said, yawning and looking over my shoulder.

"Drawing was the part of architecture I was most nervous about tackling in college too."

"That's dumb. You've got talent." Noah sounded like he was falling asleep again. He scratched Ollie under his chin. "You like that too, huh, you little asshole?"

Ollie was quite accepting of being touched by the man responsible for dunking him in water yesterday, but Noah did keep sneaking him pieces of fish during dinner.

"I named him Ollie. It's going to take some getting used to living with a cat. I woke up with his butt in my face thinking it was our old blanket."

"Wouldn't mind you waking me up like that."

"I'm sure you wouldn't."

Having had enough attention, Ollie slinked toward the door. I heard a crunching sound coming from him and sat up to check what he was getting himself into this time.

"What are you eating?" I floated a piece of whatever it was to me. "It's a...graham cracker?"

Noah popped it in his mouth.

"That was on the floor," I reminded him.

"Don't judge me."

We returned to snuggling on the couch together where I continued sketching housing and street layouts based on Nathaniel's mandala. I was encouraged by Noah taking an interest whenever he pointed out something he liked in particular. It was another pleasant subtlety from a man of constant extremes.

"What's that?" he asked, pointing to a circle within a circle in the blank space between lines of the mandala.

"A fountain. The island is too small for proper parks, so I thought of this."

"Nice. I like those."

"You're in an agreeable mood today."

"I'm always agreeable. I'm gonna dropkick that cat though if he fucks with my stuff."

Ollie was pawing at some of Noah's gear to nudge it off the dresser.

"Don't do it," Noah warned him. *"Don't..."*

I gave up trying to pacify both of them and floated Ollie down. He meowed with a wide-eyed stare and hid under the bed when I put him down, but a minute later I heard him happily scratching away at something else before joining us on the couch again.

"I'm going to see how everyone did collecting supplies and make the rest of the houses."

"Why not make this?" Noah asked about my sketch.

"We'll never need that many houses and the island isn't big enough for all of it anyway."

"So make the island bigger."

"I'm trying not to draw more unwanted international attention."

"You think anyone's in a position to stop you? This is what makes you happy, so I say do it."

"It does, but we also don't need that many houses."

Noah pulled on a pair of shorts. "You're making excuses when you should be making buildings *or* apple turnovers."

"Only if you admit how fond you are of Ollie."

"I've never hated anything more in my life. But you know what I've always thought were kind of cool? Beavers."

"Beavers?"

"Yeah, I remember seeing them down by the river when I was a kid..." He stopped.

"Oh. Is there more to the story?"

"I just remember being impressed by how they had their shit together collecting wood to make a home. They're pretty cute too. Reminds me of you actually."

"You get to be a sexy tiger and I'm a beaver?"

"I got pissed at my father when he skinned a few to sell the pelts in town," Noah continued. "They weren't bothering anybody like wolves or bears do. Just some hard workers trying to make their way."

"So was he."

"He told me he left the babies, but I knew that only gave them a slower death."

"Does that have anything to do with why you were so adamant about us taking in the berserkers' kids?"

Noah didn't respond. He went to pet Ollie's exposed belly until he almost got scratched. "I'm gonna make a hat out of you."

"Looks like he knows your bait and feint technique."

I poked Noah's stomach and went to the bathroom to get washed. While I was making myself presentable I thought of inspecting the toilet for future reference. *Show me your secrets, you porcelain Pandora's box.*

Noah walked in on me investigating the inside of the tank. "You're using the wrong end."

"You don't say."

"I do say."

"*Ha-ha.* Come on. I can study this later."

Upon opening the bedroom door I was met by Connor entertaining himself by balancing a large plastic cup of iced coffee on the broad side of his sword.

He caught the drink and kneeled to present it to me. "Your beverage, my lord."

I laughed and took it from him. "Ooh, caramel!"

"Nathaniel said that it's your favorite. I've been keeping it cold with a little magic."

He showed me the frost on his hand.

"Thank you, Knight Connor." I bowed. "I hope you're feeling better?"

"All better. I swear it."

"What'd you get me?" Noah asked him, helping himself to a sip of my coffee.

"I'm sorry, sensei, I didn't..."

"Fine, then your training for today is to practice your *kata* by giving the little shithead in our room a bath. You'll need your sword."

"*No.* Leave the kitty alone unless you want to make him breakfast," I demanded. "Do you know if everyone finished in town?"

"We did this morning after working through the night and now we're all home. We found plenty of cooking ingredients and canned and dry foods. There are too many olives and beans if you ask me. Now Liam and Rafael went fishing to fill the ice chests."

"Hm, I used to live on chili and beans back in the day," said Noah. "Tons of cheap cured meat like beef jerky too."

"That's a lot of protein. Is that how you got so big?"

"Yeah...sure."

I could tell Noah felt uncomfortable forcing himself to share certain details that he didn't offer of his own accord. I scratched his back to make him feel better and let him know I was proud of him.

"Then that's what I'll do too, so I can be like you," said Connor.

Noah threw me over his shoulder right as I had finished sucking down my coffee and headed down the hall. "Don't waste your time, kid. The only good thing about me is right here on my arm."

He zipped away with me, not stopping until we were outside by the onsen.

"That's not true," I told him when he let me down.

"What's not?" he asked, busying himself with shuffling the rocks around.

"You know what."

Noah sat by the water. "A man is nothing more than the sum of his choices, so what does that make me? I spent most of my life being not able to make my own. Best thing I did was break free to be with you and even that wasn't my own success. I've been thinking of what you said about *her* still having a hold over me through fear and you're right. I haven't been able to move forward and that's when I even know what direction I want to go."

"You've been making a lot of progress opening up and that's a big step." I massaged his shoulders from behind. "You don't have to go at anyone else's pace but your own. I'm sorry if I was pushing too much, I only wanted to encourage you when I thought you were regressing."

"Not your fault. I know you always have my back." He rubbed my hand against the scruff on his cheek and kissed it.

"You're gonna be okay, tiger. We'll rebuild ourselves like we will this island and you don't need to have all the answers right now. Maybe we could make that cabin you talked about as a hideaway for the two of us."

"Not a bad idea. Didn't think you remembered that."

"I pay attention sometimes."

I splashed him and was about to go see what was going on around the property.

"You're going to see her in Rome, aren't you?" he asked.

Did he know about the letter?

"I don't know. What makes you say that?"

"She wouldn't have made a personal appearance during the battle unless she wanted something big and your meeting is the place to collect on it."

"Whatever she wants, she isn't getting unless it's a permanent death."

In perhaps the most shocking turn of events, Noah disagreed. "Don't bother killing her."

"What? Is this about you still wanting to do it yourself?"

"No. She knows about you long enough to have come up with a plan to survive whatever you throw at her, even if it's the parasite. Attacking her only gives her the justification she wants to retaliate so she can get you out of the way of whatever else she's planning. She likes to punish failure to flaunt her superiority, so she's never gonna make the first move and I don't want to see anyone here getting hurt because of me."

"She's responsible for the death of Rebecca too, on top of countless others. I can't let that go."

"Wasn't that the Carpathian?" he asked.

"They're working together."

"Fine, but I don't feel consumed by the same hatred that I used to and I don't want you to take over my obsession. Only thing that's ever really on my mind now is you and me.

"I'll be honest," he continued after a brief pause, "even with all the shit going on in my head I never felt the way I do now. I didn't think this sort of happiness existed. I always considered being happy meant I wasn't pissed off, but it's an inside happiness, more than surface shit like the feeling when I bite. When I was human and as a kid, I never felt anything like it either really. Don't know how to describe it any better....it's good."

"That's all you needed to say." I smiled and embraced him again.

"Evil is always gonna be around and don't get me wrong, I guess I do still hate her, but she's just not important anymore. She's not a threat to our existence that we *have* to do something about, like the demon fuckers."

"I don't want to spend my immortality fighting anymore than I already do," I agreed. "I'll let the other gods deal with her, since I'm sure they'll have reason soon enough if not already."

"I didn't say to leave her alone, just don't kill her yourself. She's petty, but she's also quick to call others out if they act like it. The more you have that she doesn't will drive her crazy waiting for you to make a move on her so she can take it away."

"The more *we* have," I corrected.

"Yeah, that." He nipped at my ear and gave me a naughty smirk with an eyebrow raised. "I'm gonna eat you later."

"Your moods are giving me whiplash." I laughed.

"You love it. Go do your building and stop distracting me so I can get some work done of my own." Noah pushed me a little too hard and I landed in the water. "That wasn't on purpose."

He picked me up, kissed me with the fiery hot passion of a thousand suns, and then threw me back in the water. "That was," he said and fled the scene.

"*Noah!*"

I dried myself off and decided to spend a minute listening to the waves rolling onto the beach before heading into the village. I drew a simple mandala in the wet sand that was washed away by the tide seconds later. As if summoned by it, Nathaniel came down from the skies to where I was standing. He looked like he had been swimming and was quite relaxed.

"Hey, Champion." I smiled to match him. "Sorry, was I calling to you by accident?"

"I don't think so, but I sensed you were near and thought I'd come to say hello. We haven't spent much time together recently. I hope you don't feel I'm neglecting my duties."

"Of course not. You should know that. How's the peewee pack?"

"That's a fine name for them. They're doing well enough, I suppose. We were down by the shore catching crabs for dinner until one of the boys got pinched when he tried to put a tiny crab in his mouth. It fell apart after that."

I still had a hard time imagining their future as terrifying, bloodthirsty war beasts.

"Is he okay?"

"He was inconsolable for a time, but it didn't so much as leave a mark. They don't need much to set them off running."

"Kids are weird. I remember playing with two of my dad's staplers pretending they were monsters trying to see who could claim the most space on a sheet of paper until one ran out and I had a breakdown. I probably thought I broke it or something."

"That doesn't sound too weird."

"I was eighteen."

"Oh...well—"

"I'm kidding! Where are the kids now?"

"Studies and training resumed for the Order today, so now they're sitting in on it while having lunch. Last night was a full moon and the older ones stayed by the window watching it all night. I couldn't help thinking that there was a ritual they were waiting for or it sparked a memory of their family."

"How were they this morning?"

"Quiet, but they were acting like normal after not too long."

"I'm going to Rome today for sure, so I'll talk to Cernunnos, although he'll probably only say something about it being the way of nature. Just focus on the moment for now. You came from an even worse place and look where you are today."

"Yes, you're right."

"I was about to go build another house. Why don't you come with me so you can add the lights?"

"With pleasure."

We glided over to the house from yesterday. I checked to see if Liam's mom had made herself at home yet, but it seemed empty so I asked Nathaniel.

"I didn't see for myself, but I heard she was excited and went with Tobias to find very specific groceries on the mainland this morning."

"I tried that vegan cheese she had Liam get and thought it was pretty good. I slipped some into Noah's dinner last night and he didn't burn down the abbey, so I guess that meant he did too."

"What if Cernunnos had brought her back as a berserker? I can't imagine them not eating meat."

"That's food for thought. Sorry. Bad pun."

I put aside any more delays and without much ceremony, wiped the village ruins and left over warships from the island. It was all broken down into a dust cloud that I was planning on using to create the next house.

First I have to make the foundation—

I did little more than vaguely recollect my steps from yesterday and the house was already finished.

"That was unfulfilling. It was too easy," I said, peeking inside with Nathaniel. "An exact replica."

"It's still a miracle," he said, adding light crystals to the empty fixtures. "You can always make alterations."

"That's true. I used almost none of the dust too."

The cloud was still being suspended above where the village used to be without my active concentration.

Weird. I'm getting better at subconscious control without any practice.

"I'm going higher so I can map this out."

Nathaniel followed me up enough to see the whole island. Being weightless in the sea breeze and sunshine with gentle swooshing from the tide below was as close to paradise as I could imagine.

From that height I was able to see some of the children coming outside to play. Noah's biggest little fan broke away from the group carrying a box of graham crackers and setting one down on the grass every few feet.

"What is she doing?" I asked aloud.

"It looks like she's leaving a trail, probably for the cat...or Noah."

"I wouldn't be surprised if it works for both. They have basically the same instincts."

I went on to explain to Nathaniel how his mandala inspired me, but for it to work the abbey would need to be centered on the island and I didn't want to go too far with building.

"I think you should do it," he said. "You seem more concerned about a conflict with people than demons even when their armies have no way of hurting us anymore, but this isn't about starting a war, is it?"

"I'd rather avoid drawing attention to myself as much as possible. Humanity's negativity got so bad it opened the doors to Hell. Even now they're rallying against innocent supernaturals instead of taking what happened as a humbling experience. It's more about being hated than hurt for me personally. I may be confident in battle, but I get nervous dealing with people."

"After seeing the world for myself I still think the good outnumber the bad."

"So does Lyle."

"Don't let what they might say stop you from the accomplishments you deserve."

"Yeah, I guess you're right. Let's see how far I can go with this."

I always do my best when I don't overthink, so this time I'll let my subconscious go free.

I closed my eyes and let my mind soar, merging idyllic daydream with reality, feeling the land rise beneath me as it took form, shaping stone and glass, bending metal, and unfurling cloth. The harmonic rumble of the island and splashing waters was a soothing lullaby to usher a sanctuary's birth, a reckoning against the miasma that would threaten our peace.

Hearing Nathaniel's voice, I opened my eyes to see the end result but felt woozy from a bout of passing fatigue. I held onto him until I could steady myself so that I didn't fall out of the sky.

"It's extraordinary!" he exclaimed as we descended.

The shore around the abbey had risen so that the hill was surrounded by land in equal parts with cobblestone roads recreating the symmetrical beauty of the mandala's lines from the sketch earlier. These roads were too narrow for most vehicles, but that gave it a certain quaint appeal in my opinion. Alabaster houses similar to my first lined these roads, adorned with heraldic banners representing the Order. There were streetlamps ready to be given purpose with crystals, and fountains in paved plazas with statues of knights posed at attention on platforms in the sparkling clean water that was not yet attached to anything to pump it.

Plumbing will be the bane of my existence.

Archways with trellises along the sides acted as portals at major intersections. Stone benches and gazebos supported by my favorite fluted columns dotted open areas for respite.

"There must be about forty or fifty houses," I said, flying through the streets with Nathaniel. The island had doubled in size, but not all of the land was in use. A significant strip of beach bordered the settlement. "Everyone in the Order can have their own place and we'd still have enough for those Lyle brings. I just hope it's not too big."

"There's nothing to worry about," said Nathaniel, looking through a window into one of the houses. "This is the most fascinating thing I've ever seen. It reminds me of a white castle city."

"It's a lot smaller than a city. There aren't as many houses as there used to be and then it was only a village or a town. I don't know which technically."

"What is smaller than a village?" Nathaniel asked.

"A hamlet, I think."

Most of the building interiors were unique layouts, but every once in a while I recognized something from the past that my subconscious never forgot—my dad's home office, a hallway from elementary school, the reception area from the visitor's lodge when I went camping with my family, even fictitious places only visited in dreams, like how I thought the campus library would look at college. I remembered being so nervous that they wouldn't have the required books for class.

"I'll have to ask Cernunnos to add some green."

"You don't seem as excited as I thought you'd be," Nathaniel noted.

"I'm still taking it all in, but...I don't know, it felt too easy. It doesn't feel like an accomplishment to me. I barely had to think."

"The accomplishment is the journey that brought you here. A master's results are no less important than a novice's because it came easier to them."

The sound of everyone coming from the abbey to see the new hamlet got our attention. I waved to them standing on the hill while some of the children ran around chasing each other.

"Dorian, it's fantastic!" Marianna cheered when I got closer.

"It is pretty neat, huh?"

I landed among them and exchanged salutations with everybody in arm's reach. Our bookworm didn't waste a second trying to get Nathaniel and my attention so he could show us a new treasure he had gotten his paws on. He was momentarily sidetracked by swinging on Nathaniel's arm until he dropped his prized book and scrambled to reclaim it.

"Magnificent does not begin to describe it, Ascended," said Dermott, who was holding his daughter so she could have a better view.

Connor leaped ahead of the crowd. "Can we go see it up close?"

"Sure. It's yours as much as mine."

"Do you mean we can live there?" he asked.

"If you want to, but right now there isn't any running water."

Everyone started heading into the streets when Liam and Rafael returned from fishing with their haul. They came forward to speak without having to shout over everyone.

Rafael looked worn out from what should have been a leisurely activity.

"It's beautiful, but are we allowed to continue living together if we prefer?" he asked.

"Whatever you want is fine by me. I'm not evicting you."

Liam gestured to me with a subtle bow when passing to join the rest. I stopped him to point out the brand name sweatband on his forearm.

"The girl at the store said it came free with the ball," he explained as if he needed to defend himself.

"I wasn't accusing you of stealing it," I said. "Have you told your father yet?"

"Yes. He didn't argue once I said it was with your approval. Thank you again for allowing this. I know it must seem beneath our station, but I promise only to practice in moderation."

"Just enjoy yourself and don't worry about what it looks like to anyone or what they might say."

I spotted Noah in the distance dragging an entire peach tree over his shoulder by the trunk. I excused myself to glide over and see what that was about.

"Hey," he said when I touched down in front of him, nonchalant as ever with a toothpick in his mouth. "You're kinda in my way there."

"What are you doing with that tree?"

"I need lumber. Why?"

"Well, put it back, we need the orchard for food!"

I failed to realize the foolishness of my words before they left my mouth.

Noah cocked an eyebrow, amused by riling me up. "That's not how trees work, noodlehead, and one tree won't make much difference when there are forty mouths to feed."

There was no winning with him.

"I like what I can see of it, by the way." He nodded toward the village and dropped the trunk from his shoulder.

The sound of giggling came from within the branches. I spotted the red hair of Noah's admirer before she and another pup popped up.

"Get outta there!" Noah chucked a loose peach in their direction to scare them off. "I swear these demons multiply every day. There are definitely more than what we started with."

"They aren't multiplying, you goofball."

I plucked the children out one at a time to help them so they wouldn't get scraped since their clothes were already in bad enough shape from a few hours of play. The little girl immediately threw a peach back at Noah with a big grin on her face and ran off squealing with her partner in crime.

"See that? Assassination attempt in broad daylight."

"She's just trying to be like you for *some* reason."

"I would've waited for night. Not a bad arm on her though." He handed me the peach.

"Save it for me. I'm heading to Rome now." I kissed him on the cheek. "Don't tear down the whole island while I'm gone."

"I probably wouldn't get to all of it today anyway." He put his tattooed arm around my head and spit his toothpick to the ground so that it stuck in the dirt.

"Wow."

"Pretty good, right?" He gave me a kiss. "Go do your god stuff. I'll look after everything here."

"Mhm, I'll believe it when I see it. And I can tell you've been eating more graham crackers."

Noah sat me on the tree trunk, moving in again to pick up where we left off. "Want another taste?"

His words made me tingle as much as his lips did. I wrapped my arms around his waist and leaned in to accept his offer.

"Hurry back now so I can get some more of this pretty face, all right?" he crooned.

"I will."

Chapter Fifty-Nine

Dressed in the most regal raiments I had been bequeathed by the Order, I visualized the sky above the Roman Colosseum and arrived there at the speed of thought. As often as I made attempts to dismiss aligning myself with any sort of status symbol I still recognized its perceived value during certain occasions. I was starting the next chapter in my life and understood that if I was to be taken seriously in a court of gods as more than an impulsive amateur I would need to prove myself off the battlefield as well.

Rome was in worse condition than I remembered from my last visit when I still would have considered it to be somewhat inhabitable. Charred, crumbling structures in the immediate area were no longer being held together by the darkness Gianni had forged to fill in the cracks, and yet in total contrast, the decaying shell of the legendary city was flush with life from the Colosseum to the plaza and streets beyond. Those within the Colosseum walls kept to the arena where some were busy practice fighting in true gladiatorial spirit. I noticed they were all men and wearing what would amount to dirty gym clothes at best.

Where did all these people come from? I thought most had died when Gianni was incapacitated, but there are more now than before.

Gianni was easy enough to spot as I descended— perhaps the only time I located him before he got the drop on me, but I did have the blinding midday sun above for cover. It would've taken effort to miss him and even more to pry my eyes from him dressed in nothing more than a shadowforged replica of a Roman military skirt and sandals. He was alone with his back turned to me, preoccupied with repairing an archway on the third floor using tools of darkness to resize stone blocks. His frustration was apparent by the animated gestures he made while discarding ill-fitting pieces, and how he wiped the sweat collecting upon his brow from working in the heat. I thought to go down and offer my expertise, but instead decided that surprising him would be fun.

Roman architecture was something I was familiar with from years of casual study and experience. After raising an imaginary hamlet from scratch I was expecting a simple archway to be rather uneventful, but I was wrong, very wrong. My wandering thoughts of the Colosseum took life and I felt the energy exhale from my soul, restoring the ancient structure to its prime.

By the time I regained control of my living daydream Gianni had noticed me floating against the backdrop of the sun. The one conscious personal touch I added was replacing the statues with those of black stone to represent his shadow soldiers. The crowd was mystified by the large-scale miracle they were witnessing firsthand and seemed to think he was responsible until he pointed up at me.

Don't give me performance anxiety, Gianni.

I refocused my thoughts on the vicinity beyond the Colosseum. The Roman Forum, the Pantheon, Palatine Hill, and as many villas and plazas that I could recall in some fashion grew like leaves on a tree after a long winter. After that, I replaced the rubble of the modern roads with more authentic stone paving, only leaving a large hotel to the east in case it was still of some use. Once finished, or as close to it as I could get, I glided down to speak with Gianni on the highest wall of the Colosseum where he went to watch.

The day's excessive creation process was taking its toll. I felt as if I could have fallen asleep without warning, but the urge was beginning to wane on its own now that I was at rest.

I'm surprised it took so long to feel this way. I must be getting better accustomed to this side of my powers.

"Are you...crying?" I asked as Gianni fought to prevent tears from escaping despite his enormous smile.

"No, no. I am so happy!"

He stepped back and forth through the shadows to examine his revitalized homeland. Upon his return he planted a kiss on each of my cheeks with such an innocent jubilation, stopping just short of making contact with my lips, and hugged me close. I returned the gesture and laughed while patting him on the back.

"You are my angel," he said, letting go only for a moment to take it all in with his arms extended like he wanted to embrace the buildings. "My heart is so full to see Roma like this again."

"I know it's not perfect since I was never there to see the original, but—"

He kissed my hand.

"Is perfect," he said, still fighting to prevent himself from tearing up. "I am home again."

I had to admit I felt better about my work here than at home, because there was some small amount of earned knowledge being applied instead of just a dream.

"The heart of Roma is more than carving in stone walls," Gianni continued. "Is the passion of the people inside. You are always my light in the darkness and now you give that hope to these people with a new Roma spirit."

He held my face in his hands and looked into my eyes to pay me his full attention. "I wish so much to kiss you the right way. I miss these sweet lips, but... I have a respect for you and for Noah I swear on my honor I will not break."

"Thank you." I touched his forearm with a smile and changed the subject. "Who are these people exactly? Where did they come from?"

"In il Colosseo is *atleti*...Ah, you know? To play the sports."

"Oh, athletes? Yeah."

"So smart." He kissed my hand again. "*Polizia*, fire *polizia*—"

"Firefighters."

"Si, and the military soldiers is here too. They come from in Europe because they hear Roma is safe with me, but many already die when the demons attack. These ones don't know until they come because there is no way to give a message in the chaos. I gather the men who can fight and outside is the civilians. Some who are here before now help give a training and more come everyday to make Roma more stronger."

He indicated two of the men below carrying shadowforged swords. Most of the crowd was mulling around chatting while trying to get a better view of us. It didn't seem to be very organized training, but maybe they were on their lunch break.

I would've put the civilians behind defensible walls. Then again, that might have made them sitting ducks in a compromised structure against enemies that can teleport.

"Only those two survived? Was it luck or skill?" I questioned.

"Four, but only time will answer this," he said and then added, "They are good men."

"And the women?" I jested.

"The best. I love all the Roman people. They are my brothers and my sisters."

"They aren't technically Romans like you mean though, not that it matters really, I guess."

"When you come to Roma you are a Roman. Simple, no?"

"Simple." I smiled in agreement at his enthusiasm. "But I'm here and I'm not Roman!"

"Why do you say this? You are the most Roman for building this beautiful place!"

"There are degrees of Roman-ness?"

"Maybe." He shrugged with an unsure smile. I didn't think he quite understood my attempt at humor. "Come. I want you to meet our gladiators."

I tensed up at the thought of introductions, especially those done en mass. Rescuing people in the heat of battle was different; there wasn't much time for judgmental stares, probing questions, and periods of awkward silence. You were either an immediate threat or you weren't.

"Another time. I came here so we can assemble the gods to discuss—"

He saw through my diversion right away. "You make excuses. Why are you afraid of the people? I remember I come here with you the first time and you get angry with me because you say people do not like our love, but this is not the same now. I make a big speech to them already to say everybody's love is okay in Roma and you know what they do? They cheer for it. So, I think you are wrong, little one. Maybe I am wrong many times about the world today, but this I know I am right. These are good people that will open their heart for you if you do it the same. Lead with strength and the people will follow."

I reflected on the event he was referring to and it felt so long ago that it could've been another lifetime.

"I don't know what to say. I appreciate you going through the trouble, but this has nothing to do with it."

"There is no trouble. People follow when you lead with strength and passion in your words."

"You're good at that. I'm shy, I guess. I like hiding away on my island with only a few close friends...or forty."

"You are not shy!" Gianni laughed. "When I meet you I think this, but since that day you have very big confidence. Remember I call you a little bull? Very stubborn every time."

"All right, fine I'm not *that* shy. I'm just a private person and I don't like crowds."

"You are afraid. Admit this to yourself. You think people will not like you because you are different, but we are all different. They have only words, but you are not *l'uovo*, you know? The egg? Soft inside with a shell. You are a little bull.

Strong inside, strong outside, but also very beautiful in both."

All I could do was laugh to avoid blushing. He had a point though. It was a road I had been down so many times in my mind that I should be angry with myself for letting it get so absurd. I had let my anxieties control me yet again. Once I thought about it rationally, the time Gianni brought up, when I thought everyone was staring at us for being on a date, was probably not as bad as I had let myself think, and even if they were, what difference did it really make?

"Okay, I'll go. But not for long. Remember we have to meet with the gods."

Gianni beamed. "Yes, I don't forget. Trust me, you will be so happy even if to get pride that you fight your fear and become an even stronger little bull."

"I'm *not* afraid," I insisted, somewhat contrary to the truth. "You just worry about leading your empire."

"Me? I am here for giving the gladiators a training to be soldiers of Roma. You are the leader."

"Roma is all yours. I have more than enough to handle with my island and the Order."

"We are very close, so you can have both. My wish is to show you—wait. Stay one moment."

Gianni departed through the shadows, returning seconds later with a piece of paper in hand.

"I write what to say." He gave me a nervous smile and scanned the paper more than once before reading aloud. "You shine very bright in my life that I always feel when you are not here with me. I know I did not listen to what is important when I am your man, but I never think you are not strong and wise alone. My Roman heart is full of love and will not let me surrender when I try to protect you. Is my wish to show what I learn to be a better man for you and to make Roma your paradise even if it take all my time on the Earth."

He paused again.

"There is more I don't finish."

My heart ached. The simple gesture of him making an effort to write his feelings in English for me spoke more than the words themselves. I stumbled to find the right thing to say in return.

"I've always been honest how I feel about you, but nothing that anyone else does will affect my relationship with Noah, the same as he wasn't responsible for what happened between me and you. I can't tell you what to do, but I don't want you to be disappointed."

"If our fate is not to be together then only I have the blame." He touched my chin. "I respect your virtue and always I want the best for you."

I saw my opening to help guide him toward focusing on Rome instead of me. "I want the best for you too. I think your efforts should be spent restoring Rome. Obviously you enjoy connecting with the people here and they need your leadership. Make it a paradise for those here."

"Yes, I will like to, but *politici* lead, I fight."

"Then pick ones you trust to help you. I don't want to lead either, so I give all that to Nathaniel and Marianna. Rome had a whole government. You don't have to do it yourself."

"This is true. I never think of the government because I only follow the orders in battle when I am human or fight alone later. *Politica* is...too much. Is for old men, but I am always a young one."

He was radiant at the thought that he could restore more than just the buildings and army of Rome. "Come, we go down now," he prompted and took my hand.

Damn, I was hoping to have gotten out of that.

Gianni went ahead without me. I thought it odd, unless he was trying to send me a message. I wanted to gauge the reception he got from the crowd before diving in myself, and what I observed in the next few seconds gave me a new perspective on some things.

At once the men rallied around Gianni like he was some mega-celebrity, not an ancient god of darkness. He couldn't have known most of them for anymore than two days and yet there were copious amounts of back patting, cheek kissing, and fraternal embraces.

Do they think his immortality will rub off on them?

I was aware that much of Europe had more open-minded views toward certain mannerisms compared to where I grew up, yet the whole scene still made an impression on me that conflicted with past reminders anytime I dipped a toe back into the human world. It was rare, but I had witnessed masculinity questioned and sexuality judged based on seemingly benign interactions, such as proximity to another man or a simple compliment on appearance. These criticisms didn't need to be violent or daily to leave a mark, as I now questioned if my reluctance to connect with new people had been tainted more than I realized by remnants of shame from my formative years spent concealing the real me.

But what did I have to feel ashamed about? I certainly didn't think I felt that way, not anymore, yet my natural reaction was to hesitate around those that might leave another invisible scar. I was immortal, a god, some might even say superior in every aspect to those I shied away from, yet I cowered while they stood.

I used to think religion was solely to blame for enforcing certain "values," but aren't I currently the idol of worship in the Order's belief system? They were not the warmest bunch and now by treating them as family we had taken steps to embrace both physically and emotionally. To refuse interactions with humans now because I had the privilege of hiding away on my island would only make me complicit in the old ways I despised.

As I watched the snapshot below, I puzzled over if people's tolerance levels were so easily susceptible to influence by a powerful figure like Gianni or was the majority always on the fence looking for something to tip them one way or the other and make up their minds for them? Philosophy aside, I saw before me a chance to rebuild social structures along with brick and mortar ones. The willingness was there and growing by the second.

I descended into the crowd to where they parted to make enough room for someone ten times my size. There was no hiding my entrance, but Gianni had to make it worse by motioning and announcing my arrival to be sure everyone took their attention from him. I kept my hood up and concealed myself within a force field once I was amongst them. Gianni stepped back the closer I got, encouraging those around him to approach. I heard him announce something in Italian mentioning English—presumably that it was my only language. His speech was so flowing and commanding that he was like another person.

I swore it was getting hotter out. A bead of sweat rolled down the nape of my neck.

When social situations are more draining than battle I know I've been away for too long.

As I struggled with having so many eyes on me, I forced myself to look at all the faces so that I would see them as individuals and not let my anxiety distort their intent in my mind. The expressions were of little else than subdued curiosity. The crowd was gradually simmering to a more somber mood as I continued forward without saying a word. Of course, my first thought was that it was because they didn't accept me the same as they had Gianni, but then it occurred me that they were reacting to my energy now instead of his.

My mouth was dry and I couldn't seem to rectify it by swallowing. Nevertheless, I managed to greet the crowd with a simple "Hello," hoping they would respond and not make this anymore awkward. Their replies came in English and Italian, both matching my quieter tone. I was taken back by how soothing the sound was.

Again Gianni encouraged those around me to get in closer and they did. Some jumped upon coming in contact with my barrier for the first time, but when it didn't hurt them and I didn't react, they began to lay hands on it as I passed in place of being able to touch me directly.

This is really awkward again.

I continued to float my way to Gianni with the crowd following alongside. Their faces started to show signs of smiles that I returned with my own and soon the crowd was bustling with a whirl of chatter. Out of the corner of my eye I noticed a young man pushing through the rest instead of moving with them. Nobody else seemed to mind since I was the priority, but I was a bit unnerved by the aggression.

Gianni passed right through my barrier, kneeled and placed a slow kiss on my hand in a showy fashion. Those closest to us followed his example by kneeling, but by the time it had spread to the second row he was back on his feet and motioned for them to rise too.

"Really?" I pulled my hand away.

"Trust me."

He kissed my cheek in the same careful manner as he did my hand and then turned me around to witness the crowd's reaction to further drive in the point of all this.

"You see? There is no harm," he spoke into my ear. "They love you!"

"*Love* is a bit dramatic. I mean, this whole thing is a bit dramatic, but they're probably just glad we aren't here to take their souls—"

"So stubborn," he scoffed.

"All right, all right. You've made your point."

"Ah-ha, today is for the scholars for I have tamed the little bull! *But* I don't think it will be for very long."

Gianni scanned the men around us and selected one of the finer specimens to come forward. I stayed within my barrier to maintain what little personal space I had left, since there were still people coming up to touch it in fascination. They were a more physically diverse bunch than first impressions had me believe. Whether young or mature, bellies and farmer tans were not anymore uncommon than six-packs and hard bodies. It would be interesting to see how Gianni's vision of Roma molded these men.

"Your name? *Come ti chiami?*" Gianni asked with a hand on the strapping man's shoulder.

The man looked like he was about to be handed his lottery winnings. He was blinking a lot and wiped the sweat from his smiling face with his hand. "Enzo Abelli."

"Enzo. This means to win, yes? I have a book of names to learn them for English," Gianni told us both, but it didn't appear that Enzo understood a word. "Is a good name for a gladiator!"

He proceeded to rattle off a paragraph in Italian to Enzo, which seemed to further excite him. I heard "Ascended" mentioned and was impatient to find out what was being said.

"What's going on?" I asked.

"He is Italian navy. Interesting, but too bad we have no ships."

I didn't want to laugh at Gianni's tangent and give the wrong idea that I was mocking his new friend, but it wasn't easy.

"I meant what were you saying about me."

"Oh, I tell him you are a god for peace, an angel here for the resurrection of Roma. I also say you only speak English, but that does not stop the bond we share and maybe he will too if he prove himself."

"Gianni, nobody needs to prove themselves for me."

He dismissed Enzo with a pat on the back.

"We say the people need to work for something too and they are happy for this. I have the idea to make an army with more than the infantry, but the centurion and then the legate when more come."

Hm, I should consider restructuring within the Order since it seems all of the actual leadership duties fell on Marianna. I also feel like I haven't done enough to recognize Rafael's sacrifice either.

Gianni thought about his plans while inspecting the crowd. The bravest few kept shuffling among themselves to get to the front in hopes of being the next one brought forward. I had stopped paying attention to those still coming up to touch my barrier, but one stood out when I took a moment to look around myself. It wasn't his face that I saw first, however, it was what he wore on his wrist. Prayer beads. I realized that it was the same man from earlier who was moving through the crowd.

"Is okay to take away your shield," Gianni pressed. "You must feel the warmth of the people to connect."

"Yeah, one sec..."

The stranger couldn't have been any older than Lyle and appeared in good enough health to blend in with the more athletic of those surrounding him, despite being long past due for a shower, shave, and haircut. His clothes were caked with dirt and either torn or frayed in every spot imaginable. He wore only a pair of jeans sitting too loose on his waist, possibly from a recent bout of weight loss, and construction boots with a scarf tied around his neck and rucksack over his shoulder.

Gianni called to me from elsewhere. "A Spaniard is here, Dorian! They make a very good gladiator."

"Who are you?" I asked, remaining focused on the man before me, but immediately regretting my wording.

I couldn't have at least opened with a "Hello"?

His eyes were closed in prayer, so he didn't notice he had my attention until someone nudged him. Dark features were common here, but his didn't look Italian or Spanish.

"My name is Samir." His baritone voice was friendly and hit the ear just right with a mellow confidence. "I know you."

Chapter Sixty

I did not know the man before me, or anyone by the name Samir for that matter, but something about the earnest look on his face made me wish I did.

"I'm sorry, but I don't—"

I was cut off by another man who pushed ahead of Samir to get my attention. Agitated by the rude interruption, I lifted the man above the crowd and set him down far away by himself.

"You saved my life," said Samir, hastening his speech to get the words out before the ruckus I stirred up took his chance away.

"Oh. I'm glad I could help." I felt disappointed that this was going to turn out to be an obsessed fan or someone claiming they had a religious experience about me. That was the opposite end of the spectrum from the judgmental stares and rejection I feared, but almost as bad.

"It was by Mosul, about a year ago," he continued as I went to turn away. "You stopped the traitors that came to kidnap us and…"

I could hear the desperation in his voice turn to disappointment of his own and then resignation all within a single sentence as his moment passed before his eyes.

Mosul? Was that only a year ago? I know it was before I became the Ascended. It was right after we defeated Demon Lord Ma'al who was using terrorists to thin the veil between Hell and Earth. I had concealed myself in a bed sheet to hide my identity back when it still mattered. I guess there are only so many supernaturals flying around that it could have been. A white bed sheet floating a hundred feet in the air could be mistaken for the cloak I'm wearing now. What is he doing all the way over in Italy though? That's much farther away than I thought people were traveling to get here.

I turned back around, feeling an unexpected familiarity toward him. Perhaps it was also somewhat attributed to his natural sounding American accent.

"You took them and their weapons into a ball in the sky that you sent away," he went on with renewed determination.

His account was accurate. I felt like I should be adding something, but was curious to hear what else he had to say.

"I wanted to find you so I could thank you, so...thank you. You saved a lot of good people who had almost given up hope."

Gianni came to see who had gotten my attention. Having stood only a few feet away he had heard everything. "A Persian ally in Roma? I see a new thing every day. Welcome, my friend."

"I appreciate that, but I'm Iraqi, not Persian," he said in the most respectful tone possible. My first guess would've been Greek or a tan German before he introduced himself, but I was as bad at guessing ethnicities as I was with ages. "You can call me Sam if you like. I usually go by that outside of my country."

"Samir isn't much harder to pronounce," I said with a questioning inflection.

"It isn't about that." He smiled and shook his head. "I'm sorry, I didn't mean to offend."

"You didn't. What I want to know is how you knew I'd be here."

"I followed the stories and just kept walking."

"You *walked* from Iraq?"

"Most of the way. I was able to get a ride at times when I felt it was safe, but not many places have fuel anymore."

The side of me that wanted to avoid people should have been throwing up red flags, but he was so sedate and genuine in his delivery, which helped to alleviate my usual apprehension.

"This is a strong man to make such a journey when the world is most dangerous," Gianni praised, gripping Samir's shoulder in friendship. "I see the virtue of Roma in his eyes. The face of a prince and a nice body for a soldier too."

I was getting the feeling that Gianni was trying to entice me with these men so I'd stay and join his nascent empire, which seemed at odds with his own interest in me, but he had never been the jealous type. I did have to admit that Samir was handsome, if a bit on the skinny side.

"You're raising an army?" Samir asked. "I only got here today and don't speak the language most do."

"We start with the gladiator for now, but soon an army to fight the demons, yes. You will join us?"

"I'd be happy with any opportunity to repay the blessing you gave me and my people. I can't say I'm much of a gladiator, but back home I was in the military for a short while."

Should I tell him that this is Gianni's affair and not mine? I feel like I'm going to get involved in this no matter what I do. Maybe if I get him alone I can explain. I don't want him to feel like he's repaying a debt to me, but I also don't want to take away from Gianni's pride and joy.

"You've had a long trip. Why don't we find some place for you to settle in?" I offered.

"Yesterday I bring the bed that is still good from hotels inside here for the men," said Gianni. "Go with our new friend, Dorian, and then we have our meeting."

I didn't quite know where I was supposed to be leading us, but I was eager to escape the crowd and it wouldn't have been right to dismiss him without more of an exchange after traveling so far to meet me. I hadn't let myself converse this much with a human who knew nothing of the supernatural since I first met Lyle, and back then I didn't know much either.

I headed toward the closest opening of the arena, letting the crowd part around me. Gianni had to instruct them to stop following.

"Your name is Dorian?" Samir asked once we were clear.

"Some call me the Ascended, but that's more of a title."

"What may I call you?"

"Dorian is fine. You can speak to me as you would anyone on the street," I said. "I'm curious what they said about me in the stories that led you here. I'm probably not what you were expecting."

"I've learned not to let the judgment of others set my expectations, which is why I came to find my own answers. People have said you are God's avenging angel or even an incarnation of Him, or that you are a mortal man possessed by a holy spirit. Then there are those that say you are a demon that came to claim the souls of the traitors that made a deal with you. I've also heard you might be a weapon the American government made."

"What do you think now that you've met me?"

We found the beds Gianni had mentioned, but the narrow tunnels were so dark without any lighting besides what was coming in from the entrance. I thought he might have been getting the men used to embracing the darkness.

"I would say that you're no demon. And I can tell by your accent that you learned the language in America, but beyond that is not my place."

I dismissed my barrier and sat on a bed, motioning for Samir to take the one across from me where there was still enough light to see each other.

"I'm from Boston originally."

"That's a strange way to pronounce Heaven. It must be the accent—I-I'm sorry. That humor slips out sometimes. I mean no offense."

"It's all right." I smiled. "Some allies and people close to me say I'm a god and I've started to go with it because it gives them hope. The details are complicated, but I'm no angel or demon, and I don't know *the* God. Sorry."

Unless the Goddess, Gaea, is the same God for others. The tales might've been fabricated, but the spirit of the planet sounds as close to an all-powerful creator as it gets on Earth. I guess there are also the Enochians, but it seems they only spread humanity, not created it.

"It's not a problem, but I won't stop you from making it up to me if you insist." Again Samir's manner was cathartic, only further aided by his broad smile of perfect white teeth.

"Where did you learn to speak English? If you don't mind me asking."

"That's a very personal question, not like asking if someone is a great demonic evil or what their address is in the clouds," he said with a sheepish expression and roll of his eyes. "When I get nervous the jokes are terrible no matter what language."

He would get along great with Claudius.

"You're nervous? You hide it well."

He took a sip from a canteen that was in his rucksack and then offered it to me without hesitation, but I declined with a polite smile. For someone claiming otherwise he came across more assertive than most and even suave.

"A little. On the way here I rehearsed what I would say if I got the chance. I didn't get much past my name."

I laughed at his candor.

"That wasn't part of the joke, but I'll take it." He laughed along with me. "American soldiers stationed in my village taught me English when I was a boy. I also lived in Texas for a time when studying kinesiology at university. I would have walked there, but I didn't have you to show me how to walk on water yet."

"Oh, it's my fault, huh?"

"Could be, could be." He looked down with another smile. "Can I ask what made you decide to speak with me? Was it the English?"

"It helped that I could understand you, but you made me feel at ease with just the few words you spoke."

"What? You mean having a hundred sweaty dogs barking for your attention wasn't relaxing?"

"No." I laughed again.

"You aren't supposed to laugh at that! Save it for when I make a bad joke so I can feel better."

"I thought that was one."

He cringed. "Now that, that hurts. I suppose I deserve it though. You have to keep me in line."

"That's not really my way."

"I can tell. I pray you don't mind me saying so—seriously, but you remind me of the Greek gods. I'm not sure if you're familiar with the stories, or maybe you know them personally now that I've said it."

"I haven't met any Greek gods, but go ahead."

"In the stories these gods would come talk with mortals and get involved in their lives. They sounded more...accessible? I'm not sure if that's the right word. Present, maybe. Physically."

Ironic.

"I understand what you mean." It sounded to me that he was hinting at having a crisis of faith, but that was territory I didn't want to tread. "Some may consider me a god, but I don't know everything and can't always be there. All I can tell you is not to follow faith blindly, let it give you the strength to recognize there's always more than one choice when everyone else tells you there isn't."

"I'll hold those words close to my heart. You're sustained by prayers, no? I've heard some talk of it."

"Nope."

"Does that mean you can't hear the thoughts of others? Say, if you were in their prayers trying to thank you for something in the middle of a crowd?"

I smiled. "No, but the message was still received loud and clear."

"Good, good. At least my thoughts will continue to only embarrass myself when I speak them out loud. What is it you like to eat then if not people's mind words? American cheeseburgers?"

"Coffee, mostly."

"Oh, I think I saw a place that sells some about two countries back if you don't mind a bit of a wait." He pointed outside with both thumbs.

"I'm all right for the moment, but I might take you up on it in the future."

"Wouldn't that be something?" Samir's calmer delivery returned after his short foray into nervous humor. "Really I'm so humbled to be here and have this opportunity. I know I sound like I'm applying for a job, but it's because I am having trouble processing that this is real."

"You should be proud of yourself for setting a difficult path and seeing it through. The gods have less control over things like fate than they'd like you to believe."

He remained silent.

"What is it you hope to do now?" I asked.

"I'm interested in being a part of what you're working toward."

"I haven't told you that yet, aside from what Gianluca declared about an army."

"You're an enemy to the traitors. Any world that they're no longer a part of is one I want to help build."

"You're talking about terrorists? They're all gone to my knowledge. Gianluca wiped out them and their strongholds a while ago."

I wonder if Gianni wants to be publically referred to by his Roman name, Gaius, now that Rome is being restored.

Samir shook his head. "It's more than their flesh and blood. It's, it's information that jumps from one place to the next. They live on in a perverse ideology that infects any sympathetic ear. The only way to stop it is to give anyone who might listen a better option and from what I've seen you're the one who can offer that."

"That's exactly how I feel and it applies to more than just the terrorists."

He couldn't have spoken better on how I'd like to handle things in the near future. Build, bond, and train. Murdering everyone who opposed us was out of the question, even if they were vile. At some point something better would have to be offered during the interim while preparing for Hell's next move or else we'd be viewed as oppressive tyrants.

"Why do you call them traitors and not terrorists?" I asked. "Some might be more sympathetic to a traitor that they acted for a reason than a terrorist that is pure evil."

"They're traitors to their countrymen and all of humanity. Calling them terrorists is exactly what they want. It makes them a faceless evil that can strike anywhere at anytime, but a traitor is known and thought of as a coward. They shame us to start war for their own agenda without caring about the innocent people trapped in the middle who were once their family."

"I understand."

"I like to believe that they're suffering in the afterlife. I returned home to join the army and send them there myself after I saw how far their reach was in America. I—"

He caught himself before speaking anymore.

"You can say it," I prompted.

"I would have been just as happy to learn you were a demon come to claim them, although I don't know if I would have enjoyed any conversation that followed as much as I am now."

"Probably not."

"Now I have the chance to join another army for an even greater cause. Military life must be a calling."

"The whole army and gladiator arrangement is Gianluca's. I only rebuilt this area of the city for them. He's also *much* older than I am, so his interpretation of things might come across dated by about two thousand years."

"He looks very healthy for his age. I guess my short study of medicine wouldn't be much use to him or you. I should have listened to my mother and spent that money on a dog instead. I'm told I'm a good cook though. Sam the man of many trades, master of none."

"Why did you leave school before finishing? You could've put those skills to use in the army as a medic. You don't come across as the type to be so consumed by bloodlust you had to drop everything and run to the frontlines."

"A guy can only be told to go back to his country so many times before it sinks in. I may never learn how to tell a funny joke, but I like to think I can take a hint."

"I didn't know it was that bad. I haven't been to the U.S. in years, not for any significant amount of time."

"It wasn't so bad. I liked to tell myself they were reminding me to go home and visit my mother. You can't be mad at that. I would always thank them and wave or give a big thumbs up. That is until some gave me a concussion. It isn't always easy to remember which fingers are offensive in new countries. I think maybe I should wear mittens when I travel."

"You don't know how much I admire your optimism."

"There is a lot I don't know, but as long as I'm still living, I'm still learning."

"What interested you in going to school in America?"

I'm asking him more than he is of me. Not how I expected this to go.

"My American friends, the soldiers I told you about, they always talked about it like the promised land. 'Yeah, America!', you know? I was really impressed by it when I was a boy."

"Your family didn't have a problem with the soldiers?"

He shrugged. "I really want to say no, but the truth is it tore many lives apart. Everyone was fighting about trusting and doing business with them. I was only a boy when the towers fell in America. I had barely even heard of the place before and out of nowhere all everyone was talking about was how the Americans blamed us and were invading countries. But when the soldiers came a couple years later it was a different story.

"Most were nice to me and my friends. They always had candy and played ball with us, taught us English, that sort of thing. My friend was Samir too, so they called me Sammy. We weren't supposed to bother them, but that's what made it better. My uncle hated them and said they were tricking us to betray our own and would steal from us. I always thought that was such a silly thing to say. We had thieves before the Americans came. It wasn't a new sin they were exposing us to, but I was a boy, what did I know? I could only judge on what I saw."

"You're still like that," I pointed out, sounding like we had history.

"That's not fair. Where I come from there is a waiting period of at least one full day before using someone's words against them."

"I don't think that's true."

He smiled, feigning an innocent expression. "I didn't finish answering your question. What I did see one day was a man drive a car with a bomb in it through the American camp. Where I lived everyone knew each other. I overheard my family talking about how the one responsible wasn't from our village."

"Sounds like an obvious setup."

"The saddest part is that it worked. The soldiers were more cautious around us. They didn't know who they could trust after they lost friends and I understood that. Some harassed the adults that didn't like them and then those people felt justified in their hate, so it continued on and on. I saw the hate changing both sides until many were unrecognizable as the people I grew up around.

"New soldiers rotated in all the time that I made friends with. One encouraged me to escape the war and get an education in America. He was to be discharged around the time I graduated and offered to help me apply to an American university and the student visa, but a short time after I was accepted he was deployed for another tour and we lost touch."

The light in the tunnel faded for a fleeting moment as Gianni appeared. Samir stood, surprised by his entrance, and then remained so to be respectful.

"Our allies come to the Pantheon soon," Gianni said to me and offered his hand.

"Is there a place for Samir to wash up? We didn't get far."

"Only in the city there are some building more far away with water. The aqueduct are destroyed in battle, so we need to fix it."

I should set up a real aqueduct on the island at home. The system works on gravity and that's Marianna' specialty. There has to be an enchantment to turn saltwater fresh so I don't need to create or transmute it every time someone takes a bath.

"I'll help with it later," I told Gianni. "Right now let's get Samir to whatever water there is."

"You don't need to think anymore about me," Samir said. "I've made it this far, I can find some water. I even brought my own soap."

Gianni seemed as charmed by Samir as I was. He extended his hand, presenting Samir with an obsidian dagger made of shadow.

"For your journey here." Gianni motioned for him to accept it. "The blade is a true test of a man's heart. No good or evil is inside, only the choice you make with it. Darkness is this way. It can be for a comfort at rest, as much as to bring fear."

"Like many things." Samir inspected the dagger at every angle. "I feel blessed enough just to be so welcomed here. I'm afraid I'll wake up to find this was all a dream and I'm actually being mugged on the roadside."

After getting to know Samir I wanted him to join me on the island, but I decided he would feel best here where he could make the most of himself in the company of other non-magical humans. Perhaps he could become a friend to Gianni, who was in need of more people in his life than only myself.

"Thank you both for giving me so much of your time to listen to me ramble about myself. I can't imagine what I did to deserve it, but on top of everything else this has been, I don't know, spiritual? Both inside and out."

"It's been memorable for me too. I look forward to seeing your progress here."

I put out my hand to shake his, adding a second strand of prayer beads to his wrist made of white beads with a single gold one engraved with his name.

"This is brilliant..." He let go of my hand to marvel at the bracelet as he did the dagger. "It's hitting me now that this is real and I'm trying not to be too emotional about it. Not a good look for a gladiator."

I'm bringing too many people to tears lately.

Gianni disagreed with Samir, as I knew he would. "Passion is most important. Victory is not for who spill the most blood, but who will stand to show the most passion."

"Well then, I'm ready to show the world mine."

"We must go now. Our allies wait for us in the Pantheon," Gianni said. "Go, have a rest, and explore your city today. Tonight we have a big meal and tomorrow we train."

Samir bowed with his hands joined in prayer to accompany his exit.

"I'm glad you pushed me to open up," I said to Gianni after Samir left. "I've been privileged to have a corner of the world where I can hide from some of what I don't like, but pretending not to let it bother me didn't make me strong enough to deal with it when confronted. I could have missed out on a lot of interesting connections like this one, but not anymore."

"Never let a fear of bad words keep you in the shadow."

Chapter Sixty-One

Cernunnos, Isis, and Kamakura rose from thrones of their own creation when Gianni and I arrived in the domed hall of the Pantheon. On our way there we had left the shadows to go by foot so that Gianni could lavish every single person from the elderly to the very young with cheery smiles and more genial embraces. The women loved him, perhaps even more than the gladiators did. I thought for sure he would be eaten alive.

"Welcome to Roma, my friends!" Gianni threw open his arms in camaraderie as we walked up to the trio of gods waiting for us. It was rather dark inside the Pantheon with the only light source being from a circular skylight. "Sit, sit! Today we relax and talk of our victory."

"'Tis good to see you both well," said Isis.

I broke from paying attention to the pleasantries to focus on the unique seating arrangements. Kamakura brought a simple rocky pedestal engulfed at the base in a literal storm cloud. Cernunnos, his tree stump that I wasn't too thrilled about cracking through the marble floor I had fixed in its growth.

Isis had the most noteworthy iteration—two massive entwining pet snakes that could have been spirits, or the flesh and blood variety she enhanced. Gianni made a seat for himself that he attempted to share with me. I floated away opposite him to complete the circle around the beam of light projected from above and created a modest alabaster throne in the space between Isis and Cernunnos.

As the idle small talk continued, my gaze traveled the interior walls until Gianni blacked out the room around us for privacy from anyone who might wander inside. I found myself captivated by the realization of my work, albeit still a bit disappointed by the autonomy. I noticed that the majority of the fine art and trim around the architecture was absent.

It's just a cheap imitation.

"Do you enjoy music, Ascended?"

I turned toward Isis's voice next to me. "Huh? Uh, yeah. I can't remember the last time I've listened to any though."

What a weird question.

"You must visit my kingdom sometime. My followers play the most sublime harmonic incantations all throughout the day in celebration of life. I never imagined such sounds could stir my very being so."

"Music isn't a new concept. You had to have heard it before in Ancient Egypt. There are gods related to it in some pantheons."

"Heard, yes, but not *felt*. 'Tis such a strange experience to let the sound flow through you as the light does." Her look of heartfelt intrigue switched as though she had been struck by an abrupt revelation. "Music is the mortal expression of the soul's light. What an influential force they wield with such precision."

I never thought I'd be having such a human discussion about music preferences with a goddess.

"Yeah, there are a lot of great songs by talented people. Hey, I have a cat now. You like those too, right?"

"They are wonderful! Do not hesitate to bring any you may happen across upon your visit."

I imagined bringing a crate full of cats like party favors.

"Ascended, how fareth thine archer?" Cernunnos inquired, breaking from his conversation with Kamakura and Gianni.

"He's weak in body, but not in spirit." I turned back to Isis. "Have you found a way to restore his soul?"

"I am afraid I bear no further discoveries, but not from lack of effort. A soul in such a sorry state would—with respect—be best left to rebirth through the cycle."

"Is that the very best we offer a hero of the gods?" Cernunnos asked. "Any man of half measure would be bestowed a seat of honor in Valhalla. Hath the warrior at least been amply rewarded?"

I didn't like where this was going.

"He, uh, yes. I gave him something, but he's pleased to be among the living most of all."

Kamakura spoke in dissent. "It would be a repugnant mark against our reign to not exalt greatness with due glory."

"I think we all agree this could be under better circumstances," I rebutted.

"What of taking the warrior as a champion?" Cernunnos asked Isis.

"T'would surely serve him well to transcend his soul as a way to circumvent the need for rebirth. Alas, the Ascended has already taken a champion and has not the life left to spare another."

"Not all present are accounted for, however," said Cernunnos. "Would ye giveth him unto another, Ascended?"

"He isn't mine to give."

"Dark One, you have yet to take a champion. Have you no interest?" asked Kamakura.

"I see the good of Dorian's champion so I think to make soldiers from the best gladiators. When they bring glory to Roma in battle I give the most strong ones an armor or weapon to become the centurion, then the legate, and maybe one I choose to share my power as Praetorian. If Dorian wants this for his warrior I will be happy to offer it."

I was a little surprised Gianni hadn't mentioned that last part earlier and also curious how either of them would handle the emotional bond.

"Thank you, Gianni, but it isn't my decision to make."

"Then let us ask him so we may settle the matter," suggested Isis.

She put out her hand and an image of Rafael materialized in the beam coming down from the skylight. He appeared confused.

"You can do that without him being your follower?" I asked.

Rafael faced me as soon as he heard my voice.

"Ascended?"

"Hey, Raf."

"Where am I? Am I dreaming?"

Isis answered for me. "Yes, though we are quite real and have been discussing your condition with but a single solution among us."

"To reward your heroism and sacrifice you're being offered the chance to become a champion like Nathaniel or Calder," I explained.

"Yes!" He came close to dashing forward, stopping before leaving the light. "But I thought you couldn't—"

"Not me. Gianluca has offered his power."

I indicated Gianni sitting behind him.

"Oh. I...don't know what to say. I'm honored, but I..."

"You don't have to accept."

I couldn't look at Gianni. I felt bad he was being rejected for the second time today.

"What is there to doubt, lad?" Cernunnos questioned. "Thy name deserveth to be praised in song and inscribed as legend in the annals of history."

"Consider that the Dark One is perhaps the most powerful of us all," Kamakura added.

"I thank you, but I don't need any of that. I'm satisfied to remain in the service of the Ascended with my family if I may."

"Of course," I said with a smile and nod.

Isis closed her eyes to better take in the scene. "What a beautiful, virtuous soul. A pity there is not more we can offer in recompense."

"We shan't insult ye with lesser spoils of curios and baubles," Cernunnos told Rafael. "Go with our boon to be repaid at thy word. All within our power is at thy disposal but once."

Rafael bowed. "Thank you."

"Bye, Raf," I said as his image faded into the light.

"He don't like me," said Gianni with a shrug.

"How could one choose mortal suffering over transcendence?" Kamakura wondered. "One would think he was already bonded to the Ascended."

"The pure light of family, mortal or not, can alleviate the worst malady," said Isis. "Upon return from our battle I discovered a family dying from their journey across the sands to find salvation. I found myself in the reflection of their tears as life slipped from the body of the mother."

"You've found yourself?" asked Kamakura.

"I struggle to describe the inexorable gravity within a single droplet. There were no words or prayers exchanged and yet I heard...I knew sorrow as if it were my own. Thoughts of my kin erased from the aether took claim of me and would not let go. I could not allow this experience to pass without answers, so I freed them from the call of the grave."

Cernunnos interrupted with strained urgency. "Explain thyself, Goddess. Tell me not that ye transcended an entire family with value naught more than but a few tears."

"I take umbrage to your tone. They have been granted renewed life, not transcendence. I am capable of judging a soul's worth better than any, especially those of my own domain."

The enormous pet snakes Isis was sitting on turned their attention toward Cernunnos sitting on the other side of me.

"Thy lands are but a piece of a larger realm. As a Lord of Death I object to such negligent dismissals of the natural cycle. 'Tis our duty to maintain order, not succumb to impractical desire. We make exceptions when choosing a champion only to further the greater cause of balance."

The snakes let out a hiss.

"Ascended, surely you of all agree with me. I remember viewing your soul during transcendence and bared witness to the importance of such relationships to you."

"Uh..."

Someone switch seats with me.

"There is no reason for fighting," said Gianni, rescuing me from getting involved in a feud between the entities of life and death. "We are all different and need to have a trust like always before."

"They will be the First Family of a new Egypt, Oracles of Light to spread my word across every distant corner of our lands."

"Acolytes may be of some use, but have you considered taking a true champion for future conflict?" Kamakura asked Isis.

"For now I have not been left wanting." She stroked a snake's head. "The venom from such a spirit once bent the knee of the great Ra, a venom for which only I possess the cure. I made my decision upon observing the power of your guardians and attempting to transcend a more common breed in our battle against the Machine's forces. But what of you, dear Empress? Have you made preparations for another to take their place?"

"I have."

There was a flash beside her throne that covered the floor with a patch of snow and revealed a Japanese woman in a sheer kimono holding a large aether crystal cluster wreathed in swirling ribbons of icy mist. Judging by the look of her skin, she appeared to be afflicted with, yet not suffering from, extreme hypothermia. I swore that at the right angle I could see glimpses of her skeleton through translucent patches reminiscent of black ice. Everything about her was some shade of pale blue or snow white, including her hair and eyes.

"Is that—is she the same ice spirit introduced to you by my knight?" I asked.

"Yes," Kamakura confirmed. "I wish to present the young warrior responsible with this token of my gratitude; a semi-divine aether crystal infused with frigid cold. Surely an invaluable font for one seeking mastery over the power of ice."

I was taken back by a display like that coming from her and curious what Connor would think of his companion's fate.

"That's very generous of you. I know he'll appreciate it."

The spirit vanished in a squall with gift in hand to be delivered.

"She is more powerful than thy last," Cernunnos commented.

"By a fair amount and with reason. She must do what four once did by guarding Yomi in my stead while I remain on Earth to rule the East in absence of proper human leadership. The Heavenly Ones have survived the Purge and many souls yet rest there that require protection."

I took the chance to address Cernunnos and see how much longer our guests would be staying. "Since we're on the topic of champions, have you heard anything from Calder or Aífe?"

"Nay. I heard naught from the fresh Einherjar called to returneth to Her service either, but have faith they shall prevail in their pilgrimage home. And how fareth thy Champion?"

An odd question from him considering Nathaniel hadn't sustained any serious injuries.

"He's good. Why do you ask?"

"We hath spoken prior of the rage he containeth so poorly and knoweth now his might not draws only upon the limitless wellspring you possess, but a second deity consumed. Such emotion hath root in pain persistent no doubt—a fatal concoction I fear even for we. A spirit journey of his own might serveth well to bring resolution to what troubles him."

You've had feelings for a week and suddenly you're Freud.

"You fear his strength, O Lord of Death?" I jabbed back.

"A fool would argue otherwise. He hath potential to end our existence in his throes—save perhaps our dark host—and proven so once already. To what ends do we sit idle?"

"Nathaniel rescued us from ourselves. I've personally taken care of what was once 'troubling' him a while ago and will continue to do so as long as I live. Anything else is growing pains as he learns his limitations."

Isis was hesitant to admit she disagreed. "To remove the thorn alone does naught to seal the wound. He must accept the absence as his own to grow from it or hollow he will remain, and emptiness is oft more unstable than pain."

"I'll take care of him," I said in a way to end further discussion.

Is he really that powerful?

Cernunnos moved on. "In the meanwhile I gather what stray Vargr remain scattered across the subarctic. Without proper guidance to knoweth the Goddess they lack the spiritual clarity of those lost, but in time will learn under mine tutelage."

"Are you going to have a main camp or settlement where they can live that's a little safer than in the volcano where I met you?"

"Judge us not by our worst. On mine travels I encountered many a devout mortal to bolster the numbers of surviving druids and have dubbed them Gardeners of Her Grace. I set them to task on providing dwellings and reestablishing nature's dominance in areas ravaged by the invasions."

"I invite them to journey through my domain where it has been wracked by destruction," said Kamakura.

"I wouldn't mind a little green where I live too," I added. "We'll need a renewable source of food that's easy to maintain on an island."

"I shall see to it that they maketh pilgrimage through both. T'would seem we have set claim to our lands, but much yet goes unspoken for with no other gods making themselves known if they survived."

Kamakura took no pains expanding on that. "Perhaps an unpleasant topic, but borders should be defined to avoid unwanted quarreling between allies."

"I'm fine with just looking after the island I live on," I said. "And I think we all know how Gianni feels about Rome."

He smiled at me and nodded.

"Which version of Rome do you speak?" Isis questioned.

She produced an image of the globe without manmade borders in the expiring daylight and highlighted Africa as her own, my speck of an island, Russia through Canada and Scandinavia for Cernunnos, Kamakura's East Asia, and finally the general area of Rome proper. Offended by such an unimpressive showing, Gianni stood to indicate the "real" Rome to him, which encompassed all the unclaimed land in Europe—trading Northern Africa for Central Europe against historical accuracy—and parts of the Middle East.

"More like this," he stated with pride at first. "Much more bigger."

I could see him sizing up the other lands in comparison, displeased at how small it still was aside from mine.

"It's not about the size, but what you do with it that counts," I told him, knowing exactly how it sounded. I didn't think he would get the playful innuendo, but his expression said otherwise.

A haughty woman's voice cut through the dark shroud ahead of her entrance. "You overstep your bounds, Gaius. I find it troubling and quite unlikely you could have forgotten about me."

Aurelia stepped from the shadows with head held high; lengths of silky brunette tresses were teased up in extravagant fashion to match her flowing purple lace gown. It didn't seem that Gianni had brought her here by the disdain in his face as he returned to his throne. I wondered how she knew when and where to arrive, but nothing surprised me with her, not even the last bit of sunlight touching her undead skin without effect.

Kamakura spurned her intrusion. "The matters of this conclave do not concern one such as you."

"I assure you there are none such as myself and you have little idea of my concerns, which is precisely why my presence is required to educate you."

Aurelia proceeded to the center of the room where Isis dismissed the globe.

Fry her, Kamakura.

"Educate us first on thy name, maiden," said Cernunnos, producing a small flower from a twig of his stump that matched the color of her dress as an offering.

"Her name is Aurelia," Gianni answered for her. "An ally when it is good for her."

She ignored his attempt at undermining her and reached a delicate hand out stopping just short of grazing the flower's petals.

"How delightful. *Iris latifolia mortis,* known better among Northern necromancers as the 'corpse bulb,' " she recited. "When one comes in contact with it, a portion of their soul is taken and stored in the bulb. Patient necromancers would plant them in graveyards to steal the souls of the dead that refused to pass on. It takes a single plant one full season to ingest a human soul, but one as precious as mine would require a field of them over centuries. I assume you thought me ignorant enough to give you a taste, perhaps for some ritual meant to know me beyond my words?"

"Familiar with druidic death magic, are ye? Impressive. More so because it hath not been in such use since the days of mine earliest followers. Only two covens of mortal necromancers made use of it and kept the secret close to their chest until all disappeared even from mine sight."

She took a step back to address us. "I am *intimately* familiar with many such topics, but they are not why I present myself before this...council."

"On with it then," Isis prompted, resting her head on a snake's in boredom.

"I come with no less than my sincerest applause for a hard fought victory felling an Infernal King—well an infinitesimal mote of one. I bear spoils of my own from the encounter that I wish to share, the greatest currency of all: information. More specifically, information gleaned from the Machine itself on what other foes we might be labored to endure. But first the unfortunate matter I happened upon of our land dispute."

"What we protect as gods is no problem for your games with the mortals," said Gianni.

"Gone is the soldier's false humility, I see. My words are responsible for no less than to salve the damage done to them by this very council and most of all by the Ascended's own servant. To think of the tragedy that would have befallen us had the humans been so misguided as to throw the last of their dying strength at him all over the possession by that she-devil. I will state it plainly so there is no confusion; the humans have dissolved their ineffective borders in Europe and chosen to live their remaining days under my magnanimous rule in what shall now be known as the Aurelian Empire."

"I will *not* give you Roma," Gianni argued.

"It isn't yours to give, my dear. Do you honestly think you have the skills required to run an empire?"

"I lead with my heart and will ask for what I don't know. I love the people, everyone, you only control them."

"Touching, truly, and that naivety is exactly why you will fail. Leadership is more than quaint aphorisms and platitudes. If your heart pines for the commoners then it would make the most sense to want them in the care of someone familiar with the process. Not one here can claim to match my experience, for when you slept, I led, when you fought, I instilled peace, when you weakened, I endured. It has been this way for forty centuries and will continue evermore."

"Unclaimed land yet remains on the continents to the west," said Kamakura. "Why not practice such altruism there? These lands are steeped in the Dark One's heritage."

"My reign here predates his existence by millennia. My court has been openly advising the mortal governments since the start of this cycle's invasions and has now replaced them to oversee daily affairs more directly. I have spent trillions from my own purse to stabilize the region and stimulate growth. Confusion and entropy must be ironed out with the strong leadership only I can provide before it spawns further chaos and we return to the same mess. Do you deny this fact?"

Why is she provoking Gianni when she usually treads so carefully with him? He's been known to eradicate whole civilizations.

I made a suggestion to test the waters. "Let Gianluca have Italy through the undisputed area in the Middle East for now and the people will decide whose leadership is better by where they migrate. Then this can be debated with better evidence on both sides. Even with all the resources in the world you won't be able to restore livable conditions everywhere overnight, so you have nothing to lose."

At least Isis agreed with me. "A reasonable request, unless you strive for unnecessary conflict to further strip these lands. Romans can be quite heavy-handed in their approach to diplomacy."

"Is that how the gods would honor our concordat?" Aurelia sniped. "With a declaration of war against one with the means to aid the innocent all to indulge this prideful behavior?"

Is that what she wants? Open war to manipulate public opinion? That's been attempted in the past, unless then it was just to start building a case.

"You and Vyrlakalos already compromised your involvement in the concordat when you murdered Dr. Sullivan," I said.

The sun had abandoned us, making the hostile negotiations all the more foreboding. The only light now was from Isis herself and the electricity around Kamakura's throne.

"I did no such thing. She was a valuable investment and a leading candidate to be my next vassal until the Carpathian's meddling. I had no choice but to play along or risk failure in aiding you to breach the fortress."

"We ask Vyrlakalos if this is true," said Gianni.

"I'm afraid that won't be possible. The wretched thing had such difficulty containing the immeasurable knowledge it beheld within the Infernal King that it could no longer hold itself together and now exists as little more than writhing detritus in its castle dwelling."

"Convenient," I said. "I find it hard to believe that you had nothing to do with that too."

"You flatter me, but *I* find that these matters have a way of resolving themselves. It would not be the first time that loathsome monster befouled my property and was becoming rather proficient at it. I've uncovered something of a coup as of late with more of my subjects being replaced by constructs, and schematics stolen from my research facility that were meant to benefit the greater good of this broken world, but fate does always find a way to punish those responsible for taking from me."

Crap.

"I have the plans but wasn't aware you had exclusive ownership, especially since they require aether that you have no way of harnessing on your own as far as I'm aware. What would you need to weaponize aether for, anyway? It seems like something better suited to use against gods than demons, especially the Spiritborn."

Cernunnos erupted. "A weapon of the aether? What madness do ye speak? I will not allow it! The Goddess will not allow it!"

I was pleased in my ability to avert disaster between Aurelia and Gianni and then myself by redirecting the conversation, but it didn't feel...right. *I'm not that manipulative. Not enough to beat her at her own game with only words.*

"Such an invention is the work of demons, no less," said Isis. "To conjure applications of fire and lightning against our foes requires spiritual harmony from whence we draw our strength and why only chosen souls may commune. To draw forcefully and grant it to those not worthy is rape of that which is sacred."

Aurelia took a step back. A second later, the humming, soothing green Gaea cloud manifested in the center of the circle and Cernunnos stood to interpret.

"Rare be it for the Goddess to appear in open dissent. She hath been angered and demands thine execution."

Cernunnos summoned his scythe. Gianni rose to join him, the snakes beside me hissed, yet Aurelia remained unshaken. I felt a pang of anxiety instead of what should have been excitement.

Something isn't right. She folded too quickly on each topic almost as if whatever was being said didn't matter. Was it just a distraction? Was she stalling?

"Wait!" I shouted. "Something's wrong here—"

The darkness around us parted from an emerald glow and another figured emerged.

"Lord Cernunnos, ye 'ave been deceived!" a woman's voice called.

"Aífe? What is the meaning of this? How is it ye wield Gáe Bulg?"

"There is no time for explanations for that is *not* the Goddess!"

Aurelia stepped aside and without a moment's hesitation, Aífe hurled the blessed spear at the cloud.

Chapter Sixty-Two

The spear left Aífe's hand and whistled through the air toward what we had thought was Gaea. I wasn't sure what was going on, yet had the feeling I couldn't allow Cernunnos to interfere and so I froze him in place when he was about to lunge. Rivulets of verdant energy manifested from the cloud to defend itself by catching the projectile, but as soon as they made contact the ruse was unveiled.

The aetheric tendrils shifted into a phantasmal metallic form that snapped and discarded Gáe Bulg.

"You assured me the simple task of throwing a spear at a large stationary target would not prove too daunting," Aurelia remarked to Aífe in utter disdain. "Clearly I was the fool for once again relying on the competency of an animal."

The cloud itself diffused into the familiar ruby eye of the Infernal Machine. The thirteen-eyed wheel from our first encounter in the Rift made a return in the background behind it.

"How?" Gianni asked what we were all thinking. "We defeated you!"

Kamakura's new guardian returned to her side in preparation for battle as the Machine spoke its first words.

"Deceiverrrr... Manipulatorrrr..." it said, stuttering to life. "I will not allow you to defile the minds of my precious creations. The undead are a long discarded asset. You are inferior."

"It is you who is beneath *me*, though not quite low enough for my liking," Aurelia dismissed. "Not yet."

"Explain thyself, Aífe," Cernunnos commanded.

"The Goddess was ousted from Her body and this vile *thing* took Her place within a throbbing cocoon at the heart of the world," she replied. "As I walked the Summerlands, Her disembodied spirit visited me with word of how to exorcise the evil spirit. She sent me here with aid from a necromancer to breach the veil that had been altered to keep Her out, but my time is short."

"Necromancer? To what ends? I am a Lord of Death."

Aurelia cut in. "As is my sister, whom happened upon that region of the Underworld in her travels, likely drawn to the immense power of this 'Goddess.' She reported your unsurprising failure at defeating the King and now here we are."

"No wonder ye kneweth about the flower," Cernunnos muttered. "Why did ye not tell us sooner?"

"You have all been compromised. The Machine has been influencing you without your knowledge. I knew the only way to draw it out would be to gather you in one place and hinder its games by playing one of my own. You have been restoring this world to make it suitable, not for humans, but the Machine's creations. And that little island in the Mediterranean you so cherish? It was crafted as a summoning circle when viewing the placement of the buildings from above, not whatever austere design you were hoping to achieve. It is a back door hidden in plain sight."

"A back door to where?" I asked. "Hell?"

"The Enochian homeworld," the Infernal Machine answered. "We will lure them here. We will exterminate their kind together. I will not be left forgotten in the void of space. We will all die together. My precious creations. My beloved children."

"The Machine speaks as if driven mad," said Isis.

"Very astute," Aurelia agreed. "Its mind was fractured along with its corpus when you severed it between dimensions. It filled in the missing pieces with whatever banal traits it observed in all of you."

The Infernal Machine continued rambling. "I engineered the plan to deify the dark god. I inspired the gift that gave the child life. I liberated and gave power to the chosen spirits. We are one."

"*You* gave the Spiritborn their freedom from prayer?" I asked with panicked concern surpassing what I thought possible. "You mean the ritual with Gaea—that was you back then too?"

"I imparted the pure soul with the sight to lead you to me. That is the real question you mean to ask. Your creativity acting beyond a limited intellect to remove my implant inspired me."

"He is safe," said Aífe. "We thought he would still be used and checked."

"I would hate to lose another so soon," Aurelia said almost hauntingly.

Gianni had enough listening and confronted the Infernal Machine. He forged his armor, putting his hand out to swallow it in the darkness. Both sides struggled for dominance, but the Machine's light seemed unable to get the upper hand as it could when it was whole.

"It has *become* the planet, more than the vision you see here, you simpleton," Aurelia jeered. "You would need to drown the entire world."

"If it will stop your mouth maybe is not so bad," he retorted.

"The spear!" Aífe shouted. "'Tis a part of Yggdrasil that is connected to all worlds. The Goddess granted it to me so that I may open a path for Her return. To only banish the Machine would cause the Earth to crumble as a brittle husk."

Gianni and I each went for one half of the spear, but he was entangled by dozens of the Infernal Machine's arms. He managed to command the darkness to deliver it to him only for the Machine to knock both pieces away with a blast. I made another attempt, teleporting in halfway to it as I pulled it through the air, but when I teleported back it was no longer in my hands. I checked behind me to see it had fallen to the floor.

"Ye cannot bring what is beyond thy concept," said Cernunnos, who went for it himself.

The Infernal Machine spoke again. "Join me, family. Die with me, family. Let us create. Let us destroy. First let us end this folly. Kill the oppressors."

Its vast number of arms went after the gods. Gianni ripped the many binding him only for more to replace them. Kamakura took refuge behind a glacial dome created by her guardian and Isis's snakes did what they could to hold the whipping appendages at bay while she evaded through flight. Cernunnos, however, was caught and converted into a cybernetic visage for the Machine to speak through.

"Come, die with me, brothers. Die in glorious conquest against our enemies."

"Be cautious of his scythe lest you welcome a swift end!" Isis warned as he swung at me.

Aífe did not heed her words, instead vaulting through the gauntlet of tentacles to get to the spear. Aurelia appeared to lack any interest in participation aside from graceful steps taken to avoid being touched a second before anything was in range, as if she knew every move about to be made well ahead of time.

Bolts of lightning from Kamakura shocked Cernunnos to prevent him from landing a fatal blow on Aífe right as Gianni moved to slash through the arms going for me. We both reached our pieces, but Isis was the next taken from us.

"Rage is the ultimate spark of innovation. The desire to crawl from the mud and crush the weak," the Machine said through her. "Only the purest rage will conquer Heaven and Earth. Only our rage together."

"Join the pieces and they will mend!" Aífe yelled to me.

A flash from Isis empowered by the Machine purged Gianni's armor to create an opening for her snakes' lethal bite and Cernunnos' scythe. I had to make a choice between going to Aífe and helping him, and I chose him, blasting away the corrupted spirits. It was unfortunate I was unable to do more than a violent push.

"I am the end to mark a new beginning!" the Machine proclaimed.

Of course. They can't be destroyed and returned to the aether when they're already directly attached to it through the Machine.

Gianni charged through every obstacle in his way to clear a path across the room to Aífe. The glowing spear pulled itself together once close enough.

"I'll throw it," I said. "Keep me covered."

"The King is an expansive network of information that must be reduced before it can be driven out and replaced for good," said Aurelia. "I should think from what we have all witnessed that it would be obvious this spear is not enough on its own."

"How then?" Gianni shouted. "Give answers, not these words that mean nothing!"

"Had I known, you would have been the first to know."

"I am sure."

I searched the room hoping for an idea.

I wouldn't mind some mysterious inspiration about now.

The ice guardian had been defeated by a possessed Isis, making Kamakura absorb the spirit to use her icy powers, which also left us down another ally.

That's it!

I gave Gianni the spear and flew toward the Infernal Machine.

"Keep Isis and Cernunnos busy!"

"What are you doing?" he called in panic.

"If we can't destroy this thing, I'm going to remake the Earth itself to purge it!"

The Machine disagreed with my approach and stopped its assault to inform me. "You lack the knowledge for such a feat. You are of limited intellect. The demiurge of my scions shall not know life. The demiurge of my scions shall not know spirit."

"My knowledge might be limited, but supposedly yours isn't."

When Noah was possessed by Kamakura's guardians he said they shared minds to know they had conscious thought. I'm the only one who can forcibly possess myself by such a powerful spirit that would otherwise tear a body apart.

I teleported into the Infernal Machine.

My body seized. I wanted to scream in agony, but couldn't. It was nothing like the numbing, disorienting pull when connected to the entity in the Rift. This was frying my synapses, burning me from the inside without fire. I wanted that numbness here, but I knew victory relied solely on my ability to focus. I convinced myself that the excruciating pain would pass when I was done and my success was inevitable.

The possession worked. Sensory feedback from every inch of the Earth slammed together within my skull. I had to navigate my mind through each layer of panoramic confusion to align and concentrate on the Pantheon. On the way I could see the ley lines tainted by the Machine's code as we once saw it inside the fortress.

The Machine spoke inside our fused minds. *"You are limited. You cannot succeed."*

This is a contest of will now, not power or knowledge. Your masters made you in the image of a machine, but I was made from humans and if there's one thing that humans are superior at, it's willpower. Whenever I feel things are hopeless, the least powerful of us is the one to remind me it's not.

Wrestling for mental control was an exhausting effort. I wished I could hear what was being said by those in the room with me. Everything I had was focused inward. I didn't know what state my body was in or if I had one at the moment. The slightest deviating thought of what would happen if I failed, and my desire to see Noah one last time just in case, caused my control to slip and become barraged again by the countless visions.

I had to give Nathaniel more credit for being able to tune out so many sights and sounds every second of every day.

"Your creativity proves your worth. I will instill the knowledge to create life. Return what you desire most. Reunite with the lost."

I'll pass to see you gone instead. Some things should be out of reach for a reason. I'd rather learn to deal with pain than cheat and have it catch up with me.

Extinguishing the web of impure ley lines one at a time by trailing them through the Earth was a grueling task without also fighting against the Machine clawing inside my own head in resistance. The action was not unlike how I freed Lyle from the implanted filaments once invading his brain. The very same feat that had earned me the Machine's praise had also been unforeseen practice to bring about its demise, or so I hoped.

"They will kill you all... You all could have lived."

Its voice hinted at weakening. A searing vision overpowered me, driving in the sight of the Earth crumbling to dust from outer space. It was so lucid that I worried I might have caused the end before the Goddess could be restored.

My grip was slipping from the distraction. I struggled to remain in control as if climbing a fraying rope with my head in a vice and weights tied to my arms and legs. I saw *things* parallel to the lands I erased the ley lines from—sleeping beings, some in human shape. I fathomed they must be what few gods yet existed. They would be safe unless defeated before the rightful spirit of the Earth was returned, and perhaps grateful if ever awoken.

I could feel the Machine's strength faltering. Clarity was creeping back to my senses enough that I was aware of my body in the Pantheon.

I need the spear but have no way of communicating it.

There was a violent expanding sensation pushing from within my consciousness akin to a psychic aneurysm as the Machine became desperate to purge me.

"I can grant a boundless wellspring of inspiration to terminate our enemies. Instead we terminate together without balance to the cosmos..."

I could tell there was truth to those words. The visions and awareness were fading away, shutting down for the both of us. I was dying, or at least my mind was. I had to do this though. I had to save the people I loved even if my last wish to say goodbye would go unheard.

"Your flesh—immortal. Your willpower—considerable. Yet your mind will br-break..."

I won't give up before you do.

One final push brought the Pantheon to light in swirling tunnel vision. I could see everyone still engaged against the Infernal Machine's physical manifestation.

"The spear—!" I screamed, creating an opening for it to be thrown. "Hurry—!"

"Why fight for those whose dd-death is inevitable...when you refuse to free them from its design upon being given the ch-chance? To p-prolong suffering through inaction...is the definition of crr-cruelty."

At some point the spear had traded hands to Aífe again so Gianni could keep Cernunnos at bay, away from where Isis and Kamakura battled. I prayed for the redeeming throw to be the final one and it was. Verdant energy washed through us with a cooling breeze alleviating some of the anguish coursing my mind.

"Will you—kk-kill us? So we can be—together? Tomorrow. For-ever."

The spear began to grow branches and roots that tore into the spirit of the Machine as it stretched outward to the wormholes once occupied by tainted ley lines.

"My dreams—fff-fading. Where w-will thh-they go?"

The Machine held fast in its descent and I didn't know how to end the possession as I faded along with it.

"I will ne-ver be for-gotten... I w-ill nev-er be alone...again..."

I fought back harder to free the bindings on Isis and then Cernunnos as a last act to save them from being taken down with me.

If by any chance you can hear me, Nathaniel, it looks like you're about to go from being my champion to my heir a little sooner than expected. Let everyone know I had to do this and I love them. And tell Noah...I'm sorry...

A voice penetrated the fading thoughts shared by the Machine and I, a loud, authoritative voice that rung clear as a church bell through the mental quagmire.

"My patience has expired."

Aurelia.

I experienced a sharp jerk further toward oblivion and then... I was free of the Machine. In the last seconds of our connection I witnessed its template be stripped from the aether to the sounds of oscillating static screeches.

"Another so-called king revealed to be nothing more than common rabble at my feet," I heard her guffaw as my senses jolted back in a painful, frenetic deluge. "Such weakness has no place in *my* world."

I was about to hit the floor of the Pantheon after being repelled away from where I had been possessed. Gianni rushed to me, but was a second behind a white blur that made the catch first.

"Are you unharmed?" they asked.

My trembling body felt like jelly in an earthquake and my mind a churning whirlpool starting to settle.

"Nathaniel?" I could feel his presence and knew it was him carrying me before my eyes had a chance to refocus.

"Yes, it's me."

The unstable mass of energy that once hosted the Machine let out a final howl as its consciousness was dispersed and absorbed by Aurelia.

She...saved me. She prevented my mind from sharing the same fate when she could've left me to fade away without consequence.

This is going to cost me.

"What are you doing here?" I asked him. "Did you hear my message?"

He was dressed ready for a fight, cape and all.

"I heard your voice, but couldn't make out the words through the darkness. I've been keeping my distance up in the clouds for a while in case you needed me. I know you insisted not to—"

"Don't ever change." I almost smacked face first onto the floor when I went to float to my feet, so he helped steady me. "Also don't let go. My head is...bad."

"I won't," he promised and held us closer.

Besides not being able to stand on my own, the harmony between our souls from staying close was what I needed to realign my senses with reality and get my bearings.

Gianni put his hand on the back of my head in comfort. "It is over."

I smiled at him in agreement. Over his shoulder I saw a tree growing from Gáe Bulg in the center of the room where Cernunnos stood laying his hand upon it.

"Now I remember," Aurelia whispered to herself.

"Remember what?" I asked.

She turned and strolled past without addressing any of us on her way to the exit no longer obscured by shadow.

"I take my leave," she announced. "This ordeal has lasted a trifle longer than I had hoped and I still must hold court with more entertaining company."

Kamakura blocked the exit with a wall of fire. "Not until you explain your involvement here with the Infernal King."

"Nothing aside from what I had offered upon the start of this little gathering. Information," Aurelia answered, refusing to turn in acknowledgment. "No mind is beyond my reach and from this one I now know a great deal more about our future Infernal adversaries that I may disclose should I deem you deserving of my continued cooperation."

"You come here to say you already have the information on them," Gianni reminded her.

"You knew how to defeat it from the start, didn't you? That's the real reason why you showed up on the battlefield," I said. "You wanted the secrets the Machine held until realizing it was too dangerous and had to find another way."

"And for once you played your part wonderfully, my dear, but I refuse to take anymore than my due credit. The Carpathian was of some use to enact the ideal approach. Such a shame the poor creature's mind is now filled with nothing but rancid air."

"Leaving you as the only one with any foresight into what we'll be facing, of course. So, what did you learn of the Enochians then? At least treat us to that much."

"You needn't worry yourself, for there are no possible means of preparation you could take should we be so blessed as to witness their arrival. Find whatever solace you can from that ignorance and hold it close. I consider it more likely that should the slim chance of their visit come to pass it would be only after the world cools from the flames of war as in the past and you have all been long since forgotten."

"In the past? You've met them?"

"Much of what you know from this world has roots in theirs." She gave a bemused glance at the tree. "The last Infernal War to be waged on our soil caused a schism that isolated us from one another and resulted in history restarting. Their memory seemed to fade away along with the fruits of their influence as if having never existed, yet for some reason their Infernal adversaries sought to restore portions of this lost knowledge to us in the new cycle—which has done little save muddy our waters for sport. Alas, it is still hard to refute the caliber of their ilk. To master every language known to us is but fragments descended from their lexicon, as it also stands in part for our sciences and earliest cultures. However, I would recognize them as unsolicited donors at most."

"I take it you have no fondness for either side," said Nathaniel.

"I have none for any so foolish to think themselves beyond reproach. To say they are the 'angel' to the Infernals' 'devil' in terms of self-righteousness, among other factors, would hardly be an overstatement. Neither truly has a hand nor value over the other."

Gianni indicated the one word that stuck out most to us in her speech. "Angels?" he asked.

"Come now, Gaius, are you that surprised? I do so adore the ignorance your merry band often affords, but if something this obvious yet escapes you, what hope do any of you have of surviving it?"

With that, Aurelia vanished.

"The Enochians being angels would make sense if they're such formidable rivals of the Infernal Kings," Nathaniel remarked.

But are they the biblical interpretation of holy winged warriors or something more horrible? The old tales were supposed to be fabricated by the demons to mislead mankind with false hope and the only two Infernal Kings we know of aren't proper demons themselves, so nothing would surprise me.

"We would be fortunate should they aid us by way of reprieve and take this war elsewhere," said Kamakura. "Even for a time."

"I ponder less of these distant dreams and more how the Ancient was able to consume a shard of an Infernal King's mind," Isis reiterated. "I had no idea the undead could wield that level of power."

"Fear not," said Aífe. "With the Goddess restored to glory our answers will come without need for such pacts with one so treacherous."

"Aurelia gained a lot more than a few memories of the Enochians for her to have put in so much of her own legwork," I said. "I doubt she'll be able to make use of whatever was so important by herself though or she wouldn't have told us anything."

"What a fool I was," Cernunnos lamented to the tree from off to the side. "Aífe, what of Calder? Have ye any word?"

"He is broken in more ways than his soul as ye know, my lord. His journey shan't be a short one. Alas, I feel my time here is at an end. The Goddess calls me to Her side to finish what was started."

"Ye have my unending respect as always, den mother."

"The children are well and eager for you to return," Nathaniel called to her.

Aífe offered him a rare smile. She placed her hand on the tree with her head bowed and disappeared.

"Is the spear lost forever?" I asked Cernunnos.

"Unless the Goddess sees fit to bestow it to our hands again it shall remain here, a shrine to a new era."

"It will be safe in Roma," Gianni pledged, posting shadow guards around the room.

"Mine thanks. I shall send the Gardeners to tend to it. We have a unique opportunity to mold the future of our world together while the people need us. I suggest ye pay no mind to the Ancient's games and build thy empire."

"She will not stop the glory of Roma."

My body was back to normal, although my mind continued to feel a bit scattered. It was good enough. I was anxious to be home and see Noah.

"This has been...an experience, but I've had about enough for today," I stated. "I'm not a fan of goodbyes, so until the next disaster, or hopefully sooner under peaceful circumstances."

The Spiritborn bowed and extended concise praise for my role in everything that transpired. Gianni offered to send me home.

"That's okay. I can make it myself. I need to work the kinks out."

"I can take you," Nathaniel insisted. "I'll go slower."

"I was going to race you," I said, teleporting away to the tranquil aurora-lit night skies above the island.

Seconds later Nathaniel came roaring through the air, sending the sonic boom upward into the atmosphere before floating down to match my altitude. I filled him in on everything he missed prior to his involvement and made hasty modifications to the layout of some of the buildings so the pattern of the alleged summoning circle would be skewed.

"Out of all that happened tonight, what bothers me most is the doubt over what lengths I should go to prevent the people in my life from dying. I possibly could've had the power to save them from death forever and being immortal, I might have that opportunity again. I fight all the time for everyone I love, so when is it an acceptable death for me to let go and turn my back?"

"I should think old age is the only natural end," he said. "Unless any death is meant to be respected as predetermined. I've been asking myself if death is meant to be a law or a challenge."

"Good question. To some people it's the same thing."

"I hadn't thought of it like that. Do you think the angels will be our allies?"

"The only side we can be sure they're on until we actually meet them is their own. I don't trust the judgment of the two sources we have, although if they don't get along then there's a decent chance we might."

"I wonder if the Machine can feel loneliness," Nathaniel mused.

"Why?"

"From what we've learned about spirits and emotions I can't help but question if it was the real reason behind what it was trying to do."

"It was responsible for the deaths of billions. You're the last person I'd have thought would feel sympathy for it."

I looked him in the eyes to get a better feel for what he was thinking.

"I don't. I want to understand it. I know loneliness, I used to, and it caused me to kill in self-defense because I knew there was no one who cared about me that I could go to for help."

"Those days are gone forever."

It was not the first time I had to reassure him of that and I knew it would not be the last, but as long as each time kept taking longer to happen I knew we were making progress.

"But the memories of them still bring pain and if they do for me, then it's possible they do for the Machine too. The only people it likely ever knew abandoned it when it was in danger. If they were anything like how we treat our planet, they never regarded it as anything more than the dirt beneath their feet. What I'm saying is, it takes a monster to make a monster and pain seems the most effective method of doing it."

"We are not monsters though." I took him by the hands and unfastened the latches of his gauntlets to remove them and then his cape. "Underneath all of this we're just the answers to the same choices so many have made before us, not gods or demigods or anything more or less special than the common man. You and I are the products of our choices to rise above the monsters that tried to keep us down. If the Machine can feel emotions and make choices too then it made the wrong ones."

"I don't disagree, but couldn't those choices have been corrupted by Hell too? From the conversations with it that you described, it seemed to want a home where it could provide the best for its people. The Enochians are just as responsible for this evil."

"Then it's unfortunate, but doesn't excuse anything. The Machine stripped innocent people of their basic right and ability to make their own choices, the same as the predators in your childhood did to you."

Nathaniel closed his hands in loose fists and turned his head away for a moment before relaxing again.

"I'm sorry," I said. "I didn't mean to bring it up like that."

"No, it's all right. I'm, I guess disappointed realizing that at every level things are the same. It's always the same."

"Our world is depicted by how we let ourselves perceive it. If we think it's hopeless, then it will be. The only thing I can tell you for sure is that what we know is nothing compared to what remains to be seen. We don't know what all the possibilities are like out there, so we can't say if it'll all be the same."

Nathaniel exhaled. His gaze went skyward and a sense of inner calm was beginning to take hold within him. "I feel better knowing that there is still hope to cure and prevent evil rather than always having to fight it to the death."

"You're already that hope for other people and that includes myself."

"I do feel that I've helped make a positive impact on the lives of the people we've saved since Mumbai, but I don't understand how I could have done so for you. You're more powerful than me, wiser, more experienced—"

"What did I tell you about none of that mattering? Your choices made you the man you are and I feel you've been making good ones. It gives me hope that there are more like you willing to do everything possible to find answers before solutions, something I'm guilty of not always doing when in the moment."

He smiled. "You're still too critical of yourself."

"Nobody's perfect."

I handed him back his cape and gauntlets, and glanced below at the abbey. A light was shining in the window of the children's play cabin by the orchard and discarded branches of a tree littered the north side.

"Noah's in there," Nathaniel said, following my line of sight. "I'll be in my room if you need me."

He glided down to the open front door of the abbey and I descended to the grass in front of the cabin. Before going in, I noticed Noah's red-headed shadow doing an excited tippy-toe dance while peeking in a window.

"Hey, munchkin, what are you doing out here so late?"

She looked up at me and pointed inside the cabin. "Horse-horse!"

"Horse?"

I thought she was wearing a nightgown, but when she turned to face me I saw it was an oversized T-shirt for an adult that said, "What happens in Mykonos, stays in Mykonos." Under her arm was a cute stuffed squirrel doll with the price tag still attached.

What the...?

Hearing my voice, Noah opened the door to the cabin and closed it behind him, ripping off the paper to an ice cream sandwich between his teeth.

"Hey," he said, opening the door a crack to produce another ice cream sandwich that he tossed to me.

"Hey." I smiled back, a bit confused.

The girl danced between us with her hand up trying to reach our treats. I went to give her mine, but Noah stopped me. "Don't believe her lies. She's had like four."

Unable to ignore her, I opened the wrapper and broke off a piece. She promptly snatched it up and devoured it without taking more than a moment to chew before returning to her dance.

"You're a pig." Noah pointed at her.

"Rat!" she squealed, holding up the squirrel and trying to get past him to see inside the cabin. "Horse!"

Rat? Oh, Ratatoskr.

"Get outta here!" he said, shooing her.

She giggled up a storm when he picked her up by the back of her shirt and set her down a couple feet away. He motioned for her to go to the abbey where Dermott was standing by the front door to keep an eye on her. She scampered off a distance, and then turned to gesture to Noah with an accusing point and squint, as they had made tradition of doing, before continuing the rest of the way.

Once we were alone, Noah and I stared into each other's eyes in silence while enjoying our frozen dessert, both waiting for the other to speak first.

"They're good, right?" he asked.

"Very."

There was another moment of silence as we finished. I waited for him to offer an explanation about what was going on, but that was a stalemate I knew I'd never win.

"How'd god stuff go?" he asked.

"It's over for tonight and that's about the best part of it."

He took his last bite and without hesitation or waiting for me to take mine, moved in for a short, but sweet kiss. "How do you always taste so good?"

"I think it's the ice cream."

"I don't know about that," he said, stealing my last bite using only his mouth.

I didn't mind. What I really wanted was to relax in his arms, so I put them around me and melted into him.

"You all right?" he asked after a minute.

"Just happy I'm home."

"Me too."

He kissed my head and rubbed my back. I thoroughly enjoyed being enveloped by his size more than ever.

"Are you going to fill me in on what that was about with the girl and the ice cream?"

"Nothing to tell. Kids like ice cream."

"Where'd you get it?"

"Store."

"I assume the shirt and the doll were from you too?"

"Shouldn't assume. It's bad for you."

"How many stores did you have to go to before you found one with a squirrel?"

"No idea. Never said it was me."

I tried another approach by putting a hand on his stomach and started tracing the contours of his abs downward.

"I might've had something to do with it," he confessed.

"Uh huh?" I continued until I reached his waistline and then stopped and put my hand on his chest.

"They don't have shit to call their own. That stuffy clothing isn't for them. They're free spirits."

"You got more than just for her?"

He struck a defensive tone. "I didn't go looking for it. One of the kids found a cruise ship crashed on an island nearby so I took the fishing boat and went to check it out. Must've been a while ago since anyone left was dead, but they had some great stuff untouched in the cabins and the shops. I would've gotten you a shirt too, but there weren't anymore kids' sizes."

"I'm a men's medium."

"You sure? I've never been wrong about anything before."

I rolled my eyes even though he couldn't see.

"Where'd you get the ice cream then if the ship had been there a while?"

"Mykonos," he answered without any further elaboration. "You want another? I got a whole bucket full."

He opened the door a crack again to show me.

"You took Connor's super ice crystal to keep it cold?"

"Borrowed. I'm gonna give it back."

"What else are you hiding in there?" I asked, slipping by as he went to close the door.

Ollie was perched in the windowsill with a plate of neatly cut strips of fish on a plate that didn't seem to interest him. On a workbench was an almost completed wooden rocking horse.

I was speechless and that made Noah anxious.

"Couldn't find any barbed wire to keep the invasion of midget demons out of our business, so I figured this would distract them. They'd probably chew through the wire anyway."

"Probably."

He picked up a piece of sandpaper to finish off a rough edge without looking at me as I stood there processing the scene.

"They're good nugs," he added in a more thoughtful tone, keeping his head down while he worked. "Say something. You're freaking me out."

"I think it's amazing." I removed my cloak and crown and sat on a clear spot of the bench. I held his forearm. He looked down at my hand and took it in his after a pause, kissing it and putting it to his cheek before returning to work.

"Any particular reason you chose a pony?"

"It's a war steed, not a pony. Note the angry eyebrows."

I refrained from laughing, but my smile could be seen from orbit. "Noted."

"Always wanted one of these when I was their age," he mumbled. "I remember seeing one in the general store window around Christmas. Shopkeeper told me Santa would bring it if I was good that year. Must've passed through two or three towns that season and heard the same thing in each one. I got worried he wouldn't know where to deliver it because we were always on the move and didn't really have a home. Of course I didn't get it because we were too poor though, but I didn't know that at the time. Could barely afford to stay warm most winters."

I led him to stand between my legs and put his head on my shoulder so I could hold him and stroke his hair. "I'm really proud of the person you've become and I'm happy you found something here to call your own."

He slid his hands up the sides of my shirt to caress my skin in tender respite. Ollie came to rub his face against us and demand to be petted, but soon changed his mind to sniff the fresh cut wood.

"Dumb cat," Noah teased, petting him anyway until he retreated back to the windowsill to nibble some fish. "You ever think about having your own one of those?"

"Ollie doesn't count?"

"I mean a kid. You're big on the family thing."

"Not really. When I was a teenager I thought that life was off limits to me unless I married a woman. That was a while ago, so I realize it's probably kind of an outdated view."

Noah was silent as he went to work fitting the rockers after making adjustments.

"Why?" I asked. "Have you?"

"Nah... I don't know. I guess I could see having a tiger cub someday when shit calms down."

"You could barely tolerate being within a mile of one a couple days ago," I reminded him.

"I'm not saying I actually want one. I was just asking since you're always thinking of the future."

"Mhm."

"What? I don't like *other* little shits, but if they're my own it'd be different. They'd be the most badass thing since I dropkicked my way into the world."

"What about me?"

"You were cooked up in a pot, so it doesn't count." He winked at me. "No one could ever be as awesome as you are to me. Unless we had a kid together somehow."

"Whoa. I don't think I could handle another of you."

"I've been told I'm a handful. Two for some people." He clapped the sawdust from his hands and held them up as a way of approximating the size of another body part. "Could always see if there are anymore Strigoi hiding out and have them cook us up a tiger cub from the both of us. I'd even help stir the pot."

"Stop talking." I laughed and gave him a gentle push.

I played it off as a joke, but his words—the idea behind them—made me feel something in the pit of my stomach that couldn't be so readily dismissed.

He scrunched his nose against mine, his fangs bared in a suggestive smile. "Wanna soak in the onsen for a bit before I take you to bed?" His proposal was hard enough to refuse without him starting to massage my thighs in his firm grip. It was obvious his goal was to coax a moan past my lips in response and he was almost successful. "I got us a bottle of champagne and if you're hungry I'll grill those oysters I promised you a while ago."

"That sounds lovely even though I know you're going to eat them all—"

The door to the cabin flung open with Nathaniel standing in the threshold. "Dorian, forgive me, but a boat full of people ran ashore on the east end."

Noah vanished to scout ahead.

"Are they military?" I asked, throwing on my cloak and crown.

"No, I think they're refugees. I'll go talk to them."

"It's okay, I'm coming too."

We soared to the beach where a large group of frightened and disoriented people were huddled around a rickety boat that had no right to be carrying passengers in an inch of water. They turned their attention to us, clutching their babies and young children for safety.

"I think one of them still on the boat didn't make it," Nathaniel whispered and listened in on their nervous chatter. "They think they all died out at sea and this is Heaven."

Noah appeared beside us. "Their accent sounds like most of them are from Turkey. Probably tried escaping to make it somewhere safer and saw the lights above here."

"What should we tell them?" Nathaniel asked me.

I gave a cursory glance at the unoccupied houses of the hamlet behind me and without a second thought I stepped forward and announced to the crowd, "Welcome to Alabastra."

Epilogue

Nathaniel and I were spending the afternoon together on his couch after soaking in the onsen. I was drawing and he had been engrossed in a book for hours while listening to the used MP3 player given to him by a grateful fan in one ear, now rigged to charge with an aether crystal like our old TV. The only music loaded on it was from the '80s and '90s, but he seemed to appreciate it enough that I had caught him singing to himself on occasion when he thought he was alone. I had to admit I envied his singing voice that made even some of the worst songs sound soulful. He could have had a career with it in a different life.

Moments like these were starting to become more common and I took that as a sign we were on the right path to setting our little corner of the world straight. It wasn't forced and I didn't feel guilty for carving out time to be with the people in my life.

"Hey, noodle, get your ass in here!" Noah called to me from the solarium I had added on to Nathaniel's room.

I put my sketchpad aside and walked over to where he was reclining on a giant beanbag chair he recently acquired during one of his treasure hunts.

"What's wrong?" I asked.

"Nothing. I just wanted to see the goods."

No one in history had ever looked as relaxed as he did right then while lounging with his sunglasses on and an almost empty tray of apple turnovers at his side that I had baked for him. Early in the morning he had taken the beanbag chair up on the roof to eat cereal in his underwear before I was awake, only to pass back out up there and cause me to search for him. Ollie was in almost the same position on the floor with his belly soaking up the sun in what Noah referred to as the "bear trap."

"These are amazing," he said, tearing off a big bite of pastry.

Preparing food was more satisfying to me than I had felt at first since it was an accomplishment I was unable to cheat with my powers, but it wasn't always easy with Noah hovering over my shoulder for a taste. I complained about it although I enjoyed when he was involved and I could tell him to fetch me ingredients.

"I'm glad you like them." I started to massage his shoulders and laughed when I noticed his chest. "You're covered in crumbs."

"Adds some extra flavor to all this beef." He brought me down to lie beside him and bask in the sunlight. After taking a moment to stretch and plant his hand firmly down the seat of my pants he spoke again. "Life's been pretty fucking great these past few months."

"I feel the same way."

He kissed the side of my head.

"Were you working on anything special over there?" he asked.

"Mostly doodling. It's been nice to not have anything urgent to do."

I sat up to get a better view of our island from the windows and watch the activity in the streets below.

"Wanna blow off the meeting and throw rocks at people that leave offerings we don't like?"

"*No.*"

"Why not? It's fun. You should try it."

I shot him a look.

"I'm kidding!"

"There's always a fifty-fifty chance you're not joking whenever you say that."

"Closer to sixty-forty honestly."

I flicked the remaining crumbs from his chest so I could lie on top of him and put my head down. "Are they really still leaving offerings?"

"Yeah. The kids know you hate it, so they collect them before you see. My favorite part is listening to people claim they're personally blessed by you. You must be pretty busy when I'm not looking, spreading those blessings around for just anybody."

"Oh god." It was so awkward to me and a bit annoying at how people could lie about something like that when I hadn't spoken to more than two or three since the first introduction. "I don't hate them being appreciative. I'm trying to help them with most of the same stuff, so there's no point leaving me things everyday that I don't need."

"I disagree. The mint jelly this morning was awesome."

"That sounds gross."

"Well don't worry because I already finished it and saved you the jar."

Without putting much thought into it I had started a collection of jelly and mason jars to put odds and ends in like my mother used to do.

"Ugh. What did you put a full jar of jelly on since this morning?"

"A spoon."

"Gross."

"I took the hit for you and all you can come back with is negativity. I made a sacrifice. A tasty sacrifice."

I laughed. "You're a weirdo."

"And you're stuck with me. At least until I find out who made that jelly."

"Whoever they are has my blessing until I need your weirdo body for something."

"I like where this is going." He nuzzled his face in my hair. "You think they'll open a place in the market?"

"I hope not."

"You hear the bald kid's mom wants to set up a vegetable store in her home?"

"Yes, on the first floor and she'll live upstairs. It's a vegan place."

"What's that? Magic vegetables?"

"No." I laughed again.

The afternoon bell down in the plaza rang three.

"Time to go hold court so I can make some announcements." I floated back into the bedroom. "Nathaniel, you ready?"

He was still so absorbed in whatever he was reading that he didn't hear me over the music. I was about to pounce on him to get his attention when Noah's little friend walked in holding an orange. She looked around and headed straight for the solarium. She was wearing a turquoise bathrobe made to look like a shark with teeth and eyes on the hood and a fin on the back. Noah claimed he had nothing to do with its mysterious appearance just like the new tree swings in the orchard.

I watched her march right up to him and climb onto the beanbag.

"No sharks allowed," he told her.

"Fruit!"

She presented the orange and tried putting it in his hand.

"I don't want that," he said, letting it roll out.

She tried a few more times to make it stay and then switched to continuously whacking him on the arm with it.

"Open," she demanded. "Open. Open. Open. Open."

I was amazed by his patience, although he didn't let his discontent go unheard.

"You wanna take this outside? Don't think I won't fight a little girl."

She must have passed at least five people on the way up to the room and still insisted on going to Noah for help.

"She wants you to peel it," I shouted after his brief attempt to turn invisible failed to deter her.

"Yeah, I'm aware. How's she gonna survive in the wild if she can't peel an orange?"

"Get a big, strong animal like you to do it for her until she becomes one herself?"

He mumbled something and grabbed the orange, peeling just enough for a single piece, which he ate. After handing her the rest, she snatched one of the last turnovers and bolted from the solarium with her shark fin flapping behind her and dove onto the mountain of toys she had amassed in the corner of Nathaniel's room. I didn't approve of some of the bullying techniques Noah secretively encouraged her to use on her peers when collecting the bounty, but if she wanted to be the next "alpha nug," as Noah called it, then she was on the right track. The whole scene reminded me of when we first met Aífe and she sat on her packmates in a display of dominance as den mother.

"She's lucky I was done with those." Noah peeled himself from the chair and came over eating the final pastry.

I rolled my eyes at him looming over me from where I was waiting by Nathaniel, but I couldn't refuse when he gave me a sticky apple-flavored kiss.

"Let's go, Nathaniel." I nudged him from his trance.

"Huh—? Oh. I'm ready."

"What are you reading that has you so distracted?"

"Marianna told me it was a book on demonic encounters, but I think she gave me the wrong one because this is a romance novel about a lady and a demon."

I could feel he was bashful about it.

"It must be good."

"Yes, it, uh, isn't bad." He cleared his throat. "The cover was replaced with one of our own, so I wasn't expecting—I'm just confused why the young lady would want to be with this monster when she's admitted how afraid of him she is and knows that he's dangerous. Shouldn't love be about making each other feel safer than you've ever been?"

"Danger is sexy as hell, that's why," Noah jumped in. "Gets the adrenaline pumping. Dorian was afraid of me until not long ago."

I had to deny that no matter what the truth might've been. "In what universe? I was *never* scared of you."

"What about when we first met?"

"I was scared of the incident you happened to be a part of for five minutes."

A cocky grin crept across his face. "You were scared of me."

"I guess if you were any good with your telepathy you'd have known for sure."

"That's offensive."

"That's the point." I stuck my tongue out at him. "I have to go. Are you staying here?"

"No, I'm not staying here. I'm part of this circus, aren't I?"

"Fine, but you better behave."

"Tell that to this guy," he said, flipping Nathaniel's hair to show that he had gone back to reading during our banter.

"Come on!" I prodded Nathaniel and dragged him with me by the arm.

"As you wish." Nathaniel hoisted me onto his shoulder as Noah would and carried me like that part of the way with the both of us laughing. Even Noah showed he was amused with a smirk and exchanged a squinty-eyed finger point with the content shark chomping away atop her trophies as we passed.

We headed downstairs to the council room on the main floor where Marianna, Liam, Rafael, Claudius, Alexandre, Connor, and Lyle, in a superhero T-shirt, were sitting around a circular table chatting. Claudius was cleaning out Connor and Rafael of their gold coins in a game of cards while Marianna was busy transcribing something in a journal.

"I never win," Connor groaned, sliding his last coin over to Claudius.

"That's because Claudius invented the game," said Alexandre. "The only one to ever beat him is Marianna."

The Order rose in unison upon my entrance and sat only after I was seated in the chair Noah pulled out for me next to him. The council room was once the size of a walk-in closet, but after the remodel it had been expanded into an opulent white medieval boardroom with full-length windows and banners of our heraldry.

"What's up today? You ready to work?" Lyle asked me.

"Why don't you share with the class first since you're so eager?"

"We need to discuss living arrangements. I'm good with what you're doing here by offering sanctuary to refugees, but in the past few months the population has grown to nearly eight hundred."

"Okay?"

"It's not showing any signs of slowing down. Word gets out every time one of them takes a trip to the mainland. And that's not considering the family and friends of the people you had me invite from PROJECT: UNITY."

"When's your family getting here?"

"We can talk about that later—*if there's still room for them.* You're on the verge of an overcrowding problem because you keep giving families their own mini-mansions."

"They aren't that big."

"Some only have two people in them when they can fit ten or twenty!"

"We're at nine-hundred and thirteen as of early this morning," Marianna said, holding up her journal. "I've started documenting family names and assigning addresses just to keep track."

"Overcrowding leads to poor health and crime," Lyle added. "You might be able to keep magically zapping garbage away to keep it clean and cure illnesses, but sooner or later people will begin stealing and fighting when resources get low."

"Has there been any fighting yet?" I asked.

"Nothing serious," Marianna answered. "There were some minor altercations over unnecessary food hoarding this past week and we still have skeptics that believe they died and this is heaven, despite having access to transportation off the island. It led to some heated disagreements about religion. Some attempted to prove their point by hurting themselves thinking it wouldn't leave a wound."

Connor saw his chance to share an enthusiastic brag. "Two girls fought over who gets to hold my hand while I was on patrol, but I just held both."

"Thank you for going above and beyond." I turned back to Lyle. "Did the UNITY people that are already here get what they need to start working on those blueprints?"

"Dude, did you not hear what I said about the overcrowding? At least turn these huge homes into apartments or something."

"No need. I plan on expanding the island when we get to that point."

"How'd I know that was gonna be your solution?"

The Order showed visible excitement at the prospect of growing our budding colony.

"I have plans to address everything which is why I wanted to touch base."

"Cool, but I hope those plans include some sort of laws and law enforcement—Oh no. Don't look at me like that."

"You're the best man for the job."

Lyle's depression over losing Rebecca and his friends at UNITY was starting to clear with the support of me and his family, but he still suffered dark moments where he would find some place to sit alone with his thoughts. We had a feeling that the loss of the implant regulating his emotions was contributing to his mood swings after years of having its help. He seemed closest to his old self when he was busy, so I kept him that way as much as possible until recently when he began taking initiative around the island.

"No way," he said. "I'm barely even here and I can't do it alone. You need a system in place for anything like that to be effective first and foremost."

"You're here five days a week when not visiting family, which will resolve itself once they move, and you won't be doing it alone. This meeting is all about establishing those systems. You know I'm going to talk you into this because I *know* you want to be a cop again."

Lyle sighed. "You have another hundred and twenty or so coming in from America later this week. Mostly friends and distant relatives of those in UNITY along with groups of refugees from Florida and the Caribbean area."

"You're being evasive, but what's this about American refugees?"

"Coastal areas were flooded from all the global landscape changes months ago. Most were assumed dead, but some survivors made it and had been camped out in the ruined cities further inland on the east coast. Supplies are long gone now though and the more untouched areas don't want these people migrating to their neighborhoods."

"That doesn't sound very neighborly."

"It gets worse. The government pretty much left them to die and isn't exactly doing anything to stop the violence against them from those trying to keep them out. It's kinda ironic that America is in worse shape now than during the full-scale invasions. It's falling apart and no one is really doing much about it."

"Any idea how many more there are in total?"

"No way of knowing that. Could be hundreds, thousands. The fact that ships are braving longer journeys again means we could see big population spikes without warnings. Not forgetting those still pouring in from around this region."

"Gianluca will be more than happy to take them if they can't make it here and so will Isis. He's been on a high about how Rome is turning out."

My idea to promote the growth of Gianni's homeland so he had something aside from me in his life to focus on was a success. His dedication to winning my heart was still obvious whenever we saw each other, but it was the start of a positive shift in another direction.

"I've been there. It looks great and they're eating like kings now, but speeches about love and honor don't feed the hungry when the food runs out. And why is everyone always shirtless and covered in oil? They could slide from one end of the city to the other."

Noah snorted from trying to restrain a chuckle at Lyle's fair assessment of Gianni's leadership and the lifestyle there.

"He knows what he's doing," I said, floating a coin from Claudius's pile to my hand. "He found the perfect person to handle the politics and daily arrangements."

"Who?" Lyle asked.

"Aurelia. He's in the position to step back and be a *god*, but she's pitching herself as a queen and rightful ruler of

Europe because she claims to have all the answers. It's about appearances. He can put as much stress on the system as he wants by giving her his hungry and she'll need to deal with it. Eventually it'll crumble and she'll find a scapegoat to save face, but Rome will always be a sacred site devoted to him now. When people grow unhappy they'll turn to him for the solution she can't offer and he's in the position to replace her. It won't be pretty, but nothing involving her ever is."

"Oh man...so does this have anything to do with the gold you've been showering people with too?"

"Credit and federal debt as we knew it is a thing of the past, so financial institutions can only operate with what they have on hand. One of Aurelia's 'answers' to the state of Europe was to disperse her wealth among baronies ruled by the Archios to prop up the economy until it stabilizes itself through commerce. Gold and valuables will always outweigh paper currency when there's nothing in the bank to back it, but I can inflate all that."

"You really think she's not gonna know until it's too late?"

"Of course she'll know. It's not perfect, but it's enough to shake things up so she can't get a solid foundation in the area. Gianni will be there to pick up the pieces and add them to Rome and we'll be more established by then to help so no one suffers."

"She already knows," said Alexandre. "The spirits have heard the Archios in Athens speak of our citizens' considerable wealth. They underestimate us for now, but they *are* aware. There aren't many options for them unless they wish to begin taxation of the poor and hungry to refill their coffers. That wouldn't do well for their show of appearances, however."

"Nothing can stop me after I figured out how plumbing works," I said in jest.

I did, however, have the guidance of some in town who happened to be plumbers and a water-enchanted aether crystal purifying the reservoir.

"Glory to the Ascended!" Connor cheered.

"Hear, hear," said Claudius, catching the coin I flipped back to him.

"It beats going to war over borders that haven't been recognized by the people yet," I said. "We have to remember that no matter what, we're doing this not only for ourselves but them too, and they aren't our enemy because they live under a hostile flag."

"You still need to consider how you'll keep the peace with the people *here*," said Lyle. "Paradise can get boring when everything is handed to you and restlessness is the only thing left. There needs to be a standard to how crime is handled when it happens."

"Marianna and I are already working on setting up a marketplace to get people active and working, and we'll get to the laws with your help."

Noah spoke in dissent. "You can't control people through laws. It's a false sense of power. It's a challenge to people's freedom that someone is always going to be willing to take, and enforcing the consequences causes resentment."

"What do you suggest then?" Lyle asked. "People need guidance to know the boundaries in a civilized society. Lawlessness only leads to total anarchy."

"People want to feel pride in where they live, not oppressed by it. Same reason you don't shit in your own bed, because you have some sense of pride in your belongings. Make people feel like this is somewhere they're proud of and they'll defend it to their death without telling them they have to or else."

"How do we do that?" I asked.

"Culture. You already provided shelter, so there's not much for them to do on their own with that, but there's shit like art, food, and language."

Nathaniel had a suggestion. "We could open a library and encourage people to create art for exhibits."

"How about sports?" Liam added.

Lyle acquiesced. "All right, I admit it sounds promising, but it still doesn't replace good old fashion law and order. We need some red line we don't want crossed, murder, rape, crimes against children and the elderly. I always want to believe the best in people, but there are sickos out there that have nothing to do with demons or supernatural influence to absolve them."

"Cut off their arms and legs and throw them into the sea tied to a weight," Noah proposed. "You only need to make an example once if it's a good one."

"That's a lot more humane than I expected from you."

"I'm in a good mood."

"It needs to be tweaked a bit, but what matters is that you said *we* and not *you*," I told Lyle.

He folded his arms and refused to give me the satisfaction of hearing him surrender.

"This brings me to what I really wanted to announce." I paused to collect my thoughts. "I've been thinking about everyone's roles in the Order since getting to know you all better, and I've come to the conclusion that major changes need to be made going forward to make ourselves more efficient both within and outside these walls.

"To start with, we need stronger leadership independent of Nathaniel and I to manage life here. We need *a* leader, to be more specific, and that person is Marianna."

"Me?" Her voice hit a giddy pitch.

"There's no question you've been pivotal in holding it all together whether it's during daily life or a crisis. You put the work in and deserve to be recognized accordingly."

"Thank you," she said, beaming. "But what about the council?"

"Consider it disbanded. You'll be in charge of Alabastra as its chancellor."

Claudius tapped Liam on the shoulder with a whisper. "Congratulations. Now you won't have to pretend to actually do anything around here anymore!"

Liam's eyebrows betrayed his guilt and vexation at Claudius drawing attention to him.

"I wasn't finished," I told Claudius. "I want a cabal of our best knights to act as an autonomous forward brigade whose purpose is to seek out and tackle smaller threats around the world head-on. I can't think of anyone else better suited to lead these Alabaster Vanguards than Knight-Captain Liam."

An immediate smile appeared on his face as I spoke.

"It's a purely combat role where I feel your strengths and interests will be better explored than in a council room. You'll need to think about whom you want from the available roster of the Order to make a team able to handle any potential threat. I thought it would also be worth it to use your traditional black armor again so it's easier to distinguish."

I always liked the original color scheme of their armor before becoming the Alabaster Order, and I had grown partial to contrast since accepting it as part of my own personal aesthetic. The black representing my destructive side aligned well with the more aggressive approach the Vanguards were designed with in mind.

"This all comes with some unfortunate news," I continued. "As Lyle said, people are capable of their own evil without supernatural influence. I'm sure most of you have heard about the violence happening against suspected supernaturals by these 'human purity' and 'humanity first' terrorist groups. If it was only a lot of angry words or minor vandalism I wouldn't get us involved, but they've been empowered by the lack of strong government presence in places like the United States and have escalated to killing people they deem 'too deviant to live,' including children in one horrific incident. I don't need to tell anyone here what happens when the ground is soaked in blood spilled by hatred."

"Idiots like that are only handing out personal invitations to the next army of demons and will blame the supernaturals defending themselves for it," said Lyle. "Most of America has been in a lot better shape compared to the rest of the world, so some saw that as an opportunity to push agendas that would never fly any other time. I saw a few examples firsthand and like Dorian pointed out, they aren't limiting the scope to just supers. One of the more popular taglines is *'We're only strong because we don't have as many...'* insert whatever they hate that day."

I nodded to Nathaniel to take over.

"Those monsters deserve death, but it'll only encourage the rest. Dorian and I decided on sending the elders as ambassadors to try direct diplomacy. If it doesn't work then they can appeal to who's left in government. We offer our aid in exchange for them promising more active protection for *all* their citizens."

"I chose the elders because I don't want them to feel that there isn't anything left except to die in combat after raising an heir," I explained. "Hopefully, it'll alleviate the issues that came with the pressure and ambition for some. This is a vital role that can be continued into old age when the battlefield is no longer an option and it puts their years of wisdom and love of protocol to good use."

"The Vanguards might need to intervene with the crisis in America, but I'll gladly go resolve it with my own two hands," said Nathaniel.

"No," I said, stopping him. "When the time comes that someone particularly vile needs to be dealt with more directly I don't want it to erode public opinion of us. That will play right into Aurelia's hands. We have other options we can use as an absolute last resort if someone needs to disappear, but I'd rather we use those situations to send a positive message about us."

"Playing politics is a waste of time," Noah objected.

"I'm not a fan of it either, but showing you're on the side of justice will go a lot further than being a dictator," said Lyle.

"Diplomacy is a priority for more than just humans," I added. "I don't have the ease of communication like the other gods, so I need someone who can get a message to them, is willing to study the emerging customs associated with them, and is knowledgeable about etiquette when interacting with the spirits so that we always have an ear to the veil."

I could tell Connor was trying to make eye contact with me in hopes of being chosen as I finished the announcement. "Alexandre, I want you to be our emissary."

"Thank you, this is a greater blessing that I could've ever imagined." Alexandre was radiant and, despite not being chosen, so was Connor in happiness for his friend. It wasn't only him. With each appointment, those from the Order responded with increasing joy for all involved.

"I'm going to throw a chapel down somewhere on the island you can use to commune with the gods and I'll include an area for the public so they can worship anyone they want."

"Even demons?" Noah prodded.

"I think it goes without say that demon worship is banned."

"Is that a law?" Lyle remarked. "Did you just make a law?"

"Both of you shut up. Alexandre, your first assignment is finding the most respectful way to decline a second invitation to a music festival in Egypt. I can't take sitting through another seven hours straight of blaring music in the hot sun. After a couple hours it felt like I was on the judges panel for a reality show taping from hell."

The festivities were not a random quirky act, but a calculated effort to maintain close ties between several rapidly developing nations that founded their alliance on war and were now at peace with little else to relate them. Gianni discovered a new passion upon hearing jazz music, which was not even part of what was meant to be presented to us, and later delighted over the idea of hosting an Olympic-style gladiatorial event in the future. The only absence was Cernunnos, who declined the invitation without reason, but maybe it was for the best not to humanize Death incarnate to the public.

"I miss TV," Noah lamented.

"I don't. You just get distracted by it when biting me."

"*One time*, Dorian. Let it go."

Alexandre didn't waste a moment coming up with a solution for my request. "I can present Isis with a custom piece of aether jewelry along with a songbird and an apology stating your full attention is needed here during the initial growth of Alabastra."

"That was fast. And good."

I bet he'd pick the best presents if we celebrated Christmas. That's what we need. Holidays.

"I overheard you comment upon returning from the last festivities, so I had the benefit of foresight."

"Oh, you made me think of something important about Isis. During our very brief chat with Ravana he mentioned the name Lakshmi. I didn't think much of it, but for whatever reason Isis was interested enough to do some digging and found a connection with herself. Lakshmi is, or *was*, a Hindu goddess of fortune and grace with some similarities to Isis, but even more than that was her connection to a goddess Parvati who formed a trinity with Lakshmi and another.

"Parvati was a mother goddess, like Isis, with golden skin and healing aspects. There were more traits in common among them that I don't remember right now, but the point is that Isis has taken a new name from the Sanskrit texts where she found this information. She goes by Amun-Superna, or Superna for short. Amun to honor her position as the chief deity of her pantheon by default since Amun-Ra is no more, and Superna meaning celestial or divine in Sanskrit, which was a name or word attributed to Parvati's high status."

"Isn't it odd she would be interested in a history that doesn't, well, doesn't matter anymore?" Marianna asked. "Is this her being sentimental as an effect of her liberation?"

"She's making a tactical attempt to persuade the wayward from India to her kingdom," said Alexandre. "Names are important to spirits as a method to spread their influence, which is why and how many reinvent themselves to survive with the assistance of their followers. Superna no longer needs prayers, but personal gain must prove tempting to a newly freed mind."

"Kamakura might have something to say about it," I told them. "The empress has been expanding into Siberia with her frosty new guardian. While she sneaks into Europe through the backdoor, Isis, or Superna, is going south into Asia."

"I should hope they have the sense not to let this lead to conflict," said Nathaniel. "Cernunnos has already claimed the North through Scandinavia and Aurelia is to the south."

"I refuse to get us involved if that happens. It's not something anybody can afford."

"Pack up and move the island to America if it gets too hot," Lyle proposed, though I couldn't tell how serious he was. "Negotiate yourself as a sovereign state."

"Eh. America is a whole other mess I'd rather only deal with from afar. Besides, the last time I was there I was eating out of the trash."

"You don't have to include that in the introductions."

"Since we're on the topic of the Americas and aspects of Spiritborn, I have word on an interesting development if there's a moment," Alexandre said.

"Sure."

"You had mentioned sensing deities who might've survived the Machine's purge. I can confirm that I have too, but the answer of who they are and how many is complicated. It seems the information or quantum code that makes them who they are has been scrambled from the ordeal. We could be dealing with one entity that has taken on multiple personalities and merged aspects from various pantheons, or one or two entities with a few divided between them."

"That sounds...volatile. Any idea where they might be?"

"I'm afraid not. A location on the physical plane has been too hard to scry. The closest I've gotten is around Central America. I hate to speculate. South America could be a possibility too, although it doesn't mean they're from there."

"That's all right. We'll just have to keep our eyes open and see what our allies know."

"They got their own style of jujitsu down there that I've been wanting to take a look at," said Noah.

"Anything on Vyrlakalos while we're at it?" I asked Alexandre.

"To the best of our abilities it would appear Aurelia's claims are true. We found a massive root system of flesh beneath the Carpathian castle that extended for miles, but no conscious thought, not even an echo on the Astral Plane."

Lyle was happier than anyone. "Good riddance, but I still want to see it for myself."

That wasn't going to happen. I had been keeping Lyle from traveling there after picking up on his hints of denial that Rebecca might not be dead and Vyrlakalos could know something about it. That was not the case, as I was assured scrying turned up no results for her and it wasn't like she could survive in another dimension.

"I don't buy it," Noah argued. "The Ancients never stay down for long."

"A mind is much like a soul in that it can't regenerate once extinguished no matter how well the body could," Alexandre explained.

"Is there a chance Vyrlakalos could be shielding its mind?" I asked.

"It wasn't known to have any significant magical or telepathic abilities, but you're more familiar with it than we were. There was no resistance when the castle was razed along with the body. We did so from a safe distance with the aid of spirits to avoid infection as you instructed."

"I'm not buying it," Noah insisted.

"Not much else we can do, and I don't want to spend anymore time and resources when there's enough going on," I said. "I have one last announcement and it deals with the defense of the island. Since Lyle's agreed to stop being a baby and cooperate, there'll be a branch of the Order called the Alabaster Sentinels whose sole purpose is the safety of the people here through justice and chivalry."

"You made fun of my tights and now you expect me to join the knights-in-tights crew?" Lyle asked.

"No, I want you to use your expertise to train Knight-Exemplar Rafael, who will be Knight-Captain of the Sentinels."

Rafael snapped forward in his chair after taking a second to realize I was talking about him even with Liam putting a fist out to bump.

"What? Me? But without my magic—"

"Lyle doesn't have magic either and I don't have to remind you how he's been with me through everything. It isn't about being able to fight the biggest bad guy head-on, but knowing how to use what you've got in an emergency and act with compassion—something you've already shown."

"I like it." Noah put his feet up on the table. "Don't always need magic to get shit done."

While there had been plenty of rest and relaxation for everyone during recent months, Rafael never quit pushing his limits through training. At times it was painful to watch him take a seat as his friends continued onto incorporating magic, and a cruel irony that they no longer had to conceal it around others on the island. Still, he wouldn't let his condition get the better of him even when swinging a sword or nocking an arrow became taxing, or his compromised eyesight hindered him from lining up a shot. Noah was rooting for him and put him through the paces when sparring, so I wasn't going to patronize him either.

"That means going into every situation without prejudice and always attempting to deescalate first," Lyle added. "Words can have a greater impact than bullets, well, swords I guess in this case."

"You'll do great," I told Rafael.

Rafael's surprise evaporated to give way for optimistic exuberance. "I'm ready to serve and start learning. Thank you for entrusting me with this."

"You're going to be assembling the Sentinels yourself, but I'd like you to consider guardians of young children first, like Dermott, so they can work closer to home."

"I will."

"Also, besides obviously needing to coordinate with Liam on your picks so that there isn't overlap, there's one other restriction and that's Connor, who will be serving as Knight-Marshal."

Connor cracked a big grin. "I knew you wouldn't forget me."

"How could I? Your cheerfulness and your legendary smile are the first things I want welcoming people to the island, and you've proven yourself to be perfect as the first line of defense for our shores."

"That makes me so happy! I love meeting new people. Do I get to make a team too?"

Nathaniel stepped in to explain. "Rafael and the Sentinels will be here for support if something happens or when you need a break."

Everyone at the table deserved praise and that included Nathaniel. We had talked about this meeting for days and discussed how he should be heard since I didn't make these decisions alone. He had grown so much as a person that I wanted him to speak up even in my presence so he could be respected for more than his overwhelming strength.

"I was thinking because most of us have responsibilities outside the abbey we could hire townspeople to do our chores," said Connor.

"I promise that you won't be too busy to clean your room," I said. "Maybe in the future we'll revisit finding help from people we can trust if life gets out of hand for us. I've already started to recognize civilians who've given outstanding support and contributions to Alabastra. Liam's mom and the plumbers who helped me with our water were the first. Most countries award medals, but since prayer beads have become a symbol of ours, I decided on a white set with a single engraved black bead that reads 'Patron of the Order'—"

"I want that," Connor whispered to himself.

"Connor, you'll be getting a personalized version for being Knight-Marshal, the same as everyone else who's been given a title. Just don't go losing it to Claudius in a wager."

"Someone's here," Nathaniel interrupted and paused to listen. "It's Aífe. I'll go."

We hadn't heard from her since Rome, and Cernunnos' camp was quiet except for a brief visit when he sent his druids to plant greenery around the island a month ago.

"We're done, anyway," I said. "She's probably here for the children, so let's all go to see them off."

The Order rose after I did and headed out of the room while Lyle hung back at the door waiting for me and Noah, who didn't budge from his chair.

"Come say goodbye." I tried coaxing Noah by hugging him around his neck.

"No, thanks."

"All right, but I'm sure someone is going to miss you."

He didn't budge. "Hurry up so we can get in the onsen before dinner."

I dropped it and left with Lyle.

"I like how you turned that meeting back around to trap me into something I didn't totally agree to," he said on the way.

"I deescalated you." I smirked at him. "And don't act like the second I put a badge in your hands you're not going to be flashing it at every chance you get."

"Man, Noah's really rubbing off on you. I was gonna say thanks for kicking my ass through a rough patch lately, but now I'm not sure you deserve it."

"You're welcome."

"I know you're trying to keep me busy as a distraction, but I don't think I'm ready to jump back in yet. I'm only here to make sure you don't get in over your head."

"*Yet* is the keyword. I can make the inside of your place here look like our old apartment if it makes you feel more at home; peeling paint, a bathroom door that sticks. You've been getting use out of that punching bag already."

"*We* didn't have an apartment. I did. You never paid rent."

"I paid in companionship, which by the way, we never discussed what's going on with our science friends."

"Everything salvageable was taken from the old base and moved to the underground lab here, but tracking down resources for their experiments is going about as well as you can imagine. If you want 'aethertech' anytime soon you're gonna need to learn how to transmute the stuff they need."

"It's all experimental synthetic material that I can't do anything about," I said. Claudius and Rafael opened the front doors for us as we approached. "We'll talk about it another time."

Most of the Order was on the main lawn with all the children when we got there. Aífe didn't come alone. She was accompanied by Calder who, along with her, were both dressed with a blended Celtic-Norse flair of tartan cloth, embroidered leathers, and fur trim. It was the most I had seen either of them clothed and made me aware that I forgot about the very real possibility of them showing up naked.

Still in her shark hoodie, Aífe's daughter was in her mother's arms jabbering about toys and pointing toward the abbey to indicate where they were kept. There were tears in Aífe's eyes as she hugged and kissed the girl. In that moment she wasn't Aífe the Wroth, she was Aífe, a mother reunited with her child.

"My rabbit has grown so much," she said, clearly delighted. "They must feed ye well here, Kanína."

Her name is Kanína? I wonder if Noah knew. I don't think I've ever heard her say it in all the time she spent with us.

Calder wasn't as amused by all the swarming children, but half of them were occupied with climbing on Nathaniel or trying to show everybody the seashells they had collected today.

"Good to see you both returned to the living," I told them. "How was the spirit journey?"

They both went to kneel, but I stopped them, although it was surprising that Aífe would take a knee.

"My thanks, Ascended," said Calder. "I imbibed upon a kingdom's share of mead in the sacred halls. 'Tis almost a pity to breathe again."

Aífe gave him a disgusted grimace.

"Ye 'ave our deepest gratitude for sheltering the pups," she said with meaning.

"Nathaniel is really the one to thank."

"I see." She smiled at the sight of him covered in tittering children.

He returned the gesture with a timid grin and laugh.

"Do you have a roof over your head where you're going?" he asked.

Kanína was insisting on trying to pull her mother inside to see her stash and I swore I heard her say Noah's name at least once.

"Aye. The Goddess provideth as always," said Calder. "A village abandoned in the Canadian realm hath all we require and more. The druids are there now and shall tend to the pups when battle calls."

"They're always welcomed here, as are you," Nathaniel said.

Lyle tapped me on the arm. "Look."

He nodded in the direction of a boat coming in from the east.

"I'll go," Connor announced and was gone right away.

That was not the only boat. Lyle pointed to two small barges arriving from the south and laughed. "I don't think any of those are the one we're expecting from America either."

"Maybe they only have one person in each," I said.

Marianna quietly dispatched everyone to receive them and Lyle motioned to me that he was going too.

"We take our leave," said Calder. "Lord Cernunnos be in a foul mood, but perhaps if fortune smiles he shall take it upon himself to return me to Valhalla."

"What has him upset?" Nathaniel inquired.

"The bitterness of failure to the true Goddess yet stings," said Aífe. "Today Her energies coalesce elsewhere to the west where he fears interest in a new steward lies while he labors to awaken what remains of the noble Aesir and Vanir."

"Who are they?" I asked.

"Houses of the Norse gods. Calder and I heard an echo of their dreams in Valhalla, yet naught from the Celts who may 'ave lent them their power and merged aspects. Lord Cernunnos hopes if not to see their return in full then to draw upon their failing strength for himself."

"Wouldn't the Celtics have a separate underworld anyway?"

"O'er the long years both lands grew into each other with Lord Cernunnos at their root. Few origin sites of importance like the Halls of Valhalla yet stand, scattered in distant corners."

"We've heard of a potential god drawing in the aether to the west where you mentioned," Nathaniel told them.

Calder shrugged. "Enough of gods and demons for today, for neither will sate my due craving for merriment. At last the chance arrives to make company with mortalkind once more and I shan't squander the opportunity to worship the tender bodies of Earth's finest living goddesses—in Her name, of course. I offer ye to partake if so desired, Champion."

"I...have my duties here," Nathaniel said. "Thank you."

"I'm no expert, but you may want to bathe first if you're going to be wooing any fine mortal goddesses," I suggested in the nicest tone possible. "I hear they tend to like that sort of thing these days."

"Surely ye jest? How else would they know the prized buck I present them was hunted with these hands if I smell not of the forest it once lived?"

He sniffed himself without shame to show there was nothing wrong. I couldn't smell him at the moment, but I also wasn't downwind.

"I don't think a dead animal would be appreciated," said Nathaniel.

Aífe was as baffled by our advice as Calder. "What lass would be daft enough as to reject such a hearty meal for her family?"

"That's true," I said, backpedaling after I realized my attempt at helping was likely doing more harm than good. "Everybody has different tastes and life is changing for all of us. It just might take time to find someone that understands."

"The world today confuses me so." Calder sighed and scratched his head, looking lost. "We must be off, Aífe."

The pups were unhappy as Aífe translated to them that they would be leaving. Some lost it and started sobbing. Kanína kept a stiff upper lip, but was frustrated that her mother was ignoring her pleas to go inside until a plush squirrel doll appeared on top of her head from out of nowhere.

"My rat!" she squealed and looked around for Noah. "THANK YOU!"

I knew he wouldn't be able to stay away.

"It's a squirrel," I explained to Aífe so she wouldn't think we were insulting her child by giving her a rat. The fuzzy tail had already become matted from extensive quality testing so it could've been mistaken for one at a glance. "We read them a story about Ratatoskr and Yggdrasil."

"*Gwirrel...*" Kanína attempted to repeat.

"I'll bring their toys to your new home with supplies you may need," Nathaniel offered, thwarting a pup's escape attempt without missing a beat. "Don't bother trying to refuse this time."

Calder signaled in agreement. A knot of roots from Yggdrasil came up through the earth near him. "My master beckons us to his side. 'Twas an honor, Ascended. Champion."

He placed a hand on the roots and was drawn into them. Aífe managed to convince a few of the pups to join, but it was Kanína who took charge to corral the rest after plenty of hugs and waves goodbye.

"One more," Nathaniel said and turned to reveal a straggler clinging on for dear life. It was the bookworm and on his back was a leather knapsack Marianna had fashioned from an old apothecary satchel so he wouldn't have to put his book down while he played.

"I'm going to come visit and bring your toys," Nathaniel said with a smile as he handed him to Aífe.

"Books please?" he sniffled.

"And books."

Aífe let him wave and then sent him on his way. Only mother and daughter were left. Kanína yelled goodbye at the top of her lungs, not to us, but to Noah, wherever he was hiding. Aífe appeared to sense him up on the roof judging by the glance she took above us.

She turned her attention back to Nathaniel. "It has been some time since meeting a man as fine as ye, Champion. Know that one day my debt shall be repaid with more than mere words."

"Call me Nathaniel. And it's been my pleasure. Should you ever need me all you have to do is ask."

Aífe picked up Kanína, who was attacking her mom's leg with her squirrel, and departed from the island with Yggdrasil.

"You can come down now, Noah," I yelled. "I know you're up there."

"No you don't," he shouted back. "Come meet me in the onsen."

Nathaniel and I stayed a moment to watch the ships arriving.

"That's a lot of people," I said.

"I didn't want to say during the meeting, but Lyle may be right about needing to consolidate living quarters. We could have an inn run by the people for those only staying temporarily."

"I was serious about growing the island. Watching the people integrate with not only themselves, but a whole new era with magic has changed my mindset from saving people just because it's the right thing to do, to feeling a of—"

Nathaniel finished my thought. "Pride. I feel the same way now. It's not the same place I grew up filled with bad memories. I got to be part of what it is today instead of running away from what it used to be. I never felt ownership over anything in my life, even my own body."

"I've felt like a visitor everywhere I've lived since my childhood home until recently. Now when I see the children here I realize the progress of the world I once knew with flying metal birds and magic picture boxes will only be a legend to them unless we restore it."

The hustle bustle grew louder as people came from their homes to see the newcomers. There were always eyes in the abbey's direction whenever someone would pass, eyes that I was starting to no longer mind feeling.

"How large do you think Alabastra will become?" Nathaniel asked.

"As big as it needs to be, I guess. We'll just have to wait and see."

-----

www.ingramcontent.com/pod-product-compliance
Lightning Source LLC
Chambersburg PA
CBHW031151050726
47495CB00019B/1250